HAREM
OF
FREAKS

USA TODAY BESTSELLING AUTHOR
CRYSTAL ASH

BLURB

When I join the circus, the last thing I expect is to fall in love...

The craziest part? It's with shifters.

I ran away from my abusive home on my eighteenth birthday and never looked back. Working at the traveling carnival is my chance for escape, for joy and independence. Or so I thought.

But there's more to this circus than I expected. Monsters lurk in the shadows. Those with fangs and claws, and the men who profit from trafficking them.

Shifters are real, and they're people who need my help. The lone wolf protecting his pups. The tattooed dragon with a wicked tongue. And the prickly tiger who keeps me at arm's length.

Captured and exploited, they're furious at being paraded as circus attractions. They might be monsters, but they're also men. *My* men. Together, we must stop the shifter trade for good.

I may not have fangs or claws, but it turns out I have magic of my own. And I'm not afraid to use it.

Because these monsters? They're all mine.

Harem of Freaks is a complete paranormal reverse harem series with adult scenes, including M/M content. This series bundle includes the following volumes:

Freak Show
Abra Cadabra

FREAK SHOW

BOOK 1

PROLOGUE

THE WOLF MAN

Darkness surrounded me as I came to consciousness. The rumblings of an engine and sway of my surroundings told me I was in a vehicle. Rank smells of long stale bodily fluids of many previous victims filled my nose.

My limbs screamed with fatigue. I tried to move them, only to realize they had been shackled behind my back. I pushed myself up to my knees, only to find my head and shoulders crammed up against the bars of a cage.

Soft whimpers a few feet away sent my ears pricking forward. A heavy sense of dread filled me as my hackles raised.

Dad?

My daughter's frightened voice in my head broke my heart. *No. Not them, too.* They promised they wouldn't touch them. Handing myself over had been for nothing. I should have known better than to trust humans.

Rinna! I answered her. *I'm here, sweetie. Are you hurt?*

Daddy, my head hurts and I can't shift. Roo is sleeping and he won't wake up.

A growl of despair escaped my throat. These monsters captured *both* of my children. What kind of father was I to allow this to happen?

Is he moving at all? I asked her as calmly as I could muster. *Put your ear on his chest for me, sweetie. Can you hear anything?*

I heard a clinking of chains as Rinna shifted around and waited the longest seconds of my life for her answer.

He's breathing, and his heart's thumping, she confirmed.

So my son was still alive. That didn't mean someone wasn't about to get their throat ripped out whenever this truck stopped.

I blinked my eyes and tried to figure out which form I was in. My teeth and ears felt canine, but my senses of smell, sight, and hearing were pathetically dulled and human.

I tried to pull my wolf back and go fully human. But he was stuck. For the first time in my life, I could barely feel the predator within me. Despite having the teeth and ears and fur, it almost felt like the wolf side of me was dead.

Again and again, I attempted to transition to either human or wolf, but both sides wouldn't budge. From what I could feel, I was trapped in some in-between form.

Daddy, what's going to happen to us? Rinna's mental voice cracked with fear that no child should ever experience.

I'm not sure, baby, I confessed. *But I'm going to get us out of here. We'll be with the pack again before you know it.*

The vehicle came to a sudden, screeching halt, sending me slamming up against the bars of my cage. I growled through the pain shooting up my arms, hoping my kids didn't get as hurt as I did.

Voices outside made me bare my teeth. I heard English and then another human language I didn't recognize. When the door rolled up, the light nearly blinded me. But I was ready.

With the most fearsome growl I could summon, I lunged forward and snapped my teeth at the pudgy, skittish humans. Even with my human nose, I could smell the fear and disgust on them.

"FUCK!"

One of them stumbled back, dropping whatever was in his hand.

The other recovered quickly, his eyes dark and cold as he produced a long, electric cattle prod.

My heart sank. I wouldn't be able to touch him with that thing.

"Seems you need to learn some training, dog," he sneered in a heavily accented voice.

He jabbed the weapon toward me and the jolt felt like thousands of tiny knives under my skin. I howled and convulsed uncontrollably, but it was nothing compared to the sound of Rinna whimpering and crying.

"Get your ass in here and shut that other mutt up!" the human on me yelled at his companion.

"Please, they're just children! Do whatever you want to me, but don't hurt them." I forced my mouth to speak the words, but my tongue and throat were not human enough. It came out as garbled grunts and barks.

The human gave me one final look of disgust before he jabbed the weapon into my ribs again.

This time, the darkness swallowed me.

I

MELODY

My life didn't truly begin until my eighteenth birthday, when I ran away from home.

Every day before that was just another day in trailer trash purgatory. My morbidly obese mother scamming the government for her disability checks, bringing home equally trashy men who disappeared as soon as she got pregnant again.

And me, barely hanging on in high school to help look after all of my younger half-siblings. To be perfectly honest, I don't think any of us shared a father.

My birthday was the weekend after high school graduation. Never in my life had anything been timed so perfectly.

That morning, I woke up early. The house was quiet for once. It would've almost felt peaceful if it weren't for the piles of food containers, beer cans, toys, and everything else imaginable scattered around. I shouldered my backpack that I packed the night before, went out the front door, closed it behind me, and never looked back.

No one was awake to wish me a happy birthday, but that was okay. This was my present to myself.

I didn't have a plan aside from getting as far away from that hell hole as possible. Still, I wasn't some naïve, lost little lamb. Seeing the type of men my mom brought home made me extra vigilant about the people out in the world. I got enough creepy leers and drunken propositions to be constantly on the lookout.

It wasn't all bad, though. I was finally free. No one yelled at me to clean up or make food or get out of the way. I got some strange looks from people at greasy diners and truck stops, but that was to be expected. A skinny girl with ghostly pale skin, dark hair and brown eyes traveling on her own had to be an unusual sight.

I hitchhiked and panhandled for a good part of my trip, but by the time I made it out of my godforsaken state of Alabama, my meager change had run out and I needed to do something different, and fast.

The one positive memory of my childhood years was visiting a traveling carnival with my family. We scraped enough change together to gain entry, play some carnival games and watch a magic show.

It mesmerized me how the magician's cards appeared and disappeared. He turned silk scarves into doves and pulled a live rabbit out of his hat. My siblings and I were all allowed to gently pet the bunny and, to this day, it was the softest thing I ever touched.

The magician even pulled a coin from behind my ear and let me keep it. I never saw anything like it before. It was large and heavy, like a fifty-cent coin, with a border of silver and inlaid with gold. Instead of some politician's head, two crossed daggers were stamped into the metal.

I always carried it with me, knowing one of Mom's boyfriends would steal it if they saw it. As I got older, I watched YouTube videos and practiced the tricks on making it disappear. Just in case I needed it to.

As I walked away from the only home I'd ever known, I clutched that coin in my fist as if to draw strength from my one happy memory.

So I got out my coin and the rough deck of playing cards I bought from a thrift store and parked my ass at a popular rest stop near the freeway.

It was summer time, so it never got too cold at night. If the sightings of wolves didn't scare me, I'd sleep under the stars every night. With the plethora of families going on camping trips to the mountains, I had a steady influx of customers. Kids would shriek with excitement as I curled my fingers over the coin in my palm, then open them slowly to reveal my empty hand.

Parents at first were wary of the skinny, black-haired girl who clearly lived at the rest stop, but they could soon see I was harmless and still had all my mental faculties. I'd been away from home for two weeks at that point and did my best to regularly wash my clothes and body in the rest stop bathroom. My cleaner-than-typical-homeless appearance seemed to put them at ease. I'd entertain the children for a few minutes and their parents gave me enough tips to buy food from the vending machine.

It wasn't easy. And sometimes, when all the travelers left, I got lonely.

But I was free for the first time in my life. I saw beautiful sunsets over the mountains and watched the stars come out. I'd lay down to sleep on the bench, clutching my coin in my fist with a smile on my face. My life was my own, and I was happy. So of course, it couldn't last long.

I woke up early one morning to the sound of crackling static and crunching footsteps. My eyes cracked open and the sight before me jolted me awake. Fear gripped my chest as I sat up abruptly and began scooting away.

"Easy, easy. It's alright."

The uniformed state trooper raised his hands with open palms as his shiny steel-toed boots approached me slowly. I looked like a distorted doll in the mirrored reflection of his sunglasses. My eyes darted to the holstered gun at his hip and then to the squad car parked behind him.

"It's alright, sweetheart," he drawled. "No one's gonna hurt ya."

Did I believe him? Hell no. But while my heart crashed against my ribs, my legs couldn't seem to move.

He removed his sunglasses to peer at me with curious blue eyes. His Tom Selleck mustache twitched as he took me in, studying me.

"You been living out here a while?"

I didn't answer. Clearly, he already knew.

"How old are ya, sweetheart?"

Again, I answered with defiant silence.

"Got any family nearby?" he went on. "I bet your parents are worried about you."

I let out a dark huff of laughter. Yes, Mom would definitely be worried about her live-in maid and babysitter. How else would she be able to watch TV and fuck drunk losers all day?

"I'm eighteen," I said. "My parents don't need to know where I am."

"Ah, she does speak." His mustache twitched with a hint of a smile. "Well, that makes my job easier. Must've been a rough life to start living at a rest stop, huh?"

"I haven't committed any crimes," I snapped, although I had no idea if that was true. "If you need me to leave here, I'll go."

He crossed his arms, still studying me carefully, as if I was a puzzle he was trying to decipher.

"What're your plans for the winter?" he asked. "What are you going to do about shelter?"

I shrugged. "Head down to Florida, maybe. I haven't thought that far ahead yet."

"Obviously," he scoffed.

I bristled with annoyance. When was this cop going to stop wasting my time?

"Look, I'll make a deal with ya," he said. "I'll buy you some breakfast and give you a ride over to the next town. They have good services in place for the homeless."

My stomach chose that moment to betray me and let out an echoing growl. After living off vending machine food for a week, a real cooked meal sounded absolutely heavenly. Some hash browns, pancakes, fresh fruit, maybe even an omelet with some bacon. And a cup of fresh, piping hot coffee. And doughnuts.

The cop's smile grew wider as he watched my food fantasies dance in my head. That small gesture brought me back to reality. If I knew anything, it was that men never offered anything unless they wanted something in return.

"And what do you expect to get out of this?" I asked, trying to keep a tough edge to my voice.

He shook his head. "Just the peace of mind of knowing a young lady who reminds me of my daughter will be safe."

The curiosity in his gaze softened and for the first time, I saw warmth and protectiveness that I never saw growing up. The parental affection that I read about in books and heard rumors of, but never experienced for myself. I swore it was a myth, some kind of fairy tale.

"What's your name, sweetheart?" he asked gently.

I hesitated, but decided to answer truthfully.

"Melody."

"Nice to meet you, Melody. I'm Rick."

Rick began to turn back toward the parking lot, but kept his eyes focused on me.

"The car is warm if you want to follow me. It'll be a short ride into town. The sooner we go, the sooner we can get food in your belly and a proper bed for you to sleep on. How does that sound, Melody?"

"You can call me Mel," I said in a small voice, slowly lowering my feet from the bench to the ground.

Rick smiled affectionately. "Alright then, Mel. We'll go whenever you're ready."

He turned and began walking back to his squad car, talking in some police code into the radio clipped to his shirt.

I put both feet on the floor and considered running into the woods. He was an older guy and probably wouldn't be able to catch me. But then where would I go? He probably checked out this rest stop regularly. And while small towns dotted this stretch of highway into the mountains, I had no map or phone. I could be lost for days before finding food or safe water to drink.

It dawned on me that this cop knew that. He knew I could run off, and he'd never catch me. He never came closer than ten feet to me. He'd never even have the opportunity to put handcuffs on me if he really wanted to force me anywhere.

He gave me space, and from that I realized he was giving me a choice. Death or doughnuts? It wasn't a hard decision to make.

So I stood from my bench and touched the coin in my pocket. I picked up my bag and blanket, and hesitantly shuffled toward the police officer, patiently waiting in his car. He reached across to open the passenger door for me and I sank into the seat like a warm cocoon.

We drove in relative silence, which I was grateful for. I didn't want to answer questions.

"What kinda breakfast you in the mood for, Mel?" he asked.

"Um, anything." My stomach agreed.

"Figured you wouldn't be picky," he chuckled.

The dense forest began clearing out as we passed a sign that said "Welcome to Drowningville!"

Really? I thought. I couldn't think of a town name that sounded any less welcoming.

We stopped at a drive-thru and I inhaled my breakfast the moment Rick passed the paper bag to me.

"Slow down, Mel. You'll get sick," he warned.

Yeah, that wasn't happening. It smelled too good and tasted like greasy, piping-hot heaven.

As we drove through town and I sat back to digest my food, I noticed that Drowningville looked like a carbon copy of my hometown, Waterford. Potholes in the streets, run-down trailer parks, and graffiti on buildings galore. A tightening in my chest gripped me and I started to regret leaving my rest stop sanctuary. What was the point of returning to civilization if I was just going back to fighting for survival in another shithole town all over again?

"Here we are," Rick said.

We pulled up in front of a large, rundown house, and my heart sank. How many people just like my mother and her boyfriends would be in there?

"Now listen, Mel," Rick said, turning to me. "You're so young. You still have a long, full life ahead of you. If you take advantage of their resources and accept help, you'll be just fine."

But I barely paid attention to him. My eyes drifted over his shoulder to look at the sign on the fence across the street.

It said, "TRAVELING CARNIVAL IN TOWN FOR ONE WEEK ONLY!"

❧ 2 ❧

MELODY

"So what special talents do you have?" Mr. Fisher, the carnival manager, leered at me, not bothering to hide that he was ogling at my breasts. "What unique abilities can you add to my carnival?"

I cleared my throat and pulled my tank top up as best I could. I couldn't help the fact that it was a typical Mississippi summer, hot and muggy as the devil's armpit, nor that my top was tiny and threadbare. I had it since sophomore year and never could afford to buy more clothes since then. This stuffy, worn-down trailer with no fan or air conditioning definitely didn't help.

Still, I plastered what I hoped was a friendly smile on my face and pulled out my lucky coin.

"I can do simple magic tricks." I demonstrated by closing my fist around the coin and slowly opening my fingers to show him my empty hand. "And I'm a fast learner, so I'd be happy to shadow senior magicians and pick up more tricks by watching them."

"Ah, you have good enthusiasm dear, but you see," he leaned across the cheap plywood desk, shamelessly never removing his eyes from my chest, "magicians will never reveal their tricks. A true magician is self-taught. I'm proud to say that everyone in my carnival put in the work themselves without shadowing anyone. And I prefer to keep it that way." He leaned back, lacing his fingers together on his massive belly. "Anything else?"

I huffed in annoyance, feeling my cheeks grow warm. "Well, I can read tarot cards, too. I can look into a crystal ball and pretend I see the future. Basically, I can put on a great act."

He didn't seem convinced. My heart sank as he pursed his lips in thought while tapping a pencil on his desk.

"I already have talented people in those jobs, Miss. People that have been perfecting their acts for years. Why should I just take in a pretty girl off the street?"

"I can bring something new to the table," I insisted. "Seriously, I can improvise on the fly and put my own spin on things. I promise I can bring in lots of money for you."

He gave a smile that I couldn't read. It looked like an odd mixture of patronizing, predatory, and pitying.

"Do you *really* want to work at a carnival?" he asked.

"Yes!" I answered without hesitation.

He raised one thick, bushy eyebrow in amusement. "Why?"

I thought for a moment, wondering how much of my shitty life I should tell him. Distantly, I remembered a class in school about how to act during a job interview. The teacher said not to divulge overly personal information or something like that. I couldn't remember, but I was pretty sure I was about to break that rule.

"Because the carnival was the only glimpse of happiness during my childhood," I admitted. "The music, the games, the shows. It devastated me when all the fun and mystery and wonder came to an end. I didn't understand that it would be temporary. I wanted to live there and be happy forever."

I sat back, deflated and already sure that I bombed this interview. So why stop there? "And I want to give the attendees a reason to laugh and smile, just in case they came from the same kind of crappy life as me."

Mr. Fisher sighed and ran a hand through his thinning hair. "Look kid, I can tell you're on hard times right now and need a job. But working the carnival isn't an easy job. Every one of my performers here has very specialized skills. It takes years and years of practice to perfect these skills. You don't just wake up one day and realize you can juggle or ride a unicycle, you know?"

I nodded, lowering my eyes to my lap.

"Furthermore, it's a temporary job," he continued. "We travel for a while during summer and early fall and that's it, really. A kid like you needs stability. Something to build a foundation on so you can have a good life, you know?"

I nodded my agreement while picking at the dirt under my fingernails, wondering when he'd finish so I could leave.

"A pretty little thing like you wouldn't fit in with this freak show anyway," he laughed. "You oughta get an education, a regular job and settle down with a nice guy working in finance or some shit. Have his babies and a house with a white picket fence and all that."

I couldn't help but snort out a laugh at that. The notion of *me*, trailer park trash to a T, raising kids in the suburbs with some bland, boring guy couldn't be more ridiculous. All I wanted to do was not end up pregnant by some deadbeat drunk like my mom and older sister.

So far, I was doing pretty well for myself in that regard and had no intention of stopping. Aside from me, no woman in my immediate family made it to eighteen without getting knocked up.

"That's kind of you, sir, but I don't think that's in the cards for me," I said, holding back my giggles.

He looked taken aback. "Why the hell not? You're young and beautiful with your life ahead of you!"

"Sir, if you're not going to give me a chance at the carnival," I said, rising to unstick my sweaty thighs from my folding chair. "Then I'm heading to the strip club up the street because that's my best option right now."

His pupils dilated, and I shuddered to know what he was picturing in his mind.

"You'd make a hell of a lot more money there," he pointed out.

"Yeah, maybe," I agreed. "But I wouldn't enjoy it as much. Who knows?" I chuckled, moving toward the door. "If I learn some special moves as a stripper, I might ask you again for a job as a contortionist next year." My eyes bore into his. "That's how much I love the carnival.

I don't care how much it pays." I turned toward the flimsy plywood door of the trailer. "Thanks a lot for your time, Mr. Fisher."

My hand just turned the knob when he called out, "Melody, wait."

I paused, turning back toward him. "Yes?"

He huffed out a heavy breath before speaking. "If you're willing to be a team player, and work various menial jobs behind the scenes, I might be able to find a position for you."

"Really?" I faced him directly, my eyes daring to widen with hope.

"You won't be part of any acts, at least not the main part," he said. "But if you're willing to smile and dress a little sexy, I can make you a stage assistant. On slow nights maybe you can pour drinks at the booze tent, whatever we can find for you."

I ran forward and wrapped my arms around the large, sweaty man's neck in a bear hug. He reeled back, startled, before tentatively patting my back with his meaty hands.

"Oh, thank you so much, Mr. Fisher!" I squealed. "This is all I wanted, just a chance to show what I can do!"

"I want to reiterate that it's not easy work," he warned when I untangled myself from him. He tried to look stern, but I could see the smile playing at his lips and his face flushed a deep red. "You'll probably be driven harder than the performers. You're starting at the bottom of the ladder essentially, and if you want to climb up, expect to do it kicking and clawing and maybe throwing a few elbows."

"Oh, I'm no stranger to hard work," I said, bobbing my head in a nod. "Honestly, I'm dying to get started! When do you want me to come in?"

He flashed a toothy grin at me. "How about tonight?"

3

MELODY

I turned over rocks with my worn-out shoes as I waited outside the trailer for Mr. Fisher. After my interview, he told me to come back in four hours and meet him here. He'd "find a place to fit me in," as he put it.

I brought up my concern about proper attire or equipment I'd need. All I had were the spare change of clothes in my backpack, my lucky coin, and a deck of worn-out playing cards. He told me not to worry, that whatever position I had would come with a uniform and they'd tailor it to my size.

Another minute passed, and I sighed, growing more anxious by the minute. Should I try knocking on the door again? Or maybe a better question was, should I even be here?

Most eighteen-year-olds were applying to colleges, working part-time jobs in fast food and retail. Those kids were setting the tracks down for their life plans. But I imagined most of those kids didn't have to worry about their mom's endless string of boyfriends wandering drunkenly into their bedroom at night. The same bedroom I shared with my younger siblings, who cried in absolute terror at the huge, grunting men stumbling around our trailer at all hours of the night.

No, I didn't dream of a college experience, joining a sorority, or even having a boyfriend. The only thing that ever put a smile on my face was the carnival, so that was the only dream I chased.

With a deep breath, I raised my first to rap on the door again just as it swung open.

"Ah, Melody! Right on time," Mr. Fisher greeted with his signature toothy grin. "Come in, come in."

Yes, I had been on time. He made me wait an additional fifteen minutes.

I followed him into the dimly lit trailer and the smell of stale cigarettes and booze assaulted my nostrils. Growing up how I did, I got used to that smell, but that brief week in the fresh mountain air had spoiled me. I missed my temporary rest-stop home in that moment but remembered I wanted this job, and this life.

A busty middle-aged woman with thick blonde hair sat in a creaky, rolling office chair. Wearing nothing but stockings with a garter belt, underwear, and a bra that just barely contained her massive breasts, she reminded me of a classier version of my mother. The woman inspected me with dark, hooded eyes through the smoke clouds she blew.

"Damn, Peter," she said in a crackling smoker's voice. "I knew you liked 'em young, but this is a new leap even for you."

"I'm eighteen," I piped up. "I do have a valid ID."

The woman let out a laugh that sounded like crumbling paper.

"We ain't worried about your ID, sweetheart," she croaked. "But I ain't convinced your young eyes won't fall out your damn head when you see what goes on 'round here."

"I might be young, but I've seen plenty of things that no girl my age should see," I shot back, crossing my arms. "Trust me, I ain't no damn princess."

My defensiveness brought out my own redneck twang that I fought hard to keep at bay. Normally, I hated sounding like white trash, but with this woman, it might actually give me some credit.

She took a hard drag on her cigarette and smirked. "Ever seen two drunk dwarves fuckin' behind the tents?"

Heat rose in my cheeks, but I kept my expression bitchy. "Naw.

Seen two drunk-ass, coked out junkies fuck a hole through the carpet, though."

That got a thunderous, booming laugh from her and a nervous giggle and blush from Mr. Fisher. Something told me while he held the manager title, this woman was the one who really ran the show.

"You just might be alright, girly." She flashed a yellowed, gap-toothed grin that seemed approving. "What's your name?"

"Melody. I go by Mel."

"Nah-uh." She flicked an orange plastic lighter and lit another cigarette. "You'll be introduced as Melody. It's sexy like a stripper name. The crowd'll love it."

"Uh." I started to protest, but held my tongue. Hopefully she didn't mean I would *actually* be stripping. "Okay. So this means you're hiring me, Mrs., uh?"

"Madame," she corrected me with a wink. "Madame Tetons." She leaned forward and shimmied her shoulders back and forth, making her *tetons* sway hypnotically behind her tiny bra. A guffaw of laughter was her reaction to my reddening face, which also burned uncomfortably. Maybe I was a little unaccustomed to carnival life, but that didn't mean I still couldn't fit in.

"And sure, honey. You're hired for as long as your pretty face can handle being around this freak show." Madame Tetons grinned. "You'll get cash at the end of the night. Makes no difference to me whether or not you're here the next day."

"I'll keep coming back to work," I insisted. "Really, I'm responsible. I wouldn't just walk away from a job like that."

"We'll see, sugar," she chuckled, stubbing out her cigarette in a glass ashtray overflowing with butts. "Let's get ya fixed up then."

She stood abruptly and headed for the trailer door, shoving it open so hard it bounced off the outside wall. I looked over at Mr. Fisher who'd remained nearly silent during this whole meeting. He shrugged and motioned for me to follow Madame Tetons out the door.

"I got a show to run, sweet cheeks! You comin' or not?" she hollered from outside.

I hurriedly followed her fast, but slightly wobbly gait. Her walk reminded me of Jack Sparrow. She led me to a large circus tent and slapped back the flap, much like she did to the trailer door. I followed her in to find a group of women in various states of undress. Like Madame Tetons, some wore stockings and garter belts. Others wore corsets, tutus, and impossibly high heels.

Oversized trunks and suitcases made for temporary chairs and sofas. A pair of women sat on an antique-looking wooden trunk sharing a bottle of liquor as they giggled with their heads bowed. Portable closets on rusty wheels were bursting with various costumey clothing items. A few vanities and full-length mirrors completed the tent furnishings.

"Cherry!" Madame Tetons barked at a young woman with flaming box-dyed red hair. "This is Melody. Find her something to wear. She's Syko's dartboard tonight."

While Cherry inspected me from head to toe as if appraising me, I turned to Madame Tetons, who was already quickly exiting the tent.

"Wait!" I called after her, sticking my head out of the tent. "What does that mean, I'm a *dartboard?*"

"What's it sound like?" she cackled as she Jack Sparrowed away.

"Don't worry, hun," Cherry drawled from behind me. "Syk's a good shot. Best knife thrower on this side of the Mississippi. He won't cut ya unless he's hittin' the bottle too hard." I turned back to face her, my face white as a ghost, to find her showing me a small scar on the side of her hip. "He gave me a good nick when I dartboarded for him last summer. He was so fuckin' hammered, he don't even remember doing the show." She ran her tongue across her teeth and grinned. "He kissed it all better, though." Her expression turned venomous as she lifted her chin and gave me her best bitch stare. "And if you even look at him too long, I'll cut yer damn neck myself."

I raised my hands in a *yeah, whatever* motion. Alcoholic men were a dime a dozen, and I'd be happy to never see one again.

"Look, I just wanna get through the night in one piece so I can get my cash at the end," I told her.

Cherry nodded as if she approved of that answer and led me away from the tent flap to a rolling wardrobe stuffed with clothes and acces-sories. I squared my shoulders and took deep breaths as I followed her. Having knives thrown at me wasn't my idea of a good time, but if this

Syko guy was that good, hopefully I'd come out injury-free and be assigned a different job tomorrow night.

"What's yer tit size?" Cherry asked brusquely as she looked at me up and down.

"Um, 34B," I mumbled, knowing I was blushing. Everyone else here seemed to at least have a C cup, if not DD. I tried not to stare, but they all filled out their corsets and push-up bras perfectly. I never filled out to that curvaceous, well-fed body type that seemed to send men's tongues wagging. My mom ate and drank her welfare check the moment she got it, and the bulk of whatever little we had left went to my siblings.

Not that I *wanted* a bunch of idiot redneck men chasing after me, but I knew lots of eyes would be on me tonight. I wanted to make a good impression.

Cherry rifled through the rack of clothing as I stood there, pausing only to look at me briefly before rifling some more.

"Try this on," she said, picking out a black corset that looked entirely too small, even for my slender frame.

Still, I turned toward the nearest full-length mirror and removed my shirt and bra so she could help me into it. After a few moments of lacing and sucking in, I regretted that decision.

"It doesn't fit," I wheezed as Cherry continued tugging on the stings.

"Yeah, it does. You just need to suck it in more."

"I can't... anymore."

She finally stopped tugging as I struggled to breathe, not only with how tight she laced it but now that my breasts were shoved up into my face.

"It's a new one so you'll break it in if you stick around." She gave me a not-so-subtle side eye as she went back to rummaging through clothes.

After another twenty minutes or so, the leather corset did seem to give more room for my lungs to expand. In that time, Cherry also found me stockings, shoes, sheer gloves, a distressed tulle skirt, an elaborate choker necklace that brought even more attention to my chest and at her insistence, a goddamn top hat.

"Come on. Make up next," she said, dragging me to a nearby vanity and plopping me down.

I cringed at the amount of purple and glitter she smeared on my lips and eyelids, feeling certain that she was doing me in clown makeup. Along with my ridiculous outfit, people would be eager to throw pies at me after the knives.

Remember, you wanted this, I told myself. Maybe not this job tonight, but this life. You want to entertain and bring smiles. This is worlds better than what you ran from. And tonight, the cash you earn is going to be all yours. No one's gonna steal it for booze.

"There," Cherry said, stepping back to look at me. "Take a look but I ain't changing shit."

Bracing myself, I turned to the mirror and my purple lips fell open at what I saw.

I looked hot. Like, *damn* hot.

Yes, it was a ton of makeup and the colors were bright and dramatic, but it was perfect for being onstage at a carnival. My eyebrows were full and arched seductively. The false eyelashes fluttered like butterfly wings. And the pink apples of my cheeks glittered when I smiled.

"Uh, wow. Thanks, Cherry," I said sincerely. "It looks good. You're really talented."

She shrugged nonchalantly, but I could tell the compliment pleased her.

"Use the bobby pins to keep the hat on your head. Don't wanna lose it when you go upside down."

"Upside down?" I blinked at her.

"Damn girl," she giggled. "You really have no idea what you're in for."

4

MELODY

"Come on, let's head to Syko's tent." Cherry grabbed my wrist and pulled me along while I teetered on my sky-high heels. "It ain't rocket science, but you'll wanna rehearse the act. 'Specially since you have no idea what the fuck you're getting into."

"Uh, yeah. Makes sense." I dutifully followed her out of the tent and into the late afternoon heat.

Looking around, I realized the carnival was in full swing right at that moment. The distant sounds of laughter and music filled my senses. I could even smell the deep fried food and funnel cake. In the distance, the Ferris wheel turned slowly like the orbit of a distant planet.

Cherry and I walked through a cluster of tents and trailers on one side of the carnival, a good hundred feet or so from where families played games and ate snow cones. A string of brightly colored flags tied to two trees separated the trailers and tents from the main carnival area. This had to be where all the staff and performers stayed out of the public eye when off duty.

We didn't walk far, but my skin was already covered in a thin sheen of sweat and my stiletto heels sank into the mud. I could only pray that my caked-on makeup wouldn't start sliding off my face. Cicadas sang their song, and the air was thick with moisture each time I took a breath. Fuck, I hated the south in the summer.

Cherry approached one of the large pavilions and slapped open the flap, not bothering to hold it for me as I followed her in.

"I gotcher dartboard, baby." Her voice suddenly took on a higher pitch as she walked up to a man wearing a wifebeater tank top and pinstriped pants, which I assumed was the lower half of his uniform.

"Yeah? Let's see who's savin' my show," he drawled, taking a gratuitous grab of her ass as she wrapped her arms around his neck. But his eyes remained on me and they sent a shiver along my spine despite the sweltering heat.

This guy instantly gave me the creeps. He looked to be in his late forties, with skinny arms and a soft belly. Tufts of salt and pepper chest hair poked out from the neck of his wife-beater. His flushed face with broken blood vessels confirmed my dread that this guy was indeed an alcoholic.

And he was going to be throwing knives at me.

"Damn, she's a young one." His eyes crawled over me like inspecting a piece of meat. "What's yer name, sweetheart?"

"Melody," I answered with a smile in an attempt to hide my discomfort.

"Well, keep smilin' like that, miss Melody, and we're gonna get along just fine," he grinned, revealing yellow teeth. "I'm Syko. Drink?" He waved a hand toward a rolling cart with various bottles of liquor.

"No thanks," I said, my smile tightening.

"You sure? It'll calm your nerves." He winked. "Not that you got anythin' to be nervous about."

"I'm good, thanks. And I'm not that nervous, mainly just excited to put on a good show!" I squeaked out, my cheeks already hurting from my smile.

"I like your spirit, Melody." His tone and creepy stare indicated he liked my tits in this corset a lot more. "Maybe you could teach ol' Stilts a thing or two about a positive attitude. Eh, Stilts?"

Laughing, Syko turned to a man I hadn't even noticed in the tent. He appeared to be taking a nap on the floor, with his head and upper back propped up against a large backpack and a tattered blanket thrown over his legs.

Damn, I thought. If I wanted anyone to appreciate my tits in this outfit, it would be him. A sun-kissed tan and lean muscle covered his chest and arms. His dark brown hair was tousled as if he ran his fingers through it, his slightly pursed lips looked so kissable as he slept. A shadow of stubble peppered coated his angular jaw. If he heard Syko's comment, he gave no indication.

The creepy man marched over and nudged him with his foot, clearly displeased at being ignored.

Stilts cocked open one forest green eye and grunted out his annoyance.

"The fuck you want, Syk?" he grumbled, his voice vibrating with a low, sexy thunder.

"We have a new girl for the dartboard," Syko answered, gesturing toward me.

The sleepy green eye scanned the room but barely paused on me. "Is it show time?"

"No, I just thought we'd--"

"Don't fuckin' wake me up until it's show time or I'll break your fuckin' jaw." Stilts grabbed a beanie and pulled it down over his head and eyes, effectively ending the conversation.

I stifled a giggle. Like the pompous ass he was, Syko tried to show me off like a new prized possession, and this guy didn't give an iota of a fuck. I liked that he didn't join in appraising my body like at a meat market, although I wouldn't mind if he noticed me a little more.

"Fuck this guy." Syko waved at him dismissively. "Let's rehearse the act just me and you, sweetheart."

The sound of a throat clearing reminded both of us that Cherry was still in the tent. Syko gave her a dismissive wave too.

"Go on, girlie. I'm sure you got somewhere to be."

Her face fell and I couldn't help but feel bad for her, no matter how much of a creepy scumbag Syko was.

"I'll see ya later, right, baby?" she asked hopefully.

"Yeah, yeah. At the booze tent when the show's over. Now getcher ass out. I got work to do."

She shot me a death glare before slapping the tent flap and storming outside. My heart sank at seeing her go. I had a feeling I wouldn't make many friends in this business, but that was okay. I'd made it to eighteen years without any friends and learned to live with it.

"Come on, darlin'." Syko grabbed my hand and yanked me so hard, I nearly toppled over in my heels.

He dragged me out the back door of the tent and to a clearing where other carnival performers seemed to be practicing their acts. Two people chatted casually while juggling bowling pins and riding unicycles. A group of acrobats practiced a beautiful, flowing routine on a set of tables and makeshift trapeze hung between two branches of a tree. I covered my mouth to hold in my scream when a man flawlessly dropped a dagger down his throat and spun the handle around.

"Here we are, darlin'," Syko cooed at me. Pet names were common in the south but damn, I wished he'd stop.

My eyes fell upon what was obviously a human-sized dartboard. A round piece of wood just slightly taller than me, with slender black and white triangles pointing toward a red bull's eye in the center. Nicks, dents, and chipped paint showed just how often this board had been used. There didn't seem to be any blood on it, thankfully.

"First part of the act," Syko explained, standing too close to me, "is you just standing pretty there in front of the board while I throw. Think you can handle that?"

"Sounds easy enough." I forced a smile.

He delivered an unexpected slap to my ass, which made me jump with a small shriek.

"Then git on over there so I can warm up, darlin'." He pulled a silver flask from his pants pocket and took a long pull while I hurried away, trying to not sink into any muddy spots with my heels.

Grateful to be away from him, yet increasingly dreading the idea of this drunken lowlife throwing knives at me, I forced myself to stand in front of the dartboard. The bulls-eye met the center of my back, while the top of my head just barely grazed the top edge of the board. Only my stupid top hat gave me any extra height.

"Strike a pose and smile, honey." Syko produced a beautiful

lacquered case and opened it, revealing four eight-inch-long stainless steel blades polished to a high shine.

Fuck! He was practicing with *real* knives? In my naivete, I'd assumed he'd use dull or dummy knives at least.

But still I flashed a smile, placed my hands at my waist, and cocked my hip to the side. My heart thrummed with lightning speed despite the stillness in my limbs.

Syko made a low, throaty sound that I tried to ignore. "That's perfect, babe. Now don't move a muscle."

I was so consumed by fear and anxiety, I couldn't have moved if I tried.

He turned and walked about 25 feet away from me, about the length of a stage. His next movement was so fast and fluid, I didn't realize he threw the knife until I heard the *thunk* of that steel blade embed into the wood just above my arm.

For a moment, the creepy drunk disappeared and was replaced by a lithe, dancing figure moving with precision. Watching him was mesmerizing. His knife throws were strong and sure, but they flowed seamlessly with his spinning, graceful movements.

By the time all four blades were embedded deep in the wood, my fear—of being stabbed at least—had completely disappeared. I brought my hands together to clap as Syko took a graceful bow.

"That was amazing!" I breathed.

"Thank ya kindly, darlin'." He shot me a saccharine smile. "But you ain't seen nothin' yet."

My heart rate picked up as he came over, standing very close to me again as he removed his blades from the wood and set them in the grass.

"This next part's a doozy," he said, sneaking glances down to my chest. "But you gotta remember to trust me, alright?"

I nodded as fear gripped my stomach in knots again. Why couldn't I just *say* I didn't feel right about this?

"See that little peg there?" He leaned down, brushing the side of my leg as he pointed out a dowel about eight inches long sticking out from the board. "Step on it for me."

I did as he instructed and he pointed out the other one next to my other foot. For balance, I spread my arms wide and gripped the edges of the board, teetering in my ridiculous heels on two flimsy pegs of wood.

"You got the right idea there." Syko looked all too pleased as he pulled strips of silk from his pockets. They looked like those scarves pulled out of hats and sleeves during magic tricks, but I immediately knew that wasn't his intention here.

He knelt at my feet and swiftly tied one scarf around my ankle and then the other. I was secured to the board by him tying through two holes I didn't notice before. When he stood, he was so close that his chest brushed against mine, his foul breath coming out with lusty grunts. I turned my head and closed my eyes, praying for this practice run to be over soon.

"Trust me," he repeated, taking hold of one of my wrists and laying it flat against the board somewhere above my head. He threaded one of the scarves through the holes there, binding my wrist down tight and then the other.

I was tied to the circular dartboard, arms and legs outstretched like the *Vitruvian Man.* Syko stepped back and to the side as if to admire his handiwork.

"How long do I have to stay like this?" I asked, panic creeping into my voice. I couldn't escape now even if I wanted to. Fuck, why didn't I just speak up?

"Not long, honey. Don't worry." He picked up his knives and flashed me that predatory smile as he leaned one hand on the board, in no apparent hurry. "Just one practice run and I'll go slow." He leaned his weight into his hand and I felt my whole body tilt to the side. "Hope you don't get motion sickness."

He pressed down hard, and suddenly the world was spinning.

No, *I* was spinning.

My stomach churned, but not from the feeling of going up, down, and around again. About twenty-five feet away, Syko stood ready with his knives.

Oh, God! Oh God, please! There's no way!

I watched his figure spin, dance, and take aim, all while spinning around and around. My eyes squeezed shut. The fear of everything, plus the dizziness and disorientation from spinning, was too much.

Thunk, thunk, thunk!

I felt the breeze and vibration from the blades sinking into the wood all around me, but no pain.

Thunk! That was four. The last one.

I cracked my eyes open to see Syko jogging toward me, spinning much slower now.

"See, that wasn't so bad!" He was cheerful as he spun me upright and untied my wrists and ankles. My whole world still spun, and I held onto the board for support, my other hand pressed to my racing heart.

"Hey, listen." He grabbed my face roughly and jerked my chin up to look at him. His scowl down at me revealed at least two rotting teeth.

"You can't do that shutting your eyes and looking away shit when we're up on stage, you got it?" he growled. "Keep your eyes open. Keep looking at the crowd. And fucking smile. You gotta at least pretend you're having a good time. Otherwise we get a lower turnout and we all get paid less. You got that?"

I nodded, still trying to fight off the dizziness, but flashed him a smile just to show that I understood.

"Got it!" I chirped cheerfully.

He looked pleased again, finally letting go of my face. "Good." My jaw throbbed from where he grabbed me and I wondered if I'd have to reapply makeup.

"Show starts in an hour," he said, looking out at the sun setting behind the trees. "Families'll take their damn brats home and once night falls, the freaks'll come out to play."

He slapped my ass again, making me jump, but also too shocked to protest.

"Go on and get touched up, baby," he grinned, heading off for his own tent. "Almost showtime."

MELODY

I found my way back to the dressing tent and reapplied my makeup. After Syko kicked her out of the tent, Cherry seemed dead set on avoiding me. With a sigh, I shut my eyes and quickly spritzed my face with the setting spray. Would it do any good to explain I didn't *want* his creepy attention? Probably not.

Reaching into my backpack stuffed with my street clothes, I felt around until my lucky coin pressed into my palm and inserted it down the front of my corset. Who knew if it was worth anything of real value, but it was the only sentimental object I owned. And right then, I needed any luck I could squeeze out of it.

"Hey, new girl," Cherry snapped from across the tent. Apparently, she had forgotten my name already. "Show time. We gather at the side of the stage."

I hurried over, trying to keep from toppling in my heels. "When do I go on? I don't know when my act is."

"You go on second," she told me flatly, looking straight ahead with her arms crossed. "First the ringmaster announces, then it's Stilts, then you guys. Syk will call you out when it's your time."

"Thanks," I said sincerely.

She merely grunted, and I withered a little. Still, I followed her to the main stage at the far end of the carnival. The setting sun finally cooled off the temperatures a bit, though not by much. In the main carnival area across the trailers, tents, and gates separating us, voices chattered with excitement.

Already the feeling was different from earlier in the day. Rather than families playing games and eating corn dogs with their children, the evening patrons were almost entirely adults. They talked excitedly, but in low whispers as if this was some secret adventure.

Cherry and I joined the throng of performers and assistants gathered around the side and back of the main stage. I recognized a few of the acrobats and the dagger swallower who practiced earlier. Surely those were the later acts. They'd be far more interesting to watch than a girl get knives thrown at her.

A sudden, loud drumbeat sent my heart feeling like it would crash out of my chest. Claps and cheers erupted from the crowd, sending my pulse into overdrive. It just registered to me right then that I would be getting on stage, performing for an audience. Sure, I'd just be standing around and smiling but that thought did nothing to calm my nerves.

"'Scuse me, ladies!"

A middle-aged man in a top hat just slightly taller than mine jumped down his trailer's steps, straightened the lapels of his red tail-coat, and jogged past us up to the stage on shiny black riding boots.

He strode confidently to the center and the crowd went wild with cheers.

"Ladies and gentlemen, boys and girls!" he bellowed. "Welcome to the opening night of The Voodoo Trail traveling carnival! Prepare to watch in wonder as our performers stun and amaze you! For our entire five-night stay here in Drowningville, each show will be more jaw-dropping, chill-inducing, and death-defying than the last!"

He paused and surveyed the crowd with a wide grin as they cheered and applauded.

"Yes, indeed. We're just getting started folks! We know you'll enjoy yourselves tonight, so make sure you keep coming back until our final night." He dropped his voice and leaned forward, looking across every face with an eerie smile. The crowd hushed to a low murmur, eager to hear what he would say.

"On our last night, we'll reveal a most terrifying, exhilarating, awe-inducing, freak of nature." He removed his top hat and dramatically placed it over his heart. "If you believe in God, my good people, you will *not* want to miss this exhibition. For I can prove to you we have in our possession a true demon from the depths of Hell."

That sent the crowd into a tizzy. It was the South. Of course, God was a huge part of everyone's lives.

"And this is no ordinary demon!" the ringmaster continued, feeding off the crowd's amped up curiosity. "This is one of the most, no, *the* most vile creature I've ever set eyes on! Imagine a beast who stands upright like a man, but with razor-sharp teeth, claws like a bear, glowing yellow eyes, and covered from head to toe in hideous, mangy fur!"

"Show us now!"

"Prove it!"

"Yeah, right! Let's see it!"

The audience began shouting their demands, becoming even more eager as they hung onto his every word. In contrast, all the performers surrounding me looked completely bored. Cherry even yawned.

The ringmaster held up an index finger and waved it from side to side, shaking his head at the same time.

"Now, I know some of you may be thinking this is a hoax or that our captured beast is merely a very hairy man, but I assure you that's not the case! However," he curled his finger back into his fist and the crowd went silent again. "Friday night, you will all see for yourselves, the *Wolf Man*," he said, barely above a whisper.

"But tonight!" he raised his voice again and twirled around theatrically while placing his top hat back on his head. "We have an amazing show to whet your appetites, folks! Bring out the one, the only, Stilts, the acrobatic stilt walker!"

The drums picked up again as he exited the stage in a flourish. Running past me and the rest of the girls, he dashed back to his trailer, where I could only assume his booze, drugs, or prostitute were waiting. Maybe all of the above.

Gasps and cries took my attention back to the stage, and my jaw dropped.

It was the sleeping guy from Syko's tent. He was well over ten feet tall on his stilts and wore an intricate carnival mask, but those forest green eyes pierced me for half a fleeting second. And his act was *amazing*.

He wore long, brightly colored pants for the illusion that he really was freakishly tall. And he moved so fluidly that if it weren't for the stumps of wood at the bottom of his pants, anyone watching could easily believe those were his actual legs. He did handstands, back flips, and tons of gravity-defying moves that looked like a mixture of gymnastics and break dancing. The crowd went wild, forgetting all about the ringmaster's teasing about some freakish Wolf Man, and became just as entranced and mesmerized in Stilts' performance as I was.

The whole time I watched with my mouth hanging open, and briefly wondered why such an amazing act was the opener, and why he didn't have a better stage name than Stilts.

"That was amazing!" I cried, joining in the applause when he finished with a deep bow and headed off the opposite side of the stage from us.

"Yeah, he's good," Cherry agreed. "And a damn fine thing to look at. Too bad he's an asshole." She had produced a small silver flask from somewhere and swayed on her feet a little. Apparently, booze made her a tad friendlier, too.

"Why do you say that?" I asked, not wanting to miss the opportunity to know before she remembered she hated me.

"Psh. You saw how he was in the tent." She waved her hand and rolled her eyes. "He's always like that. To everybody. Just a rude-ass motherfucker."

Yeah, but can you blame him for being rude to a gross pervert like Syko?

I didn't say that out loud.

The crowd started up again as two assistants moved Syko's huge dartboard onto the stage. My stomach jumped into my throat again as I remembered what I would have to do.

The man himself stepped up, wearing a full pinstriped suit with a bowler hat.

"Welcome! Welcome, everyone!" he greeted the crowd jovially while casually flipping a dagger in each hand. "Are you all ready for a hell of a show tonight?"

The crowd answered back with a raucous cheer.

"Mm, he's so charismatic." Cherry was already swooning. I just looked at her like she sprouted an extra head. What on *earth* did she see in that guy?

"Let me tell ya, folks! I am one hell of a knife thrower, but I can't entertain y'all on my own," he said. I swallowed, but the dry lump in my throat would not disappear. "Allow me to introduce you to my beautiful, radiant assistant, Melody!"

He turned and beckoned me with a finger, that grin on his face boisterous and fun to the crowd, but creepy and predatory to me.

Still, I walked out under the bright stage lights on what I hoped were long, confident strides. I plastered a smile on my face and waved to the crowd. Hundreds of eyes stared back at me, cheering and hollering. The men were loudest, their tongues practically wagging at my tits, nearly bursting from my corset.

Syko took my hand and had me do a little twirl, much to the audience's appreciation. My face burned. I would have looked like a tomato if my makeup wasn't so caked on. Everything inside me wanted to run away, to retreat to somewhere dark and quiet. I felt like a piece of livestock up for auction, as if the crowd only saw what parts of me they would enjoy the most.

He led me over to the dartboard, where I did the same pose as during practice. Hips cocked to one side, hands on my hips and a massive smile.

"Melody's about to demonstrate to y'all how we like to warm up," Syko declared, twirling those knives so fast they just looked like flashes of silver light in the corner of my eye.

The whimsical music kicked up, and I remained as still as a statue, focusing on the Ferris wheel in the distance. In the fading daylight, it looked so beautiful and romantic. Inside, I froze with the realization that the magic and beauty of the carnival was all an illusion. The drunk man with the creepy leer across the stage. That was the reality.

Thunk! Thunk! Thunk! Thunk!

Dead silence filled the air for a mere second before the crowd erupted into cheers. Only then did I move, shifting my pose to demonstrate how closely Syko's blades landed without touching me.

The pinstripe-suited man approached me with a look of feigned worry on his face.

"I didn't ruin your outfit, did I, honey?"

"Good as new!" I chirped, looking out across the audience. My cheeks ached from smiling so much.

"Excellent!" Syko took my hand and raised it above our heads. "Give it up for Melody, everybody!"

An even louder cheer erupted and for a split second, I didn't want to hide. A rush of adrenaline filled me. Having sharp objects thrown at me in front of dozens of people gave me a rush, a high unlike anything else. They loved me. They were mesmerized. Maybe this illusion wasn't so bad after all. They came here to be entertained, and that was exactly what they were getting.

"Why don't we," Syko turned to me, suggestively pinning my hand against the board, "turn things up a notch, darlin'?"

"Ooh!" I shimmied my shoulders and winked at the audience, embracing the character I came up here to play. "I like the sound of that!"

He made a satisfied grunting sound, which I ignored. The audience's cheers became lewd, sending out wolf whistles and suggestive hand gestures, which I also chose to ignore. It was all in good fun. I just had to play along.

Syko produced the colorful silk scarves from his pockets with a flourish. "It ain't that kind of magic show, folks!" he bellowed, receiving raucous laughter in return.

He turned to me and I stepped on the wooden pegs sticking out from the dartboard, holding onto the edges for stability. When he came within inches of my face, scarves in hand, a coldness washed over me like being dunked in ice.

The energy in the surrounding air shifted, and I froze. This no longer felt like a harmless, playful game.

Syko pinned both of my wrists against the board and he squeezed hard. Too hard.

Oh shit, oh shit. Oh no.

I tried to wiggle but he wouldn't loosen his hold. Instead, he stepped in closer so his body pinned me to the board. His erection pressing against my lower stomach sent my mind panicking.

Then he smothered my mouth with his own.

❄ 6 ❄

MELODY

He was seriously kissing me in front of everyone! What the fuck? Why?

My mind reeled as I closed my mouth and tried to wriggle away. But he just pried my lips open again with his long, slimy tongue. He had me trapped with nowhere to run.

"Stop squirmin' and at least pretend to like it," he growled in my ear. "Or I'll give you something to bitch about later." To the audience, it probably looked like he was whispering some sweet nothings to me.

I froze like a statue again, still trying to reconcile what the actual fuck was happening.

"Smile. Laugh," he whispered threateningly. "Give them a show, you dumb slut."

Blinking back tears, I forced my facial muscles to pull my lips back into a grin that felt like a painful grimace. All I wanted was for this to be over.

The crowd continued with their suggestive cheers and wolf whistles, obviously immune to my discomfort. I searched their eyes, lingering on the women in the crowd. The wives, girlfriends, and groups of friends together. Surely they could see what just happened? They could at least tell me I wasn't going crazy and imagining things.

But none of them looked back at me. Not one person really saw *me*, but just a prop on stage.

Syko took his time tying the scarves around my wrists and ankles, helping himself to groping me at every opportunity and not even bothering to hide it. While the insides of me crumpled and dried up like pieces of paper eaten by fire, I forced the outside to giggle and smile. To go along with his act with no consequence.

No one watching even seemed to question it. Not the musicians, the assistants, nor the other performers waiting for their cue to go on after us. Everyone just watched and stood around with blank expressions while this gross older man violated me in front of a captive audience.

Every second felt like an hour as we got through the spinning dartboard part of the act. My stomach roiled, and I knew it wasn't from the spinning. I needed to get away from here. Part of me wished one of Syko's knives would land right between my eyes so this nightmare could just end.

He finally untied me without issue. The stage, the eyes, and the Ferris wheel spun around and around in a dizzying circle, but I still plastered a smile on my face and did a little curtsy to thunderous applause. The stage hands swiftly removed the dartboard, and we took our exit.

"Now..."

Syko took hold of my upper arm and started to pull me the moment we were out of sight, but I was already prepared. I yanked my arm away and took off running. I didn't know where or how far to go. I just had to get away.

But on my stupid, ridiculous heels, I didn't make it very far.

I tripped and fell, landing on soft muddy grass and couldn't hold it in any longer. My stomach heaved, and I emptied everything I ate that day onto the grass. Even after I threw everything up, I coughed and dry-heaved as if that would help purge the feeling of Syko's mouth and hands on me. If I could only throw away my body and grow a new one, I would.

Then the tears came. Ugly, wracking sobs of fear, frustration, and embarrassment. I was still on carnival grounds somewhere, looking stupid and pathetic. I was no stranger to gross men, so why couldn't I keep it together? Why'd I run away like a baby? Guys like that were part of everyday life. I had no choice but to learn to deal with them.

I wiped my mouth with a shaking hand and looked down at the muddy, vomity mess of my clothes. A wave of despair brought forth more tears. Why the fuck did I think I could come out here and be a successful bombshell carnival performer? I was homeless Alabama trailer trash. Getting paid to deal with men like Syko was probably the best I'd be able to do.

"Hey."

I jumped, so startled that I landed on my butt again. I'd been so deep in my pity party that I didn't notice anyone walk up to me.

A man walked quickly toward me, his bronzed skin illuminated by all the lights from the rides and game booths. When he got closer, I saw dark green eyes, a furrowed brow, and a serious, unsmiling face.

Stilts. The amazing stilt-walking acrobat who was an asshole to everyone. He looked angry, but I was too weak to even try crawling away from him.

"Have some water."

My eyes followed the length of his arm to the sealed water bottle he held out to me.

I accepted it with a weak, shaky hand. "Thanks."

He nodded and looked away. I suddenly felt drenched in shame. Probably the most attractive man I'd ever seen in real life, and not only because he told Syko where to shove it, was looking at me sitting in the mud next to my vomit. I wanted to sink into the ground and never see the light of day again.

"You can shower and clean up in that trailer there." He pointed to a cluster of RVs. I recognized the one I first met with Mr. Fisher and Madame Tetons earlier in the day. So I was close to the main entrance.

"Thanks... again," I said weakly. The confusion piled onto my burning embarrassment and shame. Why was this guy helping me? Did he see me run off and come after me? Or did he just happen to find poor little me puking my guts out?

He cleared his throat awkwardly, as if he'd rather be anywhere else. "Are you hurt? Do you need help getting up?"

"Um, no. I think I'm okay."

He nodded again and promptly walked off, leaving me there blinking. The whole interaction happened so quickly, I wondered for a moment if it really happened.

I twisted open the water bottle and took a few small sips. My throat felt raw as sandpaper, but the water was cool and refreshing. Feeling a tiny bit better, I pulled off my shoes and climbed shakily to my feet. Careful not to step in my vomit or any other mysterious substance on the grass, I walked barefoot to the trailer he pointed to.

A light was on inside, and I hesitated before turning the doorknob. Who did this trailer belong to?

It was clean and cozy inside, much like a typical RV when going camping. I never went camping, but I saw commercials about it on TV before. A few books and maps filled a bookshelf. Towels, linens, and a few changes of clothes filled another shelf. A pair of metal crutches were wedged between the driver's seat and the shelf. I grabbed a towel and quickly hurried to the small standing shower in the back, feeling like I invaded someone's home.

I tried to shower as quickly as I could while still scrubbing my skin raw, washing off every sensation of Syko touching me. When I finally felt clean, I toweled off and wondered what the hell I was going to do about clothing. No way was I putting that muddy, vomit-covered outfit back on. Nor was I leaving this place wearing just a towel.

With the towel wrapped around me, I located trash bags to throw the soiled outfit in and hesitantly ran my hand along the T-shirts and shorts folded neatly on the shelf.

I'm just going to borrow them for tonight. If I bring them back, it won't be stealing, I thought.

I hastily made my decision, pulling out a soft gray shirt and pair of basketball shorts. Obviously made for a man, they hung like a pair of tents on my skinny frame.

I hoisted the trash bag filled with dirty clothes over my shoulder and made out like a thief in the night. Now that some time had passed and with my head cleared from the shower, I felt a little calmer as I walked to the dressing tent. With the show still going on, no one was around, which I was grateful for.

I dumped the bag in a trash can I walked past, figuring no one would want to bother cleaning the outfit. Quickly entering the tent and locating my backpack, I grabbed it and left again within seconds. With my own worn-out but comfortable shoes on my feet, I left the carnival grounds without looking back.

The homeless shelter was dark and quiet as I crept back to my assigned room I shared with a few other girls. Collapsing on my bunk bed, I only stared at the top bunk for a few seconds before drifting off, utterly exhausted from the day's events.

A few hours later I jolted awake, still on top of my sheets and wearing a stranger's shirt and shorts. With a groan, I flipped over to rummage through my pack for my pajamas. After a minute of fumbling with my zipper, I groaned and gave up. All I wanted to do was sleep for days. I'd be washing and returning these clothes, anyway.

I pulled back the covers and settled myself underneath them. Right before falling asleep again, I lifted the gray cotton T-shirt to my nose and took a small whiff. It smelled...nice. I couldn't place the woodsy, slightly earthy scent, but it was relaxing and comforting. And the shirt felt so nice and soft. For a brief moment, I felt what could only resemble safety and comfort.

I drifted off and slept hard for hours.

MELODY

My heart crashed painfully against my sternum as I stood frozen in front of the trailer door. For some reason, my hand refused to raise up and knock.

I woke up early that morning, reluctantly peeling off the borrowed clothes that embraced me as I slept during the night. After washing them in the sink, they only took an hour to air-dry in the heat. And now, folded in my arms just as neatly as I found them, I was afraid of meeting their true owner.

I was being stupid, I knew that. But what happened with Syko had me afraid of my own shadow. Just walking across the street back to this place had me on edge. This could be nothing or it could be Syko's own trailer, and who knew if he wanted to finish what he started? If he dragged me inside, no one would be able to help me then. The thought sent my nerves into panic mode again.

Still, I couldn't just stand here forever. Nor could I keep the clothes, however soft and comfortable they were.

I raised my fist and knocked.

"GO AWAY!" bellowed the voice from inside.

I jumped at the sudden shout, but quickly recovered.

"Um, I'm just returning your clothes," I called nervously through the door. "I needed to wear something clean after I took a shower. I hope that's okay."

Some rustling and unintelligible words came through. I remained frozen, listening eagerly but still no one came to the door. I was just about to place the clothes on the doorstep and leave when the door burst open.

Deep, forest-green eyes narrowed at me.

"You're back," a familiar, throaty voice said, sounding unamused.

Stilts. Of course, this was his trailer. My face flamed at the embarrassing *duh* moment. Why else would he say I could shower here? Still, the revelation surprised me. With that intense stare and permanent scowl, he didn't seem like the type to keep such a tidy, cozy space.

And his shirt. I slept in it. That meant it smelled like *him*.

"Yeah, just to return these." I thrust my arms full of clothing out toward his chest, which I just then realized was bare and *holy shit*.

His biceps were easily as big as my thighs, maybe even bigger. Those arms and shoulders looked like they could crush a man's head, not to mention that chest and abs which looked carved from bronze itself. Of course, he had to be strong and athletic to do his performing, but I didn't expect him to be built like that. A faded tattoo was inked on the left side of his chest, the symbol familiar to me, but I couldn't quite place it. An eagle sitting on top of a globe with an anchor behind it.

He looked at the pile of clothes in my hands and cocked an eyebrow, like they were the last thing he wanted to touch.

"I washed them," I said. He didn't need to know that I slept in them. "Thanks again for letting me use your shower."

"Thanks for not being a thief," he mumbled.

Before I could react, he yanked the clothes from my hands, withdrew back inside, and slammed the door shut.

"You're fuckin' welcome," I mumbled, shaking my head as I descended the rickety stairs.

"Ah, miss Melody!"

I looked to see Mr. Fisher hurrying down the steps of his own trailer.

"Hi, Mr. Fisher," I greeted with a tight smile. Did he know what happened last night?

"Madame Tetons and I couldn't find you after the show last night," he said. "I wanted to make sure you got paid for your work." He produced a plain white envelope that was nearly an inch thick, and my eyes widened. Even if that was stuffed with singles, I didn't expect to make nearly that much.

"Thanks," I said, taking the envelope and tucking it under my arm.

"We had a record turnout last night!" he exclaimed excitedly. "It might've been the Wolf Man hype, but I heard your show got a little wild and steamy." He winked and bile rose in my throat.

"Uh, yeah." I forced out a laugh. "It was... *fun.*"

"Well, I'm sorry to say you won't be working with Syko tonight," he said. "The burlesque show is the focus tonight. We need a rowdy, tipsy crowd. You'll be helping the bartenders in the booze tent." He must have noticed my hesitation and gave me a long look. "You *were* planning on working again tonight, right?"

I opened my mouth to say no.

I didn't want to come within a hundred feet of Syko again. And if everyone else had no issues with encouraging his disgusting display, then he definitely wasn't the only one who would do it. I ran away from home to free myself from monsters, not to run right back into their den.

But my fingertips squeezed the envelope of cash, gauging the thickness of it. No matter what, I would need more. This envelope would get thinner and thinner until it ran out. I needed more, lots more money if I was going to get by.

I didn't even have a goal or a plan, I just wanted to make it to the next day. I'd have to keep working and keep dealing with men like Syko because they were everywhere. If I could hide behind a bar, that would probably be the best work day I could hope for.

So I smiled and said, "Of course! When do you need me here?"

He told me and directed me to where the booze tent would be set up. I thanked him and began walking off the carnival grounds again, but not before I saw a curtain move in Stilts' trailer window in the corner of my eye.

I went to the thrift store down the street and spent most of my money on new clothes. The last of my money I splurged on a huge breakfast at McDonald's and a prepaid cell phone. Not that I had anyone to call, but it might come in handy if I wanted to get any other jobs.

It wasn't until I was back at the shelter, relaxing on my bed and playing a game on my new phone, that I thought of my lucky coin.

"Fuck!" I sat up like a lightning bolt hit me and began tearing through all my belongings. "No, no, no..."

I dumped everything I owned out on my bed and rummaged through it five times over. Then I looked underneath the bed and began crawling on the floor. I patted myself down, even looking in my bra and underwear. Nothing.

"Goddamn it!" I threw myself on the bed in frustration and willed myself not to cry.

I couldn't explain why I was so attached to that thing, aside from that it was the only thing ever freely given to me with no strings attached. When I was little, it was magical to me. The magician pulled it out from behind my ear!

As I got older, I knew that was a trick, but it was no less special to me. It was mine and no one else's. I didn't have to share it with my siblings and no one tried to take it from me, which made me treasure it.

Rubbing my forehead, I thought back to when I last had it. I shoved it down my corset before going onstage. With a groan, I rubbed my eyes. I'd forgotten all about it during Syko's show. For all I knew, he could have reached in there and stolen it. Everywhere he touched me, I was just trying to ignore that it was happening.

And if not there, it could have fallen out while I was running. Or when I fell.

I had to face it. The only thing I owned with any sentimental value was gone.

I sighed and flipped violently over onto my stomach. It didn't seem to matter if I was back home or out in the real world. Life was shitty at every turn.

❈ *8* ❈

MELODY

"How old are ya, sweet thing?"

"Eighteen," I replied tersely.

I was getting a little tired of everyone asking for my age but thankfully Higgins, the booze tent boss or BTB as he was called, didn't look at me with the same creepy leer as Syko. Instead, he seemed disgruntled, which was perfectly fine with me.

"I ain't lookin' to get my goddamn liquor license taken away again," he snarled. "So you ain't servin' nobody til you're twenty-one, girlie. You can clean glasses and restock. Don't worry, you'll still get cash tips."

"Sounds great! Where do I start?"

His gray caterpillar eyebrows raised in amusement but I ,was being completely serious. I was great at cleaning up alcohol, I'd b.en doing it since I could reach Mom's kitchen sink on my little footstool. And not serving meant I didn't have to interact with the patrons as much. No, I was perfectly happy to keep my head down, make everything spotless, and not talk to anyone.

Higgins seemed to warm up to me as I followed him behind the bar, listening intently as he showed me where everything was stored and the proper cleaning procedures. Because we didn't have a sink with

46

running water in the tent, three buckets were set up to wash, rinse, and sanitize the various drinking glasses. A few small refrigerators powered by a generator kept the beers and chilled pint glasses. Ice was kept in a cooler, and liquor bottles lined a fully stocked cabinet behind the bar.

"And stay out of the bartenders' way," Higgins growled. "I don't need broken glass all over the damn place 'cause they keep running into the new girl."

"Not a problem," I grinned. "Does anything need washing or restocking right now?"

He directed me to two bussing tubs filled with used beer glasses. Apparently the bar back didn't show up last night, so they fell behind on cleaning. I scrubbed the glasses in the buckets, zoning out while Higgins manned the bar for the early patrons—mostly dads sneaking away for a quick beer or shot while the wives and kids rode the Ferris wheel and played at the game booths.

"Down a person again, Higgs?" asked one guy, nursing a beer while he eyed me.

"Two," Higgins grumbled. "My damn bartender is AWOL again. Kids these days, I swear to fuckin' God. At least tonight's bar back is actually doin' her damn job, but I'm not gettin' my hopes up."

It didn't take long for me to find out who the missing bartender was. A girl breezed in, who I recognized as one of Cherry's friends from the dressing tent. She wore a similar outfit as last night with a corset, short skirt, stockings, ridiculous heels, and a tiny top hat fixed to her hair. With her face full of makeup and her tits pushed up to create ample cleavage, she was sure to be rolling in tips tonight.

Her cheery smile disappeared the instant she saw me, turning down into a scowl. I bristled with annoyance. What was she so pissed about?

Higgins didn't seem to notice or care about her obvious disdain toward me.

"Yer late, Leeann," he growled at her. "Quit starin' at the bar back and get yer ass to work. I'm behind on tomorrow's order now."

"Sorry, BTB," she said flippantly. "I had to cheer up a friend 'cause some skanky bitch tried to steal her man." She stared daggers at me when she said it, and I nearly dropped the armful of glasses I carried.

Seriously? *That's* what Cherry told her? What about the fact that her man was a sleazy asshole who touched me everywhere without permission and basically threatened me to go along with it?

I saw red as I stuck the glasses in the fridge, clinking them together with more force than was necessary.

"Hey, what did I say about breakin' them glasses?" Higgins bellowed at me.

"Sorry, BTB," I mumbled, forcing myself to be gentler. I could feel Leeann's sneer like an itch on my back.

As it turned out, I excelled at staying out of the way. I made sure to put as much distance between Leeann and myself as possible while still performing all of my duties. Unfortunately, she took every opportunity to make my job hell.

"None of these glasses are cleaned properly," she complained, dumping an armful into a bussing tub. "I'm not going to sacrifice my tips because the bar-bitch can't do her job!"

Whatever. I rewashed them without complaint.

"This bar is sticky!" she whined, wrinkling her nose as she tapped her fingers down on the bar top. "Customers need a clean place to sit. What the hell are you doing?"

I said nothing and wiped down the already spotless bar again.

"Why are there still empty glasses out on the pub tables?" she demanded. "You need to bus the tables and wipe them down!"

"Because I've been busy washing the other glasses a second time," I said with all the calmness I could muster.

As dusk faded to night outside, the tent became busier, buzzing with late patrons here to enjoy the second day of the freak show. Thankfully, Leeann was kept busy tending the bar and left me in peace. It got so busy that Higgins came from the back to help out.

Without Leeann biting my ankles, I got into a good rhythm of washing, drying, and wiping up messes. Snippets of conversation floated my way as I walked through the tent to pick up empty glasses.

"He gave another whole five minutes about the damn Wolf Man again. What do you think that is?"

"It's a fuckin' hoax. Probably ain't nothin' at all. They just want us to keep comin' back and spendin' money."

"Hey, kid!" Higgins snarled when I returned. I didn't think he bothered learning my name. "You know how to pour a beer from the tap?"

"Uh, yeah," I said, confused. "But I thought you didn't want me to-"

"Fuck the liquor laws! I got a fuckin' line goin' out the door and too many fuckin' mojitos to make! Start a beer line and take care of those people!"

"What?! But she's going to get a cut of my tips!" Leeann whined over the growing noise of the crowded tent.

"She was gonna get a cut anyway, now shut the fuck up and do yer job!"

"Hey!" I cupped my hands around my mouth to yell over the crowd. "If you're in line for a beer, come and see me!"

The line branched off and veered toward me. We broke out the plastic cups for people to take outside the tent, which made things a lot faster. I worked so fast, I just threw whatever tips they left into another empty glass. By the time the line disappeared, my feet ached and my tip jar overflowed with dollar bills.

"Nice work, kid," Higgins said, snapping a dishrag over his shoulder. "You really know how to hustle and you showed up on time." He shot a glare over at Leeann. "If you want a job here tomorrow, you're welcome to it."

"Thanks!" I said earnestly, gulping down a glass of water. "I'll be here tomorrow, then."

He nodded with a grunt. "We got a couple hours left, so take it easy. The performers will be coming in as their shows finish. Help yourself to a drink but don't get sloppy."

"Thanks," I said again. *But no thanks*, I thought.

Working at a bar was fine with me, but the stuff would never touch my lips. Just seeing how my mom and older sister turned out gave me enough reason to abstain from booze entirely.

I drained the rest of my water and began cleaning up my area. When someone took the seat in front of me, I looked up with a plastered smile to find myself staring into a pair of forest green eyes and an extremely kissable pair of lips surrounded by dark stubble.

"Whiskey with ice," those lips said gruffly. "Please," he added.

I froze in my tracks for two reasons. First because my muscle memory was confused that this wasn't a beer order. Second, because the man sitting in front of me was none other than Stilts. It seemed like forever ago that he slammed his trailer door in my face. Was that really just this morning?

"Coming right up!" I chirped, unfreezing from my stupor and pulling out a whiskey tumbler.

I had no idea how much ice I was supposed to add, so I filled it about three-fourths full and topped it off with roughly two fingers of Jack Daniels. He took it from me without comment, to my relief.

"How much?" he grumbled.

"Oh, don't worry about it." I waved my hand away at the wad of cash he produced. "This one's on me."

He lifted an eyebrow while his lips pressed into a thin, tight line.

"And why're you buyin' my drink, miss?"

"For the other night," I lowered my voice. "Just to say thanks for the water and letting me shower at your place." My eyes dropped bashfully. "That was really nice and unnecessary, so thank you."

"It was nothing," he protested, his voice a low, sexy growl. "Let me pay for the drink."

"No, I told you," I argued. "It's my way of saying thanks."

"Look, I'm leaving this here." He slapped a twenty down on the bar. "Charge me for the drink or take the whole thing as a tip. I don't care. I didn't help you, so you could owe me anything in return. I'm paying for the drink, your service, or both."

I cocked my head, trying not to stare too much despite him being very nice to look at.

"I don't know what you're getting so bent out of shape for. It's *one* drink. I'm just trying to say thank you."

"You're welcome." He stubbornly pushed the bill toward me, and I made no move to touch it. With another frustrated yet sexy growl, he picked up his whiskey and took a long swig.

"My name's Melody," I offered, wiping down the counter next to him. "What's yours?"

"Stilts." He glared at me defiantly, but I swore I could see a hint of playfulness there. Just my luck that the kindest person to me in this carnival was this stubborn, curmudgeonly, but gorgeous man.

"Alright, be that way," I shot back, holding back the girlish giggle threatening to bubble up from my chest.

He rolled his eyes and returned to his whiskey, but his lips twitched as if he was hiding back a smile, too.

Rotten luck in life was nothing but second nature to me at this point. Considering today was a pocket full of sunshine compared to last night, I felt confident enough to laugh at my shitty luck tonight. Maybe even push its buttons a little.

"You in the military?" I asked, noticing the silver dog tags around his neck.

"You always ask so many damn questions?" he fired back.

"It's called having a conversation," I teased. Something told me this guy was all bark and no bite. "It's what people do when they go to bars."

"Well, excuse me, Miss Melody," he hissed through gritted teeth. "I've had a long-ass day turning tricks like a show pony for an asshole boss and hundreds of degenerates who conveniently forget that I'm a person on that stage. So if you don't mind, I'd like to enjoy the drink I *bought* in peace."

Well, shit. Clearly, I misread him.

"Sorry," I mumbled, quickly gathering up glasses to wash. "The drink is still free, though."

My confidence deflated and my cheeks burning, I hurried away from the bar to give the guy his much-needed space. But I couldn't escape Leeann's sneer as I bent over the washing buckets.

"Nice try, there. Keep at it," she scoffed. "He's an asshole so you two deserve each other."

Jaw clenched, I ignored her and continued on with my washing.

"I heard he's a fag, too," she went on. "Every girl in the carnival has tried to ride his dick, but he always tells 'em to fuck off. Plus, he's just too pretty to be straight."

"Maybe he actually has standards," I muttered under my breath. Not that I thought in a million years I had a chance with him, or even wanted one. I just wanted to learn a little about the person who extended some kindness to me.

I thought he might at least want to be friends. But again, I was wrong.

"The fuck is that supposed to mean?" Leeann screeched.

"Nothing. Shit."

She didn't escalate further, and I silently begged her to go away. A group of young guys came in, shattering the peaceful silence, and she flounced over to them, tossing her hair and making her voice high and flirtatious. I took a deep breath and forced myself to tune everything out.

After washing yet another batch of glasses, I wiped my hands dry and looked up just in time to see Stilts finish his whiskey. His forest green eyes caught mine and did not let go.

Steeling myself, I marched back over to my place in front of him.

"Another one?"

"No." He set the glass down. "Thank you, Melody." His tone was gentler than mere moments ago.

"You can call me Mel." The words tumbled out automatically, and I bit my tongue too late.

"Alright, Mel." He slid out of his barstool and paused. "It's Connor."

I looked up. "What?"

"My name," he said, "is Connor."

He turned and I watched his broad, muscle-bound back stride out of the tent.

9

MELODY

The booze tent was even more crowded the next night. On top of pouring beers, Higgins had me mixing basic cocktails. By my twentieth Jack and Coke, my tip jar was stuffed to the brim and overflowing. My feet killed me and there seemed to be constant drips of sweat running down my temples. But as long as I was out of reach of every man who leered at my tits shoved into my leather corset, I was happy to continue.

Leeann however, didn't let up in making my job miserable and because we were so busy, Higgins let one of her catty friends work behind the bar with us. One whispered remark between them and both girls looked at me like I crawled out of a sewer.

Whatever. I already accepted I wouldn't be making any friends in this place. Especially not with the girls. But I couldn't help but feel like learning Stilts' real name was a small victory.

I thought about him as I walked past his trailer on my way back to the shelter last night. His lights were on inside and I had an itch to knock at his door, just to bug him and find out what more I could learn.

But he'd likely demand what I wanted, and I didn't have an answer to give him. Even *I* had too much pride to confess he was the closest thing to a friend I had. What could I say? *Hey, I know your real name and I slept in your clothes once, so we're obviously like best pals now.*

So I fell asleep in my bottom bunk at the shelter with a small giggle in my throat as I tried out his name on my lips.

"Connor." I whispered it to my pillow like a secret, wondering if anyone else knew.

I remembered this secret, repeating it in my head like a mantra, when Leeann and her friend accidentally-on purpose began throwing drinks at me. They aimed at my legs and only did it when directly behind the bar so no one would see. To anyone sitting at the bar, it looked like they were dumping out melted ice and used-up garnishes into bussing tubs.

My legs and shoes were sticky and disgusting within minutes, but I still ignored them. I thought of the person who gave water to a girl kneeling in the mud, covered in her own vomit. If people like him existed, I wouldn't sink to the level of these two catty bitches.

A lull in customers gave me an opportunity to rinse my legs off with a hose. I sprayed myself quickly and patted my legs dry with a towel, swiveling my head around to keep an eye out for Bitch One and Bitch Two. They were at the far end of the bar, talking to someone leaning on his forearms. Leeann laughed at something he said, tossing her bleached hair over her shoulder, and my blood froze when I saw who she was talking to.

Syko. But just seeing him wasn't the only source of my shock. Someone had fucked him up.

His left eye was swollen shut and surrounded by an eggplant-purple bruise. He held a bag of crushed ice to his jaw and his lower lip was split in half. I forgot I was staring until his beady black eyes bore into mine over Leeann's shoulder and he scowled.

I sprung into action, my heart nearly exploding in my chest as I moved quickly, darting my eyes away and returning to my work with shaking hands. Time seemed to slow to a crawl as I tried to quell my panic with deep breaths.

Calm down, calm down. There's people here. He wouldn't...

I shook my head and huffed out a laugh at myself. We were in front of hundreds of people the last time he put his filthy hands all over me. Clearly, being seen wasn't a fear of his.

But the seconds crawled on as I tried my best to ignore him, and he seemed to be doing the same. The girls resumed serving customers, and he stayed put at the far end of the bar, drinking heartily from his flask. I breathed a little more freely as it became clear he had no intention of moving from his spot. All the easier to stay the hell away.

I got so preoccupied in scrubbing my glasses, I didn't notice someone took the seat in front of me until a rich, velvety voice spoke.

"No twenty here on the bar. I guess you took it after all?"

Stilts! No, *Connor*. He came back. His face was still unsmiling, but his eyes were playful.

"I donated it to the homeless shelter across the street," I said. That was the truth. I dropped it in the donation box up front before going to bed last night.

A hint of a smile cracked the rugged, hard expression on his face. "Seriously? You're just as stubborn as me, girl. You should learn to take something when it's dropped in your lap."

"So should you," I retorted. "Especially when that something is a thank you."

He groaned and hid his mouth behind his hand, but I could tell he was trying to hide a laugh.

"Anyway, what can I get you?" I offered. My heart lifted that he came back again. Maybe he wasn't as pissed off the other night as I thought.

"I'll just have a beer this time. It's hot as fuck and I'm dyin' for something refreshing." He took his hands off the bar and set them in his lap, leaning forward like he was adjusting his boots.

"There's always water for that," I teased, but grabbed a chilled glass and began pouring.

"Beer is ninety percent water, *Melody*," he shot back. His eyes narrowed, but a smile still tugged at his lips. "Do you always give customers such a hard time?"

"Just you, *Connor*," I retorted before I could think. My face heated as I turned away for a moment. Holy shit, was I flirting?

His handsome face finally broke out into a full-on grin, and my heart skipped a beat. A light blush even tinged his cheekbones pink. Sweet baby Jesus, he was even more gorgeous when smiling.

I placed the beer in front of him and tried not to read into his fingers, brushing mine. No, Mel, I scolded myself. You're not going to turn into a giggling idiot just because of a guy. Not even if he's a really hot guy.

"It's four dollars. You can actually pay for this one," I continued to tease.

"My, my. Never thought I'd see the day." He dropped a five on the bar. "Keep it, babe."

"Thanks."

My skin tingled delightfully upon hearing the pet name like it was a caress. The exact opposite reaction I felt from everything Syko called me. He could have called me every sweet name in the book and it would still make my skin crawl. These two men sitting at opposite ends of the bar seemed to perfectly illustrate the wide spectrum of humanity.

Speaking of which, Syko just then seemed to notice Connor sitting in front of me. His scowl grew even more twisted, and he hunched further over his flask, barking something at Leeann, which sounded like another drink order.

"He been bothering you any more?" Connor's gaze burned intensely into mine, the sexy smile gone.

"No. He's been staying far away, thankfully." All my flirtatious confidence zapped away in that moment. I lowered my eyes shamefully and absently wiped a glass with a cloth over and over. "So you saw that too, huh?"

"The tail end of it, yeah. I saw you run away like the hounds of hell were after you."

A thought made my hands freeze. I looked to my right again. Syko threw back a shot of something and applied a fresh bag of ice to his swollen jaw. I then looked back at Connor, his face expressionless as he sipped his beer pensively. The knuckles on his hand had faint bruises and appeared slightly swollen.

"Did you..." I lowered my voice to a whisper, angling my head in Syko's direction. "Did you have something to do with his face looking like that?"

"I ain't his dad so, no. I'm not responsible for that ugly moth-erfucker."

"You know what I mean." I narrowed my eyes.

Connor set his beer down and swallowed. His Adam's apple bobbed and my lips parted with the mental image of kissing it.

"Again, the answer is no." His expression didn't change, but his eyes danced with mischief.

"Why's your hand swollen?" I pressed.

"It's from my act. Doing handstands and swinging on bars and shit."

He wasn't going to give me a different answer, no matter what I asked. I almost wished I felt conflicted and weird about it, but I didn't.

Syko deserved it. If I was big and strong enough, I would have fucked his face up myself. I had no sympathy for him and would never condemn Connor for doing that, as much as I hated violence. The only part that confused me was *why*. But for some reason, I didn't feel ready to ask that question.

"So how'd it go today?" I said, eager for a lighthearted subject change.

"Same old shit," he mumbled into his beer. The question seemed to make him sullen, like he'd rather talk about anything else. He reached under the bar again and grimaced as he seemed to massage a cramp in his leg.

"All the stilt tricks tough on your legs?" I asked sympathetically.

"You could say that." He answered with a low growl. It didn't sound like he wanted to talk about anything regarding work. "How'd you end up in this shithole, Mel?"

My insides did a somersault upon realizing he actually asked a question about me. "A nice state trooper drove me in, technically speaking."

His eyes narrowed in confusion. "Why would he do that?"

"I ran away from home and was living at a rest stop for a week," I answered casually.

His eyebrows shot up. "Really? You're a tougher chick than you look, then." He sounded impressed and my imaginary feathers ruffled proudly. Speaking softer, he added, "Home was a rough place for you then, huh?"

"You could say that." I mimicked his dismissive answer, feeling just as eager to talk about my home life as he was about his work life.

"Fair enough," he relented.

A brief silence passed between us as both of our gazes shifted to the opposite end of the bar. Syko was nowhere to be seen, and my shoulders sagged with relief.

"Don't let your guard down yet, babe," Connor muttered under his breath. "That shifty fucker might be up to something. I wouldn't put it past him."

"You're right," I muttered back, feeling my spine go rigid again. Even though all the creepy signs were there, Syko deliberately waited to really humiliate me until I was onstage and literally tied up so I couldn't escape. Lots of men were creepy without being straight-up predators. I wouldn't make the mistake of thinking he was harmless again.

"Hey you, girl!" Leeann screeched from the back of the tent. "Get over here!"

I rolled my eyes. Of course, she wouldn't bother to learn my name.

"Coming!" I hollered back, drying my hands. "Be right back," I said to Connor.

"Won't be soon enough." He said it so softly as I walked away, I thought I must've misheard him as I pushed back the rear tent flap.

"The fuck are you smirking for?" Leeann's bitchy friend demanded.

"Nothing," I sighed. "What do you need?"

The two wore their best cunty glares with their arms folded under their breasts, staring down their noses at me through heavy false lashes.

"Stay away from Syko, you dumb whore," Leeann spat. "After all she did to help, you repay Cherry by seducing her man?"

Stunned, my jaw dropped open.

"Are you fucking kidding me?" I demanded. "This bullshit is what you dragged me out here for?"

"Why the fuck would we be joking?" Cunt Number Two shot back. "Cherry *loves* him. It's like, *real* love. She was about to tell him to stop pulling out so they could start a family. But you had to show up and shove your tits in his face!"

"Jesus tap-dancing Christ," I groaned, dropping my forehead to my palm. No matter where I went, trash seemed to follow me. "I can't believe I actually have to say this, but I don't want Syko. He's creepy, he's twice my age, and I sure as fuck did not wanting him touching me onstage!"

"Then why didn't you say no?" Leeann demanded, leaning forward into my face. "You sluts always whine about it afterward, but if you didn't like it, why the fuck didn't you stop it?"

"Are you serious?" I was incredulous, but still didn't want these bitches to know how much he scared me. "You're telling me you've *never* been in that position, Leeann?"

A glass shattering and voices yelling inside the tent made me spin around. Through the tent flap, I saw four men restraining Connor and barely at that. Two guys held back his massive arms and shoulders as he struggled. With just a bit more wiggling, he'd have one arm free.

I could only be taken aback by his strength for a split second before my panic kicked in.

"Connor!" I shrieked, running into the tent.

His green eyes, wide and dilated, caught mine as he paused for half a moment in his struggle. I saw the anger, the adrenaline pumping through them from the sudden attack, but also something else. Was that *fear* I saw?

"Get out of here, Melody!" he roared. "It's not safe! Go!"

"I'll get help!" I yelled, rounding the bar. "I'll find Higgins!"

"No! Just go!"

Running to his side of the bar, now filled with people looking to watch the fight, I noticed the figure kneeling at Connor's feet.

Syko rose to standing slowly, an evil grin spreading on his face and a wooden baseball bat resting across his shoulders. My stomach collapsed in a pit of dread.

"I'll teach y'all how to fuck with me," he said softly, then swung the bat with all his might.

"NO!" I cried too late.

He aimed low across Connor's shins. The wooden bat made a loud *clank* as it connected with metal.

Wait, *what?*

In slow motion, Connor's lower legs and shoes seemed to rip away from under his pant leg. They rolled across the floor from the force and hit the bar with a thud and another clang.

Syko and his goons laughed uproariously while I stared in horror. The four guys holding Connor up dropped him without warning. He braced himself with his forearms but still landed hard and grunted from the impact. He quickly pulled himself across the ground to his prosthetic legs and I could only stare in shock and disbelief.

This man walked in stilts when his real legs ended at his knees.

10

CONNOR

I don't know what prompted me to go back to the booze tent that night. Or why I told her my real name the first night. That girl Melody was too wide-eyed, young, and naïve. She thought the carnival world was all cotton candy and deep-fried cheesecake. She was completely unaware of the corruption that poisoned this kind of job, the poison that got me here in the first place.

That naivete was exactly the reason Syko targeted her. Dickbags like him always spotted girls like her from a mile away, circling slowly around her like vultures. The poor thing never saw it coming.

I hated people who preyed on the weak. I saw it constantly in Afghanistan, which opened my eyes to how it happened more subtly back home. So after I caught up to her and offered her water and my place to shower, I put old Syko in his place after doing that shit onstage.

Honestly, I didn't beat him that hard. Just popped him a couple of times as a warning.

"Fuckin' gimp!" he cursed at me, spitting blood. "You wouldn't be shit without those fuckin' robot legs."

"Touch that girl again," I said, "and I'll show you what I can do with no legs."

I went home after that, not sure of what I would find. Not that I would've been displeased with a naked girl in my shower, but she definitely wouldn't want to be around a man after what happened. And even if she did, she'd change her mind the moment my pants came off.

My place had been empty, the shower still wet, and a towel hung over the shower door. A mixture of relief and disappointment filled me. No one except me had been in this place since I bought it. The thought of a woman being in here using my shower felt absolutely alien.

A flash of something metallic caught my eye on the floor and I bent over to pick it up. It was some kind of coin or token, inlaid with gold and a silver ring around it. I didn't recognize the design—definitely not one of our carnival tokens.

The girl must have dropped it. Which was unfortunate, because I figured she'd never come back after that ordeal.

When she showed up at my door the next morning, my borrowed clothes folded neatly in her hands, I forgot all about returning her coin.

She looked up at me with those rich brown eyes, no longer weighed down with fake eyelashes and ridiculous makeup. Her pert, pink lips curved into a smile that no man like me would ever deserve.

And I fucking slammed the door in her face. I only took a moment to hold the shirt and shorts I snatched from her, wondering how long they touched her skin, when voices prompted me to look outside.

She was talking to the carnival manager, Mr. Fisher. Another perverted fuck, but too cowardly to actually pull shit off like Syko. He handed her an envelope and asked her a question I couldn't make out. She nodded, smiling back at him as she replied. A smile still full of naïve brightness and hope. Was this girl seriously going to keep working here? I couldn't decide if she was tougher or stupider than I thought.

I pushed my curtain back into place before they could see me. If she was sticking around, I could only hope Syko took my threat seriously.

When those big doe eyes looked at me from across the bar for the first time, you guessed it. I forgot all about giving her back the damn coin again.

She annoyed me with all her questions and attempts to start a conversation, or at least that was what I kept trying to convince myself. I was not *just* a closed book. I was a book sealed shut with a chain wrapped around it and thrown into the ocean to sink into the abyss. Nobody knew my background, my real name, and definitely not the status of my disability. Syko only knew because he drunkenly tried to stab me in the calf one time.

Classy people, my coworkers.

So I left the bar that first night, never intending to come back. She had my name now, and that already felt like too much.

But I had hers, too. She gave it to me freely, just like she gave me that drink.

Melody. Like a song.

And just like a song, I couldn't get her out of my head ever since then. All the more reason to stay far away from the booze tent.

My prosthetics were killing me after the show. I was on my way home to relax and get the damn things off when I spotted Syko making a beeline for the booze tent. I hesitated for just a second before turning around and following him.

My training in the Marines taught me to follow through on every promise I made. I told him there would be consequences for messing with Melody again and I had to see that through. It had nothing to do with how her doe eyes made my heart jump or the fact she'd been running through my head all day. A man's honor was keeping his word, and that was the sole purpose of following him.

I didn't want it super obvious to the old creep I was onto him, so I let myself talk and flirt with Melody. And goddamn it, I liked it.

I smiled for the first time in what felt like years. I even laughed a little. The girl was just as sweet as she was tough. I let my fucking guard down and just enjoyed the moment with her. It would never last, so I figured, *what's the harm in talking to a pretty girl?* By the time this shitshow of a carnival was over, I'd never see her again.

And this time, I wouldn't forget to give back her mysterious coin.

My finger traced across the face of it in my pocket. I kept it on me in the wide, bulky pants I wore during the show, which conveniently covered up my prosthetics down to my shoes. The coin never flew out during my routines, which miraculously went without any hitches in the last two nights. Maybe it was a good luck charm despite the aches in my limbs afterwards.

When Mel came back from talking to her two bitchy coworkers, I planned to flip it in the air and place it in her hand. Those doe eyes would light up and her cute little mouth would open in a gasp. I was near giddy with anticipation, waiting for her to come back. So much so that I didn't notice four of Syko's goons come up behind me and yank me off my stool.

"Well, this makes things an awful lot clearer, gimp," the ugly bastard sneered. "Yer sweet on that pretty little thing, ain't ya?"

"And you're still a big pussy," I hissed, struggling against the restraints, but they all twisted my arms behind my back. "You need four dudes to come at me? Too chickenshit to even face a gimp man-to-man?"

His smile dropped. Of fucking course he was, and he hated how I just said that in front of his boys.

He revealed the Louisville slugger from behind his back and pointed it straight at me.

"I'll teach ya to run yer fuckin' mouth on me, Stilts," he growled.

I stared him down, daring him to make good on his threat. If he cracked that thing over my head—well, the world wouldn't miss a useless gimp like me. But a man like Syko could never bear the responsibility of taking another man's life. He was too much of a weasel for that. Like I thought he would, he kneeled to the ground, laid the bat next to him, and started fucking with my prosthetics.

"Let's hear you talk shit without yer fuckin' robot legs," he muttered, pulling and twisting on the silicone sleeves that held my legs in place.

"Go ahead and keep feeling me up, Syk," I said dryly. "You only get action when your victim's restrained so enjoy it while you can."

"Shut the fuck up. At least I still have a dick to play with."

"Those tend to be pretty useless without any balls."

I still had a dick, too. I didn't know where he got the implication that I lost mine along with my legs, or if he was just really that stupid. Either way, I didn't give a shit about correcting him.

"Connor!"

Oh shit.

Melody ran back into the tent, her doe eyes wide and fearful. Fuck it all. Of all the people crowding around in this tent, she was the only one I cared about not seeing me as a gimp. We wouldn't see each other after this carnival and I didn't want to alter her perception of me. I didn't want her to think of me as lesser.

"Get out of here, Melody!" I hollered. "It's not safe, go!"

Of course, she didn't listen. She rounded the bar to get closer and saw what Syko was doing, although she didn't understand yet.

I stopped struggling then. It was no use. Syko wouldn't hurt me, not badly. All I wanted was for her to not see me, and I was powerless to stop that from happening.

He swung my legs out from under me and his boys dropped me on my face. I still weighed a good two hundred pounds from the knees up and a shock rattled my forearms when I hit the ground. But at least I didn't hit my head.

Naturally, they laughed and pointed like a bunch of schoolyard bullies as I pulled myself across the floor to my legs. I didn't give a shit about them, but the last thing I wanted to do was look up and see the expression on Melody's face.

I pulled myself up to a sitting position and quickly began putting them on again. Higgins started shouting over the din, saying it was time to get the hell out. Syko gave me one last, disgusted look over his shoulder and spit on the ground in my direction before walking out of the tent, his boys following him obediently.

I scoffed and shook my head as I secured my prosthetics back into place. Even on the ground with nothing to modify me and he still wouldn't come at me. The best he could do was try to humiliate me. What a small, stupid man. If he ever bothered to stop and think for a minute, he might realize I'd seen and heard it all before.

"Connor."

A small hand rested gently on my forearm. Up close, Melody

smelled like freshly blooming jasmine. But I couldn't bring myself to look at her.

"I told you to go, Melody," I barked as I snatched my arm away and grabbed a barstool to pull myself to standing.

"But he was going to-"

"Nothing," I snapped. "He didn't do shit 'cause he's a giant pussy. I had it handled. You should've gone."

I shouldn't have talked to her so harshly. She didn't do anything wrong. Nothing was hurt but my ego. Now she would see me as nothing more than a poor, pitiful creature. Just like everyone else did.

Who was I kidding? Vicky was right. No woman would ever want me after what happened.

"Almost forgot," I mumbled, reaching into my pocket. "Here. You dropped this."

I flipped the coin at her and began walking away before even seeing if she caught it or not.

II

MELODY

I gripped the coin in my fist, feeling like I had been standing outside Connor's door for hours. A bead of sweat trickled between my breasts, an indication I should get out of the blazing midmorning sun soon.

What am I doing here? It was not the first time the question popped into my head and I still didn't have an answer.

Last night was awful, and I just want to check on him.

Check for what? You saw that he didn't get injured. He's a grown man, he can handle some wounded pride.

The arguing with myself went around in circles. With a resigned sigh, I raised my fist and knocked at the flimsy door, making sure to squeeze my coin in my other hand for good luck.

"Go away!" came the muffled snarl through the door.

"Connor, it's me, Mel," I called.

"I fucking know that."

The words stung like acid flung at my skin. We had been getting along so well last night until Syko had to prove himself the biggest asshole in the world. Now, it was like a switch had flipped and he was treating me like I was the one who wronged him.

"We don't have to talk about what happened," I tried again. "I just wanted to make sure we're good. That you're good." I bit my lip at my concern for him leaking through.

"Perfectly fine. Now go away."

"If that's true, why are you yelling at me through the door instead of talking to me face-to-face?"

"I don't want your pity, Melody."

"I don't pity you!" I cried out in frustration, maybe a bit too loudly. "I don't care about your... condition, or whatever. Honestly, I think it's amazing what you're able to do in spite of it."

He was silent for so long, with no movement inside the trailer. I pressed my ear to the door and said more quietly, "Connor?"

"Damn it. I thought you'd gone."

"Alright, fine!" I threw my hands up. "Hide in your trailer and be a coward, just like Syko, then!"

I stomped down his steps in a huff, my blood thumping in my ears. I was so mad I didn't hear his door swing open until he called out, "Melody!"

I turned around to see him standing in the doorway, wearing the same heather gray shirt I borrowed and loose-fitting sweatpants. The shirt hugged his biceps and chest like a second skin.

"Here, isn't this what you wanted?" he asked mockingly, spreading his arms out. "Come in and help yourself to a cup of tea, why don't you?"

Part of me had it up to here with his shit and wanted to keep walking the other way. But the other part didn't want to let this opportunity slip through my fingers. Who knew when he'd go back to hiding from the world? I wanted to learn more about this man, who could be so kind and selfless, then turn around and bite my head off in the same breath. He was like a beautiful wild animal who spooked when you got too close. At the moment, he was letting me in and I had to tread carefully.

He went back inside, leaving the door open, which I approached with careful, hesitant steps. I took a moment to look at the small living space from the doorway. It looked and felt so different from the one other night I'd been in here. Still clean and orderly, but it felt far more welcoming now in the morning light.

"Thanks for giving my coin back," I said awkwardly from the doorway, still with no idea what to say or why I was really here.

Connor glanced over his broad shoulder at me. "You comin' in or
staying out? I don't want any damn cicadas in here."

Mumbling an apology, I stepped forward and pulled the door
closed behind me. The space between us and in the RV in general got a
whole lot smaller.

"You drink coffee?" Connor asked, pulling a pot out from under a
coffee maker.

"Yes, thanks."

He waved the pot toward a small table with two chairs. "Have a
seat."

I did so and accepted the steaming mug from him before he sat
across from me. He moved so fluidly. Just watching him walk about the
tiny space had me entranced. There was nothing robotic, jarring, or
unnatural about the steps he took. If he was intent on keeping his
secret hidden, he did a fine job of that until Syko exposed him.

"What's that coin mean to you, anyway?" he asked gruffly.

"It's kind of a good luck charm," I said, wrapping my hands around
the mug. "I've had it ever since I was a kid. It's just the one thing I've
had for so long." I lifted my mug to my lips. "Why, do you recognize
it?"

"I can tell it's a carnival token. Don't know where from, though."

Silence stretched between us. With every passing moment, my
anxiety grew over what he was thinking. Was he pissed at me for
badgering him again? Was he just humoring me until I finally left?

"Why'd you help me out that first night?" I asked. The one burning
question that plagued me since it happened.

"Because it was the right thing to do."

He didn't sound pissed. His voice was calm and even-tempered.

In that same tone, he asked me, "Why do you insist on barging into
my life, Melody?"

"I'm sorry," I blurted out. "You're probably the only person who's
gone out of their way to be nice to me. Not just at this carnival, but
my whole life. I'm not trying to throw a pity party, it's just that after
you did that... I wanted to learn more about you. I wanted to know

why you were different from everyone else and I don't mean your legs—"

I stopped abruptly, realizing I was digging myself into a hole. "But I can tell you don't like having me around, so I'll say hi to you in the booze tent and let that be it. I won't bother you anymore and I won't tell anyone about your... you know."

His sculpted arms crossed in front of his chest as I talked. When I was done rambling, he broke into a smile, the same one that made my heart skip a beat, and started laughing. At my confused expression, his laugh grew even louder.

"I don't dislike you, Melody," he began.

"Mel," I corrected.

"Mel," he repeated, smirking. "I gotta admit I've never met anyone like you, either. You never stop asking questions and trouble always seems to find you."

I dropped my eyes to look at my coffee. "Sorry."

"Don't be sorry, damn it."

I looked at him again, even more confused than before.

"My life has been," he paused to think of the word, "mundane. Mind-numbingly so, for the past two years. I perform, I keep to myself, I collect my cash, which dries up too fast for me to save it. Same shit, different day. But you." He shook his head as if in disbelief. "Somehow this skinny, doe-eyed girl has made my life interesting again."

"How?" I asked.

"By being *you*," he grinned. "Most people who get in my business back off as soon as I tell them to. But you keep poking the bear and won't run away when it roars at you. You're fearless in a way that's very refreshing." He cocked an eyebrow. "You're lucky I'm not Syko. Or any other of the fuckin' creeps around here."

I blinked at him. "I don't get it. You *like* me bugging you? You get so pissed off, though. And I'm definitely not fearless," I frowned. I was just desperate for work and apparently friendship, but I didn't voice that to him.

His smile dropped. "I'm not the easiest person to get along with, Mel. I've... been through some things, obviously." He gestured down to his legs. "I have a short temper. I get snappish and frustrated easily. But," he reached across the table and grabbed my hand with a surprisingly gentle touch, "I won't ever assault you like Syko did. I'll never come close to that."

"He didn't—"

"Don't you dare defend him," he cut me off with a snarl. "He absolutely did. I heard him threaten you. It doesn't matter if he didn't hurt you physically, he had no right to do that."

I swallowed and nodded.

"So," Connor sighed, "if you can handle my moodiness and don't treat me differently now that you know I'm only three-fourths of a man, I guess I'm okay with you tagging along with me."

"You're not three-fourths of a man," I blurted out.

"Watch it, kid," he said sternly. When I mumbled an apology, he playfully flicked my hand that he still held. "I'm kidding. Lighten up, Mel."

"So you don't mind me asking you questions?" I said hopefully.

"You can ask whatever you want." He said it lightheartedly, but his mouth tightened. "Doesn't mean I'm gonna answer."

I thought for a moment, sipping coffee while I filed through the many questions I had swirling in my mind, trying to pick the least invasive ones.

"How old are you?" I began.

"Twenty-five," he answered, lifting an eyebrow. "You?"

"Just turned eighteen a couple weeks ago."

"Damn," he muttered, visibly shuddering. "I figured you were young, but not *that* young. That makes what Syko did even worse."

"Where are you from, originally?" I asked, eager to get the subject off of my age.

"A little-ass town called Paris," he grinned. "Paris, Arkansas."

"I was about to say, you don't sound French," I snorted.

Connor chuckled, pleased with his joke. "How about you, Mel?"

"An even smaller town, most likely," I told him. "Waterford, Alabama."

Not that I was thrilled to talk about my hometown, but my chest still bloomed with the mere fact that he was asking me questions in return. A complete 180 from him yelling at me to go away just minutes earlier. That had to mean something.

"Let me guess." He quirked an eyebrow. "About as redneck as it gets?"

"Yeah," I admitted. "I graduated high school and haven't gotten pregnant yet. That's considered a success where I'm from."

"Yep, 'bout the same story here." Connor rubbed his jaw as his southern twang emerged. "I went to college in Florida. That was where I got some actual culture and education in me."

"I never even left the state before coming out here," I confessed, feeling a pang of envy at all the fun and adventures he must've had while in college.

To kids like me, a higher education was basically a distant mythology. A far-off dream we could never hope to have. Teachers prattled on endlessly about how important it was to get a degree for a good job, but the best I could hope for was like I said—done with high school and not yet pregnant.

"What made you leave?" he asked, draining his coffee cup.

"Just a shitty home life," I said tersely.

He nodded as if in understanding of my situation. I had no idea if he really understood, but he didn't ask any more, which I appreciated.

"How'd you end up in this place?" I asked, taking a chance on a more personal question.

He huffed out a dry laugh. "It was either this or become one of the millions of disabled veterans living on the street. Wasn't a hard choice at the time."

"So you were in the military," I confirmed, my gaze resting on his dog tags again.

"Yeah, whole lotta good that did me," he scoffed and then winced. "Well, I shouldn't say it like that. My training did me good. Getting my legs blown off and the lack of support and benefits afterward wasn't great."

"I'm sorry," I mumbled.

Connor glared at me. "What did I say about pity? I don't need or want your sorrys, kid."

I bit my tongue before another apology could tumble out. "I know. I didn't mean it like that. It's just not fair."

"Life isn't fair." He leaned back, resting his elbows on the back of his chair. "The sooner you realize that, the less disappointing life will be."

A flash of anger surged through me. "Oh, I know that well enough already. The first seventeen years of my life were completely unfair, but I got by and dealt with it until I could leave. Then I did. You're not *that* much older than me, Connor. You don't need to act all high and mighty and treat me like a kid. I get it. Probably more than you think."

My heart pounded, and I didn't even realize I clenched my fists until my palms hurt from my nails digging in. I was just tired of people treating me like I didn't know anything, like I couldn't handle myself.

Since I was twelve years old, I was essentially the only adult in the house. Cleaning, cooking, changing diapers, and paying what bills I could. Just because I was stuck in that endless loop and never saw the "real" world didn't mean I couldn't handle what it threw at me.

"Alright," Connor said quietly, rubbing his jaw with a smirk. "You are tougher and wiser than I gave you credit for. Didn't mean to assume, Mel."

I blinked, genuinely shocked at the admission. Most men didn't admit when they were wrong. If anything, they doubled-down and got even more pissed off because their precious ego was threatened. Connor was starting to surprise me in many ways.

"Having said that," I waved my hand a bit sheepishly. "I don't know about anything in this world. Carnival politics or whatever. Figuring it out on my own has been pretty disastrous so far. If you have any advice for me in that regard, I'd love to hear it."

"Hmm." Connor stroked his face, peering at me thoughtfully for a moment. "I have a pretty good idea for keeping you out of trouble."

"Yeah?" I leaned forward across the table.

His smirk returned, and butterflies fluttered inside me.

"Do an exclusive act with me."

MELODY

"Say what, now?"

"Join my act, exclusively," Connor repeated. "Exclusive means you work only with me."

"I know what exclusive means," I hissed at his teasing grin. "Doing what, exactly?"

"Performing with me, in a strictly professional sense." He turned serious. "I'll split earnings with you right down the middle. And once everyone knows, no one will bother you. I have a reputation of being somewhat of an asshole." His grin returned as if proud of that notion.

"But performing how?" I demanded. "I can't walk in stilts, I can barely make it across the grounds in those heels they give me. I definitely can't do the crazy shit that you do."

I suddenly wondered how Connor was able to walk in stilts with no feet, especially as well as he did. It seemed like it would be extraordinarily difficult to control those long pieces of wood with half the leg muscles.

"To the audience, you'll look like you're just walking across the stage, looking pretty and following my lead," he said. "But it will be a highly coordinated, choreographed routine. All you have to do is memorize the steps I teach you and keep time with the music."

Wait, he thought I was pretty?

"Okay." I rubbed my cheek like I was thinking, but really I was trying to hide my blush. "I think I can handle that. How long do I have to learn?"

Connor glanced at the clock above his kitchen sink. "About six hours."

"What?!" My eyes nearly popped out of my skull.

"I need you tonight," he said, looking somewhat apologetic. "Our fucking overlords have been wanting us to step up our shows each night." He rolled his eyes. "Something about building up hype for the wolf man display on the very last night of the carnival."

"Oh, yeah." I recalled the ringmaster's speech on the first night. "What's the deal with that?"

"Crock of shit," he scoffed. "Here's a tip for you, Mel—carnivals are scams. When everyone figures out the wolf man is bullshit and demands their money back, the company will still turn a profit because they crack the whip on us legitimate performers to jump higher and higher every night."

"Well, that's shitty," I frowned.

"It's reality." He shrugged, then his forest green eyes turned large and puppy-like. "So how 'bout it, Mel? Will you do this show with me?"

"Can I really learn the routine in six hours?" I gulped.

"I'm sure you can, babe." Just the way he said that made me swell up with confidence. "You're definitely smarter than the average chick here. We just have to repeat it a bunch of times so you have it down to muscle memory."

I thought about it for a few more moments and figured I had nothing to lose. I barely knew this guy, and yet I trusted him a hundred times more than Syko. With my whole heart, I believed he wouldn't try anything inappropriate, at least.

"Okay then," I stood from the table. "Guess we better get started."

"Seriously?" I huffed. "You didn't tell me a hiking trip was part of this lesson."

Connor, about ten paces ahead of me, tossed a large water bottle over his head. I caught it after a bit of awkward juggling and sucked down greedily while trying to keep up with him. Not that I could get too close anyway due to his practice stilts—long, slender pieces of woods slung over his shoulder. They almost whacked me in the head a few times already.

"I like my privacy when I practice," was his reply.

The carnival grounds were well out of sight. I couldn't even see the Ferris wheel behind me anymore. Connor had been leading me through a nearby wooded area that turned into a straight up forest after about a mile. After yet another mile, he showed no signs of slowing down. For a man with no lower legs, he knew how to hustle down a barely-marked trail.

I had to admit, the view of his ass made the trek just a bit more bearable. Not even the long, baggy pants he wore as part of his stilt walking getup could hide it.

"We're here," he said finally. He stopped so abruptly, I nearly got poked in the eye with his stilt again.

We came to a clearing where the grass was so short and jagged, it looked like a desert compared to the forest we just hiked through. The ground was dry and rock hard, with little water or vegetation to be seen.

"The deer population is out of control here," Connor said as he sat down on a tree stump. "They eat all the newly-grown vegetation. Sucks for the environment, but at least the ground is hard and flat. Good to practice on."

"They need natural predators," I whispered, primarily to myself. "Like wolves."

"Hey." Connor threw a small pebble at me. "You alright, Mel?"

"Yeah." I shook my head and blinked a few times. "That was weird. I spaced out for a second."

"You might be dehydrated. It's hot as Satan's balls out here," Connor smirked. "Chill out for a bit while I get ready."

I sat on a nearby tree stump and watched curiously as Connor rolled up his pant legs in preparation to put his stilts on. Right away, I saw exactly how he was able to pull off his stunts and my jaw nearly dropped.

His thighs were massive and looked to be made of pure muscle. The thin, spindly trees surrounding us couldn't compare to those trunks. His quad muscles flexed with power as he carefully removed his prosthetics. His left leg ended just below the knee and the right ended slightly lower, about halfway down the shin which was mottled with scar tissue.

Realizing I was staring, I looked away abruptly. Then curiosity got the better of me and I looked again. As he secured the stilts on, I saw he used them in place of his prosthetic legs. After wrapping his lower legs in some kind of compression fabric, he slid them into harnesses built into the wooden stilts and secured himself in with straps and buckles. Until then, I didn't notice one stilt was longer than the other to balance where he was amputated.

Then he grabbed a nearby tree and—using the trunk and the branches—hauled himself up to standing. Just like that, he was suddenly twelve feet tall and walking with the grace of a feline predator.

"Damn it. Forgot to set the music," he said. "Mel, will you grab my phone out of my pack and find the song for me?"

I rummaged through his pack while he walked around and warmed up. When I located the phone, I tried to avoid reading the message displaying on the lock screen, but couldn't stop myself. It was from someone named Vicky and read, "Are you ever going to talk to me again?"

I unlocked the phone and went directly to his music, for once refusing to give in to my burning curiosity. Snooping through his messages was wrong, especially since we barely knew each other. It didn't matter that jealousy flared up. What right did I have to be jealous? And anyway, the message seemed to imply that Connor wasn't talking to this Vicky person.

Following Connor's instruction's, I picked his performance song and set it on repeat. Over the next few hours, we practiced the routine.

Or more accurately, he yelled at me like a drill sergeant while I tried my best to follow his instructions. Some of which seemed to defy physics.

"Four, five, six, seven, eight, stop!" I froze and felt his stilt slide at an angle behind me. "Now sit down, Mel," he commanded. "Trust me, don't be scared."

"That's what you said last time when I almost fell off!"

"You won't fall if you do it right," he sighed. "Swing your legs under a bit and grip with the back of your knees. Keep your hands on either side of you for extra support."

I lowered myself carefully onto the narrow, wooden replacement for his leg, which didn't seem wide enough at all to hold me, and suddenly I was lifted in the air.

"Ahh!" I screamed in the moment there was nothing underneath me. I was falling to the ground!

Out of nowhere, strong arms caught me and held me against a broad, solid chest.

"See?" Connor tightened his grip around my waist. "You're safe."

I clung to his broad shoulders and unintentionally nuzzled my face into his neck, not wanting to see how far away I was from the ground.

"How do I get down?" I asked in a small voice.

"There's a silk rope attached to my pants," he explained. "It's rolled up now. Unroll it and brace your feet against my legs as you go down, like you're rappelling down a rock wall."

"I've never rappelled down a rock wall in my life," I grumbled, fumbling around him for this so-called rope.

At twelve feet in the air with a definite chance of broken bones if he let go of me, I was still acutely aware of his massive arm around my waist. The way his muscles bunched and flexed from holding me and keeping his balance at the same time. A bead of sweat fell into the space between his collarbones and I had half a mind to lick it.

"It's behind me," he said in regards to my fumbling for the rope.

"Of course it is," I muttered. Right above his ass.

"Don't worry, it'll hold you. You can wrap it around yourself if it'll make you feel secure."

"You're the only thing making me feel secure." I bit my tongue too late. Those words had more of an implication than I intended.

If Connor noticed, he didn't let it on. "Put your feet against my leg," he said patiently. "And hold onto the rope until it's taut. You won't pull me with you."

I did as he instructed, and screamed when he removed his arm from around me.

"Stay there!" he instructed. A grin spread on his face as his arms spread out to the sides. "See? You're fine, babe."

"It hurts," I hissed through gritted teeth. Despite the softness of the silk, I gripped so hard it was digging into my hand. I braced myself against the side of his leg and held on the rope for dear life. If I allowed slack at either points, I'd go tumbling to the ground.

"Jump straight back, push with your legs," Connor instructed. "Let the rope slide through your hand for a bit before you clamp tight again. You'll swing back and be lower to the ground. Keep doing that until you hit the bottom."

"What happened to just walking back and forth across the stage?!" I demanded.

"That's most of what you'll be doing, but this is for the grand finale," he said. "I won't let you fall. You can do this, Mel. I know you can."

Amazing how another person's faith in me could give just the courage I needed. I repeated his instructions step-by-step in my head and took a deep breath. Bending my knees deeply, I sprang off and let the rope slide through my fingers for just a split second. Then my fear got the better of me and I grabbed it again. Connor's stilts came rushing back at me and I touched my feet to the side of them again.

"You did it!" Connor clapped his hands and his voice beamed with genuine pride.

I looked up and saw he was much further away than a split second ago. My feet were firmly planted against the wood of his stilt about six feet up from the ground.

"I really did it!" I shrieked with a mixture of bewilderment and glee.

The adrenaline rush hit me right then like a drug, making me feel invincible. I rappelled the rest of the way down in two easy jumps, landing lightly on my feet and spreading my arms in a *ta-da* pose.

"Great job, Mel!" Connor praised me from high above, and my heart swelled. "Now let's do it again. We've got to make it look pretty and shit."

The sun began sinking low over the trees as we went through the routine dozens of times. By the time Connor called it good, my arms screamed with fatigue and my legs felt like jello.

"Now we've got to do all that on stage?" I panted, sitting on the tree stump.

"Yep, for one last time." Connor secured his regular prosthetics on the stump next to me. "But you know it now. Once we're cleaned up and ready, our muscles will have enough rest to give it our all. It'll be a piece of cake, babe."

I hoped he was right, but not just about our performance. Getting anywhere near Syko again had my defenses on high alert. I hoped Connor was right about no one bothering me now that I was partnered with him.

Nothing was certain until showtime tonight.

MELODY

I applied my makeup carefully in the small bathroom of Connor's trailer. After picking out an outfit in the dressing tent, I got enough dirty looks from the other girls that I opted to make myself scarce. Apparently, Leeann and her friend did plenty more shit-talking about me.

"Almost ready, Mel?"

In the mirror, I saw Connor's eyes linger on me with an intense, heated gaze before turning away.

"Yep." I smacked my lips together after a final swipe of lipstick and thoroughly checked myself over.

I was able to find a short, pinstriped dress in the dressing tent that acted like a corset but provided more freedom to breathe. My waist nipped in nicely and my tits looked bodacious, but not overly pushed up into my face. Lacey black gloves and matching tights fit snugly over my hands and legs. An elaborate black beaded choker decorated my throat, and of course, the whole ensemble wasn't complete without a top hat.

A hum of excitement filled me as I was getting ready. Already, this felt different from the first night. Having Connor as a partner made me feel two-thousand percent more comfortable than being around Syko.

During practice, he was tough but encouraging. The only times he touched me was when it was necessary during our routine, and never for longer than was appropriate. I did catch him stealing glances at me like in the mirror just now, but those looks made my stomach flutter rather than fill me with dread.

"Ready when you are," I called, stalking slowly out of the bathroom on my tall heels.

He leaned against the counter, dressed in one of his many colorful suits for the show. Tonight, his dominant colors were purple and orange with accents of black. If I had a pop of orange in my outfit, we would have coordinated perfectly.

"Damn," he muttered under his breath. His green eyes lit up like orbs against the dark kohl surrounding them. It was the only makeup he wore, as he'd be wearing a black and purple mask during the show. I had to admit it looked sexy on him. With his bright clothes, he kind of resembled an eccentric pirate.

"What? Is it too much?" I asked, looking down at myself.

"No, not at all. You look great." His voice was low and husky as he jerked his eyes up and gave me a smile that almost seemed shy. "Shall we?"

He held out his elbow like a gentleman, which I accepted, wrapping my fingers underneath and around his massive bicep. We left the trailer arm in arm and headed toward the main stage.

Crickets came out and sang their song and the evening was illuminated by all the rides and carnival lights. Attendees, staff and performers all milled about, preparing for the nighttime events and we got several curious looks our way. I felt Connor stiffen next to me. He seemed to hate unwanted attention.

I lifted my chin and lengthened my steps, exuding my pride at walking next to him. As far as I cared, he was the only decent person at this carnival. With a light squeeze to his arm, I decided to tell him what was on the tip of my tongue since we left the trailer.

"You look great too, you know."

His bicep jumped underneath my fingers as if startled. He cast a sideways glance at me with that shy smile of his.

"Thanks, babe."

I felt him relax next to me, and then the fingers of his opposite hand curling around mine.

THE BACKSTAGE AREA WAS CHAOS. We were not the only act who had to step it up for the final night, it seemed. Everyone was doing last-minute practice sessions from juggling to fire breathing to sword swallowing.

Connor calmly secured his stage stilts as the ringmaster took to the stage and began his opening announcements.

"Ladies and gentlemen, boys and girls!" he boomed. "So good to see so many familiar faces! We've got a hell of a show for you tonight, unlike anything you've seen in the past week!"

"Yo, is this wolf man shit real or fake?" someone yelled from the crowd. From where I sat, I could see an arm holding up a piece of paper. It was a carnival flyer with a cartoonish depiction of a werewolf printed on it.

"Ah, I'm so glad you asked, my friend!" the ringmaster answered theatrically. "The Wolf Man is most certainly real and a fearsome sight to behold! You may want to leave your young children at home tomorrow night, or risk nightmares of being eaten by the big bad wolf!"

He went on in dramatic fashion, avoiding more specific questions about the wolf man by urging people to attend tomorrow and see for themselves.

"Are we still all performing tomorrow?" I asked Connor.

"Nope," he answered dryly. "The wolf man scam is the only show. I hear tomorrow's tickets are almost sold out already," he added with disdain.

"Do we have to buy tickets too?"

"Nah, performers can see it for free." He cocked an eyebrow. "Don't tell me you're falling for this shit too, Mel."

"I just want to see the scam for myself," I said. "To satisfy my own curiosity."

"That's how they getcha," he chuckled, poking me playfully in the ribs. "Fine. But afterward, I get to take you on a romantic Ferris wheel ride."

Butterflies filled my entire torso to the point where even my breathing fluttered. I tried to minimize my smile as I said, "Sure, that sounds good."

The ringmaster finished talking, and our music cued up. The fluttering turned to sinking stones in my stomach and my heart threatened to beat out of my chest. Connor used the stage support to pull himself up to full, stilted height, but not before he dropped an affectionate peck to my cheek.

"You got this, babe." He winked down at me and slid on his mask. "Remember, just like we practiced."

I nodded, swallowed the lump in my throat, and steeled myself at the stage entrance. Connor strode out right on his cue. I counted carefully in my head and stepped out on my mark. If Syko taught me anything useful, it was the importance of smiling and waving. But this time, my smile felt genuine instead of plastered on. It only took a minute into our routine to realize that I was having fun.

The audience's faces were priceless as I weaved in and out of Connor's stilts across the stage. The moment it looked like he was going to step on or kick me, I did a little twirl or sidestep to show we were perfectly in sync. He walked on his hands for a minute, then touched his stilts down right in front of me in a crazy backbend. I did a dramatic pout and foot stomp when the stilts blocked my way and the crowd ate it up. I walked casually underneath his stilts as he elaborately crossed and uncrossed his legs in a crazy, tap dance sort of routine.

It went off flawlessly, and I couldn't believe how much fun I was having. Before I knew it, we were approaching the grand finale.

Connor got into position, angling his stilt like a lopsided bench, and I took a seat. Our eyes met for half a moment before he lifted his leg, tossing me through the air. I could only imagine the incredible amount of strength in his quads for him to pull that off.

Gasps and screams rose up from the crowd, now so far below me. For the briefest snapshot in time, I saw the Ferris wheel and all the carnival lights on the horizon. It was a breathtaking view, and then I was falling.

Connor caught me with ease, securing an arm around my waist and holding me snugly against him. The music ended, and we held our free arms out to the sides in our final pose. The audience went absolutely nuts, cheering and throwing fists and hats in the air.

"Holy shit," I hissed, keeping my smile on as I looked out at everyone pressing in to get closer.

"Great job, babe," Connor said with a squeeze around my waist. His voice was muffled under the mask. "You were perfect. And not only that, they're nuts about you."

I couldn't pinpoint the emotion in his voice but from the corner of my eye, I saw the stage director motioning for us to get off for the next act. I rappelled down the silk rope tied to Connor's pants, and we did a final bow before taking our leave. The reactions backstage were mixed. Some congratulated us, others seemed annoyed that the opening act came out of the gate so strongly, like we showed up everyone else.

But we didn't care. We were riding high off the crowd's energy and how seamlessly we performed. Connor wore his biggest smile I'd seen yet as he ripped off his mask and we hurried away from the chaos so he could take the stilts off privately.

I was talking a mile a minute, feeling absolutely giddy at what we just accomplished. His energy was calmer than mine, more subdued as he put his legs back on, but I could feel the rush of excitement coming off him, too.

When he stood up and looked at me with such pride and warmth, I acted without thinking.

I wrapped my arms around his neck and kissed him.

14

CONNOR

Mel's lips tasted so sweet and my body felt so starved for a physical connection, I acted without thinking.

I pulled her tight against me and opened my mouth to hers. She let me in, sighing beautifully as her soft tongue grazed across my lips. Only when her short nails raked through my hair, did I come to the rest of my senses—and my brain panicked.

"Mel, stop." I pulled away, took a step back to put space between us, and immediately regretted it.

Her big doe eyes looked up at me with confusion and hurt. It was all I could do to not kiss that pain away again.

"Sorry," she mumbled quickly, removing her arms from around my neck and stepping back. "That was... really impulsive. I wasn't thinking at all. Just... forget it happened."

Those last words almost cut me as deeply as when Vicky left me for the last time. But over the years, I'd grown to not only accept it, but expect it. Women liked to tease and flirt with me, but once they found out my amputee status, I was baggage. A burden.

It didn't matter how much I flattered them or made them laugh, no one seriously wanted a guy who was missing a couple of limbs. No one wanted to sleep next to a partner who woke up screaming from nightmares.

"It's forgotten," I said with a tight smile, my chest aching painfully. "But we should still celebrate. Follow me, Mel."

We walked for a few minutes with some awkward distance between us. Damn it. Not even an hour ago, I felt on top of the world walking to the stage with her on my arm. Not only did she look damn gorgeous in her costume, she looked proud to be seen with me. No woman ever looked that happy to stand next to me since before my accident.

"Wait here," I told her, stopping just outside the booze tent. The two bitchy girls she worked with were still behind the bar, and I didn't want them giving her any shit.

I bypassed them, ignoring their dirty looks, and went straight to the back in search of Higgins. After a minute of sweet-talking, I convinced him to sell me an unopened bottle of champagne, already chilled. We were both veterans, so he tolerated me a bit more than most people.

Mel's eyes widened when I presented the bottle. "Where would you like to enjoy this?"

"How about on the grass where we can see the fireworks?" She pointed toward the sky, where the brightly colored bursts were already firing off.

Fuck.

I hated fireworks.

All the little hairs on my arms stood on end. My heart began to speed up as my throat tightened. Usually I remembered when they were going off and planned accordingly, but Mel had me all distracted lately.

"Nah, let's go inside."

I hurried in the direction of my trailer, not waiting to see if Mel would catch up. The *boom-boom-crackle* of explosives sent my lungs tightening. I tried to keep my breaths deep and even, tried to remember when and where I was. I was *here*. Not back *there*.

"Connor, are you okay?"

She was somewhere behind me, or maybe right next to me. I

couldn't be sure. All I knew was I had to get home and get my noise-canceling headphones on before I lost it.

Shit, I hadn't had a flashback in nearly a month. I had been doing so well. Every time I did have one, it felt like I regressed further back. Five steps forward, ten steps back.

I yanked open my trailer door and jumped in, not bothering to see where Mel was. I couldn't worry about her right now.

That was just another aspect that I hated. I was trained to protect those around me. It was my duty, my purpose. When my flashbacks came on like this, I had to abandon everything to focus on myself. It was pathetic. Ordinary people could watch fireworks with no issues, but I had to stop everything just to make sure I survived the next few minutes until it passed.

I found my headphones and stuck them over my ears. Just feeling the familiar pressure and the barrier between my brain and the outside world comforted me a bit. I sat on the edge of the bed and did my breathing exercises like I was taught by my therapist, just waiting it out.

I didn't notice my hands shaking until Mel's tiny, slender fingers wrapped around them. Damn, she was still here? Why? And why did she kiss me? Did that really happen?

Real life and the flashbacks all seemed to blur together. My instinct was to shut my eyes tight, but I forced them open. I looked around, trying to take mental notes of my surroundings. I was *here*. Not back *there*.

Mel's long, slender legs in those sexy black tights stretched out next to mine, crossed at the ankles. I thought I could feel her lips on my shoulder, gently moving like butterfly wings. Was she saying something?

Eventually, the tightness in my chest faded. My pulse returned to normal and my lungs no longer felt like they were collapsing. I pulled off the headphones and let out a resigned sigh. That was exhausting. I could feel the weight of Mel's expectant gaze on me, but couldn't bring myself to look at her.

"Sorry about that," I muttered, wondering how best to explain my behavior. But my brain felt like scrambled eggs after what just happened.

"You have PTSD."

She said it matter-of-factly, but with a gentleness that showed she wasn't upset.

"Yes," I sighed. No point in lying to her. At this point, she knew more about me than all the people I met within the last three years.

Her fingers squeezed around mine gently. "Do you need anything?"

"Just a drink."

She removed her hand from mine and felt like she moved off the bed. My surroundings were still filtering in slowly, like I was coming out of a deep sleep.

I heard a *POP* that made me jump and then Mel's voice, "Sorry! I'm just opening the champagne."

In the next moment, my hands wrapped around a cold bottle, which I brought to my lips. Bubbles and a crisp, refreshing taste coated my throat. I passed the bottle toward Mel, but she held up a hand and shook her head in refusal.

She didn't want to drink. In that moment, I couldn't be concerned with why. All the better to numb myself with. After sucking down a fourth of the bottle, I allowed myself to look at her for the first time.

Her top hat was gone, but she still looked poised, perfect and elegant, sitting on the edge of my bed with her legs crossed.

"You don't have to stay with me," I muttered. "I'm good now."

"Hah. Where the hell would I go, Connor?" she scoffed. "Who else would I be with? After everything we did today?" Her hand closed around mine again. "I'm good right here, too."

Damn it. Not that I really wanted to be alone, but this girl was a whole new level of stubborn.

"What's it gonna take, girl?" I laughed bitterly. "Every day you spend with me, you learn more about how fucked up I am. How bad do I have to be before you finally run away screaming?"

"Syko bad," she answered quickly. "Which you're not and you never will be. I already know that."

I sighed wearily and leaned my head back, finally allowing my eyes to close. Every moment with this girl seemed to crack open my closed-off heart more and more. The longer she stuck around, the worse it would hurt later. I already couldn't keep my eyes off her. After our grueling practice today, I found it increasingly difficult to keep my hands off her too.

"You know what? Fuck it." Mel took the bottle from me, set it on the ground and turned to face me. "I take it back. I'm *not* sorry." Before I could respond, the sweet, fruity taste of her lips were on mine again.

"Mel..." I tried to break away, but she kept leaning into me. "You don't—"

"I *do*, Connor," she insisted. "I want this. I wanted it earlier, but I chickened out. It's just been such a good day and you're... good to me. I don't care about the other stuff."

I shouldn't have given in. Fuck, she was so young and probably expecting too much—more than I could give—from this kiss.

But she was also an adult. Not only consenting, but wanting. And goddamn, she tasted so sweet.

I allowed my arms to go around her, and her tiny hands skimmed over my pounding heart. She pressed another kiss to me, shyly this time, and I accepted.

A light moan escaped her throat as I flicked her top lip with my tongue. We opened up to each other slowly, exploring with caution and hesitancy. Intrinsically, we knew the other person had boundaries, hangups, issues. We had seen glimpses of each other's inner demons and proceeded with slowness and gentleness, lest we uncover something not yet ready to be revealed.

I felt myself turning to putty from the inside out. How long had it been since I held a woman like this, kissing her for the first time?

I cradled Mel like a fragile bird in my arms as her soft lips traveled across my face and neck like gentle rain. My hands began to grow exploratory too, running from her back to her waist, then her thighs.

Immediately, her energy shifted. She stiffened in my arms and her lips broke away from me.

"I don't want to, um, lead you on," she stammered. "Maybe I'll be ready to do more later, but I'm still kind of freaked out by, um—"

"Shh. It's alright, babe." I peppered her face with kisses. "We don't have to do anything you don't want to."

Her doe-eyed gaze filled my vision. "You're seriously okay with just kissing like teenagers?"

"You *are* a teenager," I teased.

She wrinkled her nose at me. "Not for that much longer."

"Even so," I chuckled. "Nothing will happen that you don't actively want to happen."

"Thank you," she sighed, seemingly with relief. "I'm just still shaken up by Syko touching me like that. I think I should take it slow for a bit."

Surprise filled me, but I made sure not to let it show on my face. I thought she had been freaked out by *me*. My legs, my flashbacks, or any other instance of moodiness I displayed. But none of that seemed to bother her.

No, it was that scumbag who still had a hold on her mind, making her scared to be physical with anyone else. I didn't mind that she just wanted to kiss, it was the most action I'd gotten in years. It just pissed me off that he made her feel this way and didn't give a shit about it.

I brought my hands back up to her arms, brushing light kisses across her eyelids and cheeks. Her thick, dark lashes fluttered against my lips, and she stifled a yawn.

"Do you want to lie down?" I asked.

She nodded. "It's been a long day."

Together, we slowly laid back on my mattress. Her head rested on my chest as she snuggled into my side, relaxed and fearless once again.

"Is it okay if I stay?" she asked softly after a few moments of cozy, blissful silence.

"Of course it is." I tightened my arm around her waist. My heart felt like it was leaping out of my chest with joy. But what goes up must always come down. "You can hit the light switch there."

She flicked the switch above her, and darkness surrounded us.

"I haven't felt like this in so long," she murmured sleepily.

"What's that?" I asked, almost fearing the answer.

"Safe."

15

MELODY

I woke up to solidness and warmth against my back. A heavy arm draped across me. For a moment, I forgot where I was and panicked. I shifted against the body behind me and the arm tightened around me. Fear held my breath until I looked down and saw I still had yesterday's clothes on. Not only that, my bedmate was still dressed too.

Relief swept over me as a smile came to my lips. Connor showed a really sweet, tender side of himself last night. His flashback was scary to witness, and I felt like shit for wanting to bring him out to the fireworks. The moment I saw that panicked look in his eye, I should have known.

He stirred next to me with a groan, and his arm lifted off me to rub his face. I took the opportunity to sit up and stretch.

"Making your escape already?" he asked groggily.

"No," I answered. "Just... waking up."

"Mm." He shifted, groaned, and stretched. Damn it, why did he have to be so nice to look at? "You okay?"

"Yeah," I answered, a smile playing at my lips. "I just... didn't expect to sleep so well."

"Oh, yeah?" He folded his arms behind his head, making his biceps flex. "Having regrets?"

My brow furrowed. "About what?"

"You know," he said softly. "Dealing with my shitty mental illness. Staying the night in this four-wheeled piece of shit. Kissing me."

I didn't know how to tell him a *no* that was strong enough. After everything he did for me, this guy was still convinced I wanted to walk away? So I leaned over him and smashed my mouth down on his.

He let out a groan of surprise, then chuckled against my lips before kissing me back. Just like last night, he was gentle and explorative. His arms wrapped around my back and, aside from caressing my face, strayed nowhere else. The more he held back and respected my boundaries, the more my body yearned to feel him push them. But I took comfort in knowing he wouldn't, not until I wanted him to.

"Your PTSD is not your fault," I told him. "None of this is. And I can't stop myself from kissing you, but you gotta kiss me first sometime too."

He chuckled and obliged, lifting his head up to kiss me deeply. I felt it in pleasant tingles from my lips all the way down to my toes. I'd kissed plenty of boys at school before, but never a *man*. Every touch and taste from him carried the confidence of experience. We barely knew each other, but he seemed to know exactly what my body needed. And still he stopped himself, never testing to see what he could get away with like those awkward, fumbling teenage boys.

"Why are you still here, Mel?" he asked, tracing his fingertips down my arms. "Why did you stay last night?" He didn't sound annoyed, but genuinely curious to know.

"Because I wanted to," I answered.

"But why?" The forest of his eyes made me lose sense of everything outside them. "You don't need to drag yourself down with me. You're young, gorgeous, able-bodied. Your mind isn't as... damaged as mine."

"Stop," I told him sternly. "I stayed because you shouldn't be alone when you're going through that. You looked out for me, so the least I can do is be here for you."

He sighed, leaning back on his pillow. "What are you looking for, though? I mean, what do you want out of life? I have my good qualities, but God knows I'm flawed as fuck, too. I'll never be able to watch fireworks with you. I have a temper and I'll probably hurt your feelings. I'll probably never have enough money to buy you nice things. And that doesn't even touch on the fact that I'm missing limbs and just can't do certain things."

"I don't need any of that," I insisted. "And I don't care what your flaws are. We all have them. I do too."

"You should have higher standards," he laughed, brushing my hair out of my eyes.

"Like what?" I demanded. "A rich guy who'll buy me useless shit but won't take care of me when I'm throwing up on myself? Or someone with all their limbs but treats women like Syko does?"

"You'll have more choices than that," he argued. "You can have literally anyone you want without settling."

"I'm not settling," I retorted. "I want *you*, Connor. I don't know where I'll be in five or ten years or even next week, but I'm sure I want you right now."

He sighed and didn't say anything for the longest time. For a moment, I wondered if I misinterpreted everything. Was he trying to talk me out of being with him because he didn't want *me?*

But then he broke out into a smile that lit up his handsome face. "I kept telling myself you're too good to be true. But good things rarely come my way, so I'll keep you as long as you can stand to have me."

Relief swept over me like a wave. Then lightness and joy bubbled up within me like a well. Finally, I felt like I could trust someone. Like I could relax and be myself. My life no longer revolved around me taking care of others. We could support each other.

Who knew how long it would last? Maybe it was unwise of me, but I never thought that far ahead. Even if he turned around and became a monster tomorrow, I wouldn't regret knowing him in the short time I did.

At some point, I got up and made us coffee, but we spent most of the day in bed. Hours felt like minutes as we talked, laughed, and kissed. I couldn't remember a time where I felt so at ease and relaxed. Before we knew it, the sun cast long shadows as it dipped low on the horizon.

"Damn, where did the day go?" I leaned back against Connor's chest as the sky began turning a golden pink.

"It's great to have a day off," he murmured, dropping a kiss to my shoulder. "I still owe you a romantic Ferris wheel ride."

"Damn right you do." I nuzzled his face. "Oh! That means the Wolf Man show is tonight, right?"

"Yeah." He pulled away to look at me, amusement dancing in his eyes. "You still want to go?"

I nodded. "Ferris wheel before or after?"

"Let's do it after." His lips brushed against mine sensually. "So when you're inevitably disappointed by the sham, I can still impress you with my thoughtfulness and charm."

"You already do."

He looked genuinely taken aback and confused before that infectious smile lit up his handsome face. I had a feeling no one told him that in a long time.

"Let me grab a set of clothes," I said, rising reluctantly from the bed. "And I'll be right back."

"Hurry back," he said, clasping my hands for the longest moment he could. "I have a feeling I'll miss you already."

16

MELODY

The crowd was so thick, I had to clamp down tightly onto Connor's hand to avoid losing him. Bodies pressed in all around as we slithered our way through. I caught bits and pieces of conversation as we passed people.

"What do you think the Wolf Man really is?"

"Probably just a fucking dog they taught to stand on two legs."

"I bet it is just a really hairy dude. I really want to know, though..."

"Fuckin' triple the cost of regular admission? It better be a real fuckin' werewolf."

We reached a spot near the right side of the stage, right up against the gate. Stern-looking security guards stood just on the other side of the gate beneath the stage. Their eyes traveled sharply across the crowd pressing in as close as they could to the barrier.

"They're armed," Connor muttered, his eyes falling to the holstered pistols at the guards' hips. "Something's fishy about this."

I swallowed and took a deep breath, but nothing seemed to calm my nerves. For some inexplicable reason, I had to see this, and not for the novelty or morbid curiosity that drove everyone else here. Something in my body pulled me to this spot, like my soul was on a chain being yanked here for a reason I didn't know yet.

The drums started up in time with my hammering heartbeat and the spotlights focused on the red stage curtain. Whistles and cheers rose up from the audience, followed by chants of, "Wolf man! Wolf man! Wolf man!"

The ringmaster entered from the opposite side of the stage from us, taking his place in the center.

"Ladies and gentlemen, boys and girls!" his voice boomed. "I'm so pleased you could join us tonight for our ultimate show here in lovely Drowningville. As promised, we've saved the best for last!"

"Better be worth it!" someone called out.

"Absolutely, my good man!" The ringmaster declared. "This isn't a freak show like the days of the past, with gimmicks and scams, oh no! Behind this curtain is something that, by all the laws of nature and God, should absolutely not exist."

Connor's arm slid around my waist protectively. I didn't even realize how tense I was until he rubbed my back. Squeezing his fingers, I leaned back against his chest and pressed a kiss to the closest spot I could reach, just under his chin.

"To be honest with you good folks," the ringmaster continued. "We shouldn't even be showing you this beast. The moment we captured it, we should have contacted the government. But who are we to deny what the people want?"

"Just show us already!" someone shouted.

"The second we're in danger, I'm getting us out of here," Connor growled into my ear. "I don't have a good feeling about this at all, babe."

"Me neither," I admitted. "But I have to see."

The ringmaster waved his white-gloved hand, and the curtains pulled back to the sound of thunderous applause. Onstage, a red sheet draped over a tall rectangular structure, which I could only assume was a cage. As if on cue, the security detail gathered closer to the stage, their hands resting on the weapons at their hips.

"Remember this is a once in a lifetime opportunity, folks." The ringmaster walked in a slow circle around the cage and picked up an electric cattle prod from a nearby table. "We've taken all the precautions possible, but still don't know the full strength and abilities of this beast. We made you sign waivers with your ticket purchases because we cannot guarantee your safety."

He stuck the cattle prod to the side of the covered cage and pulled the trigger.

An ear-piercing howl, followed by violent rattling and a monstrous roar unlike anything I'd ever heard, rang out into the night. With a collective gasp, the whole crowd seemed to flinch and back away as one entity. Connor held me tightly against his chest.

"What the fuck..." he mumbled.

Everyone else had a similar reaction. The heckling quieted down to a low, cautious murmur. Faces went from curious and jovial to serious, with a healthy dose of fear.

"I warned you, folks!" The ringmaster held up the cattle prod like a beacon. Whatever was inside the cage made low huffing and growling noises. "If you cannot handle looking straight into the face of Hell, I suggest you walk away now! This is truly unlike anything you have ever seen, or ever will see again!"

"Show us!" one person shouted, apparently gaining their courage back swiftly. Others quickly echoed their agreement.

Realizing he couldn't tease and titillate the thirsty audience any longer, the ringmaster took a handful of the cloth in his fist.

"Ladies and gentlemen, boys and girls! I give you," he paused dramatically, "the Wolf Man!"

He yanked the cloth down over the cage with a flourish, revealing the beast within.

A choked gasp escaped my chest, and I lifted my hands to my mouth, but not because of fear or disgust. My eyes immediately began welling with tears for the poor caged creature onstage.

The poor thing was so tall and broad, he could barely turn around in the cramped prison. He did look like a wolf standing on two legs, with hands and feet that looked somewhat like paws. The lower half of his face extended out slightly like a snout, with a long tongue that lolled out as he panted and revealed rows of glistening, pointed teeth. He was covered from head to toe in beautiful silvery-white fur, and his golden eyes were dilated and unfocused.

"He's got to be drugged," I whispered to Connor, the tears spilling freely down my cheeks. "Oh my God, the poor thing. This is fucking awful."

"What... How?" Connor blinked as if he didn't register what I said, just stared at the stage in disbelief. "How's this even possible? That thing looks *real*."

"He is!" I cried. "And look at how they're treating him!"

The ringmaster prodded the beast again with a jolt of electricity, sending him snarling, growling, and pressing against the metal bars to get away. I only then noticed all the bruises and burn marks on his ribs. The audience roared, hooting and hollering and jamming in closer to get a better look. Some were already trying to climb over the barricade and were immediately stopped by security.

"I see some of you are still skeptical!" the ringmaster yelled over the cacophony of voices. "I don't blame you, of course! But fortunately, we have further proof to the validity of the Wolf Man! If you still feel this is a hoax, then how would you like to meet," he paused, waiting for the crowd to quiet down, "the Wolf Man's *children?*"

"Oh, no..." My heart seemed to stop in my chest. "Please don't tell me..."

The wolf-man's semi-human ears pricked forward. His head jerked in the direction of the ringmaster, indicating he understood perfectly what was said.

A stagehand brought out a smaller cage, about the size of a regular dog crate, also covered with a cloth. The wolf-man pressed his face hard between his own bars, sniffing the air and making soft whimpering sounds.

"Oh my God, they can't be doing this," I whispered. Watching the scene play out before me was like watching my own heart break.

Standing between the two cages with his cattle prod raised high in one hand, the ringmaster ripped the cloth off of the smaller cage with the other.

And the wolf man absolutely lost his shit.

He went berserk, was the most accurate way to describe it. He howled at the top of his lungs, yanked and pulled and pounded on the bars with all of his might, to no avail. His cage must have been bolted into the floor because it absolutely would not move.

And the audience laughed. They *laughed* at the distraught father trying to reach his children, two miniature versions of him huddled in the small cage, shaking and whimpering with their ears flattened against their skulls as they held each other. They looked to be about the human age of five or six years old, but also with canine features and covered in fur. The boy's fur was white like his dad's and the girl's was a beautiful pattern, ticked with gray, black, and brown.

"This is so fucked up," Connor said in disbelief. "Holy shit, they're just babies."

When the father realized he could not get to his children, he looked to the ringmaster, standing pompously just out of reach of his claws. The wolf man's jaws moved as yowls, yips, and barks came out. He was trying to speak, no doubt pleading for his children to be left alone.

And the sadistic fucker nodded, raising his eyebrows as if listening raptly to the caged man's pleas, which the audience found endlessly amusing.

"Ah, yes indeed. I see what you're saying," the ringmaster said mockingly before electrocuting him again.

The howls of pain that followed radiated through my eardrums and rattled my skull. I covered my ears and Connor pulled my head into his chest, but I didn't miss the pups' reaction and that was what severed my heart in two.

They let go of each other and ran to the edge of their cage, sticking their skinny arms out as far as they could, but to no avail. They yelped and whined and cried as they swiped in the direction of the ringmaster's shoes, trying desperately to stop the torture being inflicted on their father.

His painful howls eventually stopped, and the thump of flesh against metal bars indicated he was unconscious. The audience laughed uproariously, while I could only sob into Connor's shirt, clutching him tightly. The children's screaming continued. For all they knew, their father was just murdered as part of a performance.

"Let's go." Keeping my head tightly pressed to his heart, Connor turned us away and began shoving through the crowd. "We don't need to see this disgusting shit."

My feet followed limply, without protest. A cold numbness settled over my body, but there was no escaping what played on a repeating loop in my head. And the ache in my heart felt so deep that it tore through my soul.

Connor took us all the way back to his trailer, where he laid me down on the small bed and covered me with a blanket. I curled into a ball and just sobbed, my whole body wracking with deep, ragged breaths.

Hesitantly, Connor laid down behind me and draped a large, muscular arm over my waist. I tried to take small comfort in him being there, as he rubbed my arms and placed soft kisses on my shoulder. But then I remembered those two kids, scared and alone, as they watched their dad get mistreated with no one to help.

It made what Syko did to me look completely harmless in comparison.

"I'm sorry, babe," Connor murmured, planting a gentle kiss behind my ear. "People are terrible. I wish there was something we could do."

"There has to be." I flipped over to face him. "We can't do *nothing*. Those poor kids..." My voice was raw from crying and still fresh tears spilled.

"I know." He used the pad of his thumb to gently wipe my tears away. "Trust me, I wanted to murder that fucking ringmaster and every heartless asshole in the audience."

"We have to do something." I sat up abruptly, wiping my face and nose with a shaky breath. "I hate myself for every second I'm sitting here crying and they're the ones who are actually suffering."

"I get what you're feeling, babe. But how?" Connor reached out and squeezed my knee. "What can a crippled old curmudgeon and an eighteen-year-old girl do for a... werewolf family or whatever the fuck they are?"

"I don't know yet." I hung my head in my hands.

"And here's another thing to think about," he went on. "Yes, they were being mistreated, and that's fucked up, but we still don't know *what* they are. What if they're dangerous? What if they love to eat humans? It's totally possible you want to help something that would turn around and kill you the first chance it got."

"That's not how they are." My voice grew steadier and my eyes drifted to the waning moon out the trailer window.

"Mel, how do you know that?"

My thoughts drifted back to the wolf man in his cage. His golden eyes showed intelligence and depth. He understood what the ring-master said and tried speaking to him. He didn't act like a wild animal, but a *person*. And the deepest part of my heart told me he was exactly that.

"I just know."

17

MELODY

The longer I laid there and allowed my thoughts to spiral, the more restless I became. Hours had gone by and the show was long over. If the wolf people were treated that badly in front of an audience, I didn't dare speculate how bad it was when no one was looking. Every passing second was another moment of those kids being terrified or hurt, and I couldn't stand to not do anything about it.

I tossed the blanket off me and stood from the bed. My fingers brushed against my lucky coin in my pocket for a dose of courage, then I started putting on my shoes and jacket.

"Where are you going?" Connor mumbled in the darkness.

"I'm helping the wolf family escape."

He sprang up, sliding his hand along the wall for the light switch. I pounced to stop him, straddling his waist and catching his wrists. I was nowhere near strong enough to actually stop him, but his movements paused and a low groan escaped his chest. He was rock hard beneath me and I felt my core hollow out in response. Our breath mingled for half a moment. As much as I wanted to explore this, now was not the right time.

"You can come or not," I whispered. "But I'm going and don't want anybody seeing."

"Melody." His voice was a mixture of threatening, arousal, and pleading. On an instinctual level, I wanted to hear him say my name like that again and again.

But again, not the right time. I had to focus.

"You'll get caught before you can reach them," he growled. "They've got to be heavily guarded. Who knows how many others want to help themselves to a closer look?"

"Then help me."

I released his hands and let my fingers travel up his massive arms to wrap around his shoulders. A sliver of moonlight came through the window and illuminated part of his face and one stunning green eye like a mask.

Honestly, I was scared shitless of doing this alone. He had a strange way of making me feel safer and more confident when he was at my side. Like a huge, disgruntled guardian angel, he had been looking out for me since my first day here.

And I was beginning to realize how much I wanted him at my side through everything, no matter where this crazy freak show of a life took us.

"Please, Connor." My fingers found his lips in the dark, brushing against the rough stubble on his jaw. "It's the right thing to do. You know it is."

"Fuck, Mel." His mouth captured mine savagely as his arms wrapped around me and crushed me against his chest. "You're going to get us in an assload of trouble. But the thing is, I know I won't regret a damn second of it."

My heart dared to leap with hope. "So you'll help me save them?"

"Get your sweet little ass off me." He patted my thigh. "Let me put my legs on."

Within minutes, we silently crept out the door and across the carnival grounds.

The attendees were gone, but some staff and performers were still out and winding down for the evening. The sounds of glasses clinking and multiple conversations drifted over from the booze tent, still open and lively. Others drank, smoked, and played cards in smaller, quiet circles on picnic tables. We headed in the general direction of the booze tent, and no one batted an eye.

Once out of sight, we took a hard left and walked as casually as we could behind the rows of tents and trailers. I realized vaguely this was where all the tools and equipment were stored for breaking down the Ferris wheel, booths, and everything else. It looked like a junkyard.

"This is the most likely spot they'll keep them," Connor whispered. "Out of sight, out of mind when surrounded by pieces of junk."

Before I could respond, he grabbed my arm and pulled me to duck behind the rusted shell of a car. He held a finger to his lips and looked at me insistently. I nodded and listened hard.

Voices and footsteps slowly approached, and we ducked further back, careful not to make a sound.

"Jesus, dog-sitting fucking sucks," one of the voices complained. "I could be in the booze tent right now with a bottle of whiskey and a pair of tits in my face."

"I hear ya," the other voice commiserated.

"Say." The first voice perked up as if hit with a jolt of inspiration. "What if I grab a bottle and come right back? It'll make the time go faster."

"Yes, go," Connor mouthed silently, clenching his fists.

"I dunno, man." The second voice was hesitant. "Jenkins was hard up about keeping two of us on these mutts at all times, no matter what."

"Aw, come on, you pussy. They're out cold," the first voice protested. "It'll just take a second to sweet-talk the pretty bartender and swipe a bottle."

"I know how you get around female attention," his partner snarled. "First pair of titties you see and you have the memory of a goldfish. Next thing I know, I'm out here for another two fuckin' hours by myself."

Connor and I barely breathed as we listened and waited for them to finish arguing. Finally, the first guy got his permission to visit the booze tent. The second guy grumbled angrily as his partner pranced off and he headed back to his post. Connor wasted no time and jumped on him in the blink of an eye.

With nothing more than a quick thud and a grunt, the guard went down like a sack of potatoes.

"Holy shit!" I shrieked, almost forgetting to whisper. "What was that?"

"Just knocked him out." Connor flashed me a smile as he patted the guy down. "Marine corps, baby."

"How do you know he's not dead?"

"We've got no time to find out." Connor fished a set of keys from the unconscious man's pocket and grabbed my hand. "Let's move before the other one comes back."

It didn't take long for us to find the wolf family. After only a minute, a flash of white fur caught my eye among the rusted metal and warped wooden boards of the junkyard. Connor and I made a beeline straight for them, and what I saw made me want to burst into tears again.

The children were in the same cage as before, curled up in each other's arms and appeared to be sleeping. The father had been moved to a shorter, wider cage where he couldn't stand up at all and could barely stretch out. He too appeared to be sleeping, though his breaths wheezed with labor through the crude muzzle they clamped over his snout. It looked like little more than a leather belt.

"Hey," I whispered, tapping on the bars of his cage. "We're here to let you out." He didn't move a muscle, so I tapped a little more insistently.

"We don't have time for this, babe," Connor murmured urgently.

"They must be sedated," I realized, looking up at him. "Connor, we're gonna have to drag them out of here."

His eyes widened. "What? How?"

"I'll take the kids. You carry him." I snatched the keys from his hand and proceeded to unlock the cages.

"Melody, stop!" he hissed, but I ignored him, opening the cage doors wide. He grabbed my wrists before I could do anything else and brought his face down close to mine. "Mel, what are we supposed to do with them?"

"We take them back to the trailer and hide them there."

Connor rubbed his face. I could tell his patience was wearing thin with me, but I was not about to let this family get abused again without a chance to escape or fight back. Consequences be damned.

"And then what?"

"Then we get the fuck out of here," I replied coolly. "It's the last night. We already got paid. Why bother to stick around?"

A heavy pause hung between us and for a moment, I wondered if he'd had enough. I waited for him to storm off and leave me to deal with them on my own, but he sighed and stuck his torso into the father's cage.

"I don't know why I keep going along with your crazy shit, girl," he grumbled as he began dragging the unconscious wolf man from his cage.

"'Cause you love me," I joked, reaching in and gently separating the children from each other.

Connor mumbled something in reply, but I didn't hear him over adjusting the boy's head on my shoulder before securing the girl on my other arm.

Their fur was incredibly soft with the fuzzy quality of a young puppy. Another stab went through my heart at the thought of how innocent they were, and how cruel it was to subject them to this.

With each child secured in my arms, I carefully pulled out of the cage and stood up, using all the strength in my legs. The kids sat like sandbags in each of my arms, each of them leaning limply against me like rag dolls. I wouldn't have the strength to carry them far.

Connor slung the wolf man's torso over his shoulders, carefully securing his arm and leg in a fireman carry, then stood to his full height with all the power and confidence of a bodybuilder. I only then realized how truly gigantic the wolf man was. Connor was broader and more muscular, but his prosthetics didn't make him much taller than me. The wolf man had to be at least six-foot four, made of long, lean muscles under his white fur. With how cramped those cages were, it was impossible to guess his full stature before now.

"Let's go."

Connor started off, and I followed him, keeping the kids as steady in my arms as possible. My heart crashed against my ribs and my eyes darted around for anyone being alerted to us. Running would draw too much attention, so we speedwalked through the alley behind all the tents and trailers, going behind trucks, port-a-potties, and more random storage and parts to avoid being seen.

A heavy ache settled into my arms, but spotting Connor's trailer up ahead put a renewed spring in my step. Not much farther!

Unfortunately, that was the moment the girl began waking up.

Still with her eyes closed, she squirmed in my arms, pushing away at my chest while making soft whimpering sounds.

"Shh, it's okay!" I whispered to her. "We're helping you. It's gonna be okay."

She spun around in my arms, clearly disoriented and trying to get her bearings. All I could do was keep her locked between my forearm and my chest while my feet kept moving and my other arm holding onto her brother. The poor thing must have opened her eyes and seen her dad draped across Connor's shoulders a few feet ahead, because right then she began howling bloody murder.

I pulled her face into my chest, trying as best I could to cover her mouth. "I'm sorry. I'm really sorry, little one, but you have to be quiet."

"We've got to run," Connor hissed, picking up his pace. "Someone definitely heard that."

I willed my feet to move faster, gritting my teeth against my arms begging to fall off. Through the air whipping past my ears, I heard distant voices shouting, but didn't dare look back or slow down. My eyes stayed locked on Connor's back as my panic heightened. Then the boy, stronger and bigger than his sister, started wriggling in my fatigued arms.

"Stop, stop!" I pleaded. The boy struggled so hard, I was seconds away from dropping him. "Connor!"

"Shut up!" he snapped. He was at the door to his trailer and fumbling for his keys.

I came right up on his heels, every muscle burning from running and carrying these kids. The moment I stopped, the boy began slipping out of my grasp, kicking and clawing at my shins. In his mind, he was already so close to escape and feeling the ground so close to his feet spurred him on.

"Kid, listen to me!" I brought my mouth down close to his ear. "You will die or get captured if you run from me. If you want to escape, stop fighting!"

He stopped just long enough for Connor to throw open the door and rush inside. In a flash, Connor lowered the father to the floor and sprang up to the driver's seat. I followed, quickly spinning around and slamming the door shut behind me before finally relieving myself of the weight of two incredibly squirmy children.

I dragged in a shaky breath, leaning against the door, but could not afford to relax yet. Connor already turned the vehicle on and started driving us out.

The pups ran with wobbly gaits to their still-unconscious father on the floor, nuzzling and pawing at him with soft whimpers. One of them yanked off his muzzle and his breathing seemed to grow deeper, his chest rising and falling rhythmically.

The floor swayed beneath my feet as Connor took a hard turn, then he hit the gas and sent me stumbling back toward the bed. The wolf family didn't seem to pay any mind. They were all alive and not trying to escape us yet, so I carefully moved up to the front.

Connor's shoulders bunched up and tensed near his ears. His handsome face was a scowl of concentration as he drove us like a bat out of hell off the carnival grounds.

"Can I help with anything?" I asked timidly, reaching for his shoulder.

"Get down," he barked. "Stay out of sight."

I did as he said, slinking down to the floor behind his seat and trying not to take his tone personally. Turning around, I saw the pups nestled under their father's arm. They were quiet and looked calmer, though still wary of us and their surroundings. The boy watched me with his wild, golden eyes. His lips curled back in a snarl to show me his baby wolf teeth in a warning.

I just nodded, not knowing how else to show I understood.

"We're getting far away from those bad people," I said. "You're not our prisoners. Once we're far away, you guys can go free."

The boy put his teeth away and his ears pricked forward. He did that cute puppy head-tilt as if pondering my words. Amidst all the chaos and adrenaline of this crazy day, I had to let myself smile. It was too adorable not to.

"Mel, babe." Connor's voice floated back to me, the harsh edge of it gone.

"Yeah?" I lifted my head up in his direction.

"Will you check the mirrors for me? See if anyone's behind us."

"Yeah."

I positioned myself out of sight behind his seat, but still within clear view of the mirrors. I relayed every headlight I saw as we made off like thieves in the night.

MELODY

We drove for what felt like hours in darkness and silence. Connor kept the headlights off as we put more and more distance between us and that awful carnival.

Are all of them like this? I wondered as we lumbered down the road. Did the carnival I attended as a child also treat its attractions this way? And its performers? Did every carnival have a sadistic, abusive ringmaster and a Syko in their midst?

The more I thought about it, the more it seemed like the outside world wasn't any rosier than the shitty trailer park I grew up in. For those like the wolf family, it was a hundred times worse. At least I was never treated like an animal growing up. I was treated like shit and taken advantage of, for sure. But I could never imagine going through what those three did.

No, the only good thing I had going for me was Connor, and even he seemed pissed off at me half the time. Oh, and the satisfaction of saving a family from more abuse and mistreatment, I guess.

I was still stewing in my thoughts when the vehicle slowed and finally took a complete stop. No headlights had shown up in the mirrors for the past two hours and it seemed Connor was finally ready to rest for the night.

"Should be safe here. I'll kick on the generator," he mumbled, brushing past me with barely a glance. He was careful however, to step around the wolf family still sprawled on the floor.

The father still showed no signs of consciousness. Whatever they gave him must have been a huge dose. His children looked fairly content though, sleeping peacefully and curled up against his thick fur. Who knew when they were all last able to snuggle up together? The sight tugged at my heartstrings as the inside lamps gently flickered on.

Connor walked slowly back through to collapse on the bed. He pulled up his pant legs, swiftly removed his prosthetics, then reclined back on the mattress with a heavy sigh.

After a moment, he lifted his head to look at me. "Whatchu doin' all the way over there?"

I lifted a shoulder in a lazy shrug. "I can never tell if you're mad at me or not," I admitted.

He propped himself up on his elbows and gave me a curious look. "Why would I be mad at you, babe?"

I flicked my eyes in the direction of the wolf family sleeping peacefully on the floor. He hadn't wanted to get involved, but I dragged him into it. My sense of justice was so overwhelming at times, I forgot that most people didn't feel the same way I did.

"Hey," he said softly and patted the space next to him. "Come here."

I rose to my feet and crawled across the mattress toward him, still feeling a little apprehensive. He drew me to his side and dropped a kiss to my head, knowing full well that would make me melt like putty in his arms.

"I was never mad at you, babe. The situation was just stressful and I get hyper-focused when shit like that happens. I go right back to being a soldier. A machine carrying out a mission."

"I didn't mean to take you back to that mindset," I said, chewing my lip over the guilt. It was bad enough that he had PTSD. How shitty was it of me to make him revert back to the worst period of his life?

Shit. Comparatively speaking, I was the one person in the trailer with the least to complain about.

"Not your fault, babe. That's just in my nature." He stroked my hair absentmindedly and got a faraway look in his eyes.

"What? To take command of a dangerous situation?" I propped my chin up on his chest to look at him.

"No." His gaze dropped. "To protect you."

My heart squeezed in my chest, an unfamiliar but not unwelcome feeling. Warmth and lightness spread throughout my limbs.

"Why?" I asked. No one else had ever felt the need to protect me. I was always the protector.

"Because," he paused for a moment, tightening his arm around me. "You remind me of what it was like to be happy."

The lightness and warmth in me spread all the way to my toes, and I had the unbearable urge to smile and bury my face in his side. I felt comfortable and relaxed. Was this happiness?

"When I'm with you, I think I'm starting to figure out what that feels like," I said cautiously.

He tilted my chin up to look at him, surprise and concern in his green eyes.

"You don't know what being happy feels like?"

"Well, I know what it means," I mumbled, heat rising shamefully in my cheeks. "And I kind of remember the feeling. The closest thing to happiness was when I went to the carnival as a little kid. That's why I ran away and joined. I was clinging onto that."

He said nothing for a moment, just stroked my hair absently as we listened to the wolves snore a few feet away on the floor.

"It does suck, growing up and learning what you thought as a kid isn't true," he said gently. "Adulthood is full of disappointing shit, but to be jaded and bitter about it? That's a choice." He chuckled. "I should know. I'm probably the most jaded, bitter old bastard you'll ever meet."

"You have a right to be, though," I argued. "You almost died, and then your country took a shit on you when you came home. Then you ended up in this place where you have to hide your injuries or get treated like a freak." I nodded toward the wolves. "Like them."

"Sure, but then I met this adorable spitfire of a girl who pushes all my buttons, makes me laugh, and drags me along on dangerous rescue missions." He dropped a kiss to my lips that turned all of my bones to jello. "It's all about your perspective, babe."

"So you're not wishing you never met me right now?" I had to pry my eyes away as those words, my biggest insecurity at the moment, tumbled out of me.

"Hell no." He forced me to look at him again. "You know how long I worked in that shithole?"

I shook my head.

"Two years. Two years of my life being a goddamn tap-dancing monkey because my other option was begging on the street. I couldn't even tell you why I wanted to keep living another day. Then you came along and shook everything up. You gave me reasons to smile and punch Syko in his fucking teeth. You've turned my world upside down and I wouldn't have it any other way."

"Me neither," I sighed, settling into the warm glow that radiated from being near him, and from the knowledge that he didn't think of me as some annoying little kid. I wanted to hold on to this and never let it go.

"Tell me about when you were happy before," I said, allowing a hand to snake across his chest. "What was your life like back then?"

"Well, damn," he laughed softly. "Let me see, it's been so long."

He eased back onto the pillows, his arm still snug around my waist and allowing me to lay my head on his chest. The watery thud of his heartbeat greeted my cheek as we laid together and got comfortable.

"I was a typical guy in my twenties, I guess," he began. "Going to college, working part-time, partying on weekends and being a drunk idiot with my friends. Life was simpler back then. I was busy, but I just did everything I was supposed to do and was working toward a goal. I was always a country boy, but I wanted to work in finance. I wanted to wear a fancy suit, have a corner office, get away from the rednecks and all that corporate bullshit."

"What made you join the marines?" I asked.

"Um, well," he stammered a bit. "Turns out it's hard to get a competitive job in finance right after you graduate, especially for a small-town hick like me with no connections." He forced out a laugh. "And my girlfriend at the time wanted a ring and a stable future. She wanted me to prove I could step it up and support a family, so the military made the most logical sense."

The memory of seeing the text message on Connor's phone flashed through my mind. Was that who he was talking about?

"Yeah? What did she do to prove she could give *you* a stable future?" I said with more hostility than I intended. My jealousy was showing, but I didn't care.

"Easy, tiger," he chuckled, giving me a squeeze. "That's just how things are around these parts. The man is expected to provide, so that was what I signed up to do."

"And?" I pressed. "Did you prove your worth to her?"

"I did after I completed basic and finished my first tour," he mumbled. "I came home on leave, went straight to the jewelry store and bought the ring she wanted. She said yes and everything was great." He smiled sadly. "That was until I got back from my second tour as only half the man I used to be."

"Don't say that." I smacked his chest. "You're not any less of a man."

"It's a joke, babe." He mussed up my hair playfully. "I don't take my leg situation too seriously anymore, so you don't have to, either. Perspective, see?"

"Whatever," I mumbled. "But she broke up with you because of it?"

"Not right away." His voice turned soft again. "She actually stuck by me through a lot of the hardest parts, which I'm grateful for. But in the end... she decided a life with me was not the best thing for her."

"That's a very nice way of speaking about someone who dumped you. After agreeing to marry you, no less!" My words came out harshly while a storm of emotions churned in my stomach. Anger and jealousy at a woman I never met? Oh, they were all brewing in there.

Connor shrugged, appearing utterly unfazed. "She didn't sign up for a life with a double amputee. Of course, it killed me at the time, but it's been years now. I don't fault her for wanting an easier life."

"I do," I huffed. "If she loved you, she would have stayed with you, no matter what. You don't just abandon someone you make a commitment to."

"It wasn't just the legs, babe," he said. "My PTSD was bad right after coming back. I was a completely different person than before. I pushed her away and upset her a lot. So some of the blame rests on me, too."

"You couldn't help any of that happening," I protested. "You didn't choose to lose your legs or have PTSD."

"True," he replied. "But shit happens sometimes. And sometimes it affects the people close to you, and they have to do what's right for themselves. Like you running away."

I lifted my head up to look at him. "What do you mean?"

"You did that to protect yourself after giving so much to those around you for so long."

"You're right," I admitted. "But I still want to go back at some point to help my younger siblings. They all deserve better than that hellhole."

"You will." He closed his hand around my fingers and brought them to his lips. "I mean, you're hellbent on saving *everyone,* so I'm sure you will." I felt his smile against my knuckles.

"Yeah, I can't seem to help it."

I looked over his body to the wolf family still huddled up and breathing quietly on the floor. The father had curled up into a semicircle of brilliant white fur, standing out like a ghost in the darkness. He laid like a dog would, with his jaw resting on the ground and his paw-like hands on either side of his face. His pups clung to his side, burying themselves in his fur.

"What's your next step for them?" Connor asked.

"I don't know," I answered. My entire focus had been getting them out of there. Now that we succeeded? I had no clue. "I guess rest for the night, figure out food in the morning, then see if we can communicate if they need anything else. Maybe they have a pack or something, I don't know." I returned my gaze to Connor. "Are you still worried about them hurting us?"

"No," he said. "You were right. There's something... really human about them."

"The kids stopped fighting me once I told them we were helping,"

I said. "I think letting them be near their dad shows we're not planning on using them again."

"So we figure it out in the morning, then," Connor mumbled sleepily. He was already drifting off.

I only realized then how tired I was, too. The adrenaline rush of our rescue mission drained everything out of me.

Connor flipped onto his side, drawing me against him as the little spoon. He dropped a kiss to my neck and curled around me with a contented sigh. I never went to sleep so deeply before, nor feeling so protected.

MELODY

I woke up to dappled sunlight streaming through the windows. I blinked, rubbed my eyes, rolled over, and stretched. Connor laid shirtless next to me, the sight of him making me instantly more awake.

How was it that this big, intimidating guy looked so cute when he slept? His brows pinched gently, full lips slightly parted, and the hypnotic rise and fall of his chest brought a lazy smile to my face. Especially after everything he told me last night, my body tingled in places I once wanted no one to touch. But the sight of him that morning awakened an ache deep in my core.

I leaned over him to check on our new companions on the floor. I leaned so far, unable to believe my eyes that I careened right over Connor's body and onto the floor.

"Connor!" I shouted. "Wake up, they're gone!"

"Hrm?" he mumbled groggily as I shoved open the trailer door. Sure enough, it was unlocked.

I stumbled outside, my eyes blinking as they adjusted to the morning sunlight.

Connor parked us in a small clearing of forest that resembled a campsite. I spun around in a circle, taking in the fresh, earthy scent in the air, the tall pine trees filtering out the sun, and the complete lack of human, wolf, or any other living soul.

In disbelief, I walked around the trailer, but only more trees and dense forest surrounded us.

"They're gone, babe." Connor sat on the edge of the bed wearing only his boxers as he looked out the open trailer door.

"But why?" I tore my fingers through my bird's nest of hair.

"Dad probably thought it was best," he mused. "We got them out of there, but they still don't know us. He was probably willing to risk living out in the woods rather than let someone hurt his kids again."

"I guess..." I chewed my lip. My mind thirsted for knowledge about these wolf people. I had so many questions that would now go unanswered.

"Come back in, Mel," Connor said. "Let's get some breakfast in us and figure out what the hell we're doing with ourselves."

After taking another long look through the trees and listening intently, I reluctantly obliged.

Connor sat at the small table to prepare breakfast, then hoisted himself up to sit on the counter to throw everything into a skillet. I heated up tortillas in the microwave, and within minutes we had ourselves some breakfast fajitas.

"You're still thinking about them," he observed once we finished our silent meal.

"I mean, aren't you curious?" I asked. "What are they? Where did they come from? Are there more of them out there? A few hundred people saw them. Why isn't this on the news?"

"Mel, of course they're just as real as you and I. We both know that." Connor wiped his mouth on a napkin. "But the rest of the world would probably write them off as a hoax, which is a good thing. If you think the ringmaster was a sadistic fuck, imagine what'll happen if the government gets ahold of them?"

"But I don't want to do anything like that," I protested. "I want to learn about them, help them more if they need it. I'm just so fascinated. They're intelligent, Connor! They responded like humans would."

"I know you wouldn't hurt a fly, babe," he smiled. "But like I said, they don't know they can trust you. If they're intelligent as you say, Dad wanted to do the best thing for his kids, so he made a choice."

"You're right. I know that," I groaned. "I just feel like this was a once-in-a-lifetime opportunity, to meet an intelligent species that isn't human."

"Who knows? Maybe you'll get abducted by aliens, too," Connor joked and laughed at my ensuing glare. "In all seriousness, though, you saved their lives, babe." He reached across the table for my hand and his gaze dropped shyly. "Not only do you have a heart of gold, you're brave and you're strong. Not many people are like that."

I dropped my own gaze, unsure how to handle such glowing compliments from a guy I increasingly found myself crushing on. My mind raced at how to respond and came up with nothing. Before Connor, no one had ever been good to me, as in genuinely kind and not just nice to me when they wanted something.

And just as quickly as it began, the moment was over.

"So," Connor released my hand, leaned back, and stretched his arms above his head. "What's next for us, babe?"

My heart skipped a beat. Was he referring to *us* or...?

"What do you mean?"

He gave me a funny look. "I mean in terms of money. The next job. Our food and gas aren't gonna last forever."

"Oh, right." My face heated, betraying me as I tried to play it cool. "Um, I'm not sure. What do you suggest?"

"Well, I've got two skills at this point. The main one being stilt acrobatics. I'd rather not do it forever, but the easiest way for me to get fast, legal money is to join another carnival."

"Makes sense," I nodded. "What's your other skill?"

"You might find that out later," he said with a wolfish grin.

The warmth in my cheeks flared up into a blazing inferno throughout my whole body. Heat pooled in my center like a fiery lake. The more time I spent with him, the more I wanted to let go, to let him in.

"But only if or when you want to," he added with a wink. "What about you, Mel? What are your vocational skills?"

"I don't really have any," I admitted. "I never could get a job during school because I had to take care of my siblings. This stint with the carnival has been the only job I've ever had."

"So looks like it's back to the ol' freak show for both of us," he mused, taking a sip of coffee.

"I really don't mind it," I piped up. "Aside from, you know, Syko, I actually had fun performing. If there's a traveling show out there that isn't abusive to its performers, I'd be happy staying in this business."

"Heh," Connor scoffed. "They may not be Syko but trust me, babe. All of them have some level of corruption and dirty business practices. It's kind of like pimping. When you're profiting off of human bodies, you're not usually too concerned with the ethics of the situation."

"Well, maybe we can start our own carnival," I joked. "Where everyone is treated fairly, and it's not a meat market."

Connor nearly choked on his coffee. "Ah, to be eighteen and full of dreams again," he laughed.

"Don't make fun of me, old man!" I threw my last hunk of tortilla at him, prompting him to reach around the table and tickle my waist.

After a few minutes of playful tickle-wrestling and stealing kisses in between, we got cleaned up and got ready to find work. Connor said he knew another carnival manager in a small town about two hours away, so off we went.

It was a long, slow, lumbering drive through a windy forest road. I kept looking out the passenger window, still hoping to see flashes of white fur through the trees and brush. But I eventually fell asleep with my cheek against the glass until Connor shook my shoulder gently.

"We're here, sleeping beauty," he said with a nuzzle and kiss to my neck.

I followed him out, quickly realizing we were in an RV park still surrounded by forest. But over the treeline stood a slowly moving Ferris wheel. Past the trailers and through the trees, I caught glimpses of brightly colored tents and booths being set up.

"What town is this?" I asked.

"Crying Falls, Mississippi," Connor answered as we approached a simple wooden building, the only permanent structure on the grounds. It looked to be an office or general store. "Population five-hundred-eighty in the winter and quadruple that during summer carnival season."

My stomach did a flip-flop. "A lot of people come to this one, huh?"

"Yeah, it becomes some weird hybrid between traveling carnival, Burning Man, and music festival. The sideshow scene is pretty big here."

"Sideshow?"

Connor grabbed my hand and pulled me close. "That's us, babe," he chuckled, with a kiss to the top of my head. "The freaks."

The carnival manager was a thin, reedy man who recognized Connor instantly. He pretty much ignored me, which I was honestly happy about. Any opportunity I took to not show off my cleavage to beg for a job, I happily took.

"Are you two an act together?" asked Nigel, the manager who seemed to notice me for the first time.

"Yes," Connor answered quickly, with a hint of growl in his voice. His grip on my hand grew firm and possessive.

"Wonderful," Nigel beamed. "I'll show you through the grounds, then we can get you on a schedule."

The carnival grounds were much more expansive than the one in Drowningville and seemed to have a lot more to offer. Vendors and craftspeople were setting up their booths for the coming visitors. The usual carnival games, rides, and food carts were being set up as well. A large stage for music was at the far end, hula hoopers practiced their routine in a nearby field, and the massive Ferris wheel looked over it all like an omniscient eye. It really felt more like a festival than a carnival.

Connor and I got some fresh tacos and ears of corn from a local vendor after our tour, then set up a campfire back at our trailer. Already the sky began turning pink then purple with the setting sun, and more campfires illuminated in the darkness. I didn't realize getting here and checking the place out took most of the day.

"Beer, babe?" Connor held a bottle out to me as we settled next to our fire.

"No, thanks," I answered.

"What, not a party girl?" he teased.

"Not really."

I became deeply preoccupied with roasting my marshmallow and he thankfully left it alone. I didn't want to get into explaining my alcoholic mother and the string of men just like her that came in and out of our house. If Connor could have his secrets, so could I.

Sitting together by the fire, I watched his beer intake with nervous apprehension. People drinking always made me guarded. Dealing with Syko didn't ease my nerves in the slightest.

Alcohol brought out the worst in people, as far as I was concerned. And here was someone I was starting to care about. Could he feel the tense shield surrounding me as he cracked open a second bottle?

To my relief, Connor stopped at two. He eased back in his lawn chair, staring at the flames with the same hot but scowling expression he always wore.

"What's our act gonna be?" I asked. "Same as the one in Drowningville?"

"No idea." He never looked up from the flames. "We'll figure something out tomorrow."

I left it at that. He didn't seem to be in the mood to talk.

Despite the sugar rush from my s'mores, I soon felt my eyelids drooping. Looking over at Connor, I saw he was nodding off as well. The fire went down to embers and the darkness creeped in all around us.

"Hey." I leaned over and rubbed the back of his neck. "Ready to call it a night?"

He nodded, bringing our stuff inside while I covered the fire with water and dirt from the ground. After following him in and washing my hands, I noticed him grimacing as he slid his prosthetics off. The skin just below his knee was red and tender.

"You okay?"

"I'll be alright," he said gruffly. "Just a long day of driving and walking puts pressure on the ol' stubs."

"Here." I rummaged through my backpack until I found the small sample bottle of lotion I got from the homeless shelter.

His protests turned to pleasant sighs as I rubbed it in all around where his legs ended. Just as I figured, the skin was dry and cracked.

My fingers worked deeply into the tissue around his knees to bring circulation back to the area.

"Thanks, babe," he muttered softly.

"Of course." I slid my palms up his powerful quads and tilted my chin up for a kiss.

His mouth caught mine so sweetly and so hungrily. A moan escaped his mouth as he cupped the back of my head to deepen the kiss. Our tongues clashed and danced with a heightened passion and more intensity than ever before. My skin felt alive, like the living, breathing organ it was, and it wanted more of Connor. So much more.

But ever the gentleman, he slowly, reluctantly pulled away. My body responded before my brain could catch up. I climbed into his lap, straddling his thighs, and rested my aching core over the hardening bulge in his pants. He let out a small groan of surprise as my arms wrapped around his shoulders, my chest pressed to his, and my tongue surged into his mouth for more of him.

"Mel," he rasped when our mouths broke apart. "Are you sure...?"

The question seemed to break a spell over me and I withdrew just slightly, my self-consciousness taking a front seat to my body's desires.

"I don't know," I stammered as I pulled away. "Kind of, but maybe not all the way... Shit, I'm sorry."

He caught my waist and pulled me back for another kiss before I could slide completely off his lap. Kisses peppered my face and neck as his hands slid up my back, holding me in an embrace that was just as reassuring as it was possessive. Together, we leaned over until we collapsed on the mattress. His kisses continued, and I writhed against him as his hands grew more adventurous.

"Grab my hands if you want me to stop, or just tell me," he murmured, nipping the side of my neck before his mouth traveled lower. "I just want you to relax and feel good, babe."

My nerves slowly melted away as he took his time with me, kissing and caressing until my legs parted, eager to release the heat and coiled up tension building inside of me. Lifting my shirt, his hands and lips traveled across my waist, belly, and hips in a sensual, hypnotizing pattern until I couldn't stand it anymore. I took his hands and placed them on my breasts.

Growing bolder, his hands slid under my bra cups to be quickly joined by his mouth. His tongue swirled around my nipples and flicked against the stiff peaks. It felt so good, I didn't even realize my hips were lifting off the bed to press against him. He kissed the valley between my breasts as his fingertips traveled down to tease the sensitive skin of my inner thighs until I trembled.

His palm splayed against my belly, it dipped lower and lower until he was inside my shorts. My hips bucked when he reached my core. I was too wound up, too fucking turned on to be self-conscious of my wetness that now coated his hand.

"Oh my god, Mel," he groaned and kissed me savagely as if my pleasure was his own.

Once he found my clit, it was over. I clawed at his back and bucked against his hand, my pleasure climbing higher than I ever thought possible. He pressed in hard, fast circles that showed he knew exactly what he was doing. He took my nipple between his teeth and that's when I came apart. His hot palm cupped my vulva, watching me in fascination as I rode the waves of my orgasm. Lost in the jolts shooting throughout my entire body, I forgot all about staying guarded and self-conscious.

When my orgasm subsided into warmth and relaxation, Connor kissed me one final time before dropping behind me. He curled around me and pulled me against him with an arm around my waist. Our usual spooning position, but where it felt somewhat platonic before, there was a new feeling of intimacy now.

I flipped over to face him, running my hand along his neck and jaw in the darkness.

"Do you want me to, um..."

"No, babe." He kissed the tip of my nose. "All I wanted was for you to relax and feel good. Did it work?"

I giggled and found his mouth with mine. "Yes. That felt amazing."

"Good. Don't worry about me, Mel. I've gone years without. It's more important that you can relax and trust me." He grew quiet for a moment. "I know what it's like to feel like no one is decent or trustworthy. I'm willing to prove that I'm not going to hurt you, babe."

If that orgasm left me blissfully empty, raw emotion now filled that space inside me. I was stunned, moved beyond words, but a small voice whispered a reminder that I'd fallen for pretty words before.

So I just kissed him and whispered, "Thank you. Goodnight."

He mumbled a goodnight as I flipped over again, curling my back against his chest and allowing sleep to settle into my relaxed, sated body.

I *wanted* to trust him. I wanted to believe he was the first good, genuine person I met. But every person I was supposed to trust ended in heartache. My mom. My older sister. Teachers. Counselors. Ex-boyfriends. Time after time, their actions toward me proved I was better off protecting myself than allowing someone else to protect me. Because without fail, they threw me to the wolves every time I let my guard down.

I wanted to believe Connor was different. We had common ground in being guarded and untrusting of others for good reasons. My heart and my body practically begged me to give themselves to him. But time would tell, especially if we continued doing this carnival thing together. If this business was as seedy and corrupt as he said, it would certainly test whatever this was between us. If this was a convincing act like all the others were, his true colors would come out eventually.

And if they did, I had to make sure my heart wasn't already in his hands when that time came.

Just before I drifted off in his arms, I swore I heard a wolf howling in the distance.

ABRA CADABRA

BOOK 2

PROLOGUE

I ran on all fours, light as a feather on my paws. The thrill of the hunt filled me, lighting up my steps. Tonight my mate and I would find food for our pack. The pups inside me would be nourished with the potential to grow up to be pack leaders themselves one day.

The moon rose high, lighting up my mate's silver-white fur like he was made of moonlight himself. A fierce ache grew inside me, so strong that I let out a low growl of desire. I had to wait until we took down our kill, and then I'd let him take me.

We ran in tandem, following the scent of the elk herd. My dark, brindled coat blended in with the night and dry brush of the forest. Together, we were the same, yet polar opposites. Darkness and light. He would be the diversion, the last thing our prey would see. I would be the shadow they never saw coming.

Slowing to a canter and crouching low on our bellies, we didn't have to communicate the thrill and excitement we felt. It hung between us, crackling with coiled energy as it waited to go off.

The elk were resting, the large bulls surrounding the females and their young in a protective shield of antlers. But they were relaxed. They hadn't sensed us yet.

My mate licked my muzzle before slinking away to get into position. We'd done this dozens of times before. It was like a dance. A waltz of power, blood, death, and victory.

One of the bull elks' heads turned. Tension rippled through the herd as they watched and listened closely. Internally, I cackled with delight. They always fell for it. That was why they were prey.

My mate darted out and the bull elk charged with a furious cry. The protection broke as the males charged at their silvery-white enemy. Everyone began running and bucking in the chaos.

I chose my target, a young buck, and went in for the kill. Once my mate gave the bull elks the runaround, he helped me put our food out of its misery and drag it back into the woods.

Exhausted but victorious, we threw our heads back and sang to our pack. They'd hear our call and come feast with us. Other packs would hear us as well, and know to stay away.

We dug in while waiting for the others, eating our fill until our bellies were full and round. My mate gazed at me with his beautiful golden eyes as he licked the blood from my fur. With a snapping of bones, organs, and sinews rearranging, he shifted to human form.

I cocked my head at him curiously. He was still just as beautiful as a human, with pale, flawless skin, and silver-blonde hair falling past his sculpted shoulders. His golden eyes remained the same, set into a model-esque face with prominent cheekbones and an angled jaw.

"I want to take you in this form, my love," he whispered huskily.

I shifted to human myself so I could answer him. "It feels...wrong," I mused. "Not in a bad way, but there are no humans around for miles. This isn't the time or place for this form."

He shot me a naughty grin. "That's exactly why I want you out here like this."

I returned his grin. "You're so bad."

He pounced on me—clumsily compared to our wolf forms—and we both tumbled over, laughing and groaning at the forest floor poking into our soft, human flesh.

But when he kissed me, all the discomfort and feelings of wrongness melted away. His mouth and his body on mine awakened the animal side of humans we rarely felt. Nothing was wrong or bad about this. This was nature, this was pure instinct.

Our wolves growled restlessly just underneath the surface, frustrated at our dulled human senses, but we kept them at bay. This was a moment for us to enjoy each other as humans.

We often forgot that our human side was just as precious and intrinsic to us as our animal side.

❧ I ❧

MELODY

I awoke with a start, but the howling remained.

Perhaps my groggy brain hadn't completely come out of my dream yet, but that long, haunting song at the moon continued on until it gently faded away.

The coppery taste of blood still filled my mouth. I could still feel the wind whipping through my fur as I ran on all fours.

I never had a dream that vivid before.

Next to me, Connor's breathing was still deep, even, and human. He was warm and solid, wrapped around me snugly. I turned in his arms to look at his handsome, sleeping face. He looked adorable when he wasn't scowling at everything.

From the moment he found me sitting in the mud and covered in my own vomit, I never wanted to let him go. After being groped and manhandled onstage by my show partner, Connor was the only one who went looking for me when I ran off like a frightened deer.

I felt gross, helpless, violated, frozen with fear, and the whole audience *laughed*. Syko touched me without permission because he knew he could get away with it. But Connor didn't let him. He made sure I was okay, then gave Syko a black eye for doing that to me.

As an eighteen-year-old runaway from the trash capital of Alabama,

133

you could probably figure out that I wasn't used to people treating me kindly. Once I got a taste of that, I never wanted to let it go.

And not only that, I didn't want anyone to be treated like I was, or worse.

Connor shifted and groaned, his forest green eyes cracking open to slits as he gave me a clumsy, half-blind kiss. "Morning, babe."

"Morning." I nuzzled my head under his chin. "Did you hear that howling?"

"Nope." He rubbed the sleep out of his eyes. "You still thinking about the wolves?"

"I think..." I struggled to remember the dream, but it was already beginning to escape me. Rather than visuals playing in my head, it was more like incredibly vivid senses in my body. My sense of smell, hearing, and night vision had heightened to an incredible degree. It was like my brain was still human, but my senses were pure animal.

"I think I dreamed I *was* a wolf," I told him. "And I was hunting, then I turned into a human."

"Mm-hmm," he answered groggily.

"It was crazy vivid," I went on. "I could smell and taste everything, even the blood of the kill."

"Maybe you're part wolf," he said jokingly. "And that's why you can't get them out of your head."

"Maybe," I mused, kissing under his chin. "So what's the agenda for today?"

"Coffee," he grunted. "And breakfast. I'm almost out. We can get some from the vendors setting up today."

"When does the carnival actually open to attendees?" I yawned and stretched, life and awakeness finally coming into my limbs.

"Not for a few more days," he replied. "It would be smart to check the place out and get to know the staff and other performers. See if we're dealing with a bunch of Syko-types."

I mumbled my agreement and began pushing myself up to sitting, but he knocked my arms out and made me collapse back next to him.

"I'd much rather stay in bed with you, though," he murmured, kissing sensually into my neck and shoulder.

A hum of pleasure escaped me as I arched against him, sliding my palms across his broad, solid back. He moved lower ever so slowly, skimming his lips across my skin before stopping every so often to pay attention to a certain area.

Physically, we hadn't done much aside from kissing and a clitoral orgasm from his hand. I wanted to take it slow, and he was incredibly respectful of that. We'd only met last week and were still in the process of getting to know each other. I didn't even think he liked me until a few days ago. But with every kiss and gentle touch, I found it harder to not want all of him.

He was seven years older than me and every bit a man, not a boy, and carried the scars to prove it. Some mental, some physical. He was able to hide from most people that he was a double amputee, which didn't deter me in the slightest. If anything, it impressed me because he was a survivor. Not to mention an incredible acrobatic stilt walker.

I learned just two days ago that fireworks triggered flashbacks for him. Again, that didn't put me off in the least. I grew up watching my mother and older sister faking all sorts of disabilities to keep scamming the government for welfare money. If anything, it pissed me off that my own blood took money away from people like Connor, who needed it.

But whatever flaws he had were the furthest things away from my mind as his teeth traced my collarbones. His large hands held me by the waist as his mouth traveled slowly lower, between my breasts and then my belly, as he lifted my tank top.

My belly which immediately growled so loudly, it seemed to echo off the walls.

"Hungry, babe?" he laughed, kissing me there first before proceeding to blow raspberries.

"Maybe just a little." I smacked him playfully as I giggled and squirmed away.

"Let's get some food in ya." He smacked the side of my hip and promptly rolled up to sitting, using his arms to push himself to the edge to reach his prosthetics. Within minutes, we were out and walking hand in hand through the carnival grounds.

I never had a boyfriend before, despite having a few stupid hookups in high school. The way Connor laced his fingers through mine and held me at his side sent fluttering through my stomach that had nothing to do with hunger. Just walking alongside him, looking like I was his—and he mine—put an extra spring in my step. I had to bite the inside of my cheek to keep from grinning stupidly.

This carnival looked incredibly different from the one we ran from. Drowningville, Mississippi had been a shithole town and the Voodoo Trail Carnival was no exception, down to the people that ran it. Connor drove us off in the middle of the night after we technically kidnapped a family of wolf-like people.

Although I didn't give Connor much choice in the matter, the wolf family was being treated horribly and I'd get them out of there again if I had to.

I didn't know much about the people running this place, but Connor knew the manager and they seemed to get along well. I trusted his judgement above all else.

Already I found the grounds more pleasing to the eye than Drowingville. We were in the middle of a lush, green forest. The air smelled clean and fresh, with a hint of campfires and cooking food. I could see the Ferris wheel rising over the treeline. Spots of bright oranges, pinks, blues and other neon colors dotted through the muted tones of the tree trunks. Those had to be the other rides and the typical carnival game booths setting up.

Connor and I walked through an outdoor section where people set up simpler booths for their crafts, jewelry, clothing, and other goods. Rather than foldable canopies and tents, these people used colorful fabric held aloft by wooden poles. Some even used fur blankets and what looked like animal skins.

"Check out what they're wearing," Connor nodded at some of the vendors. "Looks like this is one of those Renaissance festivals."

He was right. Most people were dressed in costumes of another time period. Women wore modest, long-sleeved dresses like what I saw in history books at school. Men wore tunics and much tighter pants than I was used to seeing. Some even wore hats with feathers in them.

Even the food booths looked like medieval kitchens with cast-iron pots sitting over open fires. Animal carcasses on long spits were turned slowly as they roasted, making sizzling sounds as fat dripped down over the flames.

We stopped at a booth advertising fresh-laid eggs, baked beans, and the thickest, crispiest strips of bacon I'd ever seen. Even the coffee was heated over a fire in a metal percolator. Connor and I each got heaping bowls of food, huge mugs of coffee, and moved on, looking for a place to sit and eat.

Long picnic benches were set out under some trees, so we settled there and enjoyed our breakfast as we watched the rest of the temporary village come to life. Nearby, metalworkers and blacksmiths worked on their crafts and set up their shops as we watched with curiosity.

They set out beautiful wares such as knives, jewelry, and chain-mail fashion. Some were engrossed in making pieces, either by welding something tiny at their table or hammering a huge hunk of metal over an anvil.

Other people hanging around nearby were clearly performers. These were the ones we'd be working with directly.

I spotted a shirtless man covered in tattoos juggling knives by one of the shops. From his legs to his neck, he didn't seem to have an inch of un-inked flesh. And that flesh covered taut, rippling muscles that made his tattoos dance as he moved. His dark hair was buzzed short and even his scalp and the sides of his face had dark, intricate designs inked in.

He moved like a cat. Not that I knew anything about knife juggling, but he seemed even more skilled at handling them than Syko. I couldn't take my eyes away as he flipped knives through the air effortlessly as he chatted with the knife shop owner, often looking away from his juggling and laughing jovially at something his friend said.

Suddenly, he tossed all his knives up in the air at once and stretched his arms out to his sides. He leaned his head back and opened his mouth to stick his tongue out at the sky. Panic gripped my heart as the knives came falling back down to earth, blades pointing directly at him.

"Oh my god!" I screamed, covering my mouth as a dagger's blade gleamed in the sunlight before falling down his throat.

I looked around in a panic. Didn't anyone else see that? But all the shopkeepers and metal workers carried on like normal, paying no mind to this man with a knife handle sticking out of his throat. Wait, why wasn't he bleeding or moving around?

"Keep watching, babe," Connor said with amusement in his voice.

The man remained standing there with his head thrown back and his knife's blade down his esophagus. His hands closed suddenly, and I realized he caught two more knives which fell from the sky. He took a small step to the side and I could barely watch what happened next.

Another knife fell directly into his waiting mouth.

He then brought both hands to his mouth and swiftly removed the knives from his throat, still shiny and without a drop of blood on them. Then he winked at me and grinned as he took a small bow.

I covered my face, embarrassed at calling attention to myself.

"He's good," Connor said with what sounded like genuine respect in his voice. "Really good. You don't see that blade swallowing stuff often anymore. Most people aren't patient enough to practice it correctly."

"That... was insane," I said, dumbfounded.

"Wipe your drool off if you're gonna keep staring," he teased, poking me in the ribs.

My face now hotter than cooking fires, I returned my attention to my breakfast. The knife-swallower guy was classically handsome, tall, and lean with a confident swagger. All the tattoos gave him a different, otherworldly appearance. From the way he winked at me, I got the impression that he liked showing off and even scaring people with his abilities. It got me more flustered than I cared to admit.

After breakfast, we explored more of the grounds with little incident before heading off to a private area of the woods to practice a new routine.

"Let's head to the bar tonight," Connor yelled down at me from high on his stilts. "That'll be the best place to get a feel for the people here. If it's shady, we'll cut and run after we get paid. If no one gives us trouble, we can stay for the whole event."

"Okay," I mumbled distractedly as I counted my steps, imagining I was waltzing across the stage. Honestly, I was excited about performing again. I couldn't wait to feel the energy of the crowd.

Just as I finished, a sudden, quick movement caught my eye, and I spun around.

A flash of white fur filled the space between the branches of the brush. And just as suddenly, it was gone.

✻ 2 ✻

MELODY

I was relieved to find out the carnival bar was in an actual building, not a tent. Despite how well-reinforced those pavilions were in Drowningville, I didn't put it past any of those wasted drunks to stumble into a support beam and send it all crashing down.

This bar was in a log cabin with a wooden sign sticking out from the side of the building with the word TAVERN painted on, along with a pair of drinking mugs. They were really playing up the medieval theme here.

Connor pulled open the heavy wooden door and stepped aside to let me in first. A smoky warmth enveloped me, adding on to the bright, cheery liveliness of the establishment. The warmth came from a large fireplace at the far wall, next to where a trio of musicians played a sultry background song on banjos and a standing bass.

"You want a coke, babe?" Connor had to yell in my ear over the music and multiple conversations. People laughed and talked animatedly like they were a few drinks in already. And the night had just begun.

I nodded at him, grateful that he remembered I'd rather not drink, and went to find us a place to sit.

"Thanks," I smiled at him as he set down two tankards in front

140

of us.

He barely acknowledged our drinks or my thanks, but pulled me into his lap, trailing kisses down my neck.

"You practiced really well today," he murmured. "I'm proud of you, babe."

My chest squeezed as I balanced on his thick, incredibly muscular thighs, the main reasons he could perform so beautifully with no lower legs. His lap felt as solid as a table.

"I have a great teacher," I replied, wrapping an arm around his neck.

This was his first time being so openly affectionate with me and I wasn't about to question it. He made me feel like he was the first man I could trust, whose intentions I didn't have to question all the time. My feelings for him were growing deeper by the minute, and I wondered if he was experiencing the same.

"Excuse me for interrupting," said a lightly accented voice, with all the depth and smoothness of molasses.

Annoyed, I looked away from Connor and my heart jumped into my throat.

The tattooed knife swallower invited himself to our table and sat down across from us like we were old friends catching up.

"I feel I must apologize to you," he said. I couldn't place his accent, although it was pleasant to listen to. "I didn't mean to frighten you earlier with my knife practice."

"Oh, that's okay," I said, taken aback by his approach. "I should have known that was part of your performance."

Up close, I could see his eyes were a pale gray, like clouds after a rain. I could also see the finer details of his tattoos, including that he had small symbols inked near the outer corners of his eyes.

"My name is Razvan," he said, holding out a hand which had three eyes peering at me from his palm.

"Melody," I answered, accepting his handshake after a moment's hesitation.

He shook hands with Connor as well, but otherwise kept his focus entirely on me. It was unsettling, if a bit flattering. Connor's arm tightened around my waist and I laced my fingers through his.

"Where are you from, Melody?" Razvan asked, smiling as he took a drink from his own tankard. He spoke to me as if Connor wasn't even there, while I was still sitting in his damn lap. Clearly, his arrogance knew no bounds.

"Um, out of state," I said dismissively.

"Of course," he replied smoothly. "Beauty such as your own could not have come from a place like Mississippi." He said the state name in a mocking southern accent.

"Look, Razvan, I'm flattered," I said, growing impatient not only by his intrusiveness but also Connor's silence. "But I'd like to have some privacy with my boyfriend, please."

He smiled again, not looking put off at all. "Of course, I only wanted to apologize for making you scream earlier." The way he said it sounded so suggestive. I couldn't help but blush as he rose from the table. Which was most likely exactly what he wanted. Damn it.

"Boyfriend, huh?" Connor chuckled once we were alone.

"Yeah, sorry." I blushed again for an entirely different reason and took a huge drink of Coke to cool myself down. "I had a feeling he just wouldn't go away if I wasn't direct."

"Why did you want him to go away?" Connor asked casually.

I looked at him in disbelief. "Seriously? I'm in your lap right now. I was just kissing you. We don't have to use boyfriend-girlfriend titles, but when I'm with you, other guys should know to back off."

He took a drink from his mug and remained silent, the fireplace making flickering gold reflections in his dark green eyes.

"Why should they?" he asked.

I couldn't believe what I was hearing. I didn't know whether to be hurt or confused.

"Are you deaf?" I demanded. "I just told you. Because I'm with *you*."

"Mel, babe," he said with a long exhale. "I don't want to be known as your boyfriend, but not because I don't want you. Other men are going to be interested in you. If you hit it off with someone else, I don't want you to pass up happiness because you feel an obligation to me."

"I don't care. I'm not interested in anyone else." Was he purposely being dense?

"Really?" He raised his eyebrows skeptically and nodded his head across the room. "Not even him?"

Of course, he was gesturing to Razvan, sitting at a round table with a few guys inked up with similar amounts of tattoos, although none were nearly as good looking. They laughed gregariously and spoke rapidly in a language I couldn't place.

"No!" I insisted, although my whole body heated to an uncomfortable degree. "He was *way* too forward."

"He's confident," Connor countered. "You gotta give him that."

"I don't want to give him anything. Why are we even talking about this?"

"I'm just putting it out there, babe," he kissed my cheek, "I can't give you everything you need. Someone else can probably give you what I can't. If you find that person, I won't be upset if you pursue something with them."

"That's crazy." I shook my head and took a long drink of my soda.

As much as I hated to admit it, I could see his point. Faithfulness was preached everywhere, but who really adhered to it? My mom always seemed to have a guy lined up after the last one left, despite her drunken rages about her dirtbag men always cheating on her. My older sister cheated on her guy just as much as he cheated on her. What did marriage vows really mean if you only said them because the church insisted on it for pregnant teenagers?

If people were at least open about it, was it really cheating?

My head swam so thickly with these thoughts, the raucous noise of the bar faded to a dull background roar.

Several boys had asked me out in school, and I even slept with a couple of them, but never expected it to progress to a relationship. Thanks to my mom, my perception of men was so skewed. I figured all they wanted was to stick their dicks in me and move on to the next girl. For the most part, I'd been right. Connor was the first one who challenged that notion. But now he was telling me he didn't want to claim me as his?

Whoa, where did that come from?

My thighs snapped shut as tension and heat suddenly built up in my core. The thought disappeared as quickly as it came, but its effects lingered. *Being claimed?* It sounded so raw and animalistic. And fucking hot.

I never thought about sex and relationships in that way before. The idea seemed to bubble up from somewhere deeply subconscious.

"Ready to head back?" Connor kissed my neck, seemingly oblivious to the sudden rush of need that overtook me.

I answered by sealing my lips over his, opening wide and surging my tongue into his mouth.

He grinned when our long, passionate kiss ended. "I'll take that as a yes."

We stood from the table together and I caught his grimace before he could hide it.

"What's wrong?" I demanded.

"Nothin'," he said gruffly. "Legs are just sore from being on them all day. I can't wait to take these damn things off." He grabbed a gratuitous handful of my ass. "And take other things off."

"Did you lotion your, um..."

"My stumps?" he laughed. "It's okay, babe, you can say it. And no, I forgot."

"Do it right when you take them off," I insisted. "I don't want you hurting."

"Yes, ma'am," he teased, kissing my temple as he threw a heavy arm around my shoulders.

Thankfully, it was a short walk to the trailer. But just as we got home, we ran into Nigel, the carnival manager.

"Go ahead, babe. I'll catch up." Connor released me. "I'm going to check in with Nigel real quick about our schedule."

"Not too long," I warned him. I knew the longer he stood, the more pain he would be in.

"It'll just be a second." He dropped a quick kiss to my lips before he jogged away. "Start a campfire for us? Just like I showed you."

Grumbling, I went inside and rummaged around for the lighter and kindling. The shitty plastic lighter was nearly out of fluid and we had a hell of a time starting the fire last night, even with Connor's Marine corps survival skills.

On top of that, our kindling was nearly gone.

I gathered up as many dried pine needles and small twigs as I could see in the quickly fading light and proceeded to build the fire.

"Come on, you stupid motherfucker," I cursed as the lighter sparked uselessly until my thumb was sore. The pine needles released smoke but ignited no flames. I blew gently, like Connor showed me whenever they caught a spark, but it would die before catching anything.

"Son of a bitch." I sat back on my heels, frustrated.

"Need some help?"

The dark ink covering his body made him nearly invisible in the fading light. His smile and pale gray eyes were the brightest parts of him, almost looking like they were floating and not attached to a body.

"Don't worry. I'll leave you be," Razvan laughed as he approached me on long, graceful legs. "But I could help you with that fire."

I shrugged, not wanting to give the impression that I was open to conversation. Where the fuck was Connor?

Razvan kneeled, balancing lightly on the balls of his feet, and grinned at me from across my haphazard arrangement of logs.

"Want to see a magic trick?"

I shrugged again, looking as bored as possible, but I was secretly intrigued.

Razvan cupped a tattooed hand around his mouth and whispered, *"Abra cadabra."*

A single flame shot from his mouth and engulfed the logs and kindling in one fell swoop.

I fell backward on my butt, stunned and scared shitless. One second there was nothing, and then *boom*, fire. From his fucking *mouth*?!

I stared through the flames at his face, calm but with a playful gleam in his eye. What the fuck kind of magic trick was that? His hands were empty, weren't they?

Razvan rose to his feet and gave me a curt, but polite nod as he turned to walk away.

"Enjoy your campfire, miss Melody."

MELODY

A beautiful pale man came to me in my dreams.

Sharp, golden eyes watched me, and silky platinum hair fell past his shoulders. His torso was covered in long, lean muscles, his pale skin making him look carved from marble.

Why did he look so familiar to me?

"I miss you," he said in a pained voice, barely above a whisper. "Every day, Roo and Rinna still ask where you are. They need their mother."

He looked at me with those sad golden eyes as he spoke, but it seemed more like he talked to himself. I felt like I was intruding on a private moment, but couldn't break away from his gaze.

"I lost the pack," he continued. "I've searched for days and can't pick up their scent. If they're no longer here, I hope they're running with you, my love."

His sadness made my heart crack into a million pieces. I felt his grief and despair as if it were my own. But why was I here? This was not my place. I wasn't meant to be hearing these things.

"It's just the three of us now," he said. "They're getting bigger and stronger every day since we got away. You'd be so proud."

Out of nowhere, his expression changed. His handsome face went from mournful to grinning. The change was jolting. His grin turned to laughter as his body leaned forward, falling to his hands and knees.

He opened his mouth to reveal a long, forked tongue, and large, scaly wings erupted from his back. I wanted to scream and back away but couldn't move. On all fours he crawled towards me, his body moving from side to side like a reptile.

BANG! BANG! BANG!

"What the fuck!"

I jolted out of my dream, sitting straight up and panting. My heart crashed against my ribs as if desperate to jump out. Next to me, Connor nearly fell out of the bed.

"Whoa! What's wrong?" he looked at me with concern as he maintained his balance.

"Bad dream," I panted, pressing my hand to my chest. The image of that man with wings and a forked tongue crawling toward me burned in my mind.

BANG! BANG! BANG!

I jumped and shrieked, then found myself pressed into Connor's chest.

"It's alright, babe. Just someone at the door," he murmured into my hair, then yelled to the person outside, "hold on a fuckin' minute!"

I curled into a ball against his solid chest while he gently rocked me and rubbed my back. Slowly I felt myself calming, but didn't want to lose the security of his arms. I curled up tighter, pressing against his warm skin.

"Must've been a hell of a dream," he observed. "You look like I did the night of the fireworks."

"It felt so real," I said, my voice shaky. I rubbed my eyes and deepened my breaths, trying to stay solidly here in the waking world.

"Dreaming about the wolves again?"

"No. Kinda. Fuck, I dunno." I leaned my forehead against his shoulder. "I'm losing my damn mind."

I didn't even tell him what happened last night with Razvan and the fire. It couldn't have been real. Whatever he did was just some trick to show off again. He was a good illusionist. I'd give him that much.

"No, you're not." He kissed my forehead and moved my hair out of my face. "A lot of crazy shit happened that night. Your brain is still processing through it."

"Connor!" A voice yelled from the outside. "We need to talk! Shit's changed since last night and I'm fucked."

I recognized the voice as Nigel, the carnival manager. He sounded panicked.

"I told you, one minute!" Connor yelled back. "You okay to get decent, babe? I gotta see what he wants."

I nodded and reluctantly pulled away from his warmth and solidness, looking on the floor for my bra and shorts.

"Let him in for me, babe." Connor pulled a shirt on as he sat on the edge of the bed, his knees hanging over slightly.

"Are you sure?" I tugged my clothing into place, eyeballing his prosthetics leaning against the wall next to him. Back in Drowningville, he had been extremely secretive about his disability, always hiding his prosthetics under long pants.

"It's alright. He knows," he answered softly. "Nigel's an army vet. He gets it."

I nodded and went to the door, pulling it open with a smile.

"Morning, ma'am," he said tersely. He looked like he barely slept. "Is Stilts decent yet?"

It took a moment for Connor's stage name to register in my still-rattled brain.

"Oh, yes! Sorry, come in."

I stepped aside to let him through the narrow door. Connor had lifted himself into one of the chairs at the small table and gestured to the other one for Nigel.

"Mornin' Nigel. What can I do for ya?" His voice was still low, gravelly, and sexy from sleep.

"I'm fucked, Stilts." Nigel sat down heavily at the table.

"Um, should I start some coffee?" I asked, feeling awkward. There was nowhere for me to really go to give them privacy.

"Coffee?" Nigel scoffed. "You got any whiskey in here? 'Cause that's what I fuckin' need."

"Coffee would be great, babe." Connor squeezed my hand before turning to the distraught man. "What's going on?"

"All but six of my fuckin' acts quit on me this mornin," he spat. "That six includes you two."

No way. I nearly dropped the coffeepot. He *had* to be exaggerating.

"What the hell?" Connor echoed my thoughts.

"You heard me right," Nigel said. "Apparently there's auditions for some big Vegas show nearby here. Everyone and their mother went off to chase the big bucks and I'm left with random freaks and shit. No offense."

"None taken." Connor narrowed his eyes at him. "Is this audition for real?"

"Probably not," Nigel spat. "Most likely Arch or one of my other competitors trying to poach my talent, fuckin' snake bastards. What the hell am I gonna do now, Stilts? Tickets are almost sold out! People fuckin' take road trips across the country for this!"

"You still got the Renaissance vendors out here, right?" Connor rubbed his chin thoughtfully.

"Yeah, thank fuckin' God. All the ride and game staff, too. What we don't have is a cohesive show, which is the main fuckin' event! Even my ringmaster up and left!"

"That sucks, man," Connor said sympathetically. "Thanks, babe." He accepted the steaming hot cup of coffee from me.

"Damn right, it sucks," Nigel lamented. "If I have to refund all these tickets, I'll be fuckin' ruined."

"Seems to me the only thing you can do," Connor rubbed his jaw, "is get everyone together to make a single, cohesive show. Make a program and put everybody up on the main stage."

"I dunno, man." Nigel rubbed the back of his neck. "Have you seen some of these weirdos? Covered in tattoos and all their freaky body mods and shit? I don't think that's what this crowd is looking for."

"They're coming here to see weird shit," Connor pointed out. "This isn't some high-class bougie Cirque du Soleil shit you're putting on.

This is a backwoods, rinky dink traveling carnival. People are coming for the freaks and the weirdos."

Nigel sighed and shook his head. "That might be the only way, but I know we're gonna have some pearl clutchers, man. I guess partial refunds are better than all refunds."

Connor reached across the table and slapped his shoulder in that encouraging, manly way.

"Come on, man. Where's that army spirit? You've put together a bunch of sad sacks into cohesive units before. Just think of this as a training exercise, sergeant."

Nigel gave a slight nod and stood from the table. "I got my mortgage riding on this shit, Stilts. I can't afford to lose." He looked between both of us. "Meet me at the tavern in a half hour. We're getting all you sideshow people together."

He abruptly left, leaving Connor and me in contemplative silence.

"Sounds serious," I mused, taking a sip of coffee.

"Mm-hm," Connor agreed. "He's an alright dude, despite the shady nature of this business. If we can help him out, I'm all for it."

"You gave him quite the pep talk." I reached over and massaged his shoulder. The muscles were tight, and he groaned as I worked into the knot.

"Seems to be what I'm good at," he chuckled, leaning into my touch.

Dare I say it?

I leaned down and brushed my lips across the shell of his ear. "That's not the only thing you're good at."

"Mm, babe," he moaned, wrapping a large arm around my waist and pulling me into his lap. "How much time do we have again?"

"Half-hour, right?" I straddled his tapered waist and bit gently on his earlobe, knowing how much he liked that.

"Well, you caught me without my legs on." His large hands glided across my thighs as he nipped the skin between my neck and shoulder. "So unless you want to move, we're staying right here."

"Here is exactly where I want you," I whispered back.

A HALF-HOUR LATER, we sat in the same spot in the bar as we did the other night. I brought my coffee mug with me, drinking it down quickly as the other performers filed in. My mind felt soft and fuzzy after messing around with Connor, but I wanted it to be sharp for this meeting.

He stood next to Nigel at the bar, talking to him and another man in low voices. Nigel and the other guy looked just as stressed and frazzled as we saw in our trailer that morning. Connor was the only one who looked alert yet calm. His arms crossed over his chest as his eyes swept between the two other men, mostly listening while they talked.

I drank him in unashamedly, remembering his skillful hands on me just moments ago. Like always, the orgasm he gave me was delicious and satisfying. A sweet release after a perfect amount of teasing and build up.

Still, my thighs rubbed together under the table. An ache for more echoed through me like a drum. He would only touch my clit, nothing more. With every attempt I made to move things further, he stopped. He wouldn't even let me touch him the same way.

I had a feeling I knew why. He wanted to prove that he respected me and wouldn't take advantage. What Syko did to me at the last carnival left me skittish and even more distrusting of men in general than I already was. But since then, Connor and I slept multiple nights in the same bed with nothing going on.

I *did* trust him, maybe more than he trusted himself.

And I was also a living, breathing woman with physical needs. And I was falling for him.

The lump in my throat wouldn't go away as that thought took hold of my mind.

It didn't matter to me what limbs he was missing or what trauma he faced. There he stood, calm and capable while the men surrounding him, who didn't face nearly the hardships that he did, freaked out like children.

Foreign words and musical laughter floating from the doorway drew my attention away from Connor. My nails dug into my palms at the now-familiar smile and dark, tattooed form of Razvan.

He looked like some kind of biker with dark pants, laced-up combat boots and a matching leather vest with no shirt underneath. Silver rings glittered across his knuckles, as if his long, tattooed fingers needed any more decoration.

Every time I saw him, I seemed to notice another detail, like he was a mystery I was uncovering piece by piece. This time it was the nude woman on his shoulder, drawn in a pinup style with a huge snake wrapping around her body in a way that barely covered her breasts and crotch.

Several of my mom's boyfriends had similar naked lady tattoos, so I usually associated them with trashiness. But on Razvan, it somehow seemed more artistic and tasteful. He covered his entire body in art and it seemed to fit his style and overall aesthetic.

A sudden flash of my dream appeared in my mind as I studied the tattoo. Something about how the snake was drawn reminded me of how the pale man crawled toward me, whipping back and forth like a reptile.

I looked at him too long and he noticed, flashing me a smile and a wink. Embarrassed, I looked back down at my coffee. He chuckled and said something to one of his friends, but thankfully didn't come over to talk.

Connor finally came back to sit beside me. His face was expressionless, but I knew how hyper-aware of his surroundings he was. He definitely saw me staring at Razvan.

He squeezed my knee as he dropped beside me and kissed my temple as if nothing was amiss. Conflicted, I just wrapped my hands tighter around my mug. I didn't want him to be right. I didn't *want* to want anyone else. Razvan was attractive in that bad-boy kind of way and he obviously knew it.

He's nice to look at, but he's not my type, I thought.

Who was I kidding? I had so little actual dating experience, I couldn't even pinpoint what *was* my type.

Nigel stepped out into the center of the room and all the side conversations died down as everyone turned their attention to him.

"As y'all know, y'all are all that's left of the performers of this show," he began. "With all the other dicks fucking us over, there's too many empty holes in the schedule now. I asked y'all here because we need to combine all y'alls acts into a single show."

He gave a slight nod to Connor, who returned the gesture.

"So all sideshow performers will be shifted to the main stage," Nigel continued. "It'll be a bigger stage and audience than some of you have ever done, which could be great for some of y'alls careers."

A low *whoop-dee-doo* type whistle sounded from Razvan's corner of the room. I'd never heard a whistle sound so defeatist and sarcastic. The man himself sat reclined in a chair, his long, leather-clad legs stretched out in front of him. His arms folded across his chest, fingertips resting on the woman and snake on his arm.

Nigel's jaw clenched at the sound, but chose to ignore him.

"I'd ask some of y'all to, uh, clean up your acts for this audience but I have a feeling that won't go over well." He glared directly at Razvan, who pursed his lips in a mocking kiss. "So you're welcome to put on what y'all have been practicing. We just gotta change the schedule and make everything flow together seamlessly. Oh, and I need a ringmaster to get the crowd amped up and make announcements. Any volunteers?"

The room fell silent for a few moments until Razvan raised his hand high like he was in a classroom.

"Not you, Raz," Nigel glowered. "Don't need you setting attendees on fire and having orgies up on stage."

"On the contrary. That's exactly what you need," the tattooed man answered with a smile.

His friends all guffawed with laughter at that, making crude hand gestures and joking animatedly in their native language.

"I need someone who can look presentable," Nigel said, turning to face everyone else in the room. "Someone with charisma and charm, who can dazzle a crowd with just a smile."

"Psst!" I poked Connor playfully on the arm and giggled when he lifted an eyebrow and gave me a very skeptical side-eye.

Nigel whipped around and his eyes landed on me, registering for a moment before a massive smile broke out on his face.

"Yes!" he cried jubilantly, raising his fists in the air.

"Huh?" I blinked. "Oh yeah, I was just telling Connor he should do it."

"No, not Connor,." He came forward, leaning across the table, and clasped my hands in his. "You, my dear."

MELODY

I laughed, certain he was joking, but his watery eyes bore into mine like I was the last woman on earth.

"Yes, you would be perfect!" he declared, then looked sheepish. "Erm, what's your name, again, hun?"

"Melody," I snapped, yanking my hands out of his grip. "And hell no, I'm not doing it! I'm part of Connor's act."

"Connor can be solo like how he's always done before." Nigel looked at him with a plea in his eyes. "Help me out here, man."

Connor rested his elbows on the table, propping his chin up in his hands as he looked deep in thought. I could practically see his brain working, going through all the possible outcomes. That alone started to make me panic.

"Connor," I demanded. "You're not seriously considering this?"

He lifted his chin off his hands and looked over at me. "I think you'd be good at it, babe."

"Yes!" Nigel cried with relief. "You're the only one here with any sense of class, miss Melody. None of these crusty folks know how to walk or speak with any kind of elegance."

I stared at him, open-mouthed and dumbfounded. *Me*, elegant and classy? Had he even looked at me?

"You do know how to capture a crowd," Connor added softly.

"She already has," Razvan said from across the room. Great. Now I realized everyone was staring at me.

"Y'all can't be serious," I protested. "I'm as trashy as they come."

"Don't say that," Connor scolded. "It doesn't matter where you're from. He's right. You have a natural ability to dazzle a crowd. I've seen you do it without even saying a word."

I remembered the rush and thrill of our first night performing together. The audience was captivated. I had no doubt we showed everyone up, and we were the first act of the night.

Even with Syko before he assaulted me, I felt a bit of that rush after I got over the nervousness. The truth was, I *liked* putting on a show and being a character. The energy from the audience was addictive like a drug, and I wanted to entertain more and more to feed off that energy.

But still, *ringmaster*? Surely that was a job for seasoned performers?

"I'm flattered, Nigel," I said, forcing a smile. "Really, I am. But I've literally been onstage twice in my life, both in the past week. I barely have enough experience in my own act, let alone leading an entire show."

"It's as good a time as any to learn." He winked at me, but then frowned when I didn't look convinced. To everyone's surprise, he fell to his knees and placed his hands in my lap. "Please, Melanie—"

"Melody," Connor and I corrected him in unison.

"Melody, my first grandchild is about to be born. I got a mortgage I'm already underwater on. If this show isn't a success, I lose *everything*." He clasped my hands again, looking up at me desperately. "Please, sweetheart. You're my one chance at this."

Damn it. It was like he knew I had a soft spot for others in need. Now I had to worry about him and his family suffering.

I looked over at Connor, who shrugged, but a smile twitched on his lips.

"You'd be great at it, babe. But it's completely up to you."

Silence fell heavily around the bar as everyone waited for my decision. I took a deep breath and released it.

"Okay, I guess."

Nigel whooped victoriously and stood to wrap me in a bone-crushing hug.

"Thank you, thank you, thank you."

"Alright, let her go," Connor growled possessively.

"Oh, dear sweet Jesus." Nigel wiped either tears or sweat from his face. "I can't thank you enough for this, Melody. You're seriously saving my ass here."

"Sure, but like," I didn't even know what questions to ask, "What do I *do*? I have to learn some stuff, right?"

"Yes, yes, of course." Nigel pulled himself together and resumed his business-like demeanor again. "You'll want to meet everyone. Get to know everyone's acts so you can entice the crowd as you announce them. Think of it like a sales pitch."

"Okay," I said blankly. I'd never sold a thing in my life before. Except drinks at the bar, and I didn't exactly need a sales pitch for that.

"We will all help you," Razvan hollered from across the room. He winked and bit his lip suggestively as he spread his legs wide. My whole body heated as if he lit me like a match. Did I *really* want to know what he wanted to help me with?

"Yes, they'll tell you what to say," Nigel agreed, apparently missing the innuendo. "Based on their strengths and how they've been announced at past performances before."

He stood and gestured to the other man he'd been talking to with Connor. "This is Herman, my event coordinator and marketing director. He'll be talking to you all about scheduling and transitioning between acts. Once that's settled, we all come together tomorrow to rehearse."

Connor groaned, and he wasn't the only one. People preferred rehearsing in private, or with their own clique of people.

Nigel ignored the grumbles and waved his hands to dismiss us. "Y'all can go back to your business for now."

Chairs scraped back against the wood floor as everyone stood and filed out the door. I remained sitting, wanting to leave last as I stared at my now-cold coffee in front of me. What the hell had I gotten myself into?

"Come on, babe." Connor ushered me up and I reluctantly followed.

Razvan and his crew approached the door just as we did. We paused to let them through, but in a flash of leather and metal, the tattooed man waved us through.

"After you, please. I insist," he smirked. I couldn't tell if he was being genuine or mocking us.

Once outside I heard a low, smooth whisper behind me say, "I never miss a chance to admire such a lovely rear view."

I froze in my tracks, my whole body burning with either desire or fury. With everywhere my mind and instincts were in that moment, it was impossible to tell which. I decided to go with fury.

After letting Syko get away with what he did, no man would disrespect me again and expect to live it down.

I turned around, snapping my head in the direction of that playful grin and steely gray eyes.

"Don't you ever talk to me like that again." I fought to keep my voice from shaking.

Razvan's eyes widened, more in amusement than surprise. My whole body quivered like a bowl of jello, but I set my jaw and clenched my fists, determined not to crumble.

"I like a woman with fire," he said huskily. "But don't worry, I'll honor your request." His grin widened like a Cheshire cat. "I'll speak to you in Romanian instead if you'd prefer that." He let out a string of beautiful, flowing sounds which sent his friends doubling over with laughter. From the mischievous look in his eye, I had no doubt whatever he said was far worse than what I reprimanded him for.

Without another word, I turned and stalked away with Connor back to our trailer. I had enough on my plate now without some foul-mouthed, tattooed pervert creeping into my thoughts.

"Damn, babe," Connor chuckled, rubbing the nape of my neck. "A little harsh, don't you think?"

In spite of how good his hands felt, I pulled away and looked at him with a stunned expression.

"Don't tell me you're defending him talking to me like that?" I felt wounded, like he wasn't on my side after all.

"He was giving you a compliment." His hand snaked around my waist and down to my hip. "And he was right. This is a very nice rear view."

I pulled away from him again, the disgust apparent on my face. "I can't believe it. Not you, too."

"What? It might've not been the romantic compliment, but give the guy a break. It's his second language."

"That's not what it was and you know it," I snapped. "He knew exactly what he was saying. It was gross and inappropriate."

"Okay, so he's rough around the edges. But you can tell that just by looking at him. He's probably lived in a gypsy caravan or whatever his whole life. You can't expect him to compare thee to a summer's day or whatever the fuck."

"Why are you so dead set on making excuses for him?" I sat in front of our campfire, pouting. But the glowing embers just reminded me of Razvan's fire trick, which only fucked with my mind even more.

"Because of what I told you earlier, babe. Guys are gonna be attracted to you. They're gonna make their interest known in different ways. Some more tactful than others. That guy didn't mean you any harm, babe. He's not a Syko."

"How do you know that? We don't know him."

"I can read people pretty well and I think you can, too. Sure, he wants to take you to bed, but he won't touch you without permission. He won't hurt you. Even if he wanted to, he knows he'd have to go through me."

I looked up at him, sitting across the fire from me with his forearms on his knees and green eyes gazing intently into mine. My soldier, my protector. Those eyes never missed anything, whether it was in our surroundings or the emotion on my face.

"You're gonna have to get to know him anyway, as the new ring-mistress," he added softly.

"He did... something the other night," I whispered like a confession.

Connor's eyes narrowed, and the muscles in his shoulders flexed with tension. Just those small indicators of his fierce protection made me want to crawl into his lap and ride him.

"What did he do, Mel?"

"I couldn't get the fire started and he..." I raked my fingers through the tangles in my hair, completely unsure how to describe it. "It looked like he lit the fire by blowing on it. Not like how you showed me but like he *breathed* fire."

Connor relaxed, a lopsided smirk emerging on his face. "I'm sure fire breathing is part of his act, babe. He was just showing off for you."

"I know it had to be a trick, but he didn't have a torch or fluid or anything." I was rambling now as the scene played over and over in my head. I saw every detail like a photograph and could not find a way to explain it.

"He's a professional. He knows how to hide his shit." Connor's smile dropped. "Did it scare you, babe?"

"A little," I admitted, curling up in my seat.

Like he said, I didn't think Razvan would hurt me. I didn't get a feeling of danger or discomfort around him. No, what really scared me was how drawn I felt to him. The fire thing didn't seem like an ordinary magic trick, but something unexplainable and otherworldly. In a lot of ways, he had a similar effect on me as the wolf man.

I was curious about him but my curiosity got me in trouble before. It made me throw caution to the wind and now that I had Connor, it put him at risk too.

"I'm going for a walk," I muttered, rising to my feet.

"Runnin' away, are ya?" he called after me, but I heard the laughter in the voice. He knew I'd come back, no matter how much I wanted to dive under his blankets and hide.

I also had half a mind to look over my shoulder, to entice him to chase me. We could find some private place away from here. Maybe a meadow full of soft grass that miraculously didn't also have a ton of bugs. We'd lay down there and I wouldn't just tell him, I'd *show* him how much he meant to me. How it was *him* I craved and no one else.

But I shoved my clenched hands in my pockets and kept walking.

A barely-marked walking trail made a loop around the fairgrounds so I walked that to clear my head. I was close enough to still see the Ferris wheel but far enough away from people that I'd be left alone.

After a couple of laps around the grounds, I started to warm up to the idea of becoming ringmistress. The role didn't require *that* much talking. The main aspect seemed to be exuding confidence and charisma. Traits that I didn't have but could probably fake well enough.

I was starting to look forward to returning to camp and getting to know the other acts. Unlike in Drowningville, no one seemed openly hostile or predatory toward me. The few other women here, the burlesque dancers and acrobats, seemed indifferent toward me, which was fine.

At this point, I wasn't expecting to make friends. Being with Connor like this was certainly the last thing I expected.

I chewed my lip as I completed my final loop and started heading back. He didn't want to be my boyfriend and while I kind of understood his reasons, hearing it still stung.

A snapping of twigs made me stop in my tracks. My breath froze in my lungs. It definitely wasn't me.

"Is someone there?" I called.

Thick brush and trees grew close to the edge of the trail. With the fairgrounds set up like a miniature village, I forgot how deep in the wild woods we were.

Another snap and a flash of white. I spun around, then nearly fell to my knees.

A man stood there, pale and beautiful, with golden eyes. Silvery-platinum hair fell past his shoulders. He watched me with an expression I couldn't read.

My throat felt like it was closing up. My heart was moments away from crashing out of my chest. I'd never been more afraid in my life, not even when Syko had me trapped onstage.

This was the man from my dreams. Was he going to sprout those wings and crawl toward me in that reptilian way?

I wanted to run with every cell in my body, but my legs refused to obey.

"Mel, babe!"

I looked ahead, Connor's voice pulling me out of my stupor. He was jogging toward me, his face looking pained as each step put pressure on his legs.

"Babe, you okay?" His eyes, green as the forest surrounding us, searched through mine with concern.

"I saw..." How could I even begin to describe it?

I turned to look where he'd been standing, and the pale man was gone.

RAZVAN

"Ooh, what does this one mean?" the blonde giggled, tracing the dark lines inside my forearm. I had forgotten her name. Sasha? Lara? Something like that.

"It means nothing," I told her honestly. "I got that done while I was drunk in Paris. Or maybe it was in Rio, I can't remember."

The girls tittered and giggled as if that was the funniest thing I'd ever said. Last night I took the blonde and her brunette friend to bed. Don't get me wrong, it was a fun night, but by mid-morning, I was tired of them.

I already finished my morning knife practice before Nigel called us all to that meeting, so I had little to do for the rest of the day. Besides, it was just so hard to get away from all the lovely burlesque girls when they fawned all over me and wanted to know the meanings of my tattoos. I'd challenge any man to pull himself away from that.

"Can I see your tongue again?" the voluptuous brunette asked me, leaning close. She was definitely Annie. No, maybe Angela. Fuck me.

I smiled and obliged, sticking my forked tongue out and wiggled both sides of it independently. She enjoyed that immensely on her clit last night while I pounded the fuck out of her blonde friend.

My tongue wasn't naturally that way. Contrary to popular belief about dragon shifters, we had normal tongues in human form. I had it intentionally split on a whim one day. My tattoo artist back in Romania knew a guy who did more extreme body modifications, and he happened to be in town that day. It hurt like a bitch for a second, but my fast healing abilities took the edge off pretty quickly.

The brunette cooed and giggled, bringing a soft hand to my face as she leaned even closer. She closed her eyes and tilted her face as her lips parted. Internally, I groaned but gave her a quick kiss with a tongue caress, like she wanted. This girl was already getting all starry-eyed with me and I could see her becoming a stage-5 clinger.

"Um, should I come back later?"

All three of our heads turned to see the new ringmistress, Melody, standing awkwardly at the edge of the burlesque dancers' camp.

Melody. Now *that* was a name I could not forget.

"Yeah, probably." The brunette snaked a hand inside my leather cut to stroke my bare chest. "We're a little busy."

She licked my ear, and I jumped. Fuck, I already told her I hated that shit.

"Actually, no." I forcibly removed her hand from me and moved away. "Now's the perfect time, miss Melody."

Her blush was adorable, but her chin lifted defiantly, and her eyes narrowed at me. Ah, so she was still unhappy about me complimenting her backside earlier.

"I was hoping to talk to the burlesque troupe about their act," she said. "I'll come around the camp and talk to your people later."

"Why not hit two birds with one stone?" I flashed her my most charming smile. "I lead the Flaming Swords. Anything you want to know about our act, you are welcome to ask me."

She shifted uncomfortably on her feet. My suggestion made sense but she was still uneasy about me. I couldn't blame her. She seemed skittish, like a feral kitten backed into a corner. The only man she seemed to trust was Connor, with how she remained attached to his hip.

"Hi, I'm Lana." Ah, that was her name. The blonde stood to greet Melody with a friendly smile and handshake. She was definitely the most down-to-earth one. "We're the Southern Belles burlesque troupe. Congratulations on becoming Ringmistress!"

"Thanks," Melody said shyly. "It's nice to meet you. I still have no idea what the hell I'm doing."

"Aw, you'll be great!" Lana waved her hand toward the folding chairs and fallen logs around their campfire. "Join us for some tea and a bite?"

"Sure, thank you." Melody gave her a smile and sat a bit off to the side of me, probably so she wouldn't have to look at me directly.

Meanwhile, Lana's brunette friend had all but climbed into my lap, shooting dirty looks at Melody the entire time.

"Let me up for a bit, hon." I patted the side of her hip. "My legs are falling asleep."

She let out an annoying whine and wrapped her arms tighter around my neck, nuzzling her face into my chest, and began kissing me there. I saw Melody look away, and I glanced over pleadingly at Lana.

"Oh, get off him already, Ally," she chided her friend jokingly. "Let the man breathe."

Ally reluctantly slumped off me, but not before pressing her mouth to mine and jamming her tongue between my lips. I didn't return it and pulled away. This girl's possessiveness was already starting to piss me off.

No one possessed me. Especially not a woman.

But Melody? She intrigued me.

She made my dragon restless, unlike any other woman before. The moment I first saw her, I wanted to do more than just show off my knife skills. The beast within me wanted to beat its scaled wings, roar loud enough to shatter these humans' eardrums, and set the entire forest ablaze just to show he was a worthy mate.

Humans pushed their animal instincts so far back into their psyche, but we shifters, or *mutaţie* as my people called them, fought a daily battle of instinct and personhood.

Still, I kept my distance as Melody settled in, accepting a mug of tea from Lana as they chatted. It would do me no good to come onto her strongly. I had to treat her carefully, just like the skittish kitten she was.

Ally settled next to me, still pressing her leg against my thigh. Still too close for comfort, but at least she was no longer in my lap. Nothing made my dick softer than blatant desperation.

I watched Melody with interest as she slowly grew more relaxed in my presence. Just like her name, her voice was musical when she talked. Nigel made the right choice in her as ringmistress. She would seduce the audience with that face and voice, even if she didn't have the confidence to believe it yet.

Despite the effect she had on my dragon, she didn't smell like a shifter. On that note, she didn't smell entirely human either. It was all I could do not to lean closer and smell that rich, ebony black hair up close.

"Why don't we go back in the tent?" Ally squeezed my thigh and tried to give me a seductive look. "Let them talk business."

"This business concerns me, too," I snarled, ripping her hand off me. "And as lovely as you are, hon, desperation is not a good look. You'd do well to remember that."

Her mouth formed an O of surprise and she finally scooted away, blinking back tears. I didn't enjoy making women cry, but it was the only way to get through to her. I had been willing to fuck her again, but now I was doubting that. From what experience taught me, she'd start talking about weddings and babies the next morning. No, thank you.

Melody finally turned those large, chocolate brown eyes on me, and my dragon startled. It was all I could do to keep excited puffs of smoke coming from my nostrils. The little fire trick from last night was risky to show her, and quite possibly an unwise move. I still wasn't sure *why* I did it, aside from the scaly beast inside dying to impress her. I hadn't met anyone in years who knew I wasn't fully human.

"So tell me about what you do, Razvan," she inquired shyly. Her eyes met mine for a moment and then darted away.

"So glad you asked," I grinned. "My crew and I are quite multi-talented when it comes to fire and sharp metal things. We do the usual knife throwing and juggling, sword-swallowing, but we add a little pyromania to it, too. One of our best acts is having a sword fight with flaming blades."

"It's a really cool show!" Lana piped up. "Kind of scary, too."

"The crowd loves a little danger," I said with a wink.

Melody chewed her lip. "Do you ever have people stand in front of a dartboard which you throw knives at?"

I tilted my head. It was an oddly specific question. "We used to with people from the audience, but not so much anymore. We've never had any unfortunate accidents but too many others have and the carnivals got sued. Now most managers forbid it to cover their own asses."

"You did it with audience members?" Her eyes widened.

"Yeah, it added a little bit of reality to the show," I shrugged. "Totally harmless as long as it's done correctly. But some dumb fucks ruined it for everyone."

Melody nodded as she mulled over what I told her. She looked especially adorable when deep in thought. I wondered if she originated from my country. With her dark eyes, dark hair, and pale skin, she had that lovely gothic look that Romanian women were known for. A look that I was a sucker for after being in the States these past few years. These cheery southern belles, while bright, beautiful, and charming, I quickly found were not my type.

"Anything else you'd like to tell me?" Melody asked.

"Absolutely." I leaned forward, those deep chocolate eyes consuming me. "Perhaps over a drink?"

I half expected her to recoil from me as if in disgust, but she didn't. Her slender eyebrows raised, but she held my gaze coolly.

"Thank you Razvan, but I'm not a drinker," she answered.

"Call me Raz." I grinned, not willing to give up. "How about over dinner, then?"

"I have plans."

Of course she did. With her man, no doubt. Anyone with eyes could tell they were together, but I had senses that were beyond human. I could smell Connor's desire for her and hers for him, but I didn't get the sense that he wanted to claim her as off limits. When I approached her in the bar, his lack of reaction confirmed it loud and clear.

He was *hers,* but he didn't demonstrate that she was *his.*

For some reason, despite his feelings, he didn't feel worthy of her.

Their relationship was intriguing, although not as intriguing as the woman herself sitting before me.

Melody was harder to read than Connor. She acted completely human, but there was something else there. I couldn't decipher her desires as easily. Maybe because of how young she was, she didn't know them entirely herself.

As much as she fascinated me, she was also blatantly rejecting me, and I was not one to push a woman past her boundaries.

I lowered my eyes and smiled, accepting her refusals as gracefully as I could. There was a difference between persistence and pestering, and I did not want to find myself in the latter category.

"How about we go for a walk?"

My eyes snapped up, unable to hide my surprise.

"You want to walk with *me*?" I asked in disbelief.

She nodded, the adorable blush rising in her cheeks. "It'll be easiest for us to talk, don't you think?"

I smiled. This girl was full of surprises. "Definitely. When would you like to go?"

"How about now?"

My dragon yearned to roar and beat his wings in victory, but I kept a cool exterior. It seemed the skittish little kitten wasn't so afraid after all.

I stood from my seat, ignoring Ally's look of jealousy, and held my hand out toward the nearby walking path.

"Shall we?"

Melody rose as well, following my lead and keeping a comfortable distance between us. That was fine with me. Being alone with her was more than I could hope for at that moment.

We walked side-by-side in silence on the first part of the trail. She chewed her lip and kept her hands clasped in front of her body. She seemed like she wanted to ask me something but couldn't spit it out.

"I would ask why you wanted to be alone with me, but I'm worried about getting another reaction like this morning," I teased, testing the waters.

She humored me with a small smile. "I might have overreacted to that. Sorry for biting your head off."

"Nothing to fear. As you can see, my head is still firmly attached."

She gave me a light, musical laugh that time. "It's an expression."

"I know. I'm just playing the adorable, clueless foreigner," I said with a wink.

"Where are you from, Raz?" Her use of my shortened name made my heart skip a beat.

"Romania," I answered. "The birthplace of Dracula."

"Really?" Her eyebrows lifted in surprise.

"Yes, Transylvania is a province in my country," I smiled. "A beautiful place actually, miss Melody."

"You can call me Mel," she murmured.

I preferred using her full name, but she was opening up to me now rather than retreating. I wouldn't ruin such a chance.

"So what else is there to your act that you wanted to tell me?" Her tone turned more business-like, but she still had that kitten-like curiosity in her voice.

I stopped walking and turned to look at her. "You want to know how I lit your campfire last night."

She swallowed nervously, but stood squarely and fearlessly in front of me. "So you're saying that wasn't an ordinary magic trick?"

"Depends on what your definition of ordinary is," I countered.

She blinked. "I'm not sure what you're trying to say. But I keep playing it over in my head. I didn't smell lighter fluid. I didn't see a match or anything to ignite a flame."

"And you still thought walking out into the woods alone with me was wise?" I flashed a flirtatious smile in hopes she wouldn't take the question too seriously.

Her fists clenched at her sides. She lowered her chin to glare at me.

"You won't hurt me. I'm not sure how I know that, but you're being evasive now, so I still don't entirely trust you."

Those last words made me bristle defensively, though I tried not to let it show. Of course she didn't trust me. This was our first real conversation together. But I had a knee jerk reaction to that statement because of how much it seemed to follow me everywhere.

People didn't trust me because of how I looked. If not my extensive body mod collection, it was rumors of my sexual escapades or my affinity for fire and sharp blades. Even though I'd never been dishonest, deceitful, or manipulated another person, I got the implication that I wasn't trustworthy.

Women loved to fuck me, but I never met one that didn't think I would cheat in some way. I was the bad boy fantasy, not the guy they took home to meet their family. Even clingy Ally saw me as a project she could improve, not someone she could take as-is. Not that I wanted to give up my freedom to fuck around as I pleased. It would just be nice if someone could see me differently.

Still, Melody had no idea of my defensiveness around the concept of trust, so I just gave her a tight smile.

"You're right, I won't hurt you," I said. "And I'm not being evasive, just bantering."

Her eyes narrowed, and she opened her mouth to say something, but the energy in the air immediately shifted. My dragon raised his defenses as I tuned into my surroundings. Another shifter was nearby. It felt like the same one I sensed earlier.

Melody's face went white as a sheet as she whipped around. She sensed it, too. Interesting.

And she was scared, but also seemed like she was familiar with this presence.

"Stay by me," I instructed, stepping in front of her and pulling her behind my back.

Her breath came out in soft puffs as her small hands rested on my shoulders, but I couldn't be distracted by that touch now.

My dragon tasted the air, sniffing out this shy shifter's motivations as Melody and I turned in a cautious circle.

When the feedback returned to me, I smiled and relaxed.

"I just saw a flash of white fur," Melody said in a hushed whisper. "It's not the first time, either. I think it's... well, it's kind of a long story."

My shoulders shook as I laughed. I took one of Melody's hands from my shoulder and turned to face her.

"You have nothing to be afraid of, *steluța*," I told her. "It seems you have a shy admirer."

⚜ 6 ⚜

MELODY

I blinked up at Razvan's steely gray eyes, though for a moment they seemed to take on a tinge of red. And maybe I imagined it, but I thought I saw his pupils narrow to slits like a reptile.

"An admirer?" I repeated.

"Yes," he confirmed. "He senses your fear and doesn't wish to scare you, so he keeps his distance. But you have my word, *steluța*, he will not harm you. If anything, he is acting like an unseen bodyguard."

His charming grin spread, almost hiding the small tattoos near the outer corners of his eyes. "You're a lucky woman, having all these admirers looking out for you."

I didn't know what to make of that. Was he including himself in that statement?

"How do you know what... my admirer is feeling?" I asked. "Do you know what it, er, he is?"

The grin faded, his expression turning serious and even intimidating in a sexy way.

"Yes," he answered. "But I'm not sure how much you know or *want* to know."

"I have so many questions," I admitted, my mind swirling with memories of the wolf man and his family. My recent dreams mixed in, almost feeling like memories themselves. "But I'm not sure who's the right person to ask."

"Right, of course. You don't trust me yet." Razvan smirked, but I felt some tension coming off him like he felt defensive about my saying that. "If you show your admirer you're not afraid, maybe he'll approach you himself, *steluţa*."

"What's that word you keep calling me?" I demanded. He said it enough times, but I had no idea if it was a pet name or insult.

"Ah, I can't tell you all my secrets now," he said playfully. "I want you to invite me on another walk in the woods."

"Is it something your friends will laugh at if they hear it?" I was still a little on edge about earlier today, but was beginning to see what Connor meant about him. This guy was different. Definitely a character, but nothing about him told my instincts to stay away.

"Not at you, no," he said softly. "But they'll give me a good ribbing for sure."

"That doesn't make any sense to me," I mumbled.

"Maybe it will one day." He winked at me. "You have a lot to do, so I won't take any more of your time, Melody."

I barely realized that we'd been walking back in the direction we came. The forest path gave way to the burlesque camp, open and welcoming with its cozy fire and tents.

I turned to Razvan, suddenly feeling shy, like this was the end of a date.

"Well, thanks for uh, looking out for me." I swallowed. "And telling me about you. Your act, I mean."

"It's been my pleasure," he said with a slight bow of his head. "Until next time, *steluţa*."

I turned down my own path to continue my way down to the other campsites, not wanting to leave my eyes lingering on him for long. He and that girl Ally seemed like they were a thing. I definitely didn't want another girl thinking I had my claws sunk into her man.

Curiosity got the better of me as I walked, and I peeked over my shoulder to look back at him. To my surprise, he went right past the burlesque tent and continued on into the woods. Why wouldn't he go right back to the woman fawning over him?

None of your business, Mel, I told myself.

Our walk in the woods left me with more questions than answers, really. I had enough buzz words to use in my ringmistress announcements, but I didn't really learn anything about him at all.

He's probably a vampire. He's from the land of Dracula, after all, I mused.

AN HOUR LATER, I returned to my own camp to find Connor practicing some crazy shit.

He was shirtless near our trailer, wearing long sweatpants covering his legs. His bronze, sun-kissed skin was glossy in a thin sheen of sweat.

He dropped backward into a handstand, kicking his feet straight up into the air. The pant cuffs cinched tightly around the metal ankle joint, keeping his pant legs from slipping down as he slowly bent and straightened his elbows.

I quickly realized he was doing push-ups with his entire bodyweight. With rigorous control and strength, he lowered himself until he nearly kissed the ground before pushing himself back up with the same fluid movement.

He did that ten times before swinging his feet down and standing right-side up again. His red face looked surprised when he saw me.

"You're back," he stated, sounding just as surprised.

"Yeah, made my rounds." My core flushed with heat as I approached him, drinking in that ripped, tan torso.

Saying nothing, he turned away and picked up a towel to wipe his face and neck.

"Practicing without me?" I teased, leaning against the trailer.

"You're not part of my act anymore, *Ringmistress*."

Maybe he meant to tease me back, but through the towel his voice came out low and gruff. And he still wasn't looking at me. My heart started to feel like it was being squeezed in a fist.

"Hey, is something wrong?" I reached out to put a hand on his arm, and he promptly pulled away.

"No. Why would anything be wrong?"

"Because you're acting like a dick."

His green eyes finally met mine, buried under a furrowed brow and a scowl on that handsome face.

"I just didn't expect you to get back from *making your rounds* so soon."

"So soon? It's been a couple of hours. And why are you mad that I'm back?"

"I'm not mad." His jaw clenched. "Forget I said anything."

He stormed off, leaving me stunned for a moment before my own anger spurred me to follow him.

"I don't know what crawled up your ass and died, Connor, but don't take your shit out on me!"

He ignored me, taking two long strides into the trailer, and slammed the door after him. I followed, yanking it open and slamming it twice as hard.

"Get out, Mel," he growled, whipping around to face me. With all his muscles coiled and flexed with power, he looked ready to tear the inside of this tiny trailer apart.

"No." I stood my ground, despite the fear creeping into my voice. Fear mixed with arousal, creating an explosive chemical cocktail inside me just from watching his abs flex as he breathed. "You don't get to be an asshole to me for no reason. You owe me an explanation, Connor."

"I don't owe you shit, Melody!" he yelled. "You have everything of mine already!"

"What the fuck does that mean?!" I shouted back.

Tears of frustration burned in my eyes. I hated yelling more than anything, but running and hiding never made it go away. I knew Connor wouldn't hurt me, not physically anyway, but I wasn't going to let him make me feel small and powerless. I was done feeling that way.

He rushed at me so quickly, I thought for a fleeting moment I was wrong about him. Fear and lifelong instincts told me to flinch and look away. I wasn't ready for him to lift me up and press me between his hard body and the wall. I wasn't ready for his lips to come crashing down on mine to consume me.

"Why do you have to do this to me, Mel?" His teeth nipped just below my earlobe, making me cry out and cling to him. He just pressed against me harder with a heavy groan.

"Do what?" I asked in a shaky whisper. A rush of wetness flooded my core so fast. I was so confused, so unbelievably turned on, I thought I was going insane.

"Make me feel this way." Pinning me to the wall with his hips, his large hands enveloped my ribcage. "Make me feel *anything* at all."

"Connor," I gasped, bringing his mouth to mine like he was the air I desperately needed to live.

Our tongues clashed in a fierce battle for dominance. He kneaded my breasts in such a way that was intense, but not painful. I shifted my legs to wrap snugly around his waist and found his erection straining hard against his pants.

"Mel," he groaned, dragging his burning hot mouth down my neck. "I don't deserve you, babe, but you're all I want."

"Stop that." I wrapped my arms around his shoulders, pressing my chest and my core to him. "You deserve so much more than me."

"No, you stop." His voice carried a light chuckle, but was still low and full of need. "I've done awful things, babe. I'm fucking selfish to want you this bad."

"Then be selfish."

I slid a hand down his chest, memorizing every muscle, hair, and scar with my palm until I reached the front of his pants. The outline of his bulge greeted me and I cupped my palm along his thick length. He shivered and moaned as I touched him, then slid his arms around my back to peel me away from the wall.

Like free-falling through the air onstage, I felt weightless as he carried me until the bed supported my back.

"Connor, will you..." I gasped during the moments my mouth was free from his to speak, "...will you let me touch you this time?"

He paused—his intense, passionate movements becoming slow and methodical.

"You're telling me to be selfish, so who am I to say no?"

I felt his smile against my skin and joy lifted in my heart. Now *I* could stop feeling selfish for a few moments and reciprocate what he gave me.

"Connor." I brushed my lips past his ear. I loved saying his name and from the way he moaned into my neck, I guessed he loved hearing it. "I want all of you."

To prove my point, I slipped a hand inside his pants and boxers. My fingers brushed past his solid, silky head to wrap around his hot shaft. In response, my molten core closed agonizingly around nothing. I needed it, needed *him*.

"Mel." His voice was thick with desire. "You have all of me here." He took my other hand and pressed it to his chest, where his racing heartbeat kissed my palm. "I want you more than anything, but you don't have to settle for *my* body to please you."

"I told you to stop it," I growled, biting down on his ear in frustration until he yelped. "I want *you*, Connor. Touch me, I'm so wet for you."

I directed his hand to the furnace between my legs, instantly sighing from the pressure of his fingers on my slick folds.

He knew me there better than anyone, despite knowing each other for such a short time. He could always tell exactly what I loved, needed, and craved, and teased me relentlessly until I went off like an atomic bomb.

"Connor," I moaned as I rocked against his palm, growing desperate to ease the mounting pressure growing inside me. "You're the only one that's ever pleased me."

He stopped suddenly and pulled away to look at me with a puzzled expression.

"So when you made your rounds earlier, what did you mean?"

I blinked up at him, equally confused. "I talked with everyone about their acts for my ringmistress speech. What did you think I meant?"

He dropped his face on the mattress next to mine. A muffled sound came from his mouth and his body shook with... laughter?

"Connor!" I twisted out from under him to look at him better. "What the hell did you think I did?"

"Fuck. I'm sorry, Mel." He wiped his eyes, and I realized he was crying from laughing so hard. "My mind went somewhere while you were gone and I didn't stop to think about how ridiculous it was."

I stared at him, agape. "You didn't seriously think I slept with the whole carnival, did you?"

"Not the whole carnival, no." He giggled as he tried to compose himself. "I figured you probably got cozy with that Razvan guy, though."

"What?! No! I barely know him!"

"You barely know me," he pointed out.

"I know you a hell of a lot better than him," I huffed. "And anyway, he has a girlfriend or fuck buddy or whatever. She was all over him at the burlesque camp."

"Something tells me he doesn't really limit himself." Connor smiled wryly.

"It doesn't matter, anyway. Nothing happened." The realization hit me like a ton of bricks. "Is that why you were so pissed off when I came back?"

"Kind of," he sighed. "More pissed at myself, really. I convinced myself you went for him since I told you I'd be fine with it. Then I realized I was jealous of you spending time with him, then pissed off at myself because I have no right to be jealous. And just, yeah. An infinite loop."

"Oh, Connor," I breathed.

I rolled over on top of him and kissed him with every ounce of emotion pouring out of me right then. No words could describe how he made me feel, how desperately I wanted him to see himself as I did.

He cradled my face sweetly as he kissed me back.

"You were right, babe," he whispered against my lips. "I shouldn't have taken it out on you. I'm sorry."

"So, you want to be my boyfriend now?" I nipped playfully at his jaw, but when the answer didn't come, I felt a sinking feeling in my stomach.

"I still don't want you to limit yourself to just me," he sighed. "I just... need to deal with my feelings about it better."

"And I still think you're making this an issue when it doesn't need to be one." I slid my leg across him to straddle his waist. "But we can talk about that later."

Our eyes met for a hot, electric moment before his mouth devoured mine again. This time, nothing stopped us or got us off track.

7

MELODY

He tore my shirt and bra off, flinging them both violently across the trailer. I lifted my hips to peel his pants and boxers down, finally revealing his glorious cock. He was hard, thick and mouth watering, and it was just as tanned as the rest of his body.

I finished undressing him, sliding his clothes past his prosthetics and the silicone sleeves that held them in place on his legs. Honestly, I found it hot that part of his body was made of metal. Like he was some kind of bionic man or sexy android. He survived horrors that made him greater than any ordinary man. If only he could see that.

But my main focus was not on his legs, but on *him*. The warmth and skin and scars that told stories and shaped this man who captured my heart, too.

He peeled my shorts and panties off and skimmed his fingertips with slow fascination back up my legs. He touched my ankles, calves, and the backs of my knees before taking a firm grip on my thighs and hips.

I loved how every touch and every kiss of his was deliberate, confident. His mouth pressed kisses to my belly while he kneaded my flesh.

He was roughness, gentleness, and intensity all wrapped into one package and I could not get enough.

My fingers tried to memorize every crevice between his muscles, every vein that pulsed through his skin. How could he not realize how incredibly hot he was? How could he really think I'd want to sleep with some stranger over him? This body needed four men to restrain him in a bar fight. This body put a huge wolf man over its shoulders and carried him to safety. This body made me feel safe, protected, and like a *woman*, not some silly, lovesick girl.

I wrapped my hand around his thick shaft again, pressing hard and hot against my leg.

"Mm," he moaned and thrust into my hand, the velvety skin gliding through my fingers. "Like this, babe."

He covered my hand with his and guided my strokes. I watched his face, fascinated and so incredibly turned on at his lip bites, his accelerated breaths, and his head dropping back in ecstasy.

"Keep doing that and I'll be off in no time," he grinned, gently pulling my hand away and bringing my palm to his lips.

"You got me almost there already," I replied huskily, resuming my position on top of him. His cock pulsed with heat against my sensitive core, my clit tingling from the hard pressure. My blood felt like liquid fire in my veins. I felt like I wanted this forever. I never knew how much I needed him.

"Hang on, babe." Connor reached above us to fumble through a shelf just above the bed. I took the opportunity to run my hands down his perfect chest and abs again. Fuck, I could hardly believe I was in bed with this sexy beast of a man.

He produced a square foil wrapper and tore it open. "Never thought I'd be using these again."

"Condoms?" I asked.

"Yes, babe." He kissed me before rolling it down his length. "You still don't want to get pregnant as a teenager, right?"

"Right. I just... figured guys hated those."

"Not as much as unexpected surprises that last for eighteen years."

Truthfully, I was taken aback that he would consider it without me having to say anything. In my experience, guys didn't care about birth control. They could just disappear and leave the woman to deal with it on her own.

But Connor wasn't like that. I had to remember that he wasn't anything like the men I knew growing up.

I leaned forward to kiss him, giving him my appreciation without words. He caressed my back and my ass, positioning his head at my slick entrance.

"You're in control, babe," he murmured into my neck. "Take what you need from me."

I needed all of him, completely. But as I started lowering myself onto him, his girth and my lack of any recent sexual activity became clear.

Connor responded immediately to my discomfort. He pressed a thumb to my clit and kissed his way down my chest to take a nipple in his mouth. His tongue and finger swirled hypnotically on those two sensitive points. When his teeth grazed the aching peak, I gasped, squirmed, and unwittingly impaled myself further down his cock.

He moved on to my other nipple as I stretched around him, my pussy already convulsing from him working my clit. It was too good, almost too much. I braced my hands on his chest as he slowly filled me, driving me to the edge with every inch of him.

When he was finally seated within me, every cell and hair follicle felt abuzz with sensitivity. He was inside me and not just physically. I felt him in every pore.

"Oh God, Mel," he groaned as I made the slightest shifting movements. "You feel so fucking good."

He filled me up so completely I didn't want to move much. He also felt so right inside me, I didn't want to be deprived of him.

Gradually, I thrust back on him harder. He began driving his hips up into me as I adjusted to him, holding my waist as we crashed together in the middle.

It felt like slow, beautiful violence. He sliced through me, but I couldn't get enough. When the pleasure teetered over the line to pain, he cupped my face and kissed me so sweetly to bring me back. When I started whimpering and my whole body quivered for release, he bucked into me relentlessly to hit my clit in just the right way.

When I came, I released so much through that orgasm. I released everything I felt about him, from the love growing in my heart to the annoyance and frustration from him being a pain in my ass. It was blissful, cathartic, and felt like a weight lifted off my chest.

"Did I hurt you, babe?" Connor brushed kisses across my cheeks. I didn't even realize I shed tears until I tasted their saltiness on his lips.

"No, you didn't." I smiled through my panting, ragged breaths. "That was just... really good."

"You're welcome," he chuckled into my neck as he lazily rolled us over, pressing my back into the mattress with the depth of his kisses.

After a few moments to catch my breath, he sheathed himself inside me with a hot moan and took my breath away all over again.

His weight on top of me felt incredible, so secure and intimate. I wrapped my arms around his wide back as he thrust into me with those powerful thighs. He lifted my hips higher as he crashed into my clit, building another orgasm through me as I barely recovered from the first one.

"God, Mel, you feel incredible," he growled, picking up speed and power as he grew impossibly stiff within me.

"Connor, you...ohh..." I lost all ability to make words as another orgasm shattered me.

His release came with one final, deep thrust into me with a powerful roar. We held each other so tightly, our skin carried matching red marks when we finally pulled away.

8

MELODY

"I swear to God you're *trying* to poke my eye out with that thing!"

"Then quit walking behind me. Get up here next to me, babe."

I ran up next to Connor and laced my fingers through his outstretched hand. He brought the back of my palm to his lips and nothing could calm the resulting fluttering in my heart.

The angry-slash-makeup sex took so much out of us, we ended up napping most of the day away. We woke up just as evening settled in, and Connor suggested I join him for practice after dinner.

Just like the first time, I followed him into the woods and far away from any curious eyes. Only this time we were under cool, silver moonlight instead of blazing hot sun. I was starting to think I could get used to being a night owl. Daytime was so overrated. Nighttime had such an unappreciated beauty and romance to it.

I had a flashlight, so we weren't just lit by moonlight, thankfully. Connor seemed oddly excited about practicing in the dark, though.

"Ever tried balancing on one leg with your eyes closed?" he asked.

"Sounds hard," I muttered.

"Exactly. You can always find new ways to challenge yourself," he said. "And the more you challenge yourself, the more you improve."

"Whatever, weirdo," I teased, giving him a sloppy kiss on the cheek.

He spent the next few minutes telling me all about the different kinds of push-ups and exercises they made him do in the Marines, when I saw an unmistakable flash of white in the corner of my eye.

At this point, I was essentially expecting it and stopped walking abruptly, turning to face the direction of the movement.

"Babe?" Connor's grip tightened on my hand. "Did you see something?"

"Yeah," I answered, remembering what Razvan said and tried to project my voice loudly. "I know you're out there. I'm not sure why you're hiding, but please show yourself. I'm not afraid and you know we won't hurt you."

I sounded way more confident than I felt. Nothing answered me for a few moments, and Connor leaned down to whisper in my ear.

"Babe, who're you—FUCK!" He grabbed my arm and pulled me back protectively when the beautiful, pale man came into view.

With his long, platinum hair and graceful stride he looked ethereal and haunting, like moonlight itself. His long, lean-muscled torso was bare except for the angry red burns on his chest and ribs. He looked incredibly tall as he approached us from the brush, at least six foot four. For a moment I wondered if he was naked, but to my relief he wore dark jeans, although his feet were bare.

The beautiful pale man from my dream stood before me in the flesh, but this time I wasn't afraid. I still didn't know why he morphed like a reptile or why he spoke to me like I was someone else, but after getting past the initial fear, instinctually, I knew he wasn't here to harm us.

Those sad, golden eyes looked at me with recognition, and I knew instantly who he was.

"Who the hell are you?"

Connor apparently did not.

"It's okay, Con." I pulled my arm gently out of his grip and stepped toward the ghostly man. "What's your name?"

"My name is Hunter." I did not expect such a deep, masculine voice to come out of such a man. "My children are Roo and Rinna."

I smiled. That confirmed it. I felt crazy, but the proof was standing right in front of me. A giddy excitedness bloomed in my chest.

"Connor," I whispered. "This is who we helped to escape from Drowningville."

He looked at me and then back at Hunter, looking more confused with each passing second.

"How... what?"

"Hunter," I said, feeling like some sort of mediator. "Thank you for coming out and talking to us. Would you like to come sit down so we can clear the air?"

He lowered his golden eyes, and I saw his lips twitch in what appeared to be a smile of relief.

"Yes. Thank you, Melody."

"Call me Mel," I said automatically.

The three of us sat around a cluster of boulders not far from where Hunter decided to reveal himself. Connor stayed glued to my side while eyeing Hunter suspiciously, not that I could blame him. Hunter kept a respectful distance away. I could tell he was trying to appear as non-threatening as possible—seemingly a challenge with his imposing frame and predatory stalking skills.

"So *you're* the fucking wolf man?" Connor demanded.

"Yes." Hunter's lip curled with distaste at the nickname. "I don't care for being called that, but I was the one on display, drugged, beaten, and electrocuted. I recognized you both from the crowd, and then in the trailer when I woke up later."

"What would you prefer us to call you?" I asked gently, resting a hand on Connor's arm to calm him.

"Humans have called us all sorts of things," he mused. "Lycan is what our kind call each other. Wolf shifter is also appropriate and a simple explanation."

"You're saying you're *not* human?" Connor said incredulously.

Hunter's eyes flashed with amusement. "Right now, I'm just as human as you are, Connor." He tilted his head as though a canine would. "And yet I'm completely different from you."

"You can... turn into a wolf, can't you?" It sounded absolutely insane coming out of my mouth.

He fixated those golden eyes on me. "Yes. My form is fully human like this," he gestured to himself, "or fully wolf. That form you saw me in was... forced. It's an in-between state and not natural for us to look like that."

"Can you tell us how you ended up there?" I asked. My heart ached with the memory of seeing him, human in stature but covered in white fur, elongated ears, and an extended snout. His kids looked the same. Goddamn, they forced *kids* to look like that for entertainment.

While the old anger and horror flooded my veins, Connor visibly relaxed next to me and rubbed my back.

"We were captured maybe three weeks ago," Hunter began. "These carnivals hire poachers specifically to hunt shifters for a massive bounty. They must have stalked my pack for months and covered their scent well. One day, they finally ambushed us and we got separated from everyone else."

He let out a heavy sigh before continuing. "It was just Roo, Rinna, and me. We were outnumbered, so I shifted to human to try and bargain with them." He swallowed. "There was a language barrier, but I asked them to spare my children if I went along willingly. They seemed to understand and agree. But they still tranquilized me anyway. The next thing I knew, I woke up tied up in a cage, stuck between my wolf and human form. My kids were right there with me."

"I'm so sorry," I choked. My throat felt like it was closing up, and Connor kissed my temple as he rubbed soothing circles on my back.

"It's okay. We're all safe now, thanks to you." Hunter offered a small smile. "I was in and out of consciousness for what had to be days. They injected all of us with something that kept us stuck between shifts. My poor kids didn't understand. I hate that I couldn't protect them."

"There was nothing you could do," Connor said sympathetically. "We saw how they treated you. It was absolutely barbaric."

"You left, I assume to be reunited with your pack," I said. "Why are you still here?"

Hunter's face fell. "Yes, I've been looking for them these past few days, but haven't picked up a fresh scent. My worst fear is they all got captured." He looked up. "With nowhere for us to go, I figured the least I could do was watch over those who saved us. I stayed hidden because I didn't know if you would understand."

"I don't know how, but... I do," I said softly. "For some reason, I *had* to see you and then rescue you. Not doing it wasn't an option."

"Clearly not," Connor teased me affectionately.

"Whatever the reason, I'll always be grateful to you both." Hunter rested his gaze solemnly on us. "If not for my own life, for my children's. This has been traumatic for them, but they'll grow up wild and free like they were meant to."

"Where are they now?" I asked.

"I made a small den for us in the woods." Hunter's eyes lit up. "If you'd like, I can bring them by and formally introduce you later."

"I'd like that," I smiled before another, less comfortable thought occurred to me. "Do they, um, have a mother?"

"My mate was killed by hunters a few years ago, not long after Rinna was born," He frowned. "Roo remembers her but Rinna doesn't, really."

An ache gripped my chest. That was who he had to be talking to in my dream. I still couldn't shake the feeling that it was wrong to be there. How would I even begin to explain the dreams to him?

"Fuck, I'm sorry. They're so young and have had it so rough already."

"They've been okay. We've always had the pack around to raise them. As for now?" He sighed, but warmth and pride tugged at a smile on his lips. "They're so strong. They've inspired me to keep going."

"That's great to hear." Warmth and relief spread through me. This family was okay. It would take time and some healing, but they would be okay in the end. That was all I wanted to happen when we broke them out.

"Are there others like you?" Connor asked. "Obviously you have your pack, but are there other... animal shifters? You talked about these poachers like they're a common thing."

"Yes. Nearly every animal you can imagine, there are shifters of," Hunter answered. "Well, vertebrates, at least. The theory is shifters developed early during evolution when the first vertebrates began splitting off into different species. Some carried only the human genes, some became only the non-human animals. Others carried both, developing abilities of two distinct animals at the same time."

He looked pointedly at me. "The one who you were talking to earlier today. He's a shifter as well."

"Razvan?" My eyes widened. Was *that* why I was so drawn to him? My curiosity toward him and Hunter felt nearly the same. Now that I knew what they both looked like in human form, that curiosity gave way to a magnetic, inexplicable attraction.

Hunter was almost exotically handsome, with otherworldly features like a model. Razvan had a unique look too, which his many tattoos just enhanced, but he was dark where Hunter was light. Still, I felt a near equally opposing pull to both of them.

"I knew there was something weird about that guy, despite all the tattoos and being foreign," Conner said. "No offense," he added to Hunter.

"Trust me," Hunter smiled. "Weird is one of the least offensive things you could call me."

"Do you know what animal he shifts to?" I asked.

"I can make an educated guess based on his smell," Hunter said with a stroke of his short beard. "But it's not my place to tell. There are so many shifters among humans staying hidden for their own protection."

I nodded in understanding. It would seem I'd be talking to Razvan again soon. His vague hints made a lot more sense now, along with his reason for being so evasive.

"He is free, which is surprising to see why he's still a performer," Hunter said with clear distaste. "Most of us in the carnival are not here willingly."

"That's horrible," I lamented. "How can this be allowed to happen? Why isn't anyone causing an uproar about that? It's basically slavery."

"Because so few believe we exist," he answered sadly. "There are no laws to protect us when we're invisible. The carnivals and circuses pay a lot of money to ensure that we don't become common knowledge. It keeps our value high when people still aren't sure we're real."

"And that's the reason for the drugs, I bet," Connor said. "To make you look like, well, a circus freak. Otherwise you're just an ordinary person or an animal, which is not as interesting."

"Exactly," Hunter nodded.

The three of us sat in silence for a moment, Connor and I absorbing this mind-blowing information while Hunter watched us curiously. Even in human form, he was a lot like a wolf in a way. His golden eyes were intense, wise, and wild. They seemed to notice things our human eyes couldn't perceive.

"Well, this has been... something," Connor breathed with a shake of his head. "I knew this business was fucked, but straight up hunting people and treating them worse than animals? It's just sick."

I looked at him. "Has Nigel ever...?"

"Not that I know of," he said. "Nigel's a decent guy. I'd be surprised if he even knows about it. In my two years in this business I've never known about this, not even rumors."

"The one you spoke of earlier, Razvan," Hunter chimed in. "I don't know him, but I can't imagine a shifter working willingly with a manager that has enslaved others like us. And I haven't smelled any others around. Those are all good signs that this one hasn't sunk that low. Yet."

He rose fluidly from his boulder, standing to his full, towering height. His muscles on his long frame were slender and lithe. Where Connor could be a bodybuilder, Hunter could've been a swimmer. I wondered how he looked in wolf form.

"I'm glad I got to meet you both, formally," he said. "I have to catch dinner for the kids so I'll leave you two for now."

"Please bring them by the camp," I said. "I'd love to meet them and see how they're doing."

"I will," Hunter promised. His smile and golden gaze lingered on me long enough to make my stomach flutter before his shift began.

White fur sprouted across his body as bones popped and rearranged themselves. He dropped to all fours as he passed the point of where we first saw him. In mere moments, all human features disappeared and a huge, beautiful white wolf stood before us.

"Holy shit," Connor breathed.

Hunter wagged his tail and approached us, closer than he'd ever been. I held my hand out, and he sniffed it with his cool, black nose and gave me a small lick.

"Wow, you're so beautiful," I said, forgetting momentarily I was not just complimenting a gorgeous animal but a *person*.

Hunter let out a high-pitched yip that sounded like a laugh. I felt myself turning beet red with embarrassment. He gave me another affectionate lick before running off into the woods. Connor and I watched his sleek, white form elegantly slink away into the darkness.

"Well, damn." Connor rubbed his face. "I don't think I can focus on practice after all that."

9

MELODY

onnor and I spotted Razvan the next evening in the tavern at dinnertime. He was alone for once, without his crew or a fawning woman in sight. Eating his plate of food quietly and drinking from his pint glass, he seemed different without an entourage. Almost pensive and introverted with no one to show off for.

"Should we go talk to him?" I asked Connor. "About, you know, shifter stuff?"

"That's all you, babe." He nudged me in Razvan's direction gently. "Go ahead, I'll hang out with Nigel."

I turned to give him a look, but he was already heading off in the opposite direction, leaving me standing there with my bowl of stew and glass of Coke.

With a sigh and a big dose of courage, I walked up to the table where the tattooed, steel-eyed man sat by himself.

"This seat taken?" I asked.

His demeanor changed immediately, his face lighting up with an electric smile. "It is now by you, *steluța*."

My pulse thrumming nervously in my veins, I stepped over the picnic bench and sat down in front of him. To distract myself, I took a long swig of Coke, suddenly feeling very thirsty.

"To what do I owe the pleasure of this dinner date?" He took a bite of his charred steak and chewed slowly, his eyes dancing with amusement.

"I met, um," I lowered my voice to a whisper and leaned across the table, "my admirer you told me about the other day."

His eyebrows lifted in surprise, and his smile faded slightly. "I see. So you know what he is?"

I nodded. "I take it you do too?"

"He smelled canine," was the answer. "So some kind of wolf or dog. Probably wolf, since no mere domesticated pooch is worthy of you."

"Yes, he's a wolf," I confirmed, brushing off the flattery.

"And you've never seen anything like him before?"

I shook my head. "Never in my life."

A corner of his mouth lifted into a smirk. "But you were not frightened?"

I shook my head again and drained my cup of Coke until it was empty. Holy shit, I couldn't believe this conversation was actually happening. My throat would not stop drying out.

"Ah, that won't do," Razvan said, referring to my empty cup. "What're you drinking, *steluța*? I'll get you another."

"Coke, thanks," I answered.

He shook his head slowly while clicking his tongue at me. "I'll get you some Jack to go with it."

"Please don't," I said. "I don't drink."

"Oh, that's right. I remember." He gave me a curious look. "Why not?"

I glared at him. "Not something I'm up for discussing."

"Now who's being evasive, *steluța*?" he teased.

"Okay, what the hell is that name you keep calling me?" I demanded. "You won't stop using it so you must find it especially fitting for me."

"That I do," he grinned. "I'll tell you what it means if you tell me why you don't drink."

There it was. That cocky attitude was back. Infuriating and also stupidly sexy, which only made me even more frustrated.

"Those two things aren't even close to being equal," I spat.

"I know that. Even so, it's just a simple exchange of information."

"Some name you're calling me does not hold the same amount of weight as my reason for not drinking."

"How do you know that?" he asked with the same infuriating calmness. "You don't know the meaning of the word."

For a moment, I forgot all about why I came over to talk to him in the first place. He wound me up like a spring just for the fun of it. And if we didn't get off this topic soon, I was going to explode. Probably by throwing food in his face.

"Let's go back to that other thing we were talking about," I said through gritted teeth, stabbing at the chopped carrots and potatoes in my stew.

"Oh no, you're not escaping me that easily."

Out of nowhere, a heavy weight pressed down on my beat-up sneaker. It didn't hurt but startled the shit out of me, to where I flung my spoon down to the floor. I couldn't believe it just from feeling it, so I had to glance under the table to see.

"Are you playing footsy with me?"

His laugh was playful, musical, carefree, and I hated it.

"I won't judge you for the reasons you don't drink, *steluța*," he said. "It might surprise you to learn that I'm a very sympathetic listener."

There was no way I was getting out of this. Damn it. Not even Connor knew, not really.

"My mother is an alcoholic," I said, lowering my voice again. Right away, Razvan's face grew serious. "She did everything she could to be as drunk as possible as often as possible. We often went without food or utilities because she spent every disability check on booze."

"I'm sorry, Melody. I didn't realize." His voice was sympathetic. It was soothing to hear and telling him was more cathartic than I expected.

"It wasn't just that." Once I started talking, it seemed impossible to stop. "She brought all kinds of men home. Alcoholics just like her. And sometimes like her, they'd just pass out after a while and be completely useless. Other times, they got violent."

Razvan growled and clenched his fists on the table. I got a distinct whiff of a burning smell and looked up. My eyes widened when I realized small wisps of smoke were coming from his mouth and nostrils. Maybe I shouldn't have been surprised, knowing he was some kind of shifter, but at the moment I was completely stunned and clueless.

He opened his hands and coughed, waving away the smoke casually.

"Sorry," he said a bit sheepishly. "I get a bit protective of innocent people who get hurt."

"It's okay. I guess I should get used to, um, not entirely *human* reactions."

He smiled again, but this time it was warm and genuine instead of teasing. "Go on, Melody."

"Well, yeah. That's kind of the gist of it. I saw what drinking did to my mom and the kids at school were sure to let me know how trashy and fucked up my family was."

"You're *not* trashy," he snarled.

"Well, that *is* how I grew up," I explained. "We lived in a trailer, not even a real house. My mom also kept getting pregnant and having more kids than she could afford. But she figured out more kids meant more money from the government, which meant more booze."

"Fucking hell," he cursed.

"In a science class," I went on. "I learned that addictions are often genetic and can be passed from parent to child. My older sister followed right in my mom's footsteps, so that was enough proof for me. I swore I'd never touch alcohol after that."

"And you've held strong I see, despite all these pesky men offering it to you," he winked. "That's admirable for someone your age."

"Something tells me you're old enough to know better." I stuck my tongue out at him.

"I'm twenty-three, so I can get away with youthful ignorance for a bit longer," he joked back, relaxing with one tattooed arm propped against the wall behind him. "But thank you for telling me, Melody," he added with a gentleness I had yet to hear from him. "That is a deeply personal and valid reason. I won't push it on you anymore." His grin returned. "Except when you deserve a little ribbing, maybe."

"I don't think I've ever really talked about my past to someone else," I admitted. "It felt good to get off my chest."

He raised an eyebrow quizzically. "Not even your man?"

I hesitated. "No, I was planning to, but I haven't yet. And he's not my man."

Both eyebrows lifted in surprise. "No?"

"It's complicated," I admitted. "We're together but he doesn't want me to limit myself to him."

He leaned back, lifting his chin as he looked at me. It seemed I was full of surprises tonight.

"And is that what *you* want?"

"I don't know," I sighed.

How did we turn to this topic? Connor grounded me and helped everything to make sense, yet confused the fuck out of me at the same time. We were clearly attracted to each other. The pleasant soreness in my body from yesterday and this morning proved that. I was falling for him, and he clearly was developing some feelings for me, too.

But then he pushed me away, saying he didn't want to label us as anything. And that stung, as much as I swallowed my pride and tried being cool with it. I couldn't figure out if he genuinely didn't feel worthy of me, which was bullshit, or he was trying to keep his own options open.

I still hadn't mentioned anything about that message I saw on his phone back in Drowningville. Someone named Vicky texted him asking, "Are you ever going to talk to me again?" He mentioned an ex-fiancee that left him, and I couldn't get rid of the nagging feeling that he'd go back to her if he could.

"Well, if you don't like limits," Razvan spread his hands out suggestively, "that's something else we have in common."

I rolled my eyes. "Not happening. So are you going to tell me what that word means now?"

"*Steluţa,*" he said again, enunciating it slowly. Watching his mouth move to speak the foreign word was incredibly erotic. "It means little star."

I blinked, taken aback. That was not what I was expecting. It sounded... cute.

"And why have you chosen to call me that, of all things?"

"Because," he said softly. "You are small but shine so brightly. It came to me the moment I saw you."

"I'd say you were sweet if I didn't know you were also a pervert."

His head dipped back as he laughed uproariously, the dark tattoos on his neck jumping as if joining in and laughing with him. "Why can't I be both?"

My face heated under his smoldering gaze. Damn it. He was flirting again, and I didn't know what to do.

"I suppose you can be," I mumbled awkwardly.

He recovered from laughing, and a calm seriousness swept over him.

"When you're done eating, I supposed you'd like to talk a bit more about shifter things."

I nodded. "If you'd like to."

He leaned forward, his eyes keeping their hold on me like some kind of alien tractor beam.

"I don't trust many humans, but I feel I can trust you, *steluța*," he whispered. "You're not shifter but you're not quite like other humans. You smell different somehow."

"I'm not sure if I should take that as a compliment," I frowned.

His lips spread into a smirk as he chuckled. "Oh, it's not a bad smell. Not in the slightest."

"That's good to know." I picked at my stew, no longer feeling an appetite. The burning curiosity to learn about him consumed me. "To be honest, Razvan, I feel like I'm starting to trust you too."

His eyes widened so much, I wondered for a moment if I offended him. Then his smirk bloomed into a full-on grin. "That means more to me than you could possibly know, *steluța*."

MELODY

Razvan and I got up to leave the tavern after a few more minutes of small talk and picking at our food. I looked around for Connor to tell him, but the place was getting so crowded that I lost sight of him.

He'll know who I'm with. He practically forced me to talk to him, I figured.

Raz was quiet as we walked side-by-side to the Renaissance fair vendors near where I first saw him juggling those knives.

"That thing you did with fire," I said, breaking our silence. "That's part of your shifter abilities?"

"Yes," he answered quietly, but didn't elaborate.

I let the information turn over in my head as we put more distance between us and the lights of the carnival.

"I don't want to frighten you, *steluța*," he said as our steps slowed to a halt. "My shift is not an ordinary animal. So I'm going to do this in small steps."

For the first time since I met him, he seemed insecure. Unsure of himself. He looked genuinely like he might have regretted bringing me out here.

"Okay," I said, trying to give a reassuring smile.

His mouth only tensed. "Please don't scream. It'll attract attention."

"I promise I won't," I answered. "Hunter—the wolf I met, told me how shifters have a high value and are exploited by carnivals. He said it was surprising that you're still performing freely and willingly."

"That is an entirely different story," Raz said dryly. "But yes, if people see me and know who and what I am, I'll be no better than a caged animal again. I'm essentially putting my freedom in your hands, Melody."

"I understand," I told him solemnly. "I won't alert you to anyone. I promise."

He still looked hesitant for a moment before nodding sharply.

"You might want to stand a few feet away," he warned.

I backed away from him a few steps, my heart thrumming with anticipation.

Razvan nervously exhaled a deep breath. "This is how I was forced to perform when I was first captured."

In the darkness, I didn't see any changes. I didn't even hear the sound of bones crunching and popping like when Hunter shifted. But when he stepped into the dim light casting through the trees, I barely recognized him.

His skin turned entirely black and was covered in a fine layer of what looked like scales. New bumps and ridges emerged on his skin like horns or spikes trying to poke through. His teeth grew a couple inches longer, poking past his lips, and all sharply pointed. And his eyes! Still steely gray but now with a slitted, reptilian pupil.

"Holy shit, Razvan," I breathed, taking a step forward.

"Don't come closer," he warned, holding up a scaly hand with long black claws. His words still came out clearly, but with a different pitch to his voice.

"You don't look that different," I said carefully, drinking in his new appearance with fascination. "Just... more modified."

He nodded. "I was first advertised as a lizard-man. Just a regular guy with full-body scales tattooed, filed teeth, and some subdermal implants. They injected me with drugs to keep my shift at this exact spot."

"You're still mostly human," I observed.

"Correct," he confirmed. "But eventually that wasn't enough. An ordinary human wasn't bringing in enough money. So they made me shift to this point and advertised me as a *real* lizard-man."

He calmly removed his vest and stood shirtless before me, displaying more of the bumps and ridges on his ribs and chest. Then I heard the bones crunching, the organs shifting, and what sounded like skin tearing apart.

I gasped, bringing my hand to my mouth only because it sounded so painful. But while the creature in front of me was unlike anything I'd ever seen, it still didn't scare me.

Razvan still retained some human features, but was mostly reptilian at this stage. Large, bat-like wings sprouted from his back. Actual horns and spikes sprouted all over his body. His black scales looked like shimmery obsidian.

Our eyes met, and I could see the apprehension in his barely human face. He opened his jaws—now elongated and slender, allowing soft wisps of smoke to gently curl out and create a type of aura around his head.

"No way," I whispered in awe, the realization hitting me like a brick. "You're... a *dragon?*"

He nodded, which looked a bit weird because of how his neck muscles rearranged, but I was too busy being utterly fascinated to care.

"That is so freaking cool!" I giggled like a high-schooler, unable to contain how thrilled I was to be seeing this happen. A goddamn dragon! An animal that wasn't supposed to exist except in mythology and folklore!

The initial shock of shifters existing at all seemed to wear off after seeing Hunter. Now I was fixated on every one of Razvan's scales, his pointy teeth, and those glorious, beautiful wings.

He finished the shift, falling to all fours as all his human features sank and disappeared into his dragon body. He grew to the size of a large pickup truck. A long, whiplike tail completed the ensemble, and I was standing in front of a real fucking dragon.

"Amazing," I breathed, unable to take my eyes off him, let alone believe what I was seeing. "Can you still understand me?"

Razvan huffed a breath through his nostrils and bobbed his head down in an affirmative.

Hesitantly, I outstretched my hand. "Is it okay if I touch you?"

He paused for a moment, as if unsure, then slowly extended his nose out to my palm.

My fingers touched armor-tough scales that were warm, almost hot on contact. It felt like holding a warm cup of coffee, if such a cup was scaly.

I couldn't stop grinning and giggling as I looked into those gray, slitted-pupil eyes. I scratched under his jaw and Razvan made a low rumbling sound, almost like a purr. Those eyes closed halfway, as if in pleasure.

"I can't believe you're real," I whispered, taking in every claw, horn, and ridge that adorned him. "This is absolutely amazing."

He grunted and settled his belly down on the ground, folding his wings against his back and curling his rear legs underneath.

"I'd love to see you fly," I told him, gazing at his wings. "That would be incredible to see. I bet you can't do it often, though. Too risky."

His head jerked down again in a sharp nod. I brought my hand back to my side and, to my surprise, he bumped it with his nose. It seemed affectionate, like a nuzzle.

"Yeah, you like that?" I laughed, scratching under his jaw again. I had to mentally remind myself again this was a person, not just an animal. Would I be okay with doing this to him in human form? I couldn't be sure. All I knew was, as a dragon, he really liked chin scratches.

With a final huff and rumble, he pulled away after a few moments and I heard the distinct, somewhat grotesque sounds of shifting again. In the next moment, Razvan the handsome, heavily tattooed human, picked up his vest from the ground without a word and slid his arms through it.

When he looked at me, it was a look of apprehension and uncertainty.

"What's wrong?" I asked. "That was incredible!"

"You really think so?" he asked in disbelief.

"Yes!" I cried, then quickly lowered my voice. "I have so many questions! Are all dragons shifters? Why are they considered a fantasy creature nowadays? How awesome is it to fly and breathe fire?"

Razvan chuckled, shoving his hands in his jean pockets and lowering his eyes to the ground. If I didn't know any better, I'd say he was being shy.

"Yes, dragons only exist as shifters," he said quietly. "We are few and far between. It's strange and gratifying to hear you say such kind words. Among my people, we are considered cursed and undesirable."

"How is that possible?" I demanded. "You're a human and yet so much more."

"Thousands of years of folklore and superstition," he shrugged. "What made it even worse for me was that I'm a firstborn son. I had responsibilities to carry on the family name. When my shifting abilities came to light as a toddler, my family saw it as a punishment from God."

"That's awful," I breathed, stepping closer to him. "I'm so sorry."

"They forced me to hide it, and I tried as best I could," he went on. "But being a shifter is like having two personalities. My dragon is a part of me, yet separate. He has strong instincts and desires apart from my own. I can always feel him, even now." He tapped his chest gently. "And he can't stay hidden for long or he'll go mad. As a teenager, the more I tried to hold him back, the more he fought me for control. I would go to bed as a human and wake up flying over the clouds."

"So you *have* to shift, at least every once in a while," I concluded.

"Exactly," he confirmed. "My dragon started lashing out. Unable to control him, I'd grow horns or wings and a tail while out in broad daylight. Eventually, my parents had enough. They felt they had to get rid of me to lift the curse off our family."

I hardly dared to ask. "What did they do?"

"They sold me to a carnival."

Fuck. Just like Hunter. A person treated like livestock. The thought made me physically ill and my heart couldn't seem to take all the pain of feeling for these people. It almost made me wish I didn't feel so much at all.

Even so, my empathy was nothing compared to what they went

through. Hunter and Razvan's story at least seemed to have happier endings.

"But you're free now," I pointed out. "But still in the carnival. How did that happen?"

He smiled at me in a way that made my heart flutter. "A story for another time, *steluța*. We should get you back before people wonder where the ringmistress ran off to."

It only then registered to me how late it had gotten. Dusk had settled into darkness with the sky brilliantly alight with stars.

"You can walk me straight home if you'd like," I offered. "We have an early morning meeting with Nigel and I want to be refreshed before showing my mad ringmistress skills." I punctuated that last statement with an eye-roll which got a laugh out of Razvan.

"You'll be great," he said warmly. "And I'll be happy to escort you home."

We took the narrow path back to camp side-by-side, closer than our first walk through the woods but still without touching. I found myself enjoying his flirty small talk and teasing, laughing as we came into the clearing a few minutes later, but still feeling unsure about touching him.

I wanted to smack him lightly for teasing me, or to simply run my fingers along the lines of ink on his skin but held myself back. Why did I have no problem touching him as a dragon but felt incredibly bashful doing so while human? Even though they were the same, my brain still separated touching another person and touching an animal.

We walked to my camp to find Connor waiting by the fire. He sat in his lawn chair, staring at the dancing flames. An empty six-pack of beer sat on the ground next to his chair. He rested one nearly-empty bottle on his knee as his eyes darted up to meet us.

"Hey babe," he said in a flat tone. "I was wondering when you'd come back."

A cold chill swept over me, and my whole body bristled with tension. If he wasn't drinking, I'd be ready to handle whatever jealous, snappish remarks he'd throw out. But just seeing those bottles made me brace myself for impact, whether that was from words or fists.

Logically, I knew Connor wouldn't hurt me. But my nervous system kicked into protection mode, anyway. My body responded to the sight and smell of alcohol like an allergic reaction. Shut down. Be quiet. Protect. Do not provoke.

It was Razvan's gentle fingertips on my lower back that reminded me he was still there.

"Go on to bed, *steluța*," he said. "I think it's time Connor and I got to know each other."

I looked at him in surprise and was met with his carefree, easy-going smile.

"We'll behave. I promise," he said with a gentle push toward the trailer door. "Sweet dreams, *steluța*."

"Um, goodnight." I glanced at Connor, who didn't meet my eyes. Great. Drunk and in one of his moods. I looked back at Razvan. "Thanks for walking with me."

"Thank you for not running away and screaming," he returned with a chuckle.

I went inside and got undressed for bed without bothering to turn the lights on. My weariness overpowered the burning curiosity to know what those two would be talking about.

I fell asleep to the deep, rumbling murmur of men's voices outside.

CONNOR

I watched warily as the tattooed man took a seat across the fire from me. He eyed my six-pack but didn't ask for one. I was a few beers deep at that point and felt surly enough to not bother offering.

"Something you want to discuss?" I asked, keeping my tone light but firm. I was willing to hear him out, but would not stand for any bullshit concerning Mel.

In the back of my mind, I knew he wasn't that bad of a guy. Hell, I practically pushed Mel to spend time with him. But after she walked off with him and the minutes ticked by with no sign of either of them, the nagging doubts started creeping in. I was only lightly buzzed, but the beers definitely made it worse.

When I saw them finally walking back, I was equally relieved and jealous that she was smiling and giggling. She was happy and unhurt, but I knew men. I knew so many of them played a nice act until they got a woman's defenses down. They wouldn't hurt her until she felt too attached to leave.

Razvan's steely gray eyes flickered from my booze to my face. "You might want to watch your consumption around her."

Oh, damn. This guy had balls.

"Fuckin' excuse me?" I demanded, keeping my voice low. "After a nice stroll through the woods, suddenly *you* know what's best for her?"

"It's not hard to see if you use your eyes," he answered calmly. "She was fine and relaxed right up until she saw you. You must know she doesn't drink."

"Yeah, and?" I challenged. "I don't force it on her. If she doesn't like me having a couple, she can say so. She's a big girl."

"She is, and yet she's like a child in other ways. I can smell her fear and anxiety around alcohol. It's an automatic reaction."

"How the hell do you know?" I challenged. "Did she tell you something?"

"A small bit, yes," he admitted.

"What did she say?" My jealousy flared up like a green-eyed monster inside me. She shared something with *him* that she didn't with me?

"That's for her to tell. Not me." Razvan's arms rested on the knees of his scuffed, dark jeans and his voice never wavered. He was utterly relaxed and not intimidated by me at all. I had to give him an ounce of respect for that.

I sank back in my chair. It was my own fault Mel hadn't completely opened up to me, as much as I didn't want to admit it. I protected her and would never harm her, but I still scared her. She watched her words around me and tried not to set me off. That wasn't fair to her.

The first time we made love, I was pissed and jealous for no good reason. She stood her ground, but I saw even her resolve weakening in those big doe eyes. And despite our beautiful, intimate moment, I saw her guard go back up. Especially when I brushed off the boyfriend title again.

I wanted to be officially hers so fucking badly. But why did *I* deserve that when she let her guard down to the tattooed punk sitting across from me?

"So you're a shifter too, huh?" I mumbled, changing the subject.

He looked up, his eyes wide with surprise. "You know?"

"Yes. Seems she didn't tell you everything after all." I quickly relayed our rescue of the wolves back in Drowningville, then getting reacquainted with them again here in Crying Falls.

"Craziest shit I ever seen," I said, draining the rest of my last beer. That would be the last one I had for a while. For Mel, I'd take his advice to heart. "Honestly, I'm not surprised by how this industry has treated y'all. It's sickening, but any chance to make a buck, they'll take."

He blinked a few times, scratching a hand over his scalp as if he still couldn't believe I knew about him.

"So you a wolf too, or something else?" I asked.

He laughed. "No, I'm not a wolf. Think more... reptilian." His eyes met mine and his smile faded into seriousness. "Forgive me for being evasive. I'm just not used to humans knowing. And my shift is, well, shocking to most people. To say the least."

"Fair enough," I answered, settling back into my chair.

"I showed Mel what I am," he said, barely above a whisper. "That's why we went away from everyone. Nothing else happened. I just shifted, and we came straight back."

"Okay." I believed him. The more we talked, the more the jealousy subsided.

"She... was not shocked. Or frightened." He seemed dumbfounded as he said that. "She was *excited*. She was smiling and laughing. I've never had that reaction from someone before. It's usually screams and running. Sometimes fainting."

I gave him a confused look. "Dude, are you a fucking dinosaur or some shit?"

He laughed again. "You're not too far off." With a smirk, he added, "I have a feeling you'll find out sooner rather than later."

"That's entirely up to you, man," I said. "But yeah, Mel is different. She seems... I dunno, *in tune* with you shifter folks. With the wolves, she knew right away they were like people. Intelligent, understanding of language and behavior, protective of their kids. Me and every other person in there obviously had no fucking clue."

"You're different too, Connor," he piped up.

"Me? How?" I asked, taken aback.

"Just the fact that you know what I am and we're still sitting here having a conversation like two normal people? You have no idea how big of a deal that is." He leaned forward emphatically. "Every human who's found out about me has either been scared shitless or tried to kill me. You smell like an ordinary human, but the fact that you've had neither of those reactions to me says there's something different in your biology."

"I have been scared shitless," I admitted. "And I... have killed."

When Razvan narrowed his eyes in confusion, I pulled my dog tags out of my shirt. Before I could rethink it, I also lifted my pant leg to show the metal rod of my prosthetic leg.

I knew a big secret about him now. I figured if we both cared for Mel, it only made sense for me to be honest with him too.

"Ah." His eyebrows lifted as he leaned back and rubbed his jaw. "That makes a lot of sense now."

"Yeah, just a walking redneck stereotype," I cracked.

"If that's what you are, I'm just a punk ass Romanian," he grinned.

"So what are your intentions with Mel?" I asked, turning serious again.

"What are you, her father now?" he scoffed in response.

"No," I shook my head. "I won't keep her on a leash. I won't snoop or get in y'alls business. But I've seen how you act with the other women here. You can't blame a guy for being protective."

"What are *your* intentions with her?" he retorted. "She's with you but said things were complicated."

"To say the least," I muttered in agreement.

He spread his hands out and looked from side to side. "What am I supposed to do with that information?"

"Does it really matter to you if a woman is taken or not?" I challenged. "You came right up to her in front of me before you knew anything about us. She shot you down hard."

"I don't like that word, *taken*. I've never felt that women belonged to men, nor the other way around." He bit back another grin. "A woman who wants me will choose me whether she has another man or not. And I can choose her in return or spend my time elsewhere."

"Mel can't be used and discarded like that," I growled. "She needs stability, people she can rely on. She has too much of a heart to be fucked and dumped."

"I know that." The dark, tattooed man grew quiet, lowering his gaze to the flames. "I want to know her better, and not just to sleep with. I want to understand why she's different, why she seems to be on the same wavelength as shifters when she has no abilities herself. She is just... full of purity and goodness. She's unlike anyone I've ever met."

"Same here," I agreed quietly. "Seems we like the same things about her."

"Seems we do," he chuckled. "If she doesn't want me like that, I'll be okay with it. I'm just happy to have met her."

My throat tightened, but I had to get the words out.

"Look man, if things develop between you two, that's great. Pursue it. I'm basically in love with her, but I'm one fucked up individual. I know myself well enough to admit that I won't be enough to make her as happy as she deserves. So if you can provide what I can't, great. Just take it slow. Don't push anything on her."

He gave me a long, calculated look. "And you're really okay with that?"

A heavy sigh escaped my chest. "I'm becoming okay with it. Little by little."

"Have you ever dated two partners at once?" he asked. "Or been with someone who was with you and someone else at the same time?"

"Nah," I answered. "Just seen lots of cheating and sneaking around between people who made vows to be faithful to each other. I figure if you're gonna fuck around, might as well be honest about it. You?"

He nodded. "I had two girlfriends at one point. They were in a relationship with each other, too."

"Yeah?" I raised my eyebrows. "How did that turn out?"

"The good times were... well, you can probably imagine," he said with a smug grin. "The bad times were awful, though. Three junkies together always ends terribly."

"I bet," I answered. "You seem pretty cleaned up though."

"Four years," he sighed. "Unfortunately, I'm the only one of the three who did clean up. One of them died from an overdose. The other is probably in a psychiatric institution somewhere."

"Tough shit," I said sympathetically. "Did they know about…?"

"No," he shook his head. "I snuck away to shift when I could. I had a few close calls, but they never knew." He paused, glancing over at the trailer door. "She's the only one I've felt I could be completely honest with."

"Yeah," I agreed, following his gaze. "You've just got to be brave enough to do it."

12

MELODY

"God fucking damn it!"

Nigel tossed his cell phone across the stage, then whipped around, looking for something else to throw while the rest of us watched silently. He settled on kicking a metal folding chair, then picked it up when it collapsed and tossed that across the stage too.

"How long is he gonna do this for?" I whispered to Connor.

At some point last night, I felt him come to bed and curl around me with all the warmth and protectiveness that made me melt in the first place. He didn't smell of alcohol anymore and he'd been cheerful and sweet this morning. His kisses and cuddles made my heart swell, but these mood swings of his always threw me for a loop. I couldn't help but wonder what was going to set him off next time.

"Just give him a minute," he murmured, rubbing a hand affectionately across my lower back. "He needs to let off some steam. He'll be okay after his tantrum."

We all met for rehearsal at the main stage a half hour earlier. The magician hadn't shown up, but everyone figured he was hungover and would come late. We carried on without him. I'd been too nervous to eat any breakfast, but my ringmistress announcements were met with glowing praise and constructive criticism. Everyone said I needed to project my voice more, even though I already felt like I was yelling. My voice felt raw after just a few practice runs.

The magician never showed up and after a few phone calls, Nigel found out he was on a plane to Vegas for the same auditions all the others had ditched him for. Hence the temper tantrum.

"The day before opening night and he said he'd be here!" Nigel bellowed at no one in particular. "What kind of show is this without a magician?! And I paid him in advance because he owed child support! Mother fucker ran off with my fucking money!"

I snuck a glance across the stage at Razvan, who was also watching the spectacle with amusement. As if he could physically feel my eyes on him, he returned my gaze and winked. My face heated, and I lowered my eyes to the ground. Even now, I felt so bashful around him. Like he was the dreamy bad boy, and I was the loser girl with a crush large enough to have its own zip code.

But you're with Connor, a voice in my head reminded me.

"WHAT THE FUCK AM I SUPPOSED TO DO!" Nigel screamed at the sky. Razvan chuckled behind his hand at the melodramatic display.

Connor wants you to keep your options open. He's said that several times, another voice argued. That was true. Despite Connor's back-and-forth mood swings, he consistently said he didn't want me to feel tied to him.

I looked up at the sexy, green-eyed man next to me. He was watching Nigel and didn't seem to notice the not-so-subtle glancing back and forth between me and Raz. Or if he did notice, it didn't faze him.

What did they talk about last night? I wondered.

Nigel finally sank to his knees, thoroughly drained of everything he let out. Connor squeezed my waist before he let go and walked to the slumped over carnival manager. He placed a hand on Nigel's back and spoke to him in a low voice I couldn't hear.

When Nigel nodded and mumbled a few words back, Connor gave him a few encouraging pats and rose to address us all.

"We're taking a break for lunch," he announced. "Then we all come back here in an hour to figure out a routine without a magician."

Footsteps stomped off the wooden stage as everyone dispersed. As Connor made his way back to me, he wore that same grimace I'd been seeing more often lately.

"Babe, you need to lotion your legs," I hissed in a low whisper. "Forget your manly pride or whatever. They're just going to keep hurting you if you don't. You can't perform when you're in so much pain."

"I can if I need to," he growled, shooting me a glare. He grabbed my hand and we walked down the backstage steps together. He hissed in a breath when we reached the ground.

"You *don't* need to, that's what I'm telling you," I argued. "After wearing them all day, you need to bring back the circulation—"

"I know, babe. But lotion and massages are not the issue. It's just a temporary solution."

"What's the issue, then?"

He remained tight-lipped until we reached our camp, out of earshot of everyone else. Then he turned to me, placing his hands on my waist as he trapped me in that forest green gaze.

"Prosthetics need to be adjusted every few years, if not replaced completely. These are my first set and I never got them adjusted because I couldn't afford it."

"How long has it been?" I asked in a soft whisper.

"Three years," he answered. "With all the movement I've been doing, these are probably at the end of their lifespan."

I swallowed. "And how much does a new pair cost?"

"You don't want to know," he scoffed.

"Tell me." I wrapped my hands around his neck. "I want to help you, babe. We're in this together."

He sighed heavily, dropping his forehead to touch mine.

"Anywhere from thirty to seventy-five grand."

"Shit."

"Yeah. The best we can hope to make at this carnival for all nights total is ten grand. And that's a high, extremely optimistic estimate."

"Can the military help you at all?" I asked. "They're supposed to take care of their veterans, aren't they?"

"I wasn't in for long when I got injured," he said. "What little benefits I had, I maxed out on my first set. I couldn't even tell you where my paperwork is now."

Anger surged through me. Why should it have mattered how long he'd served? He nearly died performing his duty to this country.

"Well, we'll figure it out." I pressed a kiss to his frowning lips. "We'll budget and keep saving until we have enough."

"I dunno, babe." He kicked the nearest tire of the trailer. "This thing costs a ton to gas up and maintain. I can only save enough to travel to the next carnival and keep myself from starving."

"I'm telling you we'll figure it out." I pressed my hands to the sides of his face and kissed him again, more insistently until his mouth finally opened up to mine.

Our lips and tongues made a slow, intimate dance until I felt like putty against him. His arms tightened around me, nearly crushing me to his chest as I tried my best to give him reassurance and warmth without words.

"Thank you, babe," he murmured when our lips eventually parted. "I'm so glad you're here with me. I don't tell you that enough, but you're the one keeping my head up."

My chest felt like bursting with the rush of emotions from hearing those words, from feeling him wrapped around me like a suit of armor no one could break through.

"I'm glad I'm here, too," I whispered into his neck. "You're the one keeping me safe."

His hands slid up my back as his lips brushed across my face to my ear. He just started kissing that spot below my earlobe that drove me crazy when we heard soft giggles nearby.

We both looked to our right to see Hunter in human form, holding the hands of two adorable, giggly children at his sides.

"Uh, hello," he smirked. "We could come back if this is a bad time."

"No, not a bad time! Perfect time, actually," I stammered, a giggle threatening to bubble out of my own chest. "Right, Con?"

He shot me a glare before putting on a charming smile directed at

Hunter. "'Course not. We were just about to have lunch. Join us, will you?"

"If we're not intruding," Hunter said, that wily smirk spreading into a grin. Damn. He looked beautiful when he was all serious and sad, but when he smiled, he was absolutely breathtaking.

"Not at all." I untangled myself from Connor and bent over to become eye level with Hunter's children. "Hi guys, I'm Mel," I offered with a friendly smile.

"You're the lady that stealed us!" the boy declared, his pale features and golden eyes a near mirror image of Hunter's.

"The word is rescue, son," Hunter chuckled, ruffling the boy's platinum hair. "Mel introduced herself. Now tell her your name," he prompted gently.

"I'm Roo," the boy said proudly. "And that's my sister, Rinna."

The girl buried her face shyly in Hunter's pant leg, but still peeked at me with one blue eye. She was not as pale as her father and brother, and had hair almost as dark as mine up in a ponytail with a bright purple scrunchie.

"It's nice to meet you both, officially," I said. "Hopefully you've had no more scary nights like that one we first met."

"No, we went hunting with Dad again!" Roo declared, clearly the more outgoing of the two. "I caught a rabbit and Rinna helped me kill it!"

"Wow, great job!" I was honestly a little squeamish about animals getting hurt and killed, especially after learning what happened to Hunter and Razvan. But I had to remember hunting prey was part of this boy's instincts and how he would learn to survive.

"Hey, why don't you two help Mr. Connor with the cooking fire?" Hunter suggested. "Then we can have lunch." Rinna seemed to perk up at the mention of fire, but Roo's enthusiasm outshined her.

"Woooo, fire!" Roo grabbed his sister's hand and darted toward the fire pit.

"Have fun with those two," I smacked a kiss on Connor's cheek and laughed at his ensuing eye roll. But he put on a smile and knelt next to the kids, gently explaining about kindling and building a fire properly.

Hunter and I stood for a moment, just looking at each other. My face heated up with every passing second as I tried to think of something to say. Thankfully, he was wearing a shirt this time.

"They're sweet kids," I said awkwardly. "You must be really proud."

He nodded, beaming as they calmly watched Connor light the kindling and gently blow on it. "They're resilient and curious. And somehow they can still trust people. That's what really amazes me."

"Yeah. That means they'll bounce back from the damage done," I said. "Hopefully anyway."

"They were really excited to meet you," he said with a glance toward me.

"Really? Why?"

"Well, I told them about what you did, of course."

"It wasn't just me," I protested. "Connor was there, too. If I didn't have his muscle, this trailer or anything, I never would have gotten you guys out."

"He wouldn't have saved us on his own," he said softly. "I'm not sure what compelled you to do it, Mel, but you're not an ordinary human."

"I'm really nothing special," I said, fighting the rising blush in my cheeks. "I just can't stand seeing people get treated like that."

"That's the thing," Hunter said. "You *knew* we were people. Everyone else thought we were just animals."

He was right. I didn't know how I knew, but I did.

"Anyway," he cleared his throat, "do you need any help getting food ready?"

"Um, sure." I turned to the trailer door and held it open for him. "Let's see what we have."

If the trailer felt small between Connor and I, it could barely contain Hunter. He bumped his head on the ceiling and had to slouch as we maneuvered around the tiny kitchen. We laughed awkwardly and neither one of us seemed eager to address the tension with a capital T.

He lived in the forest, so how could he smell so good? I caught whiffs of clean, earthy spiciness as he moved around me. His long arms reached the top shelves in the cabinets and I saw the deep lines from his hip bones as his T-shirt lifted. And why did his slender biceps have to flex so deliciously as he brought the bowls down from the cabinet?

I saw his golden eyes in my peripheral vision like the warm, gentle glow of porch lights. I noticed how he tried not to get too close and avoided touching me. But I felt his gaze travel over me like gentle, curious fingertips, and my brain felt like it was screaming.

What are you doing, Mel? You have enough on your plate juggling Connor and Razvan! Not that you're even really seeing them both, but adding a third guy to your massive crush list is most definitely not wise.

We exited the trailer carrying bowls, utensils, and ingredients for BLTs. The fresh air and open space hit me like cool water to the face after feeling *very* up close, hot and personal with Hunter.

Connor glanced at me but said nothing when I handed him strips of bacon to skewer over the fire.

"Dad, can I shift and eat my bacon raw?" Roo asked as Hunter got them settled with bowls and napkins.

"No, Roo," Hunter said sternly. "We are guests of Connor and Mel's for lunch. They're human, so we eat with them as humans."

"You're lucky nobody heard that," Connor murmured, glancing around.

"Yeah, they don't understand the importance of keeping that a secret yet," Hunter admitted.

"I want raw bacon too!" Rinna piped up.

"Guys," Hunter sighed. "I said no. No raw meat until we're back at the den, okay?"

The kids behaved as we built our sandwiches and small-talked, but after a few bites they were already growing restless. They started chasing each other around and wrestling on the open ground near our campfire, when Roo spontaneously grew triangular, furry ears and a wagging, fluffy tail.

"Roo, no!" Hunter bellowed with a roar I never heard in his voice before. Connor and I watched dumbfounded as he marched over to his son and picked him up by the back of his neck, which had sprouted into a furry scruff.

"Human. Now," he growled.

13

MELODY

Roo let out a soft puppy whimper and obeyed, sitting on the grass with a pout and a wobbly lip as his father spoke to him.

"Sorry about that," Hunter mumbled as he returned to sit with us. "I can't let them get away with even little shifts like that. It's way too risky."

"Little harsh, don't you think?" Connor asked, keeping his voice low.

I elbowed him in the ribs and gave him a look that said, *you're not a parent. Keep your comments to yourself.*

"For a completely human child, it would be," Hunter answered. He didn't seem offended by the question. "But we have to discipline our children like animals. I've had to keep both of them in line with my teeth before."

"It makes sense," I offered. "You have to keep them in touch with their animal side as well as the human one. Seems like a pretty delicate balance."

"Exactly." Hunter smiled at me. "See? You understand a lot more than you realize, Mel."

I thought of Razvan as a child and how he was forced to keep his dragon hidden, lest he be punished by his family. The thought made me incredibly sad for him, but also brought up a question.

"Can shifters be born from normal humans?"

Hunter nodded. "It's rare, but it's been known to happen. Sometimes the shifting genes go dormant for several generations before they appear again. Families can forget or just not know about their shifting ancestors for hundreds of years." He shoved the rest of his BLT in his mouth and swallowed in one gulp before continuing. "In wolf packs, when a baby is born without the ability to shift, we find it best to leave them at a hospital or adoption center. As difficult as it is, there's just no way a non-shifting human can fit into our dynamic and society."

"Other species might not be as kind, I imagine," Connor said.

"Very true," Hunter agreed. "There are rumors of those who kill their young who can't shift. Big cats, mostly. I've never seen it personally but I'm sure there's some truth to it." He gave both of us an appreciative smile as he stacked his and the kids' bowls. "Thank you for sharing your food and fire with us. On my next hunt, I'll bring a fresh kill to share. Any preference?"

"Venison," Connor said quickly. "I can't tell you how long it's been since I had a nice venison steak, goddamn."

"Sure thing," Hunter said. "Did you ever hunt your own?"

"I did," Connor answered proudly. "With a bow and arrows. I never liked deer hunting with guns. Too loud, too easy. I wanted to earn that kill, you know?"

"Absolutely! That's the best feeling."

The two of them started talking excitedly about hunting, swapping stories of their hunts, whether in human or animal form. I chewed my sandwich silently as I listened, watching the spark of brotherly bonding light up between them. The kids resumed chasing each other and playful wrestling, staying in human form the whole time.

They looked so innocent and happy, like they never went through such a traumatic, terrible ordeal less than a week ago. I envied their ability to leave the past behind so easily. Mine always seemed to creep over my shoulder, ready to drag me back to that hellhole if I even peeked back.

I knew I'd have to go back one day. I couldn't leave my younger siblings, some the same ages as Roo and Rinna, to suffer like I did. But I needed resources first. I couldn't go back until I knew I could take them with me, or get them to safety.

Connor's kiss on my cheek broke me out of my daydream.

"Hm?" I turned to him for a quick nuzzle.

"We were just talking about the state of the carnival," he chuckled.

"Congratulations on becoming ringmistress," Hunter said. "Women are rarely seen in such a position. I'm sure you'll do well."

"Thank you," I said sincerely. "I'm still nervous about it but practicing has helped."

"It's gonna be a rushed show, no matter what we do." Connor quickly filled in Hunter on everything we'd gone through, from the first group of performers ditching for an audition to suddenly not having a magician at the last minute. Hunter listened intently, looking more thoughtful with each passing second.

"Maybe," he stroked his short beard, looking far off in the distance as he pondered, "I could help you guys out."

Connor and I both looked at him curiously, waiting for him to go on.

Hunter rubbed his hands together and glanced back at his kids, now napping in the soft grass, before speaking again in a low voice.

"Because of what you two risked for us, I'd be willing to play the part of the Wolf Man. That way, your empty slot will be filled."

"No!" Connor and I cried out in unison so loudly that the kids startled awake.

"Absolutely not," I insisted in a whisper. "That was such a terrible experience for you. For *all* of you. We could never let you relive that again."

"Well, I don't want them involved." He nodded at Roo and Rinna, who were settling back down to nap. "They'll stay in the den. They know to stay put while I'm gone. But if it helps you guys out, I have no issue with doing a partial shift, and walking around and howling a little." His smirk returned. "My only requests are no cages and no cattle prods, although I figure I won't have to worry about that with you."

"Hunter, I really don't think I could stand to do it," I pleaded. "It would feel like I'm exploiting you. Just the thought of it turns my stomach. It feels so *wrong*."

"I'm offering to do this of my own free will, Mel," he said gently. "Remember, I'm a person too. I can make my own decisions. You're not forcing me into anything, but I feel like I owe you guys for saving us."

I turned to Connor. "Babe, please back me up. This is a terrible idea."

He placed a hand on my thigh, gently massaging around the knee. "He has a point, Mel."

"What?!" There was *no* way he was disagreeing with me on this.

"The Wolf Man act brought in a shit ton of money and a massive crowd back in Drowningville," he pointed out. "Because they hyped it up. If Hunter is out there with us and we start spreading the word now, it could turn things around for Nigel and us."

"So what, we're selling out our new friend for money?" I demanded.

"Mel." Hunter reached out and placed his hand on my other knee. The contact of both his and Connor's skin on mine was like an electric jolt. He clearly meant it as a friendly touch, but my body responded to it as so much more.

"I wouldn't offer to do this if I felt like you were selling me out," he said. "You two are my friends, and I want to help you. That's all this is."

"I can't," I shook my head. "When you were onstage, and they were so awful to you... they tortured you."

"But that's not what we're gonna do." Connor's strong fingers squeezed around my knee. "Babe, this could be a good opportunity. You could show the audience that the wolf man isn't someone to fear."

"You might be onto something." Hunter's eyes lit up. "Sooner or later, humans are going to know about shifters, and it's going to be a scary, uncomfortable reality for them. If we start by demonstrating we're not monsters, it could be a step in the right direction."

"Maybe," I said hesitantly, trying to avoid looking down at my knees where both of their hands were still on me.

"Here's an idea. We could have a secret signal," Hunter said. "I won't be able to talk, but we can check in with each other through a hand sign or something. You can ask me if I'm okay and I'll tell you yes or no."

"I would feel a lot better about doing it if I knew how you were feeling," I admitted. "If you seem even slightly uncomfortable, I'd want to put an end to it."

"It's a deal, then." Hunter removed his hand from my knee with a smile, though my skin still tingled all the way up to my sensitive inner thighs.

"Hold on, I haven't agreed to anything," I protested, trying to ignore the sensations in my body. "Can I think about this first?"

"We don't have time, babe," Connor said. "Lunch is almost over, and we're heading back to rehearse. We either tell Nigel this is happening or forget it completely. But we need to decide now."

Two pairs of eyes, gold and green, focused on me as they waited for my answer.

That's right, I told myself. I'm the ringmistress. I'm leading the entire show. This is up to me.

"Alright," I said finally. "But make sure Nigel knows Hunter is ours. He's not for sale. No one messes with him or they're dealing with us."

"That's my girl," Connor beamed, wrapping an arm around my waist. "You're learning this business fast."

I looked at Hunter. "Let's get that secret signal figured out. Oh, and you're getting paid an equal third of our cut. You're not doing this as slave labor."

"Yes, ma'am," he chuckled, golden eyes flashing in amusement. "I see what you mean, Connor. She's going to do great."

If only the knots in my stomach would disappear, and I felt just as confident as they did.

❧ 14 ❧

MELODY

One hour until showtime.

I swiped the large, fluffy makeup brush across my cheeks and did a final check of my clothes and face in the mirror.

Nigel was kind enough to give me creative freedom for my ring-mistress outfit. Because most of the performers had dark, edgy styles with lots of black and dark shades, I decided to go along with that theme.

Instead of a traditional red tailcoat, I found a black cropped jacket with large brass buttons. It covered up just enough of my velvet purple corset and matched the black lace mini skirt flaring out from my legs. Sheer, lacy black stockings covered my legs, and I actually found a pair of heels that fit and felt comfortable.

And of course, the look wasn't complete without a top hat. I thought the thing looked ridiculous when Cherry first dressed me up in Drowningville, which felt so long ago. Now I swore I was getting used to the damn thing.

Satisfied with my look, I left the bathroom to find Connor sitting on the bed and looking at a hand mirror. He was embracing the gothic theme as well, dressed in black with silver accents. He looked in the mirror carefully as he applied white face paint. Tonight he'd be wearing a black half-mask styled like the phantom of the opera.

His forest green eyes looked even brighter in contrast with the pale makeup.

"Lookin' good, mistress," he smiled approvingly as I approached.

"Hm, I like it when you call me that." I bent at the waist to give him a light kiss on the lips, careful not to mess up his makeup or mine. "Any updates from Nigel about how daytime went?"

"He was in a good mood last I checked," he said, returning his focus to the mirror. "Daytime numbers exceeded expectations so far and doesn't look like many people are leaving yet. Word of the Wolf Man spread fast."

Like back in Drowningville, the daytime carnival was considered the family-friendly event. Rides, games, sugary and deep-fried food, and children-appropriate shows. Except here, most of the daytime performers skipped out for that audition in Vegas, as did the head-liners for the evening show.

So with our rushed, haphazard planning and no big names on the roster, we expected many of the attendees to leave after doing their shopping through the vendors and entertaining their children. To find out most of them were sticking around was a very good sign for us.

"We just might pull this off," I breathed with an affectionate rub at Connor's shoulders.

"It's still a snowball's chance in hell, but they may see unseasonably cool temps in the forecast," he mused.

I swallowed and decided to broach the question that had been on my mind since we started getting ready.

"How are your legs?"

"Fine."

"Con, babe. Be honest with me, please."

"I am." He lowered the mirror and looked up at me. "I had them off most of the day. And I lotioned the stubs after my shower. I'm right as rain for tonight."

My heart swelled to the point of nearly bursting. For all of this man's stubbornness and grumbling, he really did listen to me. Some-times, at least.

"Good," I beamed, resisting the urge to kiss him again. "I know you did that because of me. Thank you."

"Believe it or not, I do like keeping you happy," he chuckled. "And it made sense. Being in pain tonight would affect the performance and I wanted to be in top shape."

"I just can't wait to get this over with," I sighed, wringing my hands together.

"Still nervous?"

I nodded. "My stomach's been in knots since rehearsal yesterday."

"You're gonna be fine, babe." He squeezed my waist. "Better than fine, even. You're going to be amazing."

"I just feel like this whole show is riding on me," I stammered. "If I screw up announcing the next act, the audience won't be hyped for them and it'll be my fault."

"That's not gonna happen." His eyes brightened. "Hey, where's your lucky coin? I haven't seen you messing with it much since we got here."

"You're right." I jumped up and rummaged through my backpack until I found that familiar piece of round metal.

I traced my fingers over the crossed daggers in the center, then squeezed it in my palm for a few moments. I knew it was only my mind tricking me, but I felt instantly calmer with the weight of it in my hand. I placed it in the breast pocket of my jacket and smoothed my hand over it.

"There you go," Connor grinned, cupping my chin. "Now you know you can't fail."

"Thank you," I whispered, leaning into his touch. "You're my biggest supporter. There's no way I could do this without you."

"Not true." He stroked my neck in a way that made me never want to leave the trailer. "You're amazing all on your own. I'm just glad you dragged me along for the ride."

"Hey, it's not like I held a gun to your head," I giggled.

"But that ass," his other arm wrapped around my waist and slid down to grab a handful, "these lips," his thumb brushed the corner of my mouth, "and these big doe eyes." His gaze captured mine as he shook his head slowly. "How could I have ever resisted?"

"You flatter me, handsome." I thumped his chest playfully and took a deep breath. "Ready?"

"Ready when you are, mistress."

THE CROWD WAS EASILY TWICE the size of the one in Drowningville when we saw Hunter for the first time. The massive main stage and fairgrounds easily accommodated them and only made me feel smaller as I peeked from backstage.

The scene was similar, yet so different. So many more stars glittered in the sky and out here in the sticks, the energy felt... wilder. Not that this crowd was any drunker or rowdier than Drowningville, but the forest itself seemed to vibrate with anticipation of tonight's performance. There was an untamed playfulness in the air. It reminded me of Hunter's kids playing and wrestling in the grass. Innocent and harmless, but free and undomesticated.

Hunter was waiting in a private room backstage, separated from everyone else so no one would freak out at seeing him shift. He would come out last when Connor gave him his cue. And just like before, Connor would be first on deck.

The drum music started up, and my pulse thrummed along with it. In a few seconds, when the cymbals clapped, that was my cue to go out.

A hand suddenly brushed across my shoulders and startled me.

"Good luck, *steluța*." Razvan's deep rasp purred in my ear. "Not that you need it."

"Oh, believe me, I do," I whispered back. "My legs feel like jello."

"Now, I could give you a reason to make them feel like that," he said with his signature smirk and wink.

I giggled and shook my head right when the cymbals clapped and hissed.

"Knock 'em dead, beautiful," he said with a gentle push and I took my first step into the spotlight.

Just that little bit of laughter allowed me to relax enough to stride out with the illusion of confidence, and a massive stage smile for the people waiting below.

"Ladies and gentleman! Boys and girls!" I projected as loudly as I could, even with the small microphone clipped to my jacket. "Welcome to the opening night of the Crying Falls Summer Carnival! I'm your host for the evening, Ringmistress Melody!"

The thunderous applause was shocking. I could feel the wooden stage vibrating under my feet and nearly stumbled in surprise. These people were ready to go, and I hadn't even gotten started.

"We've got a great show for you tonight and all week long!" I made sure to speak slowly and enunciate every word as I spread my arms out in a welcoming gesture.

Their unblinking eyes followed my hands as if enchanted by my gestures. A calmness settled over my limbs. I had power. I was in control.

"Our first act is a man of many talents," I said with a suggestive wink. A light chuckle and murmuring rose from the crowd, but they kept listening with rapt attention. "Handsome and strong from head to toe, this acrobatic stilt walker knows how to put on a show. Give it up for Stilts, ladies and gentleman!"

I put my hands together, and the crowd followed, sending up cheers and wolf whistles as well. As I headed off stage, I made a mental note to give Connor a better stage name. He was way too talented for something so dull.

My heart practically vibrated in my chest as I went behind the curtain, still riding high on the crowd's energy.

"Holy shit," I breathed. That went so fast, I could hardly believe it actually happened. I did it. I really fucking did it.

"Good thing your mic's off," someone remarked.

I blinked until my eyes adjusted to the darkness of backstage. Nigel stood there with a beaming grin that rivaled the sun.

"How'd I do?" I asked, feeling some panic rise.

"How do you think you did?" he shot back.

"Um, good?" I swallowed and straightened up taller, holding onto the power I just held while looking into hundreds of pairs of eyes. "Good. It felt really good."

Nigel sighed and shook his head, my confidence withering.

"Melody, you weren't just good."

"Oh... no? I—"

"You were fucking brilliant."

I blinked, thoroughly confused. "Really?"

"Girl, you cast some sort of spell out there. They were mesmerized by you. Now Connor's riding off that magic, too. Look."

Together, we peered past the curtain to see open mouths and wide eyes glued to Connor as he did flips, handstands and backbends. A sharp pang pulled at my heart as I watched him. He was doing the same amazing solo act he always did before me, but I missed performing with him.

Being ringmistress felt incredible, but it was different when I was on that stage with Connor. It was like an intimate dance, an expression of trust between us. And a testament to how well we worked as a team as long as we both put forth the effort.

Holy shit, I'm in love with him.

"Well, I suggest you tell him that, girl," Nigel chuckled.

I looked at him. "Did I say that out loud?"

"You sure did."

Thank God for thick stage makeup, otherwise I'd be as red as a tomato.

"Well, keep being the best goddamn ringmistress I've ever seen, and then tell him," Nigel laughed. "I don't want you distracted and all googly-eyed. We've still got the rest of the show to put on."

"Yes, sir," I giggled. "How's the turnout, by the way? Still above expectations?"

He hissed in a breath and closed his fists with determination. "I don't want to jinx it, but if your wolf man is legit and you keep working your magic like that, I don't think we'll have anything to worry about, sweetheart."

"That's great news!" I grinned at him. "We won't let you down, Nigel. Promise."

"Well, we still have a whole week to see if there's a drop-off. I don't want to get too optimistic but..." He trailed off, grinning uncontrollably. "At least for tonight, you've really turned this ship around, Mel. Connor's a lucky man."

"I'm the lucky one," I whispered, watching proudly as the crowd gasped at his stunts.

I didn't let him listen to my announcement about him during rehearsal. I wanted to surprise him, to shout out to the whole audience what I really thought of him. And I meant every word. I just hoped he knew that.

The crowd burst into raucous applause as he performed his finale and took his final bow. His eyes caught mine from across the stage, but I couldn't read his expression. I blew a kiss anyway before he stilted off to the opposite end of the stage. I wanted to chase after him and kiss him properly, but while his part was over, I still had work to do.

"Mic's on. You're up, mistress," Nigel cued with a wink.

I strode out into the light, all my nerves gone and my smile one of genuine pride. My confidence no longer felt like a mask. It was real, and this show was mine.

"Let's give it up for Stilts one more time, ladies and gentlemen! How incredible was that?"

Their applause sent another burst of energy into the air, a single united sound from hundreds of hands and voices. The power practically vibrated over my skin.

"Stilts is always popular with the ladies," I said, strutting across the stage like I owned it. "Now we have some lovely ladies for you gentlemen in the crowd!"

The burlesque troupe came out next, putting on a highly entertaining show full of old-school tasteful stripteases with a dash of comedy and light magic tricks to keep everyone engaged.

It was Nigel's idea to keep everyone hooked with high-energy acts, followed by calmer, more low-key performances. Every high-energy stunt grew bolder and more shocking as the evening went on.

Soon it was time for Razvan's troupe, who would combine fire breathing and sword-swallowing into one act. And then it would be Hunter's turn to shine.

I took a sip of water, already feeling the stress on my vocal cords, before stepping out once again. "I don't know about y'all," I said, turning up my country accent. "But we haven't seen much *fire* tonight yet, have we?"

The crowd screamed, mostly the men, and raised their fists in the air. Most of them were good and drunk by now and enjoying the hell out of themselves.

"That's what I thought," I said knowingly, looking out at everyone. "We're turning up the heat now, ladies and gentlemen! Our next act loves to live dangerously! Whether by flames, sharp objects, or both at the same time. Give it up for the incredible, death-defying Flaming Swords!"

I barely turned to walk off the stage when two shirtless, heavily tattooed men came running out like ninjas. They dashed onstage, juggling swords in the air while moving with lightning speed. Only when I went behind the curtain and turned back to watch did I realize they were blindfolded.

"Holy shit," I breathed. These guys were *good*.

Two more blindfolded men walked out, and the crowd went nuts with screams. These two juggled a pair of fiery torches like it was a walk in the park. They weaved in and out with the sword jugglers in perfect synchronized form. The stage lights went low to enhance the dancing fire of the torches and the flash of metal from the swords. Everyone was stunned, including me.

But still no sign of Razvan.

I watched the show feeling entranced but couldn't help the sting of disappointment. Where was the sexy, smooth-talking leader of these daredevils?

"He'll make an entrance when you least expect it," said a female voice from behind me, as if she could read my mind. "He never fails to blow everyone away."

I turned and recognized Ally, the girl who'd been sitting in Razvan's lap when I first went to speak with all the acts. Her face was heavy with makeup and she was still in her lingerie from the striptease she performed earlier with the burlesque show.

"I wouldn't put it past him," I said with a smile, biting back the unexpected jealousy that flared up. "He's great at what he does."

"He's great at *everything* he does," she purred, popping her hip out to one side and placing a hand on it to emphasize her point.

I kept my face friendly, resisting the urge to narrow my eyes into a glare. What right did I have to be possessive about Razvan? She and he were together in some way.

You're the only human here who knows he's a dragon shifter. That means something.

"I bet," I said lightly. "You're his girlfriend, right?" I kept my tone casual, despite my insides seething for reasons I couldn't explain.

"You could say that." Her lips curved into a smug, wicked smile. "He's *definitely* off limits."

I forced out a laugh. "Don't worry. I got my own man who's plenty enough to handle."

"Good." Her blue eyes flashed challengingly. "You don't seem like the type of girl to steal another's man."

Apparently, you haven't met two bitches named Cherry and Leeann, I thought.

"I'm not," I assured her. "Connor makes me really happy."

That was the truth, despite the uncomfortable tightness around my heart from learning Razvan wasn't actually available. For a moment, I was beginning to think all his teasing and flirting meant something. That *steluța* meant something. But my first impression turned out to be right. He was just a shameless flirt and sweet-talker.

I looked back out to the stage. The jugglers had just finished a routine, their swords or torches in each hand as they froze in a kneeling position. A heavy silence hung over the stage and audience. With Raz's guys like statues, everyone seemed to be holding their breath for what was to come next.

And then a *creak* came from the rafters above my head.

I looked up just in time to see a blur of inked skin fall from the stage's ceiling. A scream threatened to escape, but my throat was too dry from announcing. Razvan landed lightly on his feet, tilted his head back and exhaled a massive orange flame.

❦ 15 ❧

MELODY

People screamed and backed away from the stage, but the burst of fire from his lungs dissipated within seconds. Only the flash of heat on my skin remained. If I could feel it from back here, I could only imagine how those in the front row felt like.

With that charming grin, he pulled his hands from behind his back to reveal two long, gleaming swords. In the next moment, the twin blades lit up into flames and the fast-paced music kicked up again.

Razvan moved so quickly, my eyes could barely keep track of him. His crew resumed their blindfolded juggling, pausing only to engage in lightning-fast sword battles with him and each other.

His flaming swords cut like liquid through the air. I'd never seen anything so beautiful and entrancing. Metal clashed and clanged. Sparks flew as fire met fire.

There was no way all of this came from his shifter abilities. The fire breathing, sure. But the speed and precision with which he moved amounted to years and years of practice.

He used to be forced to do this, I remembered sadly.

Why did he keep doing it then? Why didn't he seek out other members of his kind to live freely with them? How did he go through every day not feeling like he was in a nightmare?

231

His face only showed that signature cockiness and playfulness. More women in the audience started pushing toward the front, wanting to get closer to the fire breathing, tattooed bad boy. One particularly drunk woman lifted her shirt, flashing a pair of breasts that were much bigger than mine. Razvan paused to blow her a kiss before continuing with his act, and her friends dragged her away.

Does he know her? Who is she?

I looked back at Ally, who caught my gaze and just rolled her eyes.

"He loves the attention, but he'll learn that I'm all he needs," she said.

Bless your heart. Keep telling yourself that, girlie.

I learned early on—from everyone my mother brought home—that men were creatures of habit, not change. I lost count of how many times they swore up and down they'd support her and never bail, but that was the first thing they did when she got pregnant. How I figured this out at fourteen while she never seemed to was completely lost on me.

Even knowing this, the discomfort wrapped around my heart only squeezed tighter.

Returning my attention to the show, I realized the music and Razvan gradually slowed down. He waved the flaming swords hypnotically in a figure-eight motion in front of his face, shifting his body from side to side in a way that was downright erotic.

He paused, holding one sword vertically in front of his face for just a moment, then tossed it straight up in the air.

People screamed again, some covering their heads and moving away, others keeping their eyes glued to the long shaft of metal in the air as it sailed up, and then began its return down to earth.

Razvan dropped to one knee, spread his arms to the side and tipped his head back, sticking his tongue out like a snake. Wait, was his tongue forked? I'd never noticed it before.

A perverse thought filled me for a half-second, flushing my body with heat and arousal, and then the sword dropped.

The long, fiery metal blade seemed to slide down his throat in slow motion. I couldn't believe my eyes and wanted to cover them, but at the same time couldn't look away.

Everyone in the audience reacted similarly, by covering their eyes or mouths. He remained kneeling, unmoving for a moment, with the cross-guard resting on his lips. Then he raised a hand. With hundreds of eyes tracking his movement, he wrapped his fingers around the handle and rotated the sword ninety degrees.

"Oh god, I can't watch!" someone cried out.

Razvan raised a middle finger in the direction of the voice, eliciting laughs from everyone else. It eased the nail-biting tension in the air for a moment before continuing with his act.

He raised his other hand, the second blade still alight with flame like a beacon on the dark stage. His long, tattooed arm lifted the sword as high as he could before tilting it down to point at his mouth.

"Holy shit, two swords?!" someone cried in disbelief.

His realization was confirmed as Razvan smoothly lowered the flaming blade past his lips, tongue, and throat. He made no sound, nor any movements that showed discomfort or pain. He might as well had been holding a spaghetti noodle.

I thought back to the moment I first saw him practicing, juggling those small knives, and how I screamed when he caught them in his mouth. I had no idea then, but on that stage I realized the knives had been child's play.

He spread both arms wide to his sides again and rose to his feet, head still tipped back, and two sword handles resting on his lips. The crowd broke out into thunderous applause, the loudest standing ovation I heard yet. They yelled and whooped and hollered at the top of their lungs, amazed by the human wonder standing before them.

How would they react if they knew this man could shift into a giant, flying reptile? Would they even care if he was free or enslaved?

Razvan raised his fists to his mouth and removed both swords at the same time, their flames now extinguished. With a sweeping flourish, he bent deeply for his final bow, raising another wave of thunderous applause and screams.

The click from the microphone pinned to my jacket was my cue to go out for the last time that evening. I took a few deep breaths to compose myself after what I just saw, then put on my smile and walked out.

"Give it up for the Flaming Swords, everyone!" I boomed.

The crowd was fired up. Some were even yelling, "Encore! Encore!" But we had to move on. It was time for Hunter to come out, and my stomach was in knots once again.

Razvan laughed, giving another sweeping bow and blowing kisses out to the audience as he sheathed the swords on his back. Then his arms went around my shoulders and waist so fast I didn't have time to react.

He dipped me low, supporting my back. I saw his steel-colored eyes flash intensely for a moment before he kissed me.

I kissed him back before my brain could catch up to what was going on. My body reacted on instinct and once that forked tongue flicked gently inside my mouth, I only craved more.

But then it was over just as quickly as it began.

He broke the kiss and pulled me back up to standing, a wily grin on his face as he held my hand aloft in his.

"Give it up for Melody, our beautiful ringmistress, everyone!"

The crowd cheered and whistled as I smiled and laughed. I waved and said, "Thank you so much!"

But my mind raced at a mile a minute. My heart spun in my chest with confusion and desire.

And behind me, I felt Ally's glare like a dagger in my back.

HUNTER

A gentle knock rapped at my door.

"Yes?"

It pushed open, and Connor stuck his head in. He still wore the white face makeup, but pushed the black half-mask to the top of his head.

"You're up next, Wolf Man."

"Thanks, Connor." I stood from the chair to prepare for my shift. "Sorry," I chuckled with a bit of forewarning as I made off with my shirt and jeans. "I have to undress or I'll ruin these clothes."

"Uh, right." He looked pointedly at the ceiling. "No worries."

"How's it going out there?" I asked while I could still speak.

He let out a low whistle and shook his head in disbelief. "Mel is killing it, as we knew she would. The crowd's only getting bigger and crazier with every act. We're about to be over capacity for the main floor and people are watching from the lawn." He shot me a teasing smirk. "No pressure or anything."

"I'll be fine," I said with a shrug. "I won't be watching them, just hurrrgh."

My throat and vocal cords shifted and rearranged as my teeth grew into sharp points and my tongue elongated. White fur rippled across my entire body. My ears moved up the sides of my head and pricked forward and back when I flexed the small muscles attaching them to my skull. My tail and claws had grown out, but I stopped the shift to remain standing upright.

"Ready, man?" Connor asked.

I barked an affirmative in reply, then followed his lead out the door.

He led me through a dimly lit corridor. Through the walls, I heard voices of the crowd screaming and stage hands shouting directions.

"This is a private hallway," Connor explained. "No one will see you. I'll stay with you backstage in case anyone decides to get nosy."

I softly barked my gratitude, hoping the message would get across with my lack of a human mouth. To my surprise, he chuckled and held out his fist.

"No problem, buddy. It's the least we can do."

I bumped his fist with the back of my paw and resisted the urge to lick him. He was a good human, one of the rare few I'd met in my life. The other was his beautiful lover up on that stage.

In my drugged-out haze back in Drowningville, I remembered seeing her face from the stage. While everyone else's were blurred and distorted, her face stood out clearly. Beautiful and sad. She'd been crying when she saw me, but not out of fear. It was like she saw through my fur and teeth and could feel my pain as if it were her own.

I never dreamed they would rescue us, but before I passed out, I felt an inkling of hope. There was at least one human out there who didn't see us as monsters.

And now I knew there were at least two.

Connor led me up to the backstage area. He directed me to a corner where I could remain hidden in shadows but see both the front and back of the stage. I caught the show just as the other shifter put on his fire breathing display.

"You good, buddy?" Connor asked.

I bumped his fist again and looked up just in time to see Mel walk out from the opposite side. My heart skipped a beat in my chest and my ears pricked forward. If she had any nervousness left, it didn't show. She walked out on long, shapely legs like a model on a catwalk. Her full lips and dark eyes beamed with delight and natural beauty.

Whether onstage, backstage, or the audience, there was no head she didn't turn.

"Give it up for the Flaming Swords, everyone!" she declared.

Surprise rippled through me as I watched the kiss between Melody and the dragon from my backstage spot, but I wasn't nearly as shocked as the other dark-haired girl with her mouth hanging open in shock.

"I'm gonna kill that bitch," she whined as she stormed off.

My hackles raised, and my teeth bared in her direction. No one fucked with Melody without going through me. And I knew of at least two others who would stand up for her as well. I learned of the second one just then upon witnessing that kiss.

The audience hooted and hollered like it was all part of the show, and maybe it was in a small way. But I smelled the dragon's desire the moment she walked onstage. Apparently, they had gotten better acquainted since I watched them walk in the woods together. I wondered if Melody saw his dragon form yet.

I sensed that he was reptilian, but the fire he breathed gave proof to something I'd never thought I'd live to see. A mythical shifter, here in the backwoods of Mississippi?

Running into other shifters was rare enough, but there were estimated to be less than twenty dragons in the world.

I slid a questioning glance over to Connor as Mel and the dragon breathlessly parted. He seemed even less surprised than me.

"It was bound to happen," he said with a shrug. "I'll explain it all to you later, but I'm fine with Mel seeing other people. As long as they're good to her, of course."

I nodded, letting out a soft *whuff* of agreement. It only surprised me because humans seemed so insistent on exclusive pairs.

Multiple lovers were fairly common in wolf packs. An alpha female often took several male betas as mates. Beta females could have more than one mate as well, with the permission of the alpha. My mate had me as her primary, but found comfort in others when I went on long hunts. It kept her happy and distracted her from worrying about me.

"I have a very special guest joining me for our final show tonight," Mel declared as the dragon and his men exited the stage. "Some of you may be frightened at first, ladies and gentlemen. But I assure you there's nothing to fear! My friend is gentle and kind, even if he may look like a fearsome beast. But he's also a person with intelligence and emotion. He can understand words and ideas just as well as you understand me now."

She walked across the stage with firmness and intention as she spoke, making sure to look directly into people's eyes as she did so. Damn, Connor was right. She *was* killing it.

"My dear ladies and gents, let this be a friendly reminder to not judge a book by its cover. Or a tiger by its stripes or a wolf by its teeth." She paused, letting their silence and rapt attention hang in the air like a fog. "Without further ado, I give you my incredible friend, the Wolf Man!"

"Go get 'em, man," Connor whispered with an encouraging slap on my back.

I huffed in reply and took my first steps out, letting the stage lights fall on me and keeping my eyes trained on Melody's.

I expected some anxiety as I walked across that wooden stage, hearing the gasps and cries in my ears. But as Melody's warm eyes and smile grew closer, I realized I had none at all. I'd never been on stage like this—free and not in a cage. By my own choice and not dragged in chains. By being greeted by a friend who said kind things about me.

A friend who risked her life to rescue me and my children.

Melody winked at me, our secret signal. It looked cute and flirty to the audience, but she was really asking me if I was okay. I answered yes in the way we agreed, by flicking my left ear twice.

Satisfied, she returned her attention to the audience.

"No need to be alarmed, ladies and gents. My friend here wouldn't hurt a fly. Well," she passed a grin over the dumbfounded stares, "maybe if a fly was on his dinner."

I licked my lips when she said dinner, and the crowd noticed. We rehearsed quickly earlier in the day. She would prompt me to do things or I would respond to words so everyone could get through their thick heads that I wasn't some dumb beast.

"Hmm, I'd really love a better view of the Ferris wheel." She looked out across the audience to the carnival rides in the distance. "Would you mind giving me a boost, Mr. Wolf?"

I lowered myself to her level, wrapped an arm around the backs of her legs, and raised her up to the height of my shoulder. The crowd gasped in unison, as if I was King Kong with the delicate damsel in my grip.

But Mel was completely relaxed as she sat on my bicep. She draped an arm around my shoulders and gently scratched the fur there. My pulse picked up. It had been ages since anyone but my kids touched me affectionately. I barely remembered what the touch of a woman felt like.

"Thank you, Mr. Wolf. The view is much better from up here."

I howled my agreement. It really was a beautiful view. Romantic, whimsical, and dark.

After a few moments, I gently lowered her back to the ground.

Dare I? I thought.

Before I could think too much, my tongue darted out and licked her face. That wasn't scripted, and panic jolted through me. Did I go too far?

Mel just laughed as she pressed a hand to her cheek. "Aww, you're so sweet, Mr. Wolf," she said.

The crowd finally began to relax, laughing lightly at my lick and talking in hushed murmurs among themselves.

I was amazed at how at ease she seemed. She was either an amazing actress or she really was as comfortable with me as she was acting. Being in-between shifts was often grotesque-looking to us as well, not just humans. But Mel was smiling and blushing with me just as much as she was with Connor or the dragon.

She faced away from the crowd for a moment and winked at me. I flicked my ear twice, and she nodded.

"Do I have any brave volunteers who would like to meet my friend, the Wolf Man?" she asked the audience. "Remember, he is a person and will be treated respectfully, not ridiculed. Otherwise," she stepped directly in front of me and reached up to scratch my jaw. Oh god, that felt nice. "You'll have to deal with me," she added wickedly.

Pride and warmth swelled within me that I hadn't felt in years. It brought me back to having a mate who defended me and had my back at every twist and turn.

I wrapped a protective paw around Mel's waist and let out a soft warning growl. It didn't matter if she was my mate or just a friend. If she had my back, the least I could do was have hers.

Some audience members backed away from my bared teeth. Others stood frozen. No one seemed to be in any particular hurry to join us onstage. The silence dragged on and Mel stepped away from me, standing like she was about to make her closing announcements, when a small voice piped up.

"Can I meet him?"

Everyone turned in the direction of the voice. A girl no older than eight with wide blue eyes looked fearlessly into mine. My heartstrings tightened. Her eyes reminded me of Rinna's. She pulled against the hand of her mother, who looked just as stricken with fear as everyone else.

"It's alright, ma'am." Melody smiled kindly at the mother. "My friend won't hurt your child. He adores children."

"Yeah, for breakfast!" someone called out, eliciting snickers from his companions.

Melody and I ignored them and the girl only pulled harder against her mother, who allowed herself to be dragged a few hesitant steps forward.

"I just want to pet him, mommy," the girl said. "He looks like a doggy."

"That's right, sweetheart," Mel encouraged, stepping closer to me again. "And he's as gentle as one too."

"You swear?" the mother croaked in a harsh smoker's voice, eyes narrowing on Melody. "You swear to God almighty it ain't gonna eat my kid?"

"I swear in Jesus' name, ma'am." Mel placed a hand over her heart. I didn't take her for the religious type, but she was eager to placate the mother.

The girl dragged her mom all the way through the barricade and up the steps at the side of the stage. Mom kept her hand tightly wrapped around her daughter's. Her expression of fear mixed with disgust never changed.

I stayed back as Melody went to greet them at the end of the stage.

She knelt in front of the girl and asked softly, "What's your name, sweetheart?"

"Amy," the girl answered.

"Would you like to make a new friend today, Amy?"

The girl nodded, looking over Mel's shoulder to meet my eyes again. She smelled similar to Mel. Fearless and brave. Completely human, but with a touch of something different.

I allowed Amy to approach me, lowering my head and wagging my tail encouragingly. Her mother remained at the edge of the stage and looked ready to run off, daughter or no daughter.

Mel held Amy's hand as she reached out and scratched under my jaw again with the other. Goddamn, that made me just want to stretch out in her lap and bask in her sweetness.

"You can pet him like this, Amy," she said gently.

Amy reached out with a small hand and gave me the softest scratch on my forehead. I leaned into her hand and licked her fingers, thumping my tail emphatically on the stage floor.

"He licked me!" she giggled, smoothing her hand over me with more confidence.

"That means he likes you," Mel told her.

"You're really soft," Amy said, looking directly into my smiling jaws. "Is it okay if I hug you, Mr. Wolf?"

The question took me aback for a moment. For one thing, she asked *me* directly. Not Melody. Everyone else spoke to Mel as if I wasn't capable of understanding, despite her proving to them otherwise. Everyone except this brave little girl, who was like a miniature version of Mel.

I nuzzled my face close to hers and opened my arms. Amy loosely wrapped her hands around my neck and rested her face in my fur, while I gently placed my paws on her back.

A soft chorus of "*Awww*" rose from the crowd. Maybe they were finally getting it.

I licked Amy's ear, tickling her as she giggled and squirmed away.

"Give it up for Amy and the wolf, everyone!" Melody declared as she led the girl back to her mother, who promptly whisked her off the stage.

The applause that rose was quieter and more hesitant than it had been all evening. People looked as if they were confused, unsure of whether to trust their own eyes or the knee jerk reaction of fearing the unknown.

Good. That meant they were thinking.

Mel and I stood facing the crowd as she delivered her closing announcements, encouraging people to tell their friends and come back for more throughout the week. We did our final bow and this time, people let loose on their cheers and applause. The moon hung full and bright and I let out a howl for a last little bit of showmanship. That got howls and wolf whistles in return.

Mel shot me a wink as we walked off stage together, but it wasn't a secret signal this time. Her broad, beautiful smile told me that much, and my heart skipped a beat.

We made sure everyone saw us walk off the stage together, side by side as equals.

17

MELODY

Hunter shifted to human the moment we had privacy backstage. As soon as he did, I jumped on him with a hug.

"Holy shit, that was awesome!" I laughed, squeezing my arms around his bare shoulders. "You were absolutely amazing! Did you see all their faces?! And that little girl was sooo adorable."

The discomfort on his face confused me when I pulled away.

"Hey, you okay?" I asked him, concerned.

"Um, sorry," he said, his eyes glancing down. "I can't wear clothes during a shift and uh..."

I followed his gaze and promptly jerked my eyes back up to his face, but it was too late. I saw. And I couldn't unsee.

"Oh no, I'm sorry!" I stammered as I grew uncomfortably hot. "Uh, I totally should have known."

"No, don't worry." His blush on his fair skin was beyond adorable, and it only made me hotter and more uncomfortable. Fuck a cold shower. I needed to be dropped into an ice bath.

"Here buddy, I got you."

Connor walked up out of nowhere, pushing a bundle of clothes into Hunter's arms. Both of them sighed in relief as the tension dissipated ever so slightly.

"Thanks, man." Hunter pulled on the clothes quickly while the strongest pair of tree trunk arms swept me up in a crushing embrace.

"You were incredible, babe," Connor murmured before kissing me deeply.

My mind was whirling up until that moment. Razvan's kiss confused me but set me on fire. It was at the back of my mind the whole time I was onstage with Hunter, who I also seemed to have an incredible connection with. Not to mention I just saw him naked, and what a sight *that* was!

But all that melted away when Connor lifted me up and stole my breath from my lungs. In this moment, it was just me and him. The uniquely beautiful, loving dysfunction that was *us*.

He kissed me like nobody was watching, like Hunter wasn't right next to us fumbling to get dressed and like Razvan's kiss didn't even matter. This was *our* moment.

My heart crashed so hard against my sternum, I had no doubt he could feel it. His own heart beat in time with mine through the thin cotton of his shirt. I wanted nothing more than to wrap my legs around his trim waist and find a private place. When we broke apart for air, his wild, forest green eyes told me he had similar ideas.

"I'm so proud of you, babe." He peppered kisses across my face and neck, his hands beginning to roam across my body. "I knew you could do it."

"Thank you, my love." The endearment slipped out and panic temporarily froze me.

But Connor only grinned and pulled me in to capture my mouth again. His length, already thick and hard, pressed against my hip and my core flooded with heat in response. He took a firm hold of my wrist and nipped my earlobe, eliciting a sharp hiss and then a light moan from me as he teased the spot on my neck just below it.

He began pulling me in the direction of our trailer, and I was eager to follow. I turned to say goodnight to Hunter when we saw Nigel running up to us. He wore a grin that looked like he just won the lottery.

"Amazing job, everyone!" he cried jubilantly. "Especially you, Mel!

I'm still crunching the numbers, but this was a record-breaking turnout! We've got to celebrate! Drinks are on me!"

"Uh..." Connor gave a side-eyed glance to me, which I returned with a half-hearted eye roll.

"We should celebrate and mingle, babe," I told him, then looked over at Hunter. "You should come too and bring the kids! There's food and non-alcoholic drinks in the tavern."

"Yes! The more, the merrier!" Nigel turned to Hunter as if noticing him for the first time and stuck his hand out. "Hi, I'm Nigel. Carnival manager at your service! Are you a friend of Mel and Connor's?"

"You could say that," Hunter replied with an amused smirk.

No one but Connor and I knew what Hunter looked like in human form. We figured he'd be safer that way. We just told Nigel we had the Wolf Man from Drowningville to fill in the empty slot and, because he had nothing more to lose, thankfully took us at our word.

"Well, lucky you getting a backstage view! How about that wolf man, huh? Mel really knows how to woo a crowd." He turned back to us. "Seriously, bring all your friends! Drinks are on me for the whole carnival crew and their people!"

"And he wonders why he can't afford his mortgage," Connor mumbled when Nigel darted away.

"Oh, be nice." I smacked him playfully. "He really has helped us out a lot."

Lacing my fingers with Connor's and Hunter walking on my other side, the three of us followed the crowd of carnival staff to the tavern. The guys talked excitedly about the acts and performers, even making crude jokes about the burlesque show that had me rolling my eyes. Men.

They seemed to have a rare friendship spark, those two. I looked between Hunter and Connor and saw the same animated expression in their faces, just from talking to each other. It wasn't that they were leaving me out, I was just content to listen. All the talking in my ringmistress role today drained me, and I was happy to be quiet for a while.

I also kept my head on a swivel to look out for Ally, and by association, Razvan.

Why did you have to kiss me, damn it? I demanded silently. And why right then? Your timing is sure impeccable.

I could still taste the heat of his kiss, even now after getting swept away by Connor's kisses. Raz's mouth tasted like a fresh cup of hot coffee at just the perfect temperature. Warm enough to bite, but not quite hot enough to burn.

There was no sign of either of them as we entered the tavern, and a confusing mixture of disappointment and relief swept through me.

Confused. I seemed to be feeling that way pretty often lately.

Was I reading into Hunter, pulling out a chair for me and smiling? Was he just a gentleman, or did he feel that same fluttering in his chest when our eyes met like that? It didn't matter if he was human, wolf, or in between forms. Something about those golden eyes and that lithe, strong body just captured me like prey.

"I'm going to get the kids," he said, brushing his fingertips along my elbow as I sat down. "Save us a spot?"

"Of course," I smiled up at him. "Do you want us to order for you?"

Hunter told us his requests and quickly left. The moment he was gone, Connor slid an arm around my waist and kissed my temple.

"You want him too, babe." He wasted no time in getting to the point.

I looked at him, eyes filled with guilt. "Is it that obvious?"

"With how googly-eyed you two were at each other, I think you convinced Nigel he was your boyfriend and not me."

"You're not my boyfriend. You've made it clear you don't want that," I said, more snappish than I intended. "We keep talking about this, Connor, and I feel like it's going nowhere."

"Shush, babe. This is a night of celebrating. I'm not trying to upset you." He took my chin in his hand, gently turning my face to his. "I've thought about it some more and I think I've sorted my feelings out."

I raised my eyebrows expectantly. "And?"

"I'm in love with you."

Everything went still. The crowded, noisy bar faded away to nothing, and all I saw was Connor's handsome face.

"What?" I barely spoke at all, just mouthed the word. I couldn't have heard him correctly.

"I love you, Mel." Every syllable out of his mouth carried nothing but raw honesty, straight from his heart. He meant every word, and I didn't know how to handle that. No one had ever meant it when they said those words to me before.

"I want you to be happy and to have whatever—and whoever—you want. Nothing less."

He leaned his forehead gently against mine. "You won't always want to be around me, and understandably so. I know myself well enough that I won't make you happy all the time. Even though I do love you, I'm not perfect. If you'd rather spend time with Razvan or Hunter, I'll understand."

"Hunter? I... maybe." Admitting it felt heavy and real. But who knew if that was even what Hunter wanted? "Nothing's going to happen between me and Razvan, though," I said with a shake of my head. "So you can forget about that."

Connor narrowed his eyes in confusion. "That's not the impression I got from him kissing you."

"I was talking to his girlfriend literally seconds before that happened! He basically cheated on her with me in front of a crowd of people, and now she definitely hates me. Who knows what his deal is, but I don't want any part of their drama."

Connor rubbed his jaw. "I dunno, babe. There might be more to this than you think. Maybe you should just talk to him."

"If he wants to talk, he knows where to find me," I huffed. "Oh by the way, I love you too."

He grinned broadly and pulled me into a kiss that slowly began erasing Razvan's memory from my lips. I'd never betray the dragon shifter's secret, but I didn't need him. Not like this. With Connor and potentially Hunter and his kids, my heart was full enough.

"*Now* can I call you my boyfriend?" I asked when we parted.

"Alright, fine," he sighed with mock frustration before he chuckled and kissed me again.

Our food soon came out, covering the entire table. Connor and I started digging in when Hunter and the kids showed up. I had no idea I'd been so hungry. Today had taken everything of me.

"Ooh, ribs!" Roo declared as he pulled himself up to the table.

"I want ribs too!" Rinna piped up.

"There's plenty to share," Hunter sighed with an eye roll, but smiled warmly at them.

The five of us talked and laughed into the night as we ate and drank. Rinna began coming out of her shell and told me about the butterflies she chased through the field that morning. Hunter looked overjoyed that she was talking to me without any coaxing. The poor girl probably hadn't talked to any women since getting captured.

Hunter had one beer, kept carefully out of the kids' reach, but I noticed Connor didn't order any alcohol.

My boyfriend was in a flirty mood, kissing my cheek and teasing me at every opportunity, but not possessive like he usually was. When Hunter and I got into a conversation, he engaged with the kids, telling them jokes and funny stories.

When our bellies were full and my eyelids started to droop, Hunter took the kids to the restroom. I watched them as they walked away, the family that had been through so much but still managed to look out for each other.

"So, what do you think?" Connor wrapped an arm around my waist, pulling my back against his chest and dropped a kiss to my shoulder. "Want to spend more time with the wolf family tonight?"

In that moment, there was no question of what I wanted.

"No," I said, looking up at him. "I want to go home with you."

His eyes flickered with pleasure. "You sure?"

I kissed under his jaw, pressing my ass into his crotch to make my intention known.

The time to explore something with Hunter would come. And with his children to consider, if anything progressed between us, it would need to go slowly. I was fine with that. I wanted everyone involved to be aware if things developed between us.

But right then, I didn't feel like exploring anything new. I wanted familiarity, the comfort of the man I knew and loved.

"Goddamn, girl. We have to wait and say goodbye first," he teased, nipping at my neck.

When the three wolves came back, we passed around celebratory hugs and goodnights. Hunter was so tall, I had to stand on tiptoes to reach around his neck. He squeezed gently around my waist and our embrace lingered, like neither of us wanted to let go.

"Thank you again," he whispered in my ear. "For everything."

"No, thank you," I smiled as I pulled away. "You saved all our asses tonight and gave us a reason to celebrate."

He gave me one last heart-melting smile before taking Roo and Rinna's hands in his. "See you two around soon."

Connor and I followed them out the door, our fingers intertwined between us. We barely walked ten feet when an anguished cry and a slap rang out.

Our heads snapped over to see Ally and Razvan in the middle of a heated argument. Her face red and streaked with tears, his fists clenched at his sides.

❧ 18 ❧

MELODY

"Enjoying what you've done, bitch?"

Ally turned to me, her jaws clenched with rage and heavy, sobbing gasps of air coming from her chest. She lunged toward me, spurring all three men into action.

Connor jerked me behind him, Hunter stepped up next to him with a protective growl. And Razvan grabbed Ally's arm, preventing her from getting any closer. A red mark on his cheek showed that he'd been the receiver of the slap a moment ago.

"This has nothing to do with her," he insisted, pulling Ally back by her arm. "Don't drag other people into your petty shit."

"Look at this smug bitch!" Ally screamed, gesturing wildly. "One guy isn't enough. All three of you are being fucking white knights. It's fucking ridiculous!" She turned a poisonous glare to me. "You lied to my face! Are you seriously fucking all of them?"

"Stop this nonsense. You're hammered." Razvan wrapped her in a bear hug and began dragging her away. He shot me an apologetic look. "I'm sorry about this, *steluța*."

"I'm not the one you should be apologizing to," I fired back, stepping in front of Connor. "Ally?"

"Fuck you, bitch!" she twisted in Razvan's tattooed arms to shoot me another hateful glare.

"I didn't lie to you," I said, ignoring her insult. "I don't steal other women's men. But you have to remember that men make their own decisions." My gaze flickered from Razvan back to her, trying to ignore the memory of his lips on mine and that split tongue caressing mine. "You can have him, Ally. Although I think you could do much better."

I turned to continue walking, pulling Connor by the hand with me. I didn't want to see Razvan's face. It hurt me to shut him down like that, even if it was the right thing to do. I didn't want to think about the possibility of hurting him, too.

"Was that really necessary?" Connor asked after we said a final goodnight to Hunter and the kids and continued on the path to our trailer.

Our trailer. When did I start thinking about it like that?

"Doesn't matter now," I muttered. "I don't want to think about that."

"I think it's worth it to hear him out," he said gently. "Maybe after a few days, once y'alls heads are cleared."

"You two really bonded during your late night talk, huh?" I gave him a sideways glance.

"Sort of," he muttered. "He gave me a good perspective on things I didn't think about. Even before Hunter came along, I was starting to think he'd be good for you to turn to when you don't feel like dealing with me."

When we reached the trailer, I playfully shoved him against the door before he could open it. Like a good sport, he allowed me to pin him there, humoring me with a grin.

"Well, that time is not right now," I said in what I hoped was a seductive whisper. "Not another word about Raz or Hunter."

"Yes, ma'am," he grunted, lifting me up under my thighs. His mouth claimed mine as my legs wrapped around his waist.

Now in control, he turned us around and pressed my back to the door. His hips rolled against my heated core, already revved up and ready to receive him.

"Fuck me, babe," he moaned into my neck as he fumbled with his key and the door.

"That's the plan," I whispered hotly, scratching my nails up his back like a cat scratching at a post.

We finally made it inside, and he sat us down with a heavy groan on the bed.

I paused for a moment. "You okay?"

"Babe, my legs could be bleeding, oozing stumps and with you wrapped around me like this, I'd still be okay."

"Mmm, super hot imagery for when I'm right about to fuck you," I teased.

"Call me a magician," he teased back, working my jacket off my arms. "I can bring your mind back to a state of arousal. *Abra cadabra*, just like this."

My breath caught in my throat as he pulled my hips tight against his hot, pulsing erection. The pressure and hardness made my clit explode with sensation and beg for more. Combined with his gentle sucking right below my earlobe, I temporarily forgot my own name.

"Connor," I moaned, squirming in his lap for relief.

He held my body captive and tight against him, his strong arms pinning me to his chest as he moved just slightly. They weren't thrusts, just slight rocking of his hips and we still had all our clothes on, for fuck's sake. But the pressure right on my aching clit, the friction, how hard he was and just how tightly he held me, caused the first orgasm to rip through my body.

I shook and convulsed and whimpered and only after all that subsided, did he loosen his hold and I slumped limp like a rag doll against him.

"A gentleman always makes his girl come before she's even naked," he chuckled with a kiss to my cheek.

"I thought you were a magician," I whispered breathlessly, pulling at his clothes.

"Why not both?" His voice became muffled as I peeled his shirt over his skin.

His arms slid around me to deftly pull apart the laces of my corset. With all my senses heightened from that orgasm, I glued myself to him and just drank in his bare skin on mine. Every scar, muscle, and bone told a small piece of his story. I watched my own fingers trail across his arms and chest in magnified concentration. I wanted to know this man every night down to the smallest detail.

My corset came off, breasts and ribs spilling after being caged in that thing for so many hours. Connor lovingly kissed and massaged my tender flesh, bringing cries of relief bordering on pain as circulation returned to those areas.

We untangled for a moment to remove pants and underwear. He stopped me when I went to peel off my stockings.

"Leave those on for me," he said with a soft rumble. "You look so sexy wearing nothing but lace on your legs."

"Oh? A fetishist, are we?" I teased, slowly crawling back into his lap.

"I dunno," he shrugged. "It's just hot as fuck seeing you with a little bit of clothing still on." His powerful arms went around me again, crushing me to the hot, solid wall of his chest. "I still love you naked, though."

"They're coming off as soon as we're done," I said with playful warning.

"Mm, then I might have to fuck you again." He made a trail of kisses down my neck and across my shoulder. "You know, for science."

His talking became wordless moans as my pussy rubbed against him. Heat building more heat, my soft to his hard. I lifted my hips, beyond ready to impale myself on him, when he stopped me.

"Condoms, babe," he reminded me with a kiss.

"Oh, right." Embarrassment flooded through me for forgetting.

I laid on my side, watching as he went to retrieve it from the shelf. Just enough light filtered through the curtains so I could see just the shape of him, the contours of the well-defined muscles adorning his body. They tensed and coiled with precision at every little movement he made—ripping open the package and sliding the rubber onto his length.

A fresh rush of heat flooded my core as I watched him touch himself. He gave himself a few strokes back to full hardness and tugged at his balls with a soft groan. I'd have to remember he liked that.

Without warning, he flipped me over onto my stomach and pulled me up to my knees. A sweet tingle erupted over my scalp and his mouth fanned a soft breath on the back of my neck.

"You like this, baby?" His fist wound tighter in my hair as his teeth tested the soft flesh of my neck.

I gasped, my back arching with need. I didn't even realize I backed toward him until I felt his round head kiss my slick, swollen entrance.

"Yes," I whimpered. "Oh please, Connor."

He surged forward, spreading me apart with a hot moan. His fist tightening in my hair as he pulled back, his other hand digging into the flesh of my hip.

He thrust into me so deliciously. I loved it, coupled with the light tingles of pain from his hand in my hair and his bites on my neck. He moved both hands to my waist as he fucked me, but I wanted more.

I craved it, needed it.

"Spank me," I begged. "Connor, please."

"Well, damn," he grunted, delivering a few wonderful smacks on either side.

I hummed with pleasure and begged for more, pressing back into his thrusts for more of him inside me. I couldn't get enough. He obliged until my ass stung and I felt a familiar pressure building in my clit.

Connor noticed the change in my moaning and picked up the pace and force of his thrusts. His hip bones pressed into my ass as he reached forward to soothe the ache in my stiff nipples. I saw stars when I came, my pussy closing around a rod of concrete that suddenly jerked with a convulsion of its own.

"Fuck," he groaned with his own release, fingers digging into my hip as he nearly fell forward.

The next sensations I felt were his kisses on my back, followed by the emptiness of him withdrawing from me. I wondered if I passed out for a moment.

Connor collapsed on the bed with deep, ragged breaths, and I curled up into his side. The comfort of his arms around me and his rapid heartbeat underneath my ear were everything to me in that moment.

"I didn't know you liked that rough stuff, babe," he said, smoothing his palm over the tender flesh of my ass.

"Me neither," I said with a shy giggle. "You pulling my hair just felt so good. I was craving more of that feeling."

"I'll remember that," he said with a kiss on my forehead. "Damn, we gotta get you on the pill," he sighed. "I wanna feel you bare."

The thought of feeling his orgasm spill inside me, with no barrier between us, was incredibly hot. Especially if it didn't mean an unexpected child later on down the road.

Thinking of children brought my attention back to Hunter. If we pursued this connection we had, I'd be basically dating a single father. What would that be like? How would the kids take it? Were there unspoken rules for dating men with kids? I'd never really dated anyone before, certainly not anyone I felt as strongly for as these three men.

Damn it. Not Razvan too, I cursed within my head. I had to let those feelings die. He was not someone I wanted to get involved with.

Weariness settled into my limbs and I snuggled harder against Connor, who was already breathing rhythmically. I had a feeling not many humans knowingly dated shifters, or vice versa. It was uncharted territory for all involved. We'd tackle challenges when we got to them.

One dick at a time, I thought with a giggle.

Whatever happened with Hunter and everything else on this roller coaster, I'd have Connor beside me. Even if he made me crazy, I knew now his love was genuine, and he was just as crazy about me.

EPILOGUE

RAZVAN

Fucking Ally.

Fuck her and her drunk, dramatic ass starting shit. I should have nipped that in the bud right away. Now I had a mess to clean up.

I hated having to take care of her drunk ass, but if I didn't, there would be two possible outcomes. One, she'd go after Mel and, at best, start some petty girl fight. At worst, she'd seriously hurt Mel with how fucking pissed off she was. Just in my trying to restrain her, she scratched me hard enough to draw blood. Better me than Mel on any day.

The second possibility? Some asshole, or worse, a gang of them, would take advantage of her in her drunken state. I wouldn't put it past some of these rednecks, nor would I wish that on Ally or anyone.

I couldn't allow either or both of those things to happen, so I spent the night keeping her away from Mel instead of being with Mel myself.

I saw her through the doorway of the tavern with Connor, a couple of kids, and some pale guy I hadn't seen before. One smell of the air and I knew he was the wolf. Ah, so he emerged from the shadows at last. I couldn't catch his act because of dealing with Ally, but the buzz around it was nonstop. As the attendees left, that was all they were jabbering about. Good. The final act had to be the one that stuck in their mind.

When they left the bar and I saw the look in her big brown eyes, I knew she had already written me off. And that hit me in a deep, hidden place I often forgot was still alive.

I shouldn't have kissed her. Not onstage like that.

Did I regret it? Hell fucking no.

Was I going to make this right? I was going to try my damn hardest.

The other burlesque dancers were too busy with their own hookups to babysit Ally, so I had to stay with her throughout most of the night. An exhausting, infuriating night of her throwing up, mumbling curses about Mel, then shamelessly trying to fuck me.

"I hope you remember this because I'm not coming back here," I growled, pinning her wrists away from me for the tenth time. "It's over between us, not that there was anything to begin with. I'm not fucking you anymore. I'm fucking done with your bullshit."

"Whyyyy?," she wailed. "What's so special about herrrrr?"

"She doesn't act like this, for one fucking thing," I mumbled, rubbing my temples. I could very quickly appreciate that Mel didn't drink at all.

I couldn't stop thinking about her being with Connor right then, the sounds and faces she made as she expressed her pleasure. My dragon fired up with jealousy and it was all I could do to keep him at bay.

I fucked up. Connor was who she rightfully wanted and needed at that moment. I had to set things right and then show her she had nothing to fear by choosing me.

The day was young by the time Ally passed out. When peaceful silence finally greeted my ears, nothing sounded better than an early morning flight. It was risky, of course, but still dark enough that no reasonable person would be awake.

But that didn't stop me from seeing if someone would still wake up and join me.

Cool morning dew clung to me as I took the short walk to

Connor's trailer. I didn't expect to see the light of his campfire, but also wasn't entirely surprised.

"Mornin'," he greeted from his lawn chair.

"Ah, good morning," I answered, noticing something else that took me by surprise.

He wasn't wearing the metal legs he showed me. His legs ended in stumps, one right below his knee, the other halfway down his shin.

"Close your mouth or you'll swallow a fly, Raz," he mumbled, sipping coffee from a mug.

"I'm just... even more impressed with your acrobatic abilities now," I said, running a hand over my short, buzzed hair. "I mean damn, man. Be honest, how fucking hard is it?"

"My dick? Well, give me a few minutes to refract and wake up the lady," he laughed. "The stilt shit? Yeah, took some adjustments. My training in the Marines helped, though."

I nodded. It didn't even bother me anymore that this man was fucking Mel maybe minutes ago. He lived through a hell that killed other humans and for that, he had all my respect.

"I actually came over to see if you could wake her up," I said. "I've been up all night and might as well watch the sunrise with someone I'd like to spend time with."

His eyes narrowed, and I saw that protective tension ripple over him. "You've been up doing *what*, exactly?"

"Just making sure the girl didn't get raped or come out here to fight Mel," I said, feeling just a hair defensive. "Nothing happened and there was nothing between us, really. We fucked once, and she got attached. I never promised or committed to anything. And now I let her know nothing will happen again."

Connor visibly relaxed. "I figured it was something like that, but that girl made it sound to Mel like you two were dating. She's not too happy with you, man."

"Exactly why I want to straighten things out. So what do you say, Connor?" I grinned sheepishly, trying to curb my eagerness to see those beautiful, dark eyes again. "Let me take her to see a romantic sunrise?"

He rubbed his jaw as he thought, turning his gaze to the trailer door.

"I dunno, man. Nothing against you, but I feel like she needs a bit more space. The next morning is still fresh, you know?"

Fuck.

"Sure," I said, my dragon roaring his protest inside me. "I don't want to force anything and make it worse."

"Give her a couple of days, then come back," Connor said. "Trust me, I've been keeping you in my good graces, but she's a stubborn one."

"Don't I know it." I laughed. "I get it. Thanks, man. Guess it's a solo flight this morning."

"Flight?" Connor raised an eyebrow.

"Oh, that's right," I laughed. "I never told you straight out." I took one glance around at our empty surroundings. "Well, fuck it. Hope you're not afraid of giant, flying lizards."

I began the shift before he could react. When it became clear what I was doing, he grabbed his armrests and nearly leaped out of his chair. I would've felt bad if he had fallen out because then he'd have to crawl to get around. He was nearly as accustomed to seeing this as Melody.

"A fucking dragon?" he whispered hoarsely when my shift completed, his eyes nearly bulging out of his head. "Fuck, I should have known," he laughed with a disbelieving shake of his head. "Fire breathing, of fucking course."

I snorted with laughter, smoke curling from my jaws and nostrils. With a derisive nod, I pushed off the ground and took one powerful beat of my wings to get airborne. Connor, his trailer, and the whole world became tiny versions of themselves within seconds as I ascended higher and higher.

The sky was still dark except for a creeping sliver of light on the horizon.

One day, I thought. You'll be sitting on me, wild and free. And we'll see this view together.

SMOKE AND MIRRORS

BOOK 3

PROLOGUE

Pacing back and forth in a cage is no way to live.

I could feel my muscles weakening, my mind going insane.

My rage went past the point of boiling over, but there was nothing left for me to do behind these steel bars. I gnawed at them until the humans electrocuted me, then sedated me again. Once, I was one of the most powerful predators on earth, but in here I was powerless.

The best I could do was disfigure someone if they got close enough, but it had been five long years since I've felt the satisfaction of sinking my teeth into a weaker animal's throat.

Every moment I was conscious, I fantasized about killing them all and claiming my victory, of taking ownership of my freedom to claim my mate, who I've yet to meet. I felt her out there, despite having never seen her face. What would she think if she saw me like this? I needed to be more than a caged pet to win her heart.

If Mamma were still alive, I knew she'd be ashamed of me for not only the things I've done, but for feeling this way.

"Always practice *ahimsa*, my son," she told me. "Even when we feed, we must not cause unnecessary harm. When the urge to destroy consumes you, that is when *ahimsa* is most important."

Well, I had certainly done minimal harm in my time here, although that was more out of circumstance than choice. I hadn't ripped anyone's throat out simply because I didn't have the reach, nor the strength, anymore. Maybe that displeased Lord Shiva, but I'd been in captivity here for so long, I since gave up hope of having my prayers answered.

And so I paced back and forth like the swinging pendulum in a clock. I agitated the humans in hopes that one of them would finally put me out of my misery. When knocked out, I dreamed of my mate. I felt the comfort of her presence, even though I have no idea who she is.

She's the only shred of hope I had left.

I

MELODY

I thought it was the heavy weight of despair in my chest as I woke up, but it turned out to be just Connor's arm.

He snored softly next to me as I slid out from under him and stretched. My pointed toes and outstretched arms above my head touched the fake wood paneling before I could truly get a good stretch in. Such was the reality of living in a trailer.

Sure, having an actual house sounded nice, but to be honest, I had no idea what that was like. I spent my whole life in a trailer, so traveling in one as a carnival performer wasn't much of an adjustment at all.

I shifted to a diagonal angle, stretching my legs over Connor's hips to maximize my stretch before relaxing. With a yawn and rub of my eyes, I tried to recall last night's dream.

They were different every night now and only growing more vivid. Sometimes I was running on four paws, howling at the moon. Other times I was in the dark, eerie silence of the ocean, using echolocation to navigate my way around. Sometimes I flew across cities and the most breathtaking natural landscapes. I could never see exactly what I was. All I knew while flying was that I was bigger than a bird. I wondered if Razvan experienced the same views.

No, don't think about Razvan, I scolded myself harshly.

It pained me to not think fondly of the tattooed, enigmatic dragon shifter. I thought I could read people, but he fooled me so well. I couldn't help but see the good in everyone, and I thought I saw a side of him he didn't reveal to anyone else. I even thought a unique connection sparked between us.

But he proved to be exactly the man I initially perceived him to be —an expert game player and heartbreaker. He kissed me onstage in front of everyone while his girlfriend watched from backstage. Connor saw it too, but genuinely didn't seem to mind. If anything, he encouraged me to talk to Raz again. But that deliberate deception was not something I wanted in my life, especially if I was going to entertain the idea of dating multiple men.

Last night's dream was different, though. They caged me in a different carnival, an especially bad one where the staff did little to hide their exploitation of animals. I could smell fear, death, and despair through my heightened senses. Power, strength and incomprehensible anger flowed through me, but I had no outlet to express it. All I could do was pace back and forth in a small cage.

I never felt such bleak hopelessness like that before. Not even back home in my shitty trailer park life before joining the carnival. When Connor and I saw how Hunter was mistreated back in Drowningville, I thought nothing could top that kind of sorrow. When Razvan told me he was sold into a circus by his own family, that opened the fresh wound all over again.

But that was nothing like this. This dream no longer made me an outside observer. I felt it. I *knew* what it was like to be caged, tortured, and forced to entertain. It consumed me so much that I didn't even notice when Connor stirred next to me until he pulled me back into his embrace.

"Mornin', babe," he drawled, kissing my neck lazily.

"Mornin', handsome." What was it about mornings that made us sound extra southern?

I snuggled into his heat, his warmth and protection. All I wanted to do was shake off the all-consuming sadness and despair of that dream and soak into how good he made me feel.

"How're you feeling today?" I kissed the hollow of his throat.

"Sore," he groaned. "So fuckin' glad we're not onstage today."

I hesitated before saying what was on my mind. "You should probably stay off your prosthetics today."

"Yes, babe, I know," he sighed.

"You know I'm honestly not trying to nag you." I swirled my fingertips in the soft chest hair just below his throat. "I just hate seeing you in pain."

"Pain is inevitable," he grunted, rolling onto his back and pulling me with him so I splayed across his chest.

I lowered my head to listen to the watery thud of his heartbeat, my fingers tracing the Marine Corps emblem tattooed on the other side of his chest. "It can be avoided if you take the time to rest."

"Rest is worse than physical pain for someone like me," he said with a throaty chuckle. "Doing nothing will make me even more insane than I already am."

I opened my mouth to tell him he wasn't insane and promptly shut it, knowing it would be of no use to argue. Connor dealt with his PTSD and loss of his legs through self-deprecating humor. He didn't do it for sympathy. I was beginning to see it helped him to make light of his situation.

So instead I complained, "Why do you always have to argue with me?"

He propped his head up with one arm and brushed a kiss along my eyelids. "You're so damn beautiful in the morning." With his other arm wrapped around me, he promptly slapped my ass. "See, babe? No argument here."

"Changing the subject doesn't count," I pouted.

Laughing, he shifted his broad, muscular body out from under me. I loved watching him move up close. The muscles under his skin were like a landscape of shifting sands—rising and falling, solid and rippling.

He laid on his side, facing me on the same pillow. His green eyes swallowed me up like the deepest, darkest forest.

"I'll go nuts if I don't walk around at least a little, but I promise I'll take it easy, babe."

I sighed, knowing that was the best I was going to get from my stubborn ex-Marine. "Thank you. For *almost* listening to me."

"You're lucky I love you," he chuckled, dropping a light kiss to my nose before pushing himself up to rise from bed.

"Hey." I grabbed his arm, stopping him from leaving the bed, and pulled him back to me. "You know I really am lucky to have you, right?" My mouth found his to pull a long, lingering kiss from him, morning breath be damned. "And I love you too."

Up close, I could see the conflict in his forest green eyes. Struggle and conflict ruled this man's world in ways that were unimaginable to most people. He lost so much, and not just the physical parts of him. I wanted to remind him every day that he would always be worthy of love, especially when he didn't believe it himself.

"You're so sweet to me, babe," he murmured, resting his forehead on mine. It wasn't a full acceptance of it yet, nor a total brush-off. He was trying, and that was all I could ask for.

A soft *tap-tap-tap* on the trailer door broke through our intimate moment.

"Whaaaat?" Connor groaned at the intrusion.

"Um, you guys up?"

My heart lifted in my chest when I recognized the voice of the handsome wolf shifter. Hunter!

"Only if your furry ass has coffee and bacon," Connor answered.

I stifled a giggle. He was always so grumpy in the morning, it was actually adorable at this point.

"Well, I got one of the two. Just thought I'd share."

"We'll be right out, Hunter!" I called out, pulling the sheet back and reaching to the floor for my clothes.

"Oh, *now* you want to get out of bed."

Connor's smirk told me he was teasing. He and Hunter got to be good friends in the past week. Not to mention he practically threw me at the gorgeous wolf shifter whenever we were together.

"Don't tell me you don't want any of his bacon," I said with a kiss as I stepped into my shorts. "Or his coffee, whichever he has."

"The first one!" Hunter called.

"Mmm, bacon," Connor crooned as he pulled on a shirt.

The three of us seemed to have a unique bond ever since we rescued the wolf shifter and his two children from the especially sadistic carnival in Drowningville. In exchange for saving his life, he volunteered to perform a half-shifted Wolf Man act, which earned our new ragtag team of sideshow performers some serious local buzz. Each show became bigger and more crowded than the last, and they only wanted more.

However, back-to-back nightly shows took their toll on us performers. Connor was putting so much pressure on his legs during his acrobatic stilt walking, he had intense pain the last couple of nights. Thankfully, the weekend finished and Nigel, the carnival manager, gave us the next night off. A different program would go on during the slower weekday nights.

When we were decent, I opened the trailer door and tried not to smile too brightly at the beautiful pale man with golden eyes. His platinum, shoulder-length hair was wavy this morning, probably an effect of the lovely midsummer humidity. He was dressed simply in a gray T-shirt and dark jeans but still managed to look like a model with otherworldly beauty.

"Hey, Hunt." I bit my tongue, cringing at how I shortened his name, but it was too late to take back now.

"Mornin', Mel," he greeted me with an easygoing smile as his gaze flickered downward shyly. "You look nice today."

"Ahaha, seriously? I literally just rolled out of bed." My heart fluttered like butterfly wings in my chest. "But thanks. You look nice too." Sweet baby Jesus, why did he have to be so pretty *and* polite?

"What's this about bacon?" Connor called from behind me.

"I have some." Hunter nodded to the bundle of butcher paper he held at his side. "Me and the kids took down a boar the other night. I'm telling you, Con, this is the most delicious bacon I've ever had in my life."

"Well, get a fire goin' and put the griddle on, boy!" He slapped my ass and hoisted himself onto the kitchen counter to start a pot of coffee, ignoring my glare in the process.

Hunter tried to politely look away, but I still caught his lip bite as he tried to hold back a laugh.

"Oh, don't get all shy, Hunt. I've seen you naked." Why embarrass just myself when I could embarrass him too?

"Yes, you have." His lips pulled back into a sultry smile. Damn it. I did not embarrass him at all. Not that he had any reason to be—he looked exquisite with or without clothes on. Lithe muscles covered his tall frame, and yes, *it* was very nice to look at as well. Even though I only got a quick glance because it was right after he shifted from Wolf Man to human. I hugged him after our first show together, not realizing he needed to be naked in order to shift.

It was beyond awkward at the time, but now that it occurred in hindsight I didn't mind bringing it up for flirty banter. And apparently Hunter didn't mind either.

We got the fire started, and I carefully set up the cast iron griddle over the flames, held up by two cinder blocks.

"Where are the kids this morning?" I asked.

"Sleeping in," he said, laying thick strips of bacon onto the hot pan. "It was a challenging hunt for them, but they did so well." His eyes beamed with pride and predatory instinct. "They need challenges like that to grow into strong wolves."

Another question weighed on my mind, which he seemed to sense. When he finished laying the strips of bacon, he folded up the butcher paper and moved to sit next to me. The side of his body brushed mine in a clearly intentional move.

"What if that boar was a shifter?" I said in a low voice, watching the strips of meat sizzle. "Can you tell?"

"Yes," he said, putting a hand on my knee reassuringly. He was getting bolder with touching me lately and my insides did backflips. "We can smell if another animal is also human. Most shifters can sense it in some way."

I blew out a breath. "That makes me feel better."

"It is interesting to think about," he mused. "Why other animals are okay to kill but humans are not."

"Some humans should absolutely be killed," I spat with more venom than I intended. "Like the ones who captured and tortured you. Predators like Syko. And the ones who've hurt Connor so badly."

My mind drifted to the ex-fiancee who left him, and the woman sending him messages on his phone. I still hadn't brought that up. Every time I thought about it, I felt immature and stupid to be jealous. She had him before he was injured, then discarded him. The text asked, "Are you ever going to talk to me again?" which indicated he wasn't talking to whoever she was.

And regardless, I had no legs to stand on. He was encouraging me to be with other guys. What right did I have to get upset over a text?

Hunter picked up a pair of tongs and began flipping the bacon over. "I agree with you, Mel. But there are laws that protect humans and not other animals." He ran a hand through his silky hair that could've landed him on a shampoo commercial. "And predators like me prey on other animals to live. It's not that simple."

"Yeah," I agreed, still hypnotized by his hair.

"BABE!" Connor yelled from inside the trailer. "Come get coffee!"

"Yes, sir," I said sarcastically as I jumped the two steps to get inside.

"Hmm, I like it when you call me sir." He grabbed my waist and pulled me to stand between his muscular thighs for a kiss. While sitting on the counter, he was taller than me by several inches and seemed to enjoy the perspective.

"Well?" he inquired when our lips broke apart.

"Well, what?"

A naughty grin followed. "Has he asked you out yet?"

MELODY

I blinked. "Excuse me?"

"Ah, guess he hasn't. Shy fucker needs to step it up." Connor grinned as he pushed three mugs of piping hot coffee into my hands.

"Wait, are you and him like, planning this behind my back?"

"I prefer the term 'surprising you'. Maybe 'sweeping you off your feet'." He dropped a light kiss to my nose. "Just a date, babe, not a big deal. For you to get to know each other."

"Okay, but..." I struggled to put words to my feelings. "It's kind of weird that my boyfriend is also playing matchmaker."

"He makes you happy," he said matter-of-factly. "You light up like a goddamn Christmas tree every time you see him."

"Yes, but so do y—"

"I know I do, babe. This isn't about me, though." He took back the coffee mugs, set them down, and placed my hand over his heart. "I have you. I know that, and I'm secure in that fact. That guy," he jerked his chin out toward Hunter, "is a good dude. I'm comfortable calling him my friend and I want him to be happy too. If you're feeling him and he feels the same, he deserves to feel what I do when I wake up next to you. He's suffered so much, he deserves to taste a kiss like yours, babe."

"Goddamnit, Connor." I yanked my hand away from his chest to quickly wipe the tears building in my eyes. "You going from grumpy as hell to all sappy and sweet gives me whiplash sometimes."

"I'm here to keep you on your toes," he smirked with an affectionate final swat to my ass. Thrusting the coffee mugs into my hands once again, he added, "Just wait 'til I get you to make up with Raz."

"No." I froze, all humor and smile gone from my face. "Don't talk to me about him again. That's over and I mean it."

"It never had a chance to begin," he retorted before waving toward the door. "Let's move, babe. I don't want to eat no cold-ass bacon."

Clutching the three coffees for dear life, I held the door open with my back to allow Connor outside. Even without his prosthetic legs, his movements were swift and as natural to him as breathing. Once he was off the bottom step and on the ground outside, he pressed into the ground to lift his hips and thighs up, then walked *on his hands* to the log where Hunter was sitting. His butt and legs never touched the ground.

"Jesus, Connor. Making us look like shit," Hunter joked.

"It's all in the core, man. Thanks, babe," he said as I distributed coffee cups.

"So what you're saying is I should be doing sit-ups every day. Thank you, Mel." Hunter's smile made me melt a little as his hand brushed mine.

"Nah, sit-ups are pretty ineffective, to be honest. They only target your upper abs. You gotta do planks, leg lifts, and variations of those to hit your obliques too. But hey," he slapped Hunter on the back, "keep bringin' home the bacon, boy, and I'll keep sayin' you're in perfect shape."

"Trying to get in my pants, Con?" Hunter grinned.

"Keep on feeding me and I'll do anything you want," came the reply. "Maybe I'll even show Mel how certain things are done."

"Excuse me?!" I cried. "I didn't hear you complaining last night!"

"Kidding, babe." He blew a kiss in my direction, which I pretended to brush off.

The guys continued their bantering while I curled up with my coffee and crispy strips of bacon. It *was* really good. Flavorful with just enough fat and lean meat.

I chewed, savoring the taste while I listened to the guys talk with only half an ear. Not really paying attention to what they talked about, I just enjoyed hearing their voices.

They talked and interacted as if they'd been friends for years. Normally so wary and closed off, Connor's body language was relaxed and open. Hunter, too, had been extremely cautious at first. He only watched me for a few days at first because he didn't want to scare me with what he was, even though I never feared him, not even when he was howling and roaring in his cage before we rescued him.

While quieter and more soft-spoken than Connor, Hunter laughed genuinely as he sat back, listening to Connor's stories and antics. It warmed my heart to know he trusted us and wanted to hang around, despite the fact that we were in the same business that captured, tortured, and drugged not only him but his children.

Connor was in this business because of necessity. If he didn't perform, he would be another homeless, disabled veteran on the street. Me? The carnival was my only happy memory as a child, but my first night onstage proved to be a nightmare. It was only because of desperation for money that I stuck with it, lest I be homeless myself.

Only because of Connor's strict but encouraging coaching did I discover my love to perform. Nothing was as thrilling as walking onstage and commanding a crowd. By some kind of miracle, I became ringmistress when we ended up here in Crying Falls. I still couldn't believe we were selling out tickets. Connor, Razvan, and Hunter were all brilliant of course. I just hoped to do them justice by hyping them up well enough.

And still I couldn't ignore the fact that shifters were being captured and forced to perform as exotic freaks. It sickened me and did more than shatter my dream of the carnival as a happy escape from my home life. Hunter and Razvan were just the two that happened to be in this area. How many more could there be?

My dream returned to the forefront of my mind like a punch to the stomach. I was an animal behind bars. Predatory rage flowed through me like an overdose of adrenaline. I never wanted to kill someone so badly in my life. But what stood out the most right then was the Ferris wheel peeking out over tops of tents.

I wrapped my hands around my coffee cup and closed my eyes, trying hard to grasp any more details of that place, but they were already fleeting as dreams tend to be. I was so deep in my own mind, I didn't even realize Hunter came to sit beside me until I heard his soft, "Hey."

"Oh, shit!" I shrieked, nearly jumping out of my skin. "Hey!"

"Didn't mean to scare you," he laughed softly.

"You didn't. I was just... thinking about something," I said lamely, then looked over to where the guys were sitting before. "Where'd Con run off too?"

"Said he had to take a shit, so he'd be a few minutes or thirty," he smirked.

"Of course," I groaned.

Hunter's gaze dropped to the ground. He licked his lips, an act I wished my mind could record and play it back slowly.

He cleared his throat. "So hey Mel," he began, lacing his fingers and then undoing the motion. Then his hands closed into fists.

Oh god, he's nervous, I realized. I found it endearing and utterly adorable.

"Do you want to check out the carnival together?" he asked with a lopsided smile. "You know, like normal people."

"Just you and me?" I blurted out. Even though Connor told me this was coming, it did nothing to stop that rush of jittery nerves and pure glee when a crush asked you out. My pulse jumped to a racing beat while my stomach made victorious flips.

"Yeah, if that's cool with you." He swallowed. "Connor can come t—"

"No no, that's okay." I placed a hand on his forearm to reassure him. "I'd love to. Just you and me is totally cool. I'd, um," dare I say it? "I'd love to get to know you better."

His shy smile broke into a full-out grin. "Me too, Mel. And seriously, like," he ran a hand through his hair again and how the fuck was I supposed to resist him when he did that? "Absolutely no pressure or anything. We can just eat horrible food and shoot wooden ducks or whatever. I know you're with Con and this whole situation is just kind of weird."

"I know you two have been talking," I said. "And it is weird, but so far, I'm feeling okay with it as long as you two are."

"The feeling is mutual," he replied, his shoulders sagging like a weight was off them. "And if this makes things harder for you two, just say the word and I'll back off. You two are my friends first and I don't want to hurt either of you."

"I appreciate that," I said sincerely, even though I felt in my heart it would never be an issue. Hunter was on the short list of people that Connor trusted.

The thoughts weighing heavily on my mind were the ones I was still too scared to ask. Like, what would we tell his kids if things went really well between us? And before Hunter spoke to me and Connor, I had dreams about him much like the one I had last night. I still had no idea how to tell him or even if I should.

Even more, I was scared of what those dreams actually meant. I wasn't a shifter, I knew that. Both Hunter and Razvan said I smelled human, but slightly different. I had a strong suspicion both bits of information were connected, but how?

"Want me to come get you when the carnival opens?" Hunter asked, oblivious to my internal conflict.

"Sure!" I beamed at him. "It'll be less crowded that early."

"My thoughts exactly," he grinned as he rose to his feet. "See you in a bit, Mel."

"See you," I said, looking up at him dreamily. "Oh, and thanks for the bacon!"

"Any time." He paused, lingering as if he wanted to say or do something else, but then kept on moving. "Tell Connor I said bye."

"Will do."

I watched him walk away on his tall, lean frame toward the woods. Only when he was behind the dense brush did I catch a glimpse of his platinum hair turning into snowy white fur.

I curled back up in my chair, unable to keep the ridiculous grin off my face. I had a date with a sexy wolf shifter today!

✣   *3*   ✣

MELODY

"You nervous?" Connor teased.

I checked my mascara in the mirror again, stepped back, and straightened out my clothes.

"A little," I admitted. "I've never been on a real date before."

"Seriously?" he stared at me in disbelief. "If I'da known that, I would have wined and dined you way sooner."

"You still can." I flashed a smile at him over my shoulder. "After we get your new prosthetics. Those are more important."

"Fuck that," he grumbled, sliding his hands around my waist as he pressed a sensual kiss to the back of my neck. "You're more important."

"I like you healthy and not in pain," I informed him. "You're less grumpy that way."

"I always find a reason to be grumpy," he chuckled with a playful swat to my ass. "And I need a miracle to afford new legs, anyway. I'm definitely not waiting that long to make my girl feel special."

"You already make me feel special." I spun in his arms and kissed him deeply, not caring that I'd have to reapply my lipstick. With my hands wrapped around his strong neck, my lips and tongue told him without words exactly how I felt.

277

We parted breathlessly, pausing for half a beat.

"And if a miracle is what we need, then we'll make it happen." With that, I turned back to the mirror and popped open my lipstick tube.

"Ah, to be eighteen and full of hope again," he laughed. My age was his favorite jab at me whenever I tried being positive.

"You never know," I said, carefully applying the red pigment to my lips. "We did find people who can turn into animals after all."

Right on cue, three raps came to the trailer door and my heart jumped into my throat.

"Sup, Hunter. She'll be right out," Connor greeted.

With a final check over myself as they small-talked, I swallowed my nerves and left the bathroom. *Why am I so nervous, anyway?* I wondered. It wasn't like this was a blind date. I already knew Hunter.

"Hey," I greeted, hoping my nerves didn't show through my smile. "Long time no see." Damn, that sounded a lot less stupid in my head.

"Indeed." He returned my smile, giving me every indication he didn't notice or care how lame I was. "You look really nice, Mel."

"Really? Thanks!" I was just in shorts and a tank top, but they were the nicest thrift store buys I owned. "So do you."

He traded the T-shirt for a gray button down that accentuated his tall, lean frame. The sleeves rolled up to his elbows showed off the slender, corded muscles of his forearms.

"I clean up nice when I got somewhere to be," he remarked with a lopsided grin and held his hand out. "Shall we?"

I nodded, and he took my outstretched fingers with a firm but gentle grip as I stepped out of the trailer.

"Have fun, kids. Don't do anything that I wouldn't do," Connor called after us.

"So, do everything! Got it," I shot back over my shoulder.

My boyfriend just laughed and closed the trailer door as I left for my carnival date with another man.

"Wow, he's really not bothered," Hunter mused as his fingers laced through mine. My heart collided against my ribs at the touch.

"Did you expect him to be?"

"No, I know he's a man of his word. I'm just more used to humans being so possessive of their mates. It's surprising when they don't treat their partners like property."

"I never thought about it like that," I mused as we walked through the carnival gate, waving to the ticket attendant who knew me as the ringmistress. No one recognized Hunter without his fur, teeth, and claws, and we preferred it that way.

"Hardly anyone does anymore, at least consciously." Hunter gave my hand an affectionate squeeze as we looked around at the attractions. The carnival had just opened for the day and some vendors and booth attendants were just setting up.

"Does it bother *you* being here?" I asked him. "Knowing what goes on behind the scenes?"

"In general, yes. I hate how exploitive this whole industry is, and not just of shifters. People like Connor, too." He smiled down at me. "But it's good to know this one isn't like that. And anyway, I'm here with you and determined to have a good time."

"Right. Sorry to talk about negative stuff."

"Don't be, Mel." His thumb stroked my palm. "So, what are you in the mood for? Food? Rides? Games?"

"Ooh, shaved ice!" I said, pointing. A cold dessert never sounded so good right then. At noon in the middle of summer in Mississippi, the humidity already hung in the air with a palpable thickness. Beads of sweat ran down the back of my neck like a lover's tongue and I prayed my makeup wouldn't start running.

Hunter stepped up to the truck with no hesitation and ordered for us. I got a pina colada flavored one, and he got a root beer float.

"Thanks." I accepted the frozen treat from him, swept up in the surreality of a guy buying something for me just because he wanted to.

"Thank the ringmistress. She got me a job," he winked, sticking a red plastic spoon in my cup of sugary ice.

A hula hooper danced for a small crowd not far away, so we sat down on a retaining wall to watch her and enjoy our shaved ice.

"What was your life like growing up?" I asked Hunter. "Did your pack have a lot of contact with humans?"

"We did at first," he answered, chopping at his own ice with the tiny spoon. "My pack was well known in a small town in Virginia, right on the edge of Jefferson National Forest. My father was the town butcher and liked by everybody. My mother was a teacher at the local elementary school, where I attended with all the other human children. Back then it was in our best interest to integrate with human society as much as possible, while keeping our animal sides hidden."

I hesitated before pressing. "But that's not the case anymore?"

He spooned some shaved ice into his mouth and shook his head. "Some human locals saw my parents shift and started a witch hunt, or wolf hunt rather," he scoffed. "I was in high school at the time. Our alpha pulled all of us out for our own safety and we had minimal contact with humans since then. Whenever we did, we never stayed in one place long."

He set his cup down and rested both forearms on his knees. "It's hard because we're human, too. We want comforts like a bed, a shower, and a home with a roof. We want our children to be educated, have good careers, and stable families of their own. It sounds like an easy solution to just live as an animal for the rest of your life, but we crave human lives too."

"Shit, Hunter." I chewed my lip, the sweetness of the shaved ice now cloying on my tongue. "I'm sorry. This is supposed to be a fun day and I keep making you bring up heavy stuff."

"Don't worry about it." He nudged me with his elbow and shot me a heart-fluttering smile. "That's just life for a shifter. I don't mind talking about it. And anyway," he picked up my spoon, holding a big chunk of shaved ice near my mouth, "we're making new memories, better ones."

I parted my lips and allowed him to place the spoon on my tongue, watching him watch me with those sharp, golden eyes.

"And hopefully I'm giving Roo and Rinna a better life too," he concluded, breaking the intimate, brief spell between us to return his attention to the hula hooper.

"Are they okay alone while you're out here?" Hunter's children reminded me of my own siblings in many ways. Rambunctious, curious, and far too innocent for a world that could be so dark.

"Yes, they know not to leave the den when I'm away. It's instilled in all wolf pups when the adults go on long hunts. They're generally more independent than human children because of that."

"What do you think is best for shifters in general?" I asked, scraping the edges of my styrofoam cup. "Integrating with humans or staying far away from them?"

Hunter let out a long sigh and took a moment to answer. He looked like a marble statue as he thought—still, beautiful, and wise.

"If there was a way to be among humans peacefully, with the same rights and protections, and without being hunted for what we are, I think that would be best for everyone. Because it's impossible to hide from humans forever. Even if we created our own community away from everyone else, the wrong humans will undoubtedly try to round us up for their own gains. That's essentially what happened to my pack."

It made the most sense, but would be the most difficult to achieve. Just the public knowledge of shifter existence would throw the world into chaos.

I threw my now-empty cup in the nearby trash can and wrapped my palm underneath his bicep. The slender muscle jumped at my contact.

"No more heavy conversations," I said in a mock stern voice. "Let's play some stupid games and try to win gigantic teddy bears and shit."

His face lit up immediately as he closed his opposite hand around mine.

"Shall we make it interesting?" he grinned wolfishly.

"How so?" I narrowed my eyes in suspicion as I stood from the wall, allowing my fingers to slide down his arm to his hand.

"The winner chooses what ride we go on afterward," he smirked, threading his fingers through mine as he followed. "Loser sucks it up and deals."

"Hah! Joke's on you. I love crazy rides," I declared. "Maybe I'll lose on purpose so you can give me all your spoils," I added with an exaggerated batting of my eyelashes.

"No way." He pointed at a balloon and darts booth up ahead. "That unicorn is mine."

"Yours or Rinna's?" I giggled. The plush unicorn on display was the size of a large dog, with a long golden horn and a rainbow-colored tail and mane.

"Mine," he repeated in mock seriousness before a smile cracked his face. "But will probably end up hers."

"Don't worry if you lose, I'll win it for you," I teased as we stepped up to the booth.

"Aren't you a little fox," he shot right back, his fingertips grazing my waist and lower back as he approached the attendant to pay.

It was the first time I heard anything resembling a nickname from him, and the touching only made me hyper aware of that word's implications.

"I can't tell if that's a good or bad thing, coming from you."

He caught me in that golden gaze, as I'm sure many prey animals had been before. I felt captured, frozen to my spot, but not afraid.

"Good for you. Bad for me."

"Why's that?"

He handed cash to the booth attendant and accepted a handful of darts in return.

"Because a clever fox can drive a wolf crazy."

❧ 4 ❧

MELODY

Despite several tries, neither of us won the unicorn.

"I bet all of these games are rigged," I muttered as we walked away in defeat, both of our wallets much lighter without anything to show for it.

"Just 'cause they don't traffic shifters doesn't mean they're saints," Hunter chuckled.

We tried a few different game booths, losing badly at every one. The ring toss attendant felt bad enough that he gave us consolation prizes—toy squirt guns, which Hunter and I had too much fun chasing and shooting each other with.

After a few minutes of playfully squirting each other, I asked if we could call a truce. Hunter agreed. And then I stuck my gun under his shirt to blast his bare skin.

"Ah! This is what I'm talking about, you little fox," he growled playfully as I darted away, cackling.

He got me back just as badly—wrapping a long arm around my waist, holding my back against his chest while his other hand disappeared under the hem of my tank top. I barely had time to register how much of him was touching me when I felt the plastic nozzle against my bellybutton and the icy blast that followed.

283

"Ahhh! I give, I give! You win!" I shrieked.

"Not falling for that again." His warm breath fanned against my ear, his torso a solid wall of heat against my back. The contact of him against me almost distracted me from his relentless squirt gun assault until...

"Hunterrrr! It's dripping into my underwear!"

He released me, laughing so hard he nearly fell over.

"Say that louder. I don't think the whole carnival heard you," he gasped, before bursting into laughter again.

Meanwhile, I waddled around in a circle, bending over in front and trying to look behind to see if I appeared to pee myself.

"Maybe a few rides to dry ourselves off?" Hunter suggested, still chuckling as he wiped his eyes.

"Good idea, but I pick." I glared at him although I wasn't really mad. His eyes heated as I grabbed the wet spot on his shirt to pull him closer to me. "I dunno, though. I kind of like you in a wet shirt."

His arms slid around me and, despite their warmth, did nothing to soothe the goosebumps erected on my skin.

"I can say the same thing about you." His voice was laced with huskiness.

My forearms braced against his chest, but his heartbeat didn't feel nearly as fast or erratic as mine. One of his hands pressed a warm imprint between my shoulder blades, the other traced my jaw with the lightest brush of a fingertip. My gaze fell to his lips, where I saw a smile twitching to get out.

"What?" I asked.

"I was thinking," he said with a lip bite so small I almost missed it, "that I could make a joke about wet underwear, but I don't want to scare you away."

I couldn't help but laugh at that. "Really, Hunter? I got desensitized to offensive jokes when I was a toddler. You'd need to do a lot worse than that to scare me away."

He shrugged, bringing his caress on my face to a pause. "That's not really my style, anyway. Maybe Connor's influence."

I groaned, rolling my eyes skyward. He was absolutely right that

Connor would not pass up the opportunity for an inappropriate joke. Neither would Razvan.

Stop. We are not thinking about him. Especially not right now.

"Well, whatever your style is, I want to learn about it." Feeling emboldened, I slid my hands up over his shoulders to wrap around his neck. "I want to learn all about *you*, Hunter."

His forehead lightly touched mine as his face grew closer. My pulse became a mad, rushing river in my ears as his lips filled my vision, parting as they nearly reached mine—

"OY! YOU, GIRL!"

I jumped back, startled at the voice that sounded like it yelled right next to my ear. Hunter immediately pulled me back tightly against him with a protective growl.

"Ya can do that cupcakin' later. We need to talk, girl."

The speaker was an ebony-skinned woman wearing a wraparound dress in a bright purple tribal pattern. Her hair was wrapped up in a matching purple fabric. She spoke with an accent I couldn't place and beckoned me with one long, purple fingernail.

A dark tent stood behind her with a wooden painted sign reading Madame Thembi - Fortune Teller.

"No thank you, ma'am," I smiled politely. "I'm not interested."

The woman's lips pulled back into a smile. "I'm not askin' ya, Melody."

Her jaws parted just enough to allow a long, slender, forked tongue to flick out and taste the air.

MELODY

I blinked, and the serpent's tongue was gone. Only a bright, cheery smile with a slight gap in her front teeth shined on the woman's face.

"Ya know what I am. Don't act scared, girl." She nodded at Hunter. "Ya doggy boy can rip my throat out faster than I can strike. Ya have questions and if ya come in, I can find ya the answers."

"You don't have to, Mel," Hunter growled low next to my ear. "Just say the word and we can walk away."

"She's a shifter," I breathed, barely above a whisper.

"Yes, but something's off," he snarled. "She knows what I am, but she smells human to me."

That should have spurred me to move along and quickly. But I stood rooted to my spot, unable to take my eyes off the woman. She seemed thoroughly amused by my wide-eyed stare, chuckling and shaking her head.

"Do you know what I am?"

The words tumbled out as if someone else controlled my mouth. I never voiced any of my questions to anyone, except when telling Connor about my dreams. He wrote them off as just that, dreams, but their vividness plagued my waking thoughts and sensations too. The more I tried to explain them away, the more vividly they came.

"Oh yes I do, girl," the woman's grin widened. "Never thought I'd see another one of ya in my lifetime, but here ya are."

Hearing that was enough to take one step toward her and then another.

"Mel!" Hunter hissed, pulling my arm back. "Are you sure?"

I looked back at him. "You and Razvan both said I smell human, but different. I've had... dreams and stuff involving you that I haven't told you because I don't know what any of it means." He said nothing as I wrapped my hands around his arm, just continued to eye the snake-shifter woman suspiciously. "Stay close to me just in case, but I really think she knows things about me that I don't."

His face hardened into a scowl, but he followed me to the woman's tent. She promptly flipped her fortune teller sign over to say CLOSED before pulling aside the black mesh curtain to let us in.

A spicy, smoky aroma filled my senses immediately. It wasn't bad, just incredibly strong. The dark tent was lit by dozens of small tea light candles, flickering with the slightest movement as we assembled inside.

Hunter immediately ducked to avoid hitting the various dried herbs, wind chimes, and talismans hanging from the ceiling. A low wooden coffee table sat in the middle of the tent with an assortment of crystals, incense, candles, and herbs strewn across its surface.

"Sit," the woman instructed, pointing to a pair of cushions across from the coffee table.

Hunter and I did so, his legs so long, he had to cross them at the ankles with his knees pointing straight up.

"Um, do I call you Madame Thembi?" I asked as the woman settled across the table from us.

"Thembi is fine," she said, blowing out the incense and waving her hand to dispel the smoke.

"How do you know what I am?" I asked, not caring to dance around the subject. "And what exactly is that?"

She let out a small, bubbly laugh. "Just like a shifter can sense another nearby shifter, a shaman can sense a shaman."

"A...what?"

"I couldn't sense you," Hunter growled. "But," he took a deep inhale, "you smell like Melody. Human with something else."

"Good boy!" Thembi praised with a small clap of her hands. "You're understanding now." If he'd been within reach, I'd have no doubt she would have patted his head.

Hunter's eyes narrowed and I could practically see his wolf form with bared teeth and ears pinned back.

"Fortunately for us," Thembi gestured between me and her, "we can sense shifters as well as our own kind."

"Our... own kind?" I repeated. "Are you saying I'm *not* human?"

"No, girl," Thembi huffed in annoyance. "Of course you're human. He told ya himself, ya smell like it. But," she leaned across the table, lowering her voice, "ya can give the illusion you're not." Her snake tongue flitted out again, proving her point and making me jump back off my seat.

"Not only that," she returned to sitting upright with a laugh, "ya can sense when shifters are near. If one is in need, ya can feel him pull to ya. Ya know what I'm talkin' about, ah?"

I thought back to my first night working in Drowningville, when I only knew of Hunter as the fabled Wolf Man. In reality, he and his kids had been drugged and forced to partially shift in order to make them all look like werewolves—standing upright while covered in fur, not quite human or animal.

The ringmaster hyped it up for an entire week. Connor was convinced it was all a hoax, a scam to make people part with their money, but I still felt like I needed to see them. I couldn't understand why, but something in me pulled me to that stage like an invisible leash. And when most humans reacted with horror and fear, I saw him, caged and abused, and could only feel a heart-splitting sorrow.

And again with Razvan. Despite finding him too arrogant for his own good and intimidating as hell with all those tattoos covering him, I felt an inexplicable pull to him. When we walked together alone in the woods, and when he showed me his dragon form, I was never afraid for a moment. Honestly, I couldn't understand why other humans were so afraid of shifters.

"Yes," I breathed, returning my focus back to the smoky, dimly lit tent. "I felt them pull to me and I've had... interesting dreams."

"Ah-hah, I was just gettin' to that!" Thembi slapped her knees with another cheerful laugh. With each minute that passed, I felt myself relaxing. She was no threat, and I even began to like her. "What have ya seen, girl?"

I turned to Hunter, my heart threatening to leap out of my throat. For some reason, I felt like I was about to confess a shameful secret.

"I saw you, in human form," I told him. "Before you approached me and Connor. That was how I knew you were the wolves we rescued. I recognized you from my dream." My eyes darted up to Thembi, hesitant to say the next part.

"Go on, girl," she encouraged, her whiskey-colored eyes sharp enough to see through my soul. "Tell the rest of it."

I swallowed and took a deep breath. "In most of my dreams, I feel like I *am* a shifter. I see through their eyes and experience what they're doing in animal form. And they feel so vivid, not like dreams at all but memories."

Hunter slid an arm around me, but I couldn't bring myself to meet his eyes. His lips pressed through my hair. At any point I would have been giddy, but he still didn't know. The worst was still to come.

"I think... I'm pretty sure," I choked to get the words out, "I saw through the eyes of your mate before she was killed."

In an instant, his body against me went from warm and comforting to stiff and cold. He pulled away to look at me with a harrowed expression.

"What makes you think that? How do you know it was her?"

"I was hunting with you," I explained. "I was a black wolf. You were the white one. We were stalking an elk herd."

His eyes doubled in size, and the color drained from his face.

"You were the distraction. I went in for the kill. That was our strategy," I went on. "And I... Fuck, Hunter, I'm so sorry."

"You what?" Hunter demanded.

"I knew I was pregnant."

✵ *6* ✵

HUNTER

S he didn't want to hurt me. The pained expression on her face told me that loud and clear, but it didn't stop the years-old wounds from reopening.

I saw the life leaving Audra's eyes just as clearly as I saw Mel in front of me. So much blood, and the final whispered plea she begged of me before I lost her.

"I'm so sorry, Hunter." Mel reached for me hesitantly, as if I would bite her. "I didn't know how to stop it. I didn't want to invade your privacy like that."

"I know." The words came out colder than intended, and she flinched. "When did you dream this?"

"Um." She composed herself to think. "Right before you talked to me and Connor that first time. So, almost two weeks ago?"

"How is that possible?" I directed the question at Thembi. "My mate died five years ago."

"Ah, nothin' ever truly dies, doggy boy," she waved an index finger at me. "Ya mate was taken in an abrupt and violent way. Her *yanna*, her spirit, is still earthbound. But ya cannot know or see that. Only a shaman can."

290

"So what, she's a ghost? And haunting Mel, or is Mel haunting her? And why the hell have *I* never heard of a shaman?"

The drudged-up memories and feelings I'd long since buried turned my mood sour and snappish. Mel and I had been having so much fun, too. I'd been fantasizing about kissing her for days, and it nearly happened. Now all I wanted to do was race through the woods on all fours. Alone.

"Down, boy." This woman really seemed to get a kick out of treating me like a dog. "Nah, she's no ghost. That term is too simple. And ya've never heard of a shaman because they're rare. It's a gift that is given, not inherited. Only another shaman can pass on the gift. Fewer and fewer have done so in recent years, so we are slowly dyin' out." She chuckled amusedly. "Like the dodo."

"So someone gave me these abilities?" Mel asked. "How is it given exactly?"

"Depends on the giver. You can direct your powers into an object and give that to someone. My master just did this." Thembi pressed her palm to her forehead. "Nothing happened, of course. I was a child and the gifts don't become apparent until ya turn eighteen."

"An object?" Mel suddenly slapped at her shorts and looked frantically through her pockets until she produced a coin that looked like a carnival token. "Like this?"

Thembi cackled delightedly as she slapped her knees. "It's startin' to make sense, ah, girl?"

"I still don't understand," Mel muttered. "Like, okay. Shamans have these powers and I've experienced these... visions. But what's the point? *Why* am I seeing these things?"

"A good question." Thembi adjusted her seat. "The long-held belief is that shamans are the bridge between humans and shifters. They blend in with the humans but also protect shifters from inevitable conflict with humans. Centuries ago, shamans were far more numerous. Ya could find about ten shifters to one shaman. Shifters would flock toward shamans to be their human representative, more or less." She cleared her throat and shot us a knowing grin. "Because most shamans were female, she would find herself surrounded by multiple shifter men. I'm sure ya can see where I'm goin' with that."

An unmistakable blush rose in Mel's cheeks. If my dead ex-mate hadn't been brought to the forefront of my mind, I would have found it adorable. It made complete sense as to why Razvan and I were so drawn to her, and why she never showed an ounce of fear when we revealed ourselves.

"Why have shamans stopped passing on their gifts?" I asked. "It would seem like we need them now more than ever."

Thembi's jovial face turned into a frown. "Yes, shifters are in dire straits now, exactly because of the lack of shamans for them to turn to. With no humans on ya side, the rest are treatin' ya like livestock." She ran a hand down her face with a sigh. "Shamans used to be respected among humans, until public opinion started changin'. We started bein' seen as crazy people. Talkin' to animals and havin' visions didn't belong in a world with modern science and medicine. Nobody wanted to be targeted, so they stopped passin' on the gifts."

"That's a terrible reason," Mel echoed my thoughts. "Leaving shifters to suffer at the hands of humans with no one to back them up? Just because they didn't want to be made fun of?"

"It went beyond that, girl," Thembi replied in a scolding tone. "Some got locked up in institutions back in the day. Others even got hanged and drowned as witches, goin' way back. At the end of the day, people had to save their own hides."

"That's what it always comes down to," I muttered, more to myself than anyone else. "Survival."

Small fingers gave my palm a hesitant stroke. I closed my hand around Mel's, hoping she would see that I wasn't angry. I wouldn't lash out at her. I was just consumed by things I'd rather forget.

"Why can't I sense shifters or other shamans?" she asked, her voice sounding far away from me. "I didn't sense you just now."

"A gift still needs to be developed, girl," Thembi answered. "Ya need to practice listening. Stop all those chattering voices in ya head and listen to the deepest part of ya." She pointed at her own chest. "When did ya turn eighteen?"

"A few weeks ago," Mel replied.

"Hah! I'm surprised ya've had dreams already. That's half the battle, girl. Listen to ya instincts. Humans are animals too, don't forget."

Another set of fingers closed around my bicep, and Mel's voice became much closer.

"I think we need some time to process this. Will you still be here if I have more questions?"

"Yes, girl. 'Til the end of the carnival this weekend. Take care of ya doggy boy. He's not a in good place right now."

A gentle pull to my feet and a few steps later, fresh air and sun hit my senses.

"Hey." Two hands flew to either side of my face and I found myself looking down into a pair of warm, brown eyes. "Are you okay?"

"Not really," I admitted. "You didn't mention it, so I don't think you saw what happened after the hunt."

Mel shook her head. "No, Hunter. I don't need to—"

"A hunter shot her," I said, my voice flat. "As she was dying, she begged me to take the pups and run. She was carrying two. Only one was alive." I looked toward the direction of the den, where the only two living memories of my mate remained. "That was Rinna."

"Oh, Hunter..."

Mel's arms went around my waist as she pressed her cheek to my chest.

"I'm so sorry," she murmured into my shirt. "I'll get a hang of this... gift, one way or another. I don't want to dig through your past. I don't want to bring up painful things for you or anyone."

"I know." I tucked her head under my chin and rubbed my hands across her back. "It doesn't hurt as much anymore, not like it used to. I just... didn't want to think about it again. Especially not today."

"Damn it." She looked up at me and huffed out a humorless laugh. "No matter what we do, we can't seem to have a fun, easy day, huh?"

I let out a heavy sigh, determined to get out from under the black cloud settling over me. "The day is still young, though." I stroked her face, trying to lose myself in those wide brown eyes instead of being haunted by cold dead ones.

"Let's go on some rides." I grabbed her hands and began walking us in the direction of the Ferris wheel and all the brightly lit rides surrounding it.

"You're seriously in the mood for rides?" Mel asked, catching up with my long strides.

"No, but I want to get out of this mood I'm in," I draped an arm over her shoulders, "and go back to enjoying my day with you."

MELODY

I had to admit, screaming my lungs out after a few hundred-foot drops felt incredibly cathartic. With Hunter grinning next to me, my feet dangling in midair, and the heavy ride harness secured over my chest, the day almost felt blissfully normal again. The adrenaline took over and I could forget about Thembi's haunting words for at least another few hours.

We were smart enough to get food *after* rides and walked through the vendor booths, checking out the clothes, jewelry, weapons, and other crafts as we munched on corn dogs. My stomach flipped uncomfortably as we strolled past the metalsmith tables. This was where I first saw Razvan, flipping knives flawlessly through the air like he was born to do it.

I half expected to see him here, maybe running his tattooed fingers over the array of sharp metal blades. Maybe with a girl or two on his arms as he showed off his skills for them, a preview before showing them what he could do with that split tongue.

I could still taste how that kiss felt, and thought about it more than I'd ever admit. He kissed me onstage in front of everyone on our opening night. The gentle caress on my lips from both sides of his tongue was unlike anything I ever felt before. And then it was over before I could blink. The crowd loved it, seeing it as part of his bad boy charm. But he cheated on his girlfriend by kissing me.

Maybe it was hypocritical of me, seeing as I was essentially dating Hunter *and* Connor, but I could never be with a man who kept other girls on the side. At least with my two guys, I felt like they valued me enough not to kiss anyone behind my back. And I wanted to make damn sure they knew I cared about them just as much.

The afternoon shadows grew long as we wrapped up our window shopping. Hunter kept his arm around me as we walked together, with the occasional squeeze of my shoulder or caress of my neck. I snuggled happily into his side with my arm around his waist. His long, lean muscles moved fluidly with each step and damn, he smelled good.

"What do you think, one last ride?" he suggested, looking up at the Ferris wheel.

I couldn't believe how late it had gotten already. The day flew by and I never wanted it to end.

"Okay," I said wistfully. "As long as it's a slow ride."

The moment we sat in the capsule and began the gentle ascent upward, Hunter wasted no time in getting cozy.

"No one can interrupt us now," he whispered against my hair, pulling me closer.

My heart crashing against my sternum, I turned to face him but found his eyes looking straight ahead.

Colorful lights, tents, and flags stood out against the dense, dark forest. Organ music and joyful voices echoed through the grounds, floating up to us as gentle background noise. Hunter's eyes remained fixated on the dense trees in the distance, far away from people and lights.

"Don't blame yourself," I told him, placing a hand on his knee. "If you could have saved all of them, I'm sure you would have."

"I know," he sighed. "It's a decision I made peace with a long time ago, then buried it in the past. I had to move on for Roo and Rinna. Now it just feels like all that progress is undone."

"I'm so sorry!" I took one of his hands and squeezed it as if my newfound shaman powers could take away all his suffering. "I shouldn't have kept it from you, but I was so torn on telling you for exactly that reason."

"It's okay, Mel. Really. It sucks, but it has been a long time. It's nowhere near as painful as when losing her was fresh. All I can do is let the feeling pass."

The Ferris wheel paused as we reached the top. His arm around me felt snug and secure, holding me close to him like this date had no hiccups at all. Our temples leaned against each other as we quietly watched the carnival from our place in the sky. We were untouchable here. Despite everything trying to pull us back down, this quiet place, high and alone, gave us a sense of serenity.

"In a weird way," Hunter said softly. "I'm not *glad*, but I can appreciate everything that's happened. Losing her. Getting captured, all of it."

"How can you say that?" I turned to face him, my nose brushing his cheek.

He faced me, his mouth hovering within an inch of mine.

"Because it all led me to this moment with you."

I don't know who leaned in first. All I knew was our lips met—gently, but with intention. Our kiss unfolded like a slow, partnered dance. Hunter threaded his fingers through my hair with one hand, cupping my face sweetly with the other. He tasted warm, comforting, and oh-so-delicious. It felt like everything you'd imagine from kissing a romantic Disney prince.

But in his kiss, I also felt a hot undercurrent of raw masculinity and alpha confidence. Somehow I knew it was his wolf, the animal in him, feeling the urge to claim a mate, to dominate and possess. This confidence was quiet and primal, not brash and showing off. I felt it in the way he held the back of my neck as he explored my mouth further. I felt it in the way my whole body shivered when he ran a hand down my thigh.

"Ride's over. Two bucks if you want to stay on."

The bored attendant's voice barely registered in my mind. Hunter shifted in his seat to pull out some bills and tossed them to the attendant. His lips never fully separated from mine, not even when we smiled and giggled as we began another ride up.

I don't know how many times we went around, only that I couldn't get enough of Hunter's lips and tongue. Kissing him was so intoxicating, a light soreness tingled through my lips once we parted for a breath. I opened my eyes to find daylight quickly fading, giving way to a brilliant pink and purple sky.

"So much for just one ride," Hunter chuckled with a kiss to my cheek.

"How long have we been up here?" I giggled, curling my legs under me on the seat.

"No idea. I think I threw twenty bucks at him." His eyes flickered from my lips across my face, as if debating kissing me again. "I should probably get you back to Connor soon," he added.

"Connor is not my dad," I giggled, laying my head against his shoulder. "But you should probably get back to Roo and Rinna."

"Yeah," he sighed, sweeping the lightest of kisses across my mouth before standing and pulling me to my feet.

"Hey, um." I chewed my lip nervously as he led me off the platform and down the rusted metal steps, his fingers firmly laced through mine. "Do you want to do this again?"

"Are you kidding?"

His smile was electric as he lifted our connected hands and twirled me. I spun in place, feeling like a princess as I finished the twirl with my back pressed to his chest and his arm around my waist.

He kissed me tenderly, smiling against my lips. "I'd like nothing more." Somehow my jello legs didn't give out from underneath me as he unwrapped his arms and we resumed walking like normal people. "Maybe I'll take you dancing, though. I'm feeling a little sick of carnivals at this point."

I swung our hands back and forth between us as I gathered my nerves for the next question.

"Are you going to say anything to Roo and Rinna?"

"I'm not sure," he answered after a moment of thinking. "Maybe not in a super serious, obvious way. They know you and like you. They know *I* like you." He brought the back of my palm to his lips and placed a kiss there. "If this keeps going well, I think they'll figure it out naturally just from seeing us together."

"What if they ask questions?" I pulled his arm back over my shoulders.

"Then we answer them," he said lightly. "I don't lie to them about anything and you don't have to either." He stopped abruptly in his tracks and took a deep inhale. "There's a shifter nearby. Can you sense him?"

I looked around, only seeing a sea of carnival-goers.

"Not with your eyes. He's near, but is staying out of sight. Can you tell he's here?" He spoke low and close to my ear, giving the illusion of whispering sweet nothings to those passing by.

"No," I sighed in frustration. "I don't know how to sense them like you do."

"Remember what Thembi told you," he encouraged gently. "Quiet everything else and focus on your deeper instincts."

"How do I do that?"

"Close your eyes and tune everything out. Listen to the animal part of you. Not the human."

I felt stupid but did as he suggested anyway, taking a deep breath as I closed my eyes. Focusing on the weight of his arm on my shoulders like an anchor, all the voices and music of the carnival faded to a dull white noise.

The air seemed to shift direction as I tuned out the distractions. The smell of popcorn and deep-fried sugar faded away, replaced by... smoke?

A sense of comfort passed over me as I picked up the smoky smell, like I was in a cozy cabin with a roaring fireplace. A chill tried to nip at my skin, but the heat of the fire chased it away. This wasn't the swampy, humid forests of Mississippi anymore. This place felt much colder, cleaner. It also felt... unusual in a way I couldn't explain. Almost unreal and magical, like a place out of a fairytale.

Something hot and scaly brushed against my back, then a hard, sharp point like a knife dragged down my cheek. Both touches floated across me gently, like a caress. I didn't fear them, despite sensing the burning heat and power of this shifter. Whoever it was, they only wanted it to protect me. This person cared about me.

My eyes snapped open, the recognition hitting me like a brick wall.

"Razvan," I breathed. "It's Raz. He's here."

MELODY

Raz stepped out from behind a food cart, his inked skin and all black clothing giving him an ominous, dark presence over the bright, colorful carnival decor. He wore an apprehensive look on his face as he approached me and Hunter, like he might go back on this decision at any moment.

"Hey, Mel," he greeted dryly, hands shoved in his pockets casually, but the tension in his shoulders cut through the air like swords as he walked closer to us.

My heart clenched uncomfortably. I'd almost forgotten the smooth, dark honey of his voice, clipped with that lilting Romanian accent. The type of voice that every woman fantasized about whispering dirty things into her ears.

Still, I couldn't find my voice to answer. Thankfully, he focused on Hunter for a moment and stuck out a tattooed hand.

"I don't think we've formally met. I'm Razvan. Call me Raz."

"Evening, Raz. I'm Hunter." He accepted the dragon's handshake. "What are you up to tonight?"

Raz's steel-gray eyes flicked over to me. I clamped my mouth shut, biting the inside of my cheek. I said my piece to him already. There was nothing left to say and no reason for him to approach us.

"I didn't want to interrupt your time together," he shifted uncomfortably in his lace-up motorcycle boots. "But I was wondering if I could have a word with Mel for a few minutes."

"No." The word spat through my lips like a rotten piece of food. "I'm done talking to you."

"Mel... *steluţa*." His voice strained with the plea as he stepped toward me. Hearing that name he used to call me was just another twist of the knife in my gut.

"Don't call me that," I hissed, stepping back and hiding halfway behind Hunter. The look of pain on Raz's face just about killed me too.

"Mel, please." Desperation laced his words. "This is a misunderstanding. Ally was never my girlfriend. She wanted that, but I never did. Not with her."

"So you used her," I spat from behind Hunter's arm. "She had feelings for you and you still slept with her. You lead her on. You *knew* kissing me would hurt her!"

"I..." He snapped his mouth shut and shook his head, scratching his nails through his dark hair buzzed close to his scalp. He couldn't even deny it, and that just made my heart hurt more.

"I'm not doing that anymore," he protested. "I don't want to hurt anyone, especially not you."

"I'm not hurt. I'm just fine." The lie tasted bitter on my tongue. "I have Connor. And Hunter. I don't need a man who uses girls and discards them when he's bored."

"That's *not* what I am!"

He roared the denial with enough anger to make people stop and look at us. Mothers pulled their young children close as they hurried away. Thankfully, no one was close enough to catch the smoke wisping out of the corners of his mouth, nor the glow of fire just behind his teeth.

"Okay, this isn't getting us anywhere." Hunter stepped between us with a raised hand. "Both of you need to cool off if you want to have a productive conversation about this."

"I don't want to have *any* more conversations with him." My fingers dug into Hunter's forearm, though I couldn't seem to tear my gaze away from Raz.

"Razvan, dude," Hunter addressed him in a kind but firm tone. "If she doesn't want to talk to you, you need to respect that."

"You said you trusted me," he ignored Hunter, our gazes locked. "Why are you taking the word of some girl who almost attacked you over *me*?"

"I guess I was wrong to trust you," I answered as coldly as I could muster.

His handsome face morphed from shock to a frightening scowl of rage. Hunter pushed me further back behind him, his whole body rigid as he stared down at the furious dragon shifter.

"I'm not like all the men your trashy mother brought home, Melody," Razvan leaned forward as he spat the words, until his chest met Hunter's hand, braced out to keep a distance between us. "If you weren't such a damned stubborn child, you'd be able to see that."

"Back the hell up," Hunter growled, his teeth bared and looking longer than normal. "I'm warning you."

Raz blinked, jerking his eyes away from me and meeting Hunter's as if seeing him there for the first time. His twisted scowl remained. A low, rumbling canine growl escaped Hunter's chest. For a terrifying moment, I wondered if those two would actually get into it.

Raz broke eye contact first and stepped back with his hands raised.

"We're cool, wolf. I got no beef to hash out with you." Not even sparing me a glance, the tattooed dragon shifter turned and disappeared into the fading light.

Transfixed on watching the back of his black leather jacket become smaller as he walked off, I waited. I didn't dare take my eyes away, just in case.

But there was no hesitation, not even a glance over his shoulder as he walked away from me for probably the last time. When he was out of sight, I kept watching, my hope crumbling away with every passing second he didn't come back.

"Hey." Hunter tilted my chin up to face him, his golden eyes concerned and his teeth now human sized. "You okay?"

"Yeah, fine," I mumbled distractedly. A lie and he knew it.

He pulled me against him and rubbed a warm, soothing hand down my back. "He shouldn't have said that," he murmured with a kiss on my forehead. "It was uncalled for."

"It was true, though." I continued our walk out of the carnival grounds and back toward the campsite. "He was absolutely right."

"That doesn't mean he has to throw it in your face like that," Hunter replied with a soft growl. "He did that to hurt you and that's not cool, Mel."

Razvan was the one I opened up the most to about my past. I told him details I never even told Connor, like my alcoholic mom's endless string of boyfriends who were not only drunks themselves, but abusive to me and my siblings. And the fact that I didn't drink was because I learned alcoholism was often passed down from parent to child. I saw my older sister follow in my mother's footsteps and refused to let that be me.

Just knowing the potential to become that kind of person was inside me, unlocked by a certain substance, gave me massive self-worth issues growing up. I did okay in school, but no one wanted to be friends with me because I lived in the trailer park. Boys saw me as good enough to hook up with but never date, which prompted rumors about me being just like my mom—screwing every guy that looked her way and ending up pregnant too many times. And to no one's surprise, her baby daddies always bailed.

Razvan was sweet and a good listener when I opened up about not drinking, or at least he appeared to be. He then showed me his dragon shift and said I was the only human he had shown that form to. He certainly never indicated he would throw the shame of my upbringing in my face.

I *never* wanted to be like my mom and became overly suspicious of men's motives as a result. And yet here I was, juggling my feelings for three guys at the same time. It was hard enough allowing myself to trust Connor and now Hunter. Because of them, I felt like I was finally allowed to breathe. I could relax, laugh, be myself, and fall in love.

My cantankerous soldier and the shape-shifting family man. For a fleeting moment, I thought Razvan could fit into our little band of misfits, too. But the moment his trust could be called into question, I was like a stretched out rubber band that snapped back. I regressed. I immediately went back to the mindset I knew all my life—that the only thing men cared about was getting their dicks wet.

And that was my fault. Not his.

"He did it because I hurt him first."

I didn't just see the hurt in his face. I felt it when I sensed him.

When his presence—or whatever it was I sensed—touched me, it did so with longing and sorrow. He missed me and it made me realize how much I missed him. I was right. It was wrong of him to kiss me with no warning and hurt Ally, but he was also right. I projected my own bullshit onto him, and that wasn't fair.

And I still pushed him away, lashed out at him, and for what? For no other reason than being a stubborn child, like he said.

Hunter and I walked in silence across the campgrounds to Connor's trailer, where a warm glow came from inside. My mood thoroughly soured, I hoped he wouldn't ask a million questions about this date. It seemed no matter how much Hunter and I just tried to have fun, something had to come along and ruin it for us.

"Hey, listen," the handsome wolf said softly, turning to face me in front of the door.

I peered up at him with reluctance as his arms slid around my waist and pulled me closer with a gentle tug.

"I don't care who or what tried to get in our way tonight," he lowered his forehead to mine, "I had an amazing time with you, and I can't wait to see you again."

"Hunter, it's okay. You don't have to say that," I murmured. "I'm a magnet for drama and bullshit. And I'm an immature teenager, I just make it worse—"

"Mel, stop."

He cupped one hand to my cheek and brought his lips crashing down to mine. The sudden pressure and intensity elicited a gasp from me, providing ample opportunity for his tongue to invade and deepen the kiss.

My knees wobbled under the weight of him, and his arms found their way to the small of my back, crushing me against his chest. If that kiss on the Ferris wheel was from a romantic fairy tale, this one was from a deep, dark fantasy. The charming prince had dropped his facade to reveal the hungry wolf underneath.

He left me breathless when he pulled away, and craving more than just a kiss. I clung to his shoulders, standing on tiptoe to reach his mouth again, but the kiss he returned was a soft echo of what just transpired.

He smiled against my lips, pulling away once more with reluctance. "If I don't stop now, I might not make it home to my kids."

"We wouldn't want that," I purred, pulling his head down to mine for just one more. Or maybe a few more.

Our date started to replay in my mind as I got my last few kisses in, and I remembered what he said about how shifters had human wants too. Secure homes, jobs, and schools. I suddenly felt incredibly shitty about this place with Connor, as small and junky as it was, while Hunter had to go back to the woods.

"Hey, tell me something honestly," I murmured, my hands drifting down to his chest.

"Anything," he said with a kiss to my forehead.

"Do you and the kids need a place to stay?" I looked up at him. "You know, somewhere nearby with a bed and a shower."

"We're fine, Mel. But thank you." I caught a hint of defensiveness in his voice, maybe with a bit of pride mixed in.

"Are you sure? Connor and I can pool together for a motel room or—"

"You've already done more than enough to help me." His gaze drifted across me, matching his fingertips that lightly traveled along my back. "I couldn't possibly ask you for more."

"It's no problem for us. Really," I insisted. "You and the kids deserve some basic comforts."

"And really, we're fine. I promise." His fingertips rubbed circles on my back. "We're basically camping now and they're enjoying it. When we get paid for closing night, I'll get us a trailer kind of like this one," he glanced up at Connor's RV, "probably a bit smaller, though."

I only remembered then that closing night—our final night of performing—was tomorrow. Then the carnival would close for the summer and we'd all be out of a job, left to return to a normal life or find another show to perform in.

"Where will you go after that?" I asked, fearing the answer.

He lifted one shoulder in a lazy shrug, running one affectionate finger from my jaw to my neck.

"I'll go anywhere I'm wanted."

MELODY

I didn't sleep a wink.

Connor snored softly next to me, having already passed out when Hunter and I finally parted for the night. The bottles of Vicodin and Jack Daniels next to the bed made my stomach drop when I walked in. He'd been trying to numb some kind of pain while I was away—whether in his legs, heart, or mind, I wouldn't find out until the next morning.

I held my lucky coin—my apparent source of power—above my head, alternating between turning it over between my fingers and closing my fist around it. How many times in my life had I looked at this thing, with its silver outer edge and gold inlay? With my newfound discovery, the crossed daggers stamped on both sides reminded me of grinning teeth.

A magician gave it to me at my first carnival, when I couldn't have been older than eight. He pulled it out from behind my ear, then placed it in my palm, closing my fingers around it with a white-gloved hand. As the only thing ever freely given to me, I treasured it ever since then.

In the darkness of Connor's trailer, I closed my fingers around it just as the magician did and held it to my chest. Closing my eyes, I searched hard for a clearer memory of the man who gave it to me. Did he say anything to me? Did I ever get a good look at his face?

And what confused me the most, why did he choose to pass on his shamanic gifts to *me?*

My memory of that moment was fuzzy at best. I had been distracted because of my mom stumbling around drunk and causing a scene. We may have gotten kicked out, but I wasn't sure.

I let out a sigh, released the coin from my fingers, and let it rest on my chest. It felt warm on my skin, most likely from me holding it so much. All my life, it had been the one object that held any value to me, the one thing that was mine and no one else's. It gave me comfort, strength, and confidence from dealing with my mom's drunken rages to strutting across a stage as ringmistress.

But it never felt *magical.* I certainly didn't notice anything different when I turned eighteen. I slept with it under my pillow the night before my birthday and slipped it in my pocket when I woke up before anyone else. Then, when I walked away from that so-called home for the last time, I ran my fingers across those stamped daggers and found the courage to never look back.

I remembered Thembi's forked tongue flicking between her teeth. What did she say? *"Of course you're human, girl! But ya can give the illusion that you're not."*

Okay, what is the point of that? I wondered. I had to talk to her again, hopefully before our show tomorrow, if I had time.

I held my hands up in front of my face, only their outline visible in the darkness. In my mind, I pictured them turning into paws with white fur and black nails, just like Hunter's. I stared at them until my arm muscles fatigued, then slapped them down to my sides with a heavy sigh.

How could I feel like anything *but* completely human when that was all I ever was?

I never truly felt the rush of a kill or the ground underneath my paws as Hunter did, nor fire in my lungs and the sensations of taking flight like Razvan. Only in my dreams.

My mind settled into the one I had last night, some sort of caged predator that felt completely different from a wolf. This animal was *huge* and felt powerful enough to kill a wolf with one swipe of its paw. But all it could do was pace back and forth, slowly going mad.

The humans walking by looked so smug, but I could smell their fear underneath. They had to keep me sedated round the clock just to feel safe enough, even after sticking me in this tiny cage. Gutless cowards with their tranquilizer guns and soft pink skin. One day they would pay, and they looked so damn delicious...

"Holy shit! What the—Mel?!"

Connor startled awake so quickly it jolted me out of the state I was in. He sat up in a flash and scooted across the bed away from me, as if afraid for his life.

"Babe, is that you?"

"Yeah." I blinked at him in the darkness. "You okay, Con?"

"I heard a noise, and I felt... something." He shook his head, breathing deeply. "Must've been dreaming, but *fuck*..."

I scooted across the bed to him and leaned my head against his heart, which pounded like a drum against my cheek. His skin was hot, but a cold sweat covered him in moisture.

"What did you hear?" I kissed under his chin, curling my legs up and snuggling against him.

"It sounded like," he rubbed his forehead, "an animal growling. A bear or something huge like that. I swear it was so loud, like it was right on top of me. For a second, I thought I was going to be eaten alive." He let out a long exhale as his arms wrapped around me. "I had a bit of a rough evening, as you can see." He nodded toward the pain pills and whiskey.

I peered up at him. "Your legs? Or flashbacks?"

"Both," he mumbled ashamedly, looking away. "But I've never felt like an animal was about to maul me to death and eat me before." He forced a chuckle. "I think I'm finally losing it, babe."

"Stop." I cupped his cheek to make him look at me. "That wasn't you. I'm... pretty sure it was me."

Even in the darkness, I saw his forest green eyes narrow in confusion and gave him a quick rundown of our encounter with Thembi and my latest dream.

"A shaman?" he repeated. "You mean like the old Native American medicine man type of people?"

"I don't know, maybe?" I threw my hands up. "And these powers came to me on my eighteenth birthday, from a coin I've carried with me everywhere. I think *I'm* the one losing it, Con."

"You're definitely not losing it before me," he chuckled, with a kiss to my forehead. "It *kind of* makes sense." His fingers caressed up and down my arms as he pondered on it. "You can't shift, but you can channel the shifters, sorta. Like you were just thinking of this caged animal from your dream and suddenly I feel like I need to get the fuck away or I'm dead."

"That growl you heard," my fingers worked into the stiff knots in his shoulders, "I don't remember making it but I felt so angry and powerful, like I just wanted to kill something because it was what my instincts told me to do. I felt that just now in my *own* body."

"And I nearly pissed myself in fear while in bed with a gorgeous woman. *That's* never happened to me before."

He laughed when I smacked his chest in mock anger, but turned serious when he caught me staring at the pills and alcohol again.

"Please don't tell me you self-medicate like this often," I whispered, leaning my head on his shoulder.

"No, babe. I promise." He squeezed me tighter, pressing a kiss to my neck. "I just had an especially rough day today. It won't happen again."

"Any particular reason why?" I turned my head to rest my opposite cheek and found his lips hovering over my eyelids in the dark.

"Nothing important."

"Connor."

"Honestly, babe. It was stupid of me. I just... didn't want to deal with feeling shit from the past. But I swear to you," he cupped my nape and kissed me with so much passion it left me breathless, "I'm over it. I'm not doing that shit again."

My gaze fluttered away from his, still feeling uneasy. "If you were feeling like that, I should have stayed with you. I shouldn't be out with another guy while you're struggling."

"Wrong," he said with a playful tap on my nose. "This is *precisely* why you should have someone like Hunter to spend time with. You shouldn't have to be burdened with my issues, babe. It's my shit to sort through, not yours."

"But I love you," I protested, nipping his lower lip. "And I want to be here for you when you're going through tough times. You shouldn't have to deal with that stuff alone."

"And I love you, babe. So much," he murmured, returning my kiss with a small, affectionate bite. "You help me in ways I can't even begin to explain. And you deserve better than to wade through the dark side of my mental illness. I'm not exaggerating. It's best that you don't see that side of me."

"You," I stabbed my index finger into his chest, "don't decide what I deserve, Connor. *I* do. And I'm going to prove to you I'm with you through thick and thin. Even if Hunter and I get together, I'm not gonna run to him every time you have a flashback. I'm staying by your side and helping you get through it because that's what love means to me."

I felt like a cup of water running over. The depths of what I felt for him rose to the surface and spilled over with no valve to shut it off. He opened his mouth to speak, and I raised a hand to cut him off, because there was no stopping this overflow.

"And I am *not,*" I shuddered in a breath, "going to call 911 because someone I love overdosed on pain pills and alcohol *again*. I did that for my mom, my sister, even random men at our house because I was terrified they would die, and I'm *done*, Connor. I'm not letting it happen anymore."

He stared at me for a few moments, his expression unreadable, then said nothing as he shoved me away from him and scooted across the bed. Away from me.

I watched, hurt at first, then stunned, as he grabbed both the pills and the whiskey off the shelf. With both bottles in one hand, he slid open the window with the other and chucked both items outside. A second later, I heard the distinct sound of glass shattering.

"Never again," he said gruffly, returning to me and sliding his hands around my waist. "Because that's what love means to me."

I jumped into his arms at the same time he pulled me forward. Our lips and tongues crashed together in a frantic dance to seal the promises we just made. Holding me tight against his chest, he turned to lay me down on my back. His mouth never broke from mine as he hovered above me, settling his weight on his forearms, and then between my legs.

My moans silenced by his tongue, I yanked my tank top up over my breasts before wrapping my arms around his wide, muscular back to pull him down to me. It wasn't enough just to kiss him or even feel him inside me. I wanted his skin married to mine.

"Oh, babe," he groaned, kissing a hot trail down my neck as his heart beat against mine. He helped peel my top off my arms as my thighs wrapped around his hips and shimmied his boxers down his thighs.

His hips rolled against mine, bringing his cock to full hardness as he teased my vulva with it. Every thrust of his shaft against my clit sent me gasping, digging my nails into his back as the ache inside me grew hungrier.

"Condoms," I murmured when he paused to kiss my nipples.

"Good girl. You remember."

"Shut up. Leave me alone."

He laughed, kissing me again as he reached above us to fumble on the shelf for the foil packets. After what felt like an agonizingly long wait, he pressed inside me and we both released a sigh of utmost bliss and contentment.

Connor wasn't my first sexual partner, but the first one I genuinely enjoyed it with. Even now, in this middle of the night quickie, every kiss and thrust felt like he was tailor made for my pleasure. His lips never left my skin. He murmured how much he loved me and how good I felt wrapped around him as he sank into me.

The moment my moans became whimpers, my breaths grew erratic, and the pressure began building in my core, he drew out my pleasure for as long as he could while delaying his own.

"Come with me," I pleaded in his ear. "I want to feel you."

"You first," he growled savagely at the restraint of holding himself back.

"I'm going to—oh, Connor!"

My orgasm lashed out like whips cracking along my nerves. At the same time, my pussy convulsed around him like it wouldn't let go. He shuddered and groaned, clenching his fist in my hair and grazing his teeth along my shoulder. Like coiled springs, we carried the tension to the point of no return, and then released.

But even as the tension left our bodies, we never let go of each other.

❦ 10 ❧

CONNOR

A burning hot pain pulled me out of sleep.

It concentrated around my stumps and for a moment, I was back on the black hawk minutes after being airlifted. The IED explosion itself never hurt—adrenaline and shock took care of that. It wasn't until I was laying on my back on a stretcher, looking up at the tear-streaked faces of my brothers in arms and then down at the bloody, mangled mess of my legs, that I felt the worst pain of my life.

I shouldn't have drank with the pain pills last night, least of all because it upset Mel, but they were taking too long to kick in and it was killing me. Now it all had worn off completely, and my dumbass threw them outside in the middle of the night.

Careful not to disturb Mel sleeping peacefully, I scooted to the end of the bed toward the door. My prosthetics leaned against the wall just in reach, but I looked away as if they were a bad omen. They were the reason my pain kept getting worse. After three years of wear, their custom fit had slid out of calibration. The more I wore them, the more pressure they put on the *wrong* areas of my stumps.

Fumbling on my boxer shorts, I winced as the fabric grazed over the smooth, rounded ends of where my legs stopped. It felt like knives dragging across my legs, like those masked thugs who laughed and threw rocks as I dragged my broken body across the desert—

Nope, don't go there. You're not there. You're here.

I turned to look at Mel, sleeping peacefully on her side. Her gorgeous curves made a long, sweeping line from her ankle to her shoulders. She was my anchor to reality. Thinking of her kept my head above water when the demons of my past tried to drown me. She reminded me I survived and my life now was worth holding onto.

Visibly, nothing was wrong with my legs, which only made me wonder if the pain was all in my head, too. No open wounds, no discoloration, nothing. But if it wasn't real, then the meds wouldn't have worked, right?

From the edge of the bed, I unlocked the door before lowering myself to the floor. Every brush of the floor on my legs made me want to howl in pain, so I lifted my hips up and used all the strength in my core to walk on my hands outside.

It was early enough for a chill to bite at the air, and no other performers seemed to be up yet. Even better.

I hand-walked alongside the trailer, my eyes sweeping for that orange prescription bottle. I spotted the shattered bottle of Jack right away and took care to not place my hands in broken glass.

"Fuckin' come on," I muttered, looking underneath the trailer and all around the tires. Nothing.

My mind raced as I thought about what I'd do for tonight, our closing show. I nearly passed out from the pain during my last act. I got out of my prosthetics as fast as I could and scored the Vicodin from one of Razvan's guys while Mel was busy. Yesterday's rest didn't help a lick.

I wouldn't make it through my act feeling like this. No chance in hell.

"Connor?"

Mel leaned out the trailer door, the bedsheet still wrapped around her and her big doe eyes hooded with sleep.

"Hey babe," I gritted my teeth through the burning, twisting, stabbing sensation as I rested my lower body on the ground.

"What are you doing?" She rubbed her eyes.

"Legs are killing me," I admitted. "I was looking for the pain pills I threw out here."

She rubbed her face, wide awake. "Oh, Con. Let me get dressed."

Fifteen minutes later, she had inspected every nook and cranny underneath and around the trailer. And we still turned up empty.

"Some junkie must've swiped it," I hissed, pulling myself up to the second step of the trailer so my legs could swing in midair.

"I have Midol." Mel squeezed my shoulder as she slipped past me back inside. "It's not as strong but might help."

I accepted the tablets and water from her, insisting on triple the normal dose despite her reluctance, then sat back and waited for the edge to come off, if at all. Like dark laser targets, her eyes never left me.

"How long has your pain been this bad?"

Fuck, I was in for it.

"Today makes three days."

"Three days?!" she repeated. "Why didn't you tell me yesterday?"

"Because you would have canceled your date with Hunter to be with my sorry ass."

"As I *should* have been!" She raked her fingers violently through her hair. "Connor, this is what I was talking about last night."

"What a coincidence," I huffed bitterly. "Same here."

"Con—"

"Did you have fun?"

She lifted her head from her hands. "What?"

"Did you have fun yesterday?" I asked. "With him, in spite of meeting a spooky fortune teller lady and wrapping your head around your shamanic powers."

"I... yes, I had fun. But Con—"

"Then it's a good thing you went," I told her. "Learning about yourself is just icing on top of that."

A heavy sigh escaped her as her shoulders sagged and her eyes closed. I realized I was testing her patience, but the sooner she figured this out, the better.

"Connor, there's no way you can perform like this. As ringmistress, I *do* have some sway and I will not put you through that."

"I'll be fine if this pain goes down at all. But I sure as hell am not sitting out, babe. We need the money too badly, cause who knows where we'll end up from here."

"And I need you to be *okay*, Connor." She took my hand, threading her small fingers through mine. "Can't we go to a doctor? What if it's—"

"No, babe," I said apologetically. "My benefits are completely tapped out. Even a routine visit will cost me thousands. I'll have to sell the RV if I get stuck with that, and then what? I'll be at rock bottom again and I can't do that to you."

"But it's not going to get better, is it?" Her dark eyes glittered with tears as they met mine. "You've been feeling like this for three days and it's not going away? That's serious, Connor. We need to see someone about it."

"After we get paid, maybe," I sighed. "But realistically, there's nothing we can do. We've got to pack up and drive to the next job, which is going to eat through whatever we make. Doctor's visits, new prosthetics, none of it's realistic for me. All I can do is keep kicking the can down the road."

Mel said nothing as her face hardened. Then she stood up abruptly and jumped the bottom step like she was heading out on a mission.

"Where are you going?"

"Where'd you get the Vicodin?" she asked. "If all we can do is numb your pain for now, that's what we'll do. So I'm getting you more."

I huffed out a dry laugh. "You're not gonna like the answer."

Her eyes narrowed. "Tell me."

"Razvan."

II

MELODY

Wandering through a campsite of scary, tattooed men was the last thing I wanted to do. Not to mention seeing Raz again so soon after our confrontation filled me with dread. But for Connor's pain relief, no price was too high.

Leers from Razvan's men, a group of fire breathers and knife throwers who called themselves the Flaming Swords, crawled across my skin like the legs of insects. The man sitting at the fire with the half-naked girl in his lap seemed too preoccupied to stare at me, so I chose him to approach.

"Excuse me," I said in as clear a voice as I could.

The girl looked up at me first, glaring daggers. The man slowly pulled his head away from her chest and regarded me with an annoyed expression.

"Can I help ye, ringmistress?"

His accent took me aback. I knew I'd seen him speaking Romanian with Raz and the others, but his lilt sounded Irish.

"I'm looking for Razvan."

"Aye." He threw an arm around the woman's shoulders and palmed her breast as if no one was watching. "And do ye see him?"

Of course, this guy was going to fuck with me. They would never make it easy on me.

"No." I offered a smile despite raging on the inside. "I'm wondering if you could tell me where he is?"

"In case ye haven't noticed," he replied with infuriating calm. "I've been a little busy with my pet here to keep track of his comings and goings. And trust me, ringmistress," his eyes flicked up and down my body, "if he wanted to see ye, ye wouldn't need to ask me."

Before I could wrap my head around whether this guy was insulting me or not, a string of Romanian words flowed through air like music behind me. I turned to find a familiar pair of steel-gray eyes looking back at me.

"*Steluța*," he murmured before catching himself and hardened his expression. "What are you doing here, Melody?"

Shit, shit, shit. I did *not* feel ready for this.

"Can I talk to you privately?" I could barely get the words out with my heart trying to force its way up my throat.

"I thought you were done talking to me."

His tone made me flinch, but I somehow forced myself to stand my ground, despite feeling like I would crumble at any moment.

"This isn't about me, or us." My nails dug into my palms. "It's Connor."

His eyebrows, lifting a fraction of an inch, were the only sign of emotion on his face. He stared at me for so long I began to worry he'd tell me to go.

He abruptly turned to go back inside his tent. "Make it quick." He slapped the flap open and went inside, not bothering to hold it open for me.

Steeling myself, I followed him in and took a moment to let my eyes adjust.

The inside of the tent was open, roomy, and comfortable, like a rich hunter's pavilion. A worn Persian rug stretched out across the ground, its pattern faded from years of use but no less beautiful and intricate. At the far end of the pavilion, a king-sized air mattress laid on the floor. It was haphazardly covered in sheets and pillows, like the sleeper had been tossing and turning all night. Or having wild sex.

My stomach dropped at the thought of Razvan fucking Ally in that bed. Did they ever? Had he brought anyone else here? I shouldn't have cared, but the thoughts of him with anyone else bothered me immensely.

"So, what's up with Connor?" Razvan asked tersely. He folded his arms as he leaned against a table covered in an assortment of knives and swords. I couldn't help but notice all of them pointing straight at me.

"He's in a lot of pain," I answered, lifting my eyes from the polished steel to meet his. "I was hoping you could help him."

"My boys already gave him something for that," he growled. "Try again."

"It was my fault. I made him throw it away." My cheeks flamed. "He mixed it with alcohol and I kind of flipped out."

Raz gave me a long, calculated stare. "And what happened?"

"He threw the whole bottle out the window and it was gone the next morning."

He sighed deeply. A long stretch of silence passed between us and I could only begin to speculate about what he was thinking.

"So his pain has not gotten better?" he asked in a flat voice.

"No, it doesn't seem to be."

"Then he needs more than pain management."

I glanced up. "Believe me, I tried telling him that. But you know how stubborn he is."

Razvan huffed out a breath, regarding me cooly as he tipped his chin upward. He seemed to be deciding whether to stab, burn, or kiss me. If he chose the latter, I promised I wouldn't hold it against him this time.

"And why should I help again?" He ran his tongue along his teeth. "I was already generous once. Now I'm being begged again three days later? I'm reminded of a junkie that needs a fix."

"Connor is *not* a junkie!" I finally lost my cool.

"He mixed with booze, no?" Razvan rubbed the dark stubble on his jaw.

"He was having a really hard day. The pain is unbearable to him, Raz. He's really suffering." My desperation grew like a balloon on the verge of popping. At any moment, I was ready to fall to my knees and truly beg.

"Poor human," he sneered. "Yes, nothing but a life of pain and suffering. I wouldn't know anything about that, not even if I had to beg anyone for relief."

His sarcasm bled through like acid. Like Hunter, he'd been sold to a carnival, abused and drugged for entertainment. But even worse, he was the first and only shifter in his family for generations. They had long since forgotten about their dragon heritage and saw his shift as a curse. His own family sold their son away.

I bit my tongue, fighting the urge to snap back. *You couldn't have suffered all that badly if you're still here.* But I truly didn't know why Razvan was still in this business now that he was free. And I couldn't make this about him and me again. I had to remember who I was here for.

"Raz, Connor's always been good to you. He considers you a friend. Can you please put aside whatever this is between you and me? For him? He'd do it for you."

"I'm not a pill dispensary," the tattooed dragon shifter growled. "I helped him once and was happy to do it. You fucked up and expect the same generosity again? Not happening, not without telling me what I get out of this."

"How about your full pay for closing night?" I crossed my arms, mimicking his stance. "Instead of getting cheated out of it?"

His eyes heated as his lips curled into a snarl. "What are you getting at?"

"Connor can't perform when he's in pain. If he's not part of the show, attendees will walk out. They might demand refunds. And they sure as hell won't see your act, or Hunter's, or anyone else's. His absence will make the whole show suffer, which means we all take the hit on our paychecks when this is over."

Another uncomfortable silence. He could take one of those knives on the table behind him and use it to cut the tension between us. The air in this tent felt stifling and hot. I couldn't begin to tell if it was the weather, his dragon shift heating up, or the mounting tension due to us being alone in this tent with its messy bed.

His shoulders cut through the air abruptly as he turned, rounding the table to rummage through a backpack leaning against one of the tent supports. I stood frozen, watching, not wanting to blow this chance by saying or doing something to make him change his mind.

After a moment, Raz returned to me, holding a small plastic baggie in his tattooed palm. Inside it were six white round tablets.

"This is not exactly the same, it's generic," he muttered. "But it'll do the job."

"Thank you, Razvan," I whispered, reaching toward his open palm.

Just before my skin could make contact with his, he closed his fingers around the pills and yanked it out of my reach.

"Remember, this has nothing to do with me and you," he snarled. "I'm covering my ass. And Connor owes me now."

I swallowed the dry lump in my throat. "Got it," I choked out. "I'll let him know."

Without another word, he dropped the baggie into my hand, seemingly careful to not touch my skin directly. It hurt more than I cared to admit.

"Was there anything else you needed?"

He posed the question coldly. Those gray eyes challenged me, daring me to answer a certain way.

I need you to be sorry for throwing my past in my face. I need to know you still want me and no one else. I need you to kiss me again and mean it.

"No," I answered just as coldly. "Nothing at all."

His expression twitched just slightly. For just a fleeting moment, I saw the raw, vulnerable side he revealed when he showed me his dragon shift. It passed over his face in a glimpse before the cold mask settled back over him.

"Then you may go."

He said it like another dare, but I wouldn't rise to his bait.

Clutching my prize in my fist, I turned my back on him and left.

CONNOR

"Are you sure?"

"Babe," I sighed. "My answer isn't gonna change, no matter how many times you ask me that. Yes, I feel fine."

Mel's brows furrowed extra hard as she applied her lipstick in the mirror.

"I'm just saying if you don't feel up to it, I can make something up in my announcements—"

"There's no need," I slipped a hand under her red tailcoat to wrap around the corset that defined her hourglass shape, "because I am just as fit as ever to perform." I moved her hair to drop a kiss to the back of her neck, enjoying the shiver that elicited through her.

"I just want you to be okay," she sighed in the mirror. "And I'm nervous, I guess. This is my last night as ringmistress. Who knows where we'll end up after tonight?"

"Doesn't matter," I murmured, pulling her back against me until my lips were in her hair. "I got you and you got me. And Hunter. And Razvan."

"Scratch that last one and you'd be right," she muttered, checking her makeup one last time before reaching for her top hat.

I looked at her in surprise. "You mean y'all didn't make up passionately when you went to get my pills?"

"No, quite the opposite in fact." She ran a hand along the brim of her top hat before twirling to face me. "We both made it very clear that it had nothing to do with us. We just want to see this show through, so we all get paid. And you owe him now, since he feels he was generous to you twice."

"Damn." I rubbed my jaw. "The two of you are being stubborn as fuck."

"You're one to talk," she jabbed with a playful smack to my chest.

"Takes one to know one." I slipped my mask in place and offered her my arm. "Ready, babe?"

"As ready as I'll ever be," she sighed, wrapping her hand around my bicep so we could walk backstage together.

I wished to reassure her, to tell her even bigger and better things awaited us after this was over. We'd be part of even grander shows and make enough money to not worry about anything. We'd develop our own following and people would travel across the country just to see us, no matter *where* we performed.

But we could just as likely find nothing. As much as I wanted to believe we'd come out on top, I didn't have it in me to make promises I couldn't keep. So I walked out proudly with my gorgeous ringmistress on my arm, taking in all the curious looks in our show attire. For all we knew, this would be our last night dressed up like this.

The backstage area buzzed with even more chaotic, excited energy than the past few nights. Everyone could feel this was the ultimate night and prepared to give it their all.

"I'm going to check on Hunter," Mel said, giving me a quick air kiss to not mess up her lipstick.

"Sure you are," I teased, sitting down as I prepared to remove my normal prosthetics and put on my stilts.

Our wolf boy remained out of sight until he did his partial shift for the show. It was just safer for him if people didn't know what he looked like in human form.

She paused, giving me a worried glance as I popped off my legs. "Do you want me to stay?"

"No." I smacked her playfully with my longer leg. "Go on, girl. Get some of that doggy style love. I know you miss him."

"Connor," she groaned, rolling her eyes to the ceiling, but I didn't miss that smile twitching at her lips as she walked down the hall.

I enjoyed the view of her long legs walking away in those tights until she disappeared around the corner, then fitted on my stilts.

"You're on in ten, Connor," Nigel, the carnival manager, said in a clipped tone as he walked by in a hurry. He must've been especially busy, making sure closing night went off without a hitch.

Even so, that gave me plenty of time to walk around and warm up before showtime. I grabbed the curtain to pull myself up to my full stilted height of twelve feet. Running through my mental checklist, I took a few measured steps. Balance, weight distribution, pressure on my stumps, everything felt good.

I really do owe you, Raz, I thought. Maybe he would consider the debt repaid if I talked him and Mel into making up. I loved that girl, but she wrote off a good guy before anything had a chance to blossom between them. Her instinct was to lash out defensively at the first sign of a guy being shady and with good reason. But this was the rare exception. She was wrong, and she just needed to admit that.

I hadn't seen much of Raz around either in the past week. He made good on his promise to give Mel some space, but when she hadn't come seeking him out, it sounded like things got ugly during her date with Hunter. She mentioned running into him before heading out to get my pills from him, but didn't want to talk about it further, which told me enough.

Shit. What was that?

A tingle shot up my leg, starting at my right stump, and traveled all the way to my groin. I'd been walking back and forth as I was thinking and felt completely normal up until now.

I took another few tentative steps and—*fuck!*

A zap of pain shot up my other leg. I grabbed one of the stage supports and hissed, grinding my teeth against the pain. I shifted my weight, trying to ease the pressure on my legs, which helped a little, but I couldn't do this for long. In a few minutes, I would be putting tremendous pressure on them.

Panic surged within me. Even if I had another pill, it would take too long to kick in.

The drums kicked up and all the lights onstage concentrated on a single spotlight. Shit, Mel was about to make announcements and then it'd be me. What the ever living *fuck* was I going to do?

My beautiful woman walked out from the opposite end of the stage, waving and smiling at the crowd who roared their greeting at her. Some of them had attended every single show. After being ring-mistress for just a week, Mel was already developing a fan base. She just had a natural talent for captivating an audience. Somewhere underneath my pain-frazzled mind, I wondered if that was another expression of her shaman abilities.

"Ladies and gentlemen, boys and girls!" Her voice rang out through the speakers with warmth, confidence, and clarity. "As our final show for you tonight here at Crying Falls Summer Festival, it's a bittersweet feeling for all of us."

She paused to take in their boos and protests. No one wanted this to end.

"I know, I know." She brought a hand to her chest, commiserating with them. "So let's make this the most incredible, spectacular, unforgettable night, everyone! What do you say?"

The ensuing cheers and screams drowned out my groans and grunts as I released the stage support. Hundreds of tiny knives stabbed right where my legs fit snugly into the stilts and grew worse with every passing minute. Sweat dripped down my forehead, making my mask stick to my skin. But I had to bear it. I had to get through it. I wouldn't let Mel or anyone else down.

All I could do was call on my Marine training. The pain, discipline, thirst, and hunger that I lived through years ago strengthened me for this. I just had to get through the act that I could perform in my sleep, and then get out of these stilts as soon as possible.

"Our first act knows his way around the stage," Mel winked as she began her suggestive introduction about me. "And trust me, ladies, those long wooden legs aren't compensating for anything else!"

The onstage drummer hit a *ba-dum-tss* on his drum set, and even I laughed along with the crowd.

"Ladies and gentlemen, please give it up for Stilts, the entrancing acrobatic stilt walker!"

Just stepping onto the stage made me bite my cheek against the pain. Thankfully, no one could see my face behind the mask, but I had no way to keep from screaming while they were silent.

My music started up, and I got into my routine, which unfortunately started with variations of balancing on one leg. Nothing looked different as far as I could tell, but a few jumps of one leg to the other had me seeing black dots in the corner of my vision. Fuck, this was not good. I didn't feel this bad the previous night until the end.

I switched it up, diving my torso to the floor to press myself into a handstand. Mel would notice the change in routine but hopefully not figure out why. The crowd oohed and gasped as I walked on my hands across the stage. My legs felt slightly better without the pressure of the floor, but I couldn't do this forever. Not if we were going to give them a show worthy of closing night.

I dropped my legs behind me to come back up to standing, then immediately jumped into a backflip and *god fucking damn it, holy shit!*

It hurt so badly I almost missed the landing. The crowd didn't notice me cover my stumble and burst into applause while I took a small bow to recompose myself.

That had to be the worst pain in my life. It took all my strength just to stay poised for the performance when all I wanted to do was curl into a ball and scream. And the climax of my act involved multiple backflips going across the entire stage. Right then, just reaching the end of my act felt like an insurmountable obstacle.

Bear down and do your job. You are a Marine. Just get through it.

I ground my teeth so hard against the stabbing fire in my legs, I expected to not have any left in my jaws if I lived through this. Taking a few deep breaths, I leaned into the hell, wracking my body and did a few more tricks across the stage. I couldn't think or hear anything through my brain screaming at me to stop this.

Every step felt like my legs being cut off all over again, but I pushed through. The audience had to notice me struggling at this point. I couldn't complete my act and pretend like everything was totally fine. My body could barely handle one or the other, but not both.

Time escaped me. I had no idea if seconds or minutes passed when I reached my breaking point. My vision began clouding, and I felt cold all over, despite being covered in sweat. But I had to do my finale. I had to. I couldn't let my girl down.

I stuck one leg out in front of me, preparing to throw it over my head for my final series of backflips. Throwing what little strength I had into my standing leg, I pushed off. That fraction-of-a-second moment of levitating in the air felt so peaceful. My pain briefly disappeared before the darkness swallowed me.

13

MELODY

I knew right away something was terribly wrong.

Connor changed up his routine right at the beginning and seemed more off-balance and uncoordinated than usual. My nails cut into my palms as I watched him, wishing I could read his face.

"Nigel," I grabbed the arm of the carnival manager as he tried to walk by, obviously very busy, "something's wrong with Connor."

He paused, turning to look at the stage from behind the curtain with me.

"Damn right. He's wobbling like a baby giraffe." He looked at me expectantly. "Something you want to tell me, Mel?"

I swallowed, debating frantically in my head if I should tell him. Connor would be furious. He had too much damn pride and never wanted to let anyone know he was hurting, including me. But he and Nigel had a close professional relationship. They were both ex-military and Nigel was one of the few good people in the carnival business. If anyone should know besides me, it would have to be him.

"He's been dealing with really severe pain in his legs for a few days," I admitted. "Medication has helped, but it doesn't go away when it wears off. He took some an hour ago but... it doesn't look like it's working now."

Nigel's eyes fixated on Connor, who looked moments away from toppling over.

"What the hell are you doing, boy?" he muttered to himself.

The crowd gasped as he narrowly landed a shaky somersault and vaulted a few steps to maintain his balance.

"Shit. He's going to fucking kill himself." Nigel placed a hand on my arm. "You keep watching him. I'm calling an ambulance."

The weight of those words didn't hit me until he had already gone. Panic squeezed around my heart as my eyes locked onto Connor, looking more dazed and unsteady with each passing second.

"Come on, babe. Just stop," I pleaded. "Fuck the show, just *please* stop putting yourself through this."

I grabbed the curtain to physically stop myself from running out onto the stage. He seemed determined to see this through to the end.

"Oh no," I whispered. He was preparing for a backflip.

From the moment he kicked his leg out, I knew he wouldn't make the landing. My heart stopped. He was in the air, and then he was falling.

A scream rang out so loud it hurt my ears. My legs acted on their own, but it still felt like swimming through mud to reach him. I couldn't go fast enough. Only an eternity later, when I kneeled over his lifeless body laying on the stage, did I realize the screaming came from me.

"Connor! Connor!"

I yelled his name over and over as if that would wake him up. Chaos swirled around in my peripheral vision, but my focus remained on him. I didn't touch him. Somewhere in the back of my mind, a memory surfaced of a CPR class I took. Never touch someone who hit their head. It could make a neck injury worse.

Oh God, Connor! Life was unfair enough to him with taking his legs away. If he became paralyzed or brain dead, God or whoever had a sick sense of humor.

Someone grabbed my shoulders and pulled me away from him, then a bunch of people in dark blue uniforms swarmed in like ants to surround him.

"No! Get away!" I screamed, pushing and fighting against whoever touched me. "Don't move him, he hit his head!"

"Mel, shh!" Strong arms crushed me to a chest covered in tattoos. "They're the EMTs. They'll take care of him, *steluța*." Hands stroked my hair in an effort to be soothing. This person smelled like leather, cloves, and smoke.

My brain couldn't even register who this person was. I just struggled to get a glimpse of Connor as they lifted him onto a stretcher. So many voices, so many people. But he was the only one that mattered. I couldn't lose him, not yet.

"Where are they taking him?" I demanded, struggling against the tattooed arms that held me. The team of EMTs began carrying Connor off the stage. Nigel was saying something into a microphone I couldn't understand.

"To the hospital," a deep, velvety voice rumbled against my ear. "They said we can follow."

"I need to go," I protested, pushing against the warm, broad chest to no avail. "I need to be with him."

A flash of pale hair caught my eye, and only then did my composure break. Or the shock wore off, I wasn't sure.

"HUNTER!" I cried through a rattled sob.

His golden eyes fixated on me, filled with worry and concern. Whoever held me finally let go, and I ran to my tall, beautiful wolf.

"What happened?" he asked as I crashed into him, ugly-crying into his chest. "I heard screaming and a bunch of commotion up here."

"Connor fell," someone spoke with an accent from behind me. "He hit his head and is being rushed to the emergency room."

I turned to see Razvan standing there, arms crossed, with a grim expression on his face. My mind reeled. Was he the one who pulled me away from Connor?

"We can follow them, though?" Hunter rubbed my back. His heartbeat against my cheek was the only thing keeping me from losing it.

"Yes, that's what they said." Razvan paused. "I take it you don't have a vehicle?"

"No, but I can follow the scent and run over there. I need to tell my pups where I'll be."

"Bring them. I'm sure they'll want to see Connor too when he wakes up."

Snippets of conversations drifted in and out of my awareness, but all I could do was hold onto Hunter and think back to right before the show started.

I shouldn't have left him. I should have stayed. Maybe I could have talked him out of going onstage. God fucking damnit, I knew what he was dealing with and still left him to go make out with Hunter. How selfish could I be?

"Hey, little fox." A thumb stroked my cheek and my head tilted up to gaze at Hunter's handsome, angular face. "Raz has a truck. Would you be okay riding with him to the hospital and I'll meet you there?"

"I need you." I clung to his shirt. "Please don't leave me."

"I'm not, Mel. I promise." He lowered his forehead to mine. "I need to tell the kids, then we're all coming to keep you company. You're not alone, Mel. You never will be, not anymore."

Maybe it was his tone or the fact that I could feel him speak from pressing against his chest, but his words got through to me. Everything filtered out of my frantic, worried mind, but his words cemented in there like anchors. They kept me grounded and holding onto what little control I still grasped.

A calmness came over me, and I nodded, meeting his eyes to show that I understood.

His lips curved into a small smile as he kissed me, brief but full of sweetness and comfort. "Go with Razvan," he told me gently as he stepped away. "I'll be right there. I promise."

"Okay," I whispered, watching his back jog away before turning to Raz.

He merely jerked his head to the side and proceeded to walk in that direction. "Follow me."

I did as he instructed, moving my legs robotically across the stage. Thanks to Hunter's calming presence, my surroundings began to filter in as my panic subsided.

Everyone was leaving. The crowd moved in a single massive swarm toward the exits. Holy shit, there were so many people! I couldn't catch anything but murmurs, but they had to be disappointed. Maybe

Nigel announced the show being canceled? Some audience members stayed where they were, watching us curiously as if we'd go back on like nothing happened. Not a snowball's chance in hell.

Razvan walked quickly off the stage and through the carnival grounds to his campsite. I hurried to catch up, trying not to teeter over in my heels. He never slowed enough for me to walk beside him, and maybe that was intentional. Less awkward that way. Neither of us would feel forced to talk.

"Give me a minute," he muttered when we reached his campsite. "I have to unhitch my trailer from the truck."

"Okay." I stayed by the fire, which had burned down to embers at this point.

He unhitched the truck in what had to be under a minute. I wondered if his dragon strength had anything to do with it.

"Let's go." He opened the passenger door and walked around the front to hop into the driver's seat.

I climbed in without hesitation, but stayed glued to the far side of the cab, away from him. Buckling my seatbelt, I closed the door, but left it unlocked and leaned against it. This kept me far away from Raz and would get me out faster when we arrived.

If he noticed or cared that I sat clear across the cab from him, he didn't mention it. He turned the key, and the truck roared to life.

"How far is the hospital?" I asked as we left the campsite and turned onto the main road.

"Not far," he answered. "Ten, maybe fifteen minutes."

Silence stretched on between us. I didn't get the sense that he felt angry or cold toward me, but all this empty space between us still felt wrong. I glanced at him, his face neutral and focused on the road as if he was driving alone.

"Did the EMTs say anything else?" My words felt weak. I could hear my own desperation to fill the silence with any kind of connection from him.

"Just where they were taking him, and that he was alive but unconscious," he replied flatly.

I turned to look out the window. Trees whizzed by, the space between them growing as we began to leave the forest and return to civilization. I looked for flashes of white fur, like when Connor and I first came out here. Seeing Hunter's wolf in the corner of my vision freaked me out back then. I thought I was going crazy, but now I was looking for a source of comfort. A reminder that everything was going to be okay.

"They should have worked."

Razvan spoke abruptly, startling me as I turned to look back at him.

"What?"

"The pills I gave him. They shouldn't have worn off so quickly." His jaw tense, he spat the words out through gritted teeth. I just then noticed his knuckles were white as he gripped the steering wheel. "I swear on my life, Mel. I'd never try to hurt him or sabotage his act. You and he are the only humans who know what I am."

"Raz," I breathed, unbuckling my seatbelt without thinking and sliding across the seat to sit next to him. "It's okay. I know you'd never do that."

He glanced at me once before returning his eyes to the road. "You believe me?" he asked in a pained voice. "They're going to question me, you know."

"I do believe you." I placed a hand on his arm, soaking up the heat from his inked skin. "I trust you, Raz. I--," my voice choked with emotion. So many deep emotions swirling through me for three very different men.

"I've always trusted you," I whispered, lowering my eyes. "I'm just an idiot. You were right. I'm so sorry, Raz."

He took one hand off the steering wheel and wrapped it around mine, his tattooed thumb rubbing gently across my palm.

"I am too. I'm sorry, *steluța*."

14

MELODY

We both jumped out of the truck the moment Razvan pulled into a parking space at the hospital. He grabbed my hand immediately and pulled me close as we walked up. I leaned into him, grateful for his presence now that this obstacle had moved between us. Perhaps it wasn't completely out of the way, but it had definitely moved.

Nigel was already in the lobby, standing at the counter when we arrived.

"Where is he?" I demanded when we burst through the doors.

He turned, glanced quickly at my hand entwined with Raz's, then lifted his eyes back up to me.

"They're running tests on him. X-rays and all that. I'm just finding out where our waiting room is."

After a few minutes, a nurse gave him directions and the three of us started for the elevator. Razvan pulled me tight against his chest and kissed my forehead when the door slid closed. His heart beat erratically underneath my ear and I couldn't tell which of us was more worried.

I slid my hands up his back, enjoying the momentary distraction of feeling his warmth and the contours of his body. He wasn't as tall as

Hunter, nor as muscle-bound as Connor, but a perfect balance of strength and leanness. The decorations of ink covering him only highlighted the artistic lines and shapes his body made.

Choosing not to comment on our affection, Nigel looked away politely as the elevator ascended to Connor's floor.

The elevator dinged and the door couldn't slide open fast enough as we piled out. Nigel approached the desk and told them who we came to see.

The receptionist typed at the computer for a few moments and then glanced up at me.

"Are you Victoria Miller?"

"Um, no." I narrowed my eyes, puzzled.

"Okay, well, she's listed as a domestic partner on his emergency contact form. You all are welcome to wait and we'll give updates, but if there are any life-altering decisions regarding Mr. Shaw, we can only discuss those matters with her."

"Wait," I protested. "I'm pretty sure that's his ex fiancee. They're not together anymore."

"We have to go off of what's on his current emergency contact form, ma'am. If he's lucid enough to update it later, we will surely do that. In the meantime, y'all can have a seat."

Raz gently turned me away from the desk and led me to the waiting area. He sat me down, keeping an arm around me the whole time. Nigel sat across from us and immediately picked up a magazine.

I felt beyond useless just sitting there waiting, but Raz's fingers were soothing on my arms. That gentle touch, an anchor to keep me grounded, to keep me from standing up and bursting through the door to find wherever Connor was.

Some time later, the elevator dinged as it opened and the two children running up to me couldn't help but bring a smile to my face.

"Miss Mel, don't be sad," Rinna looked up at me with her gigantic blue eyes and crawled into my lap when I opened my arms. "Mr. Connor is strong, he's okay."

"Thanks, sweetie." I hugged her close. "I know, it's just hard not to worry."

Roo placed a small hand on my knees, his brow furrowed and

golden eyes sharp. "Connor will be alright," he said in an adorably serious voice. "I know he will."

My aching heart eased just a little at how sweet these two were being. "Thanks, Roo," I whispered, fighting back tears.

"Any news?" Hunter picked up Roo and set him in his lap as he sat on the other side of me. His eyes flickered to Raz's arm around me, but his face remained cool.

"They're running tests. No updates yet."

Hunter nodded and placed a hand on my knee, gently circling his fingers in a massage. The simple gesture almost made me burst out sobbing. With Raz to lean on one way, Hunter on the other, and his two kids with their bright, adorable innocence, I never felt so supported before in my life.

Even Nigel, pointedly ignoring our affection with his nose in a magazine, was at least here for me and Connor. He seemed almost like a dad figure, from what little I knew about that.

So this was how it felt to have people there for you. A support network always sounded like such an alien concept to me. "Lean on your friends when you need them. Tell your parents when you're having a difficult time. They want the best for you." I had those ideas drummed into my head at school while growing up, and they were always so laughable. I never had anyone.

And now, since abandoning everything I knew and joining this freak show, I had people here for me. And I swore to God I would never let this go.

I threaded my fingers through Hunter's, kissed Rinna on top of her head, then leaned my head against Razvan's shoulder. I wasn't alone anymore, and neither was Connor.

The wait was long and would've felt even longer if I had no one. The guys took turns getting up and grabbing snacks from vending machines. Roo and Rinna played with some toys and picture books in the waiting room. No one said much. My eyes stayed glued to the door. I didn't want to get up for a single second.

When it finally opened, I jumped out of my seat. A tall, slender man with glasses and a white coat turned to us with a smile.

"Hi, I'm Dr. Harman. Are y'all here for Connor Shaw?"

"Yes," I answered quickly. "How is he?"

"Are you Victoria?"

I sighed, hoping this wouldn't become an issue in letting me see him. "No, I'm Melody. His girlfriend. He and Victoria are no longer together."

"I see." His eyes swept over me, still in my ringmistress outfit, then glanced to Razvan and Hunter. "Well, you can come on back so we can chat. Just bear in mind that the rooms are small."

"Go ahead, Mel. We'll wait here." Hunter gave me an encouraging smile. "Bring back good news for us."

I nodded, swallowing the lump in my throat as I followed the doctor through the door to a small exam room.

"First off, Connor is stable and not under any life-threatening conditions," the doctor began. He smiled at my massive sigh of relief. "He did sustain a concussion from his fall though, so we're keeping him sedated for the night and monitoring his brain activity."

"Thank you," I breathed.

The doctor opened a folder and flipped through some pages.

"Were you with Connor at the time of the accident?"

"Um, nearby," I answered. "He fell while doing an act onstage, you see," I gestured to my outfit. "I was backstage, watching. And I was with him right before."

Dr. Harman leaned against the hospital bed, making the sheet of paper over it crinkle. "If you don't mind, I'd like to ask you some questions, miss Melody."

I froze. "What kind of questions?"

"Questions that will help us give him the best treatment for when he leaves here." He pulled a ballpoint pen from his coat pocket and clicked the top. "I promise you, anything you tell me will be confidential."

"Okay," I said hesitantly.

He hovered the pen over the papers in the folder. "Is Connor currently on any medications?"

"Um," I chewed my lip. "He was taking some for pain."

"What was he taking?"

"Vicodin, at first. Then something else, I'm not sure."

"Did he have a prescription for this medication?"

I chewed my lip. "Um, no."

He paused and looked up at me. "Where did he get it from?"

"I don't know," I answered firmly.

The doctor scribbled some notes but didn't press any further. "Do you know what kind of pain he was having?"

"In his legs," I answered. "He also, um..."

"It's okay, Melody," the doctor said in a soothing voice. "We're trying to help Connor as best we can. It's vitally important for his recovery that you tell me everything you can."

"He has PTSD," I admitted, looking down at my feet. "He's been having flashbacks."

"I see, thank you for telling me." He jotted down more notes. "To your knowledge, has he received any treatment or therapy for his PTSD?"

"I'm not sure."

"To your knowledge, does he have a history of substance abuse? Alcohol, pain medication, other illicit drugs?"

"No."

The questions continued for another several minutes. My shoulders sagged with relief when the doctor closed the folder and returned the pen to his pocket.

"We're going to keep Connor overnight to monitor his brain from the concussion. When he wakes up tomorrow, I'll also work with him to find the source of pain in his legs and see what we can do for that."

"Can I see him?" I asked eagerly.

"Of course," he smiled. "He's asleep, but you can visit him briefly."

He led me to another room with a hospital bed propped up and an unconscious man lying in it. I barely recognized Connor, and it took everything in me to not burst into tears.

They shaved his head and placed those sticky monitoring nodes in several places. An IV was placed in his arm. Machines near him beeped and whirred. One of them showed what seemed to be a scan of his brain.

But he looked absolutely peaceful, eyes closed and breathing with deep, even breaths, as if he was sleeping right next to me.

"He's not in any pain right now," the doctor assured me. "I'll authorize a morphine drip for tomorrow when he wakes up."

"Thank you again." I looked up at him with heartfelt gratitude.

He nodded curtly. "I'll give you two a moment alone."

Except for the beeping machines and Connor's breathing, silence filled the room when he left.

"Hey babe," I whispered, approaching the hospital bed. "You're gonna lose your shit when you wake up in here."

A giggle escaped me as I took his hand. I was exhausted and still worried, but that didn't make the mental image of Connor flipping out at being in the hospital any less funny.

"I don't care if we get stuck with some huge hospital bill," I told his sleeping form. "No price is too high to have you come back to me." My hand drifted up to his handsome face and stroked his cheek. "But you've *got* to take your ex fiancee off your emergency contact form."

15

RAZVAN

Mel came out and updated us on Connor's condition a half hour later. She wanted to spend the night at the hospital, but Hunter and I convinced her to come back to the carnival campgrounds.

"You need to sleep, *steluța*," I told her. "And shower and change clothes."

"But I..." Her lower lip wobbled, and she sucked in a breath. My heart ached for her, but my dragon flared with jealousy. She cared about him so much. I had to remind the beast inside me that she had every reason to.

"I don't want to be alone," she admitted.

"You won't be." I pulled her into my arms. "We'll get your things from Connor's and then you're staying with me."

She stiffened a little, but I sensed it was more out of surprise than anything else. Then I felt her head nod against my chest. Good. I made a point of telling her and not asking.

"I'm staying with you, too!" Hunter's young son, a spitting image of the tall pale wolf, wrapped his arm around Mel's leg and hugged tightly. His daughter soon followed suit on Mel's other leg.

"Guys." Hunter kneeled beside his children to speak to them. "We're going home for the night and then tomorrow—"

"No, it's fine, Hunter," I told him. "You're all welcome to stay. I have a tent they can use."

He looked up at me, eyes sharp. "Are you sure? I don't want to impose."

"You're not imposing. Mel needs us right now. All of us."

His lip curled into the barest hint of a snarl as he stared me down. We couldn't work it out here in a human hospital, but I knew what he was doing. I returned his gaze, my own stare unflinching. Although we were completely different species, his wolf and my dragon understood each other.

Bringing his children into my territory, a foreign place without him sniffing out first, was a risk. He was letting me know what he would do if I ever compromised their safety. And I let him know that while they would be just as safe as Mel, it was *my* territory and I was the alpha there, no matter who else came in.

Hunter put his teeth away and lowered his eyes, accepting my offer and my position over him while we were there. It would be the exact opposite if I were to stay in his space.

With that settled, we all dragged our feet out of the hospital.

"The carnival is getting torn down tomorrow," Nigel told us when we reached the parking lot. "But I'll work it out with the county that y'all can stay until Connor is fit to be discharged. I know someone who'll give me wiggle room on the permits."

"Thank you, Nigel, for everything," Mel released me and went to hug our manager. He reeled back, startled, then awkwardly patted her back.

"Ah, come here you old slave driver." I pulled him into another unwanted hug as soon as Mel released him. Although he worked behind the scenes, Nigel was a hero to improving work conditions for carnival performers. Unbeknownst to him, he was an ally to shifters as well.

He literally pulled me out of a wooden crate at one of the most vile carnivals in the country. As far as he knew, he was rescuing exploited immigrant workers. He even taught me English. Little did he know how much more he was doing. At least five other shifters had been with me, but all were too proud to accept help from a human. They went their separate ways, and I often wondered if they remained free like I was. Especially Arjun, that damn tiger shifter. A powerful beast but too strong willed for his own good.

"I'll count up your paychecks tonight," Nigel said when he finally wrangled himself away from me. A grim look crossed over his face. "I'll give y'all as much as I can, but I gotta be honest. The closing show going down like this isn't gonna be good."

"I'm fine with that," Mel said quickly. "We'll figure it out."

We said our goodbyes, then Mel and I piled into my truck. This time, she didn't hesitate at all about sitting close to me. I kept my arm around her shoulder as I steered the truck back through the winding forest roads with one hand.

"Penny for your thoughts?" I quipped after we drove several minutes in dead silence.

"I feel guilty," she said after a moment of pondering. "Like I betrayed him."

"Why?"

"He wanted nothing to do with hospitals. I'm certain he didn't want me telling anyone about his PTSD or his leg pain, either. They're going to treat him, which is great, but he was right. Someone's got to pay for it and we might end up homeless because of this."

"Homeless is better than dead," I answered. "You did the right thing and so did Nigel."

"He's going to be so pissed at me, though," she sighed. "I mean, I'm glad he'll be alive to be pissed, but I just know it's going to be a fight. He'd rather be some kind of martyr than seek every possible treatment available."

"I'll back you up," I promised, stroking my thumb on her arm. "So will Hunter. He's allowed to be pissed about whatever, but we won't let him take it out on you. You did this because you love him. If he can't see that for what it is, he's a fucking idiot."

"Thank you, Raz," she whispered, snuggling into my shoulder.

I dropped a kiss on her forehead as we drove on in comfortable silence, but something gnawed at me. Was I shooting myself in the foot here? I was being an emotional support for her right now, which I was happy to do, but what about when Connor got better? Would she still need me like this? Or would she go back to hating my existence?

We pulled up to Connor's trailer, and I waited in the truck while she showered and changed her clothes. Then it was a short drive back to my campsite, where we could finally wind down and relax.

Most of my men were already breaking down tents and packing up belongings. We only gathered as a group for Nigel's carnival. Unlike me, they were humans with lives and jobs outside of the carnival world. I gave them a quick rundown of what was happening and wished them well. By morning, only my stuff would still be here.

"I didn't think I'd have company over," I said sheepishly as I led Mel into my main tent, quickly putting away my collection of knives and tidying the place up. She stood in the middle of my antique rug, a Persian relic I stole, looking uncomfortable and kept glancing at my bed.

"Raz?" she asked in a small voice.

"Yes, *steluţa?*" I approached her, fighting the urge to pull her into my arms again.

"Have you been with anyone else?" her eyes flickered from me to the bed nervously. "Since Ally?"

I almost laughed. My little star was just as jealous as my dragon.

"No," I answered, taking hold of her hands. "I've been... waiting for you to feel ready to talk to me." A grin escaped me. "Without yelling or throwing insults."

"I'm sorry, Raz." Her eyes glittered with tears. "You were right. I was just being stupid and stubborn. I didn't want to admit I was wrong."

"I'm sorry, too." She pressed her face to my chest, and I stroked her hair. "You were also right. I led her on and that was wrong of me, whether she was a crazy bitch or not. I don't want to be a man that..." I exhaled deeply. "That breaks hearts."

Her head lifted slowly as she peered up at me, and I wiped the tears that just began to escape her gorgeous dark eyes.

"Do you regret kissing me?"

My hand trailed down her cheek to cup the side of her face.

"Do you want the truth?"

"Always."

"Not for a second," I answered, my breath hitching. "Maybe the circumstances, yes. But I'll never regret kissing you if it's the last one I taste."

Her chin tilted up, lips parted. I lowered my forehead until it grazed against hers. Our noses touched, and I just felt her soft breath fan against my mouth before my own mouth opened.

"Miss Melody! Mister Razvan!"

A child yelled for us right outside our tent just as our lips touched and we jerked away from each other, already breathless and panting.

"Hey Roo," Mel laughed nervously at the boy, who poked his head into the tent. "You found us."

"Dad, I found them!" he announced proudly.

I stepped out to find Hunter just outside, holding his daughter with an amused expression on his face.

"Roo, boy. You need to knock before poking your head into tents," he chuckled, ruffling his son's hair when the boy reattached himself to his father's leg.

"There was no door. How could I knock?"

"Scratch at the flap."

I cleared my throat. "Right, I'll get a tent set up for you and the little ones."

Turning to the fire pit, I huffed out a quick breath to ignite the logs into a warm blaze again before walking off.

"Whoa! Did you see that!" Roo exclaimed.

Mel, Hunter, and his family talked in low voices by the fire while I got the smaller tent up in a few minutes. By the time I finished, a mouthwatering smell wafted in from their direction and I realized I was starving.

"I brought food," Hunter said when I rejoined the group. "It's the least I could for you offering your hospitality."

I muttered my thanks and took a seat on a tree stump next to Mel, who was already tearing into a drumstick.

"You know, some vegetables wouldn't kill you guys," she teased, wiping her mouth. "Or a little mashed potatoes with gravy..."

"Human stomachs," I joked with a jab to her ribs before helping myself to a whole, small game bird roasting over the fire. "So picky. Hunter and I are carnivores. Our tastes are simple."

All of us were apparently famished. Not long after the food disappeared, Hunter's kids began nodding off, their eyelids fluttering.

"I guess that's goodnight for us," the wolf gently patted his kids awake. "See you in the morn—"

"Hunter, wait."

He looked at Mel, surprised.

She chewed her lip for a moment without speaking. "Stay with me tonight?" She darted a glance at me, then back to him. "With us?"

Hunter's gaze moved to me, then lowered just a centimeter. Fire bloomed in my chest. Yes, the wolf knew his place. In my territory, he had to ask me for permission. But the truth of the matter was, Mel could ask for anything and I'd give it to her without a second thought. If she wanted a wolf and a dragon to keep her company all night, that was no question.

I nodded sharply, and he returned it.

"Let me get them to sleep first," he whispered, then walked to the tent with his pups in tow.

Mel immediately turned to me and, before I could open my mouth, stammered, "I just don't want to be alone tonight. I'm not in the mood for... you know. I'm sorry, I just can't stop thinking about him."

"Shush, *steluţa*. It's okay." I pulled her into a hug, feeling her shudder with relief against my chest. "You have nothing to apologize for. Besides," I pulled away just enough to look at her. "We've just gotten back into each other's good graces. We don't need to fuck each other's brains out yet."

She dropped her head back to my chest, pressing her cheek to my heart. "I just figured that was what you expected."

The words stung, but I tried not to take them personally. My reputation preceded me and Mel was still hard-wired to think that all men wanted just one thing at any cost. But with patience and time, I was changing, and so was she.

"Even if I did," I murmured against her hair. "You can always tell me no. Always and I'll listen. You understand?"

She nodded, but looked unsure. "And if I do... you won't go to anyone else?"

"Absolutely not." I cupped her chin. "I'm not going to screw things up with the only human woman who not only knows the truth about me, but accepts me for what I am." My thumb brushed against her lower lip. "As long as you want me around, my fire is yours."

Finally, her gorgeous face relaxed into a genuine smile that made my hard, scaly heart flutter. "You really do know how to be romantic. I'm impressed, Raz."

"I'm working on it," I chuckled, leading her by the hand back to the tent. "But I'm warning you now, I'm no Romeo."

"More like Dracula," she laughed, squeezing my palm. "I think I like that better."

Be still, my heart.

Hunter joined us a few minutes later, after Mel and I already changed into sleeping clothes and cuddled underneath the blankets on my king-sized air mattress.

"I'm not interrupting anything, am I?" he asked, amusement in his voice as his pale form approached us.

"No, but you're missing out on a good snuggle." Mel patted the space in front of her. "Get in. There's plenty of room."

Hunter paused by the bed, then swiftly removed his shirt and jeans, stripping down to his boxers. I felt Mel's breath hitch and her heat rate speed up as she watched him undress and climb into bed. I suppressed a grin as his arm wrapped around her waist, accidentally brushing mine on her hip.

"Sorry, Raz," he muttered.

"It's quite alright, wolf," I laughed, my breath fanning across the back of Mel's neck.. "I don't give a fuck if I touch you or not. As long as our girl feels safe and comfortable."

"Thank you, guys," she whispered, clasping her hand over mine and kissing Hunter from the sound of it. "For being here. For taking me to the hospital, just... everything. I don't know what I'd do without either of you."

"We're happy to do it, little fox." More kissing sounds and I swallowed the jealousy burning in me.

I settled with dropping a kiss to her shoulder, longing to taste her lips again, but I would be patient. She found Hunter and Connor worthy of that, but not me. Not yet.

"We just want you to be okay, *steluța*," I murmured behind her ear. "And we care about Connor, too. We're here for both of you."

She shifted between Hunter and me, turning around to face me. Without a word, her hands felt for me in the dark, finding my face. Her fingertips brushed against my lips and I kissed them before they slid around to my neck.

Then her mouth found mine, kissing me hesitantly at first, but then deeply. I fell asleep with a smile on my face and the sweet taste of her on my tongue.

16

MELODY

A tattooed arm around my waist. A pale, sculpted chest beneath my ear.

I slept so deeply, I almost forgot about last night. Looking at both of them, Hunter and Razvan both looked so peaceful, yet completely different in the morning light filtering through. And how lucky was I? Sandwiched between two gorgeous men. All I needed was my third.

Connor! He would be awake today! The thought startled me into action. I carefully lifted Raz's arm off of me and crawled over Hunter's long torso to reach my clothes on the floor. Raz groaned and rolled over, stopping inches away from Hunter. One more half-roll and those two would be cuddling.

I suppressed a giggle as I looked at them. If I had just walked in, there'd be no doubt in my mind those two were lovers. The thought sent a rush of heat to my core so fast, it made me gasp. My nipples hardened into tense peaks with no stimulation, despite it already being a hot and muggy morning.

I never thought much of two men being together, but the mental image of those two could not be erased. Down here in the south, it was definitely frowned upon, but I heard about places like California where it was celebrated more openly. I rubbed my face and went back to getting dressed, but the thought could not be unthought. And my body could not stop responding to it like it was the hottest thing since dragon fire.

I hardly dared to wake them up, but I was dying to know how Connor was doing. And I didn't want Roo and Rinna asking questions I didn't want to answer.

"Hunter," I whispered, tip-toeing to his side of the bed.

He looked like a marble statue. His platinum hair spilled across the pillows, his face turned to the side, showing off his statuesque profile as he breathed deeply. And his body. I half expected his pale skin to feel like the cold touch of stone as I gently shook his shoulder. But he was oh so real, living and breathing.

"Mmph." He turned his head and shifted, his hand clasping around mine as his eyelids cracked open lazily. "Hi, beautiful," he croaked, his voice groggy with sleep.

My heart skipped a beat. How on earth did I get so lucky? "Hi, handsome wolf," I returned.

Both of his arms reached for me. "Why're you wearing so much clothing? Come back to bed." He glanced at Razvan inches away. "I think someone else wants the middle, though."

Giggling, I pulled on his hands to bring him upright. "You should check on the kids. I want to go see Connor as soon as we can."

"Alright," he sighed, swinging his legs down to the floor. His snug boxer briefs left little to the imagination, though I'd already seen him naked.

Razvan muttered something in his sleep and rolled over again, settling on his stomach as he hugged Hunter's pillow.

"Have fun waking him." Hunter kissed my cheek after pulling on yesterday's jeans and shirt. "I'll be back when the rugrats are up."

With the blankets thrown back and the soft morning light filling the tent, I took a moment to admire the art covering Razvan's back. A single, massive tattoo of a dragon, twisting and winding through smoke and fire, covered his entire back from his neck and disappearing under the band of his boxers. From the black scales inked on the backs of his thighs, the tattoo seemed to continue over his entire backside.

The dragon seemed to inflate with smoke with every inhale and release bright burning flame with every one of Raz's exhales. It looked so alive and vivid, like it moved not just with his breaths but on its own.

Before I knew it, my hands were tracing the beast's scales, following its movement like it was a real creature that wrapped around me protectively. My hands felt warm human skin beneath them, but my mind felt armored scales that almost burned to the touch.

I closed my eyes and quieted my human mind as I was learning to do, tapping into the power that was bestowed upon me. Smoke floated around me, fire burned in my lungs, reptilian vision and instincts matched with intelligence and cunning beyond what human minds were capable. So this was what being a dragon felt like.

"Mm, Mel?"

The sensations faded as I opened my eyes. Razvan had flipped onto his back and blinked up at me.

"Good morning," I chirped awkwardly.

His gray eyes narrowed. "I swore I felt another dragon beside me, then I looked up and it was you."

"Yeah," I breathed, raking my hands through my tangled hair. "Hunter and I had an eventful date even before you crashed it."

I filled him in on what I told Connor about Thembi, quickly thinking I needed to keep these three guys together as much as possible. It was tiring repeating myself.

"A shaman, huh?" He turned on his side and propped himself up on one elbow, scratching his jaw with the other hand. "One of the shifters I'd been caged with years ago talked about shamans."

He said it so casually, but I still winced at the mention of him and others being exploited like that.

"What did he say?"

"A lot similar to what you just said. Poor cat held out hope that one would find us and rescue us. He said they looked human, but we'd just know when one of them came along." He smiled at me. "I knew you were different, *steluţa,* but it was so long ago that I never put two and two together."

"I can't stop wondering why he gave it to *me,*" I sighed. "I was a child, barely bigger than a toddler. And my drunk ass mom got us all kicked out of there."

"Maybe it's not entirely gifted," he suggested. "Maybe there's something in you that was always there. He saw it and knew you were the right one to pass this torch to."

"I still feel so clueless about it," I admitted. "I want to use it to help more shifters, but I have no idea what I'm doing. And then there's Connor—"

"Sshh." He sat up, wrapping me in a warm embrace that instantly soothed like the comforting heat of a campfire. "One thing at a time," he murmured, rocking me gently. "Connor first, and then all the enslaved shifters in the world."

"No pressure or anything," I snorted.

He loosened his hold and looked at me with wide, metallic eyes.

"You've already done the unheard of by saving Hunter and me. So many shifters have lost hope that anyone is on their side. Word will travel fast, *steluţa.* And just knowing you're out there and that you care will light a fire under so many asses."

"That's sweet." I touched his face. "But I didn't save you. You were already free."

He smiled, his thumb caressing across my cheek.

"You did, *steluţa.* In ways you can't imagine."

THE FIVE OF us pulled up to the hospital a half-hour later. Roo and Rinna had never ridden in a car before, so I sidled up next to Raz. Roo sat next to me, and Hunter sat at the far end with Rinna in his lap. Raz indulged Roo by driving over every bump and pothole in the road, making the boy scream and laugh in delight with every jump and jolt through the truck cab.

"You don't have to fuck up your tires just to keep them entertained, Raz."

Rinna immediately clapped a hand over her father's mouth and narrowed her eyes in a stern expression. "Don't say bad words, Daddy."

"Sorry, sweetie. I forget sometimes." He smacked a big kiss on her cheek and I thought my heart couldn't melt anymore.

"It's alright, Hunter," Raz returned, smirking as his eyes remained glued to the road. "I got a good warranty on these. If I pop one, I'll get a brand new one for free."

We were all in high spirits as we pulled up to the hospital. I drummed my fingers with nervous excitement in the elevator, determined to stay positive and not assume the worst.

I launched out of the elevator as soon as we reached the floor, gripping the edge of the reception desk like a lifeline.

"Hi, we're here to see Connor Shaw," I said in a single, rushed breath.

A different receptionist from yesterday typed on the computer for a few moments before shooting me a friendly smile.

"You can go right in. He's awake and already receiving visitors."

"Oh," I said, surprised. It had to be Nigel. "Thanks!" I returned her smile and walked around to the side door as fast as my legs could carry me.

Remembering where the doctor escorted me last time, I rushed past nurses and other hospital staff in my eagerness to see my grumpy Marine boyfriend. And then my feet abruptly froze when I looked through the window of his room.

He was awake alright, and talking to someone. A woman with a short blond bob sitting at the edge of his bed.

No, it couldn't be...

My feet wanted to run in the other direction, but I forced them forward as I turned the knob on his door. I had to know.

"...doll face."

Connor stopped talking abruptly, and they both looked at me as I crossed the threshold.

"Mel," Connor said, sitting up straighter. "Hey."

Mel. Not *babe*. While I swore, he just called *her* doll face.

I looked at the woman now facing me, with red painted lips and an adorable button nose. Her cropped blonde hair framed her face in sensual waves. Not just a doll face, but a goddamn Marilyn Monroe clone.

"Who are you?" I demanded, not bothering to mince words.

Connor cleared his throat. "Mel, this is Vicky. She was my, ah..."

"Fiancee," she finished for him.

17

CONNOR

My head felt stuffed with cotton, but the pain was gone. I groaned and started to move my fingers and toes. Wait, I didn't have toes.

Gingerly, I moved my head from side to side. No neck injury. The only concrete thought I could form through the fog that wrapped around me and even seemed to go through me. I cracked my eyes open to a room that was entirely too bright.

"Good morning, Mr. Shaw," a male voice greeted me.

"Where am I?" I groaned.

"You're at Crying Falls emergency hospital, Connor. I'm Doctor Harman. You had a pretty serious fall."

Hospital? Fuck.

"I can't be here." Pressing my hands into whatever surface I laid on, I began scooting my hips away. "I can't afford a hospital. This'll ruin everything. I can't do that to Mel."

"Calm down, Connor." Two hands grabbed my arms to still me. "Please calm down. We'll work out payment later. But you've had a concussion and you don't have any prosthetic legs with you."

Damn it. Fucking hell.

I relented, not wanting to fight against a guy doing his job and especially when I wouldn't get very far. I sat back, blinking to make my eyes adjust to this stupidly bright-ass room. Details began to filter in despite my head still feeling fogged up. This was a hospital, alright. A skinny guy in his early forties, wearing glasses and a white coat, stood next to my bedside.

"I promise I'll discharge you as soon as I can," he said, dragging over a stool to sit on. "In the meantime, how are you feeling, Connor?"

"Foggy as fuck," I grumbled. "But the pain's gone."

"You suffered a pretty serious concussion," he explained. "Fortunately, your scans didn't show any skull fractures or bleeding in the brain. However, your brain *is* injured and you may encounter headaches, dizziness, or sensitivity to light for the next several weeks."

"Fantastic," I murmured.

He took off his glasses and wiped them on his coat. "The young lady with you said you were in pain as well?"

Thanks, babe. Always looking out for me.

I sighed. If I couldn't get out of here, I might as well reap the benefits of having to stay. "Yes, in my stumps."

"Would you mind describing it for me and how long you've been feeling it?"

I told him every detail I could recall in my fog-addled brain. He applied pressure to my legs and even tapped them with that reflex thing they used to make your leg kick out when you were a kid.

"I'm not a specialist when it comes to amputations, Connor," the doctor mused as he finished. "But my best guess is you have some pinched or pressured nerves around your amputation points. You wear prosthetics, yes?"

"Yeah," I grunted.

"When did you last have them calibrated? They're most likely putting pressure on your nerves in a way that's triggering a pain response."

"When I got them," I muttered. "Three years ago."

The doctor's eyes widened behind his glasses. "You really need to recalibrate them, Connor. Otherwise the pain will continue and you'll prefer spending time in a wheelchair."

"Not gonna happen," I snarled. "Either of those options. I can't afford to get them recalibrated. Why do you think I'm a goddamn carnival performer? And I'd rather deal with the pain than spend my life in a wheelchair."

The doctor sighed and pressed his lips tightly together. "I'll make some calls to a few specialists I know. You're a veteran, correct?" he nodded at the dog tags around my neck. "There should be some way we can help you."

"Trust me, I hear that all the time," I answered. "And then that's the last I hear of it. I've exhausted all options, doc. You know as well as I do that I'm just one of thousands of vets this country has fucked over."

His mouth pressed even smaller, seeming determined. "I'll make those calls, anyway. You know never know what we might find." He stood to leave and quickly turned back to me. "Are you feeling up for visitors? A whole gang of people came to see you yesterday."

"Sure," I muttered, although I wasn't really feeling up to seeing anyone but Mel. Not that I wanted her to see me like this, but those big doe eyes might make me feel a little better.

"I'll let the front desk know. Just hit the call button if you need anything."

Just as he left, I spotted a TV remote next to my bed. Sure enough, one click turned on the small screen up in the corner of the room. I settled back against my pillows and found a college football game to watch. Damn, how long had it been since I did this? Kicking back and watching a football game was a simple pleasure I once took for granted.

I was so into the game I didn't notice the blonde woman outside my room until she pushed my door open.

"Connor?"

My eyes met hers, and my heart stopped. My whole body went rigid. Her hair changed, but her face was exactly the same.

"Vicky," I barked, probably harsher than necessary from the way she flinched. "What are you doing here?"

"The hospital called me," she said, hovering by the door. "I guess I'm still your emergency contact."

I leaned back on my pillows, looking up toward the ceiling. "I guess I forgot about changing that."

"Connor, what happened?" she allowed the door to close behind her and took a few tentative steps toward my bed.

"Not important," I shot back. "You shouldn't be here. They never should have called you."

"Connor, I drove all the way up from Florida to be here," she argued, coming closer still. "Believe it or not, I was worried about you. I at least deserve an explanation."

My teeth grated against each other in my jaws. I forgot how annoying it was when she ignored my requests to be alone. At first, when we were still together, I thought it was just my PTSD. In hindsight, it was just a glaring sign of our incompatibility.

Not like with Mel. My babe could get through to me even when I pushed her away at first. She understood me even when we butted heads. I wanted her here, not this woman who now felt like a stranger to me.

"I got nothing for you, Vicky," I answered, throwing my hands up. "I'm not some decorated war hero like you wanted me to be. I'm the same curmudgeonly old bastard, probably days away from being homeless again. I don't know what you expected when you came up here, but sorry to say I'm just as disappointing now as when you left me."

"I've been texting you," she said, as if everything I just told her went right over her head. "Why did you stop answering?"

"Because I'm busy. And," I paused and leaned forward, unable to help myself from rubbing it in her face, "I'm seeing someone."

Her crimson painted mouth made a little 'o' of surprise. "You are?"

"Yeah, and apparently so are you." The rock on her left ring finger nearly blinded me.

She grabbed the engagement ring with her other hand and twisted it around her finger. "It's complicated," she muttered. "I'm actually having second thoughts."

"Well, good luck with your life and whatever," I sighed, my patience growing thinner by the minute. "But it's got nothing to do with me now. And I don't care to pretend to be buddies or whatever the fuck so you can delete my number."

"Connor...," her eyes watered and her bottom lip wobbled. Oh, great. "We were together for four years. How can you act like I don't mean anything to you?"

"You. Left. Me," I repeated slowly, trying not to raise my voice despite my blood pressure shooting through the roof. "I got over you because I had to, Vick. I moved on for my own survival."

"What if it was a mistake?" she whispered, blinking rapidly and sniffling. "What if I realized... I was wrong? That I threw away the best relationship I ever had?"

I lifted both shoulders in a shrug. "Not my problem, doll face." Damn it. I bit my tongue too late. My old nickname for her slipped out like a bad habit.

Her eyes widened upon hearing the name and her ruby lips parted to respond, but the door pushed open to make both of our heads turn. At the sight of Mel's raven black hair and big doe eyes, I felt simultaneous relief and dread in the pit of my stomach.

"Mel," I breathed, sitting back against my pillows again. "Hey."

Her eyes darted from me to Vicky, wide and full of questions. The temperature in the room seemed to drop a full ten degrees.

"Who are you?" she asked Vicky, the accusation already in her tone. Oh shit. This would not end well.

I cleared my throat. "Mel, this is Vicky. She was my, ah..."

"Fiancee," Vicky so kindly finished my sentence for me.

"Ex-fiancee," I quickly corrected. "She was mistakenly called here because of an outdated emergency contact form from when I was in the Marines." I stared hard at her, hoping I was finally making myself clear. "She was just leaving."

"No, Connor. I am *not* done talking to you," she reprimanded me like a stern mother. "Your little trailer park girl can wait."

I looked at her incredulously and, in that moment, my annoyance turned to pure loathing. "Oh no, you stupid bitch. How dare you?"

But it was too late. Mel was already backing out the door with tears in her eyes and taking jagged pieces of my heart with her.

"Mel, wait!" I yelled. "Babe, stop!"

She either didn't hear me or ignored me, walking as fast as she could back down the hall.

Vicky must have worn a smug look on her face, but I didn't spare her a glance as I jabbed the call button, not lifting my finger from it until a nurse came running and burst into my room.

"Is something wrong?" she asked.

"This woman needs to leave," I said, pointing at Vicky. "Call the police if you have to. I don't want her near me."

18

HUNTER

"So," I glanced at Razvan, hunched over like me in the waiting room while we allowed Mel and Connor to have some time together. "You two have made up, I take it?"

He lifted his gaze to me, smirking. "I guess you could say that."

"Just like that, huh? When I almost thought I had to fight you the other day?"

"I never would have fought you," he whispered. "She chose you over me at the time. I respect that. I was being a dick to her." He shrugged, rubbing his tattooed hands together. "I manned up and apologized. She did the same for her part. Now," his smirk grew wider. "I guess I'm part of the pack."

"We are quite the pack, aren't we?" I huffed out a laugh. "All pawing for attention from our alpha female."

"Yeah, you'd consider her an alpha?" Razvan's eyebrows lifted. "I'm not too brushed up on wolf hierarchies."

"It's in her, even if she doesn't know it yet," I answered. "You see it in the way she steps into her ringmistress role. She thinks of it as an act, but that's really her. People just want to watch her, listen, and follow her lead. I bet the shaman powers have something to do with it, too. She's like a magnet and we can't fight the pull of her."

"Damn right," he muttered his agreement.

The moment he spoke, the waiting room door burst open. Mel flew through the room, right past us and toward the elevator.

Razvan and I sprung into action. He caught up to her first, grabbing her before the elevator opened.

"*Steluţa*, what is it?" He cradled her head against his chest and rubbed her back. "My little star, what happened in there?" From the muffled sounds, I realized she was sobbing.

I flattened my palm against her lower back and kissed the back of her head, not caring how close my face was to Razvan's.

"Sweet girl, please tell us," I murmured behind her ear. "We're here for you."

"*Her.*"

Our eyes followed where she peeked out from Raz's shirt, following an attractive blonde woman who just left the same waiting room and headed for the elevators. Her lip curled with disgust the moment she saw Mel sandwiched between me and Raz, then she turned her nose up and walked into the first one that opened.

Raz and I looked at each other, a mutual understanding passing between us. Connor either fucked up majorly or this was a perfect storm of misunderstanding.

"You go talk to him," Raz snarled protectively. "I might say something I regret. Plus, you know him better."

I nodded, placing a last kiss on Mel's head and squeezing her shoulder before I turned away. As I walked back toward the waiting room, the low murmurs of Raz speaking soothingly to her followed me.

A chuckle escaped me before I could help it. Could we be any more of a perfect yet fucked up balance? One guy hurt her, another comforted her, and another went to talk sense into the guy that hurt her.

Roo and Rinna, entranced by the toy set in the waiting room, didn't even notice the commotion around them.

"Guys, I'm going to talk to Mr. Connor real quick," I told them. "Stay here." I gave the command with an undertone of wolf growl so they knew I was serious.

"Yes, Dad," they answered.

I pushed through the door and stopped a nurse to ask for directions to Connor's room.

"Down the hall and to the left," she took in my towering frame nervously. "But um, he's not taking visitors right now. We're monitoring his blood pressure."

"It'll just be a minute," I gave her a wolfish smile, letting her know as kindly as I could that she did not want to get in my way. "Thank you."

Connor sat up in a hospital bed, with a blood pressure cuff around his arms and a nurse watching the machine. He looked fine, well, even. Just as disgruntled as usual. I pushed through his door without bothering to knock.

"You want to explain why Mel just ran out of here crying her eyes out?"

"Hey, no visitors!" the nurse snapped at me. "You need to leave."

"He's fine," Connor sighed. "You can leave us."

Her head snapped back to look at him, and he nodded, urging her to go. She promptly unrolled the cuff from around his forearm and walked wide around me to leave the room.

"Well?" I prompted when we were alone.

"Because I couldn't get that stupid bitch out of here fast enough," he groaned, rubbing his hands down his face.

"Who's the stupid bitch?" I growled, remembering the way she looked at Mel before getting into the elevator.

"My ex," he sighed. "She wouldn't leave until I called nurses to get her the hell out. In that time, she called Mel trailer trash."

"Oh, no." I rubbed the back of my neck, knowing how sensitive Mel was about her past. "Fuck, Connor. Why was she here?"

"Apparently out of concern," he scoffed with an eye roll. "The hospital called her because she was my emergency contact. But I dunno, I think she was hoping to get money or some shit. Which I have none of."

I nodded. So a misunderstanding, then. Mel saw her in here and probably thought the worst. I couldn't blame her, and it definitely didn't minimize her hurt.

"Raz is with her?" Connor asked.

"Yeah."

"Good," Connor sighed, leaning back onto his pillows. "She needs you guys right now more than me."

"Con, it's not that big a deal," I sighed. "Yeah, she's hurt right now and we're here for her. But when she calms down and we explain, I'm sure she'll understand. You didn't want your ex to be here. I'm sure she knows that."

"Nah, you don't get it, Hunter," he shook his head. "Shit like this is why she needs you two. There is so much I can't control. This hospital visit is going to cripple me, pun not intended." He flashed a smirk before continuing. "I'll have to sell the RV just to pay for them checking my damn blood pressure. And the rest of this is going to be hanging over me for the rest of my life. I can't be a good partner to her if I can't even provide a roof over her head."

"Con, dude," I held up a hand. "There's no need to catastrophize this. Yeah, hospital bills suck ass, but Mel needs you too. We all stayed at Raz's last night. He's got plenty of room, I'm sure he'll take you in, too. We'll figure all that shit out."

"It's not just that, bro," Connor gave me a sad smile. "It's the PTSD. It's the bill collectors that are going to chase me forever. It's the fact that I'm going to be an ever bigger asshole to her now from being in constant pain because I can't get new legs that fit right. She deserves better."

"Con," I said after a long, uncomfortable silence. "She loves you, dude."

"And I love her. More than fucking anything. That's why I need to let her go." He laughed humorlessly. "God, I wish I met her first. I wish I put a ring on her finger, not Vicky's. Then we might have had a real shot at something."

I cleared my throat. "But she would have been like, fourteen right?"

Connor looked at me, then burst out laughing. "Yeah, you're right. It never would have worked. She made me happy for a brief moment in time, but it was never supposed to work."

"Connor, come on," I urged. "She will *never* give up on you, so why are you giving up on her? Fuck everything you can't control, just work on what you can. The four of us will look after each other, no matter what. Well six, if you include the kids."

"I can't risk it," he shook his head. "What if I get a flashback that's so bad and vivid, I hurt her? Or one of the kids? I've shot guns through walls before, Hunter, thinking I was back *there*. My nerve pain is only going to make it worse." He looked away, still shaking his head. "No, I can't risk hurting her or anyone, for that matter. I won't abuse the ones I love."

"Con," I choked out. "What exactly are you saying?"

"I'm saying," he growled. "Take your family. Take Mel and Raz, and move on. Leave me here and forget I exist."

19

MELODY

Raz or Hunter, usually both of them, held me every moment since running out of that hospital room. My face physically ached from crying so hard. My head pounded relentlessly, but their gentle caresses over my hair soothed me at least a little.

And then I thought of *her* sitting on the edge of Connor's bed like they had never been apart at all, and the tears flowed freely again. I was so wrapped up in my heart breaking, I barely noticed the guys leading me out of the hospital and back to the truck. Rinna crawled into my lap and wiped my tears away. I hugged her tight, grateful for her, but didn't want to burden her with my pain.

The next thing I knew, someone carried me from the truck. Lips kissed my forehead, and I just clung to this person's shirt and sobbed. The tattoos on the chest and neck told me it was Raz, but my brain seemed unable to form coherent thoughts. All I could picture was *them* together in an endless, unforgiving loop.

I was laid down in a bed, offered water and tissues, then wrapped up snugly in blankets. All of these occurrences seemed to happen across a barrier, like I was in some kind of bubble disconnected from it all.

Eventually, exhaustion overtook me, and I succumbed to the darkness of sleep.

When I woke up, my eyes opened to meet a familiar black dragon gliding across the muscles of Raz's back. A long, pale arm wrapped around my waist from behind, holding me tightly. I broke eye contact with the inked dragon to turn around, meeting Hunter's sharp, golden eyes.

"Hey," he greeted softly, caressing over my back and ribs.

"Hi," I answered, my voice choked and raw.

"Do you need anything?" he lifted up to his elbow. "Food? Water? A hot bath?"

"Um," I rubbed my face, still tender and swollen. I must've looked like hell, too. "All of the above sound great, but where would I get a bath?"

The handsome wolf shot me a mischievous grin. "Turns out Raz has a tub that he hauls around when he travels. The guy likes his comforts on the road."

I let out a suppressed giggle. After seeing the Persian rugs, the knife collection, and the finest king-sized air mattress money could buy, it was clear that Raz enjoyed his luxuries.

"That's what I like to hear." Hunter stroked my face and kissed the bridge of my nose. "I love your laugh."

A shuddering sigh wracked through me. I didn't want to talk or think about what happened in the hospital. I already hurt too much and hoped Hunter wouldn't try to make me talk about it.

"Come on, let's get you in a bath," he pulled me gently toward the edge of the bed. "I'll get some food ready for you."

I followed him reluctantly out of bed and out of the tent. "That small tent," he pointed, "is where the bathtub is. It has its own propane heater and everything. Go ahead and soak," he kissed my forehead, "and I'll bring you food."

"Thank you," I murmured, leaning my head against him for a moment. Those two words couldn't even touch how grateful I felt for him and Raz.

"Of course." He gave me a final kiss and went to the main fire, where a large cast-iron pot sat on a grate above the flames.

The tub was small, although a perfect size for me, and looked to be made of a hard plastic. Probably easier to carry around that way. It was already filled with water, which felt comfortably warm to the touch. A folded towel, bars of soap, and a loofah had been placed on a wooden crate next to it.

I blinked away tears as I shed my clothing. The guys must have prepared this for me while I was sleeping. And that food smelled like it had been simmering for a while. What did I do to deserve thoughtfulness and care like this?

"Ahhh," I couldn't help but moan as I sank into the water, the heat enveloping me and sinking in my muscles like a full body massage. "You're a genius, Raz."

I leaned my head back to let my hair soak, the warmth on my scalp doing wonders for my headache. After soaking for a few moments, I picked up a bar of soap and began scrubbing it over my arms and chest.

"Mel?" Hunter scratched at the tent flap.

"Come in," I called.

His blush was adorable as he averted his eyes from me politely. While the edge of the tub just came over my shoulders, I had no bubbles to hide anything below the surface of the water.

"Is the temperature okay?" he asked, setting a bowl of stew next to the soaps. "Raz boiled the water a little while ago to purify it, then shut it off to cool down for whenever you were ready."

"It's perfect," I smiled. "Is he still asleep?"

Hunter nodded, laughing. "If I didn't know any better, I'd figure he was a cat shifter. That dude sleeps constantly."

"Reptiles sleep a lot too, don't they?" I asked, blowing on the stew to cool it. "Since they only eat like once a month."

"No idea," he grinned. "How's the food?"

"Delicious!" It really was. Although mostly meat and potatoes, I did find a few rogue vegetables as I spooned through the thick broth. So thoughtful for my human stomach. "Thank you, Hunter."

"Of course." He looked apprehensively toward the door. "Do you want me to leave you alone?"

"No," I answered. "Please stay. And you don't have to avoid looking at me, either." I playfully grabbed his chin and made him face me. "I figured you'd see me naked, eventually. It's only fair, right?" I laughed.

A grin widened across his face. "I just didn't want to be rude."

"You're the least rude person I've ever met," I told him. "These other two, on the other hand…"

He laughed with me, drifting his fingertips over the wet skin of my arm and shoulder with the lightest ghost of a touch.

"Mel," he began in a more serious tone. "Do you want to talk about—"

I shook my head, cutting him off abruptly. "It's over. That's what he told you, right?"

His face fell, confirming my suspicion. Just as my heart felt like it stopped bleeding, the wound reopened again.

"How did you know?"

"I could just see it when they were in the room together." I swallowed a bite of stew, trying to distract the pit in my stomach. "It sounds stupid, but he didn't call me babe in front of her. And then when she called me tr—"

"Hey, no. You've got it all wrong." Hunter's gentle caresses on my arm turned into a desperate squeeze. "He was trying to make her leave, and she was being a stubborn bitch, that's all. He had nurses kick her out right after you left."

"Are you sure?" I searched his gaze, hope daring to grow within me.

"She means nothing to him, and you mean everything," he said, golden eyes locked on mine.

"But why did you say—"

"'Cause he's being a self-sacrificing idiot," Hunter sighed. "With no way to pay the hospital or get new prosthetics, he doesn't want to drag you down with him. He thinks the pain is going to make his flashbacks worse and he could seriously hurt you, or even the kids. So he wants you to move on."

"But…" Confusion swirled within me, bringing my headache right back. "You don't think he'd hurt me or the kids, do you?"

"Absolutely not, if he manages all his issues," Hunter replied. "But it sounds like he's given up on trying."

"We can't let him give up!" I stood from the tub, splashing water everywhere without giving a fuck. I grabbed the towel and started wiping myself dry.

"Mel, what are you doing?" Hunter didn't bother trying to hide looking at my naked body.

"I'm going back to the hospital to talk some sense into him." Grabbing his shoulder for support, I stepped out and continued drying myself off. "Before he does anything stupid."

"Hey, wait. Calm down." He took hold of my arms, now keeping his eyes glued to my face. "He's not going anywhere. They're still keeping him to watch his concussion. And you are still exhausted and emotional. Just take a breather, little fox."

"How could I not be?!" I demanded, raising my voice. "He's trying to break up with me over the stupidest, petty shit! I don't care about money or his flashbacks, I just want to be there for him. If he has no one, then he..."

"I know, I know." Hunter pulled me into his chest as I descended into body-wracking sobs again. He shushed me and stroked my hair, not caring that it was tangled or wet.

"You're incredible, you know?" he murmured against my forehead. "For caring so much. But it takes a lot of out of you, my sweet little fox. Take care of *you* for one night. Connor will be okay tomorrow. We'll see him when we can be calm and level-headed, okay?"

I nodded just as the tent flap rustled.

"Everything okay in there?" Raz called from the outside.

"Yeah," I sniffed, rubbing my face with my hands. "You can come in, Raz."

Wearing only his dark distressed jeans, Raz's fully inked torso moved like a living painting as he stepped into the tent.

"Ah, fuck! I'm sorry." He turned away the moment he saw that I was naked in Hunter's arms. "Didn't mean to interrupt."

"You're not," Hunter assured him with a dry laugh. "I told her what Connor said. She jumped out of the tub and was about to run back there buck ass naked."

"You shoulda let her," Razvan chuckled, still with his back turned.

"Then we could chase her all the way down to the hospital and enjoy the view at the same time."

"You guys are the worst," I laughed, snuggling into Hunter's chest and returning the embrace that he wrapped around me. "This is just payback. Raz, did I tell about when I hugged a naked Hunter after the opening show?"

"No! How did that happen?"

As I retold the story, my awareness drifted to the heat and contours of Hunter's body. When I stepped in closer to squeeze him tighter, an unmistakable bulge pressed into my lower stomach. His breath hitched, and he stiffened, moving just a fraction of an inch away.

My own body ignited into a liquid heat, concentrating at my core. With Hunter pressed against me and Razvan's tattooed back watching me, thoughts entered my mind that I barely dared to voice.

I wouldn't let Connor set me free, or whatever supposedly noble way he tried to justify it. He wasn't perfect, and I accepted that about him. But I still needed him. And even if he didn't want to admit it, he needed me to keep his mind from going to dark places.

When he was low, these two lifted us back up. Sure, maybe just Connor and I would be too unstable and dysfunctional to make it together. But with the four of us? We were unbeatable.

"Razvan," I breathed in a sultry whisper while the full length of my body pressed against Hunter once again. "You don't have to turn around."

His head turned to the side, making the dragon on his back coil up as if ready to pounce on its prey. "Are you sure?"

"Please." My voice shook from either fear or anticipation. I couldn't tell which. "Look at me."

He turned slowly and his eyes heated immediately upon drinking in my curves, still wrapped in Hunter's embrace.

"You're beautiful, *steluța*," he murmured with genuine appreciation. "Conner and Hunter are lucky men."

"I feel way too overdressed," Hunter laughed in an attempt to lighten the thick tension growing in the room.

I slid my hands up his chest to wrap them around his neck. His touch drifted across my waist to my lower back, hovering just above my bare ass. An electrical intensity fired between us. I looked over to Razvan and felt the same intense chemistry from him.

Maybe it was selfish, but I didn't care anymore. For once, I wanted to forget about everything else and just feel good.

"I think both of you are overdressed."

20

MELODY

Neither of them said a word for a long moment, but Razvan seemed to get the idea first. A naughty grin spread across his face as he folded his arms across his chest.

"Have you ever been with two men before, *steluţa?*"

"No," I admitted, leaning my head against Hunter's chest. His heart pounded just as furiously as mine.

"Are you sure this is something you want to do?"

I reached out an arm to him. "Come here, Raz."

He approached me slowly, as if still trying to survey the situation. But when I cupped his face and pressed my mouth to his, he dropped all caution to the wind and kissed me back with pure, fiery passion.

His split tongue caressed both sides of mine, teasing my lips with playful flicks as he slid an arm across my upper back. When we parted, I stood on tiptoes and kissed Hunter in the next breath. He tensed in surprise but soon opened his mouth to me, too. From him I tasted that sweetness mixed with the alpha dominance that made me weak in the knees.

Just when I thought this couldn't get any hotter, Raz's split tongue danced along the back of my neck. He moved behind me, his jeans brushing against my ass as he kissed my neck, but not pushing against me. Yet.

"Now," I breathed when Hunter's kiss broke. "Did that bother either of you?"

"Not in the least," Raz whispered gruffly against my skin. "It's hot to see you kiss him, to see him wrapped around your beautiful body like this."

"Hunter?"

My pale wolf exhaled a deep breath and I could see he was trying to think with the correct head, to do the right thing by me.

"No, it doesn't bother me," he began. "I just don't want you to feel bad afterward if... this happens."

"I'm done feeling bad," I told him. "You two make me feel amazing and I just want more of that." I took his face in both of my hands. "Tomorrow, we're going to drag Connor out of a hellhole he's trying to bury himself in. But it'll be a ton of work and I can't do it by myself. I need you two with me. I need—"

He cut me off with a hard kiss, giving me every reassurance without words. As his tongue invaded my mouth, he dragged my hands down his body to stop at his pants. My fingers grazed the firm muscles of his abs before I flicked the button open, and he broke our kiss for just a moment to pull his shirt over his head.

Everyone's hesitation went out the window in that moment. Raz pulled my hips back toward him as his tongue danced along my spine. Hunter cupped my nape in a fiercely possessive hold as he captured my mouth again, all the gentleness gone and leaving only hot desire to take my breath away.

"Hey," Raz grazed his teeth along my ear. "Let's head back to the bedroom tent. Hunter, where are the little ones?"

"Home," he murmured gruffly. "At our den in the woods. They said they slept better there."

"Perfect," Raz hummed in a kiss against my shoulder. "My people have all left. No one should be around."

Hunter broke away from me to peek outside the tent. Shirtless and with his pants partially undone, he looked hot as sin and I nearly found myself salivating. He'd be right at home in a Calvin Klein ad.

"Coast is clear," he reported before stepping outside.

"Let's go, *steluța*," Raz said with a playful swat to my ass.

With Hunter already out and Raz right behind me, I darted out of the tent, cackling with laughter. The bedroom was a quick jog away and I could have taken all the time in the world with no one else around, but it still felt naughty and thrilling being out in the woods without a lick of clothing on.

Hunter was waiting, leaning back on the messy air mattress on his elbows. "Hey, gorgeous," he greeted with a wide grin as my naked form approached him.

"Hello, handsome." I got the idea to crawl across the bed to him all slow and sexy, but that was quickly ruined by Razvan.

I screamed-laughed as the dragon shifter grabbed me around the waist from behind and picked me up. Despite my squirming, he easily carried me across the tent to the bed, where he dropped us both in a freefall.

"I was going to do a sexy walk and then crawl on the bed, but you ruined it," I laughed, wiping away tears.

"Oh well. Next time," the dragon grinned. "Preferably with me *and* Hunter on the bed."

"Fine," I sighed in mock disappointment, wriggling my way up the mattress to situate myself between them.

"It's the thought that counts." Hunter grabbed my waist and rolled me toward him, kissing me deeply to continue what we started.

I closed my eyes, sighing contently as I explored him with only the senses of touch and taste. His body, so tall and lean, seemed to have muscles that went on forever. I tried to count his abs as my fingers drifted down his torso, but he started kissing my neck, which was far too distracting for such a brain activity.

Behind me, Raz did the same exploratory touches across my back and waist. I never expected him to be so gentle while Hunter took control more aggressively. I thought they'd be the opposite.

Hunter and I finally worked his jeans down his legs and behind me, I heard the distinct unzip and rustling of Raz getting undressed. Giving Hunter one last kiss full of tongue and promise to return to him, I flipped over to face my tattooed dragon.

"Hi," I said shyly to those gray eyes filling my vision.

"Hello, *steluța*," he returned, cupping my chin for a kiss.

A sharp thrill ran through me as the length of his body pressed again. This was so new to us. I'd gotten to know Hunter's body a little bit better since we spent more time together, but Razvan's was completely uncharted territory.

My fingers traced the art on his shoulders, his neck, his chest, and my lips soon followed. He groaned softly, caressing me as I took my time to explore. When I reached the waistband of his briefs, he stopped my hands.

"Before you go there," he rasped, "I want to say don't be alarmed and don't feel like you have to do anything." A playful grin twitched on his face. "I'm quite modified down there too."

"Now you've just made me curious," I giggled. After just a breath of hesitation, I dragged the edge of his underwear down. More tattoos decorated his hips and lower abs. In fact, they never seemed to stop as I slowly pulled the fabric even lower.

Turned out, they didn't.

My eyes widened as the black ink designs continued onto the shaft of his dick, decorating the thick organ with dot and line patterns like a monument. What was more, three metal balls pierced through the edge of his head just where it flared.

"Holy shit, Raz." The declaration came from Hunter looking over my shoulder, as I had been rendered speechless. "Do you get off on pain or something?"

"Nah. The pain of body mods is a rush, but it's not a sexual thing," he shrugged, his grin widening. "I just started to run out of real estate."

"What's next, your balls?"

"Yeah, probably," he remarked as casually as if he was talking about something as innocuous as a haircut. "Thinking of getting a Jacob's ladder too."

"What's that?" I asked, unsure if I really wanted to know.

"You sweet little thing," Raz teased me with a kiss. "It's a set of surface piercings down the shaft of a dick." His face went serious at my shocked expression. "*Steluța*, every dick piercing I get is with a woman's pleasure in mind. I've never had any complaints, but I realize it's strange to someone who's not used to them." He kissed me again with slow, deliberate sensuality, then pulled back with a smile. "If you want to just be with Hunter right now, I completely understand. I won't be offended."

"No, I just...," I swallowed and almost burst out laughing. The three of us were lying in bed, talking casually about Razvan's dick, which was sitting out proudly on display. "Will you show me what you like? I don't want to do anything wrong."

"Underneath all this ink, I'm a simple man, *steluța*," he chuckled, nuzzling me. "Just being touched by you feels amazing. Do whatever you're comfortable with and I'll guide you if it's necessary."

I nodded, tilting my face up to kiss him again as my hands returned to his hips. He helped me slide his boxer briefs all the way down until I was no longer the only naked one. Dragging his mouth down my neck to nibble at my shoulder and collarbone, he pulled me forward and his hot shaft brushed across my belly.

I took the opportunity to look over my shoulder at Hunter. "Stop being so overdressed."

"Working on it," he laughed softly, kissing me as he slid his own boxers down. The treasure trail of pale blonde hair led from his navel down to a partially hard cock just as perfect and unblemished as the rest of him.

I had seen it before, when we were just "friends", but nothing stopped the full-body shudder of desire as he pressed against me. He let out soft growls as his hungry kisses traveled across my back, his cock thick and pulsing as it grew harder on my ass.

Sandwiched between Hunter and Raz, both of them kissing and touching me with a feverish need, their hips beginning to roll softly in alternating rhythms against my body, I never imagined I could be so lucky.

Sensations of pure pleasure overwhelmed me. I tried to touch them, to please them too, but they each just grabbed my hand and kissed it before returning to what they were doing—making me feel beyond incredible.

Raz made me cry out when his tongue teased my nipples into stiff, aching peaks. Hunter caressed my thighs until I was absolutely trembling before he touched my clit. I jerked back so suddenly, he groaned a curse and his cock twitched against my ass.

"May I?" Raz inched his hand down my lower belly. When I moaned a yes, his hand replaced Hunter's, who turned his attention to kneading my breasts as he nibbled my neck.

"Mm, you're so wet," Raz moaned against my lips as his hands caressed my folds. "I would love to taste you, steluţa."

Oh God.

Just the thought of that inhuman tongue pleasing me *down there* sent another surge of liquid heat through my core to coat his palm.

With a savage growl, he pinned my hips down toward the bed so I laid flat on my back. Hunter scooted up higher so that my head rested in his lap as Raz positioned himself between my legs. He kissed my mouth first, soft and sweet, but that smile was anything but sweet as he worked his way down my body.

His mouth left a trail of fire, traveling over every curve of me. He hummed against my skin, sending gentle vibrations to every sensitive part of my body. Hunter teased my nipples between his fingers as Raz made his way down, alternating between gentle and rough. By the time Raz reached my soaked, aching core, his magical tongue would barely have to do anything.

But still it did. He kissed my inner thighs, circling all around my center until I was begging and bucking my hips in his face. When his mouth finally pressed to my vulva, sparks flew across my vision. His tongue flicking against both sides of my clit made it feel like *two* men were pleasing me down there.

The wicked dragon still didn't let me come, though. He looked up at me from between my legs, eyes bright and full of mischief as he danced me around the edge, watching me moan and whine and thrash like a woman possessed.

I slid my head to the edge of Hunter's thigh and reached up, wrapping my fist around his cock. If Raz wouldn't let me get off, I'd find a distraction from the torture.

"Ohh, Mel," Hunter groaned as I stroked him, squeezing his pale flesh as my hand slid upward, just as Connor showed me. "Oh, that feels so good, little fox."

"Hunter, you're so fucking sexy... ahhhh!"

Raz pressed two fingers inside me, filling the aching emptiness as he stroked my top wall with those long, skilled fingers. His lips sealed around my clit as his tongue continued to stroke it with gradually increasing pressure.

"Do you feel good, beautiful?" Hunter pinched my nipples again, harder this time, making me cry out at the shared sensation between my nipples and clit. "Is this what you wanted?"

"This is better than what I ever wanted," I panted. "I've never felt sooo... oh God!"

Raz's tongue lashed my clit a final time before the orgasm crashed through me, hurtling me into a world of pleasure I didn't know was possible.

21

RAZVAN

She quivered so beautifully when she came apart, making the sweetest moans and whimpers when her gorgeous body thrashed.

I reluctantly pulled my mouth away from her pussy to let her recover and come back down as her release passed. Damn, she tasted divine, but I knew how sensitive women were after coming. Never wanting to leave, I kissed her thighs and the beautiful lines in her hips that led down to her pussy.

She shivered some more through her ragged breaths. Her cheeks flushed with pink as she gazed up at Hunter, who looked back at her like he treasured her above all else. He smoothed his hands down her body, palming her breasts and caressing her curves while she hummed in delight.

I only then noticed she had been stroking him and he was rock hard.

"Want to switch places, wolf?" I had a feeling Mel wouldn't want me fucking her first. On top of looking apprehensive about my piercings, I was wider than Hunter—not that his dick was small by any means. She also just knew him better than me.

"Gladly," he grinned, leaning down to suck those beautiful pink nipples before scooting around to the lower half of her body.

"Did you enjoy that, *steluța*?" I purred, lifting her head to set it in my lap like Hunter did.

"Is the sky blue?" she laughed, bringing her hands up to rake her fingers down my thighs. "You felt amazing. That tongue of yours is something else."

I hissed with pleasure at the resulting tingles of her nails on my quad muscles. My dick twitched, and I ached to be inside her. My dragon roared with the need to consume her, but I shoved him down. Only she would decide if she wanted me.

"The sky isn't actually blue," Hunter quipped as he settled between Mel's thighs. "It's just the reflection of the ocean."

Mel and I both groaned in unison. "So hot to hear you talk useless facts in bed," she teased, running her fingers through his platinum hair spilling over her skin. "That's something Connor would say..."

She fell silent, growing wistful, but Hunter brought her right back into the mood with us.

"When Con's back," he kissed the valley between her breasts, "he can be the trivia master while Raz and I rock your world."

She laughed, a light musical sound that wrapped around my heart and squeezed. I couldn't wait until Connor got his head out of his ass so we could make her laugh like that every day. She was beautiful to look at no matter what mood she was in, but seeing her face light up at a silly joke made her absolutely radiant.

Hunter smothered her mouth with a kiss, turning her giggles into soft moans as his hips lined up to hers. Her arms wrapped around his back, but she suddenly jerked away and broke off the kiss.

"Wait," she said, already panting again, and looked up at me. "Do you have condoms, Raz?"

"Ah, no." I rubbed my jaw, genuinely forgetting that humans used those things.

Her face turned red as it fell with disappointment. "Then I'm sorry guys, but I can't... I'm not on any birth control."

"Mel, shifters can't get humans pregnant," Hunter said softly. "It hasn't been scientifically proven, of course, but there's ah, lots of anecdotal evidence. And unless I'm mistaken," he glanced up at me. "We also don't transmit the same illnesses. Sexually or otherwise."

"What are you looking at me for?" I demanded in mock anger. "Just because I used to, ah, how would you say it, take sexual partners indiscriminately?"

"You could just say manwhore," Hunter snorted.

"Fine, yes. I used to manwhore. And I've never caught anything. Not even a cold."

"I don't think that's how that word is used," Mel giggled, gazing up at me. "But your accent is adorable."

"Ah yes, make fun of the foreigner," I growled, but smiled as I leaned down and peppered kisses all over her face and neck. Her laughs turned to hitched breaths and moans as I went from playful to sensual, nipping her skin where it was most sensitive until she arched against Hunter.

"Do you want to continue, little fox?" he asked, running his hands across her thighs, which had wrapped around his lean hips.

"Yes," she breathed, then whispered a word in his ear that made me instantly hard again. "Please."

He didn't need any further convincing. His hips rolled forward and Mel's face upon the moment of penetration was pure bliss.

"Ohhh," she moaned so hotly, balling her fists around the sheets already.

Hunter eased into her gently, making slow, careful thrusts as her body learned to accommodate him. He pushed himself up to straight arms, watching her move beneath him in wide-eyed awe as he built up to a steady rhythm.

"Raz," she moaned, making my cock ache. Somehow it was a huge ego boost that Hunter was the one fucking her and she was moaning my name.

"Yes, *steluța?*" I stroked her hair, enjoying the glazed over look of pleasure on her face and the way her tits bounced as Hunter rutted into her.

"Do you want me to, ahh...," she trailed off in a wordless moan as Hunter changed up his rhythm, fucking her slow and deep.

"I want you to do whatever you want," I told her huskily. "I'll get my turn when you're ready."

She looked up at Hunter and tapped his arm. "Stop for a second?"

He obliged, pausing his thrusts and pulled out to sit kneeling between her legs. "You okay?" he panted, his breaths already heavy. Coated in her juices, his cock hung taut and rock hard between his thighs. I found myself licking my lips.

I highly preferred women, but every once in a while, another man caught my eye. Anyone with a pulse could see how attractive Hunter was. His pale, unmarked skin didn't need a drop of ink to look sexy. His tall, athletic figure with that long, perfect cock to match. And I loved how Mel tasted so much, I wouldn't be opposed to licking her off him...

"Mmm!" A soft tongue flicking underneath my cock head brought me out of my fantasies and back to reality, and *oh*, what a reality it was.

Mel had flipped over to her hands and knees. Her big, chocolate eyes gazed up at me as she hesitantly took me into her mouth. My heart soared and my cock stiffened to stone. She wanted to pleasure me, but still felt unsure of herself. Behind her, Hunter smoothed his hands over her back and perfect, perky ass before lining up to fuck her again.

"Yes, *steluța*," I hissed as her lips descended over my entire head. Her teeth clicked against my piercings, but it only heightened my pleasure. "Just like that. Yes."

Growing more confident with my praise, she took more of me and let out a moan that vibrated over the metal balls, tingling all the way down to *my* balls. Hunter had entered her again and thrust slowly to not jostle her too much while she sucked me. His jaw tensed and I could practically see his teeth gritting. He was dying to fuck her brains out, to take her like the animal he was, but held back to keep her comfortable.

Just like him, I clenched my fists around the sheets at my sides, fighting everything in me to not fuck her gorgeous face until I exploded at the back of her throat. With every thrust from Hunter, her moans grew louder and uninhibited. She took me deeper down her throat with no assistance, no longer bothered by my piercings.

The pressure from her mouth on them just enhanced my own pleasure.

"Fuck, *steluța*," I groaned, unable to keep my hands off her. I reached under to pinch her nipples, making her squeals even louder and more erratic. Hunter started grunting and growling as he pounded into her more forcefully, reaching around her thighs to strum her clit as he fucked her.

The sight of her next orgasm quaking over her body sent me spilling deep into her mouth. Letting out a string of curses as I released violently, I heard Hunter doing the same as he came too.

The poor girl could barely stay up on her hands and knees as the pleasure rocked through her, but she pushed farther down my shaft to swallow every drop. I didn't even realize my hands tangled in her hair, pulling her down on my cock until she patted my thigh to let her up.

"Sorry! Are you okay?" I rasped, my pulse pounding in my ears.

"More than okay," she smiled dreamily, resting her head on my thigh as she collapsed down on the mattress with Hunter laying out beside her.

"You are incredible," he murmured, his own skin flushed pink as he wrapped an arm around her waist and poured kisses over her back and shoulders.

I scooted down to recline next to them, resting my hand on her hip as it gently rose and fell with her breaths.

"Enjoy yourself?" I drawled with a lazy smile. Her bright eyes and flushed face told me all I needed to know, but I wanted to hear her say it.

"Very much." She rolled onto her belly and scooted toward me to lay her head on my chest. The gesture took me aback. Women never wanted to cuddle with me. They wanted me to fuck them senseless, to come under my magical tongue, maybe suck my dick as a half-hearted reciprocation, but they never curled up next to me like this.

"Did you enjoy yourself?" Mel looked up at me from laying over my heart. "I didn't hurt your piercings or anything, did I?"

"Is water wet?" I grinned down at her, stroking her hair out of her face. "You could never hurt me, *steluța*. And even if you did, I'm sure I'd still enjoy it."

"Oh really?" she playfully closed her teeth over my nipple. "I like a little pain too."

"Do you now?" Hunter piped up from the other side of her. "Like what?"

She blushed as she lifted her head to look over her shoulder at him. "Connor has, um, spanked me. And I got really into it one time."

"You should have mentioned it while I was behind you," he teased, nuzzling her neck as he groped the perky globes of her ass.

"I did, but my mouth was full!"

The three of us laughed, relaxed and comfortable in post-orgasmic bliss. In my experience, all threesomes were different. Some were more comfortable after doing the deed, some were awkward as hell. But none had ever felt this... *natural.* It was almost unsettling how normal this felt. Mel's fingers traced my tattoos as she chatted with me and Hunter, my arm around her back and his hand drifting across her leg and hip. It just felt so... cozy and secure.

I caught Hunter's eyes a few times looking across Mel and over to my body, reclined and stretched out with our girl snuggled under my arm. My heart quickened when I noticed it, but his eyes quickly darted back to Mel, kissing her arm or somewhere as he stared at her adoringly.

Maybe it didn't mean anything. His mind could have just been wandering, but if there was a chance he was sometimes into men too...

The thought both aroused me and filled me with dread. How would Mel feel about that? This was the south, after all. They were almost as bad as Romania when it came to same-sex unions. Of course, I wouldn't act on anything without her full knowledge and consent. And if it made her the slightest bit uncomfortable, that was enough for me to never act on it. But if there was a chance she was okay with it during any future threesomes...

"Hey," she grinned at me wickedly, sliding a hand down my torso. "Looks like you're getting excited again."

22

MELODY

az's mouth spread into a cocky grin. "Just thinking about all the ways I could give you pleasurable pain, *steluța*."

"You're thinking about something, I can see," I teased, trailing my hand down past his shaft to cup his heavy balls. He groaned as I massaged them in my palm, his pierced dick flexing as it grew harder.

"I'm good for another round." Hunter's mouth was hot against my ear, his teeth trailing along the shell of it. As he shifted his weight behind me, his semi-hard cock pressed against my ass.

"What am I going to do with you two *and* Connor?" I moaned as Raz pressed hot, sensual kisses underneath my jaw. "If we keep this up, I'll never be able to walk."

"Then we'll carry you," Raz growled against my skin. "Preferably while still on one of our dicks."

"Or both of our dicks," Hunter added. His hands palmed my ass cheeks apart, leaving no question as to what he implied.

I shivered against him, both with desire and nervousness. "I've never done that before," the confession escaped my lips.

He kissed me reassuringly. "Another time then, but not now."

"What *would* you like to do now, *steluța*?" Raz murmured as he made a trail of hot kisses down my neck. "Now that you've got me by the balls."

I giggled, releasing him there to stroke his shaft. He groaned against my neck, his cock hardening in my fist with every passing second.

"I want to... be with you," I muttered, somehow still feeling shy despite what just happened between the three of us.

He pulled away from my neck, looking at me with surprise and then delight. "Why don't you climb on top," he said in a husky whisper. "So you can be in control."

I nodded, throwing my leg over to straddle him. Still soaked from the first session, I wouldn't need much warming up. His shaft pressed against the tender folds of my vulva as I started to move against him, unsure if I was teasing myself or him more.

"Fuck, that's hot," Hunter mumbled. He propped himself on one elbow and stroked himself with the other hand. Hot, greedy need surged through me as I watched him. I'd make sure not to leave him out.

My tattooed dragon growled hot curses as I slid my pussy back and forth on his shaft, bracing my hands on his chest. He pushed himself to sit up, his back against the rigid support of the tent, and grabbed my head to claim my mouth in a kiss.

Right away, this felt different. Yes, he kissed me with just as much passion, and that wonderful tongue stroked the inside of my mouth in a hot, delicious caress. But I felt something else, like his feelings for me poured from his mouth to mine. It stole my breath away, and I gasped, kissing him again and again to chase that feeling.

Somehow I knew he was giving me something he never gave anyone else, despite surely kissing and fucking hundreds of women. The aloof, former manwhore dragon made love to me with his mouth.

"I take back what I said before. *That* was hot." Hunter's voice filtered back into my consciousness. When I looked over at him, his cock already glistened with pre-cum. His sexy abs flexed with each short breath he took, already straining to hold himself back.

"You gonna sit there and provide commentary while you jerk off like a creep, or you gonna join us?" Raz flashed a smile. I couldn't help but notice his eyes dilate even more as he watched Hunter stroke himself.

"I'm content to watch for now," Hunter returned his grin lazily. "I'll cut in when she needs a break."

"Promise I won't leave you out," I winked at him before sliding up to let Raz's wide head kiss my entrance.

He wrapped a hand around the base for me, holding himself steady as I slowly lowered my hips.

"Ahhh." A harsh breath escaped me as my pussy stretched around him. How was I able to take so much of him in my mouth? His thickness pressed against all my inner walls with no room to spare. His piercings just inside of me rubbed in an intense but not unpleasant way.

"Take your time," he murmured, moving his hands to my waist to keep me elevated.

"I might need a minute," I panted sheepishly.

"Of course, *steluța*." His smile up at me from the mattress bordered on cocky, but the warmth radiating from him calmed my nerves. Sure, he knew how big he was and couldn't help that. But he'd never want to hurt me.

A kiss on my shoulder drew my attention away for a moment. Hunter settled behind me, straddling Raz's legs and his own erection propped up against my ass. His arms slid around to cup my breasts, rolling my nipples between his fingers as he nuzzled my neck.

"Raz's hands look full so I'm helping you relax," he said, a smile in his voice. "Raz, do you mind me back here?"

"Not at all." Raz's voice was low and throaty. His eyes flickered from Hunter back to me. "Anything to keep our girl comfortable."

"You guys are the best," I sighed, arching back against Hunter as his hands sailed across my body. "What would I do without you?"

"That's not something you ever have to worry about." I felt his wolfish grin against my neck. "You're our shaman. You're stuck with us."

The retort in my throat came out a strangled moan as Hunter kissed me savagely, one fist in my hair and his other palm skimming down my belly to work my clit.

Inch by inch, I seated myself down on Razvan. His head tipped back with a groan as I lowered myself all the way, my breaths short as he filled me so utterly and completely. He dug his fingers into my hips with an iron grip, like I was his last anchor for control.

My movements started out slow and measured, just testing out the sensations of his piercings pressing into my top wall. With him guiding my hips, I found myself clutching his fingers for dear life. Every lift and lower of my body sent me chasing the most intense sensations and I couldn't get enough.

"Yes," Raz hissed between grunts and groans. "God, you feel amazing."

I leaned forward, bracing my forearms on his chest to kiss him. God, kissing him was like an addiction. Especially since that last one. He pulled me down further the moment our lips met. With our chests pressed against each other, it was a moment of just us.

His kisses were tender as he cupped my face, looking into my eyes as he began rolling his hips up to meet mine. The way he touched me, looked at me, kissed me, was so intimate it almost brought tears to my eyes. I never felt like this, not even with Connor. It was every bit as intense as his thick cock driving in and out of me, his piercings adding an extra layer of sensation as they stroked my channel.

Smack!

"Ahh!" My right ass cheek stung as I turned to look back at Hunter, who grinned impishly. "What was that for?"

"You said you liked spanking," he shrugged.

Raz shook with laughter underneath me. "She does. I felt her tighten around me when you did that."

They were right. The light sting of pain just amplified the pleasure surging through me. I felt like I walked along a razor's edge, the border of pleasure and pain.

"Want more?" Hunter rubbed his hands together as I returned upright.

"Yes," I sighed, bracing my hands on Raz's chest again. "Yes, please."

"So fucking hot to hear you say that," my dragon growled, driving his hips more forcefully to match me thrust for thrust. "I love hearing you ask for more."

The ability to form words escaped me as he filled and emptied me relentlessly. Hunter's smacks on my ass behind me sent electrified tingles to my nipples and clit. Raz's thumb stroked over that pleasure button just as my breaths grew shorter, my moans erratic and frenzied. That razor's edge was seconds away from cutting me apart, releasing everything I held back.

The combination of everything—Raz's thick cock, his piercings, his hand on my clit, and Hunter's teeth in my shoulder, sent me hurtling over the edge. Raz flexed hard inside me, spilling warmth as he roared and clutched at the sheets like a lifeline.

"Little fox," Hunter rasped in my ear. "I'm so close. Where do you want me, beautiful?"

I turned around, exhausted, panting, and still drunk off my orgasm. I lifted off of Raz, pushed Hunter down and climbed on to straddle him.

"Holy... fuck," he moaned the moment I impaled myself on him.

I rode him like a woman possessed, crashing my hips down as I chased the pleasure relentlessly. My orgasm from Raz never truly finished, and quickly began building into another.

"Yes, use me," Hunter rasped, gripping my hips much like Raz had. "Fuck me. Take what you need."

The scream tore from my throat as I came again just moments later. Hunter's cock seemed to press all new buttons, stroking inside me in a different way than Raz had. My control was no match for the previous pleasure combined with new sensations. I drowned in all of it, and happily. Hunter's release only extended my pleasure, which still felt over too soon.

The next sensations coming over me were the soft sheets, a pillow under my head, and warm bodies on either side of me. Two pairs of lips kissed me in various places. Raz's tongue tickled my earlobe, making me giggle and squirm. The last thing I heard was the chuckle from his chest, a soft rumble like thunder, before sleep overtook me.

✿ 23 ✿

MELODY

I woke up alone, delicious soreness in my body as a reminder of last night. Smiling, I stretched, taking up the entire king-sized mattress as I spread my arms and legs wide. The last few days had been exhausting. For the first time in what felt like ages, I felt truly relaxed and well-rested.

Raz sat facing the fire when I dressed and left the tent, turning to grin at me as I sat next to him.

"Hello, sleeping *steluța*," he greeted with a kiss on my cheek.

"Hi," I leaned my head on his shoulder. "How long have I been out?"

"Ten hours or so. You might be just as hard a sleeper as me," he teased.

"I really needed that," I murmured, running a hand through my hair. "I feel actually awake for the first time in days."

"You needed the sleep or what happened before?"

"Both." I pressed a kiss to his cocky grin, welcoming the caress of a tongue on my lip. I would never get tired of feeling that.

"Where's Hunter?" I asked.

"Checking on the kids." His voice grew soft as he looked away from me and at the fire. "He'll be back shortly."

I wrestled with the thought of asking him about what I noticed between them. His lustful looks at Hunter, and the way they just seemed so comfortable with each other. Should I ask Hunter first? Maybe in my own lust-filled haze, I was just imagining things?

"What?" I said to Raz's playful nudge to my elbow.

"I said," he smirked, "when do you want to go see Connor?"

"As soon as possible," I answered. "I just hope we don't run into that bitch again."

"I don't think she'll be a problem," he offered. "And if she does show up, Hunter and I will take care of her."

"That's my boys." I looped my arm through his, gazing at the flames which he undoubtedly created. I thought back to when he lit Connor's campfire with just a quick exhale of breath. I thought it was a magic trick at first. Although no trick, my dragon was definitely magical.

"If you don't mind waiting until nightfall," Raz said. "I can fly us there if you'd like. It'll be faster."

"Really?" I lifted my head. "You want me to ride you?"

"Well, always, as long as you moan so pretty like you did." He laughed when I smacked his arm. "Of course I do, *steluța*. I'd love to show you my perspective when I go on my night flights."

"It just feels a little weird to me," I admitted. "I mean, if humans knew what you were, they'd exploit you for that. You'd be like those poor horses pulling carriages around for tourists."

"I know," he said solemnly. "They'd use me for that and much worse. Think of what the Pentagon would do if they got ahold of a dragon."

"Jesus," I muttered in disgust. "You'd be a perfect weapon to them."

"Right," he agreed. "But I don't mind being your personal taxi. I trust you, steluța."

"And I trust you," I returned, lacing my fingers through his. "Completely. I won't ask you about other women anymore and... I'm sorry I assumed so much about you."

"You already apologized for that." He kissed my forehead. "It's in the past now. And..." He hesitated, his throat moving as he swallowed. The words seemed to fight their way from his mouth.

"Thank you for trusting me."

I snuggled closer to him, pulling his arm around me so I could nestle into his side. Even through his leather vest, I felt his heart racing. Trust was a big thing for him, and I'd be sure to treasure it. I still didn't know much about him, like why he had such a fragile relationship with trust and why he remained in the carnival at all. But with time, we'd get to know each other.

Just last night, even though it was sex, and hot sex at that, I could feel him open up to me on a deeper level. Some kind of channel opened between us, connecting us through the intimacy we shared and even now, just sitting together in front of a fire. It felt like the intangible parts of me and him molded together into some kind of one-ness.

"Hungry?" he murmured into my hair.

"Starving," I admitted.

"You're gonna have to wait for Hunter for that," he cracked, poking me in the ribs. "He's the master chef around here."

"You ass," I groaned, moving to jab him back before he caught my fingers with a lightning fast hand.

We fell into some comfortable domestic tasks while waiting for Hunter. Raz polished his knives before packing them away carefully. I shook out the sheets and blankets on the bed, then carefully folded them despite his teasing they would get messed up again soon.

I heard Roo and Rinna talking excitedly before I ever saw the wolf family returning through the woods. The pups squealed when they saw me and ran, attaching firmly to each of my legs.

"Hey guys!" I laughed, groaning and struggling to walk as they giggled at my plight.

"I ate a caterpillar. It was nasty!" Roo declared, wrapping his lanky arms and legs around me even tighter.

"I bet it was, dude."

Hunter caught up a few steps later, carrying a large cooler with our food in it, no doubt.

"Hey you." My heart fluttered at seeing his biceps taut and flexed under the weight of the cooler. Even while carrying supplies, he looked sexy as hell. I tilted my chin up for a kiss, smiling at him but unable to stand on tiptoes thanks to my new child leg weights.

"Hey." To my surprise, he bypassed my mouth and brushed his lips against my cheek in something barely resembling a kiss. It was how I kissed my mom when she drunkenly insisted on it, and I wanted to do anything but touch her.

I blinked, stunned at his sudden coldness when we'd been so close just hours ago. He *never* did this hot and cold thing like Connor. Ever since the day we met, he'd been slowly escalating his affection toward me. And now, after sleeping with me, he just flipped and did the opposite?

Razvan noticed too, lifting an eyebrow as Hunter began setting skewers of meat over the fire without so much as a hello to him. The only ones who seemed oblivious were the kids, still wrapped around my legs like monkeys on tree trunks.

"Walk with us, Mel! You can do it!" Rinna yelled.

"Urgh, I dunno. You guys are too big." I took a couple half-hearted steps, grateful for the distraction.

"Leave Mel alone," Hunter snapped. "Come over here and eat. Then you two can play."

They reluctantly detached from me and shuffled over to the fire, knowing better than to disobey their father's tone. I hurried into Raz's main tent, deciding to look for eating utensils and get some distance from the sudden tension.

"Hey," Raz followed hot on my heels and grabbed my arm as soon as we entered the tent. "Whatever's crawled up his furry wolf ass has nothing to do with you. I promise, steluţa."

"You don't know that," I muttered, distractedly rummaging through the shelves for plates or bowls, until he took both of my arms and made me face him.

"I do know," he insisted, his face softening. "I saw the way he looked at you last night. I saw how badly he wanted to please you and how tightly he held you while you slept. I don't know what's up with the sudden change, but I know for a fact that you give him solace from everything that's happened to him." His voice lowered, as did his eyes, to the ground. "Just like you do for me."

"I don't know, Raz. I..." my voice choked, Hunter's cold approach toward me playing on a loop in my head like a form of self-mutilation.

"I can handle Connor throwing up smoke and mirrors because it's how he protects himself. I can find my way through the fog of his mental illness and find the real him. But him *and* Hunter doing this? I can't, Raz. I just can't..."

"Shhh," Raz pulled me into his chest, stroking my hair and back. "That's not what this is, I'm sure of it. He's a single dad, remember? The kids are probably on his last nerve and pissing him off. He's allowed to feel frustrated with them, just give him space."

"I hope you're right," I sighed into his chest, although I couldn't keep the doubt from creeping into my voice.

"Trust him like you do me," he murmured. "He's not perfect. None of us are. He'll come back to you when he's ready. If not, he's a bigger idiot than Connor."

I chuckled, despite myself. We still had to convince Connor to come back to me, and that alone left a painful bruise on my heart.

With a sweet kiss and a few more reassuring words, Raz and I left the tent and headed back toward the capital of Awkward Central. Hunter pointedly ignored us, staring intently at the skewers as he carefully turned them over the fire or muttering a few words to his kids who sat angelically beside him.

Raz cleared his throat, settling on a log across the fire from Hunter.

"We're thinking of going back to Connor tonight, when it's dark," he began. "I'll shift so Mel can ride me. You all can shift and meet us there if you'd like."

"Sure, that sounds fine," Hunter muttered unceremoniously, still not looking at either of us. "Food's done. Come and get it."

"Are you eating with us?" I asked, disappointment creeping into my voice as I watched him stand and shed his clothing. He was being so standoffish I couldn't even enjoy looking at him naked.

"I already ate," he said flatly, folding his clothes into a neat bundle. "I'm going for a run. I'll be back before nightfall."

Without another word, the sounds of joints popping and organs rearranging echoed through the trees. Hunter fell to all fours, the snowy white fur covering him last. And in the next instant, he was a white blur racing through the brush.

24

MELODY

"**R**eady?"

I nodded, taking my tenth glance around to make sure we were truly alone.

"No one else is here, *steluța*," Raz chuckled as he shed his clothing. "Trust me, I could hear, see, and smell them from miles away."

Moonlight turned his bare skin a silvery hue, making his tattoos look even more magical and enigmatic. I leaned back against the tree, taking in every sleek, liquid movement of his ink as he peeled away his clothing. When he finally stripped completely naked, my core clenched around nothing, remembering how thickly he filled me and how his piercings felt.

"Like what you see?" he grinned smugly. Of course he knew the answer to that.

"Nah," I joked, unzipping the backpack I held for his clothes. "But if you hang out naked more often, I might come around to you."

"Uh-huh," he chuckled, folding up his clothes and placing them inside the backpack, which I then zipped closed and slid my arms through the straps.

"Ready when you are, naked tattooed man with a killer body and amazing dick who is totally not my type."

He cupped my chin, grinning. His eyes looked like liquid metal in the moonlight. "A kiss before we go, since I won't be able to for a whole minute."

My grin matched his as I tilted my face up, our lips melding in a smooth, passionate dance that I wished never had to end. I grabbed the back of his head to kiss him harder and felt his heart beating against mine.

Holy shit, I'm totally smitten with him, I realized. Just looking at him or hearing his voice put a big stupid smile on my face. It was similar to the nervous giddiness I felt when Hunter and I started getting close, before he went from a warm, caring puppy of a man to a cold, solid brick wall.

Like earlier in the day, he barely said a word when he got back from his run. He puttered around the campsite until dusk fell, then headed for the hospital with the kids since it would take longer for them to reach there on four legs.

Recalling his behavior that day only made me kiss Razvan harder. Now that two of my men had become moody assholes, he was the one consistency in my life. He reassured me when Hunter's behavior stung, and here he was now, holding me under a full moon and kissing me like he never wanted this to end, either.

Never in a million years would I have believed I'd start falling for the arrogant, tattooed Romanian who sampled women like free snacks at the carnival. And I never thought he'd be such a rock, a point of stability when everything else seemed to fall apart.

"Do you want to see your other man or not?" he teased when we broke apart breathlessly, kissing my nose.

"You make it very tempting to say not," I sighed. "But yes, let's go."

He nodded, placing a final peck on my lips before stepping away to shift.

At first, it looked like all his tattoos filled in to make his skin completely solid black. Then a shiny white glare reflected the moonlight as his skin turned to solid dragon scales. At the same time, I heard the same sickening pops and cracks as his skeleton rearranged itself and grew to ten times the size of a man.

Within a minute, a massive black dragon stood before me. It was no less wondrous and awe-inspiring than the first time. Razvan stretched his wings, snorting tendrils of smoke before folding them against his back again.

"God, you're magnificent," I whispered, approaching him.

He leaned his large, reptilian nose against my palm and let out a low, rumbling growl like a purr against my hand. Those metallic gray eyes were exactly the same and looked at me with the same warmth and affection as human Razvan.

"I probably should have asked the best way to get on you," I realized aloud, taking in the bumps, ridges and spikes that adorned his body.

He let out a series of huffs that could only be laughter before lowering his belly to the ground. He laid there like a loafing cat, looking at me expectantly. If only there was some way to communicate.

Running my hand down his neck and along his back, I decided to just climb aboard and see what happened. Grabbing a spike along his backbone, I braced one foot against his ribs and threw the other over.

"Hang on," I told him when he started to fidget underneath me. "Trying to not stab myself in the vagina here."

That only made him shake even more as he repeated that dragon laugh. Finally, I settled over where the spikes smoothed out into ridges. It wouldn't be the most comfortable ride, but at least I wouldn't get stabbed and not be able to enjoy that dick of his anymore.

Yes, because that's the worst that can happen when you get a dragon spike through the pussy.

"Okay," I told him. "I think I'm ready."

I was not ready.

He pushed off the ground so fast, I lurched backwards and almost lost control. I couldn't stop the scream that tore from my throat as we ascended high and fast above the treetops. I squeezed around him with my knees and held onto his neck for dear life. And somewhere under my gripping fear of falling off and dying, my brain tried to wrap around the fact that I was *riding a fucking dragon.*

I couldn't catch my breath until he leveled out, beating his massive wings at a leisurely pace. I was still scared for my life, but the beauty of our surroundings put me at ease.

The moon hung so full and bright, I felt like I could reach out and touch it. Trees passed under us like they were children's toys. Around me I could see the shapes of the hills and winding roads you could never see from on the ground. I had never been on a plane before, but I could only imagine it didn't feel nearly as free as this.

"Raz, this is amazing," I whispered, unsure if he could hear me through the wind whipping past us. "*You're* amazing." I ran my hands across his black scales like obsidian. They gave off a pleasant warmth—higher than body heat but not quite burning.

I closed my eyes just to feel the sensation of him carrying me. The air felt cool and fresh up here, his body solid underneath me. He wouldn't let me fall. On a whim, I took my focus inward. I shut out the wind whipping past my ears and listened for the dragon, the one on his back that seemed to move through me when I touched his back in bed.

I felt the heat of its flames licking the air, its powerful body wrapping around me, but this felt different. Rather than more scales and fire, this presence felt like a man wrapping around me. Strong, human arms I could practically feel encircling my waist, along with human lips and a tongue kissing my neck. A tongue split down the middle.

Razvan?

Steluța?

Hearing his voice, his *human* voice, startled me so badly I nearly lost my balance and the connection we held.

You can hear me? I thought.

Yes. You can hear me?

Yes! How is this happening? Where are you? I mean, I know I'm riding the dragon-you, but where are you-you?

I'm in the dragon, he replied. He is in control and I'm in the backseat, to put it simply. My consciousness is still here, but my human form is dormant, basically. Until I choose to change back.

So I'm talking to you telepathically? This is so weird!

I guess, his mental voice laughed. This must be another one of your shaman abilities.

Right. I'd been so consumed by Connor's fall, I forgot to see Thembi again. The carnival had broken down for the season and she was surely gone by now. Like everything else, I'd have to figure this out on my own.

Have you talked like this to others before?

Never, Raz answered. You're the first.

This is... wild. I thought. I must be able to talk to Hunter this way, too.

Probably. Although I wouldn't attempt it right away.

You're right, I agreed. Not until he comes and talks to me using his damn mouth.

That's my girl. I didn't miss the pride in his voice. We're coming up on the hospital now. I'm landing a bit farther away so we don't get seen.

He overshot the hospital, which looked like a big white Lego block passing underneath us, and landed in a wooded area just beyond the parking lot.

"Do I have to give these back to you?" I whined when Raz shifted back to human and held his hand out for the backpack of clothes.

"Not unless you want me locked up in the mental ward," he grinned, playfully snatching it from me.

His demeanor immediately changed as he started getting dressed. He grew quiet, and the smile went away. He didn't look at me once as he shrugged on his clothes.

"Is something wrong?" I asked.

"No, why?" he muttered, propping his foot up on a bench to lace up his motorcycle boots. Still, he didn't look at me.

"Not you, too," I pleaded. "Hunter and Connor are one thing, but I can't handle all three of you being weird around me."

"I'm not—I'm sorry." He put his foot down and took a deep breath, looking at the sky. "I'm just wrapping my head around the mind-speaking thing. I didn't even know that was possible."

"Me neither," I whispered. "Thembi never mentioned it. But I see it as a good thing. We can still talk while you're in shifter form."

He nodded his agreement but still looked apprehensive.

"What? Is there something else?"

"*Steluța*, could you... see anything?" His face hardened, his sharp eyes on mine. "If you can talk to me with your mind, can you also *see* what's in my mind? Or know what I'm thinking or feeling that's not in words?"

"I—I don't think so," I rubbed my forehead. "When you were laying in bed, and I touched the tattoo on your back, I could feel like your dragon was in the room with me. I felt his fire, his scales, and like his body wrapped around me. But just now, it was the opposite. I felt *you*, Razvan, like the human part of you was with me."

He nodded again as he listened, then grabbed my hand as we walked together toward the hospital.

"Forgive me for mentioning it, but there are things about me I'm not ready to talk about." He brought my palm to his lips and kissed it. "You'll probably find out eventually, but now isn't the time."

"It's okay. There's stuff in my past you don't know about, either," I slid my arm through his, wanting to touch more of him. "Although you do know a big chunk of it."

"As you do of mine," he said with a kiss to my temple.

We walked on in comfortable silence until we came around the front of the hospital, where we met Hunter and the kids already in human form. Hunter nodded at us, the barest of greetings, before turning to head inside with his family.

Raz muttered some insult under his breath, and I rubbed his arm as we followed the wolf family inside. This late at night, most of the lights were off and the hospital was nearly empty. Only a single security guard took notice of us as we headed toward the elevators.

"Excuse me, can I help y'all?" he asked, lumbering toward us.

"We know where we're going, thank you." I flashed him a smile as I hurried into the elevator, standing closer to Hunter than I intended.

"Folks, there are no visitors at this hour. You'll have to come back—"

Razvan turned and placed a hand on the man's chest, a final warning for him to stop.

"We'll be quick. And we won't steal anything. Promise." He flashed a smile, then jumped in the elevator as the man blinked dumbfoundedly.

"What was that?" I asked him on our way up.

"Old trick my grandmother taught me," he answered. "A type of hypnosis. Supposedly a talent unique to Romanian people."

"I knew it. You're a vampire, too," I teased.

He snorted with laughter while the kids giggled and playfully bit each other. Hunter remained still as a stone.

Connor's floor was equally empty and dark as the ground floor of the hospital.

"I think I want to talk to him alone," I whispered. "At first."

"We'll still come in and back you up," Raz answered. "There's probably night shift nurses who will try to stop you. Right, Hunter?"

The wolf grunted an affirmative, and I fought back the urge to snap at him. I did not need his moodiness right now, especially when I was about to be dealing with Connor's.

Sure enough, two nurses looked up the moment we opened the door from the waiting room.

"Excuse me, there's no visitors—"

"Ah, Marni! So good to see you again." Razvan squeezed my hand before shooting a charming smile at the nurse. "I've been thinking about you ever since that night. Why haven't you called?"

"Um, it's Elena. I'm sorry, but do I know you..."

I was already down the hall and rolled my eyes when I turned the corner to Connor's room. To my own surprise, I didn't feel an ounce of jealousy at Raz flirting with the nurse. He was doing nothing more than causing a distraction, and that man knew well how distracting he could be.

My feet slowed to a stop outside Connor's room. His main light was off, but he was awake. He laid back on his pillows, eyes open and bluish light flickering on his face. It took me a moment to realize it was a TV.

Steeling myself with a deep breath, I pushed his door open and let myself inside. His head lifted up at first with surprise, then a dry smile crossed his face.

"You don't know when to quit, do you, babe?"

25

MELODY

"I 'll never quit," I answered, letting the door close behind me. "Not on you, no matter what you say. Because I love you, Connor."

"Yeah?" he challenged, trying to sound tough, but I heard the emotion crack through his voice. "What if I lose control and hurt you? Really hurt you. Would you still love me then?"

"Raz and Hunter won't let that happen." I crossed my arms. "So yes, I'll still love you even if you lose control and I'll try my damn hardest to get you any help you need."

He gave me a long, lingering look, his forest green eyes examining me from head to toe. "Have you been with them?"

I nodded.

"Both?"

Another nod.

He let out a heavy sigh and let his head fall back again as he shut the TV off.

"Does that bother you?" I asked in the resulting silence.

"No," he answered. "Rather, the opposite. It gives me hope that we can still work, since you have them to balance me out. But," he shook his head, "I'm not worth it, babe. I'm just dead weight at this point. I'll drag y'all down so it's better to just cut me loose."

"I'm not doing that," I said, gritting my teeth so hard my jaw already ached. "I am tired of you beating yourself down over this shit, Connor. I love you. You love me. Let's be together. It's that simple."

"It's not, babe. And you know it." His hard stare bore through me. "I have to sell the trailer, and even then I'll still be so deep in the red, bill collectors will harass me for life. I can't perform without being in a world of pain. That pain is going to trigger worse and more vivid flashbacks. I am a *danger* to you, Melody. If you're in the wrong place at the wrong time, I could *literally* kill you. Your life is at risk by staying with me."

"I. Don't. Care," I answered, my vision blurring through the tears. "We'll find a way. I don't know how or when, but we'll figure this out, Connor. I would do anything for you. Can't you see that?"

"Why?" he demanded. "The country I fought for, and lost limbs for, had no problem discarding me after I returned home. My fiancee was happy to leave me for someone else. No one in my family could take me in because my disability was too inconvenient, plus I was another mouth to feed. Why do *you* give a fuck about me so much?"

"Because I know you would do the same for me," I cried, the tears spilling freely now. "If I pushed you away when I needed you, you'd make me come around to reason. I know you're doing this to try and protect me from yourself, but you don't need to! I have them to protect me." I shot my hand back toward the door. "But they won't need to either because I know the person you are, Connor. I know you would never hurt me..." I sniffed and wiped my nose, letting my tears fall freely to the tile floor. "You're only hurting me right now by pushing me away."

Only my sobs filled the room for several long moments. When I dared to look up at Connor, the pain on his face brought a fresh wave of tears to the surface.

"Fuck... Come here, babe."

I ran to him, burying my face in his hospital gown, and sobbed openly, letting out everything that weighed on me for the past several days. I almost forgot how thick and strong his arms were until they encircled me. I almost forgot how I could truly hide in the safety of him.

"What am I gonna do, babe?" he murmured, stroking my hair with a soothing hand. "You may love me now, but what about later down the road when you inevitably hate me for being a useless piece of shit?"

"I could never hate you." My voice muffled through his shirt. "I don't care if you lose your arms, legs, or your mind. I am here for you because you were there for me."

"What about my dick?" Of course, he couldn't resist such a joke to try lightening the mood.

I looked up at him through puffy, bloodshot eyes. "Hunter and Raz still have theirs."

"Oh, right."

My head flopped back down on his chest, neither of us saying more. His hardheadedness pissed me off so much and I felt like I was running out of strength to argue. I didn't feel like I convinced him to stay, and he sure as shit didn't convince me to leave. So here we were, at a standstill. Neither one of us giving an inch, yet unable to resist this connection between us. His arms felt like heaven around me and the way he stroked my hair told me how much he missed this. Missed *us*.

"Doesn't this feel right?" I asked him, my voice raw. "Don't you just want to stay like this forever?"

"Of course I do," he muttered. "But I feel selfish to take all this love from you when you have two more deserving guys right outside the door."

"I fucking hate it when you talk like that," I snarled, lifting my head to glare at him. "If I deserve love, Connor, then so do you. I'm nothing. I'm nobody. And I found three of you that mean the world to me and you all make me better than what I was."

"Now you know that's not true." He stroked my face and lowered his voice to a whisper. "You're a shaman, maybe one of the last ones. The shifters need you. I need you too, but selfishly. They need you to survive."

"Just because some guy gave me a coin when I was a kid!" I screeched. "He could have passed it on to anybody."

"I don't believe that." Connor shook his head. "I think he saw something in you that was already there. The power he passed on just enhanced what you already had, Mel."

Exhausted, I laid my head back down again. Round and round in circles we went, never getting anywhere. We'd already argued for too long and the nurses would burst in at any minute to kick me out. Not even Razvan could distract them forever.

When I heard the door open behind me, I squeezed my eyes shut and clutched Connor's hospital gown in my fists. They wouldn't take me away from him. I'd hold on for as long as I could. I was *not* saying goodbye. I'd show them all just how stubborn I could be.

"Doc." Connor's voice registered surprise as he laid a hand on my back. "Something up?"

"Ah, hello, Connor. And miss Melody. I hope I'm not disturbing you."

Quickly wiping my face, I looked over my shoulder to see Dr. Harman looking unkempt but happy. His shirt was wrinkled and his hair stuck out in all directions like he'd been sleeping at a desk or something, but the smile on his face shone like the sun.

"I'm sorry, Doctor." I cleared my throat, standing straight up. "I know visitors aren't allowed this late, but I—"

"Oh, no worries!" He held up a hand. "I have great news and came to deliver it straight away. It's good that you're here."

"What is it?" Connor's eyes narrowed, brows furrowing in skepticism.

"I got a call back from an old colleague of mine who is eager to meet you," the doctor bounced excitedly on his feet. "He's a brilliant guy running a non-profit for disabled vets much like yourself. He'll fit you with brand new prosthetics featuring the latest technology. They also have counselors specializing in combat PTSD, resources for job placement, housing, and the like."

My heart lifted as the room fell silent. Dr. Harman and I looked at Connor expectantly, who still wore a mask of distrust on his face.

"What's the catch?" he muttered.

"The only catch," the doctor inhaled, "is that he's in Georgia."

"Okay, but what's all this gonna cost?"

"Connor," the doctor laughed. "It's a non-profit organization! There is no cost to you."

"That's great!" I squealed, squeezing Connor's hand, but he still looked unconvinced.

"That's all good, but after I get the hell out of here, I still can't afford to make it to Georgia."

"They have programs for covering medical expenses, too. But Connor, listen." He approached the bedside, making sure to look directly at him. "I told my colleague a bit about you and he's very personally interested in helping you. I don't think he'll have any issue covering costs or whatever else you need."

Connor eyed him suspiciously. "Why? What's he so interested in me for?"

"I'm not sure myself but when I told him your full name and a bit about your condition, he essentially said he would move mountains to get you the care you need."

Connor's eyes flickered away from him, focusing on nothing as he absorbed this new information like a sponge. Or, as I knew, stubbornly trying to find a reason to refuse.

"It's a lot to process, so I'll leave you two alone to discuss it," Dr. Harman smiled, looking at both of us. "If you say yes to this, Connor, we'll be happy to discharge you in the morning and send you on your way."

"What do you think?" I asked once the doctor left, giving him a teasing poke on the shoulder. "You're all out of excuses now."

Connor sighed, knowing I was right. "It sounds too good to be true," he muttered, the best excuse he could give.

"Well, getting there won't be easy. We still have to get all the way to fucking Georgia."

"We?" he lifted an eyebrow.

"Well, yeah. There's no way I'm *not* coming with you." I crossed my arms, and he knew better than to argue. "I'm sure Raz would be along for the ride. Hunter and the kids too, maybe."

"Why's this guy so interested in me, though?" he wondered aloud. "Maybe he has a sick double-amputee fetish and the non-profit is just a front for his creepy dungeon."

"Connor," I groaned, dropping my forehead to my hand.

"It's possible, babe."

"But highly unlikely." I pinched my brow. "Maybe it's a military connection? He could have worked with you or someone you knew?"

"Also not very likely." To my surprise, he grabbed my arm and pulled me close. His mouth crashed down to mine before I had a moment to breathe, but in that instant, he was the air I needed. "You did this," he murmured against my mouth.

"What?"

"You. It's always you. The moment I'm about to say fuck it all and go off the deep end, you pull me back. And you show me it's worth it to keep going." He stroked his thumb against my cheek, the dense forest of his eyes pulling me in. "To the shifters, you may be a shaman, but to me, you're an angel."

My heart crashing into my ribs, I brought my hand up to his. "Does this mean you're not leaving me?"

"I know I'm a fucking idiot, but I'd be an even bigger idiot to do that." He lowered his forehead to mine. "I keep putting you through hell babe, and I don't know how you can stand it."

"Because I know it's not the real you doing that. It's what's been done to you." I wrapped my hands around the back of his broad neck. "And if this guy in Georgia can help you fight through that hell and bring out more of the real you, how could I not stick around for that?"

"God fucking damn it, babe. I love you so much."

He pulled me against him so tightly, I climbed into his hospital bed to reach him. We barely fit in the narrow space together, but that didn't matter. He wrapped me up in him, kissing me like it was our last day together, even though this was just the start of something new.

"I'm going to be a cranky bastard," he warned me between kisses. "I'm going to be pissed off and probably an asshole. I'll never be perfect but I swear to God, I'll try my best every day for you."

"I know you will," I told him. "You already do. Sometimes you push yourself and try too much." I gazed up at him. "Remember to be kind to yourself, too. Don't get upset if something isn't working. Try to love yourself as much as you love me."

"That will never happen," he laughed. "But I'll work on keeping my damn ego in check and letting shit go."

"That's all I want." I rested my hand over his heart, finally relaxing against him. "So we're heading to Georgia, then?"

"Guess so." He planted a kiss on my forehead. "Yee fuckin' haw."

EPILOGUE
MELODY

"What the fuck is up with Hunter?"

"I don't know," I admitted, stacking the last few boxes of supplies into Razvan's trailer. I shoved and tugged on a few things to make sure they were secure before closing the doors and latching them. Traveling light was apparently not in Raz's vocabulary.

Hunter begrudgingly agreed to come to Georgia with us, although he seemed he'd rather do anything else. He'd be driving Conner's RV since the doctor advised him not to use any prosthetics until he got fitted for his new ones.

He got discharged this morning, grumbling the whole time nurses pushed him in a wheelchair. Raz flew back to camp to bring his truck to the hospital, and Connor wasted no time hauling himself out of the wheelchair and into Raz's passenger seat.

"It's just temporary, babe," I reminded him, kissing his cheek. "Besides," I whispered breathily in his ear. "It might be fun sometimes."

"Naughty girl," Razvan chuckled delightedly, squeezing my thigh as he drove.

"We can use any regular chair for that," Connor grumbled, but I saw the smirk twitch on his lips.

"I dunno, man. Having wheels sounds like an extra bit of fun." Raz's eyes flashed excitedly at the road.

After getting packed up and hitting the road for a long journey ahead, I decided to ride in the RV with Hunter and Connor. Raz would be following us in his truck, hauling his own stuff behind him.

"Ride with me after we take a pit stop, *steluţa*," he growled, pinning me against the side of his trailer with a savage kiss that made my knees weak. "I can only go so many hours without seeing you."

"I have a feeling you'll drag me over here anyway," I teased, running my teeth along his ear. "Don't dragons like to kidnap maidens and hide them in their lairs or something?"

"If that's your fantasy, I can make it happen," he groaned, releasing me reluctantly before giving me a long look. "You gonna try talking to him?"

"I'm sure at some point, the boredom will get to me and I'll say something," I chewed my lip. "When that happens, Connor will back me up if there's a fight. But mostly, I just want to take a nap."

"A woman after my own heart," he chuckled, gazing down at me. "Have fun with them. I'll see you somewhere in Alabama."

My home state, not that I ever really had a home. We'd have to drive through on our way to Georgia, maybe even pass through Waterford, where I grew up. I thought about visiting my family and quickly shuddered with disgust. The further I stayed away from there, the better.

I climbed into Connor's RV, engine already running, to find him and Hunter talking in low voices in the front seats. They stopped talking the moment I got inside. I rolled my eyes and plopped down on the bed. Whatever. We'd have days to hash out whatever was going on.

The winding road put me to sleep immediately, but I was wide awake in another place, another body.

THE HUMANS GAVE me some shitty, half-rotten roadkill to eat for the first time in days. I still tore into it like it was a fresh, warm kill. How long had it been since I felt the satisfaction of hunting? Of bringing down prey and taking my fill? It felt like lifetimes ago.

When I finished the shitty meal, I pretended to be sedated when the human came to check the locks on my cage. He thought it would be funny to pull on my tail.

"Aaargh! Oh fuck, oh God!"

His human eyes only registered an orange blur as I swiped at him, claws outstretched and ready. I moved faster since losing so much weight, but even without the strength I once had, my claws tore through his soft human flesh like butter.

I only got his arm. He would eventually heal, but it didn't diminish the satisfaction of seeing his skin torn to ribbons, blood quickly staining his clothes a dark red. My cage was filthy, and I hoped he'd get an infection.

"Stupid fucking cat!" He grabbed a nearby cattle prod with his good arm and stuck it through the bars, the electric end sparking menacingly.

I gave him a toothy grin, even while growling through the pain of the zaps. His dominant arm was the one I injured, so he missed shocking me several times. Throwing the tool down and stomping away, I knew he'd return with the other human. The one who liked to pump me full of drugs. He'd probably give me the nerve injection again, to make my pain worse.

Oh well. It was worth it.

Hello?

I snarled in surprise. The voice rang through my head so clearly, soft and feminine. I rubbed my cheek against the bars as a deep purr rumbled in my chest. Although it wasn't a physical touch, I felt the presence of someone warm, gentle, and caring.

My name is Melody. I'm a shaman. Do you know what that is?

A shaman? I echoed. I hadn't heard that word in years. Not since Lhosten came to visit my family when I was a child.

Yes, I do, I answered. *I can't believe there are any of you left.*

I'm just getting into my powers, Melody admitted. *I've seen through your eyes in my dreams. I want to help you. Where are you?*

I don't know, I told her. *I'm kept in a cage in a shipping container when they're not making me jump through fire. I've been shipped all over the country dozens of times.*

I'm traveling now and I think I'm getting closer to you, she said. *I feel your presence getting stronger.*

I hope that's true, I replied. *The longer they keep me here, the weaker I get. I've not been performing well enough and I think they'll dispose of me soon.*

I'll find you, she said, conviction in her voice. *I promise.*

JUMP THROUGH FIRE

BOOK 4

PROLOGUE

Fire. So much fire.

I always smelled it before I saw it. Before the humans prodded me out of my tiny cage with their electric sticks just far enough to snap a chain on the degrading collar around my neck so they could drag me the rest of the way out.

What an awful, sickening, burning smell. Years ago, I enjoyed the smoky warmth of a wood burning fire. We never cooked our food, of course, but the bonfire was the center of our community. Grandparents told stories while children laughed and ran circles around the massive flames.

But this fire was all gasoline and chemicals. I prayed the fumes would give cancer to these wretched humans.

"Keep moving, stupid cat."

They zapped my flanks with the cattle prods to keep my back legs moving, but I barely felt the shocks anymore. Even the feeling in my paws had all but disappeared due to the multiple burns. But I'd be damned if I made this easy on them. I was still a 500-pound animal, and I'd make sure they'd feel every ounce of my weight as they dragged me closer to that awful smell.

At first, I thought if I went along with their demands like a well-trained pet, they'd stop shocking me. Maybe treat my burns. Or give me a decent meal for once.

I gave up on that hope years ago. If they were going to torture me regardless, pissing them off would give me a tiny amount of satisfaction.

Two of them pushed open a set of heavy wooden doors, leading me out into the ring. My usual getup, a tiny stool set in front of three fiery metal hoops, waited for me in the center.

Oohs and *ahhs* rose up from the crowd of humans in the stands surrounding us. Hundreds of different scents assaulted my nose underneath the sickly sweetness of the gasoline. That could only mean a packed house tonight.

My handlers discreetly prodded me up to the tiny stool—they wouldn't want to be reported for animal cruelty now—where I sat awkwardly on my haunches. Heat assaulted my face from the fiery hoops. The flames looked bigger and brighter tonight. No doubt the ringmaster ordered it as a punishment for maiming his assistant last night.

He stood in the center of the pit, in his stupid red tailcoat and top hat, talking me up to the crowd. I watched him through the flames like looking at prey through tall grass. A sudden thought occurred to me.

No. You will be too far gone if you do such a thing. Your soul will never be saved.

But what hope did I have left? The shaman hadn't reached out to me in over a day. I wasn't even sure if she was real or a hallucination at this point.

The ringmaster gestured to me as he completed his speech for the audience, turning his head to meet my eyes. Those cold, dead eyes that showed no remorse as he and his people abused, tortured, and starved me, plus who knew how many others like me.

Part of me thought I should have gone with Razvan all those years ago, but if it weren't me here, it would only be another shifter as a dancing puppet for these cruel masters. The ringmaster's eyes narrowed at me through the circles of flames, a warning to obey.

A roar from deep in my chest was my answer, my teeth on full display and my human head-sized paw swiping through the air. I made my decision. In the grand scheme of things, I was already dead.

I'd never see *svarga* after this life, but I was at peace with that. After all of my impure thoughts while trapped in this Hell, taking one human with me wouldn't be the worst thing. Maybe the next shifters' lives would be a bit easier until they found a new ringmaster.

I lowered my paw to the edge of the stool and lifted my rear end, coiled and poised to take my jump. So much fire. I fought back the nausea and the fear whispering at my instincts. This would be my last jump for these bastards and I had to make it count.

I focused on my prey, stilled my breath and my body, then leaped.

Flames licked painfully at my skin, singeing the fur on both sides of my flanks. I tucked my front paws as close to my body as I could. Only when I passed through the final hoop did I extend my claws.

Gasps of awe turned to screams of horror as I shredded through the ringmaster's coat. It was almost comical how his eyes bulged too late to realize what was happening. He didn't even have a chance to scream as my teeth sank into his throat.

Oh, a delicious, raw, fresh kill...

The sting in my shoulder only made me clamp down harder, tearing into the human's soft, pliable body with urgency.

So much blood. Delicious, sweet, hot flesh...

More stings pelted my body and my paws became heavy, so incredibly heavy. I smiled inwardly as the tranquilizers began circulating through my system, admiring the work I made of the former ringmaster. Now *that* wouldn't be an open-casket funeral.

I laid my head down and allowed the darkness to swallow me up. If I had any luck left at all, I would never wake up.

MELODY

I almost couldn't reach the door fast enough. The contents of last night's dinner roiled like a stormy sea up through my throat and nose, then spilled all over the concrete of the parking lot just outside of the trailer.

My stomach emptied itself, and then I dry-heaved through more coughs and gasps.

"Baby, please," Connor cried dramatically from inside the RV, "for the love of all that is holy, do not tell me you are pregnant."

"Asshole," I wheezed, spitting on the ground as I tried desperately to clear my throat.

"Here, *steluța*." A tattooed hand held out a water bottle to me, which I accepted and pulled from greedily. "Is McDonald's not agreeing with you?"

"It's not that," I gasped after draining half of the bottle. "Another vision. This one was... really, really gruesome."

"Here. Let's get you cleaned up, then you can tell us about it." Razvan rubbed my back soothingly. Since the moment we left Crying Falls, he seemed to have replaced Hunter as the sweetheart of the group. When he wasn't manhandling me and whispering all the dirty things he wanted to do to me, that was.

The tattooed dragon shifter led me, still weak and shaky, back inside to the tiny bathroom of the RV. After I brushed my teeth and washed my face, I felt slightly more human.

"What did you see?" Raz's gray eyes were wide with concern as he sat me on the bed next to Connor, who was still naked under the sheet.

"I saw through the eyes of the big predator again, the one we're getting closer to," I explained. "This time, he attacked the ringmaster. I'm pretty sure he killed him. I—" my hand flew to my throat. "I felt and tasted *everything*. The softness of his flesh, the warm stickiness of his blood. And I—no, the shifter, enjoyed it. He hadn't killed any prey in so long, and it was such a rush. But he..." My hand lowered to my lap as I recalled that feeling, the finality of it. "He had given up on escaping. He did it because he didn't expect to live much longer. Fuck, if they kill him—"

"Shh, babe." Connor sat up immediately and cradled my head to his chest. "Do not blame yourself. You can't save everyone."

"Then what the fuck is the point of me being a shaman?" I cried out in frustration. "They need me and I can't figure it out. I keep screwing up."

"You're not screwing up," Raz insisted, squeezing my knee. "You're learning. You're doing what you can."

"Eww, what's this?"

"Looks like vomit. Watch out, don't step in it."

The voices from outside the trailer indicated Hunter and the pups had returned from their early morning run, and the atmosphere immediately changed. Hunter didn't spare us a glance as he entered the trailer and took his place in the driver's seat.

Meanwhile, Raz and Connor glared daggers at his back. A full day on the road out of Crying Falls and he barely spoke a word to anyone but his kids. Oblivious to the tension, Roo and Rinna playfully wrestled on the floor.

"Don't worry, babe," Connor murmured with a kiss to my cheek. "About anything. We'll find your shifter and address the wolf in the room."

Hunter's canine hearing almost surely allowed him to hear Connor, although he made no sign that he did.

"Ready to hit the road, guys?" Connor announced in a louder voice.

"Yeah!" the kids declared in unison. Silence from the driver's seat.

Raz let out a frustrated growl as he squeezed my thigh. "Ride with me, *steluța*," he insisted.

I nodded, eager to be out of range of Hunter's cold shoulder. It was awkward enough on the drive yesterday. I didn't know if I'd be able to handle one more day without exploding.

"Now, don't get up to anything frisky, you two," Connor winked. "Eyes on the road, Raz."

"Shit, it's hard enough to focus with her just sitting next to me," Raz grinned as he pulled me to my feet, planted a kiss on me, and walked me out of the trailer, careful to sidestep over my vomit on the ground.

He turned to me the moment we shut the doors of his truck cab. "Con's gonna get to the bottom of whatever's eating wolf-boy's tail, I just know it."

"I know he will," I sighed, buckling my seatbelt. "I'm just afraid of what the answer will be."

"Don't be." He turned the ignition and the massive V8 engine roared to life. "I promise it has everything to do with him and nothing to do with you."

"You don't know that for sure," I said as we pulled out of the parking lot. My eyes flicked to the rearview mirror, where I saw Hunter maneuver the RV to follow us with Connor in the passenger seat.

"Yes, I do," my sexy dragon insisted.

"Change of subject, please." I looked out the window to the stretch of dense trees across the parking lot. We stopped for the night at a Wal-Mart out near the sticks for food and other essentials, like enough privacy for the shifters to shift. Raz didn't want to risk being seen even at night, so he slunk around in the woods in dragon form for a few hours last night. Hunter preferred early morning runs with the kids in wolf form. They caught their breakfast that way, too.

"How close are we to your old home?" Raz asked after a moment of hesitation.

I grimaced. Not the subject change I exactly wanted. Our ultimate destination was Eddison, Georgia, where Connor would be fitted with new leg prosthetics and be treated for the pain that landed him in the hospital back in Crying Falls. And if my gut was right, we'd be near this shifter whose eyes I kept seeing through in my dreams lately.

Unfortunately, our journey would also take us straight through Waterford, Alabama. Trailer trash central and my home sweet home. If a rundown trailer with an alcoholic mother and too many siblings to care for could ever be considered a home.

"Not nearly far enough," I muttered in reply.

Razvan chuckled. "You don't wish to see them? Not even at all?"

"My mom probably hasn't even noticed I'm gone yet," I scoffed. "Or if she has, it's only because her live-in maid and cook has disappeared." A question popped into my head as I drummed my fingertips on the window. "Do you ever wish to see your family again? Even after what they did to you?"

Raz inhaled a sharp breath as he mulled over his answer. He was the first dragon shifter born in his family for centuries, as the shifting gene had gone dormant. His family was so far removed from his dragon heritage, they regarded his shifting as a curse on their family. To absolve themselves of the so-called curse, they sold their son into the local circus.

"Not my parents," he answered, his voice gruff. "I would only want to see my younger siblings, to see if they exhibit any of the traits that I did. I'd want them to know they could find me, if they ever wanted that."

"When did you last talk to them?" I asked.

"Over five years ago," he sighed. "Right before I was shipped over here from Romania as cargo. I didn't even have an ID or a passport." He shot me a wry smile. "If I had come here voluntarily, I would have been an illegal immigrant."

"Oh no, not one of those!" I teased.

"Yes. It's easier to come over here as an exotic pet, it turns out. But anyway," his smile dropped as he turned the truck onto the freeway. "I think of them often and wish I could contact them. Every day that passes feels like it's too late to reach out. So I say, don't wait until five years have suddenly gone by, *steluța*."

"You're right," I breathed. "I just wish I had something more to give them. Some money or a place to stay away from her."

"You'll give them hope," he said, placing his hand on my knee. "They'll see you living your own life and answering to no one. They'll remember that. Even if they can't leave right away, they'll make plans and count down the days until they can."

I didn't answer him right away. I just squeezed his fingers around my knee, tracing the dots and lines of the tattoos on his hand. Getting away from that place had been the primary goal of my life. The thought of going back only filled me with dread.

Guilt also ate at me. I left them vulnerable to *her.* All my life, I'd been the shield between them and the wastes of life she brought home. I left to take care of myself, but no one else could defend them.

With a resigned sigh, I focused on the moving road ahead of us.

"I guess we're taking a detour, then."

❧ 2 ❧

CONNOR

"**A**lright, dude. Spill it."

Hunter's eyebrow twitched, but aside from that, he gave no indication that he heard me.

"Hunter, bro," I turned in the passenger seat to face him. "I know you didn't become deaf overnight. It's just us now. What the fuck is going on?"

"Nothing," the wolf shifter muttered.

"We both know that's bullshit. Try again."

He let out a heavy sigh, his eyes flicking to the rearview mirror to double-check that his children were indeed asleep.

"You can't tell Mel what I'm about to tell you. I mean, she deserves to know but I haven't processed it all yet."

"Sure, tell her in your own time. As long as you nut the fuck up, apologize for being a dick, and stop acting like one." I waved my hand between him and me as he drove. "And for the record, I can't believe *I'm* the one telling you to stop being a dick."

"I know," he snorted with a dry laugh. "What a role reversal, huh?"

"Spit it out, wolf-boy. I'm frothing at the mouth here."

He glanced over his shoulder once again to make sure the kids were asleep.

"After Mel and I were... together, with Razvan," he began in a voice so low I almost couldn't hear, "I went to check on the kids and spend some time with them. Rinna asked me something."

"Yeah?"

He swallowed and inhaled deeply. "She asked me if Mel would become their mom."

I rubbed my jaw. "And what did you say?"

"I don't even remember what lame excuse I said," he shook his head. "But I wanted so badly to say yes. And just the fact that I *wanted* to say that, just made me feel all guilty and pissed off."

"Why's that?" I probed, feeling like a damn therapist.

"Because my mate was her mother," he said with a soft growl. "Yes, she's dead. Yes, she wasn't perfect. But she was a wolf, a good she-wolf on her way to becoming alpha. And I can't shake the idea that's been instilled into me since I was a kid."

"And that is?"

His golden eyes flickered to me before returning to the road. "Pups need to be raised by their own kind. I can either be a single parent or I can find another pack and take another wolf for a mate. What I can't have is a shifter of another species, and especially not a human, raise my kids."

"Okay," I answered, mulling around this new information in my mind. "And this is really bothering you because you *do* want Mel in your life? As a possible mother figure to them?"

"Yes," he breathed, his fingers tightening his grip on the steering wheel. "I'm falling for her, Con. I'm falling hard."

"Obviously," I quipped. "Both of you are gaga over her. I mean, my advice would be just to get the fuck over your wolf pride hangups. The pups love her and she adores them. She may not be a shifter, but she understands you guys better than any normal human. Even if she can't teach them your wolf stuff, she can contribute to the human aspect."

"That's not all that's weighing on me." He gritted his teeth, his knuckles growing white on the steering. "In fact, that's not even the main reason I can't bring myself to talk or look at her."

I stared at him, taken aback. "What is it, Hunt?"

A long silence stretched between us. The stress and struggle to speak the words were visible on his face as I watched him.

"I am also kind of interested in another person."

"Hunter," I barked, sitting up straight. "You need to tell her this, ASAP. It's not fair to her. I'm talking the moment we stop for gas, you need to march your ass over there and tell her or I will."

"I know, but Con, it's not that simp—"

"I don't give a fuck, dude! Yes, our situation is unusual and I get that. But Mel is not anyone's side piece and I will *not* let her be treated like one."

"It's not really—"

"I don't care how you try to justify it, that's just how it is. You gotta make a choice, dude. You're either all in with Mel and us or you're not."

"But that's the thing," he said with a small shake of his head.

I barely heard him. The moment he said another person, my temper started to rise and I would have reached over and slugged him if he wasn't driving. He saw how distraught Mel was when my ex came to see me in the hospital. He *knew* how torn up she was! How could he comfort her from *that*, encourage her to come back to me, and still have a wandering eye for another woman?

"Let me guess," I spat bitterly. "You met a lady wolf shifter who is a perfect mother figure for your kids on paper, but you don't know her as well as Mel. Is that why this is so hard for you?"

"No!" he barked, glaring at me from the corner of his eye. "A female wolf wouldn't even make me look twice standing next to her."

"So what the fuck makes this person so special?"

"Look, I'll talk to her." His voice turned pleading. "The moment we stop, I'll man up and explain myself. Just please let me tell her myself. I don't want any information to get twisted."

"Hunter," I rubbed my temples. "I don't even know where you're going with this anymore. Get what twisted? The fact that you're falling for another woman?"

"It's not another woman!" he shouted before quickly glancing over his shoulder at his kids, who remained fast asleep.

I could only stare at him, dumbfounded. That was not what I was
expecting.

"Hunter?"

"It's Razvan," he sighed.

MELODY

We pulled into a gas station a few hours later, when the sun was high and sweltering. I pulled my legs off of Razvan's lap and swung them around to exit the passenger side. The moment I stepped out of the cool, air-conditioned cab, my thighs and breasts prickled from the sweat forming between them.

Damn, I wondered if the guys would be up for staying in a shitty motel tonight instead of our vehicles. Or maybe we could sneak into one with a pool.

"What're you hungry for, *steluța?*" Raz asked as he inserted the fuel pump into his car.

"Dragon," I purred, running my arm around his back and up his chest while I laid my head on his back. I couldn't help myself, I was so damn smitten with him.

"Don't tempt me," he chuckled, wrapping his fingers around mine and bringing them to his lips. "How about actual food?"

"Just a sandwich is fine," I told him as he turned to face me. "With no mayo if you can find one."

"And a side of dragon for dessert?" he grinned, stepping forward until my back met the smooth exterior of his car.

Why did I love it so much when he pinned me like this? He took the opportunity at every stop and it turned me to jello every time.

"Yes," I answered, my voice already getting breathy. "Piping hot, please."

He lowered a kiss to my mouth with a predatory growl, his upper body leaning in and pressing me hard against his truck. We must have kissed hundreds of times at this point, so much that my mouth memorized his. But when that split tongue flicked against mine playfully, it stole my breath away like the first time all over again.

"We'll have to kick those two out of the RV tonight," he voiced huskily as we untangled. "I want you in a proper bed."

"Why does that mean we have to kick them out?" I asked innocently, although my smile was anything but.

"You're so naughty and I love it," he said with a possessive squeeze of my waist. "Conner is always welcome to join but I don't want Mr. Party Pooper over there killing my mood."

I glanced up toward the RV, which Hunter pulled up to another fuel pump several feet away. He set up Connor's wheelchair just outside the door, and all of us watched as Connor handstanded his way out of the trailer and swung himself into the chair like a gymnast.

"Show off." Raz kissed my forehead before leaving me to head inside the mini-mart. "Sandwich with no mayo coming right up."

"Mel." I barely had time to enjoy the backside view of Raz walking away before a voice called my name. My heart jumped into my throat as I saw Hunter taking his long strides toward me. "Can I talk to you?"

"Um, sure," I answered hesitantly, not bothering to hide my surprise.

It seemed Connor really had gotten through to him. His expression was no longer cold and blank. Rather, the wolf shifter's brow was knitted as if worried. His golden eyes shifted around, never looking right at me. He appeared more tense and nervous than I'd ever seen him before.

I followed him away from the gas pumps, noticing Connor was preoccupied with showing the kids around the outside of the RV. He pointed at the wheels and made elaborate gestures with his hands like he was explaining how cars worked. I couldn't suppress the smile that formed. Even from a distance, I could tell he was a natural teacher.

"What's up?" I asked as casually as I could muster once we were out of earshot, despite my insides roiling like I would throw up again.

"First of all, I'm sorry for being so cold to you," he blurted. "You didn't deserve any of that, and Connor almost literally beat some sense into me. There's no excuse for me acting like that, especially after we got so much closer while he was in the hospital."

I nodded in a tentative acceptance of his apology. But I wasn't ready to let him off the hook yet.

"So what brought on the sudden change?"

He ran a hand through his platinum shoulder-length hair. "A couple of things," he sighed. "The main thing... I didn't want to admit to myself or you, or anyone. I don't know how you feel about it, but regardless, I don't plan on acting on it. So you don't have to worry about me behaving any certain way, but I am dealing with some weird feelings internally."

I blinked, just watching him talk, stammer, and ramble. I'd never seen him so nervous before. Whatever he was talking about clearly bothered him a great deal. He looked like he wanted to tuck his tail between his legs and slink away.

"Hunter, I'm not sure what you're talking about," I admitted.

"Of course you aren't," he muttered, pinching his brow. "I'm just dancing around it because I'm honestly terrified of hurting you with this information."

"Hey." I stepped closer, reaching out to touch him for the first time in days. My hand met his forearm, the contact lighting me up like an electric wire. I missed him, the *old* him. And I desperately wanted to ease the burden of whatever he carried.

"You won't hurt me if you're just honest," I told him. "Even if it's not something I want to hear, I'll appreciate you telling me. What I don't want is you hiding something because you think it'll protect me."

His arm came around me slowly, pulling me in until my cheek rested on his racing heartbeat. He lowered his chin to the top of my head and I heard his deep breaths to steel himself.

"Ever since the three of us were together," he began. "I feel like... I might be into Razvan. Physically. Maybe emotionally, I dunno."

I lifted my head to look up at him. "*That's* what you're so worried about?"

He nodded, his jaw and lips tense.

"Hunter." His name tasted like dessert on my lip as I slid my arms up to wrap around his neck. "Why would I be upset about that?"

He blinked, the shock setting in. "I dunno. Like I said, I don't know how you feel about... all that. And anyway," he shook his head. "Nothing will ever happen. He's infatuated with you and I won't come between that."

"What if he felt the same way about you?"

His breath hitched in his chest as he stared wide-eyed down at me. His mouth opened as if to ask a question, then quickly changed his mind. "Doesn't matter. We're both here for you. These... feelings don't diminish how I feel for you in the slightest."

"Have you ever felt this way about another man before?"

"No," he answered with a small shake of his head. "I can appreciate a good-looking guy, of course. But seeing him with you? There's something about him that's—never mind." He shook his head even more emphatically. "It doesn't matter. I'll get over it and I won't be a jerk to you anymore. I'm sorry, little fox."

"It's okay," I breathed, my body thrumming with fresh desire at the new fantasies dancing in my head. So I hadn't been entirely wrong when I noticed the connection between Raz and Hunter. But damn, sometimes I hated the small-mindedness of the south.

"Listen." I stood on tiptoes to stretch the full length of my body against his height. "I'm okay with you two being together if you want. I honestly think it's kind of hot."

"Mel," Hunter growled softly, lowering his forehead to mine. "You wouldn't want to see any of us with another woman, would you?"

"No," I frowned. "I wouldn't like that."

"So if things are truly equal, how is being with another guy any better?" His arms slid around my back. "I could never do that to you."

"Well, it's not just *any* guy," I corrected. "It's Razvan. He's one of us.

And if the three of us are together and I'm enjoying both of you, what's wrong with you two enjoying each other in the same moment?"

"I don't know," he murmured, although the growing bulge in his pants told a very different story. "And anyway, we don't know what Raz thinks."

"Want me to talk to him?"

"No!"

Hunter's fingers gripped the sides of my shirt, his brow growing furrowed with anxiety again. "Please don't say anything. I'm nowhere near ready to have that conversation with him. I just didn't want to keep it from you."

"Alright, I won't," I promised, gliding my fingers through his hair. "And I appreciate you telling me. I mean it when I say I'm fine with it. More than fine, even." I paused to lick my lips. "It would make me really happy to see you two together."

"You're serious?" his eyes widened.

"Of course I am!" I lifted my mouth to his, tired of waiting on my wolf for our make-up kiss, and it did not disappoint.

His long arms wrapped around my back and squeezed me against his torso, lifting me up so my toes levitated above the ground. My heart lifted and soared as our mouths molded together, chasing away all the awkwardness of the past few days as we settled back into the way we were.

Voices floating over on the breeze told me Raz and Connor were enjoying the show. I wrapped my legs around Hunter's waist and he grunted through our kisses, binding his arms under my ass to hold me securely against him.

"Was there anything else you wanted to tell me?" I asked when we parted breathlessly.

"No," he smiled. "I'm just so relieved you're okay with knowing this about me."

"I won't betray your confidence," I assured him, sliding my feet back down to the ground. "But you should talk to him. I think he might be more receptive than you think."

He glanced toward Raz, now leaning against the RV while talking to Connor, a plastic grocery bag in one hand.

"I'll think about it," he muttered.

"That's all I can ask for." I reached for his lips on my tip-toes again. "In the meantime, I have a sandwich to eat."

"You do like sandwiches," he grinned wolfishly as we walked back together, our hands swinging between us.

"Stop," I laughed, smacking his arm. "You're just as bad as those two now."

"Kissed and made up, I see," Connor observed when we rejoined them, his eyes glancing between us knowingly.

"Yeah," Hunter cleared his throat. "I owe all of you an apology. I was a complete dick the last couple of days because of my own shit. I didn't mean to take it out on all of you." He squeezed my hand affectionately. "Sorry, guys."

"If Mel forgives you, who are we not to?" Raz rummaged through his bag until he pulled out a deli-wrapped sandwich for me. "No mayo, *steluța*."

"It's a thing of the past now, bro," Connor added. "Onward and upward. No matter what, you can't unseat me as the moody asshole of the group."

"I'll know not to attempt that again," Hunter laughed, stretching upward and lacing his hands behind his head. My core heated at the sliver of taut belly that peeked from under his shirt. I was dying to make up the proper way, but it would have to wait.

Raz gave me a gentle nudge with his elbow. "Did you still want to do what we talked about?"

No. But we have to do it, anyway.

I nodded and straightened my spine as the other two looked on curiously.

"We'll pass through my old hometown, Waterford, in about two hours," I informed them. "I'd like to stop and check on my siblings, just to let them know I'm alive and okay." I looked at Connor. "Maybe give them a phone number if they need to reach me?"

"My digits are your digits, babe." He blew me a kiss. "You don't even need to ask."

"Thanks." I went to him and sat in his lap, wrapping my arm around his shoulders. "I don't really want to go there, but feel like I have to. I left really suddenly and I want them to know I didn't abandon them."

My Marine wrapped his arms securely around my waist. Here, nothing could reach me. Nothing could hurt me as long as I had them.

"We've got you, babe," he promised. "No matter how many drunk pieces of shit we have to fight in the process."

Raz and Hunter murmured their agreement, casting quick glances at each other before looking away.

4

MELODY

"*This* is where you used to live?"

The question came from Connor, mouth open and agape as we pulled up to the curb right outside the trailer park.

"Yup," I answered. "Home sweet fuckin' home."

"The bus stop I slept at was nicer than this dump." His lip curled in visible disgust.

"Yeah, why do you think I left as soon as I could?" I drummed my fingers on the RV window, remembering that day as clearly as ever. I'd never felt so scared or so free that morning of my eighteenth birthday, when I walked away and never looked back.

It had been barely a month and here I was again. The run-down mobile homes with peeling paint, rusted siding, overgrown yards, and piles of trash looked to be in even worse shape than when I left. Connor's RV was a modest apartment compared to these places. Razvan's setup, with multiple tents for privacy, a king-sized air mattress and even a bathtub, was downright luxurious.

"Which one was yours?" Hunter craned his neck from the driver's seat, looking down the narrow road between the mobile homes.

"Number eight, toward the back." I pointed through Connor's

window. "Just on the other side of that woodpile, which has never been used in years. None of the houses have chimneys, so the wood's probably all rotted out and nasty now."

"Hunter should probably be the one to go with you," Connor suggested. "Raz and I might not give the greatest first impression."

I snorted. "It's not like I'm hoping to impress my mom with y'all. Any one of you is ten times whichever man she brought home that week."

"Even so, Hunter's the calmest and most normal-looking out of all of us," Connor chuckled. "You don't need a surly wheelchair-bound Marine and a hot-headed dragon to ruin anything."

I sighed. He had a point. Even if my mom was passed out, my siblings grew to be just as suspicious of strange men as I was. One look at Connor or Raz would send alarm bells ringing and they might not be open to keeping in touch with me. Hunter would be easiest to trust based on first impressions alone.

"Alright," I breathed, moving reluctantly through the door. "Let's get this over with."

"We'll watch from the street," Connor assured. "Just yell if you need anything."

I nodded, blowing a kiss at him before stepping outside with Hunter right on my heels. His fingertips rested on the small of my back and I drew strength from his touch.

Faces peered at us from dirty windows as we walked past the trailers. Some neighbors would surely recognize me and probably already started gossiping about my return with a strange man.

When we stopped in front of the rectangular metal box that looked to be sinking into the soggy ground, Hunter gave my shoulder a gentle squeeze.

"You got this," he whispered with a quick kiss to my forehead. "We're all behind you."

I nodded, taking a quick breath to steel myself, then stepped up to the front door, despite my feet feeling stuck in concrete.

A quick knock on the flimsy, warped plywood, and the door almost immediately cracked open. A blue eye at nearly the same height as me peered through the crack, narrowed in suspicion.

"Jeanie?" I asked. "It's me, Mel."

The door promptly shut, and I heard the lock slide over on the chain.

"Jean!" I knocked again, more insistently, and waited. No answer, so I started pounding at the wood. "Jeanie May, open up!"

"Mel, should we come back?" Hunter asked as he looked around at the nosey neighbors peeking their heads out their own doors, but I ignored him and continued on.

"I'm not coming back here again!" I said through gritted teeth. "This is the *one* time I'm coming back to this shithole, so y'all better—"

The door swung wide open mid-knock, and my fifteen-year-old sister glared at me from across the threshold.

I sucked in a breath. Not even a month went by and the wide-eyed, strawberry blonde who was closest to me in age suddenly looked to be a decade older.

Jeanie wore a faded, threadbare T-shirt and sweatpants that had been mine at one point, and my older sister's before that. Her hair was piled on her head in a messy bun with dozens of strands poking out like she'd slept with her hair like that. But from the shadows under her eyes, it looked like she barely slept at all.

"Say what you need to say, then go back to wherever you ran off to," Jeanie spat, turning away from the door, leaving it wide open for us.

I stepped inside, Hunter's hand tense on my shoulder as we observed the house where I grew up. Jeanie had been sorting recycling, just like how I taught her to do. In the narrow kitchen, large trash bags were filled to the brim with either aluminum cans, glass bottles, or plastic bottles.

The rest of the trailer hadn't changed much. Piles of unsorted laundry, magazines, children's toys, and old electronics cluttered up the small space, but it was relatively clean. It seemed Jeanie had stepped up to fill my shoes as everyone's caretaker when I left.

"Um, Jean, this is Hunter," I said, waving a hand back toward him. "Hunter, my sister Jeanie May."

"Well met, Jeanie." He offered a friendly smile, carefully ducking under a ceiling light. "Thank you for letting us stop by."

Jeanie rolled her eyes toward me, never pausing as she sorted bottles and cans like a one-woman assembly line. "I just let y'all in so your knocking wouldn't wake them up."

I swallowed. By *them,* she meant Mom and someone else. Sometimes it would mean Audra, our older sister, who followed closely in our mother's drunken, stumbling footsteps. Other times, it meant the guy Mom was seeing at the time.

"Where are the other kids?" I asked.

"School," she answered curtly.

"Oh, good." I breathed a sigh of relief. "I was worried about them not getting up and going without anyone to..." I trailed off, suddenly feeling like a piece of shit for leaving.

"Oh, they missed about a week before I stepped up," Jeanie said. "There was some confusion and shit with you being gone, but shit went back to normal after that."

"I see," I said with a grimace, knowing that our normal wasn't by any means good. And I hated leaving them with that. "Hey, wait. Why aren't *you* in school?"

She stared at me like I sprouted an extra head. "Because *someone* has to take care of shit at home. With you gone, that had to be me. So here I am. Just finished cleaning puke and beer off this floor, now I gotta get this shit sorted and dropped off before I pick up the littles."

"Jean," I pleaded, my teeth biting into my cheek. "You need to stay in school, too."

"I can't, Mel," she shot back. "I can't keep this house from falling apart, *and* go to class, *and* do homework!"

"Honey, I know it's hard." I moved closer to her. "But you have to. You have to get your diploma, then you can walk out of here and apply for jobs. Real jobs. But you have to learn how the world works, how to spend your money and all of that. If you stay here, you'll be trapped."

"So what did you do?" Her eyes shifted from me to Hunter. "Looks like you found a man. Not much different from Mom or Audra, I see."

"Hunter's nothing like them," I hissed, lifting a finger at her in warning. "My situation's complicated, and it's not perfect, but I am building skills and working toward something, Jean. But I didn't want to ride off into the sunset and leave you and the others behind. That's why I came back, to let you know I'm still here for you guys."

"Yeah?" She lifted her eyebrows. "Look, I'm not mad at you for leaving. I fantasize about it every day, but if you want to help, we need more than your pep talks telling us to stay in school. The kids need new clothes and school supplies. We need new locks on all the doors—"

"The bedroom locks broke again?" Dread filled the pit of my stomach as I raised a hand to my open mouth.

"Oh, Mom broke those fuckers the first night you were gone," Jean remarked casually. "She tore this place up looking for you. It's a wonder there ain't no holes in the walls."

As if right on cue, the sounds of groans, heavy footsteps, and commotion came from down the hall. My heart jumped into my throat and I knew my time here was limited.

"I'll get you locks," I promised. "And stuff for the kids. I can't right away, but I will soon. I swear, Jeanie." I grabbed a pen from the counter and scribbled down Connor's phone number. "You can reach me here with a text or call if you need anything. We're passing through on our way to Georgia, but I can mail you the stuff you need. I can set up a bank account that only you can access."

"Okay." Jeanie's tough exterior seemed to wither away as her eyes darted nervously down the hall. Her voice lowered to a whisper. "Y'all better go. She's been—"

"Jeanie?! Who the fuck're you talking to?"

"No one, Ma!" my sister yelled back.

Hunter's hand closed around my upper arm and he moved to pull me back through the door just as Jeanie stuffed the paper with Connor's number into her shirt. We just reached the door when the shape of my mother emerged from the hall.

I never knew whether to feel sorry for her or hate her. It was usually an odd mixture of both. She was a miserable creature, that was the only reason why she led such a miserable existence. But to put me and her other children in the path of her self-destruction? I couldn't bring myself to feel any sympathy for how her fuck-ups robbed us of a normal, happy life.

So morbidly obese, she could barely walk without the use of a cane, she leaned heavily on the wall as she stared at us through glassy eyes. The skin on her face was patchy and red, her wild, unkempt hair streaked with gray stuck out in every direction. The stains on her clothes and smells coming from her indicated she had drank and passed out in those clothes for several straight days.

"Melody?" she peered at me like a mole seeing sunlight for the first time.

"We were just leaving, Ma." Every syllable shook as I fought to get the words out. I could feel myself reverting back to a terrified little girl, just trying to stay out of this woman's way. A girl who would say and do anything in the hopes of one peaceful night.

"Nah uh! You ain't leaving until you explain yourself, you ungrateful little bitch! Where the hell have you been?"

Hunter's hand tightened around my arm, a low warning growl already rumbling in his chest. I touched his other hand in an attempt to calm him.

"I don't need to explain anything to you," I replied, struggling to keep my voice steady. "I became an adult at eighteen and I moved out. Simple as that."

"Bull-SHIT! I didn't give your ass permission to move out! You wanna be an adult? You keep this place running like you used to! I went without a drink for two days because none of these dumbshits knew where to cash my disability checks!"

"Looks like you survived." I couldn't help but sneer. "Unfortunately."

"You are *my* daughter, you ungrateful little tramp! I gave you life and you should be thanking me! I gave birth to all you ungrateful shits, and you left me to suffer! You're supposed to take care of your parents!"

"And you're supposed to protect your kids!" I yelled back, the dam now bursting. Not even Hunter's presence could keep me from holding back. "But you pop them out and endanger them every single day! Do you even know how many swings I took to protect Jeanie, or Bella, or Joey? Do you even remember?"

"Oh, stop being so fuckin' dramatic. Everyone in my family was a bunch of rowdy boozehounds and we turned out fine!"

"Have you looked at yourself?" I cried out, biting back the bile of disgust. "You're *not* fine! None of us are as long as we're with you! That's why I left! Because you pushed us out, but you're no goddamn mother!"

She came at me, screaming obscenities I couldn't even decipher anymore. My throat grew raw like sandpaper, screaming back as Hunter pulled me through the door and slammed it closed behind us. He half carried, half dragged me through the park back to the street, while I could only shake, scream, and claw at my own skin to let out my rage.

HUNTER

My heart broke for Mel the moment we pulled up to that dilapidated trailer park. By the time her so-called mother hurled those insults at her, it had shattered into pieces.

She was inconsolable when I brought her back to the RV. Connor and Raz, who'd been leaning against the vehicle casually, suddenly snapped up to attention.

"What happened?" they demanded, muscles tensed and fists clenched as I wrapped Mel in a bear hug and carried her inside. They followed me, itching for a fight as I laid her down on the bed, where she screamed into a pillow and punched the mattress.

"Outside," I directed the two of them. "You too, guys. Move it," I said to Roo and Rinna, who looked at Mel with wide-eyed concern. Everyone reluctantly obeyed me and I followed them out, closing the door behind me to give Mel some privacy.

"Is miss Mel okay?" Roo asked.

"She will be," I assured him. "You guys go sit in Mr. Razvan's truck. The adults are going to talk."

"What the fuck, Hunter?" Raz demanded when the pups were out of earshot, looking around like he was looking for something to punch, too.

"Her mother was there." I shook my head. Just saying the word *mother* felt like the entirely wrong word to use. "They got into an argument."

"An argument? Why do I feel like you're downplaying what really happened?" Connor demanded. "Mel and I have gotten into arguments. She's never turned into a violent, screaming mess."

"That fucking woman," I growled, my own fists clenching at my sides. "Just came out and started calling her names. Insulting her and saying so much shit just because she was there. It was fucking insane, I couldn't believe it."

"Wow, two fucks in two sentences, Hunter. Must've been really bad." Leave it to Connor to tease me in a situation like this.

"It was," I insisted. "And God, she was so fucked up. She had to be the grossest human I've ever seen, looked like shit, smelled like shit. I can't even believe our Mel came out of *that*."

"And you just let her talk to our girl like that?" Raz turned on me, stepping in close to my personal space.

I stared him down. He wouldn't intimidate me. We weren't in his territory anymore, and he wasn't the alpha here. Still, I couldn't ignore the heat in my belly or the surging of blood to my cock when he stepped in close enough to let me inhale his smoky, intoxicating scent.

"I got her out of there, but she didn't even want to leave at first," I said, regarding him coolly. "Our girl held her own and told that piece of shit excuse for a mother exactly what was on her mind."

"I knew it," Connor chuckled, spinning his wheelchair in a circle. "That girl's got some serious bite and not just in the bedroom."

"But this can't be good." Raz lifted his arm in the direction of the RV, where we could still hear Mel's muffled screams and thumps as she hit things. "Listen to that. She's in so much pain."

"I think the confrontation caused her to let out a lot of anger that she can't put back," I said, scratching at the pale beard on my chin. "She had to put aside what she felt and put on a brave face just to come here. Now, all that's unleashed."

"Sounds like something my old therapist would say, so I think Hunter's right," Connor chimed in. "She just needs to let it out and she'll be okay."

"Fuck, I want to burn that place down to ash," Raz turned and glared at the trailer we just came out of, down at the end of the park. "It's caused her so much misery. So much pain."

"I wouldn't recommend that," I said. "Her siblings still live there. We talked to one of them before the mother came out." I gave them a quick summary of what we talked about with Jeanie, and by then, the screams had dissipated from inside the trailer.

"Let Hunter check on her." Connor reached out and put his hand on Raz's arm when we both turned to go inside. "She doesn't need you making a list of things to burn. He saw firsthand what happened."

With a reluctant nod, Raz leaned his back against the trailer and crossed his arms while I went inside.

Mel laid perfectly still on the bed except for the rise and fall of her erratic breathing. I approached her slowly, as I would an orphaned pup left behind by his pack, and sat down next to her.

"Don't ask me if I'm okay," she said, her voice low and raspy. "Don't try to talk to me about it, please."

"Okay," I responded, and maneuvered behind her. I laid on my side with my chest to her back and draped an arm over her waist. Placing a small kiss on her shoulder, I still kept a few inches of space between us in case she didn't want to be smothered.

After a few moments of tense stiffness between us, she scooted her hips back until the entire length of her body pressed against mine. She sighed and snuggled into me as I wrapped both arms around her, just dropping kisses to her face, neck, and shoulders as I held her.

I wished with all my heart that I could do more for her. But I would only give what she wanted, what she *needed*, and no less. If that was just someone to hold her while she cried, so be it.

Eventually, Connor and the pups climbed aboard, saying nothing and keeping their distance. But everyone wore the same expression of concern.

My ears picked up the sound of Raz's truck engine starting behind us. Connor folded up his wheelchair and lifted himself into the passenger seat, where he patiently waited.

I placed a small kiss on Mel's ear before asking, "Ready to go, little fox?"

She nodded and squeezed my arms a little tighter. "Thank you, Hunter."

I kissed her once more before gently unwrapping myself around her. Connor buckled up in the passenger seat and I took my place behind the wheel. With the turn of a key and no words spoken, we left that hellhole just like Mel did the first time.

With no regrets and no looking back.

❧ *6* ❧

MELODY

The further Hunter drove us away, the better I felt.

No one ever left me alone, whether Roo and Rinna kept close watch over me or Connor lifted himself up and took a nap beside me. Their presence reminded me of where I was now and what I really escaped from.

The sun faded low as we neared the Alabama-Georgia border. I sat up in bed, feeling like the dead rising as I stretched. Hunter caught my eye in the rearview mirror as he turned off the freeway.

"You okay, little fox?" he asked, lifting his chin slightly as I came up behind him and smoothed my hands down his chest.

"I am now," I answered, placing my chin on top of his head. "But I don't think Jeanie is, and that's what kills me."

He took one hand off the steering wheel and brought one of my hands to his lips. "If she's anything like you, she'll make it through. She's tough, and now she has a lifeline."

In the passenger seat, Connor spun his phone on the dashboard. "How many times did you call CPS while living there, babe?"

"Hundreds," I told him. "But they're so backed up with more urgent cases. I stopped calling when I was around sixteen because Mom threatened us. Getting split up would mean fewer dependents

448

for her, which meant less money. I'm sure she's brainwashed the younger ones into not calling, too."

"They'll get out," Hunter insisted with a small undertone of a growl. "We'll help you get them all out. Even if we have to adopt them ourselves."

"That's even more complicated," I sighed, running my fingers through his pale, silky hair. "But you guys are amazing for even offering."

We meandered through the small nameless town, looking for a place to park our two large vehicles that would attract the least amount of attention. A Motel 6 passing on our left side reminded me of my earlier desire that day.

"Hey! Do you guys want to go for a swim later?"

"I dunno if you noticed, babe," Connor laughed. "But I'm kind of missing my flippers."

"Con, your arms are strong enough to pull your entire body weight." I rolled my eyes at him. "I'm dying to just take a dip and wash this whole day away."

"That sounds good to me," Hunter agreed, circling back toward the motel, which probably thoroughly confused Razvan following us. "I'm not sure how the fire breather will feel about it."

"It's not like he'll melt," I squeezed his shoulder. "The guy pulls around a bathtub, he can't be that scared of going underwater."

"Did y'all bring your bathing suits or am I missing something here?" Connor inquired.

I climbed into his lap, facing him with a wicked smile. "Who needs bathing suits when we have birthday suits?"

"Sweet Jesus," he groaned, his large hands pawing at my waist as his pupils dilated. "I'm in, as long as there's a shallow end."

"One little naked run through the woods and she's an exhibitionist already," Hunter laughed.

"What the fuck did I miss while holed up in that hospital?" Connor demanded.

Hunter and I recounted how our first threesome began—vaguely at first, but Connor thirstily demanded more details. While we filled him in, Hunter parked the massive vehicle on a side street just behind the motel. We could get into the pool after just a short walk and a hop over the fence.

"Why didn't y'all just fuck right there in the bathtub?" Connor asked as Hunter removed the keys from the ignition.

"It was too small," I told him in a fit of giggles, my stomach flipping at discussing it so casually like this. "All three of us wouldn't have fit."

"Y'all just need to get more creative," he said with a mocking shake of his head. "I'll show you how it's done," he added huskily.

"Oy!" Razvan hollered from outside the trailer with three quick knocks to the door. "Why are we stopping here, wolf-boy?"

Roo opened the door to let him in and Hunter nodded at him from the driver's seat. "Mel wants to go for a swim. You down?"

"A naked swim," Connor added.

"How can I refuse when you put it that way?" Raz crossed his arms and sent a look my way that had me squirming in Connor's lap. Something told me that no amount of water would be putting out this fire.

"We should wait 'til it's dark, so we can sneak in easier," Connor drummed his fingertips on my hips. "Maybe grab some food first. I saw a grocery store nearby."

"Can we swim too?" Roo piped up.

"Nope." Hunter turned in his seat to face his son's pout. "It's an adults-only swim. I need you guys to stay here and guard the vehicles. It's a very important job and I'm counting on you, okay?"

"Why do we always get left out of the adult stuff?" Roo whined, stamping his feet.

"One day you'll understand, little man," Razvan ruffled his hair.

The affectionate contact surprised me. Raz hadn't had much interaction with the pups, but right then he looked down at Hunter's mini-me with an endearing expression. Hunter noticed it too, but his expression seemed more conflicted.

Regardless, Razvan's placating seemed to work as Roo stopped complaining, although he remained pouty. We all assured him how important it was to guard the vehicles before the four of us set out in search of food.

As we walked through the streets of the small, southern town and then its even smaller supermarket, I couldn't tell which one of us got the most stares. Or maybe it was our group as a whole?

Hunter turned heads with his imposing height, chiseled features and ethereal beauty. Men and women alike stopped in their tracks to stare at him. Razvan's rough-and-tumble, tattooed form put the fear of God on the faces of old ladies, brought on lustful looks from younger women, and incited jealous glares from men. Connor, running circles around us all in his wheelchair, brought on looks of curiosity, then admiration and respect when they noticed the dog tags around his neck and the strength in his massive arms.

And then there was me, the leggy, doe-eyed, raven-haired girl in the middle of this band of misfits, pushing the buggy around while yelling at my goofball men to behave. Could this be our version of reality one day? The four of us, shopping for groceries on a normal weekday evening.

The thought stayed with me as we checked out and carried our bags back to the trailer. We ate from our microwave meals while standing or sitting around Connor's tiny kitchen space. Was it a pipe dream to picture all of us having dinner together in an actual kitchen? At a table big enough for all of us to sit around, even the pups? Could we even have a bedroom one day with a bed big enough to fit all four of us?

It felt like a fantasy, but in that moment, I realized I wanted it more than anything. A normal life with my perfectly imperfect family. The family I'd chosen.

Night fell as we finished eating and put away the rest of the supplies. A giddy excitement came over me as we walked down the street, talking in hushed whispers. I felt like I was in high school again, sneaking into a house party.

The motel pool glittered like a lagoon at an oasis from the other side of the wrought-iron fence. Most of the nearby rooms were dark. Hopefully, that meant they were vacant. Not a soul was in sight. The deck chairs were still laid out and even some folded towels were piled on a table. It was our own private paradise.

"Up you go, *steluța*." Razvan lifted me by the waist so I could climb over the fence with all the grace of an elephant. He and Hunter followed me over with animal-like agility.

"Shit, wait." Hunter landed lightly on his feet, then immediately turned to look at Connor on the other side. "I'll come back over, Con."

"Boys, please," Connor scoffed, holding up a hand. "Remember who the fuck you're talking to."

We all watched dumbfounded as Connor lifted himself from his wheelchair and swung himself over the fence with even more grace and agility than the two shifters—never once using his legs.

"Alright then, show-off," Razvan laughed, peeling off his shirt. "Race ya to the pool!"

"Now I'd be foolish to accept that." Connor seated himself on the concrete pool deck as he began removing his own clothes. "Don't judge a fish on its ability to climb a tree or however the saying goes."

"Fair enough." Raz's eyes danced mischievously over to Hunter. "Wolf?"

The two of them froze in a tense moment of time, like a pair of duelists watching each other in the beginning of a standoff. In the next moment, they hurriedly undressed. My eyes doubled in size as they unzipped their jeans and hilariously hopped around as they fought to get out of their pant legs. I couldn't breathe from laughing so hard as they finally stripped down to their underwear and were neck and neck as they raced to the pool's edge.

Hunter won the race by a few inches, his height and long arms giving him the advantage as he cut through the water like a dolphin.

"Well, *that* wasn't sexual at all," Connor muttered as he pressed up and walked on his hands next to me to the edge of the pool.

✿ 7 ✿

MELODY

I looked at Connor in surprise. "You, uh, know about that?"

"If Hunter didn't tell you, I was going to do the honors." He winked up at me as he swiped a towel from a nearby deck chair.

"Get in, you two! It feels great," Razvan called. He and Hunter both surfaced and swam back across to greet us.

I lowered myself to sit on the edge and dipped one foot in the water.

"Ohh, it really does," I sighed.

"I'm headin' for the shallows," Connor muttered as he kept hand-walking to the opposite end, where the pool bottom gently sloped upward to meet the edge.

"You can ride on my back, buddy," Razvan cackled. "I won't let you drown."

"Hell no! I ain't nobody's jetpack!"

"Coming in, little fox?"

Hunter swam up next to my dangling feet, his hair spreading out around him like a halo on the surface of the water.

"Are you kidding?" I pulled my top over my head, stripping down to my bra. "This was *my* fantastic idea."

453

Raz swam up next to him and grabbed my ankle, an evil grin on his face as he looked up at me. "You need to do your fantastic idea faster."

"Don't you dare, Raz!" I kicked my legs in warning, splashing water in both of their faces. "I can't get these clothes wet. We need to find a laundromat tomorrow."

"Whatever. Hurry up and get in."

They watched like a pair of hungry sharks as I removed my feet from the water and slid my shorts off my legs. After a moment's hesitation, I made off with my bra and panties, too. Yeah, maybe I talked about birthday suits earlier, but being nude in public still made me a little nervous.

"Ahhh." The coolness of the water shocked me as I slid in. I held my breath as my entire face dipped below the surface, my toes touching the bottom a moment later.

"See?" Razvan wrapped an arm around my waist as I resurfaced. "Feels amazing."

Before I could reply, he lifted my whole torso just above the surface and threw me.

"Mel in the middle!" Hunter laughed, kissing me through my scream as he caught me, then threw me back to Razvan.

"Ha!" Supported by the buoyancy of the water, I wrapped my legs around Raz's waist, smiling triumphantly. "Can't get rid of me now."

"Like I would ever want to," he murmured before kissing me deeply, his lips cool from the water while the inside of his mouth still burned hot.

Before I could lose myself too much in kissing him, a pair of arms wrapped around my middle and dragged my upper body away from him through the water. I dipped my head back to see Hunter with a playful pout on his face.

"No fair," he grumbled before kissing me deeply. "The winner should get the girl."

"You barely won." Raz rolled his eyes. "All because of your damn height."

"You already had a head start with your shirt off! I beat you fair and square."

I found their bickering adorable. With my legs still wrapped around Raz, I alternated between kissing him and Hunter as they both drifted closer within sandwiching distance. While they shut up for the moments my lips were on theirs, they seemed more interested in trash talking than any kind of sandwiched fun.

"Screw you guys, I'm hanging out with Connor."

Raz barely seemed to notice when my legs unwrapped from him. He and Hunter were now in some heated debate about the fastest land animals.

Connor sat against the pool wall nearby, the water up to his shoulders.

"Hey, are you actually floating?" I asked as I doggy-paddled over to him.

"Nah, there's a ledge to sit on," he smirked. "Come here, babe."

I drifted over until he pulled me into his lap, the fabric of his boxer shorts teasing me through the water.

"I like watching you with them," he murmured, his mouth on my ear. "They're just what I wanted for you—good guys you can lean on when you've had enough of me."

"You know I hate it when you talk about yourself like that." I turned to face him. "So please don't. Not while I'm just trying to relax in a pool with you guys. And anyway," I wrapped an arm around his shoulders, creating droplets of water in the crevices of his muscles. "After we get to Georgia, I hope they help you see what you're worth."

"I know I'm worth more just having you with me." He kissed me long and deeply. "But I'm still skeptical of this place. I still don't know why this guy's so interested in me."

The non-profit center we were going to was headed by a colleague of Dr. Harman, the doctor who treated Connor for his concussion after his fall. His center specialized in providing services to combat veterans, including new prosthetics for Connor's legs free of charge.

"How's your pain been?" I asked him, massaging around his knees.

"Better," he admitted with a soft groan of pleasure from the touch. "Easily tolerable lately. I think he was right about pressure on the nerves."

"See? You should listen to doctors," I teased, kissing him on the cheek. "And to me."

"I'm working on it, babe." He lifted his forest-green eyes to me, bright, clear and full of adoration that made my heart skip. "I'm not used to people caring so much. Accepting help feels... weak."

"It's not," I insisted. "And you have three of us willing to help you, with no questions asked."

"I know." His arms tightened around my waist. "Believe me, I know."

His skin was cool, but quickly heated as he held my body flush to his. The mix of hot and cold sensations sent my nerves into overdrive as his firm grip palmed my ass, his tongue invaded my mouth, and he pulled me toward his growing erection.

Goosebumps erected on my skin and not because of the temperature. We were going to do this here? Now? It wasn't quite public, but close enough. The thought scared and thrilled me as Connor's rough hands enveloped my breasts in warmth before releasing them to the cold water again.

A sudden, loud splash broke our kiss and made me look over my shoulder. Hunter and Raz were roughhousing, wrestling and grabbing each other to dunk underwater. They laughed and moved aggressively, still in a competitive spirit and not wanting to let the other win. But I also saw the ways their eyes heated, and the way their fingers trailed against the other to prolong their touch.

"God, look at you, babe," Connor growled, his voice thick with desire. "You're so fucking turned on right now."

"I—" My excuse cut off with a gasp as his hand cupped between my thighs, and only then did I feel the true liquid heat building like a volcano within me, without the coolness of the water to temper it.

"Turn around," Connor instructed. "Keep watching them. They get you so hot, don't they?"

"Yes," I admitted, spinning in his lap to press my back to his chest. He cupped one hand around my breasts and sent the other down to caress my clit.

"Do you want to see them touch each other like I'm touching you?" His voice rumbled against my back and my neck, where his hot mouth nipped at my cool skin. "Do you want to see both of their cocks out, pleasing each other?"

"Yes," I gasped, arching against him. Like he had been there, he voiced every dirty fantasy in my head ever since Hunter, Raz, and I spent the night together. And as I watched them, wrestling and play-fighting for dominance, I could see it come to life before my very eyes.

Raz pounced on Hunter's back, wrapping his arms around his neck in a choke-hold and his tattooed legs around the wolf shifter's slender, pale waist. Hunter's response was to fall backward, creating a huge splash and sending both of them underwater. When they surfaced separately, Hunter swam over and captured Raz in his own headlock, their faces close enough to kiss.

Nothing about the sexual tension between them made them any less masculine. If anything, their displays of strength and playful violence made them even more masculine, and got me even hotter.

"What if I fucked you while they fucked at the same time?" Connor went on, talking low enough in my ear so only I could hear. "They'd get so hot watching you and you'd come so sweetly on my cock watching them."

"Connor..." I thrashed madly against him, the vision playing out in my head like an extension of the one happening before me. God, just the mental picture he described was as hot as his fingers stroking me, his rough kisses on my neck and shoulders.

If Raz and Hunter had any idea of what we were doing or imagining, they gave no indication of it. The two alpha shifters also showed no signs of stopping. They'd keep this up until sunrise if they could. Based on strength alone, they seemed perfectly evenly matched.

Raz's dark inked designs were a beautiful contrast against Hunter's pale, unmarked skin. For the past several minutes, they moved too fast for me to really enjoy the visual, but right then, they started to slow.

Raz clung to Hunter's back again, his arms around his neck, but instead of a chokehold, he held on loosely, his tattooed hands skimming over the top of Hunter's chest. For the briefest moment, Hunter touched his hands as if to hold them, but quickly changed his mind and let them drop to his sides with a small splash.

The dragon shifter's hands drifted over him like in a caress, but could have also been interpreted as a simple change in grip. What could not have been mistaken was how Hunter's face turned toward his. Raz's forehead touched his temple in a small but indisputable gesture of affection.

Their eyes met. All splashing and horseplay ceased for this moment of stillness, of tranquility. Hunter slowly turned to face Raz, their gazes locked on each other and standing close, so close...

"Ah-mmph!"

Connor clamped a hand over my mouth as his skilled fingers sent my thrashing overboard into an orgasm. I was so entranced by watching the shifters, the wave of pleasure snuck up on me unnoticed and took over my body like a demonic possession. Connor's words, his hands on me, and the unbearably hot images dancing in my head combined into such a perfect storm, Raz and Hunter only had to look at each other like *that* to send me over the edge.

But now, they looked at me with expressions I couldn't read. The corners of Raz's mouth tipped up in a knowing smirk, but flickers of shame and embarrassment flashed through his eyes. Hunter cast his gaze down to the surface of the water, but I thought I could see a smile playing on his lips too.

"Shit." Connor shoved me off his lap before any of us could say a word. "Somebody's coming."

"Mel already did," Raz laughed softly.

"No, lizard-brain, I feel footsteps on the concrete. We're about to get caught!"

The four of us sprung into frantic, hurried action. I climbed out and wrapped a towel around myself, praying it would stay on until we cleared the fence. Walking on his hands, Connor was the first to reach the fence, pulling himself up and vaulting over like a gymnast.

Raz and Hunter quickly swam to the end of the pool and pulled themselves up, racing to the fence.

"Hey! Stop!" someone yelled over running footsteps on the concrete.

"Come on, Mel!" Hunter waited for me as Raz scrambled over the top.

Still dripping wet and only in his boxer briefs, he grabbed my waist and hoisted me up. Raz held his arms out to catch me on the other side as I struggled to keep my towel on and also not fall like a sack of potatoes.

"Let's go!"

Hunter landed soundlessly on his feet and immediately took off running toward the RV. Connor was already in his wheelchair, speeding down the sidewalk ahead of us. Raz ran with me, my hand in his while the other clutched my towel to my chest.

One by one, we slapped the side of the RV like we were kids playing tag and it was our home base. Breathless and exhilarated, we all looked at each other between wide, wicked smiles and hushed, maniacal laughter. Maybe it was juvenile, but fuck, that was fun and risky.

"Shit!" I exclaimed, looking down at myself and then at the three guys, still dripping wet and only in their underwear, which left little to the imagination. "We left our clothes behind!"

No one said a word. After a moment of exchanging awkward glances at each other, we all burst into peals of laughter once again.

❀ *8* ❀

MELODY

After drying off and curling up snugly between Raz and Connor in the bed of the RV, I tried reaching out to the mysterious predator shifter once again. Since feeling his despair and watching him kill as if I were doing it myself, I felt uneasy about trying again. What would happen if I tried to communicate with a dead shifter? Did I want to know?

Regardless, I had to try. His presence felt stronger, and so much closer last time. Unfortunately, that meant I could feel the damage done to him in even crisper detail. He had been starved, weakened, and drugged. I got the sense that he'd been in his animal shift for so long, those predatory, survival instincts grew dominant inside him and made his human side weaker.

If his captors didn't know he shifted, I hoped that was a good thing. It meant he wouldn't be displayed as a partially shifted freak like Raz or Hunter had been. But if they figured he was just an animal, they could be treating him even worse.

I closed my eyes and took deep, steadying breaths. Trying to communicate directly with my mind was like yelling down a hallway. If I successfully reached who I was talking to, I could feel them some-

460

where in the same way, their presence amplified as if through a tunnel. Last time, the shifter felt as though he was at the other end of the hallway.

But now? I nearly gasped at his closeness. It felt like he was right next to me.

I sensed a human man nearly as tall as Hunter, with caramel skin and glossy black hair. His large eyes danced with an array of colors that took my breath away—bluish green with gold flecks, like some kind of precious stone. Dark stubble coated his angular lower jaw. He came through clearly, a shift in his energy told me he knew I was there but something was wrong.

I thought you'd abandoned me. His voice was filled with relief and longing.

I'm sorry, I answered. *It's been a rough, busy journey. But I'm so close to you now.*

It might be too late, he answered, full of sorrow.

Why? I demanded. *Why can I only sense the human side of you, not your animal shift?*

My tiger is heavily sedated. He's barely alive, he replied. *They will most likely dispose of him tomorrow. And... that will be the end of me too.*

No! I cried. *I won't let them! We're so close.*

Don't worry about me, young shaman, he said gently. *I'll die knowing there's still one of you out there. It gives me peace knowing a human who understands us. Help the poor shifter who takes my place. After these long, painful years, I'm ready to let go.*

Please, don't. Hot tears spilled down my face. Don't give up yet. I just found you. At least tell me your name.

It's Arjun, he replied. *My shift is a Bengal tiger. I'm probably the last. My family is all gone, but in case you find another one of us, tell them what I did. I want them to know.*

The man you killed? I asked.

Yes. His mental voice took on a viciousness that sent a shiver of fear through me. *I spilled the blood of my captor and it was delicious. I'll never regret it, not even if it sends my soul to Naraka. He's in whatever hell he belongs, and I want my brethren to know I sent him there.*

I'll tell them, I promised. *And I'll make sure every one of those humans who laid a finger on you gets what's coming to them. But I'll need your help, Arjun. So I need you to live.*

No response came.

"Steluţa?"

"Hm?" Hovering in the state between awake and sleep, my legs kicked out as Razvan pulled me toward the world of the living.

"You were mumbling in your sleep." Soft lips and a split tongue caressed the skin of my neck in the dark.

"I talked to him," I whimpered, the conversation flooding back. "As soon as everyone's awake, we have to move. They're going to kill him."

"Shh, calm down," my dragon soothed me. "Tell me what happened."

When I relayed the conversation and said he was a tiger, Razvan's grip tightened on me so hard it was nearly painful.

"A Bengal tiger?" he repeated, his tone incredulous. "You're sure? Did you get his name?"

"Arjun," I said. "Why?"

His fingers slowly loosened around my arm. I felt his short, buzzed hair tickle my skin as he rested his head on my shoulder. He was shaking slightly, as if holding back laughter.

"Razvan?" I felt for his face in the dark. The skin near his eye was slightly raised from his tattoo there. "What is it?"

"That striped bastard," he chuckled. "I should have known he would've had a connection to you, too. Even though it's been years since we've talked."

I couldn't believe my luck. "You know him?"

"We were forced to perform together," he answered quietly. "I set things on fire, he jumped over and through them. Poor cat was terrified of fire and had burns all over himself. I taught him to do it as safely as possible and we formed an unlikely friendship. When Nigel came and rescued a bunch of us, I went with him. Arjun went his own way. It fucking kills me that he got recaptured, although I could see his view of things. He didn't trust humans at all."

"Jesus, what are the odds?" I breathed. "That I found Hunter, you, and him all within such a short time. It makes me wonder how many shifters really walk among humans."

"It must be the shaman in you." He gave my waist an affectionate squeeze. "We just can't stop ourselves from gravitating toward you. But you're so naturally irresistible, you just happened to catch Connor first."

"Stop," I smacked his chest playfully.

"It's true," he laughed, pulling me in closer to tickle my ribs. "And don't worry, *steluţa*. We won't let anything happen to Arjun. I already have an idea."

"Oh, yeah?" I nuzzled under his chin. "Let's hear it."

"Well, seems this carnival needs a new ringmaster for one." I heard the smile in his voice. "Or ringmistress, rather."

"Raz!" I gasped, thumping his chest again, victoriously this time. "You're a genius."

"Not quite, but I have my moments," he chuckled. "And I'll audition for a knife thrower or pyro, whatever they need. We'll find our way in and get him out."

"Sounds like a plan." My fingers traced the contours of his collarbone in the darkness, then drifted down over his sternum.

"What is it?" he asked, as if he could sense a question on my mind through the way I touched him.

My fingertips paused just over his abs. "Were you and Arjun ever... more than friends?"

His breath hitched, and I felt his pulse quicken, but his voice remained calm.

"No, we weren't." His hand wrapped around mine. "We bonded over being two shifters thrown into a horrible situation. We had each other's backs, but it never went beyond that." He paused for a breath. "Why do you ask me that?"

I swallowed, my throat going dry. "I don't want to make anyone uncomfortable. But in the pool, you seemed to have chemistry with..."

"With Hunter," he finished for me in a low voice.

We both paused to listen to the slow, deep breathing of Hunter and the pups. They were curled up a few feet away on the floor in wolf form. Hunter said he found it easier to sleep that way with not enough beds to go around.

"If you wanted to pursue something with him," I whispered. "I wouldn't mind at all."

"Did he say anything to you?" he whispered back with a mixture of eagerness and uncertainty.

"I... promised not to say anything," I answered sheepishly.

"And yet you have said so much already," he chuckled, pressing his lips to my forehead. "I'll think this over," he added. "And thank you, *steluţa*."

"For what?"

"For not making a big deal of it," he answered. "For, you know, accepting us."

"He grows fur and a tail. You grow wings and scales," I giggled. "Being attracted to men isn't even half of what makes you a freak."

"Oh?" He said the word like a challenge, his arm sliding around my backside to grab a plentiful handful of my ass. "What else makes me a freak?"

"The fact that you like me," I giggled, squirming in his grip.

"I got two other men here who would disagree," he groaned huskily into my neck. "Once we get Arjun out, maybe even a third."

"No way," I sighed. "The three of you give me enough to deal with already."

"Oh, but you have so much fun with us," he teased. "And what if the wolf and I hook up and you're still craving a sandwich?"

"Thinking about that already, are you?" I teased him back, but my core flooded with heat at the thought. Connor touching me while Raz and Hunter wrestled in the pool was already too hot for words, but a threesome while watching the two of them? I couldn't imagine anything more utterly, delightfully sinful.

But the thought of Arjun was a sobering one. I hadn't even met the guy, despite talking to him and sensing his mental state. Fitting him into a threesome was beyond getting ahead of myself.

"One thing at a time, I suppose," Raz sighed, smoothing his hands along my back side. "Let's give the others a few more hours to sleep. Then we'll let a tiger loose."

9

MELODY

"Why does this story sound awfully familiar?" Connor narrowed his eyes at me. "Rescuing another mistreated animal in need? What are we, the SPCA on wheels?"

"Come on, you had so much fun last time," Hunter slapped him on the back, nearly making him spill his coffee. "It all worked out, right?"

"Barely," Connor grumbled, rubbing a hand over his eyes in an attempt to wake up. "You're lucky you came with cute kids and the natural ability to bring home bacon."

"Relax, babe." I slithered between Raz and Hunter to stand between Connor's thighs. "You won't be part of this one. It'll just be me and Raz."

"Like *hell* I won't be part of it." He set down his coffee and gripped the edges of the counter as if he would jump off. "Just from what you told me, this place sounds ten times shadier than Drowningville. You need more backup going in there."

"Remember what I told you." I returned his narrowed-eyed threatening gaze. "You need to care for yourself. Hunter will drive you on to the nonprofit center. I need you fit and mobile."

"I am!" he protested. "Didn't you see me swinging over that fence last night? I can keep up with any of you."

"I know, babe." My voice stayed calm as I circled my fingers around his knees. "But if it's really worse than Drowningville, it could have a lot of potential triggers for you. I need you in top shape mentally too."

"Jesus tap dancing Christ, Mel. I'm not some goddamn snowflake."

"This isn't negotiable." I folded my arms across my chest, holding his eye contact as I dared him to fight me. "Raz and I have this handled. You're going to where you need to go. That's the end of it."

His jaw clenched. His knuckles whitened as he gripped the edges of the counter even harder. A long, tense silence passed between us that wasn't sexual for once. I didn't move, and neither did he. Finally, he let out a long breath as he dropped his gaze.

"Fine."

Satisfied, I gave him a curt nod and grabbed my own coffee cup to fill from the pot.

"I'm so fucking horny right now," Raz muttered. A slug on the arm from Connor wiped the smirk off his face.

THE SUN just began to rise as we set out on the road. We shut off the GPS and just followed where my instincts told me to go.

"Northeast," I told Hunter. "Just start heading in that direction."

The small town faded away and turned to long, country road. We drove for hours, only stopping for gas once as the day dragged on and the miles flew past us. Not once did any of the guys question or second-guess me. They just followed where I said to go.

Arjun's presence grew stronger with each passing mile. I rubbed my fingers together, the pads feeling thick and calloused from the multiple burns he sustained. The beginnings of a roar rumbled from deep in my chest. His tiger wasn't done. He still wanted to fight and take as many of those wretched humans down with him as possible.

That will to live gave me hope as we rolled through some of the most beat-down settlements I'd ever seen. The word *town* couldn't accurately describe the decrepit shacks and trailers plopped down on either side of the road, surrounded by rusted trucks, tall, dry grass, and tarps cluttered with various debris. It was like someone took my old trailer park and decided to display our redneck poverty as a roadside attraction.

"What a dump. Can people actually live in places like this?" Connor muttered, staring out the window. "Makes Mel's old place look like a resort."

The dirt road eventually turned to gravel and then cracked pavement riddled with potholes as the structures slowly came closer together into what actually resembled a small town. A rusted sign marked with bullet holes read, "Welcome to Fulmer" as it passed us on the right-hand side.

"Looks like we found where the tiger is." Hunter nodded up ahead at the horizon, where a rusted, rickety Ferris wheel loomed over the town like a giant, bloodshot eye.

"That thing is *not* up to any modern safety standards," Connor added. "Looks like it'll fall over if you sneeze on it."

"Imagine how the rest of the carnival is," I muttered, dread filling the pit of my stomach.

We pulled over to a side street, Razvan bringing his truck right up behind us. Connor pulled out his phone and checked his GPS while the dragon joined us in the RV.

"I'll be damned," Connor declared. "The nonprofit center is only a half-hour drive from here, in a neighboring town that's much nicer than this."

"So we'll be close." Hunter crossed his arms. "That's good."

"Not close enough," Connor murmured as he pulled me into his lap in the passenger seat. "Babe, I'll never forgive myself if anything happened to you."

"Nothing will harm her, Con," Raz said with such firm conviction, it made my thighs press together. "You have my word."

"I really hope your word means something, dragon-man." Connor turned his sharp gaze to him. "Because if she even breaks a nail, I will choke out the fire from your lungs myself."

"I'd expect nothing less," Raz answered solemnly.

"You just focus on healing your pain." I wrapped an arm around Connor's neck. "Take care of this mind and body I love so much."

"Are you kidding? I won't be able to stop worrying about you for one goddamn second." He crushed me to his chest, pressing a kiss to my mouth that sent flutters all the way down to my toes.

Eventually, he released me to Hunter, who kissed me with playful nips of his teeth that left me clinging to him and gasping for more. Damn these men who knew how to make me miss them.

"Call me with an update as soon as you have one," Conner said.

"I will," I promised, lowering my mouth to his for a final long, lingering kiss. "Hopefully we'll see you before the day is over."

After hugging the pups and promising I'd be back, Raz and I exited the RV and headed toward his truck.

"Have you ever auditioned for a carnival job before?" I asked as I slid in next to him and buckled my seatbelt.

"Nope," he answered. "Before Nigel found me, everything was involuntary. After, he always had a job for me. I didn't even need to ask." His eyes slid over, drinking in the length of my legs before he placed a hand on my thigh. "How did your first audition go?"

"All I had to do was wear this," I laughed, gesturing to my shorts and tank top, "on a hot summer day. They put me wherever they needed people until Connor found me."

"Seems like we won't have much trouble at all," he grinned as we pulled away from the curb. We waved to Hunter and Connor, who turned and began driving in the opposite direction.

"Why did you stay working for Nigel?" I asked the burning question on my mind for weeks as we approached the ominous Ferris wheel. "After being forced to perform, why would you do it voluntarily?"

"What else could I do?" he replied, eyes flickering across the road. "I barely spoke English. I had no true skills besides what I was taught for the stage. I chose to cover myself in ink, which makes some people assume I'm a criminal. Plus," his voice softened, "I did leave for a bit, to return to Romania. Only to find I was no more welcome there as when they sent me away."

We pulled up to a red light, and he turned to me, cupped my chin, and pressed a soft kiss to my lips with a light caress of his tongue.

"My tongue was the last thing I did while I was there." He stuck his tongue out and flicked both sides independently. "A way to remember my homeland and my dual nature without having to see it all the time like a tattoo."

"I didn't know you could place meaning on it like that," I said.

He shrugged. "You can attach meaning to anything if you want to. Or not. Many of my tattoos mean nothing. I just wanted a certain look."

I grabbed his hand and returned it to its place on my thigh, where he gave me an affectionate squeeze.

"I'm sorry your home rejected you," I breathed, watching his side profile as he drove. "I hope you feel at home with us... with me."

"*Steluța*," he mumbled gruffly. "Being with you and the others is the closest thing to home I ever felt. I'll stay with you as long as you'll have me."

We circled around the carnival grounds, looking for a place to park. The entire place was so poorly laid out and disorganized, like the staff had been high on meth when they set up. Which probably wasn't far from the truth.

After parking, we walked around looking for someone to talk about getting hired. Raz took my hand and held me close to his side, clearly taking his promise to Connor seriously. His word meant a great deal, and he sought to prove that to my Marine.

Wandering around the back, we found a cluster of tents and trailers, much like the ones back in Drowningville. However, they weren't roped off or truly separated in any way from the main grounds. While it was the middle of the day and nearly empty, any attendee could just wander back here much like we had.

I rubbed my arms, chills covering me despite the sweltering heat. This place gave me so many similar vibes to Drowningville, if not worse. Maybe because I no longer ignored my instincts, or being aware of my shaman abilities made me more sensitive to them, but I knew deep in my bones this place was the epitome of corruption and exploitation.

Raz knocked on a few trailer doors with no answer. At the fourth one, he barely knocked once before the door slammed open and made us jump a step back.

A dwarf of a man, only about four feet tall and reeking of alcohol, peered up at us.

"Can I help y'all?" he asked in a nasal voice.

"Hi!" I answered cheerfully, plastering on a smile. "We're performers looking for jobs. Do you know who we talk to about that?"

"Me," he grunted. "But there ain't no jobs to go 'round."

I chewed my lip. If their ringmaster had died a day ago, it most likely wasn't public knowledge that the job was open yet. I couldn't act like I knew about the tiger's attack.

"Are you sure?" I pressed, sending my grin wider. "We're both very multi-talented. I'm positive we can add something to your carnival."

The small man eyed me up and down in a way that made my skin crawl, much like the way Syko had.

"What do ya do?" he inquired.

"I do ah, burlesque," I stammered. "And I was ringmistress at my last job."

Raz shot me a warning look before answering for himself. "Sword swallowing," he grunted. "And fire breathing. Often both at the same time. Anything to do with sharp objects and fire, I'm your man."

The dwarf burped and rubbed his chin. "Well," he began. "We do have one opening, come to think of it. Maybe two. I can see about doin' some quick auditions if y'all want to perform tonight." He eyed me again with a predatory grin. "You first, dollface. If I like what I see, your man can show us what he's got, too."

10

MELODY

"Sure!" I squeaked, smiling so hard that my cheeks hurt. "Whatever works. We're ready when you are."

The man grinned back, thoroughly pleased. "I'll gather some folks and get a stage ready. Come back in an hour. Name's Phil, by the way."

"I'm uh, Cherry!" I reached out to accept his sticky handshake.

"Damn ripe and sweet like one," he grunted, holding onto my hand for far longer than was comfortable before turning to Raz. "And you are?"

"Alexei," he answered without missing a beat.

"Where the hell you from?"

"Siberia," Raz answered. "A cold-ass, far north region of Russia."

"Thought you sounded Russian," Phil observed. "Alright, folks. Come back in an hour."

"Why the hell did you say that?" Raz demanded the moment we walked away from the cluster of trailers. "Burlesque? *Steluţa*, do you know what that means?"

"It's like tasteful stripping, right? Like what Ally and all her friends did."

He glared at the mention of the last girl he slept with before me, the one who nearly drove us apart for good because she couldn't handle him only having casual feelings for her.

"I have a feeling *tasteful* isn't what these people have in mind," he muttered under his breath. "Why didn't you just say ringmistress?"

"I didn't want him to catch on that we knew the last one just died," I answered. "I'm sorry, Raz. I panicked for a second. I didn't want to arouse suspicion."

"No, you're just going to be arousing everything else now."

"Jealous?" I teased, trying to make light of the situation despite my stomach churning at what I would have to do in front of these people.

"I share you with two other men," he growled. "I'm not jealous, I just don't want people looking at you like that. Whistling and yelling degrading things at you... *Steluţa*, I don't think you realize how burlesque shows get. Nigel had hard rules in place for the dancers' safety. At other places, they get really, really rowdy. Honestly, it's a prostitution front for places like this. That guy probably thought I was your pimp."

Shit.

"Shit," I voiced.

"Yeah," he agreed, running a hand over his short, buzzed hair. "We're kind of backed into a corner now. I don't know how we're going to get out of this one."

I looked around at the old worn down booths and rides that had certainly seen better days. Rusted shipping containers laid on the dry grass in the distance. My instincts pulled me there like I was attached to a long, invisible string.

"Why not see if we find a tiger?" I said, nodding my head toward the containers. "If we do, who says we have to stick around?"

"Jesus Christ." Raz ran a hand down his face. "Now I know how Connor must've felt when you rescued the wolves."

But he followed as I started heading in that direction. "Don't act like you're on a rescue mission," he growled in my ear as he caught up. "You want to not arouse suspicion? Walk slower. Meander and look around at the booths. Look at me and laugh. Smile and kiss me."

"You just can't keep your hands off me," I said in a low voice before laughing heartily and giving him a deep, full kiss.

"True," he murmured, his warm breath tickling my lips. "But they do have eyes on us. Do you feel them? With an operation this shady, they're always looking out for undercover cops trying to bust them."

"Damn it." I leaned my head on his shoulder and stuck my hand in his rear jeans pocket. "So you're saying even if we find him, we're not likely to walk out with him anytime soon?"

"I think chances of that are nearly zero." He slid a tattooed arm around my waist and looked up, craning his neck to stare at the top of the Ferris wheel. "Fuck, the thought of you taking clothes off for these assholes just makes my blood boil."

"Connor would be downright murderous." I was silently glad that it was Raz next to me and not my overprotective Marine.

"And Hunter?" Raz squeezed my hip. "What would he do?"

"He'd rip their throats out in the most calm, detached, serial-killer fashion you'd ever see."

"That's what I thought," he chuckled, his voice softening and eyes growing dreamy at the thought of our wolf shifter.

My fingers tensed in his back pocket, realizing I no longer thought of Hunter as mine, but *ours*. Warmth and comfort filled me at the thought of the two of them snuggling together, much like we were now. Already I couldn't wait for the four of us to reunite so my shifters could have their chance to become closer.

Arms around each other like any ordinary couple on a date, we slowly meandered closer to the shipping containers. I didn't even have to focus to sense Arjun inside one of them. The human side of him still felt quiet and far away, but I could've reached out and felt the dense fur and powerful feline muscles of his tiger as if he was right next to me.

With one mental touch, that power wasn't just next to me, but within me. I was so hungry. I needed to kill. I needed the comfort of a mate.

"Did you just purr?" Raz asked, amusement in his voice.

"*Hrrrrr?*"

My hand flew to my throat in shock. "Holy shit! That came from me?"

"*Steluţa.*" He stood squarely in front of me, blocking anyone from seeing my face. A smile crept across his lips. "What big teeth you have."

Trembling, my hand crept up from my throat to my chin, where two long canines jutted down past my lips.

"What? How?" I cried.

Then they were gone.

"You're okay. You look normal now." Raz rubbed my shoulders, amusement and awe in his eyes. "Your eyes were changing colors, too. That was quite something but would've raised too many questions if anyone saw."

"I don't understand," I whispered, lowering a hand to my racing heart. "I can't shift, but Thembi said I can give the illusion that I do. It's like I feel Arjun's tiger becoming part of me."

"He's the one that would be able to tell you all about it," Raz assured.

"Well he's definitely in there," I said, turning toward the shipping containers. "I can barely feel the human part of him at all. He feels almost all tiger."

"Poor guy," Raz said sympathetically. "He stayed in that form while we were together to hide that he was a shifter. People thought it was weird for the lizard-man to get to attached to one of the tigers. He must've done the same thing this time."

"So they're not even bothering to treat him like a human." The acidic taste of disgust built up in my throat. We *had* to get him out of there.

"Not if they're keeping him in there." Raz's lip curled at the shipping containers. "No light, no fresh air. No wonder he's so miserable."

Feeling brazen, I approached the large metal box and drummed my fingers against the side. A soft vibration echoed back through my fingertips and my breath caught in my throat. That was no magic. Just the simple sensation of someone moving on the other side.

Yes, we're here! I wanted to yell against the metal wall. *We're going to get you out. Please don't give up.*

But I just drummed my fingers a few more times, hoping the gentle sound gave him a clue. I wondered if he could feel me like I felt him even when we weren't speaking.

Arjun? I tried.

No response. My projected thought went through what felt like a long, empty hallway.

"Are y'all lookin' for somethin'?"

We turned to see a man with an aged, weathered face approach us with suspicious, beady eyes. His clothes were covered in old paint and oil streaks, as if he was some kind of maintenance worker. What caught my eye was the thick, white bandage wrapped around his forearm.

Yes, I'd seen this man before. Through the bars of a cage.

"Hi!" I flashed him my plastered, young bimbo smile. "We're auditioning for jobs and just killing time while they get ready."

"Well, y'all can't be back here," he snarled, bringing his bandaged forearm close to his body. "This is where the animals are kept. It's dangerous."

"Oooh, what kind of animals do you have?" I widened my eyes as far as I could while raising my voice.

"Lots. We got show horses, goats, dogs, monkeys. One tiger and we got an elephant too."

"Wow, so cool!" I exclaimed, though my stomach twisted in on itself like a knot. Arjun was the only shifter I could sense here, but those other animals surely didn't have it any easier.

"Yeah, y'all need to git," he insisted, sweeping his good arm in a gesture for us to leave.

Raz and I followed his lead, but I couldn't help turning back and staring pointedly at his bandage.

"What happened to your arm?"

"Damn tiger took a swipe at me. He's a mean son of a bitch, but it's alright," the man sneered. "I'm gettin' 'im back this afternoon."

"Oh, what are you doing?"

The man raised his good arm and straightened it out in front of him, pointing his index finger and bending his thumb like aiming a gun. He closed one eye and smirked as he looked down his finger at me.

"I'm shooting that fucker and watching him bleed."

RAZVAN

"What are we gonna do?"

Mel paced back and forth furiously, her brow tense and furrowed. I tried not to let myself get distracted by her burlesque outfit—sheer stockings covering her long legs, an under-bust corset with a matching bra on top, and her skirt, which was little more than a mass of dark lace surrounding her hips.

Every time I enjoyed the view of her legs striding out as she walked, I remembered she would be shedding clothing for these dirty rednecks and it made me want to burn down this shitty tent we were in.

"We'll think of something, *steluța*," I murmured. "We still have some time."

"He said this afternoon! It's almost one now. What if they do it while we're auditioning? We'll have come undercover for nothing?"

"You'll be able to sense his distress," I assured her. "I can light something on fire and create a diversion. Then we'll go to him."

"But it might be too late by then!"

She was right, and despite doing my best to keep a level head and think things through, my mind was completely blank at how we would pull this off. I didn't have Connor's brashness or Hunter's calm, perceptive abilities. I just knew my way around sharp, pointy things and lighting fires.

Phil poked his head behind the curtain at us, or rather at Mel. He completely ignored my presence while his tongue practically wagged at her. I wanted to singe that thirsty look right off his face.

"We're ready for you, darlin'," he told her.

"Thanks." She flashed him a smile. I couldn't understand how she could fake looking so cheery. It had to be one of those hidden talents of women, putting on a brave face around men who disgusted them. "Start my music up?"

He nodded, and his shiny bald head disappeared. She moved to her position at the edge of the stage, took a deep breath, and swallowed.

"You don't have to do this, *steluţa*." My voice strained as I took hold of her arm. "Your presence on the stage is wasted on shit like this. You're capable of so much more."

"It's okay, Raz." She reached up and touched my cheek, those large brown eyes swallowing me up. "I have an idea. I'm going to see how much I can channel my ringmistress into this."

"I just hate to see you degraded. To see the things they want to do to you plainly on their faces."

She pressed a kiss to my mouth, her soft tongue surging between my lips in search of mine, which I happily gave to her.

"If this goes like I hope," she whispered. "They'll be just distracted enough for you to go and rescue Arjun."

"Mel!" I hissed in a whisper. "I'm not leaving you here."

"Watch their faces," she told me, one foot out in front of the curtain already. "When the time is right, you'll know."

With that, she released me and walked out into the spotlight.

The claps, cheers, and wolf whistles from the small audience of carnival staff made my heart sink. They were getting a free private show and probably had every intention of doing more with her immediately after. Just the thought of any of them touching her sent wisps of smoke coming from my mouth. Still, I did as she asked and watched.

Mel stepped gracefully onto the stage, waving, blowing kisses, and no doubt smiling. Unsurprisingly, they were entranced by her already.

Her hips swayed as she began her dance to a classic burlesque music pick, some kind of lounge ballad from the 1920s. Their eyes became glued to her form as her legs, hands, and hips did the talking. She articulated each point of her toe and curl of her finger, and they didn't miss any of it.

Dancing a slow circle around a three-legged stool in the middle of the stage, she was the ultimate tease and the perfect dream all at the same time. Taking a seat on the stool, her back arched and the angle at which she sat accentuated the curves of her legs and hips. Her fingers glided from her ankle to her upper thigh, where she began the slow, torturous tease of removing her stocking.

My jaw dropped as I watched her. I had no idea she could do this. She watched the burlesque show back in Crying Falls maybe a handful of times. How could she emulate their movements so perfectly, if even better?

I blinked and quickly shook my head, feeling like I had tunnel vision while looking at her. Then I looked at the audience, and it hit me.

They were frozen like statues, all looking at her with wide-eyed, glazed expressions. No one moved or made a sound. Only their eyes tracked her movement.

My heart beat like a drum in my chest while adrenaline surged through my body. This was what she was talking about. As long as she performed, she had them captured and at her mercy. It could only be yet another aspect of her shaman abilities, but I didn't have time to speculate. I hurried off the stage and ran right past them. No one even noticed me.

I took off toward the shipping container we just visited. Pressing against the metal box, I made a slow circle around it. With a quick intention, I shifted just enough to sense vibrations in the air and through the ground to know if anyone was coming.

With the coast clear, I threw open the door and nearly retched at the smell that assaulted me from inside. Shit, piss, rotting flesh. All of it combined to make one of the foulest stenches I ever sensed, even from when I was captured.

Holding my breath, I jumped inside, still pressing myself to the wall.

"Arjun?" I whispered into the dark, rank prison. "You in here?"

I shifted a little more to gain my dragon's ability to see in the dark, and my heart sank. Among the scattered bones and half-rotting corpses of smaller animals strewn across the floor, only an empty cage greeted me at the far end of the shipping container.

"Fuck," I hissed and turned toward the exit, running my fingers across my scalp. What now? I could sense shifters when they were close to me, but I didn't have Mel's tracking abilities. I couldn't sense his location and hone in on him like she could.

I jumped down from the shipping container, feeling the ripples of vibrations up through my feet, and paused. Maybe...

Holding my breath, I focused hard. I could feel the footsteps of every human for miles around. The air across my skin gave me a blueprint of their movement. I was looking for four heavy steps, not two.

Come on, Arjun, where are you... there!

The air tasted thick with human sweat and fear, mixed with the odd-smelling pheromones of a big cat I only knew from the memory of being in such close quarters with Arjun before. Four sets of light human footsteps stumbled and pulled, trying to move the massive four-legged animal to somewhere he didn't want to go.

I followed the scent of human fear and the vibrations on the ground, which led me on a zigzagging trail behind all the shipping containers and defunct equipment at the back of the carnival. Of course, they wouldn't drag him through the main strip. They didn't want to be seen taking an endangered animal to its slow, painful death.

Angry voices and feline growls floated up to reach my still-human ears, and I ducked behind a pile of shipping pallets. They were just on the other side and, if I wasn't mistaken, just a few feet away from the small stage where Mel had the carnival staff under a spell.

Could she sense him nearby while casting her magic onstage? And could he sense her?

Arjun's growls and roars became louder, more savage and bloodthirsty. I realized he could possibly smell me, too. Would he remember my scent?

"Jesus, let's just knock him out already!" one of the humans demanded.

"Fuck no! I want him conscious when I get my shots in!" I recognized that voice as the man with the bandaged arm.

"Dumbass cocksucker, we're gonna get mauled to death before we even make it to the shooting range!"

While they argued, I saw no better opportunity and climbed on top of the shipping pallets.

"Arjun, run!" I screamed before shifting my lungs and sucking in a big breath of oxygen. The humans only had time to turn around and look at me before getting consumed by the massive ball of fire erupting from my mouth.

The blast sent them reeling back, releasing the chains around Arjun's neck and forcing them to the ground, where they rolled around with panicked, desperate screams to put themselves out.

Arjun took off in a flash of orange fur—straight toward the back of the stage where Mel was performing.

"Wait!" I hollered as I jumped to the ground and ran after him. "The shaman! Don't hurt her!" But I didn't need to worry.

He scrambled up the small stairs meant for human legs and darted past the curtain. I caught up just in time to see him leap past Mel and sail straight into the crowd as if in slow motion. He looked magnificent for the split second he hovered in midair. Twelve feet long from head to tail, claws stretched out and on deadly display. Such a massive animal weighing hundreds of pounds with the natural abilities of feline grace and lightness.

The moment he fell, sinking his claws and teeth into the unsuspecting human's fleshy body, the spell was broken.

Mel was forgotten onstage as screams and chaos rang out. People fell over their chairs and each other as they tried to run, but one swipe of Arjun's paw left them incapacitated. The smell of blood filled the air as I jumped onstage and grabbed Mel.

"We have to go," I told her. "Now!"

"He's on a rampage," she cried, eyes wide in shock at the horror in front of us. "I don't know how to stop him."

"You're a shaman, talk to him," I said, pulling her off the stage to the side. "Make him follow us, but we can't stay here!"

She nodded, following me backstage and through the maze of trailers, pallets, and shipping containers behind the carnival.

"He's not answering," she said, her voice rising in panic. "I'm yelling his name but it's like no one's home."

"Talk to his tiger, then," I said, pulling her along behind me. "You can feel what the animal feels and emulate it. Do that."

I hopped in my truck and turned it on, my foot hovering over the gas pedal as she climbed robotically in next to me. Her face wore a vacant look before I saw the flickers of tiger-like features appear. Her eyes turned a pale yellowish-green, followed by her canine teeth elongating past her lower lip.

"Mel," I said harshly. "We can't wait for him. We're fucked if we stay sitting here."

"I know, I'm trying," she answered in despair. "Just a little longer—"

Right then, a massive orange shape came loping out past the carnival trailers. In the next instant, my truck bed sagged from the weight of Arjun jumping in.

"That's it, let's go!" Mel cried. She turned and opened the rear window. "Arjun, lay down!"

The Bengal tiger met her eyes as he reclined down below the edges of my truck bed and I peeled out of there with the pedal to the floor.

12

CONNOR

"We're not in Kansas anymore, Toto," I muttered, looking out the passenger window at the lush greenery surrounding us.

"Dog jokes. So original," Hunter scoffed next to me.

"I honestly didn't mean it like that," I laughed. "There's just no other way to describe this place, aside from entering the Twilight Zone, maybe."

The complete opposite of Fulmer and the rest of the dried out, rundown parts of Georgia we'd seen, the nonprofit center shone like an oasis. Manicured lawns, carefully trimmed topiaries, and trellises with climbing vines surrounded us.

"It is... something," Hunter observed eloquently.

I looked at him. "I know you're just as worried about Mel as I am, but keep your head in the game, bro. I don't trust shiny-ass places like this. It creeps me out more than the ghetto carnival we left them at."

"Not just Mel," he admitted. "I'm worried about both of them."

Oh, right. I never had deep feelings for anyone but women, so I momentarily forgot about the flame he carried for Razvan, too.

"They'll be fine," I told him. "She's gonna be a pain in his ass but she's resourceful too." Despite myself, I checked my phone for the hundredth time. Still no call. I could only assume no news was good news.

The acres of perfect lawns finally ended and Hunter parked the RV in a nearly empty parking lot in front of a pristine white building. When we got out and I settled my ass in the wheelchair for hopefully the last time, I rolled up to the front entrance to see the words *FDR Center for Disabled Veterans* painted on the door.

"After you." Hunter pulled the door open for me, his pups clinging to his side as they blinked up at the massive, sterile building. They'd probably never seen anything like it.

I wheeled through, my tires barely making a sound over the cool tile floor. Hunter's footsteps echoed off the walls as he followed me in.

"Good afternoon," the attractive middle-aged woman at the front desk greeted me with one-hundred percent southern charm. "How can I help y'all?"

"My name's Connor Shaw," I told her. "I was told Dr. Selow would be expecting me."

"Of course, hun. I'll take you right to his office." She glanced past me at Hunter and the kids. "Would y'all care to wait here? The executive director would like to talk to Mr. Shaw privately."

"Sure." Hunter shot her a friendly smile and took a seat on one of the couches, the only thing with softness and no hard edges in the room.

"Help yourselves to tea or coffee," the receptionist told him as she rose from her desk. "Follow me, Mr. Shaw."

I wheeled slowly past Hunter. "I'm tellin' you, he's gonna harvest my kidneys," I muttered. "Or bend me over his desk. I'm not sure which is worse."

"I'll listen for the screams," he snorted, picking up a magazine. "Or moans of pleasure. You never know."

"Funny, wolf-man," I muttered. "Oh, here." I tossed him my cell phone. "In case Mel calls."

I followed Dr. Selow's receptionist past several people working at desks in an open office area. A large window on one side looked into some kind of gym or physical therapy room. Some people worked out on machines like normal. Others, mostly amputees, practiced balance or with resistance bands with trainers standing by.

She pushed open a large wooden door at the far end of the room and stepped aside to let me in.

"Mr. Shaw here to see you, sir," she announced chirpily.

"Thank you, Margaret. I'll take it from here."

As she left, I wheeled up to the large mahogany desk to get a closer look at the man who was apparently so interested in me.

He was in his forties with salt and pepper hair, dressed business casual in a polo and slacks, as he rounded the desk to greet me. And he looked startlingly familiar.

"Connor." he approached me with a smile and his hand out. "It's so good to see you again! Damn, how many years has it been?"

"Too many for me to remember, it seems," I answered, giving his hand a tentative shake. "I know your face, but I can't place from where."

The smile fell, turning his friendly expression into a mask of concern. "You don't remember how you know me? Do you recognize my name?"

I lowered my eyes to the nameplate on his desk, which read *Dr. Brian R. Selow - Executive Director.*

"No, man. Sorry."

He nodded, clenching his jaw and folding his arms as he leaned against his desk. "I see. Can you tell me what you remember about losing your legs?"

I sighed. "Not much. Look, man. Whatever history we may or may not have doesn't matter to me. I was told you can help. I need legs to work and provide for my family. Can you fit me with some or not?"

I swallowed a lump in my throat, but lifted my chin with pride. Mel, Raz, Hunter, and the pups were probably the most misfitted, wackiest family out there, but that was truly how I saw us at this point. I had my love-hate relationship with performing, but I'd earn my keep for all of us. I refused to be dead weight.

"Do you remember the unit you were with?" Dr. Selow continued. "The faces and names of the people you saved?"

Damn it. He really wasn't going to let this go.

"I didn't save anyone," I replied. "All I remember is mangled body parts strewn across the desert. I shouldn't have lived, myself. But I dragged myself a couple miles toward our checkpoint while terrorists laughed and threw shit at me. They didn't even bother shooting because they figured I'd be dead once the vultures got to me."

"But you *did* save people, Connor," he insisted, lowering his voice to a whisper. "You stopped the blast from hitting our medic vehicle en route to the checkpoint. Sargent Kelly Armstrong. Lieutenant Andrew Malkin. And me. Captain Brian Selow, US Marine doctor."

A memory struggled to surface. A man with a face much like Dr. Selow's but younger, with less gray. He injected a needle into my arm. My legs swung back and forth—legs that still wore boots on my feet— as he jokingly slapped a Sesame Street bandaid over the injection spot.

"Did you... give me a flu shot?"

"Yes!" The smile returned to the current Dr. Selow's face. "The morning of the blast. Your trauma must have kept you from retaining certain memories, Connor. But I was there, brother. You saved me, and two others."

I let out a long breath, desperately trying to locate other memories, as he picked up a picture frame from his desk and showed it to me.

"Because of you, I got to return home to my wife and little girl." His voice choked as he looked down at the smiling woman hugging her daughter. "My daughter didn't have to grow up without a father. You have a family too, you must know what that feels like."

I didn't bother correcting him. The importance of this meeting became clear in an instant.

"After our unit pulled out, I searched high and low to find you," he continued. "You were declared Missing in Action for a moment, but then found. After that, it seemed like you discharged and disappeared for good."

"I did, in a sense." The answer came out gruff. I wasn't used to being treated like a hero. "The VA could only spend so many precious resources on me, so I found my own way."

"Oh, believe me, I've had it up to here with the VA," Dr. Selow scoffed. "That's why I put everything I had into making this place. I figured if I couldn't find you, I'd dedicate my retirement to helping other heroes like you."

"I'm no hero," I argued with a shake of my head. "Just some guy the universe likes to fuck with."

"You are," he insisted. "And for your service to this country, for what you've lost and endured, you deserve financial and lifestyle compensation. That's what this place is all about." He shook his head with a small laugh. "I thought I was hallucinating when Dr. Harman called me. I told him to repeat your name like ten times. The universe works in funny ways."

"Look, Doc," I said. "I'm not a supersentimental guy, but say I believe you. What's next? What can this place do for me? I don't mean to be so cut and dry, but I gotta get back out there."

"Of course." Dr. Selow rounded his desk again. "We can get you tested and fitted for new prosthetics immediately. Are you also in need of PTSD therapy?"

"Yes," I said through gritted teeth, knowing Mel would insist on it.

"How about housing?"

"Can you fit four adults and two kids?" I asked, half-jokingly. "We're living out of two vehicles currently."

"Absolutely. We have houses with up to six bedrooms right here on campus," he shrugged. "Some military folks have large families."

The smile dropped from my face. "You serious? How much does that cost?"

"To you? Nothing," he grinned. "All services here are funded by grants and donations, Connor."

"Goddamn." A small glimmer of hope lit up within my chest. It had been years since I slept in an actual house. We wouldn't stay here forever, of course, but a real house with bedrooms? How much would Mel love that?

"And there's no catch? No price at all?" I asked, refusing to let go of my skepticism.

Dr. Selow's eyes dropped to my legs, one of which ended just below my knee and the other halfway down my shin.

"I'd say you've paid enough of a price already," he answered quietly. "I'd be just as bad as the government if I were to ask you for more."

Logically, I knew he was right. Injured veterans deserved so much more than what they got upon returning home. Still, I hated receiving charity. I hated the pitying looks while I was homeless more than the looks of disgust. That was why I chose to work instead and hid my disability from those I didn't trust.

My pride or whatever didn't want to be included in the label "disabled veteran", and therefore entitled to receive services from nonprofits like these. But then I thought of Mel, and how much my stubbornness hurt her already. She'd stick by me no matter what, but I needed to put aside my own pride and make her proud. She deserved a man worthy of her, and if she insisted on sticking by me, I'd make sure to be that man for her.

"I guess you got yourself a deal."

"Great!" Dr. Selow beamed at me. "We'll get you enrolled with our physical therapists tomorrow. I'll call the groundskeeper now and see about getting a house cleaned and ready for y—"

A loud bang startled us both. I wheeled around to see Hunter striding toward me, a serious look on his face and Dr. Selow's receptionist trailing behind him.

"I'm sorry, doctor," she cried. "I told him not to barge in but—"

"It's Raz," Hunter held out the phone to me, the screen indicating he was in the middle of a call. "They just got out, but they're in trouble. They need us."

13

MELODY

"Arjun." I made my voice as soothing as possible. "Can you please shift to human? This would be a lot easier if you were in human form."

The tiger flattened his ears against his skull and growled a low warning at me. His tail whipped threateningly back and forth in the truck bed.

"Shhh, okay!" I waved my hands frantically. "Just no growling or tail-whipping."

I looked up at Razvan, his ear still attached to the pay phone receiver outside the grocery store where we parked.

We had zigzagged all through town with a massive tiger in his truck bed, hoping to shake off the carnival people in case they followed us. Neither of us saw any, thankfully. They might have been too busy treating their injured or not willing to chase an animal they were going to kill anyway, but I kept looking around for anyone who might have followed us.

Now, in the next town over, we stopped to call Connor and figure out what to do next. My mind was at a loss for a plan for once. Getting Arjun out had been easy, relatively speaking. Now that we had him, we had no idea what to do with him.

On top of that, he never answered when I spoke to him telepathi-cally and refused to shift to human. It would be one thing to drive around with a naked man in the truck, but something else entirely to hide a five-hundred pound striped cat.

Finally, Raz hung up the phone and started back toward me.

"We're going to them," he said, pulling open the driver's side door. "Apparently Connor has a house now."

"What?" I looked at Arjun. "You're gonna have to get down again."

The tiger lowered his head to his paws, his feline eyes wide and bright on me before I jumped back up front with Raz.

"A six-bedroom, fully furnished house for the injured soldier and his large family," he chuckled. "Feels like we hit the jackpot."

"That's great and all, but what are we going to do about him?" I pointed out the back window where the tiger laid low. "I'm pretty sure they'll object to us bringing a tiger to a house owned by this place."

"He still won't shift?"

"Won't shift, won't talk, nothing," I cried in exasperation. "I can't get through to him at all. It's all tiger I feel."

"He must've been in animal form too long," he muttered. "The human side of him has grown weak and lost control."

"How do I get the human side of him back?"

"I don't know if you can, shaman," he glanced over at me apolo-getically.

Arjun wouldn't fit in the trailer we pulled full of Raz's stuff, so our next best option was covering him with a tarp and praying nobody at the organization would want to inspect our truck. The tiger thankfully didn't object too harshly when we stopped and laid the tarp over him. A few growls and teeth-baring, but he allowed me to drape the material over his head and body.

"He hasn't attacked us," I observed as Raz and I climbed back up front. "Which means he's not acting entirely like a wild animal. He must know we're not going to hurt him, so Arjun the human must still have some control."

"I really hope you're right, *steluța*," he said quietly. "I'd love to be able to talk to my friend again."

A few miles later, we drove onto the nonprofit grounds, which looked more like a resort than a center for disabled veterans. A smiling groundskeeper waved us through without making any motions to stop or inspect the truck. I released the breath I'd been holding as we drove around the pristine white building and entered what looked like a suburban neighborhood behind it.

"Con said keep going straight toward the back," Raz muttered. "They're waiting for us."

"I hope they have a plan to keep this big cat hidden," I muttered back.

The landscape turned more wild and rural the further back we went. It reminded me a bit of the forest surrounding the Crying Falls festival. I had to admit I'd grown attached to that place. I missed the fresh pine smell in the air, cooking over campfires, the starry sky and all the memories in those woods. Meeting Hunter for the first time, seeing Raz shift under the moonlight, and feeling the wild energy as I commanded the stage.

"Holy shit," Raz breathed.

"Oh, my god!" I brought a hand to my mouth in shock.

It was a gorgeous, two-story plantation house with a wraparound porch, set back amongst the trees with plenty of privacy and space. I couldn't believe my eyes. This place was *ours?*

Two wolf pups wrestled on the massive lawn, which seemed to stretch on forever. When we pulled up, they yipped and howled as they ran alongside us. Roo and Rinna never looked so happy and playful before. They looked at peace, at home.

"Welcome home, you two," Hunter greeted us from the porch, his golden eyes passing over both of us affectionately.

"What do you mean, home?" I asked hesitantly as I stepped out of the truck. "Surely, we can't actually stay here?"

"We can for as long as I'm using the center's services." Connor wheeled up next to Hunter as Raz and I approached them in a daze.

"But how?"

"Oh, the director is definitely pulling some strings since none of us are married," he smirked. "But I apparently saved his life years ago, so he's happy to do it."

"Apparently?"

He nodded. "I don't remember it. Not well. But the blast that ruined my legs narrowly missed him and a couple other people, thanks to me taking most of it."

"So..." I looked up at the house, the likes of which I'd only seen before in magazines. I never even walked through a neighborhood and saw houses like these in real life, let alone lived in one. "This is really ours?"

"It is, babe." Connor reached forward and squeezed my hands. "Maybe not forever, but I'm constantly a work in progress so we'll see."

"So they're treating your pain? And getting you new prosthetics?"

"That and more," he smiled up at me. "You deserve nothing less than a house like this and a man who strives to be better every day for you."

"Connor..."

I barely had time to wrap my arms around his neck and kiss him when Raz and Hunter started yelling in a panic.

"Kids, come here!" Hunter screamed at the top of his lungs. "Watch out for the tiger."

"Shit!"

I whipped around to see a blur of orange race across the lawn toward the trees surrounding the house.

"Con, keep the kids close!" I instructed. "Raz, Hunter, let's go after him."

The shifters followed closely behind me as I started in the direction where Arjun ran.

"Be careful, he's in hunting mode," I said, sensing the wave of bloodthirst from him through our shared connection. He hadn't hunted properly in so long. I could feel his desire to sink his teeth into soft, warm flesh and feel the hot trickle of blood across his tongue...

I shook my head. *Snap out of it, Mel.* I couldn't afford to lose myself to the sensations that already ruled him.

"He went this way," Hunter pointed. "He's not far."

"He's not moving," Razvan said after a few minutes of walking in the direction Hunter pointed. "He's just staying in one place. What's he—"

"There!" I pointed to about twenty feet ahead of us, where a naked man with dark hair and caramel skin tore into the limp carcass of a bird with his bare hands.

The three of us froze, unsure what to do. Arjun had shifted to human at some point but still tore into his prey like an animal.

"Let me," Razvan muttered, approaching him slowly.

Arjun paused and looked up at the tattooed man coming toward him with wide, multicolored eyes. His nose, cheeks, lips, chin, and chest were smeared with blood and bird guts, but Razvan paid no mind to his appearance as he smiled at his old friend.

"Hey mate," he greeted softly. "You remember me, don't you?"

The tiger shifter bared his human teeth and inhaled deeply.

"Yeah, you know I smell familiar, you big pussy cat," Razvan smirked and held an arm out to me. "This is Melody, the shaman who spoke to you. It's all because of her we got you out, man. You can hunt, be a cat or a human freely now. You don't have to touch fire anymore. You're free."

Arjun turned his gaze to me. Even with dead bird entrails smeared all over him, he was strikingly handsome. Those eyes looked straight to my soul.

"Melody? The shaman?" he breathed, a light English accent peppering his words.

"Yes, Arjun." I approached him with slow, careful steps, just as Raz had. "You're not in danger anymore. We're here to help you."

He held my gaze for a long moment where no one seemed to breathe, then stood to his full height. I kept my focus on his face, nearly at the same level as Hunter's. Like my pale wolf, his musculature was long, slender and graceful, only covered in warm, coppery skin with a dusting of dark hair on his chest.

Razvan swiftly removed his shirt and tied it around Arjun's hips to give him some sense of modesty. My face flamed at the realization that my eyes had been traveling lower down his sculpted body. He didn't need anyone ogling him right now.

"Come on, mate," Raz wrapped an arm around the naked man's waist and draped one of his arms over his shoulders. "Let's get you inside. Bet you haven't felt a bed in a long while, ah?"

With Razvan's support, Arjun took a few wobbly steps as if he hadn't used his human legs in ages. Only when we came out of the forest and reached the lawn did I notice the burn scars all over his feet. Now out from under the cover of the trees, I saw his hands and ribs carried the same scars.

"He's okay now." Hunter rubbed the nape of my neck reassuringly. "Or he will be, at least."

"We can't keep doing this." My own voice sounded far away. "They'll just replace him with another. And when that shifter drops dead, they'll just get another. We have to stop this for good. What can we do, Hunter?"

"I'm not sure, little fox," he replied sadly. "It's shocking to you, but we've been aware of these dangers our whole lives. Human entertainment is just another predator we have to look out for, and sometimes fall victim to."

"It shouldn't be," I argued. "And what about those like Raz who never knew any other shifters? They just think they're human until they start sprouting tails and fur or horns."

"Again, I don't know the answer to that."

I moved away from him, speed walking up to Arjun's other side to help Raz get him into the house. I wasn't angry at Hunter, just at the hopelessness of the situation. I didn't expect him to have the answers but there had to be another besides, *I don't know*, and, *we just deal with this*.

"*Steluţa*, go in and draw a bath for him. Then help me get him cleaned up." Raz craned his neck around Arjun's arm to address Hunter. "See about making some food in the kitchen, would ya, wolf?"

"Sure."

Hunter and I ran inside ahead of him to do our assigned jobs. Once Raz and Arjun caught up to me in the bathroom, the tiger shifter's eyes lit up when he saw the water running in the tub and practically pounced in.

"I forgot how much these cats actually like water," Razvan chuckled.

As Arjun splashed his face and hair joyously, I made a silent promise to end the cruel trade that did this to him, Razvan, and

Hunter. I may have been the last shaman left, but every human alive who raised a hand to a shifter would soon learn my name.

14

HUNTER

My ears pricked at the sound of light footsteps behind me, moving softly but still too heavy to be Mel's. My heartbeat quickened at the smoky, wild smell that accompanied those steps.

"How'd he like the food?" I asked Raz without turning away from the sink.

"Devoured it all. I suppose he was hungry," he laughed, setting the bowls next to me on the counter. "I'll wash these."

"No, it's okay. I got it." I kept my eyes focused on the soapy water in front of me, my hands scrubbing vigorously. "Where's Mel?"

"On a tour with Connor. They're exploring the grounds before he starts treatment tomorrow."

"And your tiger friend?"

"Sleeping. I expect he'll be out for a good eighteen hours or so," he chuckled, shaking his head as he turned to lean his back against the counter. He stood so close his arm nearly brushed mine. "Cats, you know how they are. Hope you and him don't chase each other like a couple of domestic pets."

"I have no intention of chasing an animal over twice my size," I

496

scoffed. "When it comes to him or me, there's no question of who would win."

"Oh? Have you gone humble on me, alpha?" Raz smacked my arm playfully with the back of his hand.

That touch, along with his use of the word *alpha*, sent heat and hardness running from my chest straight to my cock. Jesus, why did he have to affect me like this? Why couldn't Mel be enough for me?

"I'm not an alpha," I replied. "At least, I never got that opportunity."

"No?" I still didn't tear my attention away from the dishes, but I could see his face in my mind. One eyebrow cocked, gray eyes looking at me and waiting, like he expected an actual answer.

"My former mate was our alpha's daughter," I explained. "When she chose me, we were expected to become the new pack leaders. She was killed, and then I was captured before that could happen."

"Well, you're sort of the alpha now." I could see his smirk in my mind. "You're with the head female after all."

"Yeah, but so are you," I answered. "So's Connor. This whole situation hasn't exactly created a hierarchy between us."

"You're right, it hasn't," he said softly. "Does that confuse you?"

"No," I replied. "I feel like I know my place with her. You?"

"Yeah, same," he said in a soft voice. "I'm not jealous of anyone because I know what I mean to her, and what she means to me."

"Right," I agreed, turning to put plates on the drying rack and wipe my hands on a towel. "Same here."

The air was so thick with tension between us, I could barely breathe. I wanted to move away, to get space and hopefully get my goddamn cock to calm down. But his hand on my shoulder, the weight and heat of it, made me stop.

"Why are we dancing in circles around this, wolf?" Raz's voice was thick and husky. "Why not just be open about what's going on?"

"Look, Raz," I brushed his hand off of me and turned to face him, meeting his eyes for the first time since he walked into the kitchen. "It's not that easy, okay?"

"Why not?" he challenged. "No one's going to object. Mel knows. She wants us to embrace this. She just wants us to be happy."

"Because I grew up around humans too," I retorted. "Not far from here. And this," I gestured between us, "is wrong. I've been taught my whole life that being with another man in the same way as a woman is wrong. Haven't you ever seen that?"

"Hunter," he scoffed, crossing his arms. "I've been told my very existence is wrong from the moment I breathed fire for the first time at five years old. At least you had a community of other shifters like you. Me? I was told I was a curse. A punishment on my family because I couldn't control the scales growing on my skin. Fucking another man? That's the least of my sins."

I couldn't stop staring at how his biceps bulged. My gaze drifted down as his words sank in and my pulse shot up when I realized he was just as hard as me.

Fuck! I tore my eyes away. He must've caught me looking. Couldn't he see how difficult this was for me?

"What about Mel?" I said, my voice thick with desire I didn't want to feel. "Even if she says she's okay with this, her mind could change if it actually happens. I don't want to make her uncomfortable, ever."

"Neither do I," he said with a nod of his head. "So if you want to mess around, we'll only proceed when she's involved. Simple."

I nodded my agreement, relief lifting off my shoulders until the moment he stepped into my space, grinning.

"Does that mean you *do* want to mess around?"

"No." My protest was weak, and he saw right through it. "I—"

"Hunter."

He touched me again, a deliberate caress along my ribs until his hand rested on my back. It was nothing like a woman's touch, but still *so* good. Strong, firm, and warm. I knew exactly how strong he was, and it excited me just as much as Mel's softness.

"You liked playing in the pool with me," he breathed, stepping in closer until his chest barely brushed mine. "You wanted to keep going until we collapsed."

"That wasn't like this."

"Don't kid yourself, alpha." His arm tightened around me, pulling himself against me until I felt his own racing heart across from mine.

"Mel saw the whole thing, and she was so fucking turned on, Connor got her off with just his hand. If I tried to kiss you then, would you have refused me?"

I couldn't answer. My voice didn't seem to work as his other arm came to wrap around me.

"You don't have to fight it." He nudged his nose just under my chin, his warm breath fanning across my throat. "This is who you are, Hunter. Mel, Connor, and I all accept you."

His lips grazed my neck. I wanted to lean into them, to feel that split tongue that seemed to please Mel so much against my throat. I even let out a soft groan as he paused, not fully kissing me, just hovering his mouth on my neck. But years of buried shame couldn't be erased that easily.

"Raz, stop."

I pulled away, needing to put as much distance between me and the dragon shifter as possible. Stumbling out onto the porch from that hot stuffy kitchen, a run to clear my head seemed to be just what I needed.

"Hey."

I turned my head to see Connor and Mel approaching the house, curious looks on both of their faces.

"You alright?" she asked amusedly. Her eyes dropped to my waist, where I knew my erection remained at full strength. Damn, I stayed in that kitchen way too long.

"Yeah," I answered as casually as I could muster. "Just going for a run. Would you let the kids know for me?"

"Sure. You want them with you?"

"No, that's okay." I peeled off my shirt and placed it over the railing of the porch for when I'd return. "I'm going solo." My hand drifted to the button of my jeans. I didn't want to take my pants off until Mel was inside.

"Okay. Have fun."

They went in and I couldn't shift fast enough. I raced through the trees, light as a feather on my four paws. Birds and rodents scattered at my footsteps, but I wasn't hungry for them. I ran like I was trying to get something out of my system.

At the back of my mind, I knew I'd have to go back. I wasn't ready yet, but at some point I'd have to face not only him, but the person *I* was.

❧ 15 ❧

MELODY

To say Razvan looked guilty when Connor and I came home was an understatement.

"I don't suppose you have anything to do with Hunter running off into the woods with a raging hard-on, do you?"

"Who, me?" he brought his hands to his chest in feigned innocence. "You wound me, *steluţa*."

"You can't come onto him too strong," Connor added, wheeling himself through the house. "He may be a shifter, but he's also a good ol' southern boy. He's got a lot of shame around having feelings for another man."

"Don't I know it," Razvan muttered. "I didn't come on *that* strongly but yeah, maybe spooked him a little."

"Leave him alone when he gets back," I jabbed my index finger into his chest. "He won't come to you if you keep spooking him. You've got to give him space."

"And who am I supposed to harass in the meantime?" His eyes flashed excitedly right before he lunged forward, grabbed me by the waist, and covered my face and neck with kisses.

"Raz!" I squealed, wriggling in his arms, which just egged him on.

He tickled my sides and kissed me everywhere, torturing me mercilessly until I could barely breathe.

"Hey, have you guys checked this place out?" Connor called from somewhere in the house, his voice echoing off the high, slanted ceilings.

"I'm trying, but Raz won't let me go!"

The dragon released me to arm's length before he snapped out a hand, grabbed me, and pulled me back in. He just chuckled at my weak muttered protests, his feet following my steps toward Connor's voice while wrapped around me like a snake around its prey.

"Whoa." I stopped at the entryway and even Raz had to look up at the room laid out before us.

A TV screen took up nearly one entire wall, with half a dozen deep comfortable recliners facing the screen a few feet away. Shelves lined the walls, filled with Blu-ray and DVD movies of every genre imaginable.

On the other side of the room, a half-wall sectioned off a smaller area with a loveseat, an armchair, and bookshelves stacked with books. My fingers squeezed around Raz's at the thought of curling up with a book in a cozy, peaceful corner.

"Man, imagine watching the football games in here!" Connor spun in his wheelchair excitedly.

"I don't really watch American football," Raz admitted.

"Ah, Christ. You foreigners don't get it. Babe?"

I shook my head. "Not really into it. Sorry, babe."

"Damn it! *This* is why you can't scare Hunter away, Raz. I need a good ol' American boy to yell at the screen with me."

So much for cozy and peaceful.

"You guys want to watch a movie until he gets back?" I let go of Raz's hand to browse the shelves.

"Sure, but no war movies." Connor's face turned serious, and I shot him a sympathetic look. My finger skimmed past Black Hawk Down, Saving Private Ryan, and similar titles.

"You don't think we'll wake up Arjun?" I asked, pausing my browsing to look over at Raz.

"Nah, he's out like a light." My dragon came up next to me to browse more movie titles. "We probably won't see him until tomorrow morning."

We settled on Snatch, which I'd never seen, but both of the guys loved and told me I had to see it. Raz found some microwave popcorn in the kitchen and soon, two of my three men sank into the recliners on either side of me for our movie experience.

I propped my feet up in Connor's lap, relishing in the firmness of his fingers massaging into my arches. Raz held the bowl of popcorn and fed it to me, when I wasn't grabbing handfuls to feed Connor.

We munched and watched and laughed. I felt so blissfully happy, I couldn't wipe the grin off my face. It took me a moment to realize this was normal. As normal as my life could get, anyway. But this was what normal people did—watch movies with their loved ones without a care in the world.

I snuggled down lower into my recliner, stretching my legs across Connor and leaning my head on the armrest where Raz stroked my hair. I wanted to sink deep into this happiness like a bath and never leave. It wrapped around me like a blanket and I wanted to take it everywhere with me. Blissful normality. This was what I always wanted.

Not long after the popcorn ran out, the guys seemed to have other ideas.

Connor's foot massages turned into gentle stroking of my calves, which gradually reached higher up my legs. His fingers teased the sensitive skin of my inner thighs, sending my pulse racing as I tried to focus on the movie.

His light, teasing caresses became firm, kneading of my flesh, making my breath hitch. Raz tilted my chin up to make me look up at him from the armrest.

"Ever make out with a boy in a movie theater before?"

I shook my head, and then his mouth descended on me with a passionate kiss. While his tongue sent my heart racing, his hands slid into my bra cups while Connor handled my lower body. My shorts and underwear came away from my hips while I laid stretched out between them.

Kisses covered my inner thighs, my neck, my nipples. Then

Connor covered the center of my heat with his mouth, and Razvan swallowed the moan that came from me.

The movie went on, nothing but background noise and light casting across our bodies. My guys had stripped me bare, but they still wore too many clothes. I reached for Razvan's shirt, only to have my wrists pinned down as his laughter floated across my skin.

"Greedy girl," he teased. "Isn't she, Con?"

"Mm-hm," my soldier agreed from between my thighs. He pressed a finger inside me, his lips pulling back into a smile at my gasping reaction. "She's so wet. She wants to come already. But we're not going to give it to you that easy, babe."

"Did you two plan this?" I panted, looking up at their pleased faces.

"You were so entranced by the movie, it was adorable," Raz grin. "You didn't even notice us mouthing at each other right above your head."

"Sneaky bastards," I grumbled.

Raz only laughed at my pout and pried my lips open with his tongue. I swore with that split down the middle, it was even stronger than a normal tongue. Connor returned to making my pussy feel like heaven, and soon I forgot all about being annoyed.

He pinned my hip down with a strong hand to keep me from thrashing, his tongue lashing mercilessly at my clit while his finger teased me with only a fraction of the fullness I'd soon be feeling.

"So fucking beautiful." Razvan trailed his lips down my throat, his hands running across my body and breasts until that tongue reached my nipples. Each side thrashed against the sensitive peaks until they hardened like pebbles. Their sensitivity made me cry out when he grazed his teeth against them.

"She's close, Con," he murmured to my other lover against my skin. "God, I love watching her come."

Connor moaned an unintelligible reply, his voice sending vibrations through me as he carried on tirelessly. My breaths became ragged, my hands flailed along the recliner, desperate for something to grab onto. That happened to be Razvan.

My fingers bunched around the soft, worn denim of his pants, gripping hard and practically yanking them off his hips.

"Easy, girl," he teased, his tongue flicking the shell of my ear. "You'll have that pretty little pussy stuffed with cock in no time. Would you like that?"

Those words and the last few lashes of Connor's tongue sent me hurtling over the edge. My back arched off the seat just as Connor curled his fingers inside me, prolonging my pleasure. I thrashed like a madwoman and mewled like a kitten. Both guys stared in awe, running their hands across me and kissing me as the aftershocks made me shiver.

"Damn, I've never seen anything as gorgeous as that," Connor murmured, kissing my hip bones.

"Same here," Raz agreed, lifting me up so my head could rest on his chest.

"You guys..." I panted, reaching an arm up to wrap around Raz's neck.

"Yes?" Connor chuckled, laying his head on my thigh to look up at me adoringly. "Were you going to finish that thought?"

"I forgot what I was going to say."

The two of them laughed, with Connor looking as proud as a peacock.

"Just wait until it's my turn." Raz kissed sensually just under my ear. "You'll forget your own name."

"Oh, now it's a contest, huh?" Connor grinned. "Next time, babe, I'll make you forget the first letter of the alphabet."

The two of them traded boasts back and forth, growing more ridiculous every time until I wiped tears away from laughing so hard. When a door slammed in the kitchen, my laughter cut off abruptly and I peered over the top of the chairs.

"Hunter!" I called. "You're home."

"Um, yeah." The wolf paused at the entrance to the theater room, his pants low on his hips and unbuttoned as if he just pulled them on haphazardly. Carrying his t-shirt in his hand, his bare upper body flexed with deep breaths and glistened with a light sheen of sweat.

"Have a good run?" I asked, my pulse quickening.

"Yeah." His eyebrow quirked up at the sight of my bare shoulders over the tops of the chairs, as if he knew exactly what we were doing. "I was just going to shower." He turned, heading for the stairs.

"Wait."

He turned back, golden eyes already fired up. If he ran off to ease sexual tension between him and Razvan, it didn't work. Rather, it amplified it. Sweaty, tense, and breathing heavily, he looked like sex on legs. And in my current state of just coming under Connor's tongue, I wasn't going to let him walk away.

I placed both hands on the back of my chair, rising up to kneeling so he could see me from the waist up. His eyes dilated at the sight of me, no doubt taking in the redness of Raz's handprints marking my skin. My nipples pebbled again just from his lustful gaze.

I reached a hand out, a playful smile teasing at my lips.

"Come join us, Hunter."

MELODY

Hunter stayed rooted to his spot, neither coming closer nor moving away. Only his eyes moved, flickering from me to Razvan, then back to me.

"I won't touch you if you don't want me to. It can be just like the first time," Raz broke the silence, wrapping an arm around my waist. "But our girl wants to have fun with all of us."

That seemed to ease Hunter's nerves. His gaze returned to me as he stalked forward. Even in human form, he was so wolflike. Like prey, I froze—caught in a predator's trap until he stood right in front of me. His handsome mouth tipped up into a smirk as he cupped my face and kissed me.

His mouth devoured mine hungrily—more evidence that his run did nothing to diminish his desire, but only enhanced it. My hands slid down his long, lean torso, carving out the shape of his abs with my fingertips until I reached the waistband of his pants. He let out a soft growl as I shoved them down his thighs, breaking our kiss only to step out of them.

"Come here," I requested, my voice a breathy whisper.

He obliged, eyes locked on me as he came around the chairs and sat in the middle where I had been. With another growl, he pulled me into his lap to straddle him and I grinned through his sexy, possessive kiss. Such a greedy alpha.

As he kissed a fiery trail down my neck, I turned to settle my gaze on Razvan.

"*Now* will you get naked?"

"Oh, I like it so much more when you do it to me, *steluţa*," he grinned, leaning back and lacing his hands behind his head.

I leaned my head back, letting my eyes roll as Hunter nibbled the spot between my neck and shoulder. "And you boys call *me* greedy."

Reluctantly, I pulled away from Hunter, who kept his hands lingering on me until the very last moment, and crawled over the armrest to Raz. His gray eyes smoldered as I settled into his lap.

"Hello," I dropped my gaze, suddenly feeling shy under his overpowering intensity.

"Hello, *steluţa*," his sexy voice rumbled. He caught my chin and pressed a hot but playful kiss to my mouth. "The most beautiful woman who's ever sat naked in my lap."

He kissed my bashfulness away as I lifted the hem of his shirt, discarding it in some dark corner of the room. My lips and fingers trailed over the dark ink covering him as I worked my way down. Every time I touched him, I seemed to notice a new art piece, a new detail in the greater work of art that was his whole body.

His hands smoothed down my back as my mouth reached his navel, a soft groan escaping as I undid his pants. He lifted his hips for me to slide them down, and those three piercings on the flared edge of his head greeted me like twinkling stars.

I took him in my mouth, already eager to taste him, and loved watching him react. He gripped the armrests, narrowly missing grabbing Hunter's hand, and hissed in a sharp breath. I flicked the underside of his head a few times and watched him squirm before bobbing my head down to take more of him.

"Fucking...Fuck...God..."

"Forget your own name yet, Raz?"

The question came from Connor, somewhere to the right and behind me. I didn't forget him, I would make my way down there, but first—*oh God.*

A large, warm hand cupped my vulva, sending jolts through my clit at the delicious pressure. I yelped in surprise, which came out as a muffled moan with my mouth stuffed and Raz only gripped the armrests harder.

"Can't leave you to do all the work, babe." Kisses poured over my back before a sharp smack on my ass made me squeal.

"Ah, that's right," Raz grinned. "She told us she liked that, Con."

"Revealing my secrets, now? You get another one for that." A smack fell to my opposite cheek so hard, I released Raz's cock to cry out and glare back at him.

"Don't distract her too much. You're ruining my fun," Raz cracked.

"Sorry, dragon." I kissed his pierced head and lapped up the small bead of pre-come that formed. "Your turn to be teased." I slid over to Hunter, shooting Raz a wide, shit-eating grin.

"Oh, so not fair," he whined.

Ignoring him, I raked my fingers up Hunter's thighs and tilted my face up for a kiss. He was almost fully hard already, but I wanted to take my time enjoying him too.

"Melody," Hunter breathed barely above a whisper before kissing me. He said my full name almost like a plea, and his kiss was full of passion and longing.

"Hunter," I answered, a sudden flurry of emotion making my throat thick. "I love you."

He froze. "You do?"

I nodded, suddenly feeling more vulnerable than I ever had with any of them. We both murmured so softly, I couldn't even be sure the other two heard us. It was like the rest of the world just fell away.

A small smile just between us lit up his face, and he kissed me again. He didn't say the words back, but I could feel them. I felt his desire to throw his head back and howl at the moon in victory, to hold on to his mate, to me, with his teeth and fuck her savagely to make his claim.

But we were human now, and I wanted to play with all my mates.

He growled a soft protest as my lips broke away from his, kissing down his lithe, lean body until I settled between his thighs, kneeling on the floor in front of him like he was a king. Much like Razvan, he hissed when I took him in my mouth, teasing his head at first before working my way down the hot shaft.

With my mouth occupied, Connor enjoyed getting what noises he could out of me. His hands on my hips, he stroked his own cock against my entrance, teasing and rubbing with no penetration yet, no matter how much I arched and lifted my hips.

Ever the gentleman, Hunter held my hair out of my face as I stroked him with my fist, my hands meeting my lips on his length in a steady rhythm. My other hand stretched out to my left, determined not to leave my bad boy dragon out of the fun.

"Come closer, Raz," I rasped, catching his eye with my lips against Hunter's silky head. "Let me touch you too."

I didn't need to tell him twice. "Scoot over, wolf. You heard the lady."

The two of them barely fit in the same chair, but they made it work. Raz's dark ink-covered leg pressed against Hunter's pale one, but they didn't touch aside from that. I almost didn't notice their sexy, nervous glances at each other or their breaths growing more ragged now, being in such close proximity to each other. I was too busy feeling like a fucking porn star.

Returning my mouth to Hunter, I gripped the base of Razvan's dick and stroked upward. His whole body jolted as a result, and I knew he was struggling to make good on his promise to not touch Hunter.

"Holy fuck, that's so fucking hot."

I wasn't sure who said it. All three of my men moaned and grunted and cursed, the hottest sounds ever to reach my ears, heightened by all the sensations running through my body. Pulling my mouth away from Hunter, I slid over to Razvan.

"I have died and somehow gone to fucking heaven," he breathed as I sucked him into my mouth again, my hand still stroking Hunter next to him.

Connor chose right then to finally penetrate me, turning up the heat and frenzied desire in me to a fever pitch. He pulled my hips back hard, impaling me on his length as my head fell back, mouth open like I was trying to keep from drowning.

"Yes, look at you," Razvan stroked down my arms as I fought

desperately to hold on through Connor's pounding. "So gorgeous while she's getting fucked. Isn't she, alpha?"

The nickname for Hunter caught me off guard, but Connor reached underneath me to strum my clit just then and every cell in my body chased a pleasure high.

"Mm-hm," the wolf agreed. He wasn't one for much dirty talk, which was fine with me. But as my gaze drifted up to meet his, my pleasure reached a new high when I saw his face.

He couldn't stop staring at Razvan.

Raz, either because he was totally entranced by me or was determined not to make Hunter uncomfortable, looked at me like I was the only other person in the room. He stroked my face, teased my nipples between his fingers, and stroked himself for me while I sucked and licked him as best I could amid Connor fucking me.

Hunter seemed torn in two different directions. He touched me too when I turned to focus on him, but I didn't miss his golden eyes constantly flickering over to the tattooed dragon next to him. All the while, Connor spanked my ass, strummed my clit like an instrument, and marked up my back with his lips and teeth as he surged in and out of me.

Just before my next orgasm threatened to crash over me, when my pleasure crested and I was well and truly drunk on my feelings for these men, I blurted out what had been on my mind since he first walked back into the house.

"Hunter," I moaned. "Just kiss him already."

❧ 17 ☙

MELODY

My wolf's eyes widened before he looked at Razvan again, chest rising and falling with his ragged breaths.

The dragon returned his gaze coolly, neither inviting nor pushing him away to do what I asked. He left the choice entirely in Hunter's hands.

Hunter leaned over hesitantly at first, but then the desire swept over his fear and his mouth pressed to Razvan's.

Raz cupped his neck and returned the kiss passionately, sending that split tongue forward to give our wolf some of the same pleasure he gave me, and then I came like a waterfall.

"Jesus fuck," Connor groaned from behind me, pausing his thrusts as my pussy convulsed around him. I only knew it was him because the other two's mouths were occupied.

Watching them was beyond hot, and my orgasm seemed to last forever. But it wasn't just hot, it was intimate and sweet. Raz pulled away for a moment, his forehead against Hunter's, and their eyes locked. Hunter responded by grabbing his tattooed shoulders and pulling him in for another kiss.

My heart wanted to burst with everything I felt for them, and what they seemed to find between each other. If they could give each other any semblance of what they made me feel, I wanted them to have that happiness and passion more than anything.

"Fuck, alpha," Raz groaned, his back arching against the chair.

Hunter's fingers had trailed down his stomach and caressed his tattooed thighs, massaging all around that stiff, iron hard cock that flexed as it begged to be touched. I watched, entranced, as my own hands surrounded Hunter's cock.

"Go ahead. Take care of him, handsome wolf," I grinned, watching him shudder as I returned to stroking him. "I got you. Connor's got me. Take care of our dragon."

He shot me a lopsided grin, still caressing Razvan in an intimate, exploratory way. "You're sure you're okay with this?" He'd given into his feelings now, but still wanted to protect mine.

"Did you just hear me come?" I planted a kiss on his hip. "It's more than okay, my love."

My lips hovered just over the crown of his dick. I wanted to see him stroke Raz, to see the dragon's reaction to his touch.

"Ohhh my fucking God..." Raz fisted Hunter's platinum hair at the base of his skull and pulled him in for another kiss, his hips thrusting in time with Hunter's strokes.

Connor resumed his thrusts inside me, and I licked the salty pre-cum from Hunter's dick. My next orgasm was already building inside me, closer and closer with every one of Hunter's moans, Razvan's pants, and Connor's curses.

To anyone seeing us like this, it would've looked like straight up hedonistic debauchery. Four horny people chasing physical pleasure, but no one but us could see our delicate balance. How much we cared about and supported each other, whether there was sexual attraction or not.

Connor loved and encouraged me getting so turned on by our shifters. Not only that, we both encouraged them to be together for their own happiness. The walls came down today and this moment was special, intimate, and vulnerable.

"You're gonna make me come, wolf," Raz gasped in a ragged pant.

That only spurred Hunter on more, and he grew even stiffer in my mouth as his own orgasm drew near. I took him further down my throat, relishing in the fullness of him while Connor filled me from behind.

"You got me so close, babe," my soldier groaned, his fingers digging into my hips as his thrusts deepened.

Hunter's breath caught in his chest as the first spray of cum coated my tongue. I drank him down greedily just as I heard Razvan growl out his release. For the second time, their pleasure sent me over the edge.

I released Hunter's cock to let out the scream I'd been holding in, my head on his thigh as he pinched my nipples to heighten my pleasure even more. Connor's chest pressed to my back as he released inside me, sweat and sex clinging to both of us.

"Now," I panted, my heart still racing as I planted a kiss on Hunter's knee. "You can go shower."

Freshly showered, fed, and rested from our fun romp in the theater room, I decided to check on Arjun.

I knocked three times softly at the bedroom door and waited. When no answer came, I cracked the door open.

"Arjun?" I called, keeping my voice low in case he was still sleeping, and poked my head in. "It's Melody. How are you feeling?"

The simple futon bed had been freshly made with its sheets and duvet cover tucked under the mattress, but no man or tiger laid in it.

"Arjun?" I crept into the room, looking around at the bare, simple furnishings and taking slow, measured steps.

A deep, rumbling growl sent me spinning with my heart in my throat. The Bengal tiger sat on his haunches, looking at me from the small attached bathroom. His tail swished on the tile floor, inspecting me with a pinned stare, much like a house cat would.

I lowered my eyes to his dinner plate sized paws on the floor, not wanting to challenge this predator with direct eye contact.

Arjun, I'm Melody. A shaman. We've spoken before. Do you remember?

The human man within the tiger didn't answer me, but I felt his presence stronger than before. We seemed to be near each other in the same dark hallway, but without sight to know truly how close.

Would you please shift to human so we can talk properly? I would like to help you. We can take you anywhere you'd like to go. You're free now.

He pulled his lips and ears back and roared, startling me enough to stumble back a few steps. With his massive head low, he brought one paw forward and then the other. Stalking his prey.

I turned and practically flew out of the room as fast as my feet could carry me. Shutting the door behind me, I backed away and waited with bated breath.

Nothing happened.

After a few moments, I heard the distinctive creak of a box spring. The tiger apparently just wanted me out of his room so he could sleep.

Confused, I went in search of Razvan.

Bypassing the theater room, where Hunter and Connor were now watching some sports channel, I spotted the dragon shifter throwing knives at a tree on the edge of the property.

He didn't acknowledge me until I came right up next to him, juggling the silver blades through the air with casual flicks of his wrists.

"Hey," I smiled at him, my heart lifting at the memory of his pleasure from Hunter less than an hour ago.

"*Steluța*," he greeted me, taking careful aim with his knives before hurtling all four of them at the tree trunk. The sharp blades struck the wood in a perfect diamond pattern.

"I just tried talking to Arjun," I said, walking alongside him as he went to retrieve his knives. "He was in tiger form again and seemed pretty insistent on me staying out of his bedroom."

"He's most likely gone a bit feral," he mused, yanking the handles from the trunk. "It happens to shifters who stay in animal form for too long. They become unbalanced if their human sides don't take form, and they behave more animal than human."

"How can we rebalance him?" I asked, following him back to his throwing spot.

"Just talk to him like he's a person and give him time. I've had to coax him back to human a few times while we were together." He spun the knives on his fingers. "I'll pay him a visit next. A familiar face will help."

"Thank you, dragon." I grabbed his arm and stood on tiptoe to kiss his cheek, only then noticing he barely looked at me the whole time we were out here. "Hey, is something wrong?"

"No." He faced me for the first time, forcing a smile and giving me a quick peck on the lips. "Why?"

"I don't know. You seem a little distant since…" I trailed off, not feeling the need to say, *since you made out with and got stroked off by another man less than an hour ago.*

"I don't mean to be, *steluța*. Just thinking about it, I guess."

"In what way?"

"Nosy girl," he teased, tapping the end of my nose with his index finger. "Not in a bad way, I promise. I enjoyed every second of that and don't regret a thing."

"But it was different than the first time we were together."

"Yes," he breathed. "In a few ways."

"I'll leave you to think," I told him, reluctantly letting go of his arm. "But if there's anything bothering you, please tell me. You know I can't stand the silent treatment like the other two have done."

He gazed down at me gratefully before giving me a long, deep kiss. "I promise you, I will."

❧ 18 ❧

RAZVAN

"Arjun," I sighed. "Come on, shift back. You can't be a big damn pussy the rest of your life."

The tiger roared at me, his claws curling out as his massive paws kneaded the duvet cover. Damn cat was already shredding it to ribbons. He'd already scratched up the flooring, too. I hoped the nonprofit center wouldn't charge us for damages.

"I know you feel safer in this form," I told him. "But there's nothing to fear now. You're safe. I promise you that, mate. We just want to help you."

His responding growl was softer as he lowered his head to rest on his paws. Slowly but surely, he was coming around.

"Don't you want to drive a car again?" I asked him. "Walk around town without people running and screaming, go to a bar, maybe?"

Like most shifters, I preferred my animal form. The list of things more enjoyable as a human was very short. For me, driving was on that list. All the basic needs such as food, sex, and comfort could be met without being human.

At least for most animals. I'd never fucked another dragon before.

Arjun licked his paws, then stared at me. A low purr rumbled in his throat. He was hungry again.

517

"I told you the rules," I said with a shrug. "You eat human food in human form. We don't need any damn rednecks shooting at you in the woods."

He bared his teeth, which slowly began shrinking. The orange fur and black stripes sank back into his hair follicles until it morphed into a light brown tan. He shrank in size, limbs and organs rearranging until a handsome but surly Indian man looked at me from the bed.

"Good enough for you?" he asked in that musical Londoner accent. Mel would be swooning once she heard him actually speak.

"Good man," I answered, straightening up from where I leaned against the wall. "Shall I bring your food up like you're a sick child or will you get dressed and come down yourself?"

"I'll come down," he muttered, pushing himself off the bed to rummage on the floor for his borrowed clothing. "So where is she, the shaman?"

"She's with Connor at the main building. They're running tests and assessing him for new prosthetics."

"Prosthetic what?" he pulled on a pair of Hunter's sweatpants and one of my shirts.

"Legs," I answered. "I forgot, you didn't see him. He's a war veteran. Hard times turned him into a show pony like us." I clapped Arjun on the shoulder as he rounded the bed, already getting a better handle on his human legs. "Let's get some breakfast in you."

"Please tell me you have tea." I allowed him to lean on me as we descended the stairs. "Fuck me, I haven't had a decent cup of tea in ages."

"I'll see what we can do," I chuckled, pleased at hearing his old personality return.

A delicious smell and sizzling sound wafted in from the kitchen. Hunter laid out strips of bacon in a pan, while Roo stood on a footstool, carefully folding over scrambled eggs on the stove next to him. Rinna stood between them, circling around her dad and brother's legs, hoping to catch an extra piece.

"Morning, wolves." I draped an arm over Arjun's shoulders. "This is my friend, Arjun. This is Hunter, Roo, and Rinna."

"Cheers, mate." Arjun bumped fists with Roo and Hunter in greeting. "Might I ask what have you got for tea in this place?"

"Think we have some Earl Grey in the cupboards," Hunter replied, keeping a watchful eye on Roo. We hadn't spoken much since yesterday, and now, without Mel as a sort of buffer between us, it felt like the awkward morning after a one-night stand. I didn't know whether to be affectionate with him in any way or pretend it never happened.

I saw Arjun's teeth clench, but he forced a smile. "That'll do nicely, thanks."

Rinna peered up at Arjun from the floor, lifting her nose to sniff the air delicately. "Are you the big tiger?"

"That I am, love. You've got a good nose on you," Arjun smiled at her.

"Why do you talk funny like Mr. Razvan?"

"Rinna!" Hunter barked a low warning. "That's rude."

But Arjun and I burst into peals of laughter, which only confused the poor girl more. Even Hunter tried to hide a smirk as he focused on cooking the bacon.

"It's alright. No one's given me a good ribbing over my accent in years." Arjun knelt to Rinna's level. "I talk funny because I'm from a place called England. Ever heard of it?"

She shook her head, eyes wide in fascination.

"It's on an island far away from here." He placed his index fingers on the floor. "See, we're here. England is wayyy over here. And there's a big ocean in the middle."

"What ocean is that, Rinna?" Hunter asked in a gentler tone. "You know it."

"The Atlantic Ocean?" she glanced up at her father hesitantly.

"Very good!" He turned off the stove and smoothed a hand over her dark hair before bending down to kiss her head. "Now sit at the table. Food's ready."

"Now Mr. Razvan talks funny," Arjun continued, slowly easing himself into a seat at the table. "'Cause he's a damned Eastern European who didn't even speak a lick of English until a few years ago."

"Yeah, what else do you speak, you damned imperialist?" I shot back with a slug to his arm.

"Hindi," he retorted. "And Bengali. And Urdu. And *proper* English. All since birth, mind you."

"Whatever," I muttered, heaping eggs and bacon on two large plates while Hunter portioned out smaller plates for the kids. "Thanks for breakfast, Hunter."

"Of course." He touched my waist, and then I felt the unmistakable warmth and softness of his lips on my neck. His mouth connected right behind my ear, ironically right where I had a black lipstick mark tattooed. My heart crashed against my ribs while my whole body froze, and then the sensation was gone.

Unfreezing from my stupor, I turned around. The scene at the table carried on like no one noticed. Roo and Rinna excitedly asked Arjun to say words in his other native languages while Hunter attempted to settle them down to eat. Arjun indulged them and even traced Sanskrit words on the table with his fingers. The guy was truly brilliant, even if he was an English prick sometimes.

"Thanks, love." He made a kissing noise at me as I set his plate in front of him, then grinned a broad, pearly smile. "Where's my tea, then?"

"I think I liked you better as a cat," I muttered, returning to the cupboards to rummage for the Earl Grey.

"Oh, don't lie. You missed my cheeky self."

I kept my grin to myself as I prepared a tea bag in a cup of hot water. Truthfully, I did miss the big striped bastard. Even in the darkest, most bleak of times during our captivity, his cheeky attitude kept me going. Even now, after nearly seeing his own end, he could smile at the kids and give me a well-deserved ribbing.

"So we are still in the States, I take it?" he asked around a mouthful of eggs.

"Yes, Georgia," Hunter informed him.

"Ah, still in redneck central, I see."

We filled him in on our journey since meeting Mel and coming to this place. He listened with rapt attention, his blue-green eyes shifting from Hunter to me as we spoke.

"Hold on a moment," Arjun raised a hand after listening to what we knew of Mel's shaman abilities. "How old is she?"

"Eighteen," Hunter answered. "As of a month or so ago."

Arjun's eyes widened, his hand moving to his jaw that dropped open. "That is... unheard of. A shaman so young, tapping into her power already. Communicating with her mind across distances?" He shook his head. "I've known a few in my life and have never seen that."

"What's your experience been with shamans?" Hunter asked.

"My mother married one," Arjun explained. "He wasn't my sire, obviously, but he raised me and my siblings. Not a lot of great places for tigers to be out and about in London, you see, so he protected us. He could cast illusions so human eyes wouldn't notice us. A few years before I got captured, he was training a young lady shaman. I got to sit in on some of their lessons. Fascinating stuff."

His jaw clenched as he took a sip of tea. I knew his mother died when he was younger, but he never elaborated when it happened. Something told me he wasn't too happy about his stepfather taking a young female shaman under his wing, despite learning what they were capable of.

"So Mel is advanced for her age?" I asked, turning the subject back to her.

"Highly." He nodded. "She definitely needs training, though. The way she comes through my head is quite messy and jumbled. Sometimes I couldn't tell if she was another tiger shifter nearby. Her illusion powers are strong but she needs better control of them."

"I thought she was another dragon at one point too," I added.

"Connor told me, I think when she was first tapping into you, Arjun," Hunter chuckled, "that he nearly pissed himself because he heard a growl and swore there was a massive animal in bed with him."

"Can we go outside, Dad?" Roo asked, looking up proudly from his empty plate.

"Yes, you may."

"Can we shift?" Rinna slid out of her chair.

"Only if you stay behind the house," Hunter told her sternly. "I mean it. Do not let any humans see you."

"Okay, Dad!" They tore off running toward the backyard, Roo already letting out high-pitched puppy howls.

"Adorable pups, mate," Arjun beamed, glancing back at them. "You've done good."

"Thank you. They're a handful, but I try," Hunter sighed, leaning back and lacing his hands behind his head. "It's hard without a pack, but they've taken really well to our group of misfits here."

"So, now that it's only adults at the table," Arjun cleared his throat. "Perhaps you can tell me. Are all of you with her?"

"Yes, we are," I answered quickly. "It's not the most traditional situation, but it seems to be working for us."

"I see. I was just wondering because it's not unusual for shamans to form polyamorous relationships with all the shifters they keep close."

"The shaman woman we met at the carnival alluded to that," Hunter smirked. "Most of them are female and they tend to form harems."

"Well, aren't you blokes lucky," Arjun cheeked behind another sip of tea.

"We are," I agreed with no humor in my voice. "She saved Hunter and his kids. She talked Connor into getting help for his many issues. And she saved *your* ass. You're just as lucky as we are, Arjun."

"And I'm grateful," he replied, leveling his gaze to mine. "I'm sure she's a lovely woman and I look forward to speaking with her properly. But there's no way I'm standing in line behind other blokes competing for a woman's affection."

"That's not really how it is, but fair enough," Hunter remarked with a casual shrug.

Satisfied, Arjun drained his mug of tea and sat back. "Thanks for breakfast, Hunter. That was delicious. I feel my human taste buds coming back already."

"Welcome back to the world of two legs and dulled senses." Hunter laughed as he stood to clear plates from the table. "Raz, when are Mel and Connor supposed to come back?"

"Some time in the afternoon, depending on how long his physical therapy goes," I muttered, rising to help him with dishes. I avoided Mel again this morning, which I hated doing. I could only hope this ache would pass with time, or until she said the words to make it go away instantly, but I didn't hold out much hope for that.

Hunter noticed the lack of enthusiasm in my reply and lifted an eyebrow in question as I stacked plates next to the sink.

"I'm off for a catnap," Arjun said with a yawn and stretch above his head. "Catch up with you blokes later."

Hunter and I watched him go up the stairs, most of the wobbliness gone from his legs as he held the railing. He'd be at full human strength in no time.

"Something on your mind?" the wolf asked me once we were alone. His hands brushed against mine as he took dishes from me to soak in the sink.

"When is there not?" I laughed nervously, my heart returning to its violent assault on my sternum. Where could I even begin? I wanted to tell him, but where did I stand with this man?

"Are you bothered because of yesterday?" he asked, his voice low and his golden eyes fixated on the dishes in the sink.

I looked at him, watching his shoulders flex as his hands moved. "Because of you and me? No." My hand slid to the small of his back, resting in the curve just above his ass. "How could I be?" I brought my lips to his shoulder to emphasize my point. "Have you done that to another man before?"

He gave a small shake of his head as a faint blush rose in his pale cheeks. I smiled against his shoulder, breathing in his earthy scent as my arm wrapped around to skim my fingertips across his abs.

"Well, you fooled me, alpha."

"Done it to myself plenty of times, though," he laughed, his eyes meeting mine shyly. "Have you?"

"Yeah. It's been so long, though. I usually prefer women but," I stepped in closer to feel the heat of his side against my torso, "sometimes there's a rare exception."

He lifted his hands from the soapy water and wiped them on a towel before wrapping his fingers around mine and turned to face me.

"So something else is bothering you?"

I sighed. The wolf was so perceptive, he wouldn't even allow me a distraction.

"I heard what Mel said to you in the heat of the moment."

"That she loves me?" His brow furrowed with concern as his fingers squeezed around mine.

"Yeah," I admitted. "That in itself doesn't bother me, but... she loves *you*. She loves *Connor*. I'm just wondering where I fit in. If I fit in at all."

"Raz." Hunter brought his hands together around the back of my neck, lowering his forehead to mine. With a hitched breath, I brought my hands to his forearms, grateful for him being there while I didn't want to look like a whiny bitch in front of Mel.

"I thought I'd be okay with just being her toy," I admitted. "The tattooed bad boy she entertained herself with while she had more meaningful relationships with others. But...I can't."

"Raz," Hunter breathed again, his lips inches from mine. "She doesn't see you that way. She never has. She's absolutely smitten with you. Just give her time. I'm positive she is in love with you, or will be soon."

"I dunno, man. I'm starting to feel like a third wheel and it honestly fucking hurts." I released his forearms, moving to step away from him. "I don't want to get in the way of—"

He cut me off with a growl and a hard kiss, pulling my body flush against his. Fire surged through me, my dragon roaring for more from this wolf. I bit down hard on his lip and Hunter just returned it, his teeth feeling pointier than normal. This wasn't anything like kissing a woman, this was two alpha animals warring for dominance.

Hunter grabbed my wrists and turned both of our bodies to slam my back against the wall with a loud crack. It would've knocked any mere human unconscious, but he felt my dragon fighting for release. I barely registered my head bumping against the wall, only letting out a reptilian snarl from the impact. Hunter's hot erection pressing against mine held all of my attention. That and his sharp canine teeth only inches from my face.

"You're *not* a third wheel. I don't ever want you to say or think that," he growled, his words slightly muffled by the shift in his jaws. "We're individuals, Raz. Her feelings are going to develop differently for all of us. Be patient and believe that. You can't force her feelings, so don't mope and feel sorry for yourself, dragon."

"Fine," I groaned. "You're right. I just need to get my head out of my ass."

Hunter's teeth shrank back to human size and his grip loosened as he shot me a wily smirk. "You want to know something?"

"Hm?" I tried to keep my attention focused on his face, not his tall, lean body pinning me to the wall.

"I probably wouldn't have kissed you or touched you at all if she hadn't told me she loved me."

"Oh?" I lifted a brow. "What's one got to do with the other?"

"She knew about me feeling attracted to you." His eyes flickered down. "And she still loves me. Just knowing she accepted me feeling this way and loving me despite it? That was the final push I needed to act on it. To know for sure that this was okay."

"You got one thing wrong, wolf," I laughed dryly, pushing away from the wall to tease the length of his neck with my tongue.

"What's that?" he groaned, hooking his fingers in my belt loops and pulling me against him.

"Did you see how hard she came?" I grazed my teeth along his earlobe, relishing in the hot shudder that followed. "She loves you *because* of who you are, not in spite of it."

19

HUNTER

A mixture of scents filled my nose as I ran—rabbit, fox, pheasant. But this wasn't a hunt, nor a run to escape from anything I was feeling. This was a run of exhilaration and joy with two of my favorite people.

Roo and Rinna followed at my heels. I kept my pace slow enough for them to stay close, but just enough to push them. They needed the challenge to become strong wolves.

I smelled water a few hundred feet away and picked up the pace. Just a bit farther until we reached our spot to rest before heading back home.

Home. I never thought that word would consist of two humans and two other shifters of a different species. Razvan, Mel, Connor—they'd all been abandoned by their own kind. I began to see how lucky I was to grow up with my pack, that my two pups knew other wolves in their young lives. But as they grew older, those memories would only grow more distant.

I worried for them, as much as I loved how the others took to them. If our family of misfits stayed together, my pups would grow up safe, happy, and cared for. Ultimately, that was all I really wanted.

What worried me was when they'd want mates of their own. Would any pack accept them?

We reached the stream, slowing our run to a canter. The pups panted behind me as I lowered my black nose to the water, sniffing before taking a drink. They slurped at the trickling water greedily, thankfully knowing better than to drink it in human form. When we took our fill, I sat on my haunches and shifted back to human.

Sometimes I liked feeling the effects of a good run better in a human body than a wolf. My two animals just didn't feel adrenaline and excitement the same way. Right then, I was running on the high of being with Razvan in the kitchen.

The recollection brought a smirk to my mouth and a fluttering in my chest. My run felt fast and light with relief. He returned what I felt and showed me I didn't have to carry shame or guilt like a heavy burden.

And Mel... she loved me.

I loved her back. God knew I did. But the pack mentality held me in its strong jaws. I couldn't just get over it, like Connor said. Pack law dictated wolf shifters take mates of the same species. No humans and definitely no dragons.

Wolf packs weren't perfect, of course. Many of them were run by grizzled old alphas stuck in backward ways of thinking. But we had community when so many shifters had to go through life alone. We banded together and protected our own whenever confronted by humans. As a rebellious adolescent wolf, I had my issues with how much the pack dictated my personal life. But now, as an adult and father, I yearned for my pups to have that same kind of community to protect them.

Roo shifted to human after a few moments of resting on the bank of the stream. "Dad, why were you and Mr. Razvan hugging like that in the kitchen?"

I bit the inside of my cheek to hold back my laugh. He was almost seven now and so observant. Nothing got past my boy. I knew I'd have to tell them about this, eventually.

"Sometimes two males or two females like each other in the same way as a male and female do," I told him.

"Oh, like an omega."

"Kind of," I said, smoothing out his golden white hair. "Only Mr. Razvan would never be at the bottom of the pack. He's very strong."

"Yeah," my son agreed, quietly taking in this information as he looked at me. "So you like both? Since you kiss Miss Mel a lot too."

"I guess I do," I said. "Raz is the first male I like in that way, and I tried to ignore it at first."

"Why?" he seemed genuinely surprised and my heart tugged painfully in my chest.

Summer was almost over and he'd need to start school soon. I hoped he would never witness the tormenting that I saw in human schools. Omegas were a long-accepted part of wolf society. They lived at the bottom of the pack hierarchy and sometimes were sexual bottoms for other male wolves if there were no available females around. But humans were especially cruel to their own people who they speculated were gay.

"Humans don't really have omegas in their society," I explained. "Sometimes men who like other men are treated really badly for no reason. Women too. A lot of them hide it. It's not right, but it's what they have to do sometimes in order to survive."

"Humans are dumb," Roo muttered, drawing in the muddy stream bank with an index finger. "Not Mel or Mr. Connor, though."

"You're right about that." I ruffled his hair again and leaned back on my elbows to just listen to the stream. Roo shifted back to wolf to wrestle with Rinna. Their playful snarls and yelps brought a smile to my face and a sense of peace over me.

I didn't know entirely how I felt about Raz and tried to be okay with that. It was more than just physical, although those feelings didn't run as deep as they did for Mel. Not yet anyway. And I certainly liked each of them for different reasons, as I imagined she liked all of us.

I loved her sweetness, how soft she was, how she just melted under my touch. I liked his strength, that I could be rougher with him. Every little fight for dominance we had made me hard.

A good alpha never got comfortable. He was always challenged, always proving his worth of holding his position. Raz spoke to that primal part of me. As long as we had Mel and the kids to protect, he'd never let me get lazy.

But he had a softness about him too. I saw it whenever he looked at Mel, and for a moment in the kitchen when he admitted to feeling like a third wheel.

I liked that he opened up to me. He could come to me when he wasn't sure about talking to Mel, and I hoped it made him feel better. We didn't go further in the kitchen other than the hot kiss and a little slamming against the wall. Neither of us felt right about doing more without Mel around, and I was glad we were on the same page about that.

A shift in the air brought a scent to my nose that made me freeze and listen.

That scent was familiar, one I hadn't smelled in what felt like ages.

No, how could it be...

And just as quickly, it was gone.

I swiveled my head, trying to pick it up again, but all I caught were faint whiffs. The spark of hope in my chest dissipated. An old scent then, probably from months ago. The breeze just happened to carry it right under my nose.

I laid out on my back, stretching my abs and spine to get ready for the run back.

Back home, where my family was safe, and I was loved for being me.

20

MELODY

I followed after Connor in a huff. Every day he seemed faster in that damned wheelchair, despite being so averse to it at first.

"Slow down, Con." I broke into a jog, my shoes crunching on the gravel driveway leading up to our house.

I still couldn't believe those words. Our house.

"Catch up to me, babe," he laughed, pulling himself up the steps of the porch with the pure brute strength of his arms. The house came equipped with a wheelchair ramp on the left side of the wraparound porch, but of course, he refused to use it.

"Where's my bacon, Hunter?" he yelled as he wheeled inside, his voice echoing off the slanted ceiling.

"Get your own. I'm busy!" came the reply.

"Busy doing wha—Oh, I see how it is!"

"Jesus, why do y'all gotta be so loud when we have a guest resting?" I grumbled, following the cacophony into the theater room.

Someone swapped two of the armchairs with the loveseat from the reading area. Stretched out on the loveseat, watching *Jeopardy!*, was Hunter. His long legs dangled over the edge, entwined with Razvan's, who laid on top of him with his head on the wolf's chest.

"Oh my gosh, you guys are so cute," I gushed. They looked so cozy and comfortable together. A mixture of relief and a fresh burst of love for both of them made my heart lift. I was so happy to see they got over any shame or uncertainty and were comfortable enough to be openly affectionate with each other.

"Connor, where's your phone? I want to take a picture of them."

"This cuddle pile is open if you'd like to join us," Hunter grinned lazily.

"We need a bigger couch," Raz mumbled, sighing contently.

Before I could answer, heavy, lumbering steps came down the stairs, and I found myself face-to-face with a tiger.

"Hello, Arjun," I said, trying to keep my voice steady. "Have you rested well?"

Something about him made me more afraid than I ever felt with Hunter or Raz. Maybe because I saw him kill a man through his own eyes, or how he came at me when I was in his bedroom the other day. Or maybe it was just the raw, predatory power that flowed through him with every feline step.

The tiger pounced, and a scream caught in my throat.

He landed right on top of Raz and Hunter, then proceeded to just sit on them.

"Jesus fuck! Get off you bastard, you're fucking heavy!"

Arjun parted his jaws in a wide yawn and ignored the thrashing shifters underneath him, choosing to knead his massive paws on Razvan's back instead.

"Ow! Cut that out, you're not a fucking house cat!"

The tiger huffed out a breath before his form shrank down, shifting to human.

"No fun, the lot of you," he sighed disappointedly, propping his elbow on the edge of the loveseat.

"Um," I shielded my eyes, heat rising in my cheeks. "Did you forget about clothes?"

"I most certainly did not," he replied with amusement. "I heard an open invitation to a cuddle pile, which my tiger just happens to love."

"You weren't invited," Raz joked, slugging him on the arm. "Girls only."

Arjun lifted a well-defined eyebrow. "Right. Girls only invited to your cuddle party with another man. That makes perfect sense."

"Can you please put something on?" Ironically, the one man I didn't sleep with seemed to be the most comfortable sitting around nude while the rest of us were fully clothed like normal people. And damn it, why did he have to have an accent and be so good-looking too?

"My apologies. I've been a bit out of touch with my humanity as of late." The snark in his voice indicated it was far from a sincere apology, but I heard his bare footsteps pad back up the stairs again.

"He takes some getting used to," Raz chuckled. "He's English, you see."

"Really? I hadn't noticed," I stammered, flustered. I wanted to fan my face, but didn't want to give the guys another excuse to tease me.

"He's a good guy, though. And brilliant. Probably one of the few shifters left who knows a lot about shamans."

"Well then, let's hope we can get along," I murmured. Already I wasn't sure if Arjun and I would be able to have a normal conversation, let alone any kind of friendship. He seemed entirely too arrogant and rubbed me the wrong way.

Moments later, he came back down the stairs wearing a borrowed pair of sweatpants and dark green t-shirt that made his eyes pop. They looked like the bluish-green hue of a tropical ocean.

"Does this satisfy Her Majesty's requirements?" he asked, smirking as he held his hands out to his sides.

"Yes, thanks." I ignored his sarcastic remark, tearing my gaze from his as I ran my fingers through my hair. "Anyway, back to your cuddling and *Jeopardy!*-watching. Con and I are hungry so I'll see about some dinner."

"Oh, and now she's refusing the 'girl's only' cuddle invitation! I gotta say, guys," Arjun shook his head as he reclined in one of the armchairs, "I don't know about this shaman."

Connor, who had been in the room but observing silently the whole time, chuckled as he wheeled after me into the kitchen.

"Don't tell me you think he's actually funny," I whispered, opening the refrigerator with a violent pull.

"He kind of is, but I'm not laughing at that." He braked his chair abruptly. "I'm laughing at you."

"What the hell for?"

"'Cause you really are a greedy girl." His lips pulled back into a wide grin. "You want him."

"I do not!"

"You definitely do. If you didn't, you wouldn't care if he was naked."

"Yes, I would have! Connor, there are children in this house!"

"Shifter children," he pointed out. "Who would probably never be wearing clothes if they didn't have to integrate into human society."

"Well, whatever. He clearly doesn't like me." I pulled things out of the fridge at random and set them on the counter.

"He does, though. That's why he's being a pain in your ass. Or *arse*, I should say," he giggled.

"Doesn't seem very mature."

"He's a Brit, babe. Their sense of humor is different. They take the piss out of each other all the time."

"I don't even know what that means."

"They just mess with each other. It's how they show friendliness. If he didn't like you, he'd completely ignore your existence."

"I think I'd prefer that, honestly."

Connor placed his hands on the countertop and pulled himself up to sit on it, twisting around to face me.

"Do you trust my judgement of people, babe?" He pulled out a knife and cutting board, proceeding to prep what I'd taken out of the fridge.

"Of course I do. Except," I giggled, "for when you called that phys-ical therapist an asshole today."

"He *was* being an asshole."

"He was doing his job! He had to figure out which nerves your pain was coming from."

"Yeah, you think he needed to prod me fifty fucking times to figure it out?"

We bantered back and forth as our ingredients came together as BLTs. I made extras for the other guys, including Arjun, while Connor and I just ate at the counter. It was strangely nostalgic, eating and talking like this, like when we first met and it was just me and him in his trailer. Not that I wanted to go back to how things were before the other guys, but I realized these little moments were just ours, and ours alone.

"Come here," he said gruffly, pulling me into a bacon-tomatoey kiss.

"Aren't you happy for Hunter and Raz?" I whispered, my grin threatening to split my face. I couldn't get over seeing them cuddling on the couch. It was downright the most adorable thing I'd ever seen.

"I am," he smirked back. "So you love Hunter, huh?"

"Yes," I admitted. "Does that—"

"Bother me? No, of course not." He kissed me again. "What about Raz?"

"I... I dunno yet." I chewed my lip, lowering my gaze. "I have the biggest crush on him, obviously."

"Almost as big as your crush on Arjun," he teased.

"Shut up," I smacked his chest. "I mean, I like everything about him. He's so open and caring with me. I trust him and I know he takes that very seriously. Just a touch or look from him makes me all fluttery."

"But?" Connor prompted.

"But I do feel a little guarded with him," I admitted. "Because he did hurt me intentionally. Not only that, he hurt another girl intentionally. That first kiss was no accident, and he didn't regret it. I've forgiven him and I trust it not to happen again. It's just that you or Hunter would've never done that in the first place, you know?"

"Hunter and I have hurt you in our own ways," he pointed out. "I'll tell you a secret. We're knuckleheads. All men are."

"Don't I know it," I snorted, wrapping a hand around his neck. "But you're *my* knuckleheads."

"Damn right." He helped himself to firm handfuls of my ass. "We're not perfect, and we're definitely not angels. But we all love you and we're trying our best."

"And I love you." I pressed a kiss to his luscious mouth. "Raz too, I'm sure. I just need to feel right before I say it."

"And that's fine. He's trying his best to be patient and understanding, but it wounded him a little that you told Hunter and not him."

"Shit." I stiffened in his arms, suddenly feeling like the world's biggest asshole. "He told you that?"

"No, but I can just tell. I think that's why he's cozying up to Hunter right now."

"I'm so fucking stupid." I dropped my forehead into my hands. "I just blurted it out. I should have told Hunter in a more private moment. I didn't even think about Raz."

"It's okay, babe. Like I said, he understands, and I think Hunter explained it to him, too. The last thing any of us want to do is force your feelings a certain way." He lifted my chin and those forest green eyes filled my world. "There's three of us and one of you. We all love you and want your love in return, but we're trying not to make a competition about it. It's hard, babe. I get it."

"You're the best, you know that?" I sighed. "It's like you're the elected representative of our whole group. You understand all of us and know how to mediate everything."

"I don't know how my curmudgeonly ass got that job, but I'll take it."

I giggled, nuzzling him for more kisses, which he gave in spades. "I love you so much."

"I love you more," he replied gruffly, trapping me between his muscular thighs. "Damn, I can't wait to get some new legs so I can fuck you against the wall again."

"So romantic." I rolled my eyes. "How long did Dr. Selow say, a week?"

"Too fucking long," he groaned. "But yes, they'll get the first prototypes in a week. I'll try them out but it could be months of fine tuning and calibrating before I get a long term set."

"That's a good thing, though," I said. "Better to make sure they're perfect for you instead of hurting you after a couple years like the other ones."

"Right. And I'll need your help in doing some very thorough testing over those months."

"Oh yeah, like what?"

"They need to pass the fucking you against the wall tests."

"Jesus, Connor..."

21

ARJUN

T he shaman was like nothing I expected. She was so young to be so in touch with her abilities already, which was impressive enough. Even Miriam, the girl my stepfather Lhozen had trained, had been in her late twenties when she started having visions.

For being so young, though, Melody sure did seem to have a stick up her arse.

All the guys' tongue wagging and puppy dog eyes were a bit much as well. Even the non-shifter human with no feet looked at her like the sun rose and set from a twirl of her fingers.

Even so, she was the reason I was still alive, the reason I hadn't offed myself earlier despite the utter hopelessness of the situation. The least I could do was help her grasp her shaman abilities.

She and the human man, Connor, spent a while in the kitchen while Raz, Hunter and I resumed watching TV. I squirmed uncomfortably in the chair, in my soft human skin. My tiger itched to come out. He didn't understand why I needed to be a weak, two-legged human. Truthfully, I was having a hard time remembering myself.

Driving is easier as a human, like Raz said, I reminded myself. Drinking tea is also much easier without a gargantuan mouth and tongue.

Tea sounded excellent right then, so I excused myself from watching the too-bright screen and headed into the kitchen. My balance was coming back, although a tail and four legs were much easier. I barely had to lean against the wall when I rounded the corner.

Melody jumped and stared at me wide-eyed, like she'd been caught doing something nefarious. Connor was out of his wheelchair and sitting on the counter, with Melody standing between his thighs and his hands inside her shirt.

"Now, don't stop on my account," I grinned. "Just passing through for some tea."

"I got you, bro." Connor turned and opened the cabinet behind him to hand me the box of Earl Grey. Melody only blushed, her eyes darting away from me.

I itched to make a joke about where his hands had been, but bit my tongue. Melody didn't seem to need any more sticks up her bum from me, at least not right then.

"Cheers, mate." I accepted the box from him and flicked on the electric kettle for my water.

Melody cleared her throat. "There are BLT sandwiches in the fridge if you're hungry. We made a bunch for everyone."

"Lovely. Don't mind if I do." I helped myself to one as my water heated up. My tiger didn't have a taste for tomato or bread, but these simple human staples sent my taste buds into overdrive. Maybe I could get used to staying in human form yet.

"What kind of food do you like?" the young shaman asked. "We can get some more variety tomorrow."

"Assuming you mean human food," I smirked, "I'm not terribly picky. Although I'd be right chuffed to have a good lamb curry again."

"Oh, okay." She sounded unsure and looked a bit sheepish. "I don't think I've ever eaten curry before."

"Never had curry? Have you lived under a fucking rock, woman?"

"No." Her eyes fluttered away as she stepped away from Connor. "In a trailer." Abruptly, she turned and walked out of the kitchen, leaving me and her man to look at each other awkwardly.

"I meant no offense," I said sheepishly. "My mouth goes before I think sometimes."

"She's sensitive about where she's from," he replied in an even tone, indicating he wasn't angry with me. "Traveling across state lines and joining the carnival is the most culture shock she's ever experienced."

"We haven't exactly gone off on the right foot, have we?" I ran a hand through my hair, feeling like a right arsehole. "She must think I'm one hell of a prick."

He lifted one shoulder in a shrug to say that I wasn't wrong.

"I wouldn't go that far, but she is a bit sensitive and thinks you don't like her."

"Well, shit." I switched off the electric kettle a bit more aggressively than necessary as it started to steam. "I don't dislike her, but I don't even know the girl. Yeah, she saved my life but I'm not going to go all starry-eyed for her like you lot."

"She's not expecting you to be like that. She just," he paused for a moment, rubbing his jaw in thought, "she's not used to people making fun of her as a way of being friendly. She grew up being teased and belittled with malicious intent, so she takes that stuff personally."

"Shit," I muttered again, steeping my tea bag. "So I really am a prick."

"Maybe a little," he laughed, then gave me a good-natured slap on the shoulder. "We all are, though. That's what I was just telling her."

"With your hands on her tits, yeah? A likely story."

"We've all learned to multitask here," he chuckled, lowering himself off the counter and back into his chair with surprising control and strength. He never once touched the floor.

"Apparently." I stirred a sugar cube into my tea. "Pardon me for asking, but do you "multitask" with Hunter and Raz as well?"

"Nah, I'm straight as an arrow. I always had an inkling those two weren't, though, despite how they felt for Mel. Not that there were any tells, really. It was just a strong instinct I had."

"Really?" I took a sip of tea, carefully studying this American patriot without a drop of shifter blood in him. "Are you a shaman as well?"

"Me? Hell no," he laughed. "I just know how to observe people. The Marines taught me to be perceptive. When I lost my legs, it was astounding how differently people treated me. I learned how to see through facades and figure out people's genuine motivations."

"And yet this young shaman woman fell in love with you," I said. "Pardon me for being blunt. It's just that shamans often write off other humans after being around shifters for so long."

"You don't have to apologize for anything," he said, raising a hand. "I appreciate bluntness and guarantee you, there's nothing special about me. If Mel leaves me in the dust to ride off into the sunset with you shifters, I'll accept that decision. In our time together, she's made me a better man. Dare I say, a happy one. And that's more than I ever dreamed of for myself."

"Well, I'll be damned." I leaned against the counter, teacup in hand. "She's really had an effect on all of you, hasn't she?"

"She and them, if I'm being honest," he nodded toward the theater room where Hunter and Raz were undoubtedly still cupcaking. "They're good dudes. Some of the best I've ever known. We've all had shit happen to us and deserve real, genuine happiness. If that means sharing one amazing woman, it's a no brainer. She inspires all of us to be better, and we take care of her when someone's being a prick," he chuckled. "Because someone always is."

22

MELODY

"Who wants to come with me to apply for a job?" I asked at breakfast the next morning.

Six pairs of eyes stared back at me as I announced the question.

"A job where?" Roo asked me, pieces of scrambled eggs stuck to his lip.

"There's a carnival not far from here," I told him, wiping his mouth with a napkin. "In a bigger city. I can try to be a ringmistress there again."

"I want to go with you!" Rinna announced.

"No," Hunter and I both said in unison, our eyes meeting across the table.

"You don't need to work, sweetie," I said. "Not until you're older. Right now your job is to become a big, strong wolf."

"But I want to go with you!"

"Hey, shush. Inside voice," Hunter chastised her.

"I'll go with you, *steluța*," Raz offered. "I've been itching to breathe a little fire and play with my blades again."

"Thank you, dragon." I rubbed his calf with my foot under the table. Secretly, I hoped he'd be the one to volunteer. His theatrical skills would be the most likely to land us a job. Not to mention I wanted some more alone time with him.

"Tell me you're bloody joking," Arjun interjected. It took everything in me not to fling food at him.

"I'm not," Raz answered simply.

The Englishman's blue-green eyes bounced between Raz and I incredulously.

"You're seriously hoping to get a job at *another* carnival? Might I remind you, shaman, you've got three, no, five shifters here, including the little ones, who've escaped from such places. And you want to go back to another one to earn money?"

"My best skills are as a ringmistress," I answered as coolly as I could muster. "I have no other job experience and we can't stay here forever. Plus, getting inside will get me close to more shifters who need help."

"You're bloody eighteen years old! Go to uni. Get a job at McDonald's or whatever kids your age do. You're not helping shifters when you're putting money directly into these people's pockets. Even if you rescue one, the cash flowing from their new ringmistress will just replace that one with another."

"Great, Arjun. Thanks for letting me know I never should have helped you," I said, rising from the table.

"*Steluța—*"

But I was already gone, stomping through the house and fuming. Who fucking asked him for his opinion? And if he thought it was such a terrible idea, why didn't he just let those other humans kill him?

I found myself in the backyard, but not even the beautiful morning light through the trees or the fresh pine smell in the air could pull me out of my funk. Thanks to that tiger asshole, my day was thoroughly ruined.

In that moment, I wished I could turn into a wolf and just race through the woods like Hunter. I could clear my head, feel the cool earth underneath my paws, and hear nothing but the wind in my ears.

I closed my eyes and pictured it like I had in my dreams. Foliage rushed past me, all kinds of smells and sounds filled my senses but none of it was overwhelming. To my canine brain, it made sense. The rabbit's scent trail triggered my instinct to give chase. I was light and silent on my four red paws.

Wait, red?

A sudden hand on my shoulder pulled me back to human awareness.

"You look cute with those ears. What are you seeing through, a fox?" Razvan kissed my cheek and settled on the porch next to me.

"Um, I think so?" I reached up and felt fluffy triangular ears on top of my head before they disappeared. "I don't know how that happened. I was thinking of running through the woods like a wolf."

"Hm. Too bad the person who can explain that to you was a dick at breakfast."

"No shit," I grumbled. "I know he's your friend, but I think I'm better off learning this shaman stuff on my own. I can't seem to have one single interaction with him and not feel like shit."

"I'm not here to convince you otherwise." His fingers drifted across my back. "That was uncalled for, and I told him off just now. Even if he is my friend, I don't like to see you upset."

I leaned my head on his shoulder, grateful that he was just here for me and not to defend Arjun. After what Connor said last night, I was open to giving the tiger shifter another chance and try not to take his jabs personally. But this morning seemed to erase all possibilities of that.

Razvan pressed his lips to my temple. "Want a lesson in throwing knives? It's a good way to let off some steam without actually stabbing anyone."

"Sure. Can I pretend the tree is Arjun's face?"

"Arjun's, mine, your mother's. Whoever you want."

I couldn't help but laugh as he pulled me to my feet. The thought of my mother's bloated, drunk face in a tree trunk was strangely cathartic. With just a few words, my dragon shifter already made me feel better. I shook off the thought that followed, which was Jeanie still hadn't called Connor's phone.

That was just another reason I needed a job. She and my other siblings needed me.

Fuck whatever Arjun thought.

I SUCKED AT THROWING KNIVES. My first dozen or so throws went way wide of my target, which was already the widest tree in our backyard. When they did hit the trunk, they clattered uselessly to the ground with no real strength behind them.

Raz was a patient teacher, however. He reminded me of when Connor first taught me the routine to act with him onstage. The tattooed dragon spoke gently as he gave me instructions and made every excuse to touch me as he corrected mistakes in my form.

His hands tightened on mine around the handles to adjust my grip, then slid down the outsides of my thighs to adjust my feet. I didn't know how I was able to concentrate at all with his fingertips grazing over me and his breath on my ear, but eventually I sank all four knives into that trunk.

"Great job, *steluța*," he praised me with a smile as we went to retrieve them. "You're a fast learner."

"Thanks! You're a good teacher." He really was, and far more skilled than that old pervert, Syko. Really, the two weren't even comparable. I only thought Syko had skill because I'd never truly seen a gifted knife thrower before. Thank God he never did end up stabbing me.

Upon closer inspection, my knives still went wide of the crudely drawn target he made on the trunk. Two went high and the other two went low, but hey, they all landed!

I meant to pull the knives out, but decided I had a better idea.

Turning around and leaning my back against the trunk, I grabbed Raz's shirt in my fist and pulled him in with a naughty grin.

His mouth crashed to mine with a surprised grunt, then I felt his smile against my lips as he pressed flush against me, pinning me between himself and the tree.

I remembered what Connor said and kissed him harder. Maybe I wasn't ready to say the words yet, but I wanted him to know my feelings went deep and true. I didn't feel more for Connor or Hunter, I just loved them differently. These men held three equal-sized pieces of my heart, but they all occupied different chambers.

The heart has four chambers.

I pushed the random anatomy fact out of my head as my arms slid around Raz's neck, scratching the short, dark hair covering his scalp.

"Mm, I should teach you things more often," he murmured.

"I agree," I whispered, wanting to sink into this private moment between us and feel it wrap around me like a blanket. We had some alone time together while driving and back in Crying Falls, but not like this.

"You really are a fantastic teacher, you know?" I lifted my gaze to his steel-colored eyes. "And a good listener. You're just... really good to me and I appreciate you. I want you to know that."

He blinked as if dumbfounded. I wondered if anyone told him anything like that before, let alone that they loved him. Those three words suddenly found themselves on the tip of my tongue, but he silenced me with another kiss before they could escape.

"I'm a bit at a loss for words," he chuckled, lowering his forehead to mine and running his thumb across my cheekbone. "But I'm touched. Thank you."

"I knew there was a total sweetheart underneath all this ink," I teased him, wanting to lighten the mood.

"Ah, don't tell anyone. I have a reputation to protect."

With a giggle, I lifted my mouth and received his tongue surging past my lips and stealing my breath from my lungs. He pinned my hips to the tree, stepping between my legs so the fire inside him pressed against my heated core.

The energy between us turned on a dime, shifting from sweet and intimate to hot and passionate. My leg lifted to wrap around his hip and his hand found the flesh of my ass, anchoring me there as he kissed a hot trail down my jaw to my neck.

"Want to call Hunter over here?" I asked, already panting.

"No," he growled, nipping my shoulder. "I want you all to myself right now."

That was the answer I was hoping for. Right then, I didn't want to share my dragon either.

He lowered my leg off him and quickly did away with my shorts, the denim sliding down my bare legs to pool at my feet before I stepped out of them carefully. His throat made a hum of pleasure as he rubbed through my panties, already feeling my wetness through the thin fabric.

I undid his zipper with fumbling hands—too distracted, too noodley with how fucking good he made me feel already. Eventually I pulled him out, only able to stroke his thick, hot shaft for a moment before he pulled my panties aside and shoved into me with one hard thrust.

"Oh... FUCK!"

His cock knocked the breath out of me. It almost bordered on painful as I stretched to accommodate him, his piercings adding even more pressure and sensation I wasn't sure I could handle.

But my dragon lifted both of my legs off the ground and put them around his hips again. Widening my legs gave just a hair of extra room for him to fit. He grinned at my gasp for air, my eyes rolling back in my head as he surged out and then pressed in even deeper. *Good Lord.*

With my ankles locked behind his back and only his cock and impressive strength holding me against the tree, he fucked me with abandon. Gone was my warm, patient teacher. This man was splitting me apart and enjoying it from that wild, hungry look in his eyes.

If I could make sense of anything, I was probably orgasming the entire time he fucked me. My muscles just had no room to convulse and clench, but my clit felt like it was shooting off fireworks the whole time, releasing through my toes, curling so hard my feet cramped. Even my fingertips digging into his shoulders for dear life felt every centimeter of him.

He released with a roar that echoed off the trees, turning his head for a moment to allow a small flame to escape his lips without burning me.

I was covered in sweat. My clothes and bits of tree bark stuck to my skin as he gently lowered my legs to the ground. His slick forehead on mine and his ragged breathing told me the same story. Hot, rough, and probably fast, although I lost all sense of time.

Anyone looking out from the house may have seen us. Or not. I smirked at the thought. It almost felt like having a dirty little secret and I kind of enjoyed that.

No, *really* enjoyed that.

"You're a bad, bad dragon," I teased, pulling my shorts back up my wobbly legs.

"And don't you forget it," he returned with a grin.

❧ 23 ❧

MELODY

"**I**'m so nervous."

"Why?" Raz looked concerned as he helped me out of the truck.

"Just look at this place." My heels clicked and echoed in the parking garage as we walked together to the wall of elevators.

The Vaudeville Theater had loomed up in front of us when we pulled into town—a tall, glitzy building covered in lights and completely unlike the run-down, dirty outdoor carnivals I was used to. The elevator we stepped into, with a plush red carpet and mirrored walls on all sides, reflected that same vibe.

This was a classy establishment, making Money with a capital M. I was so glad Raz and I dressed up for this audition. I wore a classic ring-mistress outfit with a red tailcoat and white gloves, plus black tights, heels, a corset, and, of course, a top hat. Raz wore pressed black slacks and shoes, a black button-up shirt with the sleeves rolled to his elbows to show off his tattoos, and a black waistcoat over the top that accentuated his broad chest and tapered waist. In his hand, he carried a slim case for his knives.

"You mean, look at *us*." He slid an arm around my waist, dropping his chin to my shoulder as he stared at our reflection in the mirrored

547

walls. "We look like a million bucks and every bit like we belong here. Don't let anything convince you otherwise, *steluța*."

"I also really want this job," I admitted to our reflections. "I've never stepped on a stage wanting something that I didn't yet have. I actually have to try hard and compete against other people."

"There's no one that holds a candle to you," he murmured with a soft kiss to my neck. "I've seen hundreds of ringmasters and none of them capture an audience like you do. You've got this in the box, *steluța*."

"In the bag, you mean?" I couldn't suppress the giggle that bubbled up.

He looked confused. "Is that what the expression is?"

"Yeah. It's 'you've got this in the bag', not in the box."

"Fucking Arjun," he spat, smiling despite himself. "He taught me English expressions a few years ago, and I knew he was fucking with me on some of them."

The silly moment eased my nerves a bit when we stepped out of the elevator, but my stomach flipped on itself and twisted into knots when the main theater room opened up before us. It was *massive*.

I looked up at a glittering chandelier the size of my old trailer, hung high in the ceiling like it was the sun itself. Two levels of balconies circled around the room, in addition to the many rows of seats here on the ground floor.

A group of acrobats were onstage at the moment, auditioning to four people in the front seats with clipboards. Raz and I sat down near the back and watched. A girl stood on her hands on a platform, her feet hanging over and down, nearly touching her head. One of the other acrobats finished a floor routine of flips and contortions before grabbing a bow and arrow, tossing both items up to the handstanding girl.

She caught them *with her feet*.

My jaw fell open as she nocked the arrow and pulled the bowstring back taut, all done with her toes. She looked almost bored as the arrow loosed, sailing across the stage to hit the center of a bullseye set up at the other end.

Their music stopped, and all acrobats took a bow, the audition finished. Three of the four people in the audience clapped enthusiastically while the fourth scribbled on the paper attached to her clipboard.

"I think we're next," Razvan muttered as he nudged me.

Fuck. We had to follow *that?*

"Next! Melanie and uh, Rasman?"

"It's Melody," I said through gritted teeth, practically stomping down the aisle to the stage when all I wanted to do was sink into the floor. "And Razvan."

"Right. Take it away, you two. Whenever you're ready."

Raz and I ascended the stage. He shot me a wink before moving behind the curtain, where he'd get my music ready and wait until I called for him to come out. We worked on my announcement after our fun at the tree, then practiced a short routine together. It looked like we'd have to lay all our cards out on the table for tonight.

While waiting for my drumbeat to come over the loudspeaker, I took a better look at the people judging my performance. All of them wore dark suits. A man and woman whispered a soft conversation to each other, then glanced at their watches almost in unison. Great, so they didn't even *want* to be here.

The woman who had been scribbling while the others clapped for the acrobats was a stern-looking blonde with a dark pantsuit and glasses. She was the only one who stared straight up at me, lips pressed thin, and her pen tapping the edge of her clipboard like an impatient teacher. If Arjun thought I had no sense of humor, he would rail on this woman.

Who *were* these people? They all looked so... corporate.

My music started up and my stage smile spread across my face. It felt so natural at this point, like I was a magical doll that the stage and music brought to life.

"Ladies and gentlemen, boys and girls!" I boomed. Despite having no microphone, my voice filled the empty auditorium, even reaching some other auditioners seated in the very back rows. The two people up front whispering to each other even stopped to look at me. "Welcome to the Vaudeville Theater's opening night of our electrifying, heart-pounding, most spectacular special event of the season, A Night in the Jungle!"

I paused dramatically, the two whisperers now on the edges of their seats with their eyes glued to me. The woman in glasses had her eyes on her clipboard and scribbled madly.

"Before we take you through the jungle, dear ladies and gentlemen, we've got to warm you up!" I winked suggestively. "The jungle is dangerous, with animals and traps lurking everywhere, oh my!" My eyes widened as a gloved hand came to my mouth. Gasps elicited from audience members with their eyes glued to me, the woman in glasses scribbling as if nothing at all was being performed in front of her.

"We must arm ourselves to the teeth, boys and girls!" I continued, gnashing my teeth for maximum effect. "We must learn to handle the sweltering heat! Oh!" I held up an index finger, my smile so wide it nearly split my face. "I know just the man to show us the way."

Everyone's eyes followed me hypnotically, their tongues practically wagging as I teased them for the upcoming act. Everyone except Glasses Lady, that is. She finally looked up from her lap and stopped writing, but looked utterly bored.

"From the cold mountains of Romania, this man's fire saved hundreds of villages! He scared away dragons and vampires with his skilled blades! And he's bringing the heat to you now, ladies and gentlemen!" I paused and lowered my voice. "If you can handle him," I added with a wink. Then returning to full volume, "Ladies and gentlemen, boys and girls, I give you the amazing, the stupendous, the most death-defying sword swallower and fire breather in the world, Razvan! Leader of the Flaming Swords!"

Walking off stage, I kept my posture straight and my legs long until I could sit down, where I deflated like a balloon. Damn, it looked easy, but yelling at the top of my lungs plus giving all the right inflections and body language was downright exhausting.

Raz walked out from behind the curtain, a swagger in his shoulders as he juggled knives almost casually.

"Good evening, everyone." His eyes swept across the panel of judges with a cocky smile, his hands constantly moving.

"Hello!" chirped one of the women in suits with a giggle. I glared daggers at her.

Raz only nodded at her politely as his juggling hands quickly changed their movement.

Tossing all six knives into the air at once, he spread his arms out to the side and leaned his head back. One by one, he caught each blade *in his mouth* as it fell. Screams rang out in the auditorium, much like I did when I first saw the sharp, metal blades fall down his throat. Now it no longer phased me.

"Oh, no!" I said in feigned annoyance, rising from my seat to take my cue. Heads snapped over to look at me as I ascended the stage. "Looks like Raz got the blades stuck again."

I went to him and wrapped my hands around two of the handles resting on his lips, then pantomimed pulling on them as hard as I could.

"Ugh, Raz. You've done it again," I sighed, looking over my shoulder at our dumbfounded audience. "Knife swallowers, am I right?"

Some of them laughed at our exaggerated display, but everyone was still enraptured. At least we still had their attention.

With a final big show of effort, I pulled two knives out of his mouth and pretended to reel back, windmilling my arms from the momentum.

"Ah, glad I got those out!" I wiped my brow. "I didn't want to explain that one again to the people at the hospital."

"The knives! THE KNIVES!" audience members yelled.

"Right? Who sticks knives down their throat for fun?" I asked, pretending to be oblivious to their pointing and shrieking. "This guy, apparently."

"The knives are on fire!"

I looked down at the blades in my hands, now coated with bright, flickering orange flame.

"Aaah!" I shrieked, tossing them in the air just in time for Raz to step up and add them to the four flaming knives he was already juggling.

"Amateur," he teased me with an eye roll. "Don't play with fire unless you can take the heat."

"Oh, yeah?" I shot back flirtatiously. "How much heat can *you* take, Razvan?"

"Hold these and watch."

One by one, he tossed each knife to me, handle first. The flames extinguished before ever reaching me as I fumbled and dropped the still-smoking blades. At least that part wasn't acting.

All eyes on Raz with his hands now free, he pulled two swords from behind his back and proceeded to juggle them, teasing us all for the grand finale.

"Do I have a volunteer?" he called out to the audience.

Several jaws dropped open, including mine, as I stared at him. That was *not* something we rehearsed.

"I'm just kidding," he cracked. "No one come up here. It's extremely dangerous."

It took everything in me to not roll my eyes and slap my forehead. Damn him. Of course he'd do something off-script. Our first kiss was onstage, after all.

More shrieks rang out as fire consumed the sword blades in a slow line from base to tip.

They whirled through the air in a dazzling display, the heat warming my face as he caught and tossed them effortlessly.

"You all might want to stand off to the sides for this," he warned our audience members, who scrambled out of their seats and headed toward the aisles.

He stopped the juggling abruptly, holding each sword out to his sides like some kind of ninja assassin. Then his biceps curled, and he smirked as he tipped his head back, the flaming blades drifting slowly toward his lips.

"No! He's not!"

"Oh, my God! Is he, really?"

He really was.

With slow, careful precision, he lowered the full lengths of the blades down his throat at the same time. I thought the suited people were going to faint. My eyes drifted over to the woman with glasses, who still barely showed any trace of emotion. Her arms were crossed, eyes locked on the dragon shifter, but I couldn't get a read on her at all.

With the swords now fully inserted all the way to his stomach, Raz spread his arms to his sides again and walked forward toward the edge of the stage.

"Holy shit, they're really in there!" someone cried out.

"And he's seriously still alive!"

I saw his chest expand with a breath, knowing what was coming next as he grabbed the handles of the swords sticking out of his mouth. A pause to prepare and then... *ta-da*.

He yanked the swords out in one clean pull and followed the blades with a huge fireball that bathed the whole auditorium in heat.

People ducked and screamed, but it was over. Smirking, he took a bow as I ascended the stage.

"Give it up for Razvan, ladies and gentlemen! Our amazing pyromaniac swordsman!"

Claps and cheers rang out, and I realized more people had come in and caught the end of our audition. The suits up front had tears in their eyes and clapped enthusiastically. Raz wrapped an arm around my waist and we bowed together. He kissed my cheek when we rose and I shot him a stern look that quickly dissolved into a smile. I couldn't be mad at him. He put on an amazing show and stayed somewhat professional, at least.

"Thank you," the woman in glasses muttered, the only one to not clap, as she kept scribbling on that damn clipboard. "NEXT!"

I stood there, stunned, until Raz gently tugged me to leave the stage. That was it?

"Um, will we hear from you?" I asked once I made it to the ground floor. The next act was already shuffling around on stage to prepare.

"We'll give you a call if you're picked," the other suited woman told me with an encouraging smile. "Great job, we just have a lot of auditions to go through."

I nodded, forcing a smile as I waited for Razvan to grab his case from backstage, but as the woman in glasses forgot all about us as she focused on the next audition, my confidence went down like a lead balloon.

MELODY

I felt like an utter failure as we left, despite Raz trying his best to cheer me up.

"They can't show any preference when watching a ton of auditions like that," he told me, rubbing a sympathetic hand over my thigh as he drove. "It'll make everyone else not want to try."

"I've never seen anyone watch a performance so coldly, with no reaction at all," I mumbled, thoroughly puzzled by the woman in glasses.

"Yeah, she was a real stick in the mud, ah?" he agreed. "Made it feel like a real job interview. Maybe she represented investors or something, and all she was concerned about was how much we'd bring in. Fuck knows what kind of money goes into a place like that."

"On the bright side," I leaned against his shoulder, eager for a happier topic, "I didn't sense a single shifter in there. Did you?"

"Nope." He planted a kiss on my forehead. "You were really feeling for them? Good girl. I didn't even notice you trying."

"I've been practicing a little," I admitted. "At home, I try to identify the differences between you, Hunter, the pups, and Arjun. I can do it pretty much constantly now without thinking too much. It's like feeling different currents in the air. Hunter is a cool breeze. The pups are like little gusts of wind, probably because of how rambunctious and playful they are."

"What about me and the kitty?" he teased, squeezing his hand around my knee.

"You're always warm," I answered. "I think depending on your mood, you feel like a warm blanket or a scorching hot desert."

"Scorching. I like that," he chuckled. "And Arjun?"

I took a moment to think, trying to accurately describe the enigmatic tiger with shifting blue-green eyes.

"He's like the rush of air going past you in a car, or a rollercoaster." I rolled down the window and stuck my hand out. Yes, sensing Arjun's presence felt a lot like the air rushing between my fingers. "It's always fast-moving and a possible indication of danger."

"He would never hurt you, you know," Raz glanced at me before returning his eyes to the road. "That wasn't the first human he killed, but he's only ever attacked the ones who actively enjoyed harming us. He's a predator. It's in his DNA, but that means he only kills to eat or to survive."

"I know that," I replied. "When I sense him, it's not danger like that. It's more of a rush, a thrill. A rollercoaster like I said, or going over the speed limit."

"Ah, so he's another bad boy for ya," he teased, grinning.

"No way!" I protested, slapping his shoulder. "You're plenty bad enough for me. I'm still sore from earlier today, by the way."

"That's what I like to hear," he crooned.

We made it home as the sun was setting and shadows grew long. The truck wound down the long driveway to the house, where two small, fuzzy figures raced around the lawn at top speed. Hunter burst out onto the porch just as we pulled up, yelling at Roo and Rinna for shifting where humans could possibly see. I smiled as I unbuckled my seatbelt and slid out of the car. Home sweet home.

"How'd it go?" Hunter asked, holding a squirming half-shifted Rinna under his arm. She finally wriggled out then tore off after Roo, finishing her shift back to wolf with high-pitched puppy barks.

"Okay, I think," I muttered, approaching my tall, sexy wolf. I missed him. It felt so long since I had any alone time with him now.

"Just okay?" He pulled me into his arms, brow furrowed with concern, as he gave me a kiss. I clung to him, deepening the kiss when he tried to pull back, wanting to forget all about the audition and just curl up into him.

"She did amazing. They were going through a lot of auditions in a short time, so we didn't get any feedback either way," Raz explained. "Just said they'll call if we're picked."

"You did amazing." I looked over my shoulder at him. "It was your act, really. I was just an accessory."

"Not true, *steluţa*. You set the scene, I just followed and did my part."

"I'm sure they'll call. Go on inside," Hunter swatted my ass. "Arjun has a surprise for you."

"Arjun... what?" My brain couldn't make sense of those words. They did not compute.

"Go on. You'll see," Hunter grinned.

"Great," I muttered, dragging my feet up the porch. What could this possibly be?

Not at all eager to find out what the cheeky tiger had in store for me, I hesitated and looked over my shoulder. Hunter approached Raz, their faces close together and talking in low voices I couldn't hear. Raz's hand then shot out and grabbed a fistful of Hunter's hair close to his scalp. He pulled the wolf's mouth to his, closing the already narrow distance for a rough, hot kiss full of teeth and tongue.

Heat burned in my belly as I watched them. Hunter grabbed the sides of Raz's waist and yanked him even closer, their strong, masculine bodies flush against each other. They were rougher with each other than with me, and that only made me hotter.

Raz opened one steel-gray eye, catching my gaze over Hunter's shoulder. His lips pulled back in a grin, breaking off the kiss with the wolf.

"Can a dragon and a wolf get some privacy from perving eyes?" he teased.

Hunter turned around and made a shooing motion at me before Raz grabbed the back of his neck and directed his attention back to where it belonged, at least for that moment.

I giggled as I made my way up the porch, realizing I loved that I wouldn't be the only one sharing lovers. If anything, it made things easier. When those two were together, I could have alone time with Connor, or get to know the kids better. And then Raz or Hunter could have some space when one of them was with me.

And when all of us are together...

My mind remained firmly in a naughty daydream until I walked through the kitchen, and then the smell made my mouth water.

"What is that?" I sniffed the air, unfamiliar with it but unable to deny the growling hunger in my stomach.

"It's curry." Arjun turned from the stove, slapping a dish towel over his shoulder. "Come here, have a taste."

I narrowed my eyes suspiciously but approached him anyway, my curiosity and hunger getting the better of me.

He held out a spoon with a steaming yellowish-green sauce with flecks of spices, herbs, and whatever else was in there. I blew the steam away first, then accepted a small taste.

"Wow!" My eyes widened with the flavors exploding on my tongue. Savory, creamy, a little sweet, and a whole smorgasbord of unique spices and tastes I'd never experienced in my life before. "That is," I licked my lips, "so freaking good!"

"I didn't want to go too exotic on your bland American palate so I kept the heat down and made it with chicken instead of lamb."

I looked at him, those green-blue eyes still mischievous and full of cheek but no outright hostility. His entire demeanor was more relaxed and open than I'd seen before.

"You made this for me?" I asked, dumbfounded.

"Well, for all of us, but I wanted you to experience it, yes," he answered. "You need some culture if we're going to tolerate each other in the same household."

I rolled my eyes at that, but I could see the effort he was making. This curry was an olive branch. Not necessarily an apology for being a dick earlier, but he was making an effort to understand me, to meet me halfway. And this was simple proof he wasn't above being nice once in a while.

"Well, thank you. It's delicious." I offered him a smile. "You're going to give Hunter some serious competition in the kitchen."

"Eh, don't get too used to it," he muttered, returning his attention to the simmering sauce on the stove. "I've got simple tastes myself. A good curry is a bit labor-intensive and you've got to get all the ingredients just right. I'm content with a sausage roll and a spot of tea, myself." He shot me a dazzling white smile that threatened to send my heartbeat out of rhythm.

Thankfully, Connor wheeled in right then.

"Smells amazing, RJ. Let's all eat outside, the sunset's fucking gorgeous. Hey babe, how'd the audition go?"

He tilted his head up for a kiss, which I gave to him long and slow. "It was okay. I'll tell you about it later," I murmured, resting my forehead on his. "Also, RJ?"

"Don't ask me," Arjun said, pulling bowls down from the cupboards. "No point in a fuckin' nickname if it's got the same amount of syllables as my real name."

"It rolls off the tongue easier," Connor chuckled with a swat to my hip. "Help me set up outside, babe."

"Sure it does, with a thick American tongue like you've got."

"That's what she said!" Connor cackled, rolling through the house while balancing bowls on his lap.

"Not like that. Thick means... nevermind."

I giggled, carrying the large bowl of rice out to the back deck while Arjun followed me with the pot of curry.

"Thanks, Mel," he said when I held the door open for him.

"You're welcome, RJ." I couldn't help it.

"Bloody hell. Not you too," he groaned, but a smirk escaped as he placed the still simmering pot on the patio table.

Hunter and Raz finished their make-out session in the front yard and came around to join us. Roo and Rinna sat still enough to eat a small bowl of curry with rice each before running off to chase each other and wrestle again.

"They love the open space," Connor smiled as he watched the pups play.

"It's good for them to get their energy out," Hunter agreed, leaning back from his empty bowl. "I hated keeping them cooped up in the den back in Crying Falls. At least here I know they're safe."

We all chatted and ate like a normal family as the sun went down. I went back for seconds on the curry and almost considered getting thirds, but my belly was thoroughly stuffed as I sat back and rubbed a hand over it.

"Aw, my babe has a food baby," Connor teased as he rubbed a hand over me as well. I slapped his hand away, laughing. That was when it hit me like a bucket of ice water to the face.

We didn't use a condom last time.

No one seemed to notice me freeze up, and I exhaled the breath I held, trying to calm down. I'd have to talk to him about it later when we were alone. When did it happen? Two days ago? Hopefully, it wasn't too late to take Plan B, nor was it too hard to get it somewhere nearby.

It's probably nothing to worry about. I've had a few scares before, but nothing came of them.

Connor suddenly waved a hand to quiet everyone's conversations, bringing a finger to his lips and shushing loudly.

"Do y'all hear that?" he whispered.

Silence fell over the table. No one moved a muscle until we heard the faint, eerie sounds of howling. Goosebumps erected over my skin despite the warm air. The song was haunting, sad, and beautiful.

"Wolves here?" Connor whispered. "Man, I never—"

"Shh!" He was abruptly cut off by Hunter, whose brow furrowed as he listened hard. Then his eyes widened in shock. Color drained from his face as his mouth opened. "My god, there's no way. It can't be—"

He was drowned out by the sounds of Roo and Rinna, suddenly yipping and howling back with frenzied excitement. Roo quickly shifted to human, jumping up and down like it was Christmas morning.

"Dad, it's Uncle Colt and Uncle Gabe!" he shrieked. Rinna already ran toward the treeline and Roo shifted back and sped off after her, answering the wolf howls with his own.

"Hunter?" Raz elbowed the pale wolf, who still appeared to be in shock. "Who's out there?"

"Their uncles. My brothers," Hunter whispered. "My pack is here."

CRYSTAL ASH

TIGHTROPE

BOOK 5

MELODY

Outwardly I smiled, but my insides twisted upon themselves. I kept glancing toward the trees where Hunter and his pups had run off to.

His pack was here, his family and loved ones from before he got captured, before he ever met me and Connor. I should have been happy, like everyone else was. While Hunter froze in shock at hearing his brothers' howls, Raz lifted him from the chair and booted him toward the woods, much to Connor and Arjun's amusement.

The pups were so happy, yelping and howling as they took off toward the woods. Everyone expressed excitement and happiness at Hunter being united with his family. He deserved it after being separated from them and losing his mate.

So why couldn't I fight this dread settling over me?

Only Arjun seemed to notice something off with me, his blue-green eyes nearly glowing in the fading light.

"Penny for your thoughts?" the cheeky tiger shifter asked me.

He leaned back in his seat lazily, one arm up and resting behind his head, the other draped over his belly. All seven of us, kids included, just polished off a massive pot of curry he made. Our bellies were full, but his was still as taut and flat as ever. Come to think of it, all the guys still had their washboard stomachs, and I was the only one carrying a food baby.

And possibly a real baby.

Shit, don't think about that.

But that also weighed on my mind and might've been partially responsible for this feeling of dread. I needed to tell Connor and soon, but I wasn't about to spill all that to Arjun, even if he was attempting to not be a dick.

"I just wonder if they'll force him to choose," I voiced aloud. "Between them or us. They probably hate humans and he always made it seem like wolf packs are really strict."

And not all families were good. I got a harsh reminder of that when we visited my old home before coming into Georgia. My heart ached for my younger siblings, who had no choice but to put up with my raging alcoholic monster of a mother. I needed to get them out. We had the space now in this amazing house, but it would still be complicated to do legally.

"They can't force him to do anything," Raz said with a soft growl, leveling his steel-gray eyes at me. "He's a strong wolf. Have some faith in him, *steluța*. He'll only do what he feels is best."

"You're right," I told him with a smile. "I know you're right, dragon."

Minutes crawled, and no wolves emerged from the forest. The sun finally set, and the mosquitos came out in full force, so we packed up the dishes and headed back inside. It was still too early to go to bed, but I'd be pacing back and forth in front of the window, waiting for my white wolf to return if I didn't do something.

Arjun, the apparent perceptive one of the night, seemed to sense my need for a distraction.

"Why don't you tell me about your shaman abilities?" he suggested with a light touch to my shoulder. "And we'll see what you can work on."

I looked at him, surprised. He was really on his best behavior tonight. First making curry to make up for jabbing at my upbringing, now this. After Raz and I rescued him from that awful carnival, we kept getting off on the wrong foot. Everyone chalked it up to him being English and me not getting his sense of humor. Maybe I was sensitive, but I couldn't help that it hurt he didn't seem to like me. Not even a thank you for saving his big striped, orange ass.

His accent didn't help, nor his eyes that looked like the bluish-green of a tropical ocean. For that matter, neither did his caramel skin, his inky black hair, or his tall, powerful build similar to Hunter's.

"You're being awfully helpful tonight," I remarked, my voice laced with skepticism.

He shrugged and stepped away from me, his hands raised. "It's just an offer. You're clearly distressed at no longer being attached to your wolf's hip, so thought I'd provide some entertainment until he comes back."

"I am *not* attached to his hip," I retorted, crossing my arms. "He runs off into the woods all the time. I don't care if he's away from me for a while."

"It's a joke," Arjun sighed. "Learn to take one, for fuck's sake."

My shoulders sagged. He was right. I was being tense and uptight for no reason. Just that one time.

"Fine," I said. "Who knows when such an offer will come again?"

"It's a standing offer," he answered. "You're always welcome to come to me with questions." His mouth split into a grin. "Just a matter of whether or not you can tolerate my presence."

"The curry helped but you're on thin ice, buddy." I laughed awkwardly, pushing hair out of my face. Shit, was that really the best I could do?

"I'll behave," he grinned. "Tonight."

"That's all I can ask for. So how do we do this?"

"Let's go somewhere quiet." He nodded toward the far corner of the theater room, sectioned off by a half wall and rows of bookshelves.

"Where are you two going?" Connor lifted an eyebrow as he wheeled past us into the kitchen. I glared at him in reply. So nosy.

"Just stealing your girl out from under your nose, human," Arjun announced joyfully, throwing an arm over my shoulders.

"Not true!" I glared at the infuriatingly handsome tiger shifter, pulling away from under his arm. "Thin ice, remember?"

"Trust me, dove. I'm holding back a lot."

"We're practicing shaman stuff." I grumbled to Connor, making a shooing motion with my hands. "Go, I can't be distracted."

"Mm-hmm," he mused skeptically, as he directed his wheelchair away. Raz grinned at me, leaning against a kitchen counter as Connor approached him.

I tuned out their low voices, chatting as Arjun and I made our way to the reading corner. He sat cross-legged on the floor and gestured for me to follow suit. I stayed well out of touching range, which he didn't object to.

"So why don't you give me a rundown of what you've experienced?" he began, resting his elbows on his knees.

"It started with dreams pretty quickly after I met Hunter and the pups for the first time," I began. "I saw from the perspectives of other shifters. That's how I learned about you. Then I started feeling their animal instincts and abilities. Apparently I could take on their forms and give off their... presence or what have you."

"Like when Connor sensed an animal in bed next to him once," he said knowingly.

"Yes," I blinked, surprised. I didn't know they had been talking to Arjun about this stuff. "Before we rescued you, Raz said my eyes changed color. I grew long teeth and sprouted fur on my face. That was when I was trying to talk to you, the human, but only your tiger was responding to me and I felt... your tiger's instincts."

I didn't want to say I felt his bloodthirst, the desire to kill, and his power to do it. After seeing him kill the ringmaster from his own perspective, it still churned my stomach.

"When did you start communicating with your mind?" he asked, his blue-green gaze curious and focused on me.

"Back in Crying Falls," I replied. "I rode on Raz in dragon form, and just directed a thought to him and he answered. It was crazy."

"Very interesting," he mused, stroking the dark stubble that began to appear on his jaw. "A shaman's abilities are usually separated and very distinct from each other. Yours seem to have them all blended together."

"What do you mean?"

"When my stepfather trained his apprentice, he focused on only

Sight for the first year," he explained. "That's the ability to see through a shifter's eyes. The next year was Sense, being able to feel the instincts and desires of the animal you're focusing on. And it took a whole three years to master Semblance, the ability to throw the illusion that you are an animal as well."

"What about the mind communication? Telepathy, or whatever."

"It's called Speak," Arjun said softly. "Not every shaman has it. In fact, it's incredibly rare."

"Seriously?"

He nodded slowly. "My stepfather's grandmother was the last known shaman to Speak."

"That's... crazy." I rocked back, placing my hands behind me on the floor. "I might not have been able to save you in time if I couldn't talk to you."

"You are correct." He mimicked my posture, leaning back with his hands behind him. "Quite serendipitous, isn't it?"

"Seems that way," I admitted. "Like I was supposed to find you to figure all this shit out."

"The universe has a funny way of unfolding on us," he grinned.

✿ 2 ✿

HUNTER

I ran in the direction of those howls, my heart crashing against my ribs. Even in wolf form, my human emotions bled over. I felt the tension in my stomach, the all too human hope of seeing my brothers again daring to rise.

Colt, Gabe. Can it really be you guys?

I had to prepare to be wrong. The disappointment would be too great if I dared to hope too much.

My paws carried me soundlessly to a boulder, where I paused and let out a warning howl. The pups, who had raced off ahead of me, came back to wait under my rock. Roo whined. Rinna's tail wagged rapidly. They missed their family too and were dying to see them. But they had to stay by me.

I growled a warning at them to emphasize staying near me before I jumped off, loping at a slower pace toward the howls.

With a quick sniff in the air, my pulse went into overdrive. Yes, those were their scents. The scents I picked up temporarily while out in these woods the other day. They had been so faint then, I thought it was an old trail. But now the scent was fresh, bringing back powerful memories of playing together as pups and running proudly with our pack.

I followed the trail carefully, my nose to the ground to pick up any possible scents of danger. Roo and Rinna whined and pawed at me, running in circles and through my legs. They were eager to see their uncles, but I would not take any chances of endangering them again.

We reached the stream where we drank and rested the other day, and across the water, I saw two canine silhouettes that looked remarkably like mine. Their smell was overpowering, the scent of family, warmth, and familiarity. I wanted to run over and hug them, but I stood my ground and let out a warning growl.

Their shapes, dark and shadowy in the fading light, shifted and stretched tall as they took on their human forms.

"Can you believe it, Gabe?" one of them said. "He doesn't even recognize us, but the pups do."

"Uncle Colt!" Rinna squealed. The pups shifted too and practically vibrated with excitement.

God damn it.

I shifted to human myself, already splashing across the stream before I even had fully formed human feet.

"You goddamn sons of bitches," I choked out, clapping my arms around Colt in a rough bear hug before turning to Gabe and doing the same.

"Glad to see you too, bro," Gabe laughed, slapping my back. "Thought I was going nuts when I picked up your scent out here."

"Christ almighty, look at you." Colt grabbed the back of my neck, ruffling my hair with his other hand. As my oldest brother, he often took a fatherly role with me and now was no different.

He examined my face, affectionately slapping my cheek with a wide grin. "You look good, little ghost. I'd even venture to say you look happy."

"A lot has happened," I said, my own grin threatening to split my face. "Jesus, I never thought I'd see you two again!"

"Uncle Colt!" Roo shouted from the ground, practically wrapping himself around Colt's leg like he did with Mel.

"Ah, I've missed you, little man." Colt picked him up and settled him against his side. "Have you been taking care of your dad?"

"Yes, sir!" Roo bobbed his head emphatically. "And Miss Mel, too!"

"Oh really, who's that?" Colt cast a questioning glance at me while Gabe picked up a squirming, giggling Rinna and proceeded to tickle her.

"She's a human," I said quickly, before Roo could blurt out anything else. "And a shaman. She rescued us from the carnival and we've been with her ever since."

"A shaman?" Colt's eyes narrowed.

"Been with her?" Gabe asked at the same time, turning Rinna upside down. "What do you mean?"

"Traveling with her," I said lamely, although with one look I knew they could see through it. "She's a carnival ringmistress. After she freed us, I stuck around and filled in a spot in a carnival for her."

"You *what?*" Colt growled, disdain in his eyes.

"I volunteered. She didn't want me to," I replied, holding his gaze. "But she saved all of us, so I felt like I owed her. She's a good person, amazing even. And I—" my voice choked, and I swallowed. "I didn't have anyone else. I couldn't pick up any of your scents and thought I lost you all for good."

"Sounds like you're in love with her," Gabe observed. "A *human.*"

"A shaman," Colt repeated, folding his arms under Roo's legs. "That certainly makes things interesting."

"You know about them?" I asked.

"Not much." He looked over at Gabe. "We met our first one recently."

Gabe snorted, setting Rinna down on the ground. "And what a fuckin' brat she is."

My eyes shifted between my two brothers. Clearly, they had some disagreements about this subject.

Colt chuckled a bit patronizingly. Gabe was younger than me, and Colt often made sure he knew it.

"I for one think they can be useful," Colt said. "Miriam's saved our asses a few times."

"Our instincts would have done the same," Gabe retorted snappily. "I say let's keep it simple and not trust any humans. Then we'll never run the risk of getting hunted or sold to carnivals! How easy is that?"

"It's not that simple," Colt replied. "You're still a human yourself, runt. A true wolf pack would have left you for dead, but thanks to our humanity, you're still around to be a pain in my ass."

"I'm no runt," Gabe snarled.

"You overcompensate like one," Colt muttered.

"Guys, guys." I stepped between them to interrupt their growling and teeth gnashing. "This is supposed to be a happy reunion, right? It feels like years since I've seen you both."

"The middle child is right," Colt laughed. "Enough talk of shamans for now, let's hunt! Let's bring down a kill and feast like we used to." He looked between Roo and Rinna, bouncing Roo on his side like he used to when my boy was an infant. "What do you guys say? Want to hunt with your dad and your old uncles?"

"Yeah!" the pups cried in unison, already shifting as Colt set Roo down.

My older brother looked at me while the pups yipped excitedly around our ankles.

"We've got a lot to talk about," he said solemnly. "About you, us, and the state of the pack right now, but all that can wait." Colt's jaws elongated, his teeth already snapping with the anticipation of a kill. Before losing his ability to speak, he added, "Right now, let's just celebrate being alive."

MELODY

With my head resting on Connor's brawny chest, and the heat of Razvan's skin pressed against my back, I couldn't feel any more comfortable, safe, and secure.

But sleep wouldn't come. My eyes stayed glued to the moon out the window in the dark sky. I kept the window cracked so I could listen to any howls. The clock read 1:22 am, but I was wide awake. And I knew I'd remain awake until Hunter came back.

I thought about using Speak or Sight to get a sense of what he was doing, just to check that he was okay, but I resisted. I would know if something bad happened to him. He deserved private time with his family.

But we're *his family,* a stubborn voice in my head reminded me.

Raz groaned in his sleep behind me, shifted his position, and wrapped an inked arm tighter around my waist. His cheek brushed against my back like a soft, sweeping kiss.

You have to come back, Hunter, I thought, lacing my fingers with Raz's at my belly. *For both of us.*

He shifted again behind me and rubbed his thumb across my palm.

"Still awake, *steluța?*" he asked groggily.

"Just can't sleep," I whispered. "Don't worry about me. I'll fall asleep, eventually."

"You saying that is automatically going to make me worry about you," he chuckled, gently pulling me away from Connor so he wrapped around me even tighter with my head resting on his bicep. "What's on your mind?"

"I'll give you three guesses."

"Hunter, Roo, Rinna," he murmured, nuzzling at me sleepily.

"Congratulations, you win a prize."

"Heh, I already have my prize." He ran a hand over my hip and down the length of my thigh. "Are you afraid he's going to leave us?"

"I don't know. Maybe subconsciously?" I wondered. "Rationally, I don't think he would. But aside from you guys, every man in my life has left me at some point."

He said nothing for a few moments, just tenderly ran his hands over my skin. Honestly, that was enough. He listened, and he was there.

"I wish I could tell you that won't happen," he whispered. "But I've been proven wrong about people many times. I've had friends who let me down badly. I've had people who barely knew me accept me like one of their own." He squeezed me for a brief moment. "Like you."

"And you're stuck with me," I teased, looking at him over my shoulder. "I'm not letting you go no matter what."

"There's no one else I'd rather be stuck with," he replied. "If it came down to choosing, I want you to know that I would always choose you over Hunter."

I flipped around to face him, my fingers tracing the contours of his neck and jaws in the darkness.

"I'd never make you choose. You know that, right? You're all so amazing to me, I could never choose in a million years. How could I ask you to do what I can't?"

"Just in the event that Hunter forces a decision," he explained. "Or whatever other unforeseen circumstance happens."

My fingers found his lips, and then my mouth did. He kissed me hard as he pulled me tight against him, bringing my leg over his hip.

"Can you stay quiet?" he whispered, his split tongue caressing the side of my neck.

"What—ah..."

His hand secure on my ass, he rolled his hips against me. The motion was slow, almost lazy, but his flesh was hot and growing harder as he pressed against me. I clung to his shoulders, matching his movement as his heat lit me ablaze.

"Don't want to wake up sleeping beauty over there," he chuckled, pressing against my slickening core as his cock grew stiff and thick with every breath.

Behind me, Connor slept like the dead, snoring softly.

"He's going to be pissed he didn't get to join in," I giggled.

"I don't care," Raz whispered with a soft growl. "As hot as it is to share you, I like having you to myself."

With that, he pressed inside me, and I bit my lip to hold in the moan. I lifted my leg higher on his side and he muffled his own moan into the pillow as he surged into me deeper.

"Bite me when you want to scream," he rasped. "I want to feel how good I'm making you feel."

My teeth immediately found the taut skin of his shoulder, the hard muscle moving under my mouth as he thrust into me.

When my first orgasm came, turning me into a hot, shuddering mess from his effortless thrusts, I wondered if I ruined one of his tattoos from biting him so hard. My teeth still clamped down on him, he rolled me over on my back and fucked me with same slow, rolling thrusts.

He moaned so hotly into my neck and the pillow under my head. Seemed I wasn't the only one having a hard time keeping quiet. I could feel how much he was holding back from the tension in his body. He wanted to fuck me until the headboard slammed against the wall and made Connor literally fall out of bed.

But I liked this quietness too. It was naughty and intimate. I loved hearing the variance in his breathing, feeling his restraint, and letting him know my pleasure in ways other than noise. He hummed as my nails dug into his back. My teeth in his shoulder made him curse under his breath and deepen his thrusts. He kissed my neck so deliciously every time my head fell back with a gasp.

I came one more time when his cock turned to iron inside me, right before his own release with a shuddering growl. Then only the sound of our heavy, panting breaths filled the room.

"That was more difficult than I thought it would be," he laughed under his breath as he slid out of me, pulling me against his chest where his heart hammered like a drum.

"Hotter than I thought it would be," I said, curling up against his side.

"Mm, and I have the marks to prove it," he agreed, his fingers drifted over my hair. "Think you'll be relaxed enough to sleep now?"

"Oh, was that your plan all along?" I teased, circling a finger around one of his nipples.

"Maybe." He grabbed my hand. "Stop, that tickles."

"You seduced me with your ulterior motives!" I laughed quietly, reaching for his other nipple with my free hand. He caught that one too, and soon we were wrestling playfully as he tried to keep my hands away. Connor only groaned once and flopped onto his side, facing away from us. I swore that man could sleep through a hurricane.

Unsurprisingly, I stood no chance against Raz, and he had me pinned within a minute. He somehow crossed my arms over my chest, then held them down with his arms as he settled back into cuddling, holding me against him and sighing happily.

"Hey," I whispered, wriggling against my bonds. "Let me turn around. I want to tell you something."

"Hm, I don't know about that," he said with a playful kiss on my neck. "You've got tricks, woman."

"I'm serious, Raz."

He loosened his hold enough to let me spin in his arms to face him again. My hands rested on his chest, where his heart began slowing down to normal. He caressed my hair out of my face as he waited for me to speak.

"What is it?" He tried not to sound concerned, but I knew he was.

"I love you, Raz," I whispered. "I have for a while. I'm sorry I wasn't able to say it earlier."

Underneath my hands, his heartbeat sped up like an animal breaking into a run. In the darkness, I still saw his smile break out, so beautiful and unrestrained.

"And I love you, *steluța*," he returned. "So utterly and completely. Don't be sorry. I don't ever want you to tell me something before you're ready."

Our mouths found each other again, pressing in a warm, sensual dance as we sank into this glow, this love we didn't have to hide anymore. I was so grateful to him for his patience and sweetness that lived beneath his hard, tattooed exterior. Even then, I still loved his roughness and the way he took my body without apology, without treating me like I might break.

He also successfully got my mind off of Hunter, which I appreciated.

My hands drifted in the midst of our kiss, caressing down his chest now that his guard was down.

And his nipples ripe for tickling.

"Ah! You little—!"

He batted my hands away and reached to pin me again. Laughing, I let him grab me and pull me against him. While he muttered curses about my sneakiness, I snuggled in his warmth, utterly content.

Sleep must have taken over me eventually because the next thing I knew, soft light filtered through the window and voices murmured in the kitchen downstairs. Some voices I didn't recognize.

I lifted my head to find Raz gone, but Connor still sleeping. He rested on his stomach, arms under his pillow. His sculpted shoulders and back rose and fell with his breath.

"Hey," I whispered, sliding over to him. "You're getting your first prototypes put on today." I kissed his neck and the top of his back until he stirred and groaned beneath me.

"Mmm. Mornin', babe."

Not a minute passed before the deep breathing resumed.

"You're always so slow to get up," I teased, swatting his perky ass before climbing out of bed to get dressed.

"Hmm?" he rolled onto his back to look at me with one sleepy eye. "Why would I get up when I have this amazing view from bed?"

"Stop." I rolled my eyes but hid my grin as I pulled my shirt over my head. Raz inside me during the night and Connor admiring me first thing in the morning? How did a girl like me get so lucky?

My Marine lifted his head from the pillow and squinted as if he was concentrating.

"Is Hunter back?"

"I don't know," I admitted, my stomach fluttering nervously. "Someone's here, though."

He sat up, pushed back the covers, and stretched. "Hand me my clothes, babe? I'm going down with you."

I grabbed him clean underwear, shorts, and a tee and handed them to him, taking note that he chose to ask me for help. On any other day, he'd get out of bed and walk on his hands to get to his clothing himself. But it was easier to ask me. My stubborn Marine was trying to not be so stubborn, bless him.

We headed for the stairs together. I recognized Hunter's voice immediately upon leaving the bedroom, along with two others I never heard before. His brothers, most likely.

I paused, reaching deep into the shaman side of me to gather more information. I sensed dense gray fur, long slender snouts filled with canine teeth. Silent paws and sensitive black noses. Yep, definitely wolf shifters.

Connor gave my leg an affectionate caress with his hand as he walked himself down the steps. A simple reminder he was there for me, no matter what.

I descended the stairs to find all the shifters in the kitchen, Raz, Arjun, and the pups included. Two men I'd never seen before stood next to Hunter. The older one had his same golden eyes and tall, slender build, but dark wavy hair that reached his shoulders. His hair had a few streaks of grey, like he was in his mid-thirties.

The younger one was shorter, but still not *short* by any means. His height matched Razvan's. I stopped at the bottom of the stairs because he gave me an unmistakably dirty look. His dark auburn hair was straighter, like Hunter's. If it weren't for his scowl pointed in my direction, he would've been handsome, with freckles dotting over pale skin and sharp green eyes.

"Ah, the two-legged specimens arise," Arjun announced. "Mornin' to you both."

"You're hilarious, RJ." Connor settled into his wheelchair and breezed into the kitchen, ignoring the two strangers and heading straight for the pot of coffee. He would be an insufferable grump until he got a couple of cups in him and didn't care who knew it.

"I didn't mean anything by it, mate," Arjun giggled. "Not my best though."

"Connor, Mel." Hunter cleared his throat awkwardly. "This is Colt," he gestured to the older man next to him, "and Gabe. My brothers."

"Nice to meet you both." I offered a smile despite Gabe's frown and Colt staring at Connor's legs like he was growing aliens from his stumps. Nothing better than killing with kindness, right?

Gabe merely grunted at me before turning away to play with the kids on the floor.

"Hey, man." Connor whipped around from the counter. "I'm only saying this once. I get that y'all aren't the biggest fans of humans, but you're in *my* house and Mel's the shaman who saved your brother's ass. The least you can do is be respectful. If you're not, I'm kicking y'all out."

An uncomfortable silence hung heavily over the kitchen. Even the kids stopped playing and froze. Raz and Arjun tried to hide their smiles behind their hands.

Finally, Colt let out a soft laugh as he thumped Hunter on the chest. "The human with no feet has the bite of an alpha. I like it."

"I'm waiting, dude." Connor ignored the compliment and remained staring pointedly at Gabe, whose eyes shifted toward Colt as if waiting for instruction.

"My apologies," Gabe said, returning his gaze to me. "It's nice to meet you, too."

"It's alright." My smile didn't waver. If there was one thing I was good at, it was smiling through awkward situations.

"We hunted last night," Hunter announced. "We brought down an excellent buck and have been skinning and preparing it all morning. The first cuts are in the smoker outside and they'll be ready soon."

"We helped!" Roo added proudly. "We hunted like a real wolf pack again!"

"We sure did, buddy. We got him like this!" Gabe picked him up and growled menacingly as he tickled and kissed his nephew, while the pup squealed with laughter.

Colt struck up a conversation with Connor while Gabe proceeded to tickle attack Rinna as well. With his brothers occupied, Hunter made a beeline straight toward me.

"Sorry about Gabe," he muttered, lowering his forehead to mine. "My brothers have run into another shaman who's helped them, but he's still resistant to having any involvement with humans."

"It's okay." My heart fluttered at the closeness of him, his strong, lean body towering over me. It felt like so long since I felt him and only him this close, it took a moment to register what he said. "Wait, another shaman?"

"Yeah, I could hardly believe it myself." He slid his arms around my waist. "Her name is Miriam."

"I'd like to meet her if possible."

"I'll ask Colt," he smiled. "He seems fond of her."

My fingers trailed up his arms, tracing the long, slender muscles. "I missed you last night. I wish you told me you were going to be gone the entire night."

His handsome face fell. "I'm sorry, I didn't plan on it. I didn't believe it was really them until I saw them with my own eyes. We hunted to celebrate coming back together."

"I understand." I smiled up at him. "I just didn't know when I'd see you again."

My wolf pulled me tight against him with a soft growl, the sides of my shirt clenched in his fists.

"I'll always come back to you," he whispered, his eyes burning into mine. "Always."

"It's not just me you have to come back to, you know." My eyes shifted over to Razvan, who talked quietly with Arjun.

He took my chin in his hand to return my gaze back to him. Those golden eyes looked at me with all the sharp brightness of two suns.

"No one replaces you for me," he insisted. "Not even him."

❧ 4 ❧

CONNOR

I wasn't sure how to feel about these new wolves. Part of me wanted to give them the benefit of the doubt because they were Hunter's brothers. Not to mention his kids just adored and idolized their uncles.

But the younger one just pissed me the hell off. Mel made an effort to be nice, and he was just a rude piece of shit. They wouldn't have a fancy-ass smoker for the deer they killed if it wasn't for her getting me to come here.

I guzzled down my coffee in the now too-crowded kitchen, then wheeled toward the front door, eager for some fucking peace and fresh air.

"Let's go, babe." I pulled the door open and propped it against my chair, waiting for her to finish up with Hunter.

He gave her a long, lingering kiss and whispered something, to which she smiled and gave a small nod before coming to join me. As he turned to watch her go, I looked at him and made sure he saw me. His smile faded, and he returned my serious expression. The pale wolf was a perceptive guy. He'd get the message.

Satisfied for the moment, I left with Mel to walk the path leading to the main building of the FDR Center for Disabled Veterans.

"What was that about?" she asked once we were a few yards from the house. "You joining the wolf pack in some staring contest for alpha or something?"

"Nah," I answered. "Just reminding our wolf boy what's important."

"And what's that?"

"His brothers are guests in our house. *My* house, which I only have thanks to you. Which Hunter and his kids live in comfortably, thanks to you. They have one chance to shit on our hospitality, and Gabe already blew it. One more act of disrespect to you or any of us and they're fucking gone. I don't even care if it makes the kids cry. And Hunter needs to know not to tolerate that shit. If he makes excuses for them treating you like shit, I'll kick him out too."

"Damn," she breathed as if in disbelief, but smiled down at me warmly. "I don't often see your Marine side come out anymore, but I guess he's still in there."

"My only mission now is eliminating threats to your happiness." I released one wheel to grab her hand as she walked alongside me. "Plus, I only had one cup of coffee so I'm still fuckin' grumpy."

"I knew that had something to do with it," she laughed, threading her fingers through mine. "And I love that my grumpy Marine still defends my honor so valiantly."

"You are never the cause of my grumpiness, babe." I brought her palm to my lips and kissed it. "It's every other limp-dicked piece of shit out there."

"Oh my god, Connor," she groaned, slapping her other hand to her forehead but couldn't prevent the smile from escaping. Nor the shake of her shoulders as she tried to hold in her giggle.

I chuckled, pleased with myself as our scenic walk neared its end and the stark white building loomed up in front of us. Little did she know that I said that ridiculous shit for her reactions. She rolled her eyes, groaned, and *Oh, Connor*'d me, but I knew she secretly found it hilarious.

We said good morning to the physical therapy staff as we entered the building. At this point, we'd gotten to know most of them pretty well. The male therapists' eyes lingered a little too long on Mel and they greeted her enthusiastically, while greeting me cordially at best.

I almost gave them a piece of my mind the first time—she was *not* a piece of meat and not up for sharing outside of who she chose, but it wasn't necessary. She always responded politely, while holding my hand like now or her arm around my shoulder. Last time, she even sat down on my lap as I wheeled us to my therapy session.

It filled me with pride that I didn't need to get all territorial and claim her. She claimed me all on her own.

This time, Dr. Selow himself waited for us in our usual spot.

"Connor! How are you this morning?" He clapped me on the shoulder with a broad grin, looking more excited than I was. "Ready to try on some legs?"

"Man, I've been waiting to hear those words all week," I told him.

It was true, but a nugget of fear nestled in the back of my brain. It had been ages since I used what little leg muscles I had. Would I even have the strength to walk upright on my own?

"Right on, man! I'll be right back. I wanted to do the honors myself."

He left the room, and I lifted myself out of the chair to the bench against the wall. It was higher off the ground and would allow enough room to adjust the legs on me if necessary.

I gripped the edge of the bench, swinging my stumps back and forth like an anxious kid at the doctor's office. My nerve pain that put me in the hospital had been completely nonexistent for several days. Aside from not being able to walk, I felt right as rain.

I was nervous about the pain coming back from the pressure of the prosthetics, but Dr. Selow assured me after multiple tests that it wouldn't. And anyway, I knew not to push myself again like last time. I scared the hell out of my girl, pushed her away, and almost succeeded in losing her. I wouldn't make that same mistake again.

Mel came up next to me, leaning against the bench, and placed a small kiss on my shoulder.

"What're you thinking about?"

"Honestly?" I replied, nuzzling my forehead against hers. "Fucking you in a standing position."

"Connor..."

Dr. Selow returned with another man in a white lab coat, each of them carrying something wrapped in gray cloth, and Mel jumped away from me as if we got caught. I smiled inwardly. *Babe, we haven't even gotten started yet.*

"Connor, Mel, this is Dr. Lawson, the prosthetist who designed these prototypes for you. He's going to see how they fit and take note of any discomfort you have to make adjustments on future designs. Sound good?"

"Great." I drummed on my thighs, more out of anxiety than anything else. "Let's do it."

Dr. Selow smirked and paused before lifting the cover off of the prosthetic he held. Dr. Lawson followed his lead like they were unveiling priceless antiques at an auction or some shit.

But the pieces they held made my jaw drop. Even Mel let out a soft gasp. Smooth and sleek carbon steel laid across their palms. I knew they were using the latest technology, but those things looked straight up from the future, like robot legs. In short, fucking sweet.

"Nice and light, for less stress on your hip and knee joints." Dr. Lawson gently tossed his leg, my right leg, up in the air a few inches and caught it again. "I also equalized the weight between them so even though they're different lengths, one won't feel heavier than the other."

"There are sensors here too that'll detect when certain muscles flex," Dr. Selow pointed inside where my thigh would fit, "which will make the toes and ankle portions flex and move as if it were a real foot. Your balance will feel a lot more natural this way."

"I'll be damned," I laughed lightly, unable to take my eyes off the sleek, beautiful limbs. "You got my hopes up so high now, I'm almost scared to put 'em on."

"Remember, these are just prototypes," Dr. Lawson reminded me. "They may not work perfectly right out of the box, but we'll tweak and adjust whatever we need to."

"Put 'em on, babe." Mel squeezed my arm excitedly, shooting me a smile that made my heart flip-flop in my chest. My woman, my love. The one who never stopped believing in me. I couldn't be happier that she was at my side for this.

"Alright, Docs," I waved my arm, gesturing them forward. "Let's see how they fit."

Only ten minutes later, after a bit of adjusting and securing, I looked down at my robotic feet. With Mel's hand still on my bicep, I pushed off the bench and stood up.

I turned around in a small circle and looked at her.

"Hey," she grinned up at me, standing on tiptoes. "You're taller than before."

"The longer limbs assist with better range of motion," Dr. Lawson explained.

"Walk around a bit, Connor," Dr. Selow suggested, beaming.

I held my arms out at my side as I took more steps around the room. My balance was already excellent from my stilt-walking, but I'd still have to get used to these. I felt almost too teetering, like on the verge of losing my balance but not quite. Mainly, I was distracted by all the sensations. I could feel the ground beneath my feet, only I felt it in my thigh muscles. It didn't entirely make sense to me, but then again, I wasn't a fucking prosthetic limb engineer.

"Try balancing on one foot, then roll your ankle around on the other foot," Dr. Selow suggested.

I did as he said, realizing that I could sense how much weight I was putting into one leg. My foot rotated around as if it was actually connected to my body.

"How is it doing that?" I said in an awed whisper.

"Your brain is still connected to the leg muscle you have here," Dr. Selow pointed to my quad. "The prosthetic legs' sensors are so sensitive, they identify the muscle fibers you use for certain movements and when they're activated, the computer chip inside then tells the leg to do that motion, as fast as if it were coming from your brain."

"Amazing," Mel whispered. "It's like magic."

"Almost," Dr. Lawson chuckled. "It's science."

I walked a few more laps around the room, practicing squats, kicks, and other motions the doctors suggested.

"Any pain, Connor?" Dr. Selow asked. "Or discomfort?"

"None at all," I said, bouncing on the balls of my new feet. "Balance was a little off at first, but I'm getting the hang of it now. Feels great, actually."

"Excellent," Dr. Lawson grinned. "You're welcome to take this set home today and see how it feels after a few hours of wear. You still don't want to overdo it. Use the chair as your primary means of moving and gradually work up to these over time."

"Sure," I said dismissively, doing a few high-knee jumps. *I wonder if I can do a back flip in these...*

"Connor," Mel said in that adorable stern voice with an equally adorable stern look.

"I know, babe." I leaned over to plant a kiss on those pouty lips. "I'll listen to the doctors. God knows you'll give me hell if I don't."

"Smart woman," Dr. Selow chuckled. "Alright, you're welcome to exercise here or head home to try them out. Call us if anything's off with them."

"Thank you, doctors," Mel and I said together as they left the room.

"What's that naughty look for?" she demanded as soon as we were alone.

"What?" My smirk widened into a grin. "I just want to try something."

"Connor, what—"

I stuck one leg out and vaulted it over my head, the other one following. The world spun in a quick circle, and then my feet touched down less than a second later. A thrill I hadn't felt in ages surged within me.

"Backflips already?" Mel crossed her arms, but her eyes shone with pride.

"I landed it, didn't I?" I crossed the room to her and pulled those sexy hips against mine. She let out a little gasp, which I silenced with a kiss.

Damn, it felt so fucking good to kiss her like this. Her body flush against mine, standing on tiptoes to reach my mouth. I knew she didn't care about me having legs or not, but I felt like a man again holding her like this. Finally, I could dominate my woman again in the way I craved.

She let out a soft moan as my tongue pried her lips apart, her soft body molding to my hard torso as I pressed her against the wall. I broke the kiss only to lower myself and grab under her thighs, lifting her legs off the ground to wrap around my waist.

"Connor," she said in a breathy whisper, her face flushed. "Here?"

"I told you I wanted to conduct these very important tests as soon as I got legs," I reminded her, my mouth between her neck and shoulder. "The fucking you against a wall test."

"Con, anyone can walk by and see." She glanced nervously at the floor-to-ceiling window covering nearly the entire wall. The hallway on the other side was mostly empty since it was still early in the morning, but there would be the occasional client, doctor, or physical therapist milling about.

"Let them see," I rasped against her neck before sucking the tender skin there. "Or let's make it fast."

"Con..." she moaned a weak protest as I sucked on her earlobe, my hand kneading her soft breast as my hips rolled against her.

"Tell me something," I whispered, kissing the column of her throat. "Was I dreaming or did you fuck someone in bed next to me last night?"

Her red face and shocked expression told me everything.

"Razvan," she admitted.

"That sneaky. Fucking. Dragon." I punctuated each word with a thrust of my rock solid shaft against her clit. "Thinking. He can hoard. My pussy. Right. Next to me?"

"Wait." Her eyes widened. "Are you really mad about that?"

"No." I kissed her lips to reassure her. "But I'm going to fuck you so hard, he won't get a chance to do that shit again tonight."

"Connor." Her eyelids fluttered, and I knew she was torn between giving in to her pleasure and keeping the rational side of her brain. "I need to tell you something else."

"I'm listening, baby." I kissed her neck some more to tease her, but stopped my thrusts. She hesitated, and I pulled away to look at her, realizing this was serious. "What is it, Mel?"

"Um," she chewed her lip nervously. "Remember the last time we had sex? When Hunter and Raz first got together?"

"Yeah. What about it?"

BZZZZT!

Of course, my phone chose that moment to go off. I pulled it out of my pocket to silence the call, but Mel grabbed for it.

"Wait! It might be my sister."

"Shit. Sorry, babe." I handed it to her, and she answered, hitting the speaker button as well.

"Hello?"

"Hello, may I speak to Melody, please," a crisp woman's voice came from the phone.

"Melody speaking." She glanced up at me nervously.

"This is Angela Dyer from the investor's board at the Vaudeville Theater Company. I'm calling in regard to your audition yesterday."

MELODY

I stared at the phone, unable to talk due to my throat feeling closed up. *Shit!* In the midst of everything since last night, I had completely forgotten about my audition. I certainly didn't expect them to call back so soon.

"Are you still there?" Angela asked. From her sharp, no-nonsense tone, I could only gather she was the woman in glasses who seemed wholly unimpressed by my and Raz's audition.

"Oh, yes! Sorry, I'm here," I answered.

"Is this a good time?" Her crisp voice was jarring over the phone speaker.

"Yes! I'm sorry. I just uh, didn't expect to hear back so quickly." I settled on the bench while Connor remained standing. "What can I do for you?"

"After reviewing your audition with the other investors, we decided to go with a different act for our local theater," she informed me robotically. Yup, she was definitely Uptight Glasses Lady.

"I see..." My heart sank. Of course, it was a rejection call. Raz and I performed our hearts out, and she didn't even smile at our audition.

I really wanted that gig. Even though we had it good now with a house and plenty of land, Connor might not need the services of the

FDR Center forever. We needed to plan toward the future, and I needed every dollar I could scrape together to get Jeanie and my younger siblings out of that trailer. They deserved so much more than struggling to adulthood like I did.

"Well, thank you for the call," I said, now eager to get off the phone.

"However, I do have another offer if you're interested," Angela continued.

Connor, who had been pacing around the room on his new legs, suddenly stopped and turned to look at me, his eyes wide and bright.

"Oh. Uh, yes?"

"A brand new Vaudeville Theater location will be having its grand opening next week. The performers we initially booked have broken their contract to chase another opportunity." Her monotone voice was laced with irritation. "If you are able to make it to the opening, we'll simply fill you in for the existing contract. Frankly, we don't have time to draft a whole new one for you."

"Oh! Uh, okay." I ran a hand through my hair, feeling drastically out of my element. "Where is the location?"

"Miami, Florida."

Connor cleared his throat and leaned in close to the speaker. "Good morning, ma'am. My name's Connor Shaw and I'm Melody's booking agent. Would you be so kind as to outline the terms of the contract?"

"Certainly," she quipped. "We'll pay a flat fee of thirty-thousand dollars for opening night to be divided among the performers at their discretion. Additionally, we'll also pay ten percent of ticket sales for the event."

My hand slapped over my mouth to prevent anything stupid from coming out while Connor and I exchanged wide-eyed stares. That couldn't be right. Thirty-thousand dollars?! I never imagined I'd see that much money in my lifetime, let alone on a single night.

"I see," Connor replied, keeping his voice calm. "So this is a one-night only event, correct?"

"Yes, although depending on the success of the show, we may offer more long-term contracts in the future."

"I see," Connor repeated. "We'll definitely take this into consideration. By when do you need our answer?"

"As soon as possible," Angela said. "If I don't hear from you by the end of the day tomorrow, I'll have to pass the offer onto someone else. We *need* performers for this show as this has been a highly anticipated event and we're nearly sold out of seats."

"We'll have an answer for you before then," Connor lifted his eyes to me. "May I have a copy of the contract so we can look it over in greater detail?"

"Certainly. I'll email it to you."

Connor gave her his email address and then we both said goodbye as I ended the call. We both leaned back and just stared at each other while the information sank in.

"That's a lot of money." I broke the silence first.

"A *shit ton* of money," he agreed, rubbing his jaw. "This must be one fancy-ass theater."

"The one Raz and I went to was super-fancy," I said, remembering the massive chandelier, plush seats, balconies and private boxes, and that huge stage we auditioned on. "What do you think I should do?"

"Take it," he said with no hesitation. "I'm no lawyer, but I'll look over the contract for anything crazy. But damn, thirty grand for one night? There is not much I would say no to for that amount of money."

"Same," I agreed. "But all the way in Florida?"

"Where I went to college," he grinned. "And in Miami, at the very fucking tip of Florida. It'll be a drive, but we can do it, babe. Especially for 30K."

"We?" I lifted my eyebrows. "So you're coming with me if I say yes?"

"Hell yes, I am." He slid his arms around my waist, nudging my legs apart to stand between them. "Anywhere you go, I go."

"Babe, you haven't been on stilts in weeks," I warned. "You still have to get these legs adjusted."

"I'll practice. They already feel tons better than my old ones, so they shouldn't be a problem." He dropped a kiss to my forehead. "Raz will go with you, too. Arjun probably won't, but whatever. He can house-sit. As for Hunter, jury's still out on that one, but even with just us three, it'll be a hell of a show. "

I stared up at him. "Do you really think we can pull it off? Do you think we're worth that much money?"

"Baby," he cupped my face, his forehead on mine, "just you alone are worth so much more than that. You're priceless."

"To you, maybe." I wrapped my hands around his forearms, my eyes lost in his. "But to thousands of strangers who've never seen me before? When my only worth to them is my entertainment value?"

"We could ask any random person who's seen you on stage before," he said, "and I'm positive they would say the same thing. You have an impact on people, and not just those of us lucky enough to have your love."

"I don't understand it," I said with a slight shake of my head. "I definitely don't see it like you do. I feel like a different person onstage. Is it because of my shaman powers or is that really *me?*"

"They're one and the same," he insisted, directing my gaze back to him.

"I wouldn't have that kind of presence if it weren't for—"

"I don't believe that for a second," he cut me off. "I don't know anything about all this magic shit, but what I do know is you're such an incredible person. Personally, I don't think it matters one bit whether some guy gave you a gift or not. You've always had a gift."

He pulled his face away to look at me. "You became a mother figure when you were just a child yourself. You stepped up and protected your siblings like a shield, even if it damaged you. And the moment you could save yourself from hell, you did."

"I feel like I gave up on them by leaving," I admitted.

"You didn't." His hands lowered to my shoulders, where he gave an affectionate squeeze. "To give up would've been to stay, to keep perpetuating that cycle. Do you realize how brave it is to break away from that? Do you have any idea how strong a person has to be? Your environment could have broken you, but it made you this strong, resilient, amazing woman instead."

I didn't know how to respond. Even after spending all this time with him and the other guys who showered me with love and adoration, I didn't feel like anything special. Maybe my brainwashing of being told I was worthless growing up still had a hold on me, but it was hard seeing his words as truth.

"What I'm trying to say is," Connor said, wrapping his arms around me and pulling me into his chest. "You can absolutely do this. You're ready, you're worth it, and you've been through hell and back. You can do any fucking thing you want."

MELODY

On the way home, Connor walked beside me with his new, long strides. He almost got away with leaving the wheelchair at the FDR center until I insisted on bringing it with us. The doctors' orders were to not overuse the new prototypes, so I'd make damn sure he didn't.

"Hey babe," he shot a naughty grin at me as the house came into view. "Get in the chair and I'll push you the rest of the way."

"No way!" I shot back. "You'll go super fast like a maniac."

"What happened to the girl who loved scary rides?" he teased, swatting my ass as he pushed the empty chair in front of him with the other hand.

"Even the scariest rides have safety features," I replied. "But nothing will stop me from falling out of that thing and getting trampled on if you come to a sudden stop."

"I won't do anything that would hurt you," he said, his voice tinged with offense. "Promise. I won't even go that fast. I just want to see how well these legs can bear weight and resistance."

"Fine," I sighed, taking a seat in the chair, gripping the armrests and setting my feet up on the footrests.

Connor moved behind me, and I felt him grip the handles on the back of my chair. "Ready?"

"Not real-*aaahhh!*"

The damned liar took off like a fucking sports car. I heard his feet crunch on the gravel path like he was sprinting for a gold medal. The whole chair rattled as the world rushed by, as did my teeth, while I held onto the armrests for dear life.

"C-c-c-c-Conner! S-s-s-stop!"

"You'll fall out if I stop!" he laughed behind me.

Just as the house came rushing up to us and I was afraid I'd crash right into that beautiful wraparound porch, he gradually slowed until we came to a walk, and then a complete stop in front of the first step.

"Don't look at me like that," he said in response to my expression upon getting out of the chair and turning around to glare. "That was fun. Admit it."

"It would be more fun if I wasn't close to dying."

"But you still had fun."

I had a terrible poker face and couldn't keep it up. My glare cracked and the damn treacherous smile shined through. Yes, that scared me to death, but it was a thrill and a half that I hadn't felt in a long time.

"See! I knew it." He leaned across the chair to kiss me, then lifted each of his knees to examine his prosthetic feet. "These things really are crazy, though. They grip and push off the ground like real feet. Most of the power came from my quads but these puppies did an awesome job of assisting."

"Remember why we brought this thing in the first place," I said with a hand on the chair. "I know you want to push to the limit but no overdoing it, seriously. You should probably take those off soon for a break."

"Yes, ma'am." He leaned down for another kiss, this time pulling me around the chair and crushing me to his chest. Damn, I missed him doing that.

"Hey," he said when our lips parted. "What did you want to tell me? Before the phone call?"

Shit.

"Oh, yeah. Um..." I'd been working myself up to telling him all morning, finally found my inner lady-balls and just about did it when that phone call fucked up everything. Now this job was the only thing on my mind and I didn't have the mental focus to deal with that and a possible pregnancy scare. Shit, shit, shit.

"It's not important right now," I forced a smile. "We'll talk about that later."

He lifted a skeptical eyebrow. "You sure?"

"Positive." I swatted his ass, enjoying that it'd be up for grabs and not parked in a chair all the time now. "Let's tell everyone the news."

"Maybe not everyone," he muttered, following me inside. "Just the ones who need to know."

We had nothing to worry about in that regard. The house was silent and empty, the complete opposite of the crowd we had this morning.

"Where the hell is everyone?" I wondered, wandering from room to room.

"I see Raz and RJ," Connor pointed out the sliding glass door to the back deck, where the dragon and tiger shifter hung out in the backyard.

"No Hunter?" I asked, jogging to catch up. It didn't matter if he had feet or wheels, my Marine was always speeding ahead.

"No wolves in sight, babe."

Raz and Arjun talked quietly near a tree, the same one he taught me to throw knives at and fucked me against like an animal. I grinned at the memory. Raz seemed to have the same idea, smirking and shooting me a wink as we approached.

"Nice legs, mate." Arjun gave Connor an appreciative nod as we joined them. "I'm sorry. There's no way to say that without sounding homosexual. Believe me, I've been trying to think of something since you came outside."

"Thanks, RJ! Pretty sexy, aren't they?" Connor spun in a circle, then did a goofy catwalk strut, much to the guys' amusement.

"Goofball." I rolled my eyes and nestled into Raz's side, where he slid an arm around me and kissed my temple. "I have news," I said, lifting my eyes to his. "The Vaudeville called me back."

"Oh?" His eyebrows lifted. "What did they say?"

"We didn't get picked for the local show, but they want us to do a grand opening show for a different location," I paused, "in Florida."

"Fuck Florida," he spat. "That was where I first landed in the US. I'll be happy to never set foot in America's swampy asshole again."

"Wait 'til you hear about the money, Raz," Connor chuckled.

"Thirty-thousand dollars," I said. "Plus ten percent of ticket sales. For *one* night."

His mouth fell open, then promptly shut again. "Guess I should've held my tongue," he said sheepishly.

"You don't have to come with me if you hate it so much," I said earnestly. "I don't want you to—"

"*Steluţa*, are you kidding?" His arm tightened around me. "If you're jumping on this, of course I'm coming with you."

"But you just said—"

"It's America's swampy asshole, I know," he chuckled. "But that's *a lot* of money. You can get all your siblings out of that hellhole for that much, easily." He cupped my face, staring inquisitively down at me. "You *are* going to accept this offer, right?"

"I don't know," I admitted. "It's... a lot to think about. Yes, the money's tempting, but it's *next week*. Can we put together a show worth thirty-grand in that time? And we'll be leaving the FDR center so soon after settling in."

"You know, for such a powerful shaman, you do lack a lot of self-confidence." The observation came from Arjun, who returned my narrow-eyed glare with a passive stare.

"This doesn't concern you, but thanks for your input," I snapped. "It's not like I don't have enough on my plate already."

"Arj, now's not the time," Raz added. "She's got a lot to think about."

"The hell do you mean, this doesn't concern me?" Arjun kept his gaze focused on me, ignoring Razvan. "You brought me into the Brady Bunch here, Mel. What, you don't want my input because we haven't fucked?"

"It's got nothing to do with that," I hurled back at him. "You've made it clear you don't approve and want no part in any ongoing carnival business, so why should I listen to your opinion?"

Arjun rolled his gaze skyward, chewing his lip and crossing his arms as he let out a long sigh. I fought to ignore how hot and flustered just looking at him made me feel. God, I hated how much his words got under my skin.

"Look, if you're so concerned about putting on a show that's worth the dollar amount attached to your contract, I'd be willing to go, too. Not that you need me to increase the perceived value."

He could have slapped me across the face and it wouldn't have shocked me as much. I just stared, dumbfounded. Connor and Raz said nothing, so I only imagined they were as dumbstruck as me.

"You can't be serious," I breathed. "You can't mean—"

"Look, I hate fire, alright? But what I hate more is being fucking caged for days on end and starving on old roadkill." He nodded at Raz. "Lizard boy here knows how to keep his flames cool enough to not burn me, as long as I'm careful. And seeing how all these wankers adore you, I can only assume you don't treat them like, well, circus animals."

"Why?" I asked with a slow shake of my head. "Why would you put yourself in that environment again?"

He shrugged. "Why did Hunter?"

"Because I rescued him. And his kids."

He inclined his head toward me. "There you have it."

"Arjun," I breathed, my thoughts whirling too fast in my brain for me to catch up. "You don't have to—"

"I know, Mel," he sighed, as if exasperated. "You made that clear. I have a choice. I don't have to help you. I also know I'm a cheeky bastard and it's hard for me to properly express myself. So let me just do this, please."

A silent pause passed between us like we were the only two people present. His eyes glowed with an unnatural beauty against the dull, muted colors of the forest.

"Okay," I said finally. "Thank you, Arjun."

"I quite like Florida, actually," he quipped lightheartedly, shooting a grin at Raz. "Reminds me of some of the forests in India where my mum's from. Much warmer and less dreary than London."

"You'd hate Romania, then," Raz muttered. "Damn, I'd fucking love to feel cold mountain air again."

"Well, look at you, babe." Connor beamed at me with pride. "We just might put on a million-dollar show yet."

"Let's aim for the modest goal of thirty-grand first," I scoffed before looking back up at Raz. "Hey, where is Hunter?"

"Who knows," he said with the undertone of an annoyed growl. "The whole pack took off again soon after you two left. They're out here somewhere, doing whatever wolves do."

I leaned my head on his shoulder and he kissed my forehead sympathetically. Disappointment washed over me as I looked through the dense trees, not a wolf in sight. What he told me this morning already felt like empty words. Maybe it was an overreaction, but it already felt like he was choosing his wolf family over us. Over me.

They were his original family. Before he ever met you, they would always come first, I reminded myself.

Still, it didn't shake the feeling that I was slowly losing Hunter. And what if, after this grand opening in Florida, they wanted us to stay and do more shows? What if we never came back here?

One thing at a time, Mel.

The four of us slowly walked back to the house. Connor brought up the contract from Angela on a computer and looked over it with a fine-toothed comb. When he felt confident there were no loopholes or pitfalls, I called Angela back and confirmed we would accept the job.

"Great!" she chirped over the speaker, the most emotion I heard from her yet. "We'll start advertising the new lineup right away. Will you need accommodations?"

"Um, yes?" Less than a week in this house and I already felt spoiled by having a wonderfully spacious master bedroom. I didn't want to go back to sleeping in the RV, even if it was just for one night.

"We'll set you up in the hotel down the street. How many rooms?"

"Um. Two, please. How much will that be?"

"It's on us, Melody. Remember, we're investing in you."

That last sentence caused a jolt of panic to surge through me. If a thirty-grand paycheck wasn't enough pressure, the expectation of being an investment sure was.

"Oh, right! Thank you," I replied, not wanting to give off the impression that this treatment was completely alien to me.

We finished the call and the four of us began brainstorming a show and choreography around the kitchen table. Connor ordered pizzas, and we practiced into the afternoon and evening. As each hour passed with no sign of Hunter and the pups, the feelings of disappointment and being let down ate away at me.

I tried to throw myself into the routines, imagining myself onstage before a massive ballroom full of people. I imagined their energy, their screams, cries, gasps, and thunderous applause as I led my men through their acts. The stage, as volatile and terrifying as it was, was my second home. I craved it again, the chance to tell stories and exhibit the talents of my acts without exploiting them.

But my vision didn't feel complete without Hunter.

It wasn't like I needed him as a half-shifted Wolf Man for a good show, I just missed him being here. I wanted his support, to see his sexy smile again. I wanted to see him and Raz being cute together, either with me in the middle or not. Like me, my dragon periodically looked to woods, letting out a small displeased sigh when no wolves emerged.

We called it a night long after the sun had set and only Razvan's fire illuminated the darkness. Stumbling upstairs on tired, shaky limbs, we said goodnight to Arjun, who muttered something about sleeping for fifteen hours and I didn't think he was joking.

Connor, Razvan and I showered together in the massive walk-in shower in the master bathroom. While they enjoyed soaping me up and I returned the favor to them, we were all too tired for anything especially naughty.

It was just before midnight when we settled into the king-sized bed, the entire house still and quiet.

"Damn wolf's gonna get an earful from me when he gets back," Connor muttered, his voice vibrating against my cheek on his chest.

Raz muttered an agreement as he snuggled against my backside.

I only hoped Hunter's return would be a matter of *when* and not *if*.

❦ 7 ❦

MELODY

I couldn't place exactly what woke me up. The bedroom was pitch black, and both Raz and Connor's chests fell and rose with deep, even breaths.

Then a sound.

It was so faint, I couldn't even discern what it was. But it came from downstairs.

Now wide awake, I slid out of bed, careful not to disturb my sleeping men as I pulled on a tank top and pajama pants.

A light was on in the kitchen as I crept down the stairs. Soft, rustling noises and the clink of silverware floated up to me. I rubbed my eyes and blinked to force my eyes to adjust.

"Hunter?"

He looked up at me, gorgeous as ever. His hair was disheveled like he hadn't brushed it in a day or so. Those golden eyes looked wild, more feral and animalistic than I'd ever seen before.

"Hey little fox," he greeted me in a hushed voice. "What are you doing up?"

"Where have you been all day?" I ignored his question as I approached him, my body physically aching for his touch.

601

"I'm sorry," his face fell. "We went with Colt and Gabe to visit their shaman. I didn't expect it to go on all day."

"Why?" I folded my arms in front of my chest, suddenly feeling the most insecure I ever felt since dating multiple men. "What did you do? You have a shaman right here."

"Mel, it wasn't like that." He closed the distance between us, his hands on my bare arms. "I went to learn more about you. Maybe I could find out something that would help you decipher between your powers."

"Arjun's already started on that," I answered tersely. "I have Sight, Sense, Semblance, and Speak."

"I see." His mouth ticked up, my attitude having no effect on him. "Miriam doesn't have Speak. She's nowhere near as gifted as you."

"Hunter, I missed you." My arms flopped down to my sides, my voice taking on a whiny tone, but I didn't care. "So much happened today, and I didn't get to share any of it with you."

"I'm sorry, little fox." He cupped my chin, pressing a kiss to my mouth that I couldn't help but return, despite not wanting to. His kiss was like precious water I'd been thirsting for. "I really am. I'm not trying to neglect you. We're just trying to make up for lost time. The pups are ecstatic to spend time with their uncles again and I don't want them to miss out on that bonding."

"Even though one of them hates humans," I remarked.

Hunter let out a tight-lipped sigh and I could see the conflict in his face.

"Gabe is harboring a lot of pain, a lot of resentment, but he's coming around. I can tell he likes Miriam more than he'll admit. He's a proud, stubborn wolf."

Before I could reply, he scooped me up in his arms and carried me toward the theater room, where he settled us down on the loveseat.

"Now tell me everything that happened today," he said, his lips ghosting across my forehead. "I missed you too, little fox. So much."

I began, reluctantly at first, talking about Connor's new prosthetic legs and how much better they were than the old ones. He didn't have stilts in this house, but still did some impressive acrobatics while we practiced. When I got to the phone call and the money we'd earn, I almost forgot about being annoyed with him.

"Mel, that's amazing!" He kissed me hard, golden eyes beaming. "I knew you and Raz could pull it off."

"Hunter," I voiced his name softly. "Will you come with us?"

His face fell again, and I quickly rambled before he could answer.

"Not to perform. I'd just love for you to be there. Connor and Raz, and now Arjun, I guess, are such a storm. You're the calm in that storm. I need you to keep me sane while those three drive me crazy." My hand trailed from his shoulder down the center of his chest. "I miss you, Hunter. I miss... just being with you."

"I miss you too. I swear to God, Mel, I was thinking about you all day today. I hate being away from you for so long." He hesitated and my heart dropped into my stomach.

"But?" I prompted.

"But I should probably stay here," he finished. "I'll be thinking about the kids constantly. I'd rather not drag them along. They want to spend all their time with their uncles, but I don't want to be away from them, you know? Even if it's just for a night."

I nodded my understanding, even though it hurt.

"There's a possibility," I added. "That they'll want us for more shows if the grand opening goes well. If they offer that, we'll probably say yes. It'll be more money for my siblings, for whatever therapy Connor needs and such."

"And that would involve living in Florida permanently." He said aloud what I didn't dare to. It was getting too far ahead of myself but a strong possibility all the same.

"Yes," I confirmed.

I waited for him to repeat what he told me so emphatically this morning, that he would always choose me. That he wouldn't hesitate at all to bring himself and those kids, who I almost began to love as my own, to Florida or Timbuktu or wherever the hell I ended up. The fact that he was just one of three men I loved didn't even matter. I needed *him* and what only *he* could give me.

But he didn't.

"It's so fucking hard," he said instead. "As much as I'd love to follow my heart, to follow you to the ends of the earth if need be, I can't do that, Mel. I have to think of what's best for Roo and Rinna."

"And what is that?" I asked, my voice threatening to crack.

"I don't know," he admitted, resting his forehead on mine. "They love you. Rinna wanted to start calling you Mom. But with their uncles here... I've never seen them so happy. Not since before we were captured."

He pulled me tight against him, his arms bracing against my back and pressing me to his chest. "Please know, this is the hardest decision I've ever had to make. Not even my mate dying did this to me. I love you, my little fox, so fucking much. More than I ever loved her. Please don't ever doubt that. Even though you're not a wolf, I know in my heart you were meant to be mine."

"Then come with us." My arms circled around his neck. "Bring the kids. Bring your brothers, too. I don't care. I just don't want to be without you—all three of you."

"Oh, Mel," he whispered gruffly. "I want to, so badly. But my brothers found home in these woods. They've been cut off from the rest of the pack, so it's just them and their shaman now. If I were to take the kids and go with you... I'd be separating my family all over again."

"We're your family, too."

"I know. That's why this is so hard."

His mouth fell to mine, and I kissed him with every fiber of my being. Every kiss was a plea, a desperate cry for him to choose me. I couldn't force him to make the choice. I wanted him to *want* to follow me with those two kids in tow.

I wanted him to forget his life before being captured, as selfish as that was. The carnival became such a turning point in all of our lives. But if I couldn't fully let go of my life before, what right did I have to ask him to do that?

I clung to him only more desperately as he laid me out on the loveseat, settling his weight on top of me while his hands roamed under my tank top. His touch was sweet, sensual fire, and I craved him even more, trying not to think it could be one of our last times together.

Clothes peeled away as I sensed the need in both of us to hold on, to cling to what we knew and enjoyed so much. We didn't want to face the unknown even if it was best for those most vulnerable among us—Roo and Rinna.

His hot flesh pressed flush to mine, his mouth on my neck as my fingers sailed across the length of his back—we wanted to be selfish, to hold on to this and savor it because we knew it couldn't last forever.

He pulled his hips back, holding the side of my thigh as he aligned himself and pressed forward—filling me up and splitting me apart at the same time.

A whimper escaped my lips at the first penetration, not because it hurt, but because it was almost *too* good. I realized this was our first time truly alone together without the other guys involved. I pressed my feet into the cushions and lifted my hips to meet his, wanting to savor every inch of contact.

"I love you, Mel," he groaned as he surged deeper. "I'll always love you, even if I don't have you."

"Then come with me," I panted. Tears prickled at my eyes and my nails dug into his back as the first jolts of a building orgasm shot through me. "If you love me, don't leave me."

"You're the one leaving," he said with a dry laugh. His fingers dug into my hips, the impact of his cock pressing me down hard into the loveseat cushions. "Stay. Don't leave, my love. Stay with me."

"I can't." My whole body seized up as the orgasm rocked through me, my thighs pressing to his sides and my arms locked around my wolf as if he would disappear at any moment. "You know I can't."

He slowed his thrusts, pushing up to his hands as he gazed down at me beneath him. God, he was so fucking beautiful. And he was *mine*, but for how much longer?

He looked almost ghostly in the darkness. Pale and flushed, breathing raggedly with exertion, his abs flexing on his long torso as he continued filling and emptying me. Loving and leaving me.

His hands traveled up the sides of my body, palming the curves of my waist, filling his hands with my breasts. Each touch was exploratory and intentional as his golden eyes took me in, like he was creating a memory to look back on.

He fell back down to kiss me when his hands cupped the back of my head, his hips picking up pace as he crashed against me. The tears I'd been fighting finally spilled when my next orgasm convulsed around him again.

He released with my name on his lips, and his fists locked in my hair. The tiny loveseat grew uncomfortable, but we stayed there all night, unwilling to let go.

✵ 8 ✵

RAZVAN

I woke up early and came downstairs to find Mel and Hunter entwined in each other on the loveseat. *Huh, looks like wolf boy came home after all.* I covered them with a blanket, then went into the kitchen for coffee and a bite to eat.

Not fifteen minutes later, I heard movement coming from the theater room and then watched as Hunter, with pants on but still shirtless, carried a blanket-wrapped Mel up the stairs. He treaded softly, careful not to wake her.

I regarded him as coolly as I could when he came back down, determined to not be distracted by his long, lithe muscles and ghostly pale skin. Mel may have let him off the hook, but not me.

"Morning, Raz," he greeted, trailing a hand against me on his way to the fridge.

"Wolf," I returned, stiffening against his touch. "Have a fun night?"

He stopped and turned to look at me, his face conflicted. At least he had the self-awareness to feel bad.

"No, honestly. Mel told me about Florida and everything. And I've been feeling shitty ever since."

"Poor you," I sneered. "Can't have your venison and eat it, too."

"It's not about me, Raz," he growled, his shoulders squaring up to me. At any other time, it would have been sexy. Now it just pissed me off. "It's about my kids. I can't uproot their lives and rip their worlds apart again. They need stability. You think I don't want to go? If I did, *then* I'd be having my venison and eating it too."

"So you'd rather raise them with your own kind, even with someone who hates humans?" I shot back. "You wolves and your pack mentality is just as bad as humans, I think."

"What, like you never hated humans at one point?" he retorted. "Like Arjun doesn't? Gabe is coming around, but he needs time."

"Too fucking bad. He's out of time. He doesn't get multiple chances to disrespect our shaman."

"I would *never* let him." Hunter stepped in close to me with a growl, his teeth already elongating. "I love her. I'll rip his throat out myself if he even looks at her like that again." With a blink, he paused and stepped back out of my space. "I don't think he would, though. I know you all don't trust him, but he's my brother. I know him. He knows not to mess with what's important to me."

I rubbed my jaw, debating for a moment to bring up what else was on my mind.

"What about us, then?" I wondered aloud.

His gaze flicked to my lips and then back to my eyes. "What do you mean?"

"Wolves don't look too kindly upon interspecies relationships, do they?" I crossed my arms. "How would your precious brothers feel if they knew about you and me?"

He let out a long sigh, dropping his gaze. "I don't know, Raz. It hasn't really come up yet. They're still getting used to having a shaman around and I've been trying to make them see not all humans are bad."

"Right," I scoffed. "And if we settle in Florida and you never see me or Mel again?" I spread my arms to the side. "Will you have your happy wolf pack with no regrets?"

"No," he breathed. "Any choice I make will have major regrets, Raz. I love Mel with all my heart. You mean the world to me, too. But they're my family, my blood—"

"Blood isn't everything," I countered. "You saw that with Mel's mother. I'd say the same for my own family. You, me, Mel, and

Connor? That's the family we've made, the one we've chosen. Hell, Arjun's pretty much stuck with us too now."

I stepped in close, just like he did to me, my face inches away from his. "And if you won't kiss me in front of them? If you make excuses for them disrespecting the woman you love? If you use your own children as the reason to not follow where your heart wants to go? Are they really worth keeping around?"

A flash of movement out of the corner of my eye nearly made me turn my head, but Hunter caught my chin. He made me face him, eyes boring into mine for one passionate moment, then his mouth crashed to mine. Hard.

With a rough pull of my body against his, the sharp points of his teeth grew long and my cock did the same. I moaned, loving the pleasurable pain he gave me, and fisted his hair at the nape of his neck. Heat soared in my body at the wolf's taste and I fought to control my dragon's fire.

"Um, whoa. Okay."

Hunter slowly broke our kiss, but kept his forehead on mine. He turned his head to exhale a small plume of smoke that escaped my lungs and found its way into his mouth.

"Hey, little brother," he remarked casually, stroking a hand across my chest.

Gabe's eyes flitted between us, his face nearly as red as his hair as he tried to reconcile what he just saw.

"Uh, something you care to explain, Hunter?" he asked.

"No." My pale wolf smirked, turning back to face me as he planted a gentler kiss on the bridge of my nose. "Not really."

MELODY

The days leading up to Florida passed by too fast. We practiced day in and day out, perfecting a routine like we never had before. Arjun was surprisingly easy to work with. He made his usual sarcastic jabs but never complained about the boring, monotonous work of repeating his part over and over and over. If anything, it almost seemed like he enjoyed it.

We were so busy, I barely saw Hunter or the other wolves. They came and went as they pleased, sometimes bringing meat from a hunt, other times just stopping by the house to rest. Gabe never gave me any issue again. This morning, he even smiled when he said hello to me. But it wasn't his attention I wanted.

Hunter seemed to keep his distance from both me and Raz. Our dragon shrugged it off and acted tough, but I knew he was bothered by it, too. Hunter seemed happiest when focused on the pups. He rolled around on the lawn, wrestling and playing with them, laughing and smiling like any proud dad. But he seemed sad when he looked over at us.

He probably can't wait until we're gone, I thought bitterly. So we're not around to kill his mood and remind him of the choice he made.

I was lost in thoughts like those when I headed for the kitchen during a break—so much so that I ran straight into a hard chest I didn't recognize.

"Oh! I'm sorry, Colt." My face flamed as I looked up at the smirk of Hunter's older brother.

"Head in the clouds, Mel?" he asked, stepping aside for me. His voice was deeper than Hunter's, but other than that, he could have been a dark-haired, slightly older clone of my wolf.

"Nose to the grindstone is more like it," I chuckled, pulling the fridge open in search of something cold to drink.

"I've been watching y'all a bit," he remarked, leaning against the door frame. "Pretty impressive. I'm sorry we'll miss the main event."

I paused, my arm halfway out of the fridge with a can of Coke. We'd barely talked since we first met and I couldn't get a read on him. His expression didn't tell me if he was being genuine or sarcastic. I expected him to react like Arjun did initially when I auditioned for ringmistress—outraged that I'd keep performing with shifters.

"No need to look so frightened," he said with a smirk. "I'm a big bad wolf but I don't eat humans."

"I just couldn't tell if you were actually complimenting me or not." I shut the fridge and cracked open my can, holding his gaze.

"I was," he insisted. "Best of luck to y'all down there. I really mean that."

"Well, thanks."

He must have sensed my apprehension, because his smile widened as he folded his arms.

"I'm in favor of shifters doing whatever they want, as long as it doesn't hurt anyone. You've obviously given them the choice and are making sure they get paid and treated well, which is all you can do. My youngest brother may disagree but he's more of a pack traditionalist."

I couldn't stop what rolled off my tongue next. "Does your view include shifters of different species seeing each other?"

His eyebrows lifted slightly, but he seemed overall unsurprised. "You're talking about Hunter and the dragon shifter."

"Yes, his name is Razvan," I said defensively.

"You've got some bite, girl. I like it," he chuckled. "And yes. I see nothing wrong with interspecies dating. A few months ago, though," his voice softened, "I probably would have answered differently."

"Yeah, what changed?"

His gaze lifted away from me, focusing on something far away. "Miriam." He said her name in the same affectionate way my guys called me by my nicknames.

"Your shaman."

"Yes." His gaze returned to me. "She's changed everything. Not in a bad way, but," he ran a hand through his mane of black hair, "times are different now than how they used to be. We shifters *need* shaman. After years of trying to handle stuff on our own, we just keep getting killed and captured. We need humans on our side." His eyes shifted toward the window, where Roo and Rinna climbed all over Gabe like a jungle gym. "Some just aren't ready to face the reality of that yet."

"I'd like to meet Miriam," I said. "After Florida, I guess, but maybe we can—"

"I'll bring her by the house tonight," he said quickly.

"Oh," I blinked. "Uh, sure."

"You two would get along, I think," he said, leveling his gaze at me. "She's also had trouble fitting in with other humans." His brow furrowed. "Sorry. Hunter's told me a bit about you."

"It's alright." I waved it off with a smile. "Sounds like Miriam and I have a lot in common already."

We were all winding down after dinner when Colt brought Miriam to the front door, but I sensed her before they even walked onto the property line. Her presence felt like a warm, dull pulsing in my veins, on a different beat than my own pulse. Before ever seeing her face, I knew she was powerful.

She wore a long maxi dress and walked in a way that made her look as if she floated over the ground. Long, dark hair framed vibrant green eyes and petite facial features. She appeared to be a few years older than me, maybe mid-twenties. Her skin tone was a medium tan, similar to Arjun's. The tiger in question stood from the table so suddenly, he knocked his chair over.

"Miriam!" he cried in disbelief. "What are you doing here?"

"She's our shaman," Colt answered for her with a protective growl.

"Your shaman was my stepdad's apprentice," Arjun shot back. "I haven't seen her since I was in London."

"It's good to see you again, little brother." Miriam finally spoke, her accent just as American as mine. She offered a small smile to Arjun. "What a small world it is. I hope you're well?"

"Better now than I was for the last four years," he muttered. "What brought you this way?"

"This is where I'm from," she answered with a lighthearted laugh. "I came back with Lhozen two years ago."

"Lhozen? He's here?" Arjun's eyes grew wide.

"Not here, but he's in the country." Her eyes flicked over to me. "You'll probably run into him at some point."

Remembering my manners, I stepped forward and cleared my throat. "Thank you for coming over, Miriam. I'm Mel. I've been eager to meet another shaman." I offered her a smile, which she returned. "We've just finished dinner, but did you want anything to eat or drink?"

"Just some tea, maybe. That's one of the things I've missed most about the U.K."

"I'll get that for you." Colt pressed a kiss to her temple, and I didn't miss the love and adoration sparking between them.

The guys cleaned up their dishes and slowly filed out of the kitchen to allow us girls to talk.

"So you've known Arjun for a while?" I asked, sitting across the now empty table from her with a cup of tea of my own.

Miriam wrapped her hands around her own mug. "We were never that close," she said hesitantly. "I mean, I've always adored him but I don't think he's ever liked me much."

"Why's that?" I was surprised. Something about this woman made her instantly likable to me. Like she could be a real older sister, unlike the shitty one I grew up with.

Her eyes flicked up apprehensively to me. "His stepfather Lhozen took me as his apprentice not long after his mother was killed. I lived with them and Lhozen spent all of his free time training me. Arjun was unhappy about that. I think he saw it as his father replacing his mum with a much younger woman."

She reached across the table for my hand, her eyes practically begging me. "But it wasn't like that, I swear. Lhozen and I were strictly teacher and student. And he was a *hard* teacher. I think putting everything into teaching me was his way of grieving his loss."

"I believe you," I told her with a gentle squeeze of her hand. "And I'm sorry to hear Arjun judged you like that. But it must have been difficult for him too." A small twinge of envy passed through me. Arjun's mother must have loved him for him to miss her so much. I wondered what that was like.

"Yes, he was crushed. Poor thing." She gave a small shake of her head, then cast a curious look my way. "So he's in your harem, then? You've got a very good-looking group, I must say."

"Uh, not exactly." I laughed nervously, hiding my reddening face behind my mug of tea. "He has no interest in being one of four mates to a shaman, though he is helping me distinguish between my abilities. I wouldn't say we're friends but slowly warming up to each other, I guess."

"Oh, it'll happen." Miriam steeped her tea bag casually. "Has he told you about the variation of abilities from person to person?"

"No, it won't," I groaned, rolling my eyes. She and Connor should've started a matchmaking business with how insistent they were about this. "And no, he hasn't."

"A shaman's powers are as unique as the person carrying them," she explained. "It's like a fingerprint. No two shamans have ever been recorded having the exact same abilities." She spread her palms on the table. "We all have common threads, of course, and that is we can sense shifter-kind and have a better understanding of them. Just the way we're able to do that is always a little different."

"I have Sight, Sense, Semblance, and Speak," I told her. "Arjun told me that last one is rare."

"It is," she confirmed with a slight lifting of her brows. "Sight and Sense are fairly common, but Lhozen's grandmother was the last known one who could Speak." She leaned toward me and lowered her voice to a whisper. "I have Sight as well, along with a second type of sight."

"What do you mean?"

Her eyes lowered to her fingers stretched out on the table. "Your dreams are through the eyes of a shifter, yes? Usually in the past or in present time? My dreams are glimpses of the future."

"The... future?"

She nodded slowly. "I never remember it all, just random flashes and scenes. And it's always changing. Sometimes only in minor ways, like a single word being said, or the color of someone's shirt. Sometimes in huge, drastic ways." Her fingers squeezed around mine. "Do you want to know what I've seen about you?"

My head nodded yes before I could really think about it. Was this wrong or dangerous somehow, to know my future? I had no idea, but I felt the urgent need to know.

"You will be loved, happy, and fulfilled, Mel." A smile spread across her lips as her eyes lowered. "You and the baby."

My heart stopped as one hand jerked down to my stomach. *Shit!* It had been nearly a week, and I still hadn't told Connor or anyone. We were so busy all day and just collapsing into sleep exhausted at night. But yes, I was also completely chickenshit about bringing it up.

"Life will be good to you," Miriam went on. "But my dear Mel, you will go through Hell first."

An icy shiver went down my spine and I had a feeling she was being literal.

"You'll feel every ounce of their pain, hear the anguish in their voices, but you must remain strong for them," she went on, her hand squeezing around mine. "You must not succumb to it, Mel."

"Succumb to what? Whose voices?" I demanded.

"Lean on Arjun," she continued, as though I didn't say a word. "Your other men will try their best to help you, but they will not be what you need. You'll need Arjun the most."

𝕊 10 𝕊

ARJUN

The next morning's mood felt about as far from a sunny vacation in the Keys as one could get. Mel sulked. The white wolf looked depressed. Raz was pissy. And Connor was in a foul mood because Mel and everyone else was too. A goddamn chain-reaction of sourpusses. And people wondered why I didn't care to be part of a shaman's harem.

I stifled a yawn and choked down another cup of coffee. I hated the stuff, but apparently Mel and Miriam went through all the tea whilst chatting last night. I already couldn't sleep a wink after seeing my stepfather's mistress for the first time in years. Now she was becoming old chums with the shaman who saved my life. Just lovely.

Thankfully, Miriam was gone by morning, as were Hunter's brothers and the wolf pups. Despite only leaving for one night, apparently the pups would be too upset at seeing Mel leave. So Hunter employed his brothers to be a distraction and allow for some romantic goodbyes.

However, the tension in the kitchen was anything but.

Hunter and Mel barely spoke to or looked at each other. Raz did much of the same. I grew bored of this and wanted fresh air from the

616

stench of coffee, so went out to the RV where Connor was checking it over for the long drive ahead.

"Need any help, mate?" I asked, approaching as he fiddled under the hood of the gargantuan vehicle.

"Hah," he scoffed. "Still awkward as fuck in there, huh?"

"How did you guess?" I groaned, scrubbing a hand down my face. "It's one night we'll be gone, two days max. I'm not sure I understand why they're acting like teenagers being apart for a whole summer."

"They're in love," he answered simply. "And there is the possibility of us staying out in Florida permanently, which puts a serious damper on things if Hunter insists on staying here."

"It's quite a big *if*," I remarked. "Really, what's the point of getting our knickers in a twist over what might or might not happen?"

"Again, love," Connor smirked, flipping over a wrench in his hand. "You act like you've never been in love before."

"I haven't," I answered truthfully. "Although I was engaged."

He paused in his work, looking me over quizzically. "So was I. The love part usually comes first, though."

"Arranged marriage," I sighed. "My mum grew up in a region of India where it's still common. Pretty old school by today's standards, but these traditional folks swear it's better that way."

"They still do that in Afghanistan. Shocked the shit of out us American military kids," he chuckled. "So what happened?"

"I was captured and shipped over here," I shrugged. "Got thrown in a cage with a hotheaded dragon and the rest is history."

"Well, that's one way out of marrying someone you don't love."

We laughed together at that. The more I talked to Connor, the more I liked him. He was a good bloke.

He shut the hood of the RV, then jumped down from the bumper on his new robot legs. "She's all set to go. Now it's just dragging those two out of the house so we can get moving."

"Lovely," I groaned, but my complaint was premature.

Mel and Raz came around to the side yard with Hunter between them, the three of them talking quietly. Hunter paused, turned to Mel, and cupped her cheek before leaning down and kissing her passionately. She returned it with just as much reverence, wrapping an arm around his neck and holding onto him like she'd never let go.

A twinge of heat and something else ran through me, and I found myself looking away. This private moment wasn't mine to gawk at.

When I glanced up again, Mel had stepped to the side and now Hunter and Raz were wrapped up in each other. Seeing them together made me smirk to myself. Mum would have a fit, God rest her soul. She hated any kind of openly sexual deviance. Any time she complained about seeing same-sex couples together, I suggested she go back to India. I thought I was clever, but my tigress mother was not amused.

After their long, lingering goodbyes, Mel and Raz trudged up the into RV with all the enthusiasm of children going to back to school.

"Y'all got everything?" Connor asked as he started up the engine. Those two just remained with their faces pressed to the windows.

"Remind me never to fall in love," I mumbled, taking the passenger seat and bucking myself in.

Connor just chuckled as he carefully drove the vehicle out of the side yard and onto the road. "That's a little dramatic, isn't it? Falling in love is a beautiful part of the human experience."

"If it makes you act like that? No thanks, mate. Give me a belly fully of meat, some tea to wash it all down, a place to sleep the day away, and I'm settled."

"Simple pleasures are great," he agreed. "But you're human too, bro. That big ol' human brain loves to make everything complicated. It's never satisfied with the simple things, not for long. Once you have everything you want, you always want more."

"Yeah?" I propped my feet on the dashboard and laced my hands behind my head, settling in for the long ride. "What do you want more of?"

"I'd like to go a whole three months without triggering my PTSD, for one." He lifted an eyebrow at me. "You've seen some shit too, RJ. Might want to get that looked at."

"That's where I'm thankful for my simpler cat brain," I answered. "Spending most of my time as a tiger made my years in captivity a simple predator versus prey situation. Sometimes I was one, sometimes the other."

"Animals experience psychological trauma, too. Even I know that, but fair enough," he replied. "Everyone processes it differently."

I ground my teeth in my jaw. Connor was not one to be underestimated. I couldn't be certain that he saw me snarl and turn when the occasional door slammed in the house. He certainly couldn't feel the spike of adrenaline rushing through me when Raz breathed fire during our practices. I made sure not to give any physical tells of fear, but Connor was especially perceptive for a human.

"And once you cure yourself of your own trauma?" I asked, returning the subject back to him. "What will be next?"

He lifted his eyes to the rearview mirror. I didn't see them, but Mel and Raz were silent behind us. Their scents intermingling—hers light and floral, his deep and smoky, indicating they were physically wrapped up in each other as well.

"It'll never be cured," Connor murmured in a low voice. "It'll always stay with me, but when I have it more under control, I don't want anything too crazy. Kids and a wife. You know, stability."

I stared at him as he drove. "And how do you expect that to work with... you know, all of you?"

He shrugged, smirking as he glanced over at me. "However my woman wants it to. I have my place with her and that's plenty enough for me."

"Mate, you're not even a shifter," I said with a shake of my head. "What's your excuse for being under her spell?"

"Ain't no spell, man," he answered. "It's just love."

THE JOURNEY TURNED long and uneventful. Raz took over driving after Connor started feeling soreness in his legs. I napped in the passenger seat, paced around the vehicle, shifted, then napped on the floor. This long drive was making me feel antsy and caged in again.

"RJ." Connor looked up at me from the small bed pushed against the wall. "Grab some Midol from the cabinet in the bathroom? Mel's got a killer headache."

He sat up with his back against the wall and Mel leaning against his chest. Her eyes were shut tight and her brow pinched as if she was in pain. His fingers moved in soothing caresses over her temples and forehead.

"Sure, mate." I retrieved the pain medicine and a bottle of water from the mini-fridge and handed them over.

Connor had her take a few pills with some water, kissing and murmuring to her as he rocked her gently in his arms. Just like when she was kissing Hunter, something uncomfortable and unfamiliar passed over me while I watched them, and I excused myself to return to the passenger seat.

"What's going on?" Raz asked from the driver's seat.

"Mel's got a headache."

"Hm." He glanced over at me. "You know how to drive this thing?"

"Fuck no," I shot back. "Connor's got her. Keep your eyes on the road."

His inked knuckles turned white on the steering as his lips pressed into a thin line. For fuck's sake, why did all of them want to rush to her side so badly? She had a bloody headache, not fucking gunshot wounds.

Another hour passed. My ears picked up soft whimpering from the back of the trailer, followed Connor's voice still trying to be soothing, but it carried an underlying tremor of fear. In the next moment, he took a few long strides up to us.

"Something's really wrong. We've got to pull over and find a hospital," he said, tapping Raz's shoulder.

"What's going on with her?" Raz made a sharp turn off the interstate at the next exit, too sharp for a such a large vehicle and we all struggled to stay upright.

"Careful, dude!" Connor barked. "I don't know, but her head is killing her and it keeps getting worse." He tapped my shoulder next. "Arjun, can you stay with her? I gotta give Raz directions with my GPS."

"Me?" I looked up at him, knowing he was dead serious because he didn't use my stupid nickname. "The fuck you want me to do?"

"Just sit with her so she's not alone." He smacked my shoulder more insistently. "Move it."

"Alright, Marine," I grumbled, rising from my seat reluctantly and moving toward the back of the vehicle.

Even my heart twinged at seeing Mel curled up in a fetal position, her hands pressed to her ears and her red face streaked with tears. Still, I knew nothing about how to comfort a woman in distress. I could charm women, yes, but that came from quick-witted banter and keeping an emotional distance. This vulnerable, nurturing stuff was not my forte.

"Hey," I said softly, lowering to sit on the mattress next to her. "Your guys are finding a hospital. You're going to be okay, Mel."

"Arjun, help me," she whimpered, thrashing on the bed like a fish out of water. "There's too many of them. I don't know how to make it stop."

"Mel," I choked out helplessly. "It won't be much longer—"

"You don't understand," she sobbed. "You can't hear them."

"Mel, what—"

She grabbed my hand and pressed my palm to the burning, sweaty surface of her forehead. A sharp flash of sensation flooded over me so quickly, I almost thought I was on fire again. The feeling passed, then captured me again in an icy grip of pure horror.

I saw everything she saw, all in quick, vivid, and gruesome flashes. Cattle prods, whips, and batons. Fists, kicks, and BB guns. Cages, limping figures, and broken bodies. Weapons of every kind imaginable and the dozens of shifter species they inflicted upon.

I tore my hand away from her forehead and looked around for a place to vomit. Someone pushed a water bottle into my hand and I gulped it down, which helped settle my stomach a little.

"Did you hear them?" Mel asked in a weak voice. "Their screams. Some of them are barely alive."

I shook my head. "I could only see. You can hear too?"

She nodded, squeezing out a few more tears. "And I can feel... everything. In my body."

Just then, I noticed the red marks on her arms from where she had been scratching at herself.

"And it's getting worse?"

She nodded. "I've never felt it like this. Not even when I felt you." With an anguished whimper that tore right through my heart, she clapped her hands over her ears. "I don't know how to make it stop. I just want it to end…"

Before I could think of doing anything else, I slid my arms around her back and pulled her to my chest.

11

MELODY

I had never been in so much pain in my life. Not even when one of Mom's exes broke a bottle across my back and Jeanie spent the whole night picking glass shards out with tweezers.

What started as a simple headache not long after we left home turned into the most horrific visions in my head and sensations in my body. I wanted to jump out of the RV and prayed a semi-truck would hit me. It hurt so badly, but if I closed my eyes at all, what I saw haunted me.

"Listen to my voice," someone with an English accent said. Maybe Arjun? I had no idea if it was someone right next to me or one of the hundreds of voices in my head. "Focus on the sound of my voice and nothing else, Mel. You can do this."

I tried. Good lord, I tried. But the voice sounded like it was at the end of a long tunnel, and all the pain and abuse I felt was slowly drag-ging me away.

"I can't," I whimpered out. "You're too far away."

Hands touched me, some with gentle caresses and others with fists. I wondered if this was what Connor's PTSD felt like, not being able to discern between reality and how my mind was just fucking me over.

"Stay with me, Mel. You're right here, love. You're in your own body. You are your own person. No one is hurting you. You're with me and your men. You're safe. Listen to me and focus on that."

The voice continued in a warm, soothing tone, and I tried desperately to hold on to it like a lifeline. But sometimes the screams drowned it out and I couldn't hear all the words.

I saw through the eyes of a small animal, shaking with fear in a dark corner. Humans dragged a struggling black bear with a chain around its neck. One of them pressed a handgun into the bear's shoulder and squeezed the trigger. The bear roared in anguish and tried to swipe at the human, but its other paw hung limply at its side. The animal I was seeing through, her cub, cried out a desperate plea and pressed against the bars of his cage, tiny paws swiping desperately at nothing.

"I can't stand this," I sobbed, forcing my eyes open to not witness more scenes of torture. "I don't want to see any of this."

My hands found a smooth, solid wall, and I scrambled closer to it. Then I slammed my forehead into the wall as hard as I could. I didn't want to die, just pass out. I was so desperate to get these images out of my head and I knew none of my guys would hit me in the head to knock me out. Sweet unconsciousness, please take me away from seeing and feeling all of this...

But then what if I still dreamed?

It didn't matter. I could only smack my head on the wall twice before someone dragged me away.

"No, please," I begged, feeling for the smooth, solid wall again. "I can't be awake. I can't do this."

"Listen to RJ, babe. You can fight this but we're not letting you hurt yourself."

Connor? Was he here?

"I'm right here, *steluța*. We're all right here. You're safe, my love. Come back to us."

"Raz..." I squeaked out, trying to make sense of the faces that morphed between my lovers and the cruel, hard faces of strangers.

The bite of a whip on my back felt like a kiss. A gentle caress became a closed fist punch to my gut. Everything bled over and between each other in blurry, dreamlike images. Jesus, when would it end?

A low rumbling started up, faintly at first, then growing louder and stronger. I saw through one of many caged parrots on a truck, and figuring it was the engine roaring. But it continued even when my vision shifted to something else.

The rumbling stayed constant, a repeating rhythmic noise that vibrated gently across my skin. I found it comforting and clung to it. After a moment, the visions faded. The windows and walls of Connor's RV slowly returned with full clarity. The sounds of torture faded away, as well as the pain, except for a dull ache in my forehead.

And the rumbling remained at its loudest volume yet, soothing like a balm to my sore brain.

"Jesus tap dancing Christ," Connor sighed. "You scared us to death, babe."

The rumbling nearly drowned him out. I could barely hear him and I was so tired now.

"What is that noise?" I murmured, rubbing my aching forehead. "It finally made everything stop but I can still hear it."

"Take a look and see, steluţa," Raz grinned. He sat on the floor in front of me, his hands resting on my legs. My dragon's eyes looked heavy and tired, but also full of relief.

I sat up from where I'd been reclining and looked behind me.

A massive Bengal tiger with the most striking blue-green eyes looked back at me. I had been leaning against his side, where I felt the deep rumble of his purr vibrate through me.

He continued purring, sounding like a small jet engine as he gazed back at me.

"Arjun," I breathed. "You saved me. I literally felt like I was dying several times."

Lay back down and rest, he thought to me. *The visions could come back while you're sleeping, so lean on me and I'll keep them away.*

He sounded so stiff and formal in my mind. I also realized for the first time that his accent didn't come through in my thoughts. But thinking about it too much made my head hurt.

"Thank you," I said. My eyelids drooped heavily, but I still reached a hand out. "May I touch you?"

His large head tilted as if confused by the question, but then pressed his forehead against my palm where I scratched him. My hand all but disappeared in the dense orange fur, my fingers barely stretching from one of his ears to the other. Those eyes closed slowly, as if in utter relaxation, and his purring volume only increased.

"I'll get you an ice pack for your head, steluţa." Raz rose from the floor and gingerly kissed me where my head throbbed. Shit, that was going to be a hell of a bump.

"Are you really okay with me lying down on you?" I asked Arjun. "I know we're not all that close—"

The tiger huffed, pausing his purring for a moment to shove me down against his side with his head and one large paw. I noticed how careful he was not to get his claws anywhere near me.

"Alright," I laughed, lowering my head to rest on the fur right above his ribs.

I curled my legs up close to me, shifting around a little to get comfortable before finally resting my hands near my face on Arjun's side. His purring immediately started up again, and he lowered his giant head to his paws.

My brain was too wiped out to think much about what just happened, but as I drifted off, cozy and secure against one of the most dangerous animals in the world, I mumbled, "Seriously, thank you, Arjun."

The tiger shifted slightly underneath me and I felt the tickle of his whiskers as he gently nuzzled my leg.

12

MELODY

I woke up to cold water dripping in my eyes.

"What the—"

As I moved to get up, that was when the melting ice pack tumbled off my forehead down to the blanket covering me.

I sat up, stretched, and tried to make sense of the world again.

Arjun still laid behind me, although his purring stopped. He breathed deeply, whiskers twitching slightly in his sleep. My eyes traveled over his form, taking in the beauty and strength of the tiger curled around me protectively.

He was beautiful in human form too, but up close the tiger seemed like such an otherworldly creature. Books and movies could never do justice to this powerful force of nature that was somehow related to the chubby tomcat that hung around my old trailer park.

The RV was quiet and still. A quick look up toward the empty driver's seat told me Connor and Raz had gone somewhere.

I pushed the blanket away and swung my legs to the floor. My head no long throbbed, but a quick poke with my fingers told me I still had one hell of a bump. Hopefully, my top hat would hide it during our show.

A grunt behind me made me turn around. Arjun opened one eye

lazily and then stretched, his claws the size of Raz's knives as they extended long on those paws the size of my head. He then lifted his head and yawned, his mouth big enough to swallow one of my legs whole.

"Good morning," I greeted groggily before blinking up at the light still streaming through the windows. "Or afternoon, whenever it is."

"Sorry to disappoint, dove," Arjun's mouth shifted back to human while he was still mostly a tiger, which was a little freaky to see, "but we did not spend a romantic night together, despite what your jumbled memory may tell you."

He finished his shift, then made a big point of covering his naked lap with the blanket, those blue-green eyes teasing me. The first time we ever truly spoke, he had just shifted and didn't have any clothes on. I did not want to deal with looking at a naked man I wasn't sleeping with, so refused to look at him until he got dressed.

Now, it was all I could do not to look at him. His warm, brown skin was unblemished except for a few burn scars on his ribs and arms. A light dusting of dark hair swept across well-defined pecs. Like Hunter, he looked built for swimming or long-distance running. A long, slender torso carved with abs that disappeared under the blanket in his lap. His musculature looked slightly bigger than Hunter's, though not as beefy as Connor, with arms and shoulders that looked powerful and swift.

"With you gawping like that, I'm starting to know what my prey feels like," he joked, poking me with an elbow.

"Fuck! Shit, I'm so sorry." I forced my eyes away as my face heated up like the sun. "I didn't mean to stare, I just zoned out. I'm still so out of it from before." A lame excuse, but still a plausible one.

"That was one hell of an ordeal," he remarked, the humor gone from his voice.

"My head just started hurting and then it all came on at once." I stared at my hands, remembering the tiny, helpless bear cub paws sticking through the bars of a cage. "It felt like dozens, maybe even hundreds of shifters coming through me at once. And all of them were being hurt, caged, or watching it happen to others. I've never seen anything so horrible."

"You are highly empathetic," Arjun stated matter-of-factly. "Have you always been able to feel what others felt physically? Even before you knew you were a shaman?"

I thought for a moment and nodded. "Yes. When I wasn't able to block my siblings from getting hit, I felt their pain when they cried. Not just the physical pain either, I could feel their heartbreak and confusion about it. Sometimes Mommy was nice to them, but other times she was so mean and they didn't understand why."

"Fuck me," Arjun muttered, his brow knitted as he listened. I remembered he didn't know my past like the other guys. He wasn't there when Hunter and I confronted my piss poor excuse for a mother.

I shrugged at his response. "It's just what I've always known. When I was younger, I pretended I could absorb all their pain like a sponge so they couldn't feel anything. I don't think it really works that way, though."

"Unfortunately not," Arjun sighed. "Even so, many shaman have given themselves as martyrs for shifter kind. But the thing about martyrs is they're no good once they're dead." He gave me a stern look, his eyes resting on my forehead.

"I wasn't trying to kill myself," I said defensively. "I was just trying to knock myself out to make it stop. I didn't know what else to do."

"Well, it's a good thing you weren't near an open door," he remarked. "If you had jumped out while we were moving? All bloody three of us fools would have jumped after you without a single thought and this old bucket would have gone careening across the highway."

"Aww. I'm so flattered, Arjun." I mockingly batted my eyelashes at him.

He snorted in reply, folding his arms across his chest. "Just because I don't like to watch anyone suffer doesn't mean I'm in love. An easy concept for an eighteen-year-old girl to get confused."

"Oh yeah? How old are you?"

His lips twitched with the beginnings of a smile. "I'm twenty-two."

"See, you're not that much older than me." I propped my elbow on my knee and rested my chin in my hand, feeling like this was the most productive conversation I had with him yet. "Speaking of the men who are in love with me, where are they?"

"Getting food. And tea," he answered. "God, I hope Razvan got through his thick head that I need English breakfast, not that Earl Grey bullshit."

"So when you talk about martyrs, do you mean you've seen that happen to other shamans too?"

"Well, every shaman communicates with shifters a bit differently," he began, running a hand through the black hair that began to fall in his eyes.

"That's what Miriam told me," I said. "Their abilities are as unique as a fingerprint."

He made an odd face at the mention of her, but nodded his head in agreement. "Right. My stepfather had episodes of overwhelming shifter visions that drove him to drink a lot. I still don't think he saw them nearly as vividly as you."

"My mom drinks a lot too," I replied, feeling a strange sense of solidarity with him. "Well, even a lot is an understatement. That's basically the reason I ran away and," I waved my hand through the air, "here I am."

As Arjun looked at me while I spoke, I felt a softness filtering in around him. Like he had always been slightly on edge, defensive and ready to strike if need be, but right then it gave way just slightly.

"Lhozen didn't get too bad until after my mum died," he said. "Then he was hitting a full bottle of Johnnie Walker almost every night when he wasn't sticking his sad, grieving prick in *her*."

I remembered Miriam's words to me, how she thought Arjun didn't like her, despite that she never got involved with his stepfather. She had probably tried to explain it to him before, so would it do any good to say anything now? From the way he spoke, he seemed utterly convinced that Lhozen fell deep into drinking and this much younger woman immediately after his mother passed.

Honestly, I barely knew either of them and it didn't feel right to try to convince him that something he believed so deeply was wrong. Even if my gut told me Miriam was telling the truth.

"What happened to your mom?" I decided to ask instead.

"Poachers happened," he answered with a heavy sigh. "The only place we could shift in London was a wildlife park. Humans could still get buy entry and drive around like they were on safari or some shit. Mum and I spent a couple nights a week there, hunting, stalking, napping. Just getting the tiger out of our system, you know."

I stifled a giggle at the thought of using shifting as an excuse to take long naps. Such a cat shifter thing to say, not that I knew any other cat shifters.

"One day, this lot gained entry and smuggled guns in." His eyes took on a faraway look. "They were looking to get as many exotic hides and trophies as they could get away with."

"Fuck," I whispered. "Arjun, I'm so sorry."

"They got a rhinoceros, chopped its horns off and left it there bleeding," he continued. "Tusks from an elephant. A few ibex heads to mount on their walls. Skins from zebras and jaguars." He let out a long breath. "And Mum, of course."

"Jesus. How old were you?" I hardly dared to ask.

"Fourteen," he answered.

My hand reached out and took hold of his before I knew what I was doing. "That's terrible. I'm so sorry for everything you went through."

He looked at our hands clasped together as though he didn't know what to make of them, but didn't pull away. After a moment, his thumb slowly stroked over my palm.

"I could say the same to you," he replied.

13

RAZVAN

"Connor!" I craned my neck, looking around the store for the man with robotic legs. "Where the fuck are ya?"

"Ugh, language!" A middle-aged woman shot me a dirty look as she breezed by me, holding her wide-eyed daughter close to her body.

"What?" I glared at her. "I'm speaking English."

"There are children in this store, you brute! Watch your profanity!" Her eyes inspected my tattoos disapprovingly as she mumbled some bullshit about the devil and saving my soul.

I rolled my eyes, muttering a half-hearted apology while I looked around again. "Connor!"

"What?" he demanded, popping up out of nowhere and coming toward me with an armful of things to dump into the grocery cart.

"God bless you, sir! Thank you for your service!" The same bitch who gave me the stink-eye practically swooned as he walked past her. His dog tags were visible like usual, but so were his prosthetic legs, which he didn't normally show off in public.

"Thank ya, ma'am!" He shot her a winning smile, which immediately dissolved into a groan and an eye roll once he reached me. "She's the same person who would spit at me if I was sitting in the street with a cardboard sign. I guaran-fuckin'-tee it."

"Heh. Can you remember what fucking tea Arjun wanted?" I asked, making sure to make my *fucking* especially loud as I turned to the rows of boxes on the shelves.

"I dunno dude, just grab something."

"No, he wanted something specific. You know these English pricks and their *fucking* tea."

Smothering his laugh as we heard the woman's audible gasp in the next aisle over, Connor pointed to a box. "I think it's that one."

"Sure, whatever. Looks familiar." I snatched it off the shelf and threw it in the cart, eager to get back and see how my steluța was doing. "If it's the wrong one, the big pussy will just have to deal."

After going through the ridiculously long checkout line—seriously, why did Americans buy so much damn food at once?—we made it to the RV, parked along the furthest row of spaces in the parking lot.

"*Steluța,*" I breathed a massive sigh of relief when I saw she was awake and no longer seemed to be in pain.

"Hi, my dragon," she smiled at me.

"How are you feeling, my love?" I took her face in my hands and kissed the bump on her head. It already shrank considerably, but we got another large bag of ice for it just in case.

"Better," she murmured before her soft lips found mine.

I let out a groan at the sweet contact of her mouth, pulling her to me and kissing her like I hadn't seen her in days. Connor and I had been so worried, and so helpless to do anything for her. If Arjun hadn't been there and thought so quickly, who knew when her torment would have ended?

I paid him no mind on the bed next to her, easing her back down on the mattress with one hand cradling her head as I devoured her mouth. Even if he didn't want a taste of her, which I didn't believe for a second, he'd have to get used to seeing it.

Someone grabbed my shoulders forcefully and yanked me away from my woman. I turned with a growl when my lips disconnected from hers, nowhere near ready to be done kissing her.

But Connor, with his insane strength for a human, tossed me aside like a rag doll and took my place, his arms enveloping Mel and kissing her neck as she laughed.

"Wait your turn, asshole," I snarled, smiling despite myself.

"You had long enough. I was worried about her too, lizard boy." His voice was muffled against her skin. Mel looked up at me apologetically, but her smile was too wide.

I smirked back. Of course she would enjoy this, her men fighting each other over her.

"That's how it's gonna be, ah?"

I grabbed Connor's shirt in my fists and pulled up. He batted my arms away and went back to her, but I grabbed him around his middle and pivoted around, judo-tossing him to the floor.

"Nuh uh, man!" He rose to his feet quickly and shook his index finger at me. "I'm not Hunter, you can't do this gay wrestling shit with me."

"Aw, you're no fun, Con," Mel pouted adorably from the bed.

"You'll wait your turn then, robo-legs," I laughed, dropping back down to the bed beside her.

"Boys, you know there's plenty of me to go around," Mel giggled, stroking a finger down my cheek.

"Fucking neanderthals, the lot of you," Arjun muttered. He'd been scooted to the edge of the bed amid our skirmish and quickly pulled on a pair of pants before getting up. "Please tell me you got my tea, Raz."

"Mm," I mumbled distractedly as Mel dragged her nails across my scalp. "There's a sandwich for you," I told her. "Without a wolf, unfortunately."

"Thanks, dragon," she kissed my cheek, then leaned back and looked at me. "You miss him?"

"A little," I admitted. "A little pissed, too. I wish he'd get his head out of his ass and see what's right fucking in front of him."

"I can see his perspective though." She propped herself up on her elbows. "It's hard for him, choosing between what he wants and what's best for the kids."

"You're an angel to be so patient with him, and that alone means he should choose you."

"Us," she corrected me, stroking a finger across my lower lip. "Choose us."

"While this is all romantic and lovely," Arjun interjected, tea in hand like the English prick he was, "Mel and I need to work on putting up shields in her mind, lest she get hit by another wave of information like that."

"Yeah, what exactly was that?" Connor piped up, stirring up some instant coffee.

"I caught a glimpse when I touched her forehead," Arjun said, looking at me. "It looked a lot like the compound where they first held us, Raz."

"Fuck, those poor bastards," I muttered. "I can still hardly believe we got out alive and relatively unscathed. So many shifters died because of the horrible conditions or were injured badly to the point of being disfigured."

"There were so many children there." Mel curled her legs up to her chest. "I saw through the eyes of a bear cub as his mother was tortured."

I pulled her close and rubbed my hands down her arms, sensing the tremors through her body.

"What the fuck?" Connor's eyes darted between Arjun and I. "What the hell is this place?"

"Think of it like a distribution center," Arjun explained. "It's the first place we get dumped at after being captured. Hunter was probably in a similar place. We get evaluated, experimented on, all that lovely stuff before a price is put on our heads. Sometimes they hold auctions. Once someone buys us, we're shipped out to our new homes. Usually a circus, sometimes a zoo or a fucking foreign cosmetics company. Sometimes just a rich, sadistic fuck who likes owning a person who can turn into an animal."

"They're constantly crying for help," I murmured, tightening my arms around Mel. "You're probably the first person in ages who's heard them."

"Not only that. Remember, she can feel everything being inflicted on them," Arjun pointed out. "She needs to learn how to block it out, otherwise next time she'll have much worse than a lump on her head."

"Yeah, don't go doing that again, babe," Connor said. "I got enough brain damage for all of us."

"You guys are totally missing the point," Mel huffed, wriggling until I loosened my grip on her. "This trip isn't about the show anymore. Those shifters need us. I can't just ignore them after feeling their suffering like that."

"Lawd," Connor groaned, rolling his gaze toward the ceiling. "Jesus, you've blessed me with an amazing woman, but why in the Lord's name does she insist on saving everybody?"

"Because I'm a shaman." She leveled her gaze at him. "And it's the right thing to do."

"Wasn't talking to you, babe. I was asking Jesus."

"*Steluţa*," I said while Arjun laughed into his tea, and Connor continued pleading with his imaginary god in the sky, "the compound is nothing like sneaking into a carnival. It's a massive warehouse with top-notch security. I'm talking armed guards posted twenty-four seven, cameras everywhere, only one way in or out. They see it as guarding millions of dollars worth of merchandise, so they're serious about keeping it secure."

"So?" Her warm brown eyes lit up with a fire I'd never seen in her before. "You're a fucking dragon."

"You flatter me, my love," I kissed her temple. "But you'd need a whole fleet of dragons to take on this place. And even if we just light her up, there's the matter of getting the shifters out safely and discreetly."

She sighed, leaning back against me. "We have to do something. Even if it's a long shot, imagine if we succeed. We could stop the shifter trade for good!"

"But if we fail," Arjun said, "Not only do Raz and I risk being enslaved again, we could lose one of the most powerful shamans alive."

"What do you mean?" Mel demanded. "They'll kill me?"

"Or worse," he replied. "They'll capture you too. And force you to use your abilities to control *us*."

❧ 14 ❧

MELODY

After more long hours of driving, night had just fallen when we reached our hotel in Miami.

"Oh my god, we're right on the beach!" I pressed my nose to the window, unable to believe I was looking at the real world outside and not a postcard.

"Let me guess, never seen the ocean, either?" Arjun teased. "I'm still not convinced you haven't lived under a rock your whole life."

"If by a rock you mean my morbidly obese, alcoholic mother, you'd be right."

He laughed softly at that, brushing past me with the lightest of touches on my waist. I froze in place, unaccustomed to this new affectionate side of him but not entirely hating it.

He spent the last few hours teaching me how to meditate, taking ideas from his Hindu upbringing and integrating them with lessons he saw his stepfather teaching other shamans. I got frustrated quickly, not seeing the point at all in sitting with my eyes closed and breathing, but he was surprisingly patient with me.

By the time we reached Miami, I could feel the presence of the shifters clouding my consciousness again. They came through even more vividly, like we must have been closer. My heart sped up and my stomach churned at feeling those wounds and thoughts again, but I remembered how Arjun told me to create shields in my mind.

"Use whatever imagery resonates the most with you," he told me. "Maybe a castle with walls surrounding it. An island surrounded by ocean where nothing can touch you. A wild sex party with all of your men, it's completely up to you."

I did use mental images of my men, but not in the way he suggested. The first line of defense in my shield was Connor, standing at attention like the proud Marine he was. He protected me from the first moment I ran into trouble at a carnival, so it made the most sense to me. To focus on my breath, I pictured Razvan breathing fire and imagined the strength in his lungs. What gave him life also gave him the power to destroy. To remember what I loved most, I pictured Hunter and the pups playing together, laughing and smiling. Love and protecting the innocent, those were the most important things, the reasons why I was doing this at all.

And if I ever lost focus, I pictured a Bengal tiger with blue-green eyes watching me with its silent wisdom. The guide and the teacher who pulled my mind out of a dark, hellish place and showed me how to defend myself.

Keeping these mental barriers firmly in place, I followed the guys out of the RV and into the fancy beachside hotel. My fingers flexed with tension at my sides as the cool, salty breeze washed over us. There were tons of shifters in this city. I sensed all of them easily now.

My feet carried me stiffly into the lobby and I hardly dared to breathe for fear if I lost focus and my mind became consumed with suffering again.

"You're doing great," Arjun whispered with a gentle touch to my shoulder. "It gets easier the more you practice."

I didn't know he was still behind me, but mumbled my thanks as I followed Connor up to the front desk. As if sensing my discomfort, my Marine wrapped an arm around my shoulders and pulled me close with a kiss to my head.

Closing my eyes, I leaned into him with a shuddering breath. I dared to relax just a hair and my mental shields stayed up, thanks to my protective Marine.

"I'm sorry, we've overbooked and the two rooms held for you are no longer available," the woman at the front desk said after a few moments of typing on her computer.

"Ridiculous," Connor huffed in his fake manager's voice. "I'm calling Angela Dyer right now and—"

"Not to worry, sir. We've upgraded you to make up for the inconvenience," the woman said, not looking up from her screen. "You'll be in a suite but I'm afraid we only have one available."

"I suppose that'll do," Connor grumbled with a heavy sigh.

After receiving our room keys, Connor led us to the elevator like he knew exactly where to go. He practically skipped down the hallway as soon as we were out of sight of the front desk.

"Wait til you see this, babe," he grinned, kissing me. "Ever seen a hotel suite before?"

"I've never even been in a hotel room before," I answered. "What's the difference between a room and suite?"

"Check it out." He swiped his key card through the door and pushed it open, revealing what looked like a luxury apartment on the other side.

"Oh, my..."

I walked through breathlessly, feeling like I was in a dream. A floor to ceiling window with an amazing view of the beach, along with a spacious balcony and deck chairs. Marble tiles covered the floor with columns to match. The furniture was sleek, modern, perfectly coordinated, and spotless.

"It's not as big as our place," Connor slid an arm around my waist and dropped a kiss to my shoulder, "but there's a living room, kitchen, and two bedrooms. Arjun will still have his own room."

"Have you stayed here before?" I looked at him over my shoulder.

"Not here, but I rented a suite with a bunch of college buddies once. Like ten of us in one place like this, it was nuts." He spun me in his arms and kissed me long and deeply. "I've always wanted to pamper my woman by staying in a place like this. It might be on someone else's dime now but here we are, babe."

"Connor." I placed my hands on his biceps and broke off the kiss abruptly. I couldn't ignore it or hold back anymore. I already delayed things to the point of no return and couldn't afford to chicken out like this. Every day that passed without telling him just made it a bigger lie.

"What's wrong?" Those deep green eyes conveyed hurt as they bore into mine. "You don't like the room?"

"No, it's not that at all. I love it." I looked past him to see Arjun and Raz meandering from room to room, pointing out fixtures and talking softly to themselves. "Can we talk somewhere in private?" I asked, returning my eyes to Connor.

"Of course," he said immediately and pulled me to the nearest bedroom. It was relatively small, so probably not the master, but still had a gorgeous view of the ocean and its own bathroom that looked like a spa. "What's going on, babe?" he asked, seating us both down on the bed after shutting the door.

I clasped my hands in my lap to try to stop them from shaking. My heart felt firmly lodged in my throat and I didn't know if I'd be able to speak at all.

"I want to say I'm sorry first." I lowered my eyes to the bedspread, focusing on the embroidered palm trees. "You're probably going to be pissed, and it's completely my fault I didn't tell you this sooner, when we could have done something about it."

"Baby, you are the love of my life." He took my hands and brought them to his lips. "I could never be pissed at you. If you're struggling with something, all I want to is to be here for you. Now, please tell me what's going on."

"I think," I choked out, then swallowed and tried to take a breath. "I think I might be pregnant."

I didn't dare look up at him, but felt his hands squeezed around mine.

"Babe... you serious?" His forehead pressed gently to mine.

"We didn't use a condom last time, remember?" The words tumbled out like shaking leaves. "You always reminded me to be so careful before. And I just got so caught up in you, Hunter, and Raz... I wasn't thinking straight. It didn't even occur to me until later. I wanted to tell you so we could get a Plan B pill but then the theater called back and Hunter's brothers were there...."

"Shhhh." He quieted my ramblings by pulling me close and rubbing his hands up and down my back. "My silly, sweet girl. You don't have a damn thing to apologize for. It's just as much my responsibility as it is yours."

"You're not mad?" I looked at him to see a smile and bright green eyes staring back.

"Do I look mad?" His smile only widened, and his kiss that followed was full of giddiness and excitement.

"But you said before," I swallowed, "that you didn't want any, you know, accidents dragging us down."

"That was when our broke asses were living in the RV and I walked on legs that nearly killed me," he pointed out. "Now look at us, babe." He spread his arms wide to indicate the whole suite. "We're about to bring home over thirty grand for one show, and that's just the beginning." His arms dropped as he studied my face. "How do you feel about it?"

"I don't know," I admitted. "I'm relieved that you're not mad, but now it feels like I have so much to protect. The shifters here, my siblings. I was almost starting to think of Roo and Rinna like my own kids, but now I might have this one, too. I just want to keep them all safe and I don't know if I can do that."

"You're not alone," he told me solemnly, running a protective hand across my abdomen. I couldn't deny the rush of heat to my core at the thought of him as a father. A *real* father at that, and not just a sperm donor. "You have all of us. Plus the simple fact that you're so much stronger than you think you are. We can protect them all, babe. No one will ever fuck with our family and live to see the next day."

My hand traveled up his arm, taking in the hard, corded strength like a tree trunk. Strength he would use to protect those smaller and weaker than him.

"How do you feel about this?" I asked him. "Tell me honestly."

"Honestly?" His hand on my belly drew me closer, the other brushed my hair off my shoulder to cradle the nape of my neck. "I'm fucking overjoyed."

"Really?"

"When I was with Vicky," he paused to chuckle at my glare, "I always had this nagging doubt about her being the future mother of my kids. She was always a bit selfish and didn't respond to stress well, so I figured the bulk of the child-rearing would fall to me and I was okay with that. But you," he massaged my neck as he gazed at me adoringly, "I can't imagine anyone better. You're perfect for me, Mel, and I just know you'll be an amazing mom." He brought his lips to my ear. "And the thought of your belly growing big? Knowing my woman is carrying and nurturing my baby inside her? It gets me so fucking hard."

≈ 15 ≈

MELODY

Connor guided my hand to the front of his pants, where his hot whisper against my skin proved to be true. His lips fell to my neck, groaning as his cock filled my palm through the fabric.

"I don't know for sure if I am or not," I said, trying to not be distracted by his mouth gradually moving lower. "I haven't taken a test or anything."

"We can get one while we're here," he murmured against my collarbone. "But you know how I feel. Just tell me where you want me in the meantime."

His hand moved between my thighs, pushing them apart as he kneaded the sensitive flesh growing so hot near my core. Another groan escaped him as my fingers closed around his shaft, beginning some light, teasing strokes through his pants.

"God, Mel," he groaned, shoving me down flat on my back and pressing himself right against my core. "It feels like forever since I've had you to myself."

"I want you so bad," I gasped at the heat and pressure between my legs. "You and *only* you right now."

He hummed with pleasure as he lifted my shirt to my bra line,

643

kissing my ribs and belly with slow deliberation. Then a pause and a smile as those gorgeous green eyes looked up at me, his fingers hooked in the edges of my shorts and panties.

"You've made me so happy, babe," he murmured, pressing more kisses to my lower belly as he peeled my clothes down my legs. "You've made me a better man. I can't wait to meet our baby, whether that's in months or years."

"Connor." I reached for him, blinking away tears. When his lips returned to mine, I didn't need to say anything else.

I needed his kiss more than I needed air. As I fumbled impatiently with his pants and took his cock, thick and pulsing in my hand, I never wanted to lose the taste of him. We only barely broke apart when I pulled his shirt off and then mine. When he aligned himself and pressed forward, filling my aching emptiness, I never wanted him to leave.

He barely exerted himself when he slid his hands underneath me to grab my ass, then lifted us both off the bed. My back met a hard wall, and he held me there, impaling me with his cock as I secured my arms around his shoulders. Our kiss never broke, and his body never left mine. We were locked, connected, and meant to be this way.

I loved the strength in his body and clawed my hands across his back and arms to let him know. Nothing about him made him lesser. He could be missing all his limbs and still be twice the average man on the street. Every person who judged him, degraded him, or turned him away, he was better than. And he was mine.

He pulled me away from the wall just as my first orgasm convulsed around him. I whimpered and shook in his arms and he just held me—one arm around my waist, the other caressing my neck as he kissed me. Strong, solid, and unyielding, he walked us across the bedroom to the vanity and gently removed my legs from around his waist.

"Turn around, babe," he said in a husky whisper, gently facing me toward the mirror. "Watch us. See what you do to me."

I watched him in our reflection, for some reason embarrassed to look at myself. His arms flexed as his hands slid down the sides of my body, then gripped his cock in his fist to enter me again. My eyes closed at the return of the sweet, delicious fullness of him, then I felt his mouth on my ear.

"Open your eyes, babe," he commanded. "Look at how fucking gorgeous you are. I want you to see yourself how I see you."

My eyelids slitted apart, catching his gaze in the mirror's reflection. His jaw tightened with restraint, his fingers dug into my hips, and every muscle in his upper body flexed so hotly as he fucked me.

Me, with my pale skin flushed rosy. With my hair fucked up and my mouth hanging open to release the sounds of my pleasure from every one of his thrusts. Me, with my hands scrambling to hold on to the vanity like I would fall off the edge of the world if I didn't. That was who he wanted, who he loved. Not only him, but two men just as incredible as him.

My eyes rolled back in my head as I came apart for the second time. But my vision returned just as Connor's whole body went rigid and his cock turned into a steel rod inside me.

"Babe, so close," he panted.

"Don't stop. Let me feel you," I pleaded, reaching back to grab his thigh.

I watched his release in the mirror. Feeling his cock flex inside me and the spreading of warmth while watching his own tremors and facial expressions nearly got me off again. I'd never seen anything hotter and couldn't get enough.

"I wasn't sure about this mirror idea," I breathed, kissing him when he leaned forward over me. "But fuck, that was hot."

"Hm, noted," he grinned, resting his head on top of my back. His rapid pulse matched mine, along with our deep, ragged breaths. "I hope our bedroom has more fun angles."

"You mean this one isn't ours?"

"Hell no. We've got the master suite." He brushed lazy kisses along my neck and back. "Gotta make room for the dragon."

We cleaned up and got dressed to return to the living room, but not before he grabbed me for one more long, lingering kiss.

"I meant what I said," he murmured. "I want a baby with you so much. But it's up to you when the right time for that is."

"Well, just now might have sped things up. If that wasn't set in motion already." I chewed my lip nervously, the weight of being pregnant now hitting me like a ton of bricks. I wouldn't be able to perform in a few months. We still didn't live anywhere permanently. Connor would stay by me no matter what, and I felt confident Raz would too, but Hunter? Things were still so up in the air with him.

I missed the hell out of him and it hadn't even been twenty-four hours yet. Did this time apart affect him like it did me? Did my absence solidify his decision at all? I was both desperate to know what choice he made and scared to death of hearing the answer. Even if he chose me, would he want a role in raising a human child?

"You're thinking too loud again," Connor teased, stroking his thumb affectionately across my cheekbone. "Don't worry, babe. Whatever happens, we'll figure it out."

"You sound like me when we first met," I scoffed.

"And you were right back then, no matter how much my negative ass tried to drag us down." He cupped the back of my neck. "Ever since you came to my trailer and ignored me when I told you to go away, everything has worked out. Hasn't it, babe?"

"It has," I chuckled at the memory. "That'll be a story to tell our kids."

"Damn right it will." He squeezed my nape and gave me one more kiss. "Now let's head back out before your dragon boy steals you from me again."

I giggled as the door opened, Connor's hands still on me as Raz and Arjun spun around from looking out at the ocean.

"Oh, for fuck's sake," Arjun whined. "Don't tell me you just shagged in my room? You've got the damn master!"

"Sorry, man." Connor draped an arm over my shoulders and unapologetically groped my breast, clearly not sorry at all. "Been a while since the lady and I had any alone time."

"Connor!" I slapped his hand while Raz smothered his laugh with a fake cough, turning away so Arjun couldn't see him smiling.

"Now I've got to call downstairs and get the sheets changed," the tiger shifter huffed, heading straight for the phone.

"If you're doing to do that, might as well have them wipe down the vanity too," Connor smirked, all too pleased with himself.

"The vanity?! Fucking hell..."

"And the wall next to the bed," I added, unable to stop myself from joining in the teasing.

"The wall too?! Fuck me, you lot are a bunch of animals."

The next sentence tumbled out of my mouth faster than I could stop myself.

"If you can't beat 'em, join 'em, Arjun!"

16

HUNTER

Normally, I could handle one day apart, or even a few. But the possibility of never seeing Mel again was too much to bear.

Seeing Colt and Gabe with Miriam made the longing for her even worse. I already knew Colt was smitten by their shaman woman, but seeing stubborn, surly Gabe warm up to her made the fierce ache in my chest cut even deeper.

The pups and I spent the day with them in their cabin, tucked back into the woods. It didn't feel right to stay in the house at the FDR Center without Connor there. They loaned it out to him after all, not me.

After spending the day in the woods and then enjoying a fresh kill for dinner with my family, I should have been content. I should have patted my full belly while looking over at my pups, safe and exhausted from living more like wolves than humans in the last few days. I should have felt grateful beyond measure that my two brothers were still alive —that my pups had more strong wolves to look up to, even if we weren't a full pack.

Before meeting Mel, I might have been content with all that.

But if I hadn't met her, I probably wouldn't be alive to see my pups content, well-fed, and happy. I might not have reunited with my brothers at all. And I certainly wouldn't be looking across the table at Colt, smiling at the human woman in his lap and missing my doe-eyed little fox with every bone in my body.

I should have gone with her. I was foolish to stay. And now I might never see her again.

When the three of them said goodnight and headed off to one bedroom, I scooped up my kids and headed for the second bedroom, grateful it was on the other side of the cabin. I didn't need their noises to rub salt in the wounds of being away from my woman.

And Razvan. I didn't realize until after kissing him goodbye how much I would miss him, too. We still hadn't established any explicit relationship between ourselves, but he was a solid fixture in our arrangement. I couldn't miss Mel without missing him as well.

I wanted more than sex with him, which I realized when he confronted me in the kitchen and I kissed him, knowing Gabe would walk in and see. I wanted Gabe to see, and I wanted Raz to know I wasn't ashamed of the connection we had. He deserved better than that.

The moment I laid my pups down and tucked the blankets around them, Rinna stirred with a whimper, then woke up crying softly.

"What's wrong, sweetie?" I pulled her close and smoothed out her hair, letting her curl up against me.

"When are we going home, Dad?" she asked between sniffles.

I hesitated, not knowing exactly how to answer. "Which home, sweetie?"

"The big house with Miss Mel, Mister Connor, and Mister Razvan," she sniffed. "And the big tiger shifter who talks funny."

My heart splintered in two. "We can go back tomorrow, honey. But Mel and the others won't be back for a little while. It'll just be us. But we can always visit your uncles."

"Why did they go away?" my daughter demanded with a trembling bottom lip. "Don't they like us anymore? Did we make them mad?"

"No, sweetie. Of course not." I kissed the top of her head and hugged her tightly. "Actually, we could have gone with them. But you had so much fun with your uncles, I thought you guys would rather stay."

"I miss Mel," she whimpered, burying her head in my chest. "I love visiting Uncle Colt and Uncle Gabe, but I want Mel back."

"Me too, honey." I blew out a long breath as I rubbed her back. "Me too."

HOURS AFTER SOOTHING Rinna back to sleep, I still couldn't doze off myself. After tossing, turning, and staring at the ceiling, wishing I had Mel's soft, feminine body and Raz's hard, tattooed one wrapped around me, I got up from bed.

Knowing sleep wouldn't come, I crept out the back door as silently as I could. I didn't feel up for a run, but certainly couldn't lie still. I just needed something to keep my mind off the two aching holes in my heart.

"Come to howl at the moon?"

I turned to see Gabe, shirtless and leaning against the wall with a cigar in his hand. Even in the dim light, I could see the scratches down his chest. That and his smug, satisfied expression told me all I needed to know about his evening went.

"Sure, you could say that."

He handed me the cigar, and I accepted it without question, taking a few short puffs before handing it back.

"What's eating your tail, brother?" he asked. The smoke pouring lazily out of his mouth and nostrils reminded me of Razvan.

"I miss her," I confessed, leaning against the wall next to him. "I should've gone with them."

"Yeah, you probably should've," he agreed.

I looked at him in surprise. "You've really changed your tune toward humans since we met up again. What gives?"

He lifted one shoulder in a lazy shrug. "The human woman who was riding me a few minutes ago, I suppose."

"How did you two meet her?" I asked, eager for a distraction from my own love life.

"After you got captured, the pack got separated," he began. "They were trying to round up as many of us as they could, so we split up. Colt and I got chased to the edge of our territory to a small town. They set out traps and tracked us for weeks. It was safer for us to stay close to humans in the town. Our tracks were covered and we could stay together."

He took a hard pull on the cigar. "But we were forced to scavenge since we couldn't go in the woods to hunt. We came out at night and dug through garbage cans like fucking raccoons. One night, she saw us." His lips turned up at the memory. "She worked in a grocery store and was throwing out cuts of meat. For an entire week, we waited for her at the end of every shift and she saved the best cuts for us. Finally, she came up to us and said, 'I know you guys are shifters'."

"Huh. How did that go?" I accepted the cigar from him again.

"I wanted to bolt," he admitted. "You know how it was growing up. If a human knows what you are, they might as well be putting a gun to your head. That's what Dad always said. But Colt wanted to trust her. I almost took off without him, but no way could I live with the fact that I possibly left my brother to die at the hands of a human."

"And now you're sharing her," I concluded.

"Yeah," he breathed with a small shake of his head. "It's a tough pill to swallow, you know?"

"What, sharing a mate?" I asked. "It's not unheard of among us."

"Not that," he replied. "The fact that we *need* humans on our side. Strong packs with good alphas aren't enough to keep our pups safe anymore. We have to turn to the same species, rounding us up like cattle and profiting off our abilities. I still can't fully wrap my head around it."

"Shamans aren't the same," I said. "They smell different. I'm sure you've noticed."

"Yeah," the smirk returned. "And they magic their way into our big bad hearts."

"There used to be more of them, from what I understand," I said.

"So it's not a new thing to be involved with shamans, but not as many shifters know they're around."

"Miriam told us something else that makes me worry," he glanced at me hesitantly.

"Yeah, what?"

"Not all shamans can be trusted."

17

MELODY

"Barring any highly negative feedback from attendees, I fully expect the investment board to approve a long-term contract for you in the near future."

"That's... wow," I breathed, trying not to move my mouth too much and risk frustrating the makeup artist.

Angela Dyer sat across from me in my dressing room, tapping out messages on her phone and scribbling notes on a memo pad. All business as usual.

In the meantime, I could scarcely believe I had a dressing room at all. After crashing for the night in our suite, the guys and I showed up the next day at the time we were told, only to be ushered into separate dressing rooms. A girl offered me wine and tiny sandwiches the moment I sat in the makeup chair. I declined the alcohol but helped myself to the snacks offered.

"We've completely sold out and still have attendees scrambling to get in," Angela went on as she scrolled through her phone. I swore I heard a hint of delight in her voice. "People are posting on our Facebook page saying they're big fans of yours. Some are coming all the way from Mississippi to see you."

"Seriously?" I completely forgot about keeping my face blank. "People from Crying Falls are coming to see us?"

"It appears that way. Seems you made quite an impression in your previous work."

I sat back in the chair, utterly flabbergasted. Some attendees came to every single show back in Crying Falls, but after Connor's accident, I figured that fanbase had been too disappointed and washed their hands of us.

"I had no idea people would follow us from that far," I whispered in disbelief.

"You need your own social media pages," Angela declared, scribbling on her memo pad. "So your fans can continue to follow you. We can hire someone to manage the accounts for you."

"Oh, okay." I didn't even know that was a thing. I wished Connor was in here, pretending to be my agent or whatever again. He knew this business stuff way better than I did.

"Um, how soon after tonight would you want a new contract signed?" I asked. That had to be important information, right? I mainly just wanted to know if I'd be able to go back to Hunter and the pups again.

Angela tapped her pen on her memo pad as she thought. "It'll be a few weeks to a month before the board drafts an offer for you. Then I'm sure you'd want to negotiate the terms with your attorney, so that will add on a bit of time."

"Ah, right. Of course," I nodded like I knew what she was talking about.

"Once the contract is signed, we'd love to schedule weekly shows in time for the Christmas season. So with all the planning and negotiation involved, it'll be another few months before you're onstage with us again."

"I see." That would allow plenty of time to see Hunter again. And depending on how much money we made from this one night, I could get my siblings out of that hellhole in time for Christmas, too.

But if I was pregnant and started showing in a few months?

"How long does a contract typically last?" I asked.

"Six months to a year," she replied. "After the first run, we can arrange a traveling show if that interests you. We have plans to open more Vaudeville theaters in Texas, the Carolinas, D.C. We'd even love to have a spot right in Times Square in New York."

"Sounds great!" I forced a tight smile. "I'll have to talk it over with the guys, but I'm sure we can figure something out."

"The board is absolutely willing to be flexible with your schedule and other commitments," Angela said, leaning forward and looking over her glasses at me. "You're reliable, you put on an entertaining show, and you already have an established fan base. I'd say you're one of the wisest investments we've made in years."

Was that a compliment? It kind of sounded like a compliment.

"Thank you," I responded, keeping my smile up.

"I'll leave you to get ready," she said, rising from her seat. "If you need anything, don't hesitate to buzz me."

Not a minute after she left, a knock came to my dressing room door.

"Come in," I called nervously.

All my nerves melted away when Connor, Raz, and Arjun walked through the door. Even my dutiful makeup artist had to stop and stare at the three gorgeous men who walked right up to me.

"Man, am I glad to see you guys," I breathed.

"You clean up quite nicely, ringmistress," Arjun observed, his ocean-colored eyes taking me in from head to toe.

To fit in with the Vaudeville's corporate, polished image, they put me in a simple black leotard and jacket. For stage makeup, my look was fairly subdued, with just purple-magenta eyeshadow and lipstick to stand out against the black clothing.

"Thanks," I said, hoping my foundation and contouring covered up my blush. "Too bad I can't say the same about you."

"Oooh, burn," Connor muttered under his breath, while Raz just chuckled.

The two of them were dressed up to entertain, with Connor in a form-fitting tank top and baggy jeans, and Raz in his biker getup with a leather vest and pants, and motorcycle boots. Arjun, on the other hand, was still in the borrowed clothes that he came to Florida in. He wouldn't be gracing the stage in human form.

"Ouch," Arjun brought a hand to his chest, but his smirk told me he wasn't really offended. "I'll be happy to remain in my birthday suit, seeing as that's how you prefer me."

I gritted my teeth and dug my fingers into the handles of the chair. Ever since I blurted out the suggestion that he join us, he never stopped teasing me about it. I said it without thinking and it was a total accident. Now I couldn't stop mentally kicking myself.

The makeup artist held back a snicker as she dusted my face with setting powder. I suddenly felt annoyed that she was partial to this moment between me and my guys.

"Can you give us a minute if you're done?" I asked.

"Yeah, totally," she answered, but looked disappointed as she gathered up her brushes and left the dressing room.

"Angela said there's a pretty good chance of us getting a long-term contract," I told the guys as soon as we were alone. "People who saw us in Crying Falls have been dying to get into this show."

"That's great, steluța," Raz beamed, the pride clear in his voice. "You entrance people. We've seen this all along."

"Yeah, but," I shifted my gaze to Connor. "That thing we talked about earlier might not bode well for any long-term deals."

"What thing?" Raz and Arjun looked between me and Connor.

Connor met my eyes calmly as he leaned against the vanity. "I can say it or you can if you want, babe. But since you've brought it up, we might as well tell them."

"Tell us what?"

I closed my eyes and took a deep breath, remembering that everything had worked out since these men came into my life. "I might be pregnant."

"Pregnant?!" Raz gasped.

"Might be?" Arjun lifted a skeptical eyebrow.

"I haven't taken a test yet but we," I nodded to Connor, "might have forgotten to use protection the last couple times."

"Ah, ah, the last one wasn't being forgetful," Connor teased me with a smile. "I distinctly remember you telling me not to stop."

"I've heard enough already." Arjun covered his ears with his hands and turned around.

"So you were all but, ah, planning this?" Raz asked. I couldn't read his expression.

"No," I protested. "Not the first time, but I only told Connor yesterday because I was scared and we'd been so busy. We had our alone time, and he assured me everything would be okay, so it... kind of happened again." I reached for Raz's hands and pulled him close. "Are you upset?"

"I'm not upset," he muttered, stroking his thumbs across my palms. "I just would have liked to have known. Been included in that decision, maybe." His eyes flicked up to mine. "Because it affects me too, you know."

"I'm sorry, dragon," my hands wound around the back of his neck. "We should have told you right away."

"It's my bad too, Raz," Connor clapped him on the shoulder. "Since it would be biologically mine, I didn't think of you or Hunter right away. I just got so caught up in the idea of making a baby with the woman I love. Sorry, dude. We're still finding our way around this being in a harem thing."

"It's alright. I get it," Raz grunted.

I slid off my chair and kissed him hard, pouring every ounce of my love for him into it and not giving a fuck that I ruined my lipstick. "I love you, Raz, and I'd love to have your dragon babies too if I could."

That finally got a smile out of him as his arms slid around my waist. "Any baby you have, I'll love as my own. Just tell me if you're trying. Or you know, not preventing it from happening."

"I will. I promise." I kissed him again. "I brought it up because if I am, I'll have a serious bump in a few months, and they probably don't want a pregnant ringmistress onstage."

"Scheduling can get moved around," Connor said casually. "Things happen, girls get knocked up, everyone's used to it. If they're serious about us, they'll give us time. If not, we'll be in demand enough to go somewhere else that will accommodate us."

"This is why I love you guys," I sighed, staring at him while I leaned my head on Raz's bare chest. "You make me feel better and talk so much common sense when all I do is worry."

"Is that the only reason?" Raz teased, kissing my forehead.

I lifted my gaze up to him. "You support me, believe in me, and take care of me in ways I didn't know was possible. I would really be lost if I didn't have you, and I mean that."

"Love you, *steluţa*," he growled with a possessive kiss and stepped out of my reach all too soon.

"Where are you going?" I whined from my chair as they all headed toward the dressing room door.

"Almost showtime, babe." Connor winked as he followed the shifters. "And you need your lipstick fixed."

18

MELODY

Several small acts of local talent took the stage before us. All four of us would perform together last as a single act, the head-lining event.

My nerves grew with every peek I took behind the curtain. The auditorium was massive, easily twice the size of the one we auditioned at in Georgia and it was absolutely packed. They filled every seat from the floor to the upper decks. I even saw security guards stop people in the lobby and turn them away.

Since the first time I ever stepped onstage, I wondered if I'd be too nervous to take that first step out into the spotlight. It was always the hardest, but now it felt nearly impossible.

We'd never put on a show like this before, combining all our talents into one cohesive performance. We only had a week, but we practiced our hearts out. Nothing should stop us from nailing it, nothing except ourselves.

When the final act finished and my drum beat started up, so did the crowd. They finished their polite applause and then got serious. Feet stomped the floor. Hands clapped together. Voices shouted our names. It still boggled my mind to hear how thousands of people could sound like a single organism. They all wanted the same thing, and that was us.

The first step is always the hardest. Do that and this show is yours, I told myself.

Feeling somewhere between fainting and vomiting, I stepped out past the curtain and my other foot followed. The spotlight bathed me in brightness, and like magic, the anxiety disappeared. Cries, cheers, and applause rang out, and a genuine stage smile grew across my face.

"Ladies and gentlemen! Boys and girls!" My voice boomed with omnipotent power through the speakers. "I see some familiar faces tonight!"

The audience only grew louder, shouting and chanting my name. Humbled, I brought a hand to my chest and smiled down at my feet.

"Thank you. I've missed you all too," I replied. "For those of you who don't me, I'm Melody, your host for this evening. Tonight, you will all meet new friends and perhaps see familiar ones, but this is unlike any show you've ever seen before. You won't believe your eyes, ladies and gentlemen! Your mind will question what is real and what is even possible. And tonight," I paused, surveying the crowd from left to right, "We dare you to believe in the unbelievable."

The stage grew dark, and I walked on my tall heels to the edge of the curtain. Low murmurs and whispers rose up in anticipation of the first act. From my place at the side, I took deep breaths, feeling just as anxious as the crowd.

When the hip hop instrumental music kicked on and the first light shone on Connor at the top of a platform, the screams and cheers hit me like a splash of cool water to the face. He didn't have stilts for this show, but he didn't need them.

He moved too fast for anyone to get a good look at his prosthetics, not that it mattered. They'd be even more in awe of him, but he insisted on not being showcased as an amputated acrobat. His routine consisted of flips and handstands like a typical acrobat, but also incorporated break-dancing and, dare I say... stripping?

Women screamed as he slowly eased down the edge of the platform to the stage floor, rolling his hips as he gripped the edges with his hands and knees. I crossed my arms as I watched, smiling with a bite to my lip as his shirt came off when he reached the floor. If I didn't know any better, I'd think this was a *Magic Mike* show. Everyone went nuts, and I was grateful as hell for my earplugs.

He front and back-flipped, cartwheeled, handstanded, danced across the floor, a dazzling charismatic smile on his face the whole time. My heart nearly burst for him. He actually looked like he enjoyed himself. It always seemed like he performed just because he had to. It was a job and he got it done. Now he was having fun at it, too.

The stage darkened again, concentrating a small spotlight on him, but he carried on as if oblivious. Some of the observant members of the audience noticed the small flame hovering above the platform where he began.

Connor's music faded away as the flame grew bigger, nearly the size of a person. People gasped and shouted, "Fire! Look out!"

He turned and looked up, the blaze now creating most of the light onstage as a man's silhouetted figure stepped into the flame and drew a sword from his back. Everyone grew silent and sat on the edges of their seats as figure and flame jumped down from the platform as if they were one, and then a heated battle ensued.

The flaming swordsman swung, jabbed, and stabbed his blade at Connor, who flipped, backbended, and vaulted off the platform's vertical surfaces to dodge the attacks. Fast-tempo music accompanied the duel as Raz chased Connor around the stage.

Grabbing my prop sword from the side, I switched my mic on.

"Connor, you need a weapon against the flaming sword!" I declared. "Take this!"

Tossing it to him like we'd practiced thousands of times, he caught the handle in one hand while doing a handstand with the other. Returning to his feet, he blocked Raz's blow at just the right moment. Gasps and shrieks arose from the crowd as the human flame grew dangerously close to Connor's skin, swords crossed and pushing against each other. Even from where I stood, it looked completely real.

"I have a new plan," Razvan declared menacingly, the flames disappearing across body. His clothes and body completely unburnt, his fire concentrated along the length of his sword. Pulling the fiery blade away from Connor, he vaulted over both of us as if carried by some unseen wind and landed on his feet behind me.

Everyone screamed and shouted, "No!" when he pulled me close to his body and held the flaming sword in front of my face. I widened my eyes to show fear, watching the flames dance inches away from my face. His fire's heat was nothing more than a gentle warmth like a candle.

"Let her go, Razvan!" Connor cried out. "Your fight's with me!"

"Take her from me!" Raz cackled, walking us toward the edge and center of the stage where everyone could clearly see. "Is there anyone brave enough to free Melody? Come down and fight me if you are!"

Several men shouted back from the audience, and Raz taunted all of them.

"Ah, you've already pissed yourself in fear. I can smell it from here. You? Boy, you haven't even grown all your pubes yet. Sit back down!"

While talking shit to the crowd, Connor took the opportunity to snatch Raz's sword away. Now, with one naked blade and one on fire, he pointed both of them at us.

"You're unarmed, Razvan! No choice now but to let her go."

"Silly man," Raz sighed, lifting a hand toward his mouth. "You shouldn't play with toys unless you know how to use them." He blew across his palm, sending a stream of fire past my face and across the stage. Now both of Connor's swords were on fire.

He swung them back and forth a few times, creating a dazzling display of light which made the crowd awestruck. "I think I can handle it, you pyro."

"Come at me then!" With one hand still tight around my waist, Raz reached the other into a hidden pocket and pulled out four knives between each of his fingers. He tossed them to the other hand, juggling the knives inches away from my body. One by one, each of those blades caught fire as well.

Looking more apprehensive now, Connor approached us warily with his two flaming swords. A fight with incredible optical illusions ensued. Every jab he took looked as though it was blocked by a knife as it was tossed in the air. But Raz's juggling rhythm never broke, he just carried on. This took us nearly the whole week to get down perfectly and I couldn't be more proud and relieved that my guys were so on it.

On and on it continued, neither one of them gaining an advantage. It would have carried on forever if another small spotlight didn't appear at the top of the platform and a large feline face stepped into it.

"A tiger! Oh my god, it's a tiger!"

Raz and Connor looked up together, both of them dropping their weapons in mock surprise.

"It's Dawon!" I cried. "Here to save me!"

Arjun jumped down from the platform, eliciting gasps of shock and awe at his powerful feline form. Landing gracefully on all fours, he lowered his head and roared at me and Raz. Even though we practiced this and I knew he wouldn't harm me, the fear on my face was genuine. A tiger's bare teeth in its roaring, open mouth might as well had been looking death in the face.

"Fine, you want her?" Raz said. "Go ahead and eat her!"

He shoved me away, but the tiger remained focused on him, stalking forward to his prey. I ran dramatically behind Connor and peeked over his shoulder like any good damsel in distress.

"You don't scare me, cat," Raz told the snarling feline. "I have more skills with my blades than you have teeth!"

With that, he kicked one of his knives that he dropped to the stage floor. It hurtled toward the tiger, who batted it away like a toy. The crowd gasped, and Raz wore a look of shock on his face. He kicked up another knife and this time, Arjun caught it in his mouth. Twice more and all his knives were gone. The only thing left to do was run.

Everyone now burst into laughter and cheers as Arjun chased Raz around the stage, the dragon's knees kicking up high in an exaggerated gait, while Arjun loped around lazily just on his heels. The tension grew higher as Arjun got closer and began swiping at Raz's feet. When Raz finally got some distance, he turned around to face his pursuer and blew a massive fireball across the stage.

Laughs turned to screams as Arjun jumped right through the flames and pounced on the fire breather. Raz screamed as the massive animal knocked him to the ground. With the evil, damsel-kidnapping fire breather subdued, Connor ran up behind him for the grand finale.

He raised the two flaming swords above his head and shoved them all the way down Raz's throat.

The crowd went absolutely nuts. Even through my earplugs, I heard their cries and screams. Some were standing up in their seats and looking over as if they couldn't believe what just happened.

Raz's eyes bugged out. His hands clasped to his chest. And with a final gurgling breath, his head fell back, and he laid still. Arjun approached me and head-butted my hip, circling around me with a loud purr that radiated through the speakers. Then the stage went dark.

Just as we suspected, the audience was too shocked to clap. Without the light, you wouldn't even know the theater was packed with people. Everyone was silent, most likely holding their breath as they wondered if we actually killed a man in front of a live audience.

The four of us remained posed onstage as the lights returned. Raz was the first to move, coming to his feet with his head back and the sword handles still resting on his lips. With one hand followed by the other, he swiftly removed the now-flameless blades and held them at his sides as he gave the audience a charming smile, then took a deep bow at the waist.

The silent theater erupted into thunderous applause as the rest of us stepped next to him and took our bows as well. Even Arjun lowered his head, much to the delight of the crowd. We spent the next minute smiling, waving, bowing, and saying thank you, but crowd would not let up. Everyone was on their feet, clapping, cheering and taking photos. It felt like the applause would go on forever.

Checking to make sure his mic was off, Connor leaned over and whispered in my ear, "I think that thirty-grand just got a *lot* bigger, babe."

19

MELODY

We were rich. Or at least we would be in a few days when the Vaudeville cut us our check. For the next few hours, we signed merchandise, posed for photos, and chatted with VIP attendees. Only Arjun made himself scarce, as the theater had strict rules about animals outside of performances and we weren't about to reveal his shifter status.

Somewhere around my ten-thousandth photo with fans, a familiar pain struck the back of my head like a hammer. A vision of a woman covered in white feathers restrained under heavy shackles filled my head. In the next moment, I saw through her eyes.

"Do it, or we'll shock your kids again," said a man in a while lab coat, *wielding an electric cattle prod in front of him. "Shift back until you only have feathers on your arms. Let's see our pretty angel."*

"It doesn't work like that," she said through gritted teeth. *"I can't just—"*

Her words were cut off by the sensation of hundreds of needles digging under her skin. I gasped in pain, clutching my side as I doubled over.

"Steluța!" Raz wrapped a protective arm around me. "What's wrong?"

"I see them again," I gasped. "They're hurting kids..."

"Remember what Arjun told you," he murmured, running a soothing hand across my back. Then to someone else, "Sorry, she's not feeling well. We have to cut this short."

"Oh, okay! Can she just sign my—"

"Leave," Raz hissed. "Now."

After exerting myself in tonight's show, it took all my mental strength just to keep the pain away. The visions and sounds came through just as strong, but at least the pain was just a dull ache. Raz and Connor guided me through the backstage area with their arms around me. I could barely make sense of anything, but vaguely recognized my dressing room door being pushed open and the handsome man waiting in my chair.

"For fuck's sake! Took you all long enough playing celebrities—"

"She needs you," Connor cut him off. "The shifter visions are hitting her hard."

Through blurry vision, I saw Arjun's face close to mine. His blue-green eyes were wide with compassion as he touched my face gently. I wanted to lean into his hand, into him. He was warm, solid, and felt good...

"I can't shift here. It's too risky," I hear him say over the cries in my head. "We have to go back to the suite."

The next few minutes or hours, I couldn't tell, went by in a blur. I felt like I was drifting back and forth between two places at once. There was darkness, and then blinding bright light. I looked up at one point, realizing I was on an operating table. A man holding a sadistic-looking dental tool smiled down at me. When I screamed and tried to get up, it was Connor holding me and kissing my face.

At some point, I heard the rumbling, the sound that was so nice and comforting. I went toward it, heard it get louder, and wrap around me with warmth and safety.

I woke up as I often did these days—my head on a man's chest and someone else snuggled up behind me. My sigh of relief was short-lived.

The suffering of those shifters was never ending. Even right now, while I didn't feel them, there were scared children huddled up in cages, their parents hurt and experimented on right in front of them.

I nuzzled my head over my man-chest pillow as I rubbed my eyes, slowly returning to the waking world. A familiar tattooed arm wrapped snugly around my waist, and I looked behind me to see Raz, fast asleep and looking adorable.

With a smile on my lips, I turned to face him. Not ready to face the world yet, I sank into his warmth. Wrapping my arms around his sides, I kissed the tattoos on his throat and collarbone until he gently stirred.

"Mm, I love waking up with you," he muttered groggily. "How are you, *steluța?*"

"Better for now," I whispered. "But I feel awful for being here while all that is going on."

"We'll find them," he answered, pulling me in closer. "Now that the show's over, we can focus on that."

"Four of us against an entire compound? I'm simply dying to hear that plan of attack."

I froze upon hearing not only the voice, but the accent behind me. No fucking way! Was I just...

Almost too afraid to find out, I looked slowly over my shoulder. And my heart went into overdrive when my eyes confirmed my fear. I had been sleeping on Arjun's chest.

"Morning, dove," he greeted me lightheartedly, muscles flexing as he pushed himself up to sitting. "You know I don't care about this sharing business, but I must admit you are a good cuddle."

My eyes nearly bugging out of my head, I looked panicking between him and Raz. "Why... what?"

"Relax, *steluța,*" Raz chuckled, kissing my cheek. "You were drifting in and out of visions in your sleep. Arj kept you grounded with his purring but seems he shifted to human at some point."

"Sometimes I go to sleep as a tiger and wake up as a human. Does that ever happen to you, Raz?" Arjun got up from bed and I buried my face in Raz's chest, but it was too late. I already saw *dat ass.*

"I've never slept in dragon form," Raz answered casually. "Not intentionally, anyway. Too risky being seen."

"I miss your dragon form," I murmured, nuzzling his neck. "Feels like forever since I've seen him."

"Yeah, it sucks not being able to shift often," he replied, then swatted my ass playfully. "But you're a shaman. You can see him any time you want to."

Hesitantly, I looked over my shoulder at Arjun. He put on pants, thankfully, but it was all I could do not to stare at his torso, which was carved better than the marble columns in the suite.

"If I do, will I be vulnerable to feeling all the other shifters again?"

"I don't think so, as long as you keep your mental shields up." He turned to leave the room, but hesitated and added, "They're getting stronger. Your mental blocks, I mean. You're doing good, Mel."

"He likes you," Raz teased once he left the room, planting kisses on my neck.

"He does not," I retorted.

"Lies," he chuckled. "Do you like him?"

I remained silent, unsure how to answer. I didn't dislike Arjun anymore. If it weren't for him, I'd probably be braindead or in a coma by now. And I appreciated that as a friend. He was nice to look at and listen to, but that didn't mean I *liked* him.

"I knew it," Raz chuckled at my silence.

"He's been a good friend," I relented, but he wasn't getting any more out of me than that.

"Sure," he grunted, moving his kisses down to my shoulder.

"Stop distracting me!" I giggled. "Let me feel your dragon."

"Is that code for something else?" he grinned against my skin, but stilled as I mentally reached out for the animal within him.

It was effortless this time. I was shocked at how easy it was. The beast roared as he felt my presence. He missed me, too. He longed to feel me on his back as we flew under the moonlight again. Hot, smooth scales wrapped around me in a protective embrace. I felt the wind on my face from the powerful beat of his wings, and smelled his smoky, earthy scent.

Gradually, the scales became skin, and the wings dissolved into tattooed arms that wrapped around me. But my dragon was still here. He was always here.

"I'll never get tired of that," I smiled up at Raz. "You're simply amazing."

"You are, my love," he sighed contentedly, sinking into the mattress next to me. "I'll take you to Romania one day. With all our riches, we can rent a castle out in the black forest where no one will bother us. I can let my dragon out anytime I want and fly you to the moon every night."

"Sounds romantic," I murmured, my lips against his.

"I have my moments," he chuckled, kissing me.

"One day," I sighed. "When no shifters are mistreated anymore." It felt so wrong to be here, in a luxurious suite, wrapped up in my man's arms while this compound existed. I couldn't ignore it, no more than I could ignore seeing Roo, Rinna, and Hunter that first time.

God, I missed them.

"Well, we're not getting anything done staying in bed." He kissed me once more and moved to get up.

I admired the sight of his inked physique for a moment before getting up myself. Thankfully, I was in a camisole and underwear. I'd probably die of embarrassment if I cuddled with Arjun naked.

"You say that like you know where to go," I remarked, finding a pair of shorts and pulling them on.

"I don't," he admitted, pulling on his own clothing. "But the beach is a good place to start."

"The beach?" I repeated.

"Have you been able to follow the presence of the shifters?" he asked. "Like you did when we found Arjun?"

I hadn't realized it but shook my head, frustrated. "No, I can't pinpoint a direction for them. The visions got worse as we got closer to Miami, but I have no way of locating them."

"Arjun mentioned that last night," he said. "He's afraid another powerful shaman is working at the compound. Someone who can block you from finding it, while also projecting those visions into your head."

I couldn't believe what he was saying. "Another shaman? Letting shifters be treated like that?"

"It's possible he or she is a prisoner as well," he said. "They might be forced to do this. But if that's true, we've got another issue on our hands."

I stared at him, the realization hitting me as we said the same thing out loud.

"They already know we're here."

20

MELODY

"We just put on a show for thousands of people," I realized with increasing horror. "We were probably on the news. We'll be in newspapers and magazines. All over social media. If these are the same people who held you and Arjun, they'll definitely recognized you."

"All the more reason for us to go to the beach," Raz replied calmly. "It's public, it's crowded, we'll blend in. We'll be able to scope things out. Maybe we'll even find shifters blending in with the humans who can give us information."

I nodded. It made sense. "I don't have a bathing suit, though."

A wily grin spread across his face. "I might have gotten someone from the hotel to do a shopping errand for us."

"What?" I demanded. Then, "Wait, you can do that?"

"Dunno, but I did," he shrugged, his smile growing wider. "Do you want to see what they picked out?"

"I guess so," I shrugged back, my own smile growing despite myself. "Over thirty-grand per show, hotel staff going shopping for us. This is my life now."

We went out into the living room to find Arjun and Connor

inspecting dozens of bikinis. Every style, cut, and color imaginable laid out on the coffee table and surrounding couches.

"Jesus, how many did you make them get?" I demanded.

"Might have bought out the whole store," Raz coughed into his hand.

"Not those, babe." Connor wagged a finger at me as I went to look at a pile of swimsuits in an armchair. "Those have been rejected. These are the ones you have to choose from." He waved his hands over a smaller pile on the coffee table.

"What? But these are cute!" I picked up one with a navy blue and red paisley pattern that would cover up my chest but show off my shoulders nicely.

"Not slutty enough," Arjun quipped, nodding his head toward Connor. "His words, not mine."

"Connor, what—"

"We need to blend in to the Miami crowd, right? So you've got to wear Miami bathing suits." He picked up a stringy scrap of clothing with one finger. "Try this on, babe."

"Is that... a thong?" I looked at him in disbelief. "Connor, my entire ass will be hanging out!"

"It's what every woman in Miami is wearing to the beach." He coughed. "Not that I've been looking."

"No freaking way! I mean, wearing a bikini at all is a compromise enough. I'm not going out in a crowd of people basically naked."

"*Steluța*, you wear those stockings and corsets and shit onstage. A bikini isn't that much different."

"It's completely different!" I whipped around to face Raz, who was trying too hard to look innocent. "You didn't even want me doing burlesque onstage back in Georgia! But you're okay with this?"

"The lads do have a point," Arjun remarked. "Every woman at the beach will be wearing nearly nothing. Covering yourself up won't do you any favors if we're trying to blend in."

"Jesus, not you too," I turned on him with a glare. "You're supposed to be the brilliant one! How do I blend in without my ass and boobs hanging out everywhere?"

"Sometimes the most genius plans are the simplest, dove."

"Traitors, all of you," I muttered with a pout. "Have you ever thought maybe I don't want my body out on public display?"

"We'll all be right there with you, babe," Connor assured. "No one will look twice at you and get away with it. If someone tries to touch or catcall you? We'll knock motherfuckers out. I'm not kidding."

"Because that definitely won't draw attention," I retorted.

"Where's the free-spirited girl who jumped naked into the pool?" Raz came up behind me, gliding his hand along my lower back.

"Only you guys saw me, plus it was at night!"

"Minor little details." Raz pressed a kiss to my cheek. "We won't force you to do anything, *steluța*. But I have a feeling part of you secretly wants to show off."

"And what the hell makes you think that?"

"The lady doth protest too much," Arjun smirked.

"You like to take risks," Raz whispered seductively into my ear. "You like a little bit of danger. And you love being surrounded by your strong, handsome men."

"Don't flatter yourself," I muttered, now being argumentative just for the sake of it and they knew it. Raz kissed the spot between my neck and shoulder and my back arched in response, eliciting a pleased chuckle from him.

Damn him. Damn them all. At what point did they start to know me better than I knew myself?

"I'll try on the ones that *I* like," I relented. "But none of you get to say if it's showing off enough or not. That's for me to decide."

I got no argument from them as I pawed through the sets of tops and bottoms in search of one that, hopefully, wouldn't be downright humiliating.

A half-hour later, I left the suite wearing a little burgundy number that thankfully covered most of my ass, even though it tied at the sides of my hips in thin strings. Who said I wasn't willing to compromise? The top was a classic bikini style with triangular bra cups and strings that tied at the bra line and around my neck. My chest felt a bit more exposed than I was comfortable with, but there wasn't much I could do about that.

The guys filed close around me like bodyguards in the elevator, with Connor and Raz on either side of me, and Arjun behind us.

"Where's your swimwear, now?" I asked my Marine with a quizzical eyebrow.

"I ain't gettin' near that water," he replied. "Don't want anything to rust. Honestly, getting near sand is probably a bit dicey for me."

He wore baggy jeans covering his legs and sneakers over his prosthetic feet. On top he wore a breezy, tropical shirt completely unbuttoned, showing off his washboard stomach and pecs that could crush walnuts if he tried.

"Oh, so *you* can cover up, but I can't?" I teased.

"I have a medical condition," he replied in a mocking, nasally voice. "Take it up with my doctor, missy."

I swatted his chest affectionately and stood on tiptoe to kiss him, during which he took a gratuitous handful of my ass.

"All this sun is gonna make my ink age faster," Raz grumbled on the other side of me. He wore nothing but blue swim trunks and flip-flops, a large beach towel draped over his shoulder. I pulled away from Connor and nestled against my dragon's side.

"I'm sure we can find some sunscreen to rub all over you," I purred, tracing my fingers across the images and lettering across his abs. It felt like a while since I really poured over the art on his body.

"God, I hope so," he grinned, draping his arm over my shoulders. "You'll need some too, *steluţa*. You'll look like a lobster if you're not careful."

"Am I the only one actually looking forward to the beach?" Arjun voiced from behind us. He too was only in swim trunks and sandals, which made me grateful I couldn't see him. "The water down here is perfect. It's clean, warm enough to jump into, but cool enough to be refreshing. We can see fish, coral reefs, maybe even some dolphins."

"I don't mind the beach part," I answered. "It's the crowds of people I'm not looking forward to."

"You got nothing to worry about, babe," Connor said gruffly, stepping closer to me as the elevator doors opened to the lobby. He placed a hand on the small of my back as we stepped out. With how close all of them, even Arjun, walked with me, it felt like nothing short of a security detail.

After obtaining a few sample-sized bottles of sunscreen at the front desk, we headed out in the direction of the ocean. It really was a breathtaking view, despite the throng of people, towels, and umbrellas dotting the white sand.

Raz's arm slowly dropped from around my shoulders and he took a firm grip of my hand, threading his fingers through mine. Seconds later, Connor did the same with my opposite hand. I didn't notice anything as we walked until I heard Arjun's chuckle behind me.

Every woman we walked past, decked out in their neon-colored bikinis much smaller than mine, checked out my men, then their faces fell with disappointment as they noticed our hands. The few who looked past them to me shot me dirty looks.

"Ignore them." Arjun's voice, surprisingly close to my ear, made me jump. "Jealous cunts." Then, to my complete shock, I felt the warmth of his hand on the nape of my neck, followed by a soft kiss at the juncture between my neck and shoulder.

"What are you doing?" I turned to look at him, utterly dumbfounded, and my pulse skyrocketing.

"Relax, dove," he shot me an easygoing smile. "They won't stop gawping, so just giving them something to gawp at."

"Well, shit. I'd appreciate a warning next time," I huffed.

"Sorry," he muttered, the laughter gone from his ocean-colored eyes as he gazed downward. "I didn't mean anything by it."

I opened my mouth to tell him it was okay. It just surprised me, but didn't bother me. It felt really nice, in fact. My skin still tingled with the ghost of his lips and his hand on me. But I just faced forward and kept walking. I didn't want to deal with the rush of thoughts and implications if I actually allowed something to happen between us.

We found a partially shaded spot to lay out the towels and formed a sunscreen-applying train. While Connor sunscreened my back, I rubbed the white cream into Raz's back until the black dragon running from his shoulders to his waist absorbed it. He let out a sigh as I rested my cheek on his back while running my hands around him to rub more sunscreen into his chest.

"You miss him?"

"Yeah," he grunted, rubbing the sunscreen into his legs. "More than I thought I would."

"Me too." I planted a kiss on his shoulder. "It just doesn't feel the same without him here."

"I miss those damn pups too," he laughed lightly. "Never thought I was one to get attached to kids, but all their energy and happiness is infectious."

"I know. It's probably good they're not here, though. Especially if this compound is as big and dangerous as it seems."

"Yeah," he agreed. "The more I think about it, the more I can't be pissed at him for not coming. We're more or less a shifter rescue squad now and got to keep our own asses safe. It's just too unsafe for kids, especially if you're a single parent."

"You've been pretty quiet about the whole Hunter situation," I said to Connor, turning around to face him. "What do you think?"

He shrugged, peeling his shirt off so I could sunscreen his shoulders. "Neither choice is clear or easy. But he's trying to make the best choice for his kids and not himself, which is commendable. He's a great dad and a selfless person, and I'll always call him a friend whether or not he's with us. My first priority is your happiness, babe, but his will always be the pups. I can never fault him for that."

Connor's eyes flicked over my shoulder to Raz, who scooted up behind me so his chest pressed to my back and I sat between his legs. Always had to be spooning me, that one. And I loved it.

"Our check will clear in the next few days, and we'll hear about future jobs soon after that," Connor said. "The real question is, how will Razvan survive living in America's swampy asshole?"

"Heh. For thirty-grand per show, I suppose I can get used to it," Raz scoffed.

"It won't be that much at every show," Connor answered. "We can expect that much for special opening nights, but a typical show will net us somewhere between ten and fifteen if we stay with this company."

"How do you know all that?" I asked.

"I've been researching," he shot me a knowing grin. "Planning ahead, you know. For our future." Our eyes fell to my belly at the same and a nervous flutter went through me. I hadn't missed a period yet. It was probably too soon, but I was dying to know.

Raz just grunted after Connor finished rattling off numbers. "Ten, fifteen, whatever. We won't be broke anymore. It's not having those damn wolves around that bothers me more."

I leaned back against him and kissed his jaw in sympathy. He squeezed around my waist, the look in his gray eyes somewhere far off and distracted. My chest ached for him, knowing better than anyone what he was going through. He was falling for Hunter.

"Bro, you want any of this?" Connor held up a sunscreen bottle to Arjun, who remained standing and silent while the three of us lotioned up on the towels.

"Nah, I don't burn," the tiger shifter muttered. "I'm going for a swim." He started off toward the water on those long legs without another word, earning plenty of looks from bikini-clad women along the way.

"Someone's a grumpy pants all of a sudden," Connor muttered, rubbing the last of the sunscreen into his arms.

"And why do you think that is?" I asked in my best talk show host voice, only half-joking. But really, I was dying to know his perceptive insight into Arjun's behavior.

"He likes you. He touched you and you told him off. Now he feels bad for misreading things and also rejected because you told him off. So he's off to get some space and clear his head."

"Shit. You're good, Con," Raz breathed.

"And I'm never wrong," Connor added with a wink.

"Damn it," I groaned. "I really hope this one time you're wrong."

"Why?" The inquiry came from Connor. "I saw this coming a mile away. I think you did too, Raz."

"Knowing him and knowing you, *steluța*, I figured it was only a matter of time before you two would be into each other."

"Ugh, everyone knew it but me, apparently."

"Babe, you can take four lovers or four hundred. I don't care, as long as you're happy and every one of these knuckleheads treats you well."

"Same here," Raz murmured against the shell of my ear. "As long as you still have a place for me."

"Neither of you are replaceable to me." I looked between both of them. "Not ever."

"We know."

Connor grabbed my ankles and stretched my legs out across his lap. With him at my feet and Raz at my back, it reminded me of our time in the theater room before Hunter joined in. Before my dragon and my wolf gave in to their feelings for each other.

Oh, Hunter.

My heart wasn't ready to let him go. I refused to. He was just as much my mate as the two men sitting with me now. Connor and Raz had no issue with me being with Arjun, but how would my wolf feel? If we settled here, would he really be so opposed to moving himself and the kids here?

Or was he already moving on? Building a new life without me or Raz in it?

The thought stung as I wondered what he was doing right then. Had he found a new pack with his brothers? Was he meeting females to replace the mother of his pups?

Just sitting there, stewing in those thoughts, made me so uncomfortable. I had to move. I needed a distraction.

"Think I'm gonna swim for a bit too," I muttered, rising to my feet and heading toward the water.

21

MELODY

I was able to find a somewhat secluded spot near some rocks at the water's edge. Some rocks made shallow pools that filled and emptied as the waves came in. I spotted a few couples making out in these pools and steered clear of them, looking for a private one to call my own.

Finally, *jackpot!* A near-perfectly round pool deep enough to sit in, with the surrounding rocks creating a barrier of privacy. I sank in and closed my eyes at the perfect temperature water washing over me. The sand and dry rocks had been nearly too hot.

I barely soaked for more than a few moments when I felt the presence of a shifter nearby. It came to me so quickly my feet kicked out in surprise, splashing like I'd nearly fallen asleep. But it was unmistakable, the first one I felt here at the beach. And even more surprisingly, this one wasn't under distress.

I reached out to feel it even more, and was surprised by what this shifter projected. Happiness, playfulness. A sense of joy, fun, and family. I felt warm sun on my skin and tasted salty water. The smile it brought to my face was infectious.

Hello? I attempted.

Oh, hello! A surprised, feminine voice answered. *Who are you?*

My name is Melody. I'm a human shaman.

A shaman? Well, isn't that interesting!

I stood from my pool and looked out over the rocks. Turning in a slow circle, I searched for the source of the voice. My senses tugged me in the direction of the water, the open ocean.

Looking for me, are you? the voice asked playfully.

Yes, I admitted. You don't have to show yourself if you don't want to. I know shifters are—

Here I am!

Out of nowhere, a dolphin broke the surface. Her tail fin slapped the water, splashing playfully as she let out a squeal before diving back underwater. A memory suddenly resurfaced of a dream I had. I saw through the eyes of some marine mammal, even used echolocation to communicate and find food.

Wow, that was amazing! I projected to her.

Aww, thank you! Sorry, I can't do it too much or more humans will come around to take pictures of me.

That's okay. Do you mind telling me your name?

I'm Waverly! Nice to meet you, Melody, the shaman.

It's nice to meet you, too, I replied. *Have you talked to other shamans before?*

Not for a long time, since I was a calf.

I picked up a sense of apprehension immediately after she said that.

My pod told me not to talk to any humans after that, but it's boring only talking to other dolphins!

I'm sure they're just trying to protect you, I told her. *Not all humans are good. And don't worry, I won't tell any other dolphins that we've talked.*

Pinky swear?

A slender hand emerged out of the water with all the fingers closed but the pinky sticking up. I reached down to it and saw a smiling teenage girl's face below the surface. Strawberry blonde hair spread around her head like a halo, drifting delicately in the water. Light brown freckles dotted over a petite nose and emerald green eyes looked back at me. She reminded me of my sister Jeanie, once so bright and full of laughter.

I curled my pinky around Waverly's until her hand dipped below the surface again and the smile of a young bottlenose dolphin grinned up at me.

Can you tell me about the other shaman you met? I asked her. There's not many of us around anymore.

Hmm, I don't remember him super well, but he was so nice! He brought me treats all the time like cupcakes! I never had a cupcake before and they were sooo good! I was so sad when my pod told me not to talk to him anymore.

Why did they say that? Just because he was human?

I think so, Waverly nodded her head back and forth. I heard the adults say he caught another pod with nets, but he would never do that! He was so nice to me!

Oh, wow. That's serious. My pulse picked up. Could this other shaman be affiliated with the compound capturing shifters? It sounded like he was trying to lure Waverly into trusting him when she was young. And from the sound of it, it worked.

I know! And it's not fair, she cried.

Did he tell you anything about himself? His name or his job?

He told me his name, but I can't remember. It was a weird word. She swam just under the surface in a lazy figure-eight pattern as she thought some more. *He told me he was very powerful. He trained other shamans to use their powers.*

I wish I had someone like that, I told her. I have some help, but I've mostly learned everything myself.

Oh, he told me had a school for shifter children! Waverly recalled excitedly. But he said to keep it a secret because shifter parents don't like their kids being taught by humans. We're too proud, he said.

Oh, don't worry. I'll keep that secret too, I told her, my heart now pounding wildly. It was all I could do to keep my mental voice calm. *Did he tell you where the school is?*

Here in Miami, but it's hidden. Shifters and even other shamans can't sense it, she giggled. He said it was like Hogwarts.

Oh, wow! I wonder if you'll get a letter, I teased her. Would a penguin deliver it to you?

There are no penguins here! Maybe by pelicans, she laughed, then her tone turned sad. *I'm probably too old now. Anyway, I'm homeschooled by my pod. It's true they really don't like humans involved in our lives.*

A small vibration bounced off my skin, and Waverly suddenly turned and began swimming away at high speed.

Oh no, I gotta go! I'm going to be in so much trouble, but it was nice talking to you, Melody!

You too, Waverly! I responded, as her presence grew fainter. *And hey, listen to your pod! You'll understand when you're older, but they're just trying to protect you.*

I felt her response as a sassy click through the water, and then she was gone.

My mind reeling, I sat down in my pool with my back against the rocks. I didn't want to perpetuate anti-human feelings, but it sounded like her pod had good reason to be cautious. If there was a compound of captive shifters, it only made sense to groom the young ones. Everything Waverly told me about this shaman guy gave me creepy vibes.

And if he was luring shifters to be captured, he definitely wasn't a victim himself.

The thought was inconceivable to me. Someone gifted him his powers, probably trusting him to do good with them and protect shifters from harm. And instead, he lured children to a fake school with cupcakes.

"Hey, baby doll. Want some company?"

Shielding my eyes against the sun, I peered up to the source of the voice that pulled me out of my thoughts. A balding, middle-aged man with a large belly and covered in dark hair smiled toothily back down at me.

"No thanks. I'm good," I answered, but he was already lowering his spindly legs into my pool and seating himself on the edge of the rocks.

"Aw, come on, pretty little thing. We can go party on my yacht if you want. You like Cristal?" At my non-answer, he clumsily slid into my pool, making a large splash as he purposely tried rubbing up against me. "Or we can have a private party in here," he added huskily.

"Ugh, I said no already." I recoiled and moved away, grabbing for a hold on the rock wall to get out, but the pervert wrapped a hand around my arm and yanked me close.

"Don't play hard to get, bitch," he snarled with his rank breath in my face. "How much do you charge? Five hundred? With your attitude, that's fucking generous."

"Let me go." Rage filled me like boiling water in a kettle. "Or you'll regret it." The audacity of this man made me want to turn the water red with his blood.

"Girl, you're gonna regret opening your damn mouth." His next insult was choked off with warbling gasp and a wide-eyed stare of fear.

Because I did open my mouth, pulling my black lips back to reveal the pointed canine teeth of a wolf. And a low growl of warning rumbled in my throat.

"Learn to take no for an answer," I told him. "And I might let you live."

"What the fuck is going o—"

"Say it," I snapped, my teeth now elongating past my lips to resemble a tiger. "You will never touch anyone ever again after they tell you no."

"I'm sorry," he blubbered, now scrambling to escape back up the rocky wall. "Please don't hurt me!"

"Say it or I'll cook you slowly." Glancing down at my arms, I watched the shiny black scales cover me like armor. While no actual fire burned in my lungs, I blew out a few wisps of smoke for dramatic effect.

"I will take no for an answer," he whispered meekly.

"Louder," I demanded.

"I will take no for an answer!" He began sobbing, and I knew the dragon horns on my head made him believe all his sins had come back to haunt him. "I'll never fuck another girl again after she says no! Even if I pay her! I'm so sorry, please..."

I pulled back all the illusions I threw out, looking once again like a normal girl in a bikini. "I'll know if you go back on your promise. And next time, I won't be so kind to you."

Leaving the whimpering, pathetic man curled up against the rock, I lifted myself out of the pool and nearly ran headfirst into the center of Arjun's chest.

"Well," he remarked, looking past me at the man. "My tiger felt a pull like you were in trouble, but it seems you've got things handled."

MELODY

"Uh, yeah." The sight of the powerful tiger shifter knocked me off my high horse and back to feeling self-conscious. I nearly crashed into that solid, sun-kissed chest, and the fleeting memory of sleeping on him flashed through my mind. I was so consumed with teaching that old pervert a lesson, I didn't even notice Arjun's presence get closer. "Guess I did."

His blue-green gaze flicked amusedly back to me. "How will you know if he sticks to his promise?"

A smile played at my lips as I walked past him, following the length of the beach and returning to the throng of humans enjoying themselves. I walked until Arjun caught up, striding next to me on those long legs to answer.

"I won't. But he doesn't know that."

"Clever girl," he chuckled.

"More importantly," I said in a low voice, "I spoke to a young dolphin shifter who told me some pretty useful information." I repeated to him what Waverly told me, feeling a pang of guilt that I betrayed her secrecy. I never did like breaking promises, but what she told me was just too important.

"A shaman luring unsuspecting shifter children," he spat bitterly. "I can't say I'm surprised. It's the oldest fucking trick in the book."

"How the hell can someone hide an entire so-called school in plain sight?" I wondered. "Who's powerful enough to do that?"

"No one," he answered. "No one person, at least. But if multiple shamans consolidated their power? Who knows what's possible."

"I didn't even know you could do that."

"I have no idea, honestly. I'm just speculating."

We continued walking along the beach in silence, each of us wrapped up in our own thoughts. To anyone looking, we might have appeared to be a couple. We didn't touch, but why else would anyone be walking along the beach together?

Arjun only looked straight ahead or down whenever I glanced at him. He seemed to have forgotten that I was there, but he walked slowly, matching my pace as our feet sank into the warm sand as if he was in no hurry to leave.

I should have looked anywhere else, but his side profile was too attractive to tear my gaze away. Long obsidian lashes framed those striking eyes. His straight nose, high cheekbones, and angular jaw were so classically handsome, it was almost unfair. His jet black hair, reflecting the sunlight, was pulled away from his face in waves like he dipped his hands in the ocean and pushed it all back with his fingers.

"I'm sorry for snapping at you earlier," I blurted out. "I was honestly just surprised when you did that. I wasn't angry." Still, I didn't want to outright say, *I didn't mind that you kissed my neck*, for fear of making it sound like more than it was—a simple display to piss off onlooking women.

"You did nothing wrong. It was me," he muttered, still looking just ahead of his feet. "I took it too far. I realized it as soon as it happened. You don't have to worry about it happening again."

"It's really not a big deal," I told him, his admission stinging my ego more than I wanted to admit. Had Connor read him completely wrong? "I mean, we've reached a point now where there's flirting and banter between us. It's just kind of an extension of that, I guess."

"To you, maybe. But not to me." He let out a soft chuckle. "I realize multiple partners is common between shifters and shaman, but that's not something I've ever been a part of. My mum was an old-school Indian and raised me as such. Hell, I was engaged to a girl I barely knew because our families knew each other and deemed us suitable partners. So to you, a kiss may be just be messing around, but to me, it carries a lot more weight. I acted without thinking and that's not the type of person I am."

We continued on in silence for a few moments as I processed his words.

"That's not to say I've never kissed anyone. I'm not a total prude," he tacked on before I could respond. "I'm just saying I'm from a culture where arranged marriage is common, and all of that stuff tends to happen behind closed doors after everything is official. So the whole harem thing doesn't really appeal to me, even though I'm happy for the lot of you. You're all good together, which is rare."

"So what kind of life do you see for yourself?" I asked. "Married to a suitable tigress? A family with a dozen cubs?"

"No," he scoffed. "The whole arranged marriage thing is rubbish. But truthfully... I don't know. My whole life was planned out for me. Outside of minor things, I never really felt in control. My mum and grandparents ran the show, as is customary. Then they died, and I got captured. And my whole life became focused on surviving to the next day."

"And here you are," I said. "The world is your oyster now. Or your deer kill, or whatever."

"Right," he laughed dryly. "And if I said *adios* right now? Struck it out on my own to leave you and your lovers to deal with imprisoned shifters?"

"We'd be badly disadvantaged," I admitted. "We probably are already, who knows. Not to mention the visions would be killing me without your help, but it's your choice. You owe us nothing, and you're free to do whatever you want."

He said nothing for a few moments, just chewed his lip as he squinted at the horizon.

"I never did say thank you, did I?"

"For what?"

"For that view of your arse as we walked down here," he shot me a cocky grin before saying in a quiet, more serious tone, "No, for saving my life."

I lifted one shoulder in a shrug with an accompanying sigh. "So much has happened since then, I honestly don't remember."

"Well, thank you, Melody." His hand grazed against mine and our shoulders nearly touched as we walked alongside each other. "Thank you for giving me a second chance to live."

"You're welcome, Arjun." The back of my palm lingered against his before I had to pull away, before either of us would read too much into the contact. "Even if you were a dick to me at first, I never regretted it."

"Good," he chuckled. "I don't know where my life is headed anymore, but all I know is I'm not leaving you."

WE RETURNED to where the guys camped out on the beach towels—Connor avoiding the sand like it was lava, Raz avoiding the sun like a vampire. Neither of them commented on Arjun and I walking together, thankfully.

"So what do we do next?" Raz asked after I gave the rundown of what Waverly told me.

"Honestly, I'm fuckin' stumped, mate," Arjun muttered, lowering himself to lie on the towel. "Mel can't follow anyone's presence to where the compound is. There's probably loads of shaman working to disguise the place in plain sight, and they're recruiting kids right out from under their parents' noses."

"Not to mention this has gotten shifter parents really protective over their kids interacting with humans," I added. "I'm sure Waverly's pod isn't the only family unit that homeschools them and outright forbids any contact with humans because someone they knew went missing."

"That rules out just talking to any shifter adults we come across," Raz sighed.

"Maybe not. You guys are shifters." I looked between him and Arjun. "Would they trust you more based on that?"

"Of different species? Not likely," Raz answered. "Plus, just look at me, *steluța*." He gestured to his tattooed body and I could see his point. My bad, sexy dragon was probably not the most approachable when it came to talking with strangers.

"When am I not looking at you?" I purred, rolling toward him.

His smile lit my heart up as he dropped a playful kiss to my nose. "You know what I mean, my love."

"I have an idea," Connor declared, sitting squarely in the middle of the second towel. "It's stupidly obvious but might also be risky."

"Let's hear it," I said, spinning around to face him.

He hesitated a long time, looking at me with a grave, intense expression. "You can sense the captured shifters, right? See through their eyes and all that?"

"Yeah, I just can't pinpoint where they're located."

"So you can communicate with them? Speaking mind to mind?"

"I imagine so. I just haven't tried it."

"Don't tell me you're suggesting what I think you are," Arjun said with a soft growl.

"You're the expert on this, RJ, not me. But what if Mel talked to them? If they gave us clues, anything. If they saw a building or went through a series of doors or something, we might be able to pinpoint their location."

"It's far too risky," Arjun replied with a quick shake of his head. "She had dozens, maybe even a hundred shifters in her head at once. If they all realize she's there and tried to answer her, she could sustain permanent brain damage."

"Can you filter them out or something, babe? So you can talk to one person at a time, maybe with RJ's help?"

"I don't know, maybe. Sometimes it was a bunch at once, other times it felt like I was hopping from head to head."

"Mel, I don't recommend this at all." Arjun placed his hand on my leg, a sign that let me know he was serious. His color-shifting eyes narrowed in concern. "My stepfather was knocked unconscious for days when he tried to communicate with multiple shifters at once. Your brain physically can't handle it."

"What if I could stay focused on one person, though?" I asked him. "If your purring helped me to block out everything else, it would be just like Speaking with you or anyone."

"And if that doesn't work?"

My hand covered his on my knee. "We have to try. It's the best chance we have."

MELODY

The four of us went back up to the suite to make the Speaking attempt. At Arjun's reluctant instruction, Raz and Connor closed up all the windows and turned off every light source they could find. Focus would be best achieved with darkness and silence.

We pushed the coffee table out of the way and sat on the floor in the middle of the living room.

"What do we need to do?" Connor asked, sitting across from me.

"Say nothing and do nothing unless Mel appears to be in distress," Arjun said. "And if she does, physical touch will be most effective in pulling her back to her own mind. Raz, don't try to reach out to her with your dragon. More shifters in her head will just be confusing."

"Got it." Raz took a seat next to Connor.

Arjun sat behind me, still bare-chested and in his swim trunks.

"Skin-to-skin contact works best," he mumbled awkwardly. "I could shift to my tiger if you prefer, but then I'll have to direct you via Speak, which just adds one more shifter voice to the noise in your head."

"Oh, okay." My pulse sped up nervously, though I couldn't explain why. I already woke up this morning with my head on his chest. "I get it. You can stay human."

I pulled off the T-shirt I just threw on and slowly leaned back until the warmth and gentle contact of Arjun's chest met my skin. The only barrier between us was my bikini string, and I wondered if he could feel how fast my heart was going from back there.

"Close your eyes," he instructed, his voice a gentle vibration on my spine. "Picture your mental shields, the ones that guard you and keep your mind safe."

"I see them," I answered, visualizing all four men at their positions.

"Now, release them one by one. Let them fall away slowly in layers. If you feel too much getting through, stop."

Panic filled my body, sending my heart into overdrive. The pain of those visions was still fresh and raw. Rather than lower my defenses, I wanted to fortify them. I knew letting the shifters through was the only way to help them, but it still scared the shit out of me. I nearly felt like dying the first time.

Just as I opened my mouth to tell him I couldn't do it, I felt the low, unmistakable rumble of a purr from his chest. It kept me anchored to this room with these three supportive men who would never let any harm come to me. With that vibration running through me, I found the strength to let go.

My first layer of defense fell away, and I stopped, waiting to see what filtered through. I saw and heard only ghostly shapes and faint whispers, so I carried on. The visions became clearer then but still felt like looking through a mask. My view was obstructed, but I knew the next phase would be startingly clear.

"You're doing great," Arjun's voice echoed over the rumble of his purr. "Take your time, dove."

Almost unconsciously, I leaned further back against him, wanting to solidify the sensation of him in my body before my mind went somewhere else. The bare skin of my back seared to his torso until I felt the tickle of his coarse chest hair and the watery thud of his heart beneath his purr. I swore I could feel his hands on my hips, but I couldn't be sure.

"I'm here, dove. You're safe." Warmth tickled the side of my head.

Was he speaking right against my ear? "You can come back or proceed. Whichever you want to do."

My body wanted to pull back. I wanted to explore Arjun physically, to be present in the room while he let me lean against him like this. I wanted to feel those fingers trail across my skin and find out what those lips tasted like...

"Focus, Mel. We're doing this to reach out to the shifters."

I thought I heard laughter and faraway voices, but couldn't be sure. I brought my attention back to the obstructed view of horror I allowed to filter through. Arjun's purr grew louder, and I drew on its strength to peel back another layer of defense.

"Remember, you're here, Mel. You're safe. We're all here with you. What can you see?"

"Cages all around me," I muttered. "Most are empty."

"You're doing wonderfully, dove. Can you hear or feel anything?"

"No, I just see."

"Good. Can you try to change perspectives? See through another shifter but only one at a time."

Different views before my eyes came and went like unrelated scenes from movies. Some were similar, but each one was slightly unique.

At first, it just looked like random rooms and corridors to me. But after a few moments of flipping through different shifter perspectives, I began to piece together what the whole place looked like. The only thing was, I didn't know what to look for.

"Look for light," Arjun's voice came through like an omnipotent entity. "A window or a door looking outside, maybe."

"I don't see one..."

Not a single window was to be seen in the place. It just looked like a maze of corridors and rooms that I struggled to keep straight. All light sources were from overly bright florescent lights, or dim, single lightbulbs in dingy dark rooms full of cages.

Then... *wait!*

I saw clear blue sky just for a half-second, and then familiar grimy walls. This shifter was paralyzed but conscious. I felt its fear and confusion, its inability to move. He or she had just now been captured and brought to this place, which made my heart ache with helplessness.

"I think I found one that can help us." My lips moved slowly, as if numbed. "Give me a minute."

Sinking deeper into the shifter's perspective, I realized this one had four legs and fur.

He was male and a young adult, but smaller than a wolf or tiger. The paws stretched out in front of me looked puppy-sized in comparison to Hunter's.

I waited, taking note of every detail I could through his unblinking eyes as two humans carried his cage through a set of hallways and doors. One, two, three, four doors away from the brief glimpse of the outside I saw. Then the humans tossed his cage like a sack of laundry against the wall, making a loud echoing clatter. From the corner of the shifter's eye, I saw other figures wince at the noise before huddling back into themselves in their own cages.

He was panicked, but his heart thudded slowly from the effects of the tranquilizer. Everything felt wrong. His mind was in fight-or-flight mode, but his body would not cooperate.

"I'm going to attempt contact," I reported to my guys through my physical body. Speaking with my own lips felt sluggish and laborious, each word a struggle to say. But I had seen through only this shifter for a few moments, and was eager to reach out.

Don't be alarmed. My name is Melody. I'm here to help you.

No, no, no! Get out! Not again! Get out of my head! Oh God, just please let me go!

I physically flinched, taken aback by the shifter's mental cries and whimpering. A soothing pressure rested on my chest, enhancing the vibration of Arjun's purr in my own body.

"Keep trying. He's just scared. Just be calm and patient." The tiger's voice was right next to my ear and yet so far away at the same time.

I will not hurt you, I promised the shifter. *I want to get you out. I want to help everyone get out, but you have to work with me.*

He talked in my head too! Why should I believe you?

I know you're scared, and you don't know me. But this is the only way I can try to get you out.

He didn't respond in words, but I felt the fear and racing anxiety in his brain. His instinct was to lash out and run, but he had no choice at the moment.

I'm Melody, I repeated. *What's your name?*

Julian, he replied softly.

Thank you, Julian, for trusting me.

What are you? he demanded, the panic in his mental voice returning. *How can you and him talk to me like this?*

We are both shaman, humans who are in tune and closely connected to shifters. We're supposed to protect you, and I'm so sorry he did this. It's not right and I'm going to do everything I can to fix it.

You're not shifter? he sounded surprised.

No, we're a rare class of humans. There aren't many of us, I answered. *I can see through your eyes, but I can't see you. What species are you, Julian?*

Coyote, he answered. *Nothing special.*

That's where you're wrong, Julian. You are special. I'm talking to you because I desperately need your help.

What can I do? I can't even move!

That's okay. Can you tell me where you were just before getting captured? Please be as specific as you can.

I was at La Hacienda to meet a guy for a lunch date, he muttered, shame creeping into his voice. *I waited at the bar and had two drinks before I figured he stood me up and got up to leave. But then I saw him looking straight at me near the back of the restaurant, so I went over to confront him.*

What happened next, Julian? I prompted gently when he went quiet.

He started going toward the back, and I followed him. I'm a lightweight, so I was a little tipsy and not thinking straight. Then he shoved me into a room and tazed me with this stick he had. It hurt so fucking bad.

I'm so sorry, I told him. *Can you tell me what happened next?*

He was in there with some other guys, and they kept yelling at me to shift. I didn't want to, but they kept saying they were going to kill me, so I did. Then they kept trying to inject me with something. I fought back, but I'm not big and strong like a wolf, you know. They hit me and tazed me some more until I stopped fighting. Then they injected me with the stuff, threw me in a cage and here I am.

Julian, you have been so incredibly helpful, I said. *And believe me, you are so brave and strong. Those men are monsters and I'm going to bring them down.*

I hope so. I'm starting to get some feeling back and it really hurts.

His pain became mine as I cemented my consciousness in his body. His jaw was swollen and tender, with the taste of dried blood on his tongue. Pain along his ribs made it difficult to breathe. I took in every sensation in his body and made it my own. Julian's pain was my pain, and he would not suffer any worse.

Julian, I need you to tell me a bit more if that's okay. About how far from the restaurant did they take you to this place? Did they get in a car? A highway?

No, they walked. It was definitely less than a mile. Tons of regular humans saw me. I think they were disguised as animal control or something? Their uniforms kind of looked like it.

Great, that's super useful! How about the man you were supposed to meet? Had you gone out with him before? What did he look like?

No, it was our first Tinder date. He was clean shaven with salt and pepper hair, blue eyes, dressed nicely in a suit. His profile said he was 51. I, uh, kinda have a thing for older men.

No judgement here, Julian. I allowed a soft chuckle. *But seriously, you're amazing for recalling all of this in such vivid detail. I have to go now but—*

Wait, you're leaving? No, please don't go, Melody!

Julian. I could feel his panic rising, his heartbeat now elevating as his nervous system began to wake up from the tranquilizers. *I'm not leaving you alone. I just have to tell my mates—*

Don't leave me! Oh, please don't leave me! They're going to hurt me, I just know it!

Julian, please calm down. Be strong for me. I know you can.

His pleas turned into unintelligible whimpers, and cries as he pawed at the wires of his cage. Through his eyes, I saw other shifters began turning their attention to him. I smelled their curiosity and suspicion of this once-silent captive now causing a ruckus. As much as it broke my heart to do so, I had to leave him and return to my own body. But I couldn't help but try to soothe him with one final message.

You'll be freed, Julian. I promise you.

WHO IS THAT? WHO ARE YOU?
A SHAMAN? COULD IT BE?
HELP US! GET US OUT OF HERE!

All at once, it felt like ten people were yelling at the tops of their lungs directly next to my ear. I couldn't even feel the vibration of Arjun's purr anymore, it was so loud. A sudden, stabbing pain threatened to split my head apart, and the noise became too much, a deafening roar of too many voices. I clasped the sides of my head, which did nothing to muffle everyone out considering they were already in my head.

Hands grabbed at my arms, legs and waist, but I couldn't come back. I couldn't hear my guys over the voices in my head. All the shifters screaming and pleading for my help felt like they were sucking me into a black hole.

"Mel... Mel... please..."

Lips covered mine, smothering my breath in a kiss that tasted unfamiliar, but too good not to kiss back. A soft tongue caressed mine, followed by a hand pressing to my cheek.

"She's coming back..."

Why was I so tired? I could barely open my eyes.

The voices began to fade, but that searing, splitting pain remained, even when the world went dark.

✤ 24 ✤

MELODY

The pain never went away. Somehow, I was aware of it even while passed out. Like the antithesis of Arjun's purr, it was a constant reminder of suffering, not soothing.

My head swam as I returned to consciousness. Light felt like needles stabbing my eyelids, so I shut my eyes tightly and pressed my face into the pillow, down into comforting darkness.

"Babe?"

"Mmugh."

"She's alive, at least."

"Stop talking so loud."

"What? I'm talking at my normal volume."

"She's sensitive to noise right now. Just turn it down a notch."

"Is this better?"

"Not really," I groaned. Even though I knew the guys were whispering, it still felt like screaming directly into my ear.

No one said any more, thankfully. Someone pressed a piece of paper into my hand and I cracked open one eye to read it.

Do you feel well enough to tell us what Julian told you? -A

I couldn't help but smile through the pain. How considerate of him to ask me without using noise.

698

"Testing. Mic check. One, two, three." I murmured into the pillows.

Light, muffled laughter followed, and I knew the guys were trying to keep from making as much noise as possible. My own voice didn't bother me nearly as much, so I repeated everything Julian said before the other shifters somehow heard me. After a few moments, another note pressed into my palm.

Thanks. Your consciousness was so deeply entwined with Julian's that when he started to panic, you did too and lost focus. The other shifters began filtering in and that's how they heard you. -A

"Sorry," I murmured into the pillows. "He was so scared, and I was just trying to comfort him. I didn't mean to make you all worry."

I got no words back, but a soft kiss accented by the caress of a split tongue danced across my shoulder. Another kiss, this one with a normal tongue, pressed to the exposed skin of my waist. Someone moved on the bed next to me, and then stopped as if hesitant. I thought everyone had left until a hand gently caressed my palm.

"Thank you, guys," I sighed, weariness settling over me. "You're all the best. Even you, Arjun."

THE PAIN in my head faded to a dull, throbbing ache when I woke up again. The curtains had been pulled across the windows, sending the room into darkness. When I dared to push them back an inch, darkness greeted me from outside as well, with street lamps as the only illumination.

Murmured voices floated through the closed bedroom door, along with a bright strip of light peeking through the crack at the bottom. I moved toward the door slowly until my ear pressed to it, testing my sensitivity to light and noise. When the pain didn't worsen, I cracked the door open slowly, allowing the outside light to spill into the bedroom.

"There she is."

Four pairs of eyes looked at me as I blinked to allow my eyes to adjust. Wait, *four?*

I rubbed my eyes and blinked harder, then an ugly sob escaped my throat.

"Am I dreaming?" I asked no one in particular as my gaze settled on the gorgeous man with shoulder-length platinum hair and golden eyes.

"No, you're not, little fox," Hunter answered, a smile playing on his lips as he rose from the couch and strode over to me.

"What... how..."

"Shh." He pulled me into his chest when I just stood there dumbfound, stroking my hair with a soothing hand. "God I missed you, my beautiful girl."

"I missed you," I whispered, coming out of my stupor to send my hands up his long, solid back. Nothing ever felt so right.

He tilted my chin up to look at him, those eyes as deep and endless as amber. "Can you forgive me, Mel? I was so wrong, my love. My place is with you, and it always will be."

"But the pups?" I blinked up at him. "Roo and Rinna? Don't tell me you—"

"They're back home with my brothers," he assured me with a hand on my cheek. "It's just temporary. Whatever the group decides, whether settling here or going back, I'll get them when we make a decision."

"But are you sure they're okay?" I demanded. "You didn't want to leave them even for a day before. And who knows how long—"

"Colt, Gabe, and Miriam will protect them with their lives," he said, conviction in his voice. "I have no doubt of that. And Miriam has a phone, so we can video chat and check in whenever."

"What about the fact that they're your pack? Your family?" I asked, eager to squash the last nagging doubt in my mind. "They're wolves, like you. You don't feel like your place should be with them?"

"They are my family," he agreed. His hands then fell to the curve of my waist, where he pulled me flush against him with such dominance and possession that my knees turned to jello. "But *you* are my mate," he growled. "My place is at your side."

"Hunter..." His name rolled off my tongue like an erotic moan, and we weren't even naked yet. My brain just couldn't process seeing him again after fearing I never would, and craving him like he was my first meal in days.

"They filled me in on everything, little fox," he told me, his lips hovering barely an inch from mine. "The compound, a shaman kidnapping people," he paused, a smirk forming on his lips as he cupped my chin, "and I heard you may or may not be trying for a baby."

"Well, ah." His eyes, that mouth, his smell, were all too intoxicating for me to focus. His body too hot and pressing hard against me. "One thing at a time."

I stretched on my tiptoes to reach his lips. He closed the distance and lifted me up, allowing my legs to wrap around his slim hips. Our kiss was a desperate, hungry clash of teeth and tongue. I swore the lingering pain in my head floated away as his fingers dragged sensually across my scalp. His growing erection pressed against the center of my heat, sending jolts through my clit.

After feeling like I got hit by a truck, he was exactly what my body needed. Not that my other men didn't feel good, but no one else was my wolf. He was my missing piece, the reason why I felt so complete and right and just better.

In a tangle of arms, legs, and kisses, we dropped to the couch and I couldn't hold back the moan from his resulting thrust against me.

"We'll give ya some alone time," Raz chuckled to the left of me.

"No, wait." I broke the kiss and reached to grab his arm. "Stay with us, dragon."

HUNTER

az's eyes raked lustily over me, much like they did when I showed up at the door. But now our gorgeous woman was included in his field of vision.

"Are you feeling better, *steluța?*" he asked her, his voice thick with desire. "You're not in pain anymore?"

"Just the pain of not having you right now," she smiled at him wantonly, her temple resting on my forehead and her arm around my shoulders.

The dragon dropped all hesitation and leaned over, kissing her deeply right in front of my face as the other two made themselves scarce. Arjun immediately went to his room and closed the door, while Connor looked ready to leave the suite.

"Connor?" I inquired with a lifted eyebrow.

"Y'all have fun. I'm gonna throw back a couple and watch the game." He pulled on a jacket and dropped a kiss to Mel's head as he walked by.

"I might meet you down there after we're done," I said, leaning my head back against the couch.

"Sounds good, wolf man. Love you, babe."

"Love you too!" Mel called to him as he left the room, freeing Raz's mouth to crash down to mine.

I released a groan at the first hot, smoky taste of the dragon shifter. My mouth opened to him and savored his snakelike tongue caressing over mine. God damn, I didn't even realize how much I missed him. How much I craved his taste almost as much as Mel's.

As I wrapped a hand around his neck to deepen the kiss, Mel's soft plush lips made a trail of kisses down my neck. Another moan escaped and my hips rolled in an upward thrust as if they had a mind of their own.

With no pause in her kisses, Mel slid halfway off my lap to straddle one of my thighs, giving Raz ample room to move in closer. And he did just that, now kissing down the other side of my neck as he slid a hand up my thigh, moving increasingly closer to the bulge in my pants that begged to be freed.

"Fuck, I am never leaving you two again," I growled, writhing between my two lovers as they teased me.

"You better not," Raz growled, pulling away and meeting my eyes with a smoldering gaze. "And if you do, do us a favor and never come back. You can't fuck with our hearts like that."

"Never again," I repeated solemnly, holding his gaze before turning to Mel. "I promise. You're my mates. Both of you."

Raz let out a small gasp of surprise, but Mel just smiled as she kissed me sweetly, her small fingers trailing with aching slowness down my chest. The moment her mouth broke away from mine, Raz turned my head back to face him.

"You mean that?" he demanded, eyes now wide with disbelief. "Mates? You and me?"

That word carried a lot of weight in the shifter world, and I used it purposely. A mate was so much more than a hookup or a fling. It was a partner. A lover and friend wrapped up into one, often for life. A close, unique bond that was rare to find.

I thought I found that in my pups' mother, but that bond didn't hold a candle to what I felt for Mel, or this dragon shifter that knew how to light me on fire. I was the luckiest fucking wolf in the world to have two mates, and for the two of them to have each other.

"I mean it, Raz. Trust me, I thought about it on the long-ass bus ride here." I took one of his tattooed hands and placed it over my heart. "You're my mate just as much as Mel is."

The look on his face was unreadable before his mouth crashed to mine and Mel made an endearing, "Awww," sound.

"I'll show you *awww*," Raz growled against my mouth, then pulled her across my body as she squealed.

His kisses to her were as rough as mine, manhandling her as he tore off her top. He swallowed her moans and mewls as he rolled her nipples between his fingers until they were tight little buds. I followed suit with her lower half draped across my lap, dragging her shorts and pants down her long legs.

My cock turned to iron at the sight of her gorgeous, heart-shaped ass so close. Listening to the sounds of Colt and Gabe being with Miriam while my woman was hundreds of miles away was downright torturous. Now she was here in the flesh, and I couldn't stop running my hands over her delicious curves.

A moan and a soft slurping sound drew my attention up toward her head. Raz was just peeling his shirt off his tattooed arms while Mel's head moved in his lap. His jeans were unzipped and shoved haphazardly down his thighs, like she wanted his cock so badly she couldn't wait until his pants were off. He shot me a lazy smile as he stretched his arms across the back of the couch.

"Welcome back to heaven, wolf," he sighed happily.

"It's good to be back," I said, trailing a finger between Mel's thighs to gauge her wetness. "Fuck, she's soaked."

She twitched and squirmed as I rubbed her slit, her moans muffled by Raz's cock, when I circled around her clit. My own erection pressed so hard against my zipper, it was nearly painful. With one hand still playing with her, I used my free hand to work myself out of my jeans.

"Need a hand there, wolf?" Raz's eyes danced hungrily as he watched me.

A nervous thrill zipped through me. *Dare I say it?*

"A hand would be great," I told him. "But your mouth would be even better."

The pleasure lighting up his face was absolutely priceless.

With a bit of scooting and adjusting, our dragon got into position and took his time. First he kissed me, slower and more sensually than before. I sensed he was giving me room to change my mind, knowing I never had another guy do this to me before. But I kissed him back hard, shoving my tongue in his mouth and letting him know what I wanted. I said he was my mate, and I fucking meant it.

He began kissing a trail down my chest and I took the opportunity to take in his tattoos, to inspect the art I never got such a close look at before. My fingers skimmed over the black dragon covering his back, the nude woman on his arm, the knives on his ribs. When his mouth reached my navel, my fingers dragged across the flowing lines on his scalp, barely visible through the density of his dark, buzzed hair.

And when he pulled my jeans away from my hips and flicked both sides of that tongue against my cock, all I could do was press my head back against the coach and let out a wordless, animalistic moan.

His voice vibrated against my shaft as he took more of me in mouth, and only then did I remember Mel was still sucking him too. I pulled my gaze away from him to watch her, my cock swelling as his piercings slid past her lips. Letting him pop out of her mouth, she continued stroking him with her hand as she looked over her shoulder at us.

"Fuck," she breathed, her eyes glued to Raz, now taking more of me down his throat.

"You got that right," I rasped, my fists clenching as his lips easily reached my balls. Jesus, how many other guys could say they got sucked off by a hot, tattooed sword swallower?

To distract myself, I returned to playing with Mel's pussy. Her beautiful ass was still draped over my thighs, but her heat and wetness only walked me closer to the edge where Raz was taking me. Her moans and whimpers, with her face stuffed full of dragon cock, didn't help either.

She ground her hips against my hand as I rubbed her clit. Her moans grew louder, more frantic, her thighs quivering as she neared her release. My balls felt like lead as Raz teased that tongue along my shaft, my cock bordering on painfully hard as our perfect circle of pleasure heightened, nearing its peak. When his hand squeezed around my balls, I knew it was over.

My release exploded in his mouth with a force that was nearly violent. With the way he jerked and moaned as he swallowed me, I knew he just gotten off too.

"Stop touching her for a second, wolf," he instructed once his mouth release me.

"I'm so close," she whimpered.

"I know. But I can't let Hunter have all the fun," he grinned.

He got up and sat on the other side of me, letting Mel's legs stretch out over his lap. After smoothing his hands over her ass for a moment, his finger stroked along her slit, making her shiver a few times before inserting them.

"Now you can play with her clit again," he told me.

With his fingers stroking inside her, and my firm pressure on her clit, we made our woman orgasm at least six times until she told us she physically couldn't anymore.

 26

ARJUN

I turned the volume on my TV all the way up to drown out the noises from the living room. A knock pounded at my door after about an hour.

"Yeah?" I called, muting the TV.

"It's Raz. Let's go out, Arj."

I pulled open the door to see the dragon shifter surprisingly fully dressed. "Thought you had plans for the evening?"

"We ah, had a nice little reunion," he flashed a grin. "But we've got a restaurant to scope out. So why don't you and me hit the town?"

I hesitated, feeling an intense push-pull within me. On one hand, I wanted to stay curled up and hidden in my room. On the other, I was dying to get out of this suite and put as much distance as possible between myself and Mel, at least temporarily.

"Yeah, alright," I relented.

I followed him out to the living room, the smell of sex and sweat drifting in the air like a breeze. A human nose wouldn't pick it up, but it made my tiger growl and stretch his claws out. He needed a mate and was convinced she was the one. She smelled right. She was strong, kind, and a sight for sore eyes. I knew and understood the pull he felt —it was animalistic and instinctual. But it could never happen.

The woman in question stood next to the door, a rosy blush on her cheeks and a relaxed, blissed-out look in her eye as the only evidence of what just happened here.

"Hey," she greeted with a shy smile. "Sorry to, uh, make you run off to your room like that."

I shrugged as casually as I could muster. "As long as you bleach the couches and whatever other surfaces you've tainted, I'll forgive you."

She laughed, giving me a playful smack on the arm. Part of me was glad she didn't have such a big stick up her arse anymore, and was coming around to understand me. The other part wished she would still huff and throw a fit. This would be a lot easier to deal with if she still clearly detested me.

"Where are you lot off to?" I asked when Hunter emerged from the restroom and joined her by the door.

"Meeting Connor down at the bar to watch the game," Hunter answered, squeezing Mel's nape. "Maybe see about some food and video chatting with the pups."

"Yes, let's go! I'm dying to talk to them," she urged before turning to Raz. "Be careful. Both of you. Keep us updated."

"Of course, *steluța*," he murmured, nuzzling and kissing her as the four of us left the room. He kissed Hunter as well, then we parted ways with Mel and the wolf taking the fancy, winding staircase down to the lower levels, while Raz and I heading to the elevators.

"You don't have to make this so difficult for yourself, you know," he said, looking straight ahead as our elevator doors slid shut.

"I don't know what you're bloody talking about," I sighed.

"Come on, you big pussy. Do I have to say it? You and her."

"Sorry, did you say something? Because I swear you just spouted a bunch of bollocks that doesn't exist."

The elevator ride was blissfully silent until the moment we reached the ground floor.

"So, are you going to tell her it was you kissing her that brought her back?"

With a soft ding, the door slid open, and I walked out into the lobby without answering him.

"She deserves to know," the pesky lizard continued as he followed, hot on my heels.

"And what good would that do?" I said with more snarl than I intended. "Nothing else was working to bring her back."

"That's bullshit, Arj. I know you better than anyone here, so I definitely know a kiss means more to you than most. You wouldn't have done it without a reason."

"The reason was to prevent from her brains from becoming scrambled eggs."

"Right," he huffed. "Next you're gonna tell me there was a legitimate reason for that skin-to-skin contact?"

"I could catch glimpses of her visions while touching her, so I could guide her and keep her focused. Plus, she could feel my purr better that way. Now where the fuck is this place?"

"I looked up the address. Follow me." Raz took a hard left out the hotel doors and turned to face me, pushing them open with his back. "We're not done talking about this, by the way."

Finding La Hacienda, the restaurant where Julian had been set up, was easy enough. It was at the center of Miami's night life, complete with flashing neon lights, human men wearing too much cologne, women in the tightest dresses I'd ever seen, and loud club music blasting from neighboring establishments.

I followed Raz's lead up to the bar, quietly surveying the dark corners and clientele of the place.

"Two fireball shots," Raz ordered, flashing me a smile. "Drink this and you'll get a small taste of what it's like to be a dragon."

"Ugh, I'd rather not." My stomach churned at the sickly sweet cinnamon smell that poured from the liquor bottle.

"Come on, you big prick. Just one."

"Hey, aren't you that one guy?" the bartender looked dumbfoundly at Raz, nearly spilling as he poured the shot.

"Depends who's asking," Raz answered.

"You were in that show last night! The sword swallower, fire breather guy!"

"That's me," the dragon chuckled amusedly.

"Well, shit, that was amazing! These are on me tonight! Where's the rest of your group? We'll treat them too!"

"Enjoying a quiet night at home. Just me and my boyfriend here tonight." He threw an arm around my shoulders and slapped my chest affectionately, ignoring my glare.

"Well, you boys just flag me down and I'll take care of whatever you need." The bartender winked suggestively and I only then noticed the rainbow-colored wristband on his smart watch.

"For fuck's sake, Raz," I groaned when he walked away, rubbing my forehead.

"What? Live a little! You're a free man now, no need to brood and pout." He clinked his fireball shot against mine. "Drink up. To beautiful women *and* men."

"You're in a good mood since the wolf returned," I observed, choking back the shot.

He nodded as he swallowed his drink, his face flushing red from either the alcohol or what I said. "It's a fucking rollercoaster, man. First, Mel scares us to death and we're all worried about her becoming a vegetable. Next thing we know, she's okay and our missing lover shows up." He leaned heavily against the bar with a sigh. "Can't make this shit up."

Over his shoulder, I noticed a shadow flicker across the wall. To human eyes, it looked like nothing but my tiger perked up. Alert, ready, and dying for a hunt.

"Don't make any sudden moves," I told Raz, leaning in closer and speaking in a slow voice. "But looks like someone just headed to the back room where our boy Julian got fucked up."

He gave the barest hint of a nod and drummed his fingers on the bar top. I knew he was using his reptilian senses to pick up the vibration of the man's footsteps, gauging distance, direction, and movement.

"Excuse me," I raised a hand to get the attention of the bartender, and he came eagerly running over. "Where's your restroom?"

"Down the hall and to the left."

"Thanks." I leaned close to Raz's ear before leaving. "Meet you around back."

He grinned, chuckling to himself as if giddy with my display of propositioning him, but I knew he was genuinely amused. I could play the part if need be.

Making my way down the hall, I quickly picked up the scent of the man who headed back here a moment ago. He smelled like blood and tranquilizers, a cocktail of scents I was all too familiar with. More faintly, I picked up a mixture of scents I didn't recognize. Probably all the shifters that got dragged back here.

The hallway and scents dead-ended to an unmarked door painted black. I tried the handle, but it didn't budge. I could've broken it down, but figured that would draw too much attention at this stage. Mel did warn us to be careful.

Retracing my steps down the hall, I exited the restaurant through a side door to find Raz waiting for me in the alleyway.

"He's moving fast," he warned, taking off at a spirited, but still leisurely pace.

"It's alright, I can smell him," I replied, walking alongside him. "Julian said he was in walking distance, so we'll find it soon enough."

We walked a few blocks following our respective trails when the scent suddenly disappeared. I stopped, did a double-take, then walked a few steps back the way we came. Yes, still a strong trail there. Then a few steps forward and nothing.

"What the fuck?" Raz growled in frustration. "I can't feel shit anymore. It's like he just became a statue. Can't even feel a breath."

"Yeah, his scent stops right here." I pointed at the sidewalk, drawing an imaginary line with my finger.

"How is that fucking possible?"

"An illusion," I realized, lifting my face to the sky. "A fucking magic trick."

"Arjun," Raz stared at me. "What do you mean?"

I picked up a pebble and tossed it straight up in the air. About a foot above our heads, it hit something unseen with a metallic clang sound and shot back down to the earth.

"We're dealing with a shaman who can cast illusions not just over themselves but entire areas of space. Fuck, I should've known..."

The world spun around me and I felt violently ill. I didn't feel this sick after eating roadkill for the first time. All the signs were there. A hidden "school", a man in his fifties. Oh Shiva, how could I have been so blind. I leaned against a lamppost and tried not to lose the contents of my stomach.

"Arjun?" Raz grabbed my shoulder and attempted to shake me back to my sense. "Should've known what?"

I couldn't meet my friend's eyes to say it.

"That my stepfather, Lhozen, is behind this."

CURTAIN CALL

BOOK 6

PROLOGUE

JEANIE MAY

I shut the door behind me as quietly as I could, then grabbed Bella's tiny hand as we descended the rickety, rotting porch steps.

"Grab Joey's hand, Bells," I told my younger sister.

"Got it," she replied, in a voice that sounded too confident for one being so young—for why we were sneaking off like thieves in the night in the first place.

"Where are we going?" Riley mumbled, still half-asleep. The youngest of my siblings, a toddler of three years old, curled up against my chest with my arm holding her securely to my hip.

"We're going on an adventure, Riley." I kissed her forehead and tucked her hair under her hood before quickly glancing in both directions. We took off out of the park and across the street. Bella and Joey kept their hands clasped and trailed after me like a row of ducklings following their mother.

I wasn't their mother. Neither was Mel. But when raising the little ones fell on us, we had no other choice. We had to be strong and protect them.

Mel looked after me and the others until she couldn't take any more and left. Maybe she knowingly passed on that responsibility to me, then again, maybe not. Just that morning, we all woke and realized she was gone. I promised myself a long time ago that I wouldn't leave unless I took all the little ones with me.

That day came this morning.

The sun wasn't even up yet and a chill hung in the air. Later, it would feel like the end of summer again, but the coolness of the night was settling in longer throughout the day.

"Walk fast, you guys," I said in a hushed whisper, trying to keep my steps slow enough for Bella and Joey to keep up. The wild crashing of my heart felt like it would explode. I fought the urge to look over my shoulder, to look back at the hell hole we just left. Mel never looked back. I was sure of that.

"Where are we going?" The plea came from Joey this time. He had slowed to a stop and was pulling back on Bella's hand, which slowed all of us down. "I'm tired. I wanna go back to bed," he whimpered.

"Joey." I stopped and turned, dropping to his eye level. "You'll go to bed soon, buddy. But we have a new home now. We just have to walk to it first, okay? Then you can sleep in super late, I promise."

"Why are we going to a new home?" His big brown eyes, so much like Mel's, shined like amber under the streetlight.

"We're going somewhere you guys won't hear Mom yelling anymore," I told him, trying to make my voice sound excited. "You won't have to hide under your beds. You won't be scared anymore. And you'll get to see Mel again, all the time! Don't you miss her?"

"Really?" His wide-eyed gaze broke my heart. His six-year-old mind probably couldn't grasp the thought of a house without yelling and not being scared. Neither could I, until I met my boyfriend Dustin's family.

Ex-boyfriend, I reminded myself.

My first thought was to run to his house, but I couldn't burden his family with all of us. He was so sweet and kind, I hated burdening him with any of the shit I dealt with at home. As much as it killed me, I broke up with him, because he deserved better.

"Yes, Joey." I rubbed some sleep out of his eyes that still lingered. "But we have to get there first. You gotta be a brave boy and walk with me, okay?"

He nodded solemnly and took Bella's hand again. I turned to her, rubbing my thumb across her small fingers. "How are you doing, Bells? Feel good, okay to keep going?"

She bobbed her head yes, sticking her chin out proudly like she wasn't even aware of the dark bruising settling in around her eye. For the first time, something got thrown, and I wasn't fast enough to block it from hitting one of the kids. But Bella was.

"Good girl." I booped her nose and returned to standing. "Let's go, gang."

I didn't let out a breath until we left the shitty, rundown neighborhood and entered the downtown area of Waterford. The sky was just beginning to light with the dawn, and the first cars on the road for work passed by us.

Drivers rubbernecked like they never saw a teenage girl hauling along three kids before. It was a common sight around these parts, but people never tired of staring like I was a goddamn zoo animal.

Riley was getting antsy, and the other two were starting to fade when we still had a mile or so to go. I allowed us to stop and rest at a bus stop, but only for five minutes. Every minute we lingered gave *him* more time to catch up to us.

Finally, we made it to the downtown Waterford homeless shelter. I checked us in, but the regretful look on the volunteer's face filled me with dread. When she told me the situation, I knew it was time to make the call. I had to swallow my pride and ask for help.

I had to set Riley down, thanks to my arm being thoroughly numb, and gave them all snacks from my backpack while I made the phone call. I dialed the one number I had committed to memory and put the receiver to my ear.

The one she gave me when she came back, right before Mom got in her face and made her leave again.

My heartbeat started going crazy again as the phone on the other end rang and rang and rang.

MELODY

"We miss you, Mel! When are you coming back?"

"Aww, I miss you guys too!" Holding the phone out in front of me so Connor and Hunter could clearly see Roo and Rinna on the screen, I smiled back at the adorable pups. "We'll be back soon. We just need to finish some work down here."

"Well, hurry up! You're missing all my big kills! I took down a buck all by myself!" Roo declared, puffing himself up proudly.

"You did not, that was Uncle Colt and Uncle Gabe!" Rinna ratted him out, much to our amusement.

"Well, I helped!"

"Alright, guys," Hunter removed his arm from around my shoulders to take hold of the phone. "It's past your bedtime. Be good and do what your uncles tell you, or I'll drag you by your scruffs when I get back."

"We will!" they sang in unison. "Goodnight, Dad! We love you!"

"Goodnight. Love you guys too."

The warmth and love in his voice made me melt into a puddle. I placed my head on his shoulder and curled my legs underneath me, leaning on him heavily. We'd been eating dinner and catching up in our Miami hotel restaurant, but I still couldn't believe my wolf was back.

His brothers showed up out of the blue to our house in Georgia, right around the same time we got a job offer hundreds of miles away in Florida. For thirty-thousand dollars, we just couldn't say no. However, we had a strong possibility of working long-term for the Vaudeville Theater, and Hunter wasn't sure if he'd be willing to leave his family so soon after being reunited.

He had Raz and I in limbo for a few days—we didn't know whether to treat this like a breakup or some kind of long-distance relationship when Hunter showed up in Miami. He chose us. His mates.

He left his pups in the temporary care of his brothers and their shaman, Miriam. We would soon return to the Georgia house and weren't sure what the Vaudeville would offer us yet. But there was still the massive shifter compound to deal with.

On the other side of me, in the round booth table, Connor stroked my calf and leaned over to kiss my shoulder.

"I'll be back in a while, babe. Meet you guys back in the suite."

"Where are you off to?" I asked, watching him slide out the opposite side.

"You'll see," he answered evasively. "Keep her safe while I'm gone, Hunter."

"She's never been safer," Hunter replied, draping his long arm over me again.

"My knights in shining armor," I huffed, rolling my eyes.

Hunter chuckled, dropping a kiss to my head. "You just bring out the animal in all of us. In more ways than one."

"Naughty wolf," I teased, wrapping an arm around his waist. I could still feel the effects of the orgasms he and Raz had given me hours earlier. The three of us had quite the reunion when our wolf returned and told us he was staying.

Thinking of Raz made me lift my head off Hunter's chest. When we joined Connor for dinner, he and Arjun went to scope out the restaurant where they captured Julian, a young coyote shifter I was able to Speak to psychically. Over an hour had passed now, and I wondered if my dragon and the tiger were okay.

"What's up?" Hunter noticed the shift in my body.

"I was just thinking of Raz and Arjun," I told him. "I hope they haven't run into any trouble." I didn't want to voice my fear of them being captured. If they were caught, the chances of us finding the shifter compound were slim to none, not to mention getting in and freeing everyone.

"I'm sure they are." He massaged my hip soothingly. "Why don't you check in with them? Can you use Speak when they're in human form?"

"Not sure. I've never tried it."

I closed my eyes, picturing my handsome tattooed dragon in my head, and decided to try.

Hey, Raz. Can you hear me?

Steluța, he answered immediately. Yes, you're loud and clear, my love. What is it?

Just checking in. How are you guys?

He hesitated for a moment before answering.

Physically, we're fine. We've found a way into the compound and have learned some new developments. We're heading back to the hotel now and will give you a full update.

Okay, I replied. See you soon.

"They're okay and heading back," I reported to Hunter, lifting my head off him and sitting up straight.

"You don't seem all that happy," he observed, locking those golden eyes on me.

I chewed my lip, mulling over Raz's choice of words. "He said they were physically fine, implying they're *not* okay in other ways."

"Hm." Hunter pursed his lips thoughtfully. "I guess we'll find out when they get back."

"Now I'm going to worry until the moment I see they're alive and well," I muttered, sliding out of the booth and straightening my clothes. "Especially after all the mind shit I had gone through. I wouldn't wish that on anybody."

On our way down to Florida, I started having increasingly worse headaches. The pain kept growing exponentially until I saw horrific visions of what the compound shifters were going through in real time.

Not only could I see through their eyes, I heard their cries and felt all of their pain in my own body. To say it was unbearable was putting it lightly.

What got me through it was Arjun, much to my surprise. He'd really saved me in so many ways while we were down here. Maybe it was my imagination, but I could swear we were getting closer. The guys insisted he liked me, but he always kept me at arm's reach. Except for the times that he didn't.

"Arjun and Raz are strong. I'm sure they're fine." Hunter rubbed my back as he followed me out of the booth and back to the hotel lobby. "Seems like the tiger's got a thing for my little fox," he teased, pulling me to his side.

"Don't start," I groaned. "I mean, I'm not opposed to the idea, but one minute Arjun's firmly against it, and the next, he's touching my hand and shit. I've talked about it with Connor and Raz and it's... complicated."

"Aw, what's throwing one more shifter into our little love triangle?" he laughed. "Or I guess we're a love square, actually. With Arjun thrown in, what does that make us? A love pentagon?"

"Stop," I giggled, poking him in the ribs. "Speaking of love triangle, I'm really happy you claimed Raz as a mate."

"Yeah?" His cheeks flushed and an adorable smile played at his lips. "I probably should have talked about that with you, since it was you and me first. But I was thinking about it the whole trip down here and it just... felt right."

"Then it is right." I wrapped an arm around his waist as we ascended the winding staircase to our suite level. Sure, we could have taken the elevator, but this gave us more time to talk. "And I have two other mates, for Christ's sake. You don't need my permission to have one more."

"Still, I don't ever want you to feel disrespected again."

His fingers squeezed around my shoulder. He was referring to his brother Gabe, shooting me a dirty look back home. It wasn't a huge deal to me, but my guys seemed to take it as a major offense. At that point, I fully understood why shifters held such a deep hatred for humans. Though Connor and Raz were ready to chase some wolves back into the woods.

I looked up at Hunter, smiling broadly. We were all new to this multi-person relationship and still figuring out our way around it. He wanted to keep me aware of his intentions and I appreciated that, but the way he claimed Raz and me was just perfect.

"You know, I don't think Raz has felt loved by anyone before this," I said. "I mean, he knows he's sexy and charming. His adult life has always been about surviving and occasionally having meaningless sex."

"Now he has two people that love him," Hunter agreed softly.

"Yeah," I answered. "Being someone's mate. I think it means a lot to him."

We reached the suite to find Connor waiting for us, a small plastic grocery bag in his hand.

"Gonna tell us where you ran off to, now?" I asked, eyeing the bag.

"Babe, you can see plain as day where I ran off to," he remarked, holding up the bag. "The question is what did I get?" He shook it at me tauntingly.

"Don't keep me in suspense now." I rolled my eyes, crossing my arms. "Did you get me a Walmart engagement ring?"

"Please, we just made like forty-grand in a single night! The rock I get you is going to be worth at *least* that much."

"I'm telling you right now, don't waste our money," I laughed with a shake of my head. "But really, what did you get?"

He shot a sneaky glance toward Hunter before reaching into the bag and holding its contents out in his hand. My heart leaped into my throat when I saw what laid across his palm.

"Pregnancy tests?!"

"Yeah, I got a bunch of different ones." He shook the bag in his opposite hand.

"Connor, uh..." Why did my face feel so hot? Why was I suddenly so fucking nervous? "I think it's too soon to tell. My period isn't due for a while so I'm not sure if I'm going to miss it."

"I remember you saying that, so I got some early detection ones too." He rummaged through the bag and pulled out one to read it.

"Yep, here we go! As early as a week after conception, it says." He held it out to me, his forest green eyes lit up like a Christmas tree. "Babe, don't you want to know?"

"Of course I do," I told him. "I just think we're jumping the gun a little."

"She knows her body best, Con," Hunter added.

"Well, try this early one and if it's negative, we'll try again when your period is due. And if the red tide rolls in, I guess that'll be our answer."

That sounded like a reasonable request. I just couldn't figure out why it felt like he was asking me to jump out of a plane.

I took the box from him with slow, hesitant hands. I turned it over to read the directions, but the small writing just blurred together.

"I love you, babe." Connor pulled me close and kissed my temple. "No matter what the results are. We're all here for you."

While I didn't know whether to be excited or scared to death, Connor was an electric ball of excitement. He was trying to be calm and strong, but I saw the hope in his eyes. He wanted me to be pregnant, to grow big and round with a product of our love. And I wanted to give that to him, more than anything.

I wanted to give him a baby so badly, I didn't know if I could handle the disappointment of a negative test. Sure, we could try again later. Still, so many aspects of our lives were up in the air—the compound shifters, my siblings, finding a forever home and being able to afford one for our big, mixed-species family.

All of these thoughts jumbled through my head as I marched like a zombie to the bathroom. My hands pulled down my shorts and underwear as I sat on the toilet mechanically.

A random statistic popped into my head, as they often did when my thoughts wandered all over the place. Something like a third of all pregnancies don't ever fully develop. Many women miscarry before they even realized they were pregnant.

It hit me just as I started to open the packaging on the test. My hands froze as my mind became clear. Then, just as quickly as I sat down, I stood up and pulled my clothes back on.

When I returned to the living room, Connor crossed his arms and arched a skeptical brow at me.

"Now I know you women are speedy about this shit, but you did *not* just take a leak, babe."

"I'm sorry," I told him, placing the unopened pregnancy test back in the bag. "But I can't do this. Not right now."

❧ 2 ❧

MELODY

A look of hurt crossed Connor's face before he put on a mask of neutrality. "Why not?" He posed the question casually.

"Because if I take that test and find out that I *am* pregnant," I swallowed. "You guys would do everything in your power to protect me and keep me, *us*, out of danger."

"Naturally." Connor narrowed his eyes, now confused. "Of course we would, babe. Why's that an issue?"

"It's not, not normally," I answered. "But we have to take risks in order to save the shifters at the compound. We're all going to risk our lives, most likely. If something happens to me—"

"Babe!"

"If something happened to me or the baby," my hand drifted over my stomach. "I'd rather not know I was carrying. Not this early. With everything else going on, I couldn't live with knowing I lost—"

"Shhh." Hunter pulled my head onto his chest, his hands soothing over my back and in my hair. "I get it, little fox. I understand."

"You do?" I looked up at him, resting my chin on his chest.

He nodded, looking sad. "Roo and Rinna were not our first attempts at conceiving. My former mate lost our first pups early in her

726

pregnancy, but it was no less devastating. We almost wish we hadn't known."

That floored me. I had no idea Hunter dealt with such a loss. He lost his pups, his mate, his entire pack, and had been captured. And while he wasn't perfect, my pale wolf was still an amazing mate and father. He could have let the events of his life destroy him, but he didn't.

"We're protecting you regardless if you're pregnant or not," Connor said. "No one is letting you get hurt by those sick fucks."

"All I'm saying is, there's going to be risks we can't predict," I told him, now wishing I had Miriam's ability to see a glimpse into the future. "If we find out I'm pregnant, y'all probably won't let me leave the suite and that's a no-go from me. I won't let you guys risk your lives while I'm locked away in an ivory tower."

Connor rubbed his jaw, a grin threatening to emerge on his lips. "I have half a mind to tie you to the bed, anyway."

"I'd be in favor of that," Hunter agreed.

"I know you guys are joking," I sighed, "but seriously, this is my decision. I'll take the test after everything is done. I don't want to be treated differently, and I don't want to grieve a loss if something were to happen. Maybe that's selfish, but it's how I feel."

"Of course it's your decision, babe." Connor's serious face returned. "I'm bummed because I was dying to find out, but it's totally up to you. However you feel is more important."

"Thank you," I told him, feeling several pounds lighter. I approached him and unfolded his arms to put them around me, where they belonged.

Just then we heard the sound of a keycard sliding through the electronic lock on the door.

"They're back!" I breathed, spinning in his arms to watch eagerly for Raz and Arjun to come through the door. The moment they did, it was like all the air got sucked out of the room.

Arjun headed straight for his room, not even making eye contact with anyone, before slamming his door shut. The sound reverberated throughout the suite like he had used all his strength. We all turned to Raz with silence and wide eyes for an explanation.

With a sigh, he leaned his back against the front door and looked toward the ceiling, displaying his sexy throat tattoos. "Shit is fucked," was all he said.

"What happened?" Hunter asked. He reached forward and took a light hold on Raz's hand, gently pulling our dragon toward us.

"Are you okay?" I grabbed his other arm as he came forward, looking for my answer in those steel-gray eyes.

"I'm fine, *steluța*," he gave me a reassuring smile before lifting his eyes toward Arjun's room. "He's not."

"Why?" A rush of emotions overcame me. If it weren't for Connor wrapped around me, I might have marched over to Arjun's door to check on him. If he wasn't okay, he shouldn't be alone. He'd basically saved my life on this trip. The least I could do was be there for him, too.

"Let's all sit down," Connor suggested.

Hunter and I sandwiched Raz between us on the couch while Connor took the oversized armchair to himself.

"We went to La Hacienda," Raz began. "Arjun spotted a guy right away, heading toward the back room where Julian was taken. He said he smelled like blood and tranquilizers, and he could also faintly smell other shifters who had been back there before."

"Oh God," I whispered, my stomach churning. How many had been baited to go back there just like Julian?

"The door at the end of the hall was locked, but we followed the trail outside and behind the restaurant. Arj stayed on his scent trail, and I could feel the guy's footsteps," Raz continued. "We followed for a few blocks and then it was gone. The scent dead-ended and I couldn't feel any vibrations of movement in the air. It was like he disappeared, or turned into a statue and covered up his trail."

"How is that possible?" Connor wondered aloud.

"Shaman illusions," I answered. I couldn't explain how I knew, but it somehow made sense to me. It was a simple game of opposites. Cover up movement and you have stillness. Cover up the scent and you remove the trail.

"Yes, exactly," Raz looked at me. "But this was nothing like what I've seen you do. Arjun picked up a rock and threw it above our heads.

It bounced off something that sounded like a metal door, even though we couldn't see anything there."

"Whoa," Hunter leaned back in his seat. "So this place is really hiding in plain sight. This shaman can cast an illusion to hide an entire compound?"

"Yes, and apparently there's only one who can do that," Raz sighed. "Arjun deduced it must be his stepfather, Lhozen."

"*What?*" the three of us demanded in unison.

"Isn't this the guy who raised him?" Connor asked.

"He was married to a shifter, Arjun's mom! How could he do this?" I demanded.

"He taught Miriam everything she knows, and she wouldn't hurt a fly," Hunter voiced. "I trust her as much as my brothers, which was the only reason I left my kids with them."

"I asked him a lot of the same questions," Raz answered sadly. "He's convinced that he's right, but naturally, he's all torn up about it now. He was silent and brooding the entire way back, like he just tuned me out. I think he needs to be alone for now."

"Damn." I leaned back on the couch, mirroring Hunter. "Poor Arjun. What a terrible thing to find out."

"Jesus tap-dancing Christ," Connor groaned, rubbing a hand down his face. "So what the hell are we dealing with here?"

"Someone who knows both shifters and humans very intimately, and is powerful enough to fool them both," Raz muttered. "A goddamn fucking magician."

"Something tells me that doesn't make our chances any better," Connor replied.

"I'm really going to need Arjun's help," I realized, folding my hands in my lap. "He knows Lhozen better than anyone. If anyone knows how to see through his illusions, it's him. He proved that already with the rock and the invisible door."

"Sure, but how much will he want to help?" Hunter asked. "I'm not sure how close he and Lhozen were, but this must be a monumental betrayal to him. It's his father... stepfather. Is he going to have his head in the game? We have to beat him—Maybe even kill him?"

The room was silent for a moment, all of us deep in our own heads as we pondered those questions. But nobody could answer them, except for the tiger shifter locked away in his room.

MELODY

We decided to leave Arjun alone for the night, and try gauging his feelings in the morning. As the four of us got ready for bed, the space issues in our love square became clear.

"How the fuck are we all gonna fit?" Connor demanded, looking between all of us and the king-sized bed. "I'll tell y'all right now, I'm not cuddling with anyone besides Mel."

"It'll be a bit of a squeeze, but the wolf and I can snuggle up close." Raz kissed Hunter's neck before peeling his shirt off. "You should have plenty of room to spread out like a starfish, Con, on your side of the bed."

"I do not spread out like a starfish. I sleep like the dead. That's the only reason you got away with it that one time ... fucking our girl right next to me, you sneaky bastard."

"You told him about that?!" Raz demanded, his mouth hanging open in mock betrayal.

"He had me pressed against a wall!" I shot back defensively. "I didn't mean to, but he'd just gotten his new legs and I couldn't think straight."

"Wow, when did I miss this?" Hunter chuckled. Now shirtless

himself, he came up behind Raz to wrap his arms around the dragon's tattooed shoulders. Pulling him close, he dropped kisses to Raz's neck and shoulder, making the dragon visibly shiver at the contact and heat pool between my legs.

"When you were off with your douchebag brothers," Raz murmured in reply, leaning his head back to kiss Hunter's ear and jaw.

"What are you staring at, babe?"

Connor came up behind me, his firm hands gliding along my waist made me jump. I didn't realize how entranced I was watching the shifters being sweet to each other. It almost felt perverse, getting so turned on by them just expressing their love and affection.

"*Steluța*, you must know by now that we love putting on a show for you," Raz grinned. "We are performers, after all." His breath hitched as Hunter turned it up even more, caressing sensually over the dragon's chest and abs. His kisses became more passionate, slow and open-mouthed, with a hint of teeth.

"Did your little reunion still leave you wanting more?" Connor's stubble was rough on my cheek and neck, his lips just grazing over my tender skin. "Is our woman just that insatiable?"

"Not that it wasn't good, but I would have liked..." Connor's mouth found my earlobe, making all words escape my breath as I arched against him, the intense sensation too good to ignore. He immediately pulled my hips back, limiting my movement and letting his bulge nestle against my ass.

"What would you have liked, little fox?" Hunter and Raz sat together on the edge of the bed, Hunter's chin resting on Raz's shoulder as his hands now massaged down the dragon's thighs. "Tell us." Raz leaned back against him, much like how I was with Connor, lifting his hips off of the bed so his jeans began sliding down from the wolf's touch.

My pulse thrummed in my veins, hotter by the second and moving fast. We hadn't even done anything yet. It was the teasing, the antici-pation of watching what played out between the shifters that turned me into an instant puddle of sex-goo.

"I would have liked your cock, Hunter." The words sounded so dirty, yet empowering, coming from my mouth. "Inside me."

"Boys, did you deprive our woman of cock?" Connor held up a finger and wagged it disapprovingly. "That is *not* how you keep her satisfied. Shame on you."

"I was hoping you'd say that," Hunter grinned wolfishly over Raz's shoulder. "Because that was exactly what I wanted to give you. What happened earlier was just a warmup."

"Oh, she's warmed up alright." Connor ran his hands from my waist up over my breasts, my nipples practically stabbing his palms through my bra and top. "She barely needs any foreplay, just watching you guys."

"Come here, *steluța,*" Raz ordered, his voice low and husky. "Let me make sure you're properly warmed up."

My legs already like jello, I walked over to him, with Connor following close behind. Before straddling his legs, I helped Hunter pull his jeans the rest of the way down. Our wolf kept kissing and teasing him, his hands playing along the waistband of his snug boxer briefs. Raz's thick head poking out of the top and his hot grunts and groans told me all about how warmed up *he* was getting.

Together, Connor and Raz helped me out of my clothes, and the feel of two pairs of hands on me was almost too much to bear. Raz's tongue made a burning trail from my lips to my nipples, the two sides flicking the stiff peaks into aching buds. Connor's mouth sent shivers along my spine, his hands and face rough on my back. It contrasted with Raz's smooth jaw and the delightfulness of his split tongue on my most sensitive areas.

I felt the bed depress behind me as Connor sat down. His chest and abs, a strong impenetrable wall, pressed against my back. Always shielding me, my protector. I turned to kiss him over my shoulder, sighing into his mouth at the feel of Raz's lips and tongue caressing my exposed neck and throat.

All four of us leaned to the side until our bodies hit the mattress. Connor and I never once broke our kiss, his firm grip holding the curve of my waist as he spooned me from behind. His cock, hot and rock hard, pressed between my ass cheeks.

In front of me, Raz and Hunter must have switched places. As I kissed Connor, soft wolfish growls vibrated along the skin of my chest.

Sharp teeth closed around one of my nipples, making me gasp with a soft moan.

"Hello, little fox," Hunter murmured, his mouth traveling from one breast to the other.

"Hello, my handsome wolf," I breathed, running my fingers through his gorgeous platinum hair while I waited for his lips to return to mine.

When his lips captured mine in a savage kiss, my hands often met with Razvan's as we both explored our wolf's body. Raz nibbled at his neck and shoulders, eliciting more soft growls from Hunter. While Hunter also gave light, teasing bites to my lips. My fingertips skimmed down his long torso to wrap around that iron hard shaft pressed between us.

He groaned at the contact and surged his hips forward, pressing hard against my clit, which made my own hips buck in response. Behind me, Connor slid his mouth along my shoulder as he pressed two fingers between my legs.

"Oh my God," he moaned into my neck, dipping those fingers into me and stroking my inner walls. "You are so ready for him, babe."

"I've been ready," I answered, my voice a low, lusty whisper. I couldn't take my eyes off Hunter's face. His golden eyes were hooded and his mouth hung open in soft, sexy pants as I stroked him from base to tip.

He looked away from me for a moment, glancing over his shoulder at Raz, who fiddled with a small bottle of lube. Raz kissed him and murmured something that sounded like, "Relax, wolf. I won't hurt you."

Taking hold of his chin, I turned Hunter back to face me, kissing him with all my pent-up need and frustration at their teasing.

"I need you," I murmured against his lips, my lower body thrashing against Connor's fingers, still pumping in and out of me.

Hunter grabbed my hips to line himself up with me and Connor's fingers withdrew, leaving me achingly empty. My wolf pressed into me slowly, letting me savor every delectable inch of him. I seemed to forget how to breathe, like he pushed all the air out of me.

Hunter seemed to lose his breath too, but not because of being inside me. Behind him, Raz kissed him and murmured in his ear. I couldn't see everything, but the dragon's hands seemed busy near Hunter's ass.

His expression shifted from being blissed out with pleasure to mildly uncomfortable. I pressed my hands to his face, knowing he was adjusting to the new sensations Raz was giving him.

"We love you, Hunter," I whispered against his mouth. "All we want is for you to feel good."

A shudder and a hot moan escaped him before he started thrusting against me. Connor held me in place, keeping me sandwiched between them so I could only absorb the impact of Hunter's body on mine.

"That's it," Raz rasped against his ear. "Just let go. Let yourself enjoy it." His tattooed arm flexed as he played with Hunter's ass a bit more vigorously, applying more lube as needed with his other hand.

"Fuck," Hunter choked out, fucking me more erratically as his control began to slip. "Why is that so fucking good?"

"It's a little-known pleasure center for a man," Raz grinned, his eyes dark with lust as he watched our wolf's pleasure build and his control unravel.

Without warning, Hunter suddenly pulled out of me. He sucked in deep, ragged breaths. His cock jutted out, wet and glistening and flexing with more tension than a tripwire.

"I need a breather," he gasped, shooting me a sheepish grin. "Or I'll be done too fast."

"Mind if I take over, babe?" Connor was already rubbing his head over my slick, sensitive entrance.

My moans and whimpers were all the permission he needed. He pressed inside me, filling the emptiness that Hunter left behind. Still spooning me from behind, he lifted my leg for easier access to my clit while he fucked me with abandon.

"Watch them, babe," he whispered in my ear like a devil on my shoulder. "Watch your mates please each other and I dare you not to come."

Hunter and Raz made out passionately—all teeth, tongues, and rough manhandling by two alpha males. Hunter jerked Raz's thick cock, which was already slick with lube. His own cock still jutted out hard and straight as a steel rod. I could now clearly see Raz's well-lubed fingers sliding in and out of Hunter, giving our wolf pleasure that he'd never known before.

"Connor," I panted, not knowing what I was pleading for. He pinched one of my nipples, making me buck even harder against his other hand pressed firmly to my clit. My orgasm was building up so fast, I felt like I was drowning. I couldn't catch a breath, I was chasing pleasure so hard and climbing a mountain so fast.

Just when I was about to crest that peak, he released me. His cock slid out of me, feeling like a hot iron against my thigh.

"Ready to go again, Hunter?" he asked.

"Ugh, I hate you." My teeth nearly chattered, I was such a frayed bundle of nerves. He merely shot a shit-eating grin at my glare.

"I think so." Hunter rolled on his side toward me again, with Raz settling behind him. This time, I saw Raz nudge his cock toward Hunter's ass.

I scooted forward and practically impaled myself on Hunter. Call me greedy, but I wanted to see his pleasure up close and make it my own. With my hands cradling his neck, I kissed him hard. I raised and lowered myself, taking my fill of him and chasing that pleasure again.

I kept my eyes open, watching his gorgeous face in fascination as Raz slowly eased himself inside of him.

"Fuck," he gasped, abruptly cutting off our kiss. "Fuck, you're big, Raz."

"Thanks," the dragon chuckled, nuzzling his neck. "That's why I'm going slow. Just tell me if you want me to stop."

"No, it's good." Hunter's eyes fluttered in pleasure, his lips pulling back into a lopsided smile. "Enjoying this, little fox?"

"Immensely," I said. "I'm so close and it's mainly because of you two."

"Oh?" He looked over my shoulder at Connor, who propped himself up on his elbow as he gently stroked himself. "Did someone deny you an orgasm over there?"

"Yes." I shot another glare back at my Marine, who just laughed.

"I'm just teaching you to appreciate delayed gratification, babe," he returned. "Like I could have blown my load already but it's going to be so much better when I'm back inside you."

Before I could reply, Hunter let out one of the hottest moans I ever heard from him right against my throat. Raz's fingers dug into his hips, his teeth buried in his shoulder, and his cock seated all the way inside our wolf.

When Raz thrust gently, he pushed Hunter forward to thrust into me.

"Oh God," Hunter choked out, wrapping around me tightly until I was crushed to his chest. He was delirious with pleasure, and Raz and I exchanged a glance that shared how much we loved it.

While they were rougher with each other, Raz was just as sweet and attentive to Hunter as he always was to me. He kissed him and kept checking in to make sure he was feeling good. He applied a liberal amount of lube and carefully watched our wolf for any signs of discomfort. My heart wanted to burst with how much I loved them both, with how much love and care they showed each other.

Hunter looked over his shoulder to kiss Raz hungrily, wrapping an arm around the back of our dragon's head to pull him even closer. As Raz's thrusts grew deeper and more intense, so did Hunter's.

I'd been teetering on the edge for so long, I was amazed they didn't set me off instantly. Raz controlled the movement and the power, pushing Hunter into me and making my pleasure climb high with a slow, steady build.

Time seemed to slow down around us. Every look, every kiss, every thrust carried meaning. I was drowning again, but every beat of pleasure was longer, dragged out like the most luxurious morning stretch.

Every nerve in my body crackling with pent-up energy, my pleasure crested again just as Raz broke a kiss with Hunter. Their foreheads pressed against each other as each of their beautiful eyes locked.

"God, I fucking love you," Raz choked out first.

And that's when I crashed, convulsing so uncontrollably that tears came to my eyes. I didn't know if Hunter said it back. I couldn't hear anything over my blood pounding loudly in my ears. His warmth spilled inside me within seconds, his face buried in my neck, his cock still pounding into me as Raz pounded him.

His orgasm, longer and more intense than anything he had ever felt, seemed to feed my own. Our pleasure rode on each other for what had to be several minutes until the world stilled around us.

"Well, goddamn." Connor's arms came around me to gently tug me from Hunter's tight embrace. "That might have been the hottest thing I've ever seen."

I shivered at my Marine's touch, full-on body tremors from how sensitive I still was. Hunter did the same as Raz caressed him.

"Look at these two, Raz," Connor quipped. "I think you literally fucked their brains out."

"Mm. Still in there, wolf?" Raz teased Hunter, staring at the wolf adoringly. He was still hard and now nestled against the cleft of Hunter's ass.

"I just... fucking wow," Hunter panted, slapping Raz's hand over his heart. "I had no idea I could come like that."

"See what you've been missing all this time?" Raz grinned, dragging his fingertips across Hunter's pale skin to elicit even more shivers.

Returning the grin, Hunter rolled onto his back and grabbed Raz's arms, pulling him roughly on top and wrapping him in a bear hug.

"Now it's your turn," he whispered before crashing his mouth to his in a savage kiss.

"Mm, you want more of me, do ya?" Raz scooted into position so that his cock lined up with Hunter again. Running one hand down the wolf's taut body, he sat back on his heels and applied fresh lube as he stroked himself.

"Always." Hunter licked his lips as he watched.

I playfully smacked Connor, who almost looked more transfixed by their show than I was. "Hear that? Your turn now."

"Mm-hm, you caught me," he chuckled, giving me a kiss. "Get on your knees, babe. I have a feeling you want a front-row seat to this."

He stood from the bed and I took a moment just to look at and appreciate him. A solid wall of muscle, pure strength and masculinity. His cock jutted out from that strong body like a weapon, surrounded by those powerful thighs like tree trunks. His prosthetic legs put him at the perfect height to fuck me from behind while standing.

I scooted on my knees to the edge of the bed, closing my eyes for a moment just to enjoy his hands on my hips and waist. His round head kissing my slick, sensitive entrance, but not penetrating yet.

A deep groan made my eyes open. Raz was buried deep in Hunter again, but this time, the sight of them made me want to look away. Not because it wasn't hot, it definitely was. They wrapped around each other in an intimate embrace, kissing and staring at each other, chest to chest. Anyone could tell the world melted away, and they were aware of nothing except each other. They were making love, and this was their moment.

I flipped over, staring up at my handsome Marine. He was my first love and the future father of my children, as he gave me a quizzical look.

"Come here." I crooked a finger at him with a smile. "I just want to see you and feel you right now."

I felt his smile through his kiss as he lowered to his knees and lined up with me at the edge of the bed.

"Damn, I didn't know I could love someone so much," he said in an awed whisper.

"Me neither." I locked my ankles behind his back and wrapped my arms around his neck. "Or so many people."

"I always knew your heart was too big for just me," he groaned as he pushed inside, filling me to the brim.

"But I still love you completely," I whispered, arching and leaning my head back at the wonderful fullness. "I love all of you, with all of me."

He surged in and out of me with a deep intentional rhythm. Soon the world melted away for me too, until there was nothing but his incredible body and those forest green eyes.

❧ 4 ❧

MELODY

I woke up early the next morning with an overwhelming urge to check on Arjun. The only question was how I'd get up without waking anyone else.

The eyes that stared back at me belonged to the black dragon on Raz's back. For once, he ended up as the little spoon. He and Hunter were tangled up in a mass of arms and legs like they would never separate. Connor wrapped tightly around me from behind and I struggled to get loose from his ever protective hold.

The room was still dark. It couldn't have been past five in the morning. But I slept like the dead and now felt wide awake.

After carefully extracting myself from the cuddle pile, I dressed myself in clothes that had been taken off the night before.

Hey, now that we have money, maybe I can afford some nicer clothes, I thought. *From Target or a mall, maybe.*

I walked out to the silent living room, taking a moment to stare at the ocean in the distance. Florida really was beautiful. I found it hard to believe this tropical paradise was only two states away from the shithole where I grew up. The two places might as well had been different universes.

I wouldn't mind settling here, but only if all the guys agreed. And

740

once we got rid of that awful shifter compound hidden right under our noses.

Before approaching Arjun's room, I went to the kitchen to prepare him a cup of tea. However moody he was feeling, tea always seemed to cheer him up. Such an Englishman thing. And if I was truly honest with myself, my heart went pitter-patter at the thought of seeing his handsome face light up. I wanted to make him happy.

I opened a tea bag and plopped in a cup of water from the tap. Then stuck it in the microwave and turned to look at the ocean again while I waited.

It was too quiet now. Too much of a... *not* home. I missed the rambunctious pups and the forest surrounding our house in Georgia. My heart ached at the thought of everyone living under the same roof again. Even having Colt and Gabe around didn't immediately fill me with dread. They seemed to have warmed up to me before we left, so we could hopefully be close neighbors. I was eager to talk to Miriam some more. Had her other Sight changed since she caught a glimpse of my future?

The microwave beeped, and I carefully removed the mug, holding it by the handle as my bare feet padded across the cool tile floor to Arjun's room. I pressed my ear to the door. Total silence.

I knocked softly. "Arjun? It's Mel."

Nothing answered from the other side, so I grabbed the doorknob to find it was unlocked. I waited five more seconds before turning the knob and pushing the door open.

"Arjun?" I poked my head in. "I brought you tea."

He sat on the bed with his back against the headboard, still fully dressed in his clothes from yesterday. With his legs stretched out in front of him, he stared at nothing. The room was dark except for his bedside lamp. His TV was off. It was like he'd been sitting there, staring into empty space all night.

"Arjun?" I placed the cup down on the nightstand and moved closer. He didn't even react to my presence until I touched his shoulder.

"I don't understand it," he whispered. "I've been trying to connect the dots, but they simply aren't there."

"Arjun..." I didn't know what to say. His face was blank, but I felt the emotional anguish coming off him in waves. He looked up to this man, Lhozen. He trusted him and saw him as a father figure. Only to find out that same man profited from treating others—like him—like cattle.

I didn't know how to help him make sense of it, or to ease the feeling of loss and betrayal, so I just asked him, "Can I sit with you?"

He didn't answer, so I invited myself on the bed next to him, climbing up and taking the same position as him, back against the headboard and legs stretched out. When I reached for his hand, his fingers gently curling around mine were the only indication he knew I was there.

"I'm so sorry, Arjun," I told him, feeling like I was speaking to an empty room. "It's selfish of me, but all I can think about was how horrible my mother was. She never should have had kids. That was clear from the start. The best thing she could do for us was to be an example of how not to live our lives. How to not treat other people."

He didn't respond, but his thumb moved back and forth across the inside of my palm.

"But I was lucky in a way," I continued. That got a small huff of breath from him, like a scoff, so I kept going. "Since the day I was born, I knew what to expect. I knew exactly who and what she was, so I never felt disappointed and betrayed by her. She wasn't a mother, so I didn't hold her to any standards or expectations. I always knew she was just someone I had to avoid. I had to stay out of her way until I turned eighteen and I could be free."

I looked at him, all light and spark gone from those gorgeous ocean-colored eyes. I didn't even know Lhozen, but I hated him in that moment. Not even for all the shifters who suffered, but just for hurting this man sitting next to me.

"I can't even imagine how it must feel, to have someone tell you they love you, to be an actual parent who guides and protects you, and then rip that all away." I leaned my head to the side until it touched his shoulder. "Lhozen is even worse than my mother because of that. I'm so sorry that he did this to you."

He let out a long sigh, the first true sign of life since I came into the room.

"I never suffered like you," he said softly. "I never wanted for anything growing up. We weren't wealthy and mum was pretty old-school about a lot of things, but my childhood was happy. For that, I'm grateful. I can't hate him for giving us a good life when I was young. It wasn't until she died that everything got all fucked up."

His hand tightened around mine, and I felt the gentle pressure of his temple resting against my head.

"Hindus believe in reincarnation," he went on. "That the deeds of your current life determine how you will be reborn in your next life. If mum were here, she'd tell me to do nothing. That he'll answer for the suffering he's caused in his next life."

"But you don't want to do that," I speculated, and felt his confirming nod against my head.

"I want to watch him die a long, suffering death," he muttered in a low, predatory growl. "I want to taste his blood and let every shifter he's captured get a taste as well. But," he paused, "wanting such things and doing them will not bode well for my own rebirth into the next life."

"Why's that?"

"The concept of *ahimsa* is very important to Hindus," he explained. "It means do no harm, not only in actions but also in thought. Although it's moot for me. My next life is probably already determined because of all the harm I have done. It's just hard to let go of that guilt." He chuckled. "You didn't expect to come in here and listen to me ramble about my religion, did you?"

"Doesn't it make a difference if you're only harming those who've harmed you?" I asked, lifting my head off his shoulder to look at him. "You were tortured, Arjun. For years. And now you've learned this man who raised you is part of that, and torturing others. Suffering in their next life isn't enough. That ringmaster you killed deserved it. And Lhozen deserves to feel the pain he's inflicted on others in this life."

"You would make a terrible Hindu," he muttered.

"Thanks."

We both chuckled at that and he closed his other hand around mine, fingertips gently caressing the skin of my wrists and palms. It made me want to purr and curl up in his lap.

"I used to be afraid of you," I admitted, watching his hands envelop mine. "I felt every ounce of your anger and desire to kill, like it was my own. But now I know it was only aimed at those who caged you. It must be hard balancing your tiger's instincts with your peaceful beliefs."

His eyes searched mine, eyebrows lifting slightly in surprise. "Yes, it's been a lifelong struggle," he admitted. "We're told to do no harm, but we must kill for food. I spent four years in a cage and I'm supposed to just pray to Shiva. I learn my stepfather is a monster and I'm expected to let his next life be punishment enough."

"I don't know what's going to happen in your next life, or if there even is one," I said. "But you're nothing like him, Arjun. You've never harmed anyone who didn't deserve it. You deserve happiness and peace after everything you've been through."

He gave me a long, lingering look. "Why did you come in here, Mel?"

"I just wanted to check on you." Suddenly remembering, I pulled my hand from his. "And look, I brought you tea."

"So you did. Thank you, dove." He smiled for the first time, accepting the warm mug from me and taking a sip. Immediately after swallowing, he made a face. "How did you prepare this?"

"Just water and the tea bag," I answered, puzzled at his expression.

"How did you heat up the water?"

"In the microwave."

"The microwave?!"

"Well, how else am I supposed to heat it up?!"

"In a damn kettle, like a civilized human being, you muppet. And where's the milk and sugar?"

I tried to hold back my laughter, but it came spilling out as soon as he called me that name. Here we were, depressed and upset about something serious, and he was giving me shit about the tea I brought him.

"It's not funny, Mel." He tried to a keep a straight face, but the smile was breaking through, the brightness returning to his eyes. "We take our tea very seriously in England."

"I know, but..." My shoulders shook with the giggles and tears threatened to spill out of my eyes.

"I appreciate the gesture, dove, but you've fucked it up royally," he continued in a deadpan voice. "Let me show you how to make a proper cup before you attempt something like this again."

"Okay..." For some reason, the way he talked about it made it even funnier and fresh peals of laughter burst from my throat. I guess I finally got his English sense of humor.

"Come on now." He set the mug down, his grin wide and beautiful as he wrapped his arms around me. "What have you done, you silly woman?"

I didn't understand his question, so I looked up at him, my gaze captured in those eyes as deep and clear as the ocean.

Slowly, his arm dropped from around my shoulders, fingertips trailing down my back until he reached my waist. His large hand nestled in the curve there, pulling me closer. Not that he needed to. I was already close enough to see the iridescent flecks of color in his eyes, to feel the soft warmth of his breath fan across my lips.

We leaned in as if pulled magnetically toward each other. His dark lashes flickered downward, obscuring those eyes as he gazed at my lips. My hand found itself drifting up to graze across his cheek. He leaned into the touch, a catlike gesture of affection that was so uniquely him.

I tilted my head in the opposite direction, my own eyes fluttering closed as my mouth parted. His lips looked so soft and I could nearly taste their warmth as they hovered over mine.

Bang, bang, bang! *"Steluța, you in there?"*

I jumped away, startled, nearly flying out of my own skin as Raz burst into the room. He was dressed only in his boxer briefs haphazardly, like he pulled them on in a hurry and ran over here. His face looked concerned, but not at me or Arjun.

He held out Connor's phone, the screen lit up and indicating it was in the middle of a phone call. "It's your sister. She needs you."

MELODY

"Hello?"

"Mel?" Jeanie May's voice sounded small and far away.

"Yeah, it's me." I stood from the bed and headed for the living room, the thrill of the near-kiss with Arjun still pounding through my veins. "Where are you, Jean? Are you okay?"

"We're okay. We're at the downtown Waterford shelter." Her voice carried over calmly through the speaker, but I heard the underlying fear she swallowed down to put on a brave face for the kids.

"We?" I repeated. "Is everyone with you?"

"Yeah, we're all here. We're safe for now but we can't stay here forever." A small voice filtered through the background that sounded like Bella. "Yes, I'm talking to Mel, Bells. You can say hi in a minute."

"Jean, what happened?" I demanded, my pulse and mind racing. There were closer places to get away from the house if shit went down. If they were at the downtown shelter, it meant they walked over five miles and had zero intention of going back. They were hiding.

"It started off like any other night," she muttered. I knew she was keeping her voice low to prevent the kids from overhearing. "Mom's latest went ape-shit and started throwing glass bottles at the wall, right above Riley's crib."

"Oh no," I covered my face with my hands, the image burned behind my eyes. "Is she okay?"

"She's fine, nothing hit her," Jeanie answered. "But I was in the back bedroom helping Joey with homework. By the time I got out there, he ran out of bottles and was looking for any random shit to throw."

She paused and I heard ruffling and scratching through the phone like she was covering the mouthpiece.

"Bella was out there," she whispered. "He threw a shoe and aimed low. It got her in the face because she climbed into Riley's crib to protect her."

"Oh my God..."

"I'm okay, Mella!" Bella piped up in the background. She liked making our names sound similar, so she called us Mella and Bella. "Riley was scared and crying but I protected her."

"Yes, you did, Bells," I choked out. Someone came up behind me and rubbed my shoulders as they kissed my head, but all I could think about were my helpless baby sisters. "You're such a brave girl. But that's never going to happen again."

Jeanie repeated the message to Bella and resumed talking to me normally on the phone. "This place is crowded as shit, Mel. They don't have enough beds and our time is limited, but there's no fucking way we can go back."

"I know, Jean. I know." I rubbed my forehead, struggling to think straight. "I can send you money in a day or two for a hotel. But I can't come get you yet, I'm in Florida right now."

"What the hell are you doing down there?"

"Um, a job," I answered. It was close enough to the truth.

"If we scrape the money together, can we meet you down there?"

"No!" I barked louder than I had intended. "No, Jean. I'm sorry. I hate to be vague right now, but it's not safe for all of you here. I can't risk you or the kids."

"What the hell? Are you okay?"

"I'm fine, but... I'll have to explain it all later because it's too much for one phone call."

"Well, we might not have two days here, Mel." Jeanie's calmness cracked for just a second, but she recovered quickly. "They're trying not to kick three young kids out to the street, but they may not have a choice. People are already double-bunking and sleeping on the floor here."

"Shit." *Come on, Mel. There has to be a way.* But no clear solution came to me and I felt like I was failing them all over again.

"Babe." Connor sat next to me on the couch, looking at me with a soothing calmness. "If they need to get out now, I'll pick them up. I can take them to the house at the FDR Center and stay with them there until y'all take care of business down here."

My mouth dropped open to refuse, to say, *No, I need you here,* but I realized how selfish that was. My siblings were a day away from living on the street, and I was in a luxury suite overlooking Miami Beach. I had three other men here who would protect me with their lives, and Jeanie had no one.

So instead I asked, "Are you sure?"

He nodded. "Arjun is your best bet on beating this guy. The other two will help you win over the shifters too if need be. As the token human, I'm more likely to get in the way. But I'm there for your family, babe. They'll be safe and we'll wait for you to get back." He grabbed my hand and squeezed. "Because you *will* succeed and you *will* come back to us."

"Mel?" Jeanie asked. "Are you still there?"

"Hang on, Jean. I'm figuring something out." I muted the phone so she wouldn't hear us, then looked back at Connor. "You're absolutely positive you want to do this?"

"Yes, babe," he chuckled. "You don't need me to protect you, not like how you used to. You're a badass and you've got the other guys. But it sounds like your siblings need someone and I'm happy to be that person."

"If you're completely sure," I rested my forehead on his, "I can't thank you enough. I love you so much."

"No need to thank me. I take care of my woman and her people." He kissed me warmly. "When should I leave?"

"Right away. Like, now." I bit my lip. "They're in an overcrowded homeless shelter and could get kicked out at any time. They're in downtown Waterford, my hometown."

"I'll get the ol' bucket warmed up." He kissed me again as he rose from the couch. "Tell your sister I'm coming."

Releasing a breath, I unmuted the call. "Jean?"

"Yeah?"

"My, uh, boyfriend is coming to get you," I told her. "He'll take you all to where we're staying and I'll meet you there after I'm done with the job here."

"Okay. That pale guy with the long hair I met?"

"No, that's Hunter," I said. "Connor is coming to get you. He'll show up in a big RV."

"Oh, damn. You're going through 'em fast." She was joking, but I heard the disapproval in her voice. Our mom went through boyfriends like bottles of Mickey's.

"No, it's not like that. I, ugh..." I pinched the bridge of my nose, not wanting to explain this to her now. "Hunter and I are still together, too. Everybody knows about each other. I'll explain later," I said lamely.

"Wait, what? You're with two guys?"

"Three, actually." And possibly a fourth, eventually.

"Mel, what the—"

"I'll explain later!" I couldn't help the giggle rising in my throat. "When I see you, which will be very soon. I promise, Jean."

"Mel, be honest with me. Are these guys—"

"Don't even finish that sentence," I told her. "They're great men. Amazing men, actually. They love me and want to protect me and my family. That's why Conner stepped up to get you. I trust them with my life. The little ones are in good hands with them, Jean. Connor won't let anything bad happen, I swear to you."

"Okay," she said after a long silence. "I believe you, sis."

"Thank you." I sighed a massive breath of relief. "Connor's leaving soon. He'll get there as soon as he can."

"Alright. I guess I'll see you soon."

"You definitely will," I told her. "And I'll explain everything when I see you guys. Give them kisses for me, I love you all."

"Love you, Mella!" the little ones shouted from the background before the line clicked dead.

"Goddamn, *steluţa*."

I looked up, not even realizing that Hunter and Raz stood together in the kitchen the whole time.

"Guess everyone's awake," I muttered. "Did y'all here the whole thing?"

They nodded in unison. "Having Connor get them is smart," Hunter said.

"I agree," I said. "I just hate the idea of us being separated again, especially after you just got here."

"It won't be for long." Raz came up to me and pulled me into a strong embrace. "We'll string Lhozen up by his balls, free the shifters, and go home."

"If only it were that simple," I chuckled, laying my head on his shoulder.

"It definitely won't be."

The remark came from Arjun, who breezed out of his room and into the kitchen. "There's a high probability that my dear old stepfather will enslave or kill us all, and there will be no going home." He raised a glass of water with a bitter smile. "Cheers to us."

✤ 6 ✤

MELODY

"What should I tell them?"

I just shrugged and nuzzled my face harder into the center of Connor's chest. I didn't want him to leave me, as selfish as that was. He'd been at my side since the beginning. And now he was about to be hundreds of miles away. The RV's engine rumbled like a fearsome beast, echoing off the concrete walls of the hotel parking garage.

"They're going to see the pups, and Hunter's bros, and Miriam, most likely," he said, rubbing his hands down my back. "Your sister's going to ask questions and I'd rather not lie."

"Then tell them the truth," I answered, inhaling his sharp, masculine scent.

He squeezed around me tightly, dropping a kiss to the top of my head. "I'm gonna miss you, babe, but I'm not worried for once. Lhozen has no idea what's coming to him."

"It's the opposite," I groaned, placing my chin on his chest to look up at him. "We have no idea what we're up against because everything is an illusion."

"You'll figure it out. You always do." He cupped my face, holding me in a long sensual kiss that I never wanted to end. "I gotta head out,

751

babe," he murmured reluctantly, "if I'm gonna be there before tomorrow."

I nodded, slowly releasing my hold on him like we were stuck together with superglue. "Be safe. Tell them I love them and I'll see them soon."

"Absolutely." He kissed me again, a final time. "I love you, Mel. You better bring this sweet ass home to me."

"You know I will when you say shit like that." I laughed despite the dread in my chest and tears threatening to spill over. "I love you, Connor."

I stole one, two, three more last kisses before he bro-hugged all three other guys who stood around me, clapping each other hard on the back and exchanging well wishes. Hunter and Raz each held my hands as we watched Connor slowly back the RV out of its space. The tears didn't spill until he drove out of sight, and I could only hear the roar of the engine before it faded away.

Hunter and Raz held me between them as we got back in the elevator, kissing me and wiping my tears away. Arjun stood a polite distance away, looking in the opposite direction. All of us were silent as we came back to the suite. My tears dried quickly and a new feeling settled over me.

I had to do this. I had to beat him. Connor stepped up to do what he could. Now I had to do the same.

"Arjun."

"Yes, dove?" He turned to me with a curious look. He seemed to snap out of his shock from this morning, but I wondered if the uncertainty and doubts he expressed still weighed on him.

"What do I need to do?" I asked. "What is our best possible chance of taking him down?"

He took a deep breath. "Your Semblance needs to be at his level. You need to cast illusions not only over yourself but other people, objects, and locations. And they need to be strong enough to fool even him. That is our best possible chance."

"Okay. And how long will that take?"

"For an exceptionally gifted shaman as yourself?" He tapped his chin as he thought. "Years. Optimistically, three to five years if you practice daily."

"Years?!" I repeated, panic making my voice screech. "We don't have that kind of time!"

"Exactly," he said with mock cheer. "Therefore, we are well and truly fucked."

"What can you teach me in, like, two days?"

"Not anywhere close to enough," he replied. "You must understand, Mel, Lhozen has been a practicing shaman for over thirty years. Longer than any of us have been alive. And who knows how long he's held up the illusions around the compound. The longer they're cast, the more realistic they appear to be."

"So what can we do?" I cried with exasperation. "Besides give up?"

"I'll tell you what we *should* do," he said, his voice taking on a predatory growl. "Run down the street waving our arms in hopes that Connor sees us. We did our job. We've been paid. We went to the beach. The smartest thing we can do now is get the hell out and save our own arses."

I stared at him, half expecting him to morph into Lhozen himself or some other stranger, because it was the last thing I had expected Arjun to say.

"We can't leave," I said, fighting the tremble in my voice and the urge to scream. "They have no one to help them besides us. They need us. I promised Julian—"

"You should break that promise, dove. Won't be the worst thing in the world. He might even understand."

"Are you listening to yourself?" I demanded, my control shattering. "It already *is* the worst thing in the world for them, Arjun! They're suffering! They're dying! How can you say things like that when you went through the same?"

"You keep talking about *them*. I'm talking about *us!*" His words now echoed off the marble columns, as I could physically see his anger rising. Eyes wide, lips pulled back to show his teeth, fast movements meant to intimidate.

"Lhozen knows what Raz and I look like. He's probably waiting for all of us to waltz in on some daring, amateur rescue mission just so he can resell us. I'm not joking around, Mel. We *need* to save ourselves."

"We have to try." My teeth ground painfully against each other as I fought back the angry tears. "We can't just leave them."

"Mel, dove," he said in a gentler tone. "If you want to see Connor and your siblings again, then I'm afraid we must do exactly that."

"No," I crossed my arms defiantly. "There has to be a way we can save them *and* ourselves."

"What the fuck do you think I've been awake all night thinking about?!"

The outburst came from him so loud and suddenly, it made me jump and shrink back. No one had yelled at me like that since I left home, and all my defensive instincts kicked in.

"Arj," Raz barked, stepping up to him and pressing a hand to his chest. "Take it easy, mate." Hunter approached him from my other side like a watchful bodyguard, golden eyes sharp.

The wound-up tiger shifter looked at each of them in turn before focusing on me again. "Mel, you have a good heart and you want to do right by the captive shifters. That's admirable," he said, sighing like he was tired. "But I know what Lhozen is capable of. We cannot win, dove. I'm sorry."

"Then why did you help me?" My voice cracked with helplessness. "Why even guide me through Speaking with them? We knew the risk was high. Why do all that just to give up now?"

He kept silent for a moment before lifting his eyes and saying sadly, "That was before I knew exactly who we were dealing with."

"So that's it, then?" My hands flopped to my sides. "Our ride just left and he's heading to Georgia. Not back here. So we're stuck here, anyway."

"You forget we have money now, Mel." The asshole dared to smirk. "We can catch a plane and be out of here in an hour."

I just shook my head. "I can't fucking believe you."

"It may be callous, yes." The smile dropped. "But Mel, it's the only way to preserve everything you've earned up until now. If Lhozen captures you, he will be the only shaman in the world with such a massive influence. You can do great things for shifters, but you must pick your battles."

A dry laugh escaped as I dropped my forehead into my hands. "And you don't stop rationalizing it. I really didn't expect this from you."

"What do you mean, Mel?"

I lifted my gaze back up to Arjun, then quickly turned toward the master bedroom. I couldn't stomach looking at him. I needed a pillow to punch and scream into.

"I never expected you to be such a fucking coward," I yelled over my shoulder before slamming the door.

❈   7   ❈

ARJUN

I swirled the Scotch in my glass as I looked at the sunset over the beach. Our suite came well-stocked with expensive booze, but the Scotch just tasted like a bag of peat moss to me. I couldn't bring myself to enjoy anything after that argument with Mel.

She called me a coward, then stormed off to her room hours ago. And here I was, hoping to enjoy the sunset with some company. Maybe even have a chance to finish that kiss so rudely interrupted this morning.

And now the chances of that were essentially zero.

I didn't enjoy upsetting her. I especially hated seeing the heart-break on her face when I told her we should leave. But it was the cold, uncomfortable truth as far as I could see. We couldn't save everyone. But we might be able to save a few more if we survived ourselves.

It was an argument that would've kept us going around in circles. At this point, she must've seen me as utterly selfish. And I couldn't understand how she could be so bloody selfless. How had she not gotten herself killed yet? Or gotten someone else killed? She wanted to storm into battle like the most ill-equipped soldier and yell, "Free-dom!" at the top of her lungs while getting hacked to death. No thanks.

The sliding door opened behind me and I immediately picked up Razvan's smoky scent.

"Not having a romantic evening with your mates?" I asked.

"Eh," he muttered, leaning his forearms on the balcony railing beside me. "The mood isn't very romantic right now."

"Wonder why." I stared into my glass. "So are you here to convince me we should die as shifter-heroes that no one will remember?"

"I'm not here to convince you of anything," the dragon replied briskly. "I see your point. I see hers too. But we have to come to a decision, one way or the other."

"Explain her view to me, then." My hand tightened around my Scotch glass until it was nearly painful. "Is she just suicidal? Does she want to let the enslaved shifters see a friendly face before they're all dead?"

"She's a rescuer," he said with an easygoing shrug. "If someone is suffering, she has to help them. It's that simple."

"But it's *not* that simple. Surely she must see that?" I downed the rest of the glass, choking it back. I didn't care much for Scotch after seeing how much Lhozen depended on it after Mum died. Still, I needed something to take the edge off before I lost my shit again.

"She understands that, logically," Raz replied. "It doesn't matter to her, though. If someone needs her help, she will give it to them. It's just how she is."

"But why?" I tore my fingers through my hair, endlessly frustrated by this woman. "Why can't she think about preserving her own life for one damn second?"

"My guess is because of how she was raised," he mused. "She never had the luxury of taking care of herself. Since she was a child, taking care of others always fell on her. Walking away from it all and joining her first carnival was probably the only selfish thing she ever did. And even then, she did it to find a way to support her siblings." He shot me a sheepish grin. "That's what I think, anyway. Connor could probably tell you more and in a much better way."

"No, that makes a lot of sense, actually," I sighed, feeling the anger leave like letting the air out of a balloon. "What if I wasn't here, Raz?

You went through the same shit as me. Would you go along with her on a rescue mission or try to talk her out of it?"

"I'd go with her," he replied without an ounce of hesitation. "Not because it's the best thing to do, necessarily. But if no one goes with her, she'll do it alone. And I'd never save my own skin to leave her behind."

"Because you're in love with her," I stated. "Of course you wouldn't."

"Even if I wasn't," his eyes bore into mine, "you don't just let someone walk into danger like that. I don't think you're a coward, mate, but that shit *is*. I'll turn the question back on you. What if *I* wasn't here? Nor Hunter? Would you let her walk into the compound by herself? Because that's exactly what she'll do."

"No," I muttered. "But I'd stop her before she got anywhere near it. Maybe tie her up if I had to."

My cock swelled unexpectedly, and I turned to subtly adjust it. Just a flashing image of Mel, naked, tied, and writhing on a bed, sent my tiger roaring. *Yes, she is our mate. We must take her!*

No. No, she's not. We must remember that.

Thankfully, Raz didn't seem to notice.

"That might not work." His mouth lifted into a smirk. "She's a tricky one."

"Whatever. I'd prevent it from happening and force her to watch videos on the importance of self-preservation. Put your own air mask on before helping others, that kind of thing."

"It won't matter," he said softly. "It's in her blood."

"Well, if she nearly gets herself killed another time, she may think twice and thank me."

"Arjun, man." Raz stared at me with a slight shake of his head. "Do you even know why you're fighting her so hard on this?"

"Because I'm trying to keep us alive, Raz." I returned his stare. "That's what I've been bloody saying this whole time."

"That's not the only reason," he breathed. "You're fighting your feelings for her, too."

"Oh, for fuck's sake..."

I turned to head back inside, thoroughly done with this bullshit psychoanalysis, but Raz caught my arm. And I couldn't find it in myself to fight him as well.

"You see it now, you big pussy?" He pulled me back to the railing with a shit-eating grin. "You see why we're all crazy about her because you are too."

"I am not. That's ridiculous."

"Arjun." He said my name slowly, like trying to placate a child. "It's okay. You're already one of us, anyway."

"I don't want to be like... that."

"Sharing her." He nodded knowingly. "I understand it's weird to think about. Especially with your upbringing. But you know us all, mate. We get along and we all just want her safe and happy. And she's so giving, so loving. You know she does all she can to make us happy, too. You can see that."

"I've heard quite enough of this bollocks."

I pushed off the railing, and this time he didn't try to pull me back. The animal inside me only roared and pawed at the edges of my human skin. He agreed with the dragon and found it infuriating that I was resisting. *She is our mate! We must take her! Her other mates have given permission.*

It took all my willpower to hold him back. When I reached my room, I even checked the mirror to make sure I hadn't partially shifted.

All I could do was pace, well, like a caged animal. She felt right. She smelled right. It wasn't just my tiger side that wanted to make her mine. And if I asked myself honestly, I didn't even mind sharing her with the other men.

But to love such a stubborn woman hellbent on saving all shifter-kind, was to surely lose her.

❧ *8* ❧

MELODY

"**I**'m hungry," I whined, rolling over so my head rested on Hunter's stomach.

"Hi, Hungry. I'm Hunter," he snorted, tickling my side.

"Leave it you to make dad jokes," I giggled, squirming away.

"Want to go out for dinner?" He ran his fingers over my calf and I shivered under the touch. "Or get something delivered?"

I looked up at him. "Arjun is probably still out there, isn't he?"

He gave me a pointed look and tapped his index finger on my nose. "You'll have to face him eventually, little fox."

"I don't wanna," I sighed. "He's the only one who can help with my abilities, but won't. Just thinking about it pisses me off."

"If you think about it another way, he cares enough about you—about all of us—to not want to risk our lives."

"By walking away from those who are already *at* risk!"

"I know, love." He dropped a kiss to my nose. "I'm just saying, I see his perspective too."

I laced my fingers through his and held our hands over my belly. Where I possibly had a child growing.

No, don't think about that.

"What do you think I should do?" I looked up at my wolf. "Is it really stupid of me to even attempt this?"

"Of course I don't think you're stupid." He raised our hands off my belly and kissed the back of my palm. "It's important to look at all the risks and try to mitigate as many as possible, but I think you should do what feels right."

"I just know doing nothing is wrong."

"Then nothing is what we won't do."

"What?" I looked up at him, unable to hold back my giggle.

"Don't not laugh at my double-negative," he teased, tickling my sides again before swatting my hip. "Come on. Let's get food, then figure out how we're going to rescue some shifters."

I stalled, dragged my feet, and whined some more. We eventually left the bedroom to find Raz in the living room, alone. He had his feet up on the coffee table, flipping through the TV channels with a bored expression on his face. When we came out, his eyes lit up.

"Hey, my loves," he greeted us, accepting a kiss from Hunter first, and then me as if we hadn't seen each other in days rather than the past hour.

"Hungry, Raz?" Hunter called from the kitchen, flipping through various menus while I slid in next to our dragon.

"Always," he replied, draping an arm over my shoulders and pulling me into his side.

"What're you in the mood for?"

"A sandwich," I blurted out, much to their amusement.

"God, you're insatiable, and I love it," Raz growled with a nuzzle to my cheek.

"Little fox, I'm still recovering from last night." Hunter came up behind the couch and pressed a kiss to my other cheek. "You can have a sandwich later, though," he added in a seductive whisper before returning to the kitchen.

"Worth a try," I sighed, stretching my legs over Raz's lap. A sudden pang of missing Connor hit me squarely in the chest at that moment. He usually had my legs, while Raz supported my back.

My dragon must have noticed the sudden shift in my demeanor. He cupped my chin, turning my gaze to meet his.

"We'll be with him soon, *steluța*," he assured me, pulling me snugly into his lap. "Our big happy family will be even bigger and happier after our work is done."

"I wish he didn't have to leave," I admitted. "Of course, I don't want my siblings to be homeless, but he'd be able to see something I can't. We could use an extra brain to figure out how the hell to get into this place and get everyone out."

"*Steluța*," Raz said with a gentle tone that almost sounded scolding. "You would not have gotten off the phone with your sister saying there was nothing you could do. That's not how you are."

"I know, of course not. Shit, I'd probably go pick them up myself, but—"

"You made the best choice for them," he said softly. "Now we have to decide how to proceed with the resources we have left."

"Which is apparently nowhere," I said with an exaggerated look around the suite. "Did he up and leave already?"

"Arjun? He's brooding in his room again." Raz frowned. "He wouldn't just leave, you know that."

"That's not what he said this morning," I huffed.

Before Raz could reply, the sound of Arjun's door opening reached every corner of the living room like an omen. Even Hunter paused in flipping through the takeout menus.

The tiger shifter emerged from his cave, shoulders square and moving stiffly as he headed for the armchair next to our couch. He sat down mechanically, staring at his tented fingers and resting his forearms on his knees.

"To cast Semblance on something besides yourself, you need to start with small details that you can focus on," he said abruptly. "Your focus is what holds those illusions and makes them believable. Something like eye or hair color."

"Wait, hold the phone," I held up a hand. "What's going on here?"

"From what your mates tell me, and what I've gathered from our... conversation this morning," he lifted his gaze coolly to me. "You will insist on carrying out this rescue mission despite the heavily stacked odds against you and us. So I will teach you to cast better, more effective illusions in order to make this slightly less of a suicide mission."

"So… you'll help me?" I asked in disbelief after a long silence.

He shrugged. "My guidance in the limited time we have won't get you very far. But again, if you must put yourself and those you love in danger, I might as well give you a chance to say goodbye before you meet your end." He straightened up to look at Hunter in the kitchen. "Now, how about some tea, then? Actually, never mind," he rose from the armchair, "I'll get it myself."

Once he was settled in with his tea and Hunter called in our dinner order for delivery, I drilled him with questions.

"So I can cast illusions that aren't… shifter-related?" I wasn't sure what to call it. Up until that point, I only knew how to give myself shifter features like Razvan's dragon horns or Hunter's teeth. While seeing through the eyes of a fox shifter once, Raz had caught me with furry, red ears on top of my head.

"It's possible, yes," he replied after a hearty sip of tea. "It depends on the shaman and how strong their innate Semblance ability is. Lhozen's was always exceptional. He pranked me often by creating doors and such that weren't really there. The more complex an illusion you're casting, the more skill and focus it takes, which is why I suggest starting small."

"Like hair or eye color," I repeated, focusing on the depths of Arjun's irises. In my head I pictured the endless blueish-green darkening to a warm chocolate brown like my own. It was a feature I knew well and figured it would be the easiest to try out.

"Whoa! Arjun, holy shit!" Raz leaned forward, squinting like he couldn't make sense of what he saw. "Look in the mirror, mate."

Arjun obliged, standing to look at his reflection in the gilded mirror next to the door. "Ah. Well done," he said, sounding unimpressed. He still looked handsome. Dark eyes suited his complexion well, but he didn't have that breath-taking brightness to his face without his natural eye color.

"That was clearly easy for you, so you can drop the illusion now and try something more difficult," he said, returning to his seat.

"Hm." I tapped my finger on my chin, feeling sassy. "I don't know. Maybe I'll keep it up and see how much my focus can shift. You said the longer the illusion remains, the more realistic it becomes, right?"

He glared at me, which no longer seemed as intimidating with dark eyes. "Yes, the longer you keep an illusion up, the less focus you need. Your train of thought is correct."

I returned his glare with a smile, enjoying myself perhaps a little too much. "Don't worry, Arjun. I'll give you your eyes back. Just let me test what else I can do."

"Alright," he grumbled a little petulantly. "Keep my eyes the color of shit while you do something else. Give Hunter a perm, maybe."

I ignored his dig at my eye color and looked at Raz instead, a different idea forming in my mind.

"Oh no. What's that look for?" he teased, gray eyes twinkling with curiosity.

My eyelids closed halfway to concentrate as I pictured him in my mind while still keeping awareness of Arjun's new eye color.

"Holy shit!" Hunter exclaimed from the kitchen, coming up behind the couch in two long strides. He tugged at Raz's collar to get a better look at his neck, wide golden eyes traveling all over our dragon. "Raz, look at your hands."

Holding his palms out in front of his face, Raz nearly jumped out of his now un-tattooed skin when he saw them.

"What the..." He lifted his shirt to reveal smooth, unblemished skin without a drop of ink in sight.

"Look in the mirror, mate," Arjun couldn't hold back his laugh. "You look like a damn church boy."

I watched him get up and look, holding the illusion with relative ease as he stared at himself, touching his face, turning around, even undoing his pants to see that his more adventurous tattoos and piercings were gone.

"*Steluța*, why would you do this to me?" he lamented, although he shot me a playful smirk in the mirror's reflection.

"I've wondered what you looked like with naked skin," I shrugged. Like Arjun, he still looked sexy as hell without his tattoos, just different. My illusions took away their uniqueness in a way and made them more normal, if even a bit bland. My dragon just wasn't himself without all his ink.

"I've been getting tattoos since I was thirteen. I would never look like this," he said, still looking at himself in disbelief.

"Let's hope Lhozen thinks that too," I replied. "By the way, open your mouth."

He obliged, wiggling a now perfectly intact tongue at the mirror.

"Now I know you won't keep that illusion up," he grinned, turning to face me. "You enjoy my tongue too much."

I nearly shrank back under his gaze. The illusion was almost too real already. It felt like a stranger was looking at me too suggestively.

"Let's move on," Arjun snapped. "Now, you'll also need to disguise inanimate objects. You can make them look like something else or disappear entirely. This should be easier than creating illusions over people, since objects are more simple to create and manipulate. Try making the coffee table disappear."

I did so easily. I also turned it into a billiards table when he asked. And then turned the couch into a hot tub and made that disappear. I turned the ceiling lights into elaborate chandeliers and the floor tiles into plush carpet. And on and on and on for what felt like hours. Everything Arjun told me to do, I did. All the while, I kept up the illusion of his brown eyes and Razvan's choir boy look.

By the time he told me to turn an end table into a fire pit with the illusion of heat as well, my focus faltered and my head began to pound painfully.

I rubbed my temples as I curled up on the couch. Strong arms pulled me into an embrace, and a soothing kiss dropped to my forehead.

"Well done, little fox," Hunter murmured. "Looks like you're about tapped out."

"I've never seen anything like that." Raz curled up behind me, his now-tattooed hands and arms wrapping around me. "You really are fucking magical."

"She's going to need to do a lot more if we have any chance of beating Lhozen," Arjun said snappily. I cracked an eye open to see that his ocean-colored irises had returned, and they captured me from across the room. "Sure, you're exceptionally gifted, Mel. But look how drained you are. To Lhozen, everything we did just now would be child's play. Our chances of beating him are still slim to none."

"Hey, that's enough," Hunter barked with a soft warning growl. "She's doing the best she can. You can only push her to do so much."

"He's right, Arj," Raz added. "You can't force her to be powerful enough to win in a single day."

"Guys, it's okay," I said, sitting up between them and looking at Arjun. "Thank you. Seriously."

His eyebrows lifted in surprise. All three guys just looked at me like I sprouted an extra head, so I elaborated.

"I don't want you to go easy on me. I don't want any sugar-coating on how hard this is going to be. I might not be as powerful as him, but I want to go in as prepared as possible, and that means my limits need to be tested. So thank you, Arjun, for pushing me to my limit and not holding back."

Again, no one said anything. But Arjun inclined his head toward me in a sign that he understood and that was plenty enough for me.

9

CONNOR

I parked the RV in a lot across the street from the shelter and hopped out, keeping my guard up and taking in my surroundings as I jaywalked to the front entrance. It was only two blocks away from the main downtown strip, with trendy restaurants and shops, but far enough that it seemed like an entirely different country.

Giant trees lined the block, cracking and uprooting the street and sidewalks. Clearly, the city hadn't bothered to come out and trim them in years. The rundown state of the houses and yards showed barely any care or money went into them. This area of Mel's hometown was just as forgotten and crumbling as her old trailer park.

The homeless shelter itself looked like a large house that was one storm away from crumbling to the ground. It had no signage and looked completely unassuming next to the other houses on the block. Mel told me it catered toward women and kids escaping abusive situations, which explained why it was kept hidden like this.

I entered the front door to be immediately met with a suspicious glare from a woman sitting behind a desk.

"Can I help you?" she asked shrewdly.

"Good evening, ma'am." I offered her a smile, which she didn't return. "I'm here to see Miss Jeanie May."

"Is she expecting you?"

"Yes, ma'am, she is."

"Are you family?" Her eyes narrowed at me. "How do you know her?"

"I'm her sister's boyfriend. My name is Connor Shaw. We've arranged for Jeanie and the younger ones to stay with us."

"Why isn't her sister with you?"

"Melody couldn't get away from work," I explained. It was mostly true. "I'll be happy to wait, ma'am, while you verify everything with Jeanie."

I took a seat on a folding chair near the door, trying to keep my posture relaxed while still alert. I understood why they were suspicious of men coming here, but the suspicious looks and questioning still irked me just a little. Whether on my legs or my gender, it felt like I was going to be judged no matter what.

The woman blinked in apparent surprise, like I was one of the few guys who didn't throw a fit at the immediate suspicion.

"I'll be right back." She rose from her desk, never taking her eyes off me as she slipped through another door.

Once alone, I leaned my head back with a sigh to rest it on the wall. It had been barely twelve hours, and I already missed Mel something fierce. The world felt so different without the one person who accepted all of me at my side.

A good ten minutes passed before the door opened again and a teenage girl stepped out. She had strawberry blonde hair up in a messy bun and crystal blue eyes, but her nose and face shape were nearly identical to Mel's.

"You're Connor?" she asked in a small voice.

"Yes, ma'am." I stood from the chair. "You're Jeanie, I presume."

She nodded, those large eyes studying me from the doorway as if surveying a threat.

"If there's anything you want to know, ask me." I spread my hands out, palms open. "I know I'm a stranger to you, and it's a lot to ask for you to come with me. I don't want you to be afraid."

"No matter what I ask, you could just lie," she pointed out.

I held back a smile. She had the same fire as Mel.

"But my sister trusts you," she added. "That's the best assurance I'm going to get. So let me pack up the kids and our stuff."

I nodded, feeling a huge swell of relief in my chest that I wouldn't have to convince her to come with me. "Y'all need any help?"

"No. I'll be right back." She went back through the door and returned a few minutes later, holding a curly-haired toddler on her hip. Her other hand gently guided two other children, a boy and a girl, in front of her.

They all looked completely different, but with enough similarities that you could guess they were related. The three younger children openly stared at me with wide-eyed curiosity.

"Hi, guys." I lowered to a squat to be at their eye level. "My name's Connor. I'm a friend of your sister, Mel. We're gonna see her real soon, okay?"

"Mella?" the dark-haired girl piped up. "We gonna see Mella?" Only when she looked straight at me did I notice the faint bruising around her eye. Like a reflex, my fist clenched at my side, but I put on my best non-threatening smile for her.

"That's right, little lady. What are your names?"

As they often did, the kids went shy and clung to Jeanie's legs as they looked up at her.

"This is Bella," she introduced, putting her hand on the dark-haired girl's shoulder. "She likes to rhyme with her name, so she calls Mel Mella. This is Joey." She ruffled the hair of the boy with medium brown hair.

"He's Jella," Bella giggled.

"And this is Riley," Jeanie bounced the toddler girl on her hip. "Say hi to Connor. He's a friend."

Riley just smiled shyly and buried her face in Jeanie's neck.

"Nice to meet all of you. And you can call me Connella if you want," I said to Bella, who giggled into her hand. "If y'all are ready," I said to Jeanie, rising back up to my feet. "The sooner we go, the sooner we can get y'all set up."

"Ready when you are," she nodded curtly. "We don't have much. Kinda had to get out of there in a hurry."

Just then I noticed she, Bella, and Joey carried small, worn-out backpacks and nothing else. After hearing everything Mel said about her life growing up, they probably didn't own much more than that.

"Alright, I'm just parked across the street. It's an RV, so there's plenty of room. Are y'all hungry?"

"We just had dinner, so we should be good," Jeanie answered, following my lead with the kids in tow.

"Sounds good. We can stop anytime on the way. Just let me know."

All five of us barely made it out the front door and onto the sidewalk when Bella screamed and immediately began crying and babbling hysterically. Concerned, I turned to her and kneeled down. I didn't notice the man approaching until her small, shaking hand lifted and pointed over my shoulder.

"Shit," Jeanie hissed, pulling the kids close. "I knew he'd find us."

The guy was about my height, bow-legged and with a beer gut hanging over his pants. He swung his arms as he walked, bald head forward and beady eyes narrowed. This motherfucker was looking for a fight.

"Relax," I murmured, rising up to standing. "I got this. Y'all go back inside for now."

"Inside?" she asked. "But what're you—"

"Just in case it gets ugly, the little ones shouldn't see this. Hopefully, it won't get to that. Now go on."

"Connor, he's—"

"Jeanie. Inside," I said, raising my voice just slightly.

She listened that time, dragging the kids back through the front door and slamming it shut just as the shithead stopped in front of the house. And me.

"Fuckin' move, asshole," he grunted at me, his speech slurring.

"Nah, man," I replied with a calm that I must've channeled from Hunter, folding my arms in front of my chest. "That ain't gonna happen."

He got in my face, forcing me to hold my breath against the rank smell coming from him. "I dunno who the fuck you are, but you need to mind your own fuckin' business. Those are my kids in there and I'm gonna take their ungrateful asses home."

"Funny. They don't look too eager to go home with you." I lifted an eyebrow. "I wonder why that is. Something to do with the little girl's bruise, I bet?" I knew I was goading him but I couldn't help it. What kind of disgusting piece of shit came to a homeless shelter drunk like this?

"I told you to mind your own fuckin' business!" His hands shot out and gave a weak shove to my shoulders. Even if I didn't have awesome balance on these new legs, he had no power behind his push and I remained standing like a boulder. The guy looked intimidating enough to go around picking fights, but he was fucking weak. Apparently, nobody had put him in his place before.

"Look, man. You're lucky I'm a nice guy," I said, keeping my voice calm despite the rage simmering underneath. "But if you touch me again, you'll wish you never came here looking for a fight. This ain't the place for that, so I'm giving you this one chance to turn around and leave."

"Fuck no, I'm not leavin'! Those kids are my fuckin paycheck, so they're comin' the fuck home! And I'm givin' you this one chance to get the fuck out of my way! Who the fuck are you, anyway?" he sneered at me. "You fuckin' Jeanie? I knew that dumb bitch had a sugar daddy."

"Changed my mind." I smiled cheerily at him. "You don't get another chance." With that, I drove my metallic foot straight up between his legs, connecting with soft flesh.

His mouth dropped open to scream, but only a pathetic whimper escaped. He held himself as he doubled over, slowly crumpling to the ground as the pain set in. I actually put some effort behind that kick, so I was pretty sure I ruptured at least one of his testes.

I pushed open the front door of the shelter, meeting four pairs of wide eyes.

"Coast is clear. Let's go," I said.

"What did you do?" Jeanie demanded, holding the young ones tightly as we walked past the guy, rolling around on the sidewalk in pain.

"Don't worry, he won't go picking fights again," I told her. "And I'm pretty sure he won't be able to have any more kids."

"He's acting like a baby," Bella laughed.

"I called the cops," Jeanie said, tugging Bella's hand to keep her close as we crossed the street.

"Oh, good," I said cheerfully, looking both ways for traffic. "He can tell them whatever he wants."

We boarded the RV, and I started it up while Jeanie secured the kids. When she buckled up in the passenger seat next to me, I paused before putting it in drive.

"Any other loose ends to tie up?" I asked her.

She looked at me and gave an emphatic shake of her head.

"Nope. Get us the fuck out of there."

10

ARJUN

Mel grasped Semblance faster than any of Lhozen's students that I'd ever seen. It wasn't easy, and I could see how much effort she put into practicing the illusions. It made me respect her even more, though I found myself constantly shoving it down and giving her even more to do.

Under any other circumstances, it was too much. She was mentally and physically exhausted, and I just kept pushing her. But she never asked for a break. She never wanted to stop. Whenever Raz or Hunter suggested she take it easy, she just demanded more. *What next, Arjun?* she asked, her brows knitted with the headache she surely felt. And so I kept giving her more illusions to practice.

I kept hurting her when all I wanted to do was hold her.

After an evening of practicing in the suite, we upped the ante the next morning. She cast illusions over Raz and Hunter, giving them disguises so they could scope out La Hacienda. This time, they'd hang out in the cafe across the street and watch how people entered and left the compound.

For today's illusions, she erased Raz's tattoos again and gave him dark eyes and curly brown hair. She made Hunter a foot shorter and slightly overweight, with darkened features and hazel eyes. They were both so normal and average-looking, no one would give them a second glance. Even my cynical arse had to admit their disguises were good.

"Remember, the illusion is only a shift in perception, not reality," I told her when they left. "Hunter still *feels* tall, and he is. If someone touches him above his illusion's head, they'll feel the real Hunter's body. The risk is always there. Even humans may be able to see through your illusion, the perceptive ones anyway."

"Connor would," she sighed wistfully. "I wonder how he's doing. He should have picked up my siblings by now."

"Don't let yourself get distracted," I warned. My tiger yearned to comfort her, to rub his big striped face against her side and let her be soothed by his purr. I fought him down, despite those instincts feeling like they were taking over me with each passing day.

"Keep your focus."

She nodded, her eyes half-closing as she resumed concentrating on Raz and Hunter's illusions. Weeks, maybe even days ago, she would have rolled her eyes and gotten huffy with me. I would've said some remark that made her bristle and she'd storm off to one of her mates with a red face and a stick up her arse.

Now, her back straightened, and her chin lifted. She trusted my word and never once complained. Even with no formal training at all, she looked like a proud shaman. Like the ones Lhozen used to tell me about in my childhood.

I shook my head at the memory and stared out the window at the ocean, partially so Mel wouldn't catch me staring. Also, because I still couldn't reconcile the man who raised me with the monster who kidnapped shifters for profit.

Was it all a lie? That was the question that I kept coming back to and had no answer for. For as long as I could remember, he took me to school every day. He encouraged me to read and think critically, even with things I didn't agree with. He adored my mother and treated her with the utmost respect. Was it losing her that triggered this shift?

If by some miracle of Shiva we survived this and had him at our mercy, he could not be allowed to live. It was the one thing I was sure of in this whole mess.

A soft thump prompted my head to swivel back to Mel, who had slumped over on her side. Her head leaned against the armrest of the couch, her half-closed eyelids fluttering rapidly.

Before I could control myself, my legs carried me to her, and I gently leaned her back upright.

"Here, dove," I murmured, taking a seat next to her and allowing her to lie back down again with her head in my lap. I stroked her hair away from her face. Not knowing what else to do in this intimate position I found myself in, I allowed my tiger to purr at the contact with her.

She smiled dreamily, resting her hand on my thigh near her face. "You're being nice, now. I never know when I'm going to get nice Arjun or grumpy Arjun."

My chest felt tight, and I swallowed a dry lump in my throat. Even now, she could be lighthearted and sweet.

"I have been hard on you, and wish I could take it all back now," I confessed. "You shouldn't bear the burden of this alone. I know him better than anyone. It should be me carrying the weight of this plan."

"Stop, Arjun," she murmured, tightening her hand ever so slightly around my thigh. Regardless of her gentle grip, it sent a rush of heat and desire straight to my cock. "I have to do this because I'm the only shaman among us."

"I know," I sighed. "And you're an incredible shaman. Not just because of your abilities, but what you're using them for. I haven't told you that enough."

"It's because of you. Don't you realize that?" she gazed up at me. "If it wasn't for you, I wouldn't know how to block the shifters out when we first came here. I'd have one hell of a concussion, and that is, if I didn't die from trying to make it stop. You gave me the mental shields to deal with them."

"You had them all along." I gave her a weak smile. "I just helped you find them."

"Arjun." She sat up, now incredibly close to me. We'd been in close proximity before, but not like this. Her hand still rested on my thigh. "Where is all this humility coming from?" She allowed a tiny smirk on those rosebud lips. "It's not like you to be humble."

Unlike her, I couldn't find the humor in this situation. Not right now.

"When we get in there," I said, "I'm going to have to face him. Me and no one else. And I'll have to ask him why." I looked away from her, returning my gaze to the ocean. "I have to know, for my own peace of mind, why he did this to me? To Raz and all the others. Guessing is driving me insane."

"I understand," she whispered. "And it's because of you we have a fighting chance of getting in there at all. Don't diminish your role in this, Arjun. None of it would be possible without you."

"I have to kill him." I returned my gaze to her, fighting the urge to look away. She was just too lovely. "You realize that, right? Once I have my answer, I have to do it. And it has to be me and no one else."

Her expression flickered before returning to its blank gaze of concentration, and she nodded. "I do understand, and I won't stop you. I'm sure everyone in that place will want the same thing, but you're right. It has to be you."

"The thing is, Mel," I covered her hand with my own, wrapping my fingers tightly around hers. "I don't know if I can do it."

She looked at me as if about to say something, then did the complete opposite of what I expected. She kissed me.

It took me by surprise, but I kissed her back as if I'd been waiting to do so for years. And truthfully, maybe I had been.

Her arms wrapped around my neck and my tiger released a growl of pleasure at the sensation of her nails running across my scalp. She tasted perfect, absolutely delicious. Her mouth opened up to me delicately and let out the softest moan at my invading tongue, claiming her.

Just as quickly as she started, she broke away.

"Sorry." Her breath came out in soft pants. "I was doing good for a while but started to lose focus."

I could only blink at her, my brain trying to catch up and reconcile what just happened. She sat halfway in my lap, her fingers in my hair. Her chest pressed to mine, my arms holding her there and wrapping around her back. I could still taste her on my mouth and I was hard as a steel beam.

"The guys are talking to me up here," she tapped her temple, smiling shyly with her cheeks flushed pink. "Raz saw one of his hand tattoos coming back and let me know."

"Right," I cleared my throat. "How are they doing?"

"Good. They're noticing a pattern with how people are entering and leaving the compound. No one has given them any extra attention."

"Good. Yes, that is good." Apparently, kissing her had robbed my brain's capacity for everything but repeating the same words.

We sat like that for an incredibly awkward amount of time. When she pressed her forehead to mine, my hand drifted up to brush her hair off her shoulder. Her soft lips skimmed a trail down my cheek, breath gently fanning across my skin. My heart crashed like a drum as she inched closer to my mouth.

"I thought you needed to focus," I murmured, my lips just barely in contact with hers.

"I am," she replied playfully, pressing another kiss to the corner of my mouth. "But I also need my focus tested by distractions, so..."

Gods above, I didn't want to fight this anymore. Clearly, neither did she. Still, I had to, albeit for different reasons than before.

"You don't want to make a habit of this, dove," I murmured, turning my face away.

"Why not?" The rejection in her voice was like broken glass in my skin. "The guys have talked to me about this. I'm sure they have with you, too. Arjun, is it—"

"Your heart is too big," I told her, carefully sliding her off my lap. "Too pure. I can't be the one to break it. I'm sorry, Mel. It has nothing to do with sharing you, but I can't do this."

"Then what's the matter?" she demanded. I hated myself for causing the pain she felt at that moment, but it would be better in the long run. It killed me to refuse her, but I'd always choose that over breaking her heart later.

"Lhozen," I said, barely above a whisper. "He's more likely to kill me than I am to kill him."

11

MELODY

After watching the hidden entrance to the compound outside of La Hacienda for most of the day, Raz and Hunter felt confident they knew how to get in.

Arjun and I mostly avoided each other after the awkwardness on the couch. He gave me tips on holding up the illusions from across the suite, and I took his advice while doing other things to distract myself in order to test my focus.

When housekeeping came, I turned them away and cleaned the place myself, only staying out of Arjun's room. The master bed and bath were immaculate. I swept and swiffered the marble floors until they were spotless. It was incredibly tempting to hide under the bed out of shame and embarrassment from Arjun rejecting me.

My thoughts and emotions were so mixed up, it was all I could do to keep Raz and Hunter's disguises up as they made their way back to the hotel. I wanted to call bullshit on Arjun's excuse, though he had no reason to lie to me. As far as I knew, he had never lied to me once.

Deep down, I knew the truth of it was I didn't want to believe Lhozen could kill him. I didn't want to face the fact I was bringing three amazing men to their possible deaths. Knowing that, how could

I carry this out? Was I just kidding myself on this rescue mission like what Arjun had been telling me all along?

You can't just stumble around and figure your way out of this one, I told myself. This isn't some shitty carnival anymore. All of our lives are at risk.

A click followed by the sound of a door opening let me know that my boys had returned.

"*Steluța!*" Even Raz's voice sounded different. "Please drop the illusions now, I feel like the victim of a damn body snatcher."

Letting go of that concentration felt like an enormous weight off my mind. My wolf and my dragon, now with their familiar handsome faces, wandered into the bedroom.

"Why're you hiding in here, little fox?" Hunter asked with a curious look at me. Those sharp eyes missed nothing.

"How did it go?" I stood from the bed to greet them both with kisses, purposely ignoring his question.

"Perfectly," Raz answered with pride. "No one suspected a thing and we've got the entryway down. It seems like not all the compound workers fully grasp the illusions, so we even have a bit of wiggle room when we attempt to get in."

"How are you?" Hunter tugged me against him possessively. "Everything okay while we were gone?"

"Yeah," I sighed. "Took some Midol for the headaches. I'm just a little foggy right now."

"Does that have anything to do with Arjun?" Hunter kissed the top of my head before I looked up at him. How did he know?

"I can smell him on you," the smug wolf answered.

"And it's clear you're avoiding him," Raz added.

Damn them. It must've been Connor's influence, making them so perceptive. The thought only made my chest ache for my Marine even more.

"I kissed him," I admitted. "And he rejected me after that."

"Oh, my love. Don't let him get to you." Raz stepped into Hunter's embrace around me and gave me the most passionate, reassuring kiss I needed. "If he kisses you too much, he'll feel compelled to marry you next. It's just the way he is."

"He did mention that." I remembered our walk on the beach a few days ago. He came from a culture of arranged marriages and all inti-macy happening behind closed doors. It was difficult for me to see from that perspective, especially since I was so open and affectionate with my three. But I *wanted* to understand him. I wanted him to know I accepted all his quirks, just like the other guys.

"In any case, it's probably best to worry about this if we're still alive after tomorrow," I muttered.

"We will be," Hunter said firmly. "Not one of us can do it alone, but the four of us can manage together. And you've got your Marine and your siblings to see after this is over."

"You're right," I breathed, leaning my ear against his heart. "Sur-viving is the only option."

The next morning, all four of us met in the living room and went over our plan. I slept like the dead the previous night and still felt groggy until I got some coffee and breakfast in me. Raz and Hunter filled us in on how to get inside, and Arjun made sure to repeat our plan several times.

"Mel." His gaze lasered in on me. "You're the only one who's seen the inside. We're essentially going in blind and you have to be on top of your Semblance. If your focus wavers just a little, it could be the end for us. If you have any doubts about this, please let us know now."

"No doubts," I told him. "I won't let any of you be discovered."

"It's not just keeping up the illusions," he said. "You'll be right at the source of all the visions that have plagued you since we left home. Since they appear to get stronger the closer you are, you'll have to block all of them too." The intensity of his gaze softened, along with his voice. "A lot is riding on your shoulders, dove. I wish we could do more, but we all have to count on you."

His words echoed the sentiment of what he had said last night, right before our kiss. He didn't want me carrying the lion's share of this mission, but there was no way around it. Only I could cast the illusions to get us inside. The guys' muscle might help us once we were in, but we truly didn't know.

I felt the yearning from him like it was my own. Maybe it was his manly pride wanting to step up and do more, or possibly his feelings for me. Though I still had no idea what those honestly entailed. My own feelings were a swirling mix of confusion. The kiss felt more than good. It felt right.

But I had to focus on the life-or-death situation at hand.

"I understand," I told him flatly. "I can't pretend to know if I'll be able to do both at once, but my number one priority is to keep y'all hidden and safe. Even if the shifters get through my mind, I'll be focusing on you guys no matter what."

Arjun gave a curt nod, the other two said nothing. I could only imagine what they were thinking. Maybe they just wanted to go home too. To live happily ever after as freed shifters despite so many others trapped in the same situation they had once been in. Maybe it was selfish of me to drag them into this just, because I couldn't stand to see suffering. People and animals would always suffer. It was part of living after all.

But if I *could* do something about it, then why wouldn't I?

And if I was lucky enough to find one, let alone three or even four men who cared enough to stay by my side no matter what, why wouldn't I ask them for help in doing the right thing?

All four of us slowly rose to standing. It felt oddly ceremonial, a *this is it* type of moment.

"Ready when you are, little fox." Hunter wrapped an arm around my shoulders and lowered a kiss to my forehead. I looked up at those golden eyes and remembered the first time I saw them—through the bars of a cage.

"I love you," I blurted out, my heart speeding up into overdrive like this could be the last chance I had to tell him. "You didn't have to come here or stay for this, but I'm so glad you're here with me."

"And I love you." He cupped my face and kissed me with all the heat and dominance of an alpha claiming his mate. "My place is by your side, no matter what."

We released each other, and I took a deep breath to cast an illusion over him. Again, I made him appear shorter and softened his physique to a normal dad-bod. I darkened his hair, eyes, and skin tone just enough to make him unremarkable before turning to Razvan.

"I know you love me, *steluța*," he chuckled, pulling me into a possessive embrace. "Don't act like we're saying goodbye. This is not the end of anything, okay? Besides our trip to America's swampy asshole."

He made me giggle, forcing me to put extra focus on Hunter's disguise so it would hold. His handsome face grinned at my reaction before giving me a long, slow, lingering kiss full of sensuality. He ensured I felt every part of that split tongue and took my breath away.

"I can't wait to taste you again when we're done being heroes," he smirked, running his thumb along my lower lip before he stepped back and proceeded to shift.

It felt like forever since I'd seen his dragon form in the flesh—all obsidian scales and fearsome horns, teeth and claws. I could only stare in awe as this creature the size of a large horse wrapped his tail around his feet and tucked his wings close to his body. He'd have a hell of a time leaving this suite without damaging anything.

Hunter's and Arjun's eyes widened in awe at the sight of him.

"Fuck me sideways, mate. All these years later and I still can't believe you're real," Arjun breathed.

"We're just waiting on you," I reminded the tiger shifter before reaching out to scratch Raz's scaly forehead. "Maybe you could fly out onto the balcony and meet us outside, dragon? Rather than going through the hotel."

Raz snorted two small plumes of gray smoke from his nostrils and jerked his large head up and down in a nod. *Might as well use these wings for something,* he thought, nuzzling against me.

With my dragon carefully following behind me, I went to open the sliding glass door to the balcony. If Raz crouched down and tucked his wings close, he could just squeeze through.

When I looked back at Arjun, a beautiful Bengal tiger returned my stare. He sat on his haunches, the tip of his tail flicking absently as he waited. Hunter stood patiently by the door, not even a flicker in his illusion.

I took a final deep breath to cast the next set of illusions—making

Arjun and Raz invisible. Only a gust of wind told me that Raz left the building, and the sensation of a large furry head bumping my hand told me Arjun was close.

While looking as if we were alone, Hunter and I left the room for possibly the last time.

12

RAZVAN

Damn, it felt so good to fly again. And it was completely surreal flying over people's heads without them ever looking up. The gusts from my wings might as well had been another ocean breeze.

I knew it would take a minute for Mel, Arjun, and Hunter to leave the hotel, so I took my time soaring high. The sun felt wonderful on my scales, and the swells of hot air lifted me higher. The only thing better would be having Mel and Hunter on my back.

If we really did survive this, I'd have to bribe my *steluța* into making me invisible more often. A half-dozen orgasms from my tongue should do the trick. I never realized how much I missed flying or my dragon form until I was in it. Around people I had to shift so sparingly, but with her abilities I might be able to more often.

I drifted lazily through the air until I spotted Hunter's disguise coming out of the hotel. I had to do a double-take at the woman he was with. Mel disguised herself as a shorter, curvy woman with blonde curls and an ample chest. She and Hunter walked with some distance between them, indicating to me that Arjun walked there, unseen to those around him.

Did you do that just to torture me, steluţa? I asked her, circling down closer above their heads. *I can see down your shirt and just want to run my tongue all over you.*

Behave, dragon, she teased back, lifting her eyes just slightly as she smiled. *Just thought I'd play around. I've never had a body like this.*

You could disguise yourself as a four-hundred pound man and I'd still want you, I answered. *Because I'd know it's really you under there.*

Romantic, she scoffed.

I have my moments.

She and Hunter continued down the street toward La Hacienda, careful to not let people walk between them. I followed just hovering above until we reached the alley behind the restaurant to carry out the second phase of our plan.

I still don't understand why I have to be a damn raccoon, Arjun whined.

Nobody will look twice at a trash panda, I reminded him.

A raccoon isn't even a cat, he complained. *At least you're still somewhat related to a dragon.*

An iguana eats only vegetables, can't fly or breathe fire, I retorted. *I think we're about even.*

Maybe it was inappropriate to be cracking jokes at a time like this, but who knew when we would laugh at each other again?

"Guys," Mel muttered, biting her lip to keep from laughing. "Get in here so I can focus."

I sensed Arjun following her, then landed softly to ensure no nearby humans could feel the impact of my landing. To fit in the alley, I had to suck in my breath and hold my wings flush to my body. Thankfully, there was no one else in there or else they definitely would've felt my wings or possibly my scales.

Raz?

Right here, steluţa. I nuzzled against her side with my still-invisible head.

She turned toward me with a tense smile—even now she was trying to stay positive—and closed her eyes to cast the next set of illusions.

"Alright," she whispered. "Lead the way, Hunter."

Nothing changed from my perspective. I was still a dragon and

Arjun was still a tiger, but to anyone else looking, Hunter and Mel were a couple of uniformed animal control officers carrying a surly raccoon and a large green iguana in metal cages.

You don't look that different to me, mate, I said to Arjun, now a fraction of his tiger's size as he peered through the bars of his cage with black, masked eyes and nimble, human-like hands.

Oh, shut your bloody mouth, lizard boy.

I resumed flying just overhead as the others walked the next few blocks to the hidden compound entrance. For me, that was the easiest way to not bump into humans and shatter the illusion. At about ten feet above their heads, my own head abruptly crashed into something solid and metal. And it made a shit ton of noise.

Fuck!

"Raz!" Mel hissed in surprise, stopping in her tracks and looking up at the seemingly empty sky above.

Don't look up! Arjun warned. *Nothing is there. You'll draw attention to yourself.*

Are you okay, dragon? Mel asked me with her mind.

Yeah. Fuck, sorry about the noise. There's an invisible barrier here. Must be part of the compound. The entrance is just at the next block, so it makes sense.

Are we good to keep going? Uncertainty crept into Mel's mental voice.

Yes, a few humans looked around, but they're back to minding their own business. I'm going to walk behind you guys now.

I landed softly on the sidewalk behind Mel and Hunter's heels, lowering my snout to sniff the ground. Like Arjun that first time, I could smell that many shifters walked this same path. Some scents were old, others as recent as a few hours ago. And just after the next intersection, the scent just disappeared.

Here we are, I said. *Now, do exactly as I say, steluța. Turn straight to your left and walk ten steps.* She did as instructed, walking toward a fence between two buildings. The fence was a typical chain-link over wooden slats that didn't allow anyone to see to the other side. There were no gaps in it either, to the untrained eye.

Good. Now left again, three steps. Now right, five steps. Lean forward and you'll see a gap in the fence. Go through it.

She did so and paused. *I can barely squeeze through it. Will you be able to get in, dragon?*

Yes, the small doorway is just an illusion, too. It's actually huge, like a warehouse door. You'll see.

In the next moment, she was gone.

After double-checking to make sure no humans would be passing by, I walked through the same opening. In the next moment, Mel, Hunter, Arjun, and I stood at the entrance to a large, square building made of concrete and metal. Aside from the two double doors in front of us, the building had no windows.

It's all you now, dove, Arjun told her gently. *We're all here with you.*

Just tell her you're in love with her already... I wanted to say to him, but kept the thought to myself. I was quite certain Mel could not only hear us, but that it was her Speak ability that allowed us to talk amongst each other.

After a moment of pause, she stepped confidently up to the door and pushed it open. Following her, Hunter held it open long enough for Arjun and I to slip through.

You good, wolf? I gave Hunter a soft nudge on his shoulder, noticing he'd been silent since we left the hotel. He nodded sharply, but the tension in his body was palpable.

The hallway seemed to stretch on endlessly like a long, metallic tube with only fluorescent lights and the occasional unmarked door on either side. We didn't pass by anyone else, but I was ready, the fire swelling in my chest in preparation for any threat.

You know where you're going? Arjun asked Mel after a minute or so.

I think so, she answered. Her confident stride didn't betray any uncertainty, and Hunter simply followed her lead.

The hallway ended by splitting in two opposite directions. Mel turned to the left without any hesitation, nearly running headfirst into a woman wearing a white lab coat.

"Oh, I'm sorry!" Mel forced out a dry laugh while I hurriedly glued myself to the opposite wall.

"It's alright. Ugh, more vermin species, huh?" The woman shook her head at the caged raccoon and iguana. "I feel bad for you guys having to go out and catch these. It's like, why bother? I keep telling him we need the exotic animals, not another pest."

"I know," Mel sighed, doing a convincing job of commiserating with the woman. "Just doin' what we're told, ya know?"

"I hear ya." The woman rolled her eyes before continuing down the hallway. "Hope you land a big one soon! I'm dying for another dolphin, personally."

"I'll keep that in mind," Mel called after her, then visibly shuddered when she turned out of sight. Hunter approached her like he was going to put his arm around her in comfort, but she picked up the iguana cage and resumed marching down the hallway.

"Lhozen is yours, Arjun. But that bitch is mine," she growled through gritted teeth.

On any other day, I would have pinned her against the wall and taken her sweet little body right then and there. I loved when my woman got aggressive. Seeing that fire in her got me hard, unlike anything else. But we had to survive this first.

The right wall of this new hallway soon opened up to a bay of windows looking over a large, open room below. And what I saw, I'll never be able to unsee again.

Rows of cages crammed up against each other and stacked precariously high on top of each other. Each one held some different kind of creature. I didn't want to say animal, because many were partially shifted, obviously stuck between forms from the drugs they'd been given. These poor shifters were beyond freakish, if even nightmarish in appearance. Some of them looked deformed due to injury or trauma, or possibly because they were simply the victims of sick experiments.

Melody, Arjun barked, his mental voice ringing like a bell in my head. *You're losing the illusions. Stay focused. Shut them out.*

"How can they...?" Mel whispered, staring through the glass as her eyes welled up with tears. "Oh my God. How can they do this? They're *people.*"

A glance down at the floor sent my pulse into overdrive. I could see my own black scales and claws turning opaque, while the iguana and cage in Hunter's hand was fading into nothingness.

Steluţa, I'm going to be seen, I told her. *You have to focus, or we have to leave.*

"We can't leave them." A choked sob escaped her throat as she raised a hand to the glass. On the other side of her, orange and black stripes became more clear and solid with each passing second.

"Mel! Little fox!" Hunter, now at his normal height with his skin slowly becoming paler, grabbed her arm and turned her around to face him. He clapped his hands to her cheeks, forcing her to look at him. "Mel, if we're seen, we're done for. We *need* you to hold up the illusions—"

The sound of clanking metal overpowered his words. Like in some kind of sci-fi movie, a heavy door slid out of the wall from the direction we just came from, cutting off our way out. Up ahead, a similar door cut off the opposite end of the hallway.

Just like that, we were fucking trapped.

"I daresay, the ones with the bleeding hearts are always the most gullible," a clipped English accent announced cheerily.

We all turned to see the same woman we passed in the hallway, smiling as she casually leaned against one of the many unmarked doors.

"Lhozen," Arjun voiced, barely above a whisper. I didn't even notice he had shifted to human.

"I'm sorry for not saying a proper hello, my dear stepson," the woman chuckled in the same English accent, now with a man's voice. "I thought I'd try a new look."

Her form shifted before our eyes, stretching up to the height of a man in his fifties, with salt and pepper hair, blue eyes, and an expensive tailored suit on a slim build. I recognized him immediately. He spoke fluent Romanian to my parents right before he purchased me, then personally shoved swords down my throat until I learned to take them without flinching.

My jaws opened, ready to spill the fire that raged inside me at this man for years. I knew he was Arjun's to kill, but none of that mattered now. We would either die or never leave this compound if he wasn't eliminated right the fuck now.

Lhozen held up a hand in front of my snout, palm open and completely unafraid.

"Not so fast, Razvan. Don't you feel like you're getting sleepy?"

What the...

"Why don't you take a nap?"

The last thing I saw was my reflection in his shoes, polished to a high shine before my head hit the floor.

13

CONNOR

The drive to Georgia was mostly silent. I didn't try to force small talk between Jeanie or the young ones. I was still a stranger to them and had no desire to make them more uncomfortable.

Whenever Jeanie requested stopping for bathroom breaks or food, I agreed without question. It was only in the last hour to the FDR center she started talking to me unprompted.

"How did you meet Mel?" she began.

My knuckles whitened on the steering wheel as my hands clenched at the memory. I never imagined I would think of Syko again.

"A guy was trying to take advantage of her," I answered. "It was her first time onstage at a carnival, which made it even worse. Poor thing was like a deer in headlights up there. At her first chance, she bolted."

"And let me guess. You were her knight in shining armor," Jeanie remarked sarcastically.

"Not exactly," I laughed. "You'll see I'm not that type at all. But she slipped and fell in the mud, then threw up all over herself. Don't let her know I told you that."

"Wow. That must've been sexy."

"Love at first sight," I cracked. "But no, actually, I did feel bad. So I gave her water and let her use my trailer to shower in, while I stayed far away. I tried to keep staying far away, but she never left me alone."

"So when did y'all fall in love?"

"Hm, for me?" I took a moment to think about when exactly it happened. It was crystal clear to me, but I felt a little unsure about spilling that to Jeanie.

"I guess it was when I had a bad PTSD episode." Fuck it, why not? She was Mel's family, and would figure it out when she saw the FDR center, anyway. "Mine gets triggered by noises like gunshots or fireworks sometimes. Mel stayed with me the whole time and just calmed me down. No one had really done that for me before, so that was when I knew she was special."

"PTSD?" Jeanie asked.

I nodded and reached down to lift up my pant leg.

"Holy shit," she breathed.

"It's not my place to tell you what to do with your life, but I don't recommend joining the military," I snorted. "It worked out alright for me, but I wouldn't wish the hell I went through on anybody else."

Except maybe Lhozen.

My heart tightened uncomfortably in my chest. *Lord almighty, please keep my babe and those three knuckleheads safe.* I wished more than anything I could hear her voice in my head like they could. Only two days away from her and I was already fighting every instinct to turn this bitch around and run to be at her side.

Maybe Jeanie was onto something, and I was more of a knight in shining armor than I cared to admit. Or maybe falling in love with Mel made me that way.

"So Mel's a circus performer or whatever now?" Jeanie said. "That's why she couldn't come get us herself?"

"She's a ringmistress, yes," I said evenly. "But that's not why she couldn't come."

"Y'all said it was because of work. Like, I get that she's trying to provide for us. Be the mother we never had or whatever, but we were about to be homeless. The kids miss her more than anything. They don't even want any birthday presents, they just want to see her. And she couldn't get out of work to see them?"

"I get it, Jeanie. I really do. But it's not as simple as that. You don't know the whole story."

"So what is the whole story?"

"Mel should be the one to tell you."

With a scoff and an eye roll, Jeanie crossed her arms and turned to look out the passenger-side window, in typical teenage fashion. I was her age not too long ago, so it didn't bother me much. We drove on in silence until we came onto the grounds of the FDR Center.

Home sweet home. But it wouldn't feel like home until I had my woman back in my arms.

"You live *here?*" Jeanie forgot she was pissed at me as she pressed her nose to the glass, taking in the colorful flower beds and topiaries that flanked the driveway to the main building.

"Not in there," I chuckled, following the road around the main building as I waved to one of the landscapers. "But we live on campus. You'll see."

"What is this place?"

"It's a non-profit center for disabled veterans," I answered. "I'm pretty certain your sister and this place have both saved my life. They custom-made these legs for me." I knocked on my metallic left shin as the road turned to gravel and the landscape grew wilder.

Jeanie's knuckles whitened as she gripped the armrests of her seat. I could guess what she was thinking about this guy driving her and three small children deeper into the woods. I couldn't think of how to reassure her. Like she said earlier, I could lie about anything. I just had to wait it out and prove that we weren't abusive or axe murderers.

The plantation house soon came into view, but that wasn't what captured the attention of Joey and Bella as they pressed their faces to the windows.

"Puppies!" Bella squealed. "I see puppies! Two of them!"

"What? I want one!" Riley demanded, squeezing between her siblings to see.

"Hey! Sit down and buckle up, the car's still moving!" Jeanie barked at them.

I rubbed my jaw as we pulled up to the house, where Colt, Gabe, and Miriam relaxed on the front porch while the pups ran wild. I forgot that they might be even more rambunctious without their father around. It seemed I'd have to explain some things to Jeanie before Mel got back.

"I want you to know something," I said, slowing the RV to a halt and turning to grab Jeanie's hand before shutting the engine off.

"What?" She looked surprised, even put off a little by the contact, but she didn't pull away.

"You're safe here," I told her. "The kids are safe here. You're not in danger. You're going to see some shit that's weird, but I promise you no one will hurt you or the young ones anymore."

She gave a strange, squinty-eyed look with a tilt of her head. "What the hell are you talking about?"

"I know me saying that just set your alarm bells ringing," I patted her hand before letting go and standing up. "But you can trust me and anyone here. Just remember what I said."

"Oh. Kay..." She got out of her own seat and marched back to gather the kids. "Come on guys, hold hands. I know you want to meet the puppies, but Connor's going out first."

Here goes nothin'.

I popped open the door, wincing slightly at the impact of the ground. I definitely over-wore my legs on this road trip and needed a few days without them, or I'd never hear the end of it from my doctors and Mel.

"Connor!" Colt and Miriam approached the RV, arms around each other in an affectionate embrace. "We didn't expect to see you back so soon. Where is everyone?"

"Still in Florida," I answered before lowering my voice. "I had to get Mel's siblings out of a bad situation. They're all completely human. As in, they have no idea about any of this."

"Leave it to me," Miriam winked before releasing her wolf shifter's arm and looked past me to Jeanie wrangling the young ones. "Hi! You must be Mel's family."

"Uh, yeah. Hi." Jeanie's eyes darted around as she pulled Bella and Joey close, securing Riley on her hip.

"I'm Miriam, and this is Colt. You'll meet the others later. Can I help y'all bring in anything? Are you hungry?"

"Uh, I think we're okay—"

"Here, let me get that for you." Before Jeanie could protest, Miriam marched over and took the backpack sliding off her shoulder. "I can show you the bedrooms and you can pick which ones you and the kids would like."

"Uh, thanks. How many people live here?" Jeanie looked up at the two-story plantation house, as if noticing it for the first time.

"Mel, her guys, and the pups make seven," Miriam said. "I live with Colt and Gabe in a cabin a bit deeper in the woods. We're just house-sitting and watching the kids while Mel and everyone's away."

"Kids? What kids?"

"Hunter's pups." Colt cocked his head toward the lawn where Roo and Rinna chased each other and wrestled playfully.

Jeanie forced an awkward chuckle while Miriam and I glared at Colt. "He loves his puppies enough to call them his kids. That's cute."

Just then, the pups took notice of me and ran over as fast as their four legs could carry them, mouths open in wide smiles and tongues lolling out.

"Shit," I muttered under my breath, but forced a smile as they ran closer.

Just as I feared, they began shifting to human mid-run.

"Mr. Connor, you're back!" Roo called as soon as he had a human mouth.

"Holy fuck! What the—" Jeanie clapped a hand over her mouth before pulling Bella and Joey close to her side.

"Jesus," I muttered, pulling off my shirt and tossing it to Colt to cover Hunter's now-naked children clamoring around us. "Hey," I placed a hand on Jeanie's shoulder, "remember what I told you, okay? You're not in danger here. They're just kids... who also happen to be wolf pups."

"What the fuck is going on?" she stared at me wide-eyed. "What are they? What are *you?* How the hell did my sister get involved with all of you?"

"I'll tell you everything," I promised her. "As for me, I'm nothing special. Just a surly ex-Marine missing a few limbs and brain cells."

"Hi."

At our feet, Bella walked right up to Rinna, who now wore my shirt around her like a huge tent of a dress. "Are you a girl or a puppy?"

"I'm both!" Rinna declared proudly. "My daddy is a man and a wolf. My name's Rinna. That's my brother, Roo."

"I'm Bella," Mel's younger sister giggled. "Can I call you Rella?"

"Sure. Do you want to play tag?"

"Okay!"

"Rinna," Colt crouched low to the ground to talk to his niece. He spoke in a low, gentle voice about ground rules like wearing clothes and staying in human form when playing with humans. She listened with rapt attention and nodded, clearly excited to play with someone other than her brother.

"Wait, hold on," Jeanie's arm shot out and yanked Bella back to her side. "No one is playing with anyone until someone explains this stuff."

"Come inside, Jeanie," Miriam suggested gently, holding her arm out. "I'm a regular human like Connor. I can't shift either. We'll explain everything and answer any questions you have, I promise."

Jeanie's wide, panicked eyes darted from me to Miriam as she struggled to make her choice. I understood how difficult it was for her to trust and knew we shouldn't push her. She came all this way with me having no idea what she was getting into, and had certainly not expected anything like this.

"Okay," she said finally.

With that, we all turned to head into the house. I gave Miriam a quick glance and she returned it with a small nod and smile. It might take some time, but we were making progress. For all we knew, Mel and the others would come home to find her siblings completely at ease and feeling at home with shifters in their new family

❧ 14 ❧

MELODY

My eyelids felt like they weighed ten pounds each as I fought to open them. My throat felt like a desert and my head swam in a fog, but I didn't feel pain anywhere.

When I finally forced my eyes open, my body wanted to tense up, but it wouldn't obey. My limbs felt heavy and too relaxed. In fact, whatever I was lying on was soft and comfortable, like the loveseat at home where I would happily curl up for a nap.

I looked up at a dark ceiling with a simple chandelier, casting warm yellow light throughout the room. The walls were dark wood paneling lined with bookshelves. An antique wooden desk sat in the corner, its feet rested on a large area rug with an intricate design. When I pressed myself up to sitting, I realized I had been reclining on a loveseat. It felt plush, soft, and expensive.

Something was all wrong about this. I was in someone's cozy office, not a prison for shifters.

"Ah, good. You're awake."

All too slowly, my head turned to the voice. The man I now knew was Lhozen smiled cheerfully back at me.

"You must be parched, dear," he said in a charming English accent.

"There's a glass of water on the table next to you." At my suspicious look, he added, "Oh, there's no need for that look. I haven't put anything in it. Why would I want to harm the next most powerful shaman besides me?"

"The guys," I croaked through my dry mouth. "My shifters. Where are they?"

"With the others," he said dismissively, walking over to the desk to rifle through some papers. "Drink up, Melody. Are you hungry as well? My kitchen can prepare anything you'd like. We have much to discuss and I want you in top shape, love."

"The others?" I demanded, my voice growing stronger as if everything he said after that never even registered. "You mean caged and brutalized? Disfigured and tortured? What makes you think I would ever want to cooperate with you?"

Lhozen let out a patronizing sigh. "What you saw through the window, dear, was merely another illusion." He waved a hand theatrically in front of his face. "But I can certainly make it a reality should you decide not to cooperate." The charm never left his smile, but I saw something dark and sinister in his eyes for the first time.

So the monstrosities I saw weren't real? That was a relief, albeit a tiny one. The visions in my head and what I saw through Julian's eyes weren't much better though.

"What do you want from me?" I demanded. "What's the point of this place and why do you even need my cooperation?"

"Because you are like a daughter to me, Melody." The charming grin grew wider. "The young protege I've always wanted but could never find. Miriam showed promise, but unfortunately she was not very intelligent or strong enough."

"What?" None of what he said made sense. I never met this man before in my life, and even what he said about Miriam puzzled me. She had future Sight, how could she not be smart or strong enough? But I kept my face blank and tried to absorb whatever information he might tell me. Who knew if it would be useful to getting the guys out of here.

"You don't remember me, do you?" He looked disappointed and clicked his tongue at me. "Here, maybe this will jog your memory."

He waved a hand, now encased in a white glove, over his head, where he now wore a silky black top hat. I flinched when he reached that hand out to touch me, but his gloved fingers only gently grazed the shell of my ear. Just as quickly, he pulled his hand away, holding a coin between two fingers.

The realization made my heart drop into my stomach.

No way. Please no. It can't be.

"You've made me proud, Melody. You took the gift of my powers better than anyone else I've ever seen." He flipped the coin in the air and it landed next to me on the sofa, the crossed daggers shining up at me. They reminded me of Razvan and my gut twisted into a series of tight knots at my confusion and dread.

"Why?" I squeaked out. I didn't even know what I was asking. Why me? Why was he doing this to shifters, including his own step-son? What sick, twisted purpose did he have in mind for me?

"Oh, the decision was easy," he said lightheartedly, the gloves and top hat illusions now gone. "Even as a seven-year-old child, you had magic in you. I saw it in the way you calmed your sister down and distracted her from your horrible beast of a mother."

"Don't," I threw up a hand, my temper going from zero to sixty within seconds, "say one goddamn word about my mother. You raised Arjun like your own son and then did *this* to him? He couldn't fucking walk, because he'd been in tiger form for so long. He trusted you! And the whole time, you're treating shifters like lab mice?!"

"My dear, you are young," he said with that same dismissive, patronizing tone. "You're not seeing the big picture, and I'll forgive your ignorance for now. You still need training to build your powers and—"

"Forget it." I crossed my arms defiantly. If he was going to treat me like a child, I was happy to act like one. "I don't give a shit if you gave me my abilities, I'm not training under you."

"You may want to rethink that, Melody." His voice took on the undertone of a threat. "Believe it or not, I take no pleasure in the pain of others. But if you do not go along with my plan that I have so carefully constructed over the past eight years, there will be consequences."

When I said nothing, keeping my arms crossed, he gave a curt nod and said, "Very well." He snapped his fingers, then two men in dark green, military-style fatigues marched through the door and took hold of my arms.

"What the—! Let me go!"

"I warned you, Melody." Lhozen almost sounded apologetic. "But perhaps it's best that you learn what I'm capable of. Oh, Renson?"

"Yes, sir?" asked one of the men holding my arm.

"Give her lovers metamorparfizan before you let her have some time with them. Make sure she sees."

"Yes, sir."

The guards began dragging me out of the room, not roughly, but firm-handed enough that I couldn't get my feet under me.

"Jesus, stop it. I can walk on my own," I protested.

They humored me, slowing enough for me to regain my footing and walk between them. Each man's fingers dug into my biceps like vice grips, which I tried to ignore. It sparked a memory of my mom leaving bruises when she grabbed my arms and shook me to scream in my face, but I swallowed it down. I had to keep it together for the guys.

The hallway outside of Lhozen's office looked exactly the same as the one we stood in before getting caught. I couldn't tell if it was the same anymore since he apparently illusioned the shit out of this place.

I craned my neck to the right side, looking through the large bay window to the open area down below. The same cages still lined the floors and stood stacked on top of each other, but everyone was in animal form as far as I could see. No partially-shifted or mutated freaks.

A chill ran through me. How did Lhozen know seeing shifters like that would throw off my focus? Did he just assume I'd be freaked out by that, as most people would be? I had a nagging feeling he knew more than he let on.

Aside from the compound humans talking in low voices and the hum of machinery, I also realized no one was screaming. Bears, owls, coyotes, bobcats, foxes, and more all sat quietly in their cages. Their blank, glassy-eyed stares made me wonder if they were sedated.

My guards led me down a flight of stairs to the cage area. A few people in lab coats worked on computers at a metal table in the center of the room. Around the perimeter of the room, I noticed heavy metal doors with small square windows in them. Squinting through, I could see some people in hazmat suits through those doors, but the windows were too small to see what they were doing.

"Hold her," one of my guards said to the other. One man now crushed both of my biceps in an uncomfortably tight grip.

My eyes darted around the room as he held me, trying to take in as much information as possible. Were there any exits to the outside in this room? Could I cast any illusions in here to distract the humans and get the shifters out?

"Don't even think about it, missy," my guard sneered as if reading my mind. "Lhozen will know the second you try to fool us."

My teeth gritted in my jaw. Come on, Mel, think. Lhozen isn't all-powerful. He isn't a god. There's got to be a way.

"Got 'em," my other guard called from behind us. "Bring 'em out."

The one holding me spun us around just as a large cage began moving toward us on some kind of pulley system. It was in a dark, back corner of the room, slowly coming out toward the center on a track in the floor. This cage was huge—big enough to hold a dinosaur or a—

"Raz!" I cried out, trying to bolt toward the cage, but the guard held me still.

Steluța!

My dragon barely had room to turn around in his barred prison. His wings pressed against the top, unable to stretch out fully. The moment he saw me, he let out a terrifying roar and reached for me, stretching one clawed hand through the bars and nearly swiping the lab coat off a nearby human.

Underneath Raz was an unmoving mass of white fur. My dragon stood protectively over the white wolf and somehow, the sight of Hunter's still form allowed to me to break free of my guard's hold.

"No, no, Hunter!" I pressed my face between the bars, grabbing hold of Raz's claw as it caressed over my face. "Hunter, get up!"

He's alive, but he bit someone, so they gave him a huge dose of sedative. I can barely feel his heart.

"Fuck..." I looked up at my dragon's face, covered in obsidian scales and horns, but those same steel-gray eyes were so human as they looked back at me.

Raz, can you breathe fire? If you torch someone and get them to panic, they'll be distracted and I can—

I can't, steluţa, he told me mournfully. They stuck me with so many injections when Lhozen knocked me out. Every time I try, I feel like I'm choking.

I leaned my forehead against his clawed hand, despair swallowing me up like quicksand. I couldn't even bring myself to cry, so I just watched Hunter breathing weakly.

What about Arjun? I asked Raz. Have you seen him?

No, my love. He's not in a cage. I don't know where they're keeping him.

"Alright, time to move this sweet reunion along," someone muttered behind me.

Before I could react, something shot past my head and struck Razvan's arm. He let me go with a scream and began thrashing wildly against the cage bars.

"What did you do?!" I cried, trying to reach for him, but someone grabbed my arms again.

I watched helplessly as my dragon roared in pain while he spasmed, hitting his head against the bars and nearly stepping on Hunter's lifeless form as he seemed to lose control of his body. Someone else was screaming too, and only when a hand clapped roughly over my mouth did I realize it was me.

After what felt like hours, but had to be only seconds, I noticed Raz's form was shrinking. His tail and wings disappeared into his body, his arms and legs rearranged to be roughly human in shape. His head shrank down to human size, but he still kept a layer of black scales over his skin. His horns and dragon teeth remained, giving him a demon-like appearance.

And there the forced shifting stopped.

"Still wanna kiss your lizard boy?" a mocking voice asked. "Go ahead."

The door to the cage opened, and in the next moment, I was flying through. The tears fell freely now as I wrapped my arms around Raz's neck, sobbing uncontrollably into his shoulder. He cradled my back, gently stroking my hair as if it was his duty to comfort me after what had just been done to him.

My hand drifted down his scaled arm until it met the injected needle they just shot at him. I yanked on it with all my strength, making him flinch and grunt with pain. What I pulled from his arm was at least four inches long and thicker than a toothpick.

"Thyrrr." Raz attempted to speak, but his jaws were still too dragon-like. A soft chuckle floated around us from the observing humans, and it made my blood boil. They did this to humiliate him.

They strengthened their needles since I was last captured, he told me sadly. Now they can penetrate my dragon hide instead of sticking me when I'm human.

"Dragon, I'm so sorry." I curled up against him, laying my head on the black scales of his chest as sobs wracked my body. "I'll get you out of here. I don't know how, but I will."

A mocking, "*Awww,*" rose up from around us. My body immediately tensed and I moved to lift my head, but Raz pulled me tightly against him, a clawed hand cupping my face.

Do not try to bargain with Lhozen, he said. Don't believe his lies. If he offers to set us free in order to keep you, it's a trick. Everything he is, is an illusion, steluţa. Don't make deals. Don't trust him.

A cocking sound made us both look up.

"No, don't!" I moved to cover Hunter with my own body, but wasn't fast enough. The fired injection stuck him on his flank.

Grab him, Raz ordered. He's going to seize like I did. Make sure he doesn't hurt himself.

Together, we held Hunter's body as still as we possibly could while the onlooking humans chuckled and made their insulting comments. We ignored them, but I took note of everyone, making sure to remember every face and name tag.

I held our wolf's head in my lap while Raz held down his spasming arms and legs. There must have been some amount of adrenaline in the forced-shifting drug, because Hunter's golden eyes shot open, wide, and dilated.

"I'm sorry, my love," I leaned down and kissed his forehead as he grunted and struggled through the forced shifting. "I'm so, so sorry."

Hey, handsome, Raz said, lacing his clawed, scaly fingers through Hunter's human-like paw. *You look just like when I first saw you.*

"Rarrz?" Hunter blinked and began looking around—first at me and Raz, then down at his body stuck between wolf and human.

I didn't give a fuck that humans were looking at us like animals in a zoo and laughing. All I wanted was to stay with my wolf and dragon, but someone grabbed my arms and dragged me, kicking and screaming, out of the cage.

MELODY

"You can take me back to Lhozen," I murmured in a daze, my feet no longer working like they were supposed to. My guards actually had to drag me across the floor this time. "I'll do whatever he wants me to do, just don't hurt them anymore."

"Not so fast, sweetie," one of them chuckled. "We have one more for you to visit."

Arjun. Oh god, Arjun.

I tried twisting my head around to look back at Raz and Hunter, but my left guard jerked on my arm. Pain shot through my shoulder as I yelped. The asshole had nearly yanked my arm out of my socket.

At least my dragon and my wolf had each other. I found the smallest possible comfort in that fact.

My guards dragged me to one of the metal doors in the walls with tiny square windows. One of them waved a card over a panel next to the door, which beeped and a small green light turned on. The door slid open and there was my tiger.

Human and naked, his back pressed against the rear wall of the tiny room, no bigger than a walk-in closet. His ocean-colored eyes, wide with fear, didn't notice me. Right away, I knew why.

Hoops of fire lined the floor like some kind of hopscotch layout from Hell. The flames jumped and crackled, sending sparks in the air. But something wasn't right.

My guards shoved me before I could process and think. With a scream, I teetered forward, heat enveloping my body as I swung wildly in midair for something to hold on to. Bracing myself for the pain of being burned alive, I crashed to the floor on my hands and knees.

"Melody!" Arjun screamed.

Immediately I rolled, instinct taking over. I must've rolled five or six times across the floor before it hit me: I wasn't on fire.

I stopped, my heart going a mile a minute, and held my hands out in front of my face.

Another fucking illusion. *I'm not really burning.*

My lips moved rapidly as I repeated the mantra over and over, trying to calm the panic response in my body. *This fire isn't real. I'm not burning.*

When I sat up, Arjun's head was in his hands. His fingers gripped so tight in his thick black hair, I was afraid he'd pull it out.

"Arjun?" I scooted across the floor and touched his bare shoulder. Only then did I realize he was trembling.

"Arjun, it's okay." I kissed his hair and his brow as my hands slid over his, gently trying to unlock his fingers. "The fire isn't real."

"Nothing is okay," he muttered. "None of this is fucking okay."

Any determination I had to get us out withered away into nothing at that moment. I collapsed into sobs right there, my forehead pressed to his and my fingers locked in his.

"I'm so sorry." How many times had I said that already? I felt like the most pathetic idiot on the planet. "You were right. I should have listened to you. Everything we planned, everything you taught me. None of it mattered. Now he's hurting all of you and this is all my fault."

At some point, his hands wrapped around me. He held me against his chest and, for once, I didn't care that he was naked. I kissed his neck, his collarbone, his mouth. I didn't know what else to do, how else to convey how much I regretted putting him and the others in this place.

"We should have gone home," I whispered mournfully. "We'd be with my siblings, with the pups, with Connor, at our beautiful house. Oh god, at least Connor isn't here."

He held me wordlessly for a few moments, fingers grazing along the nape of my neck. I couldn't tell if it was absent minded or if he was intentionally touching me in one of my most sensitive areas.

"If we did that, would things have gone back to the way before?" he asked with surprising nonchalance.

I paused to let a few ragged breaths, and sobs escape my chest. "What do you mean?"

"I mean this." He cupped my chin roughly and kissed me. Those lips and tongue seemed to take my breath away and give me new life at the same time. My world spun, and I was soaring. My arms ached from my guards manhandling me. My heart was shattered at how my men and every shifter in here were being treated. Maybe that was why Arjun tasted so fucking good and I couldn't stop.

"Would I have you like this?" he murmured gruffly, teeth trailing down my jaw to my neck, "if we weren't trapped in a fucking metal box? Would you be here, soothing me away from what I fear most, if we weren't close to death?"

"Arjun..." His hand closed over my breast, tugging on my nipple through my clothes as his mouth sent nerve endings tingling through my neck. Oh god, was I getting wet? My brain spun with confusion. How could I be getting turned on right now, of all times?

"Answer me," he growled, though I wasn't sure he really wanted an answer. "Do I want you so fucking bad because I might not be alive tomorrow? Do you feel so good because I'll never get another chance to touch you again?"

"I don't know, Arjun." Tears escaped my eyes, but he raised his face to kiss them away, his mouth soon capturing mine again. My lips felt delightfully bruised when he pulled away softly.

"Or is it because you're meant to be my mate?" he whispered. "Like my tiger believed the moment I first heard your voice in my head, and I've been too fucking stubborn this whole time to admit it?"

"I think... the second one."

He pulled away, his eyes meeting mine, and blinked. "Well, *that* was anticlimactic."

I let out a dry laugh. I actually *laughed* despite this horrible situation we were in. How adorably cliche to admit one's feelings right before almost certain death?

"I knew I wanted you before all this happened," I whispered. "But it probably took a while for me to admit it, too."

The handsome tiger inhaled deeply, caressing my nape again in a way that made me forget everything outside of his touch.

"Well, aside from our delightful parents, there's another thing we have in common."

A smirk played on his lips, and I found myself smiling back. My pulse thrummed in my veins, but not from fear or adrenaline this time. For a moment, it was that euphoric feeling upon first pouring your heart out—somewhere between awkward embarrassment and uncontrollable happiness. Just for the briefest moment in time, it was just us basking in that feeling.

Then someone banged on the metal door, followed by yelling and whistles from the other side. Of course, they were watching us like a spectator sport too.

"I don't suppose you want our first time together in front of an audience," Arjun mused.

"And if it's our last time, too?" I wrapped my hands around his neck. "Let them watch. I don't care."

My lips descended on his, never separating, as I shifted my legs around to straddle him. He let out a hot moan as I leaned into his erection. If his cock was the last one I ever rode, I'd die a happy woman. My fingers drifted down his taut chest and abs to wrap around the base. He was deliciously thick and curved upward slightly when hard. By the way he had touched me already, I knew he wasn't a selfish lover.

"Mel, dove." His lips broke away from mine, sucking between his teeth as his hand stopped my upward strokes on his shaft.

"What's wrong?" Goddamn, I was already panting. Was I ready to die so quickly?

"I'm not making love to you here in a filthy prison cell." His heated gaze kept an air of playfulness but also determination. "If you want this, you've got to get us out of here, love."

"What? You're not seriously rejecting me again?"

"I am, but not because I want to," he said huskily. "I don't want some rushed half-assed fuck. I want to savor every piece of you after all this is over."

I blinked at him. "But you just said—"

"I know what I said, love." He pushed my hair away from my face, cupping my cheek as he kissed me deeply again. "The odds are still against us. But if anyone can beat them, Melody, it's you."

"How?" The noise outside our cell rose, and I knew our time was limited. Our captors weren't getting the show they originally wanted, and now they were bored. "Arjun, if anyone can tell me how, I know it's you."

"No, my beautiful dove. It's all you," he said quickly as we heard the telltale beep of someone scanning their card to open the door. "You're not just a shaman, you're a ringmistress. Command the stage. You own it."

His gaze bore into mine as the guards' brutal hands dug into my arms to drag me away. I didn't struggle against them, but my mind raced at his words. I knew he was speaking in a metaphor, but why? And what was he trying to tell me?

"Now you can go to Lhozen," my left guard sneered at me. "He'll have a whole army of half-animal freaks to fuck you. Isn't that what you like?"

I would have spit at him, maybe tossed out a *fuck you* and gotten my arm dislocated as a result. And it would have been worth it. But I had more important things to worry about now.

I had to figure out what the hell Arjun meant. And fast.

CONNOR

"So what you're actually telling me is, there are people who can turn into animals?"

"Yes," Miriam answered Jeanie's question calmly. "And your sister Mel is like me, a shaman. We have a close connection with shifters. We sense them and communicate with them in ways normal humans can't."

"But most humans are like you and me," I told Mel's wide-eyed sister. "We're stuck with the bodies we have and we're as magical as a can of beans."

"I know it's a lot to take in," Miriam added to Jeanie's stunned silence, keeping her voice warm and soothing. "But you get used to it after spending more time with them. And you realize they're just people like anyone else." She affectionately poked Colt in the ribs, who grabbed her finger and pretended to bite it.

"It's so weird, it's like... I can't explain it," Jeanie shook her head. "Like, I am shocked and I'm not all at the same time. Like I always *knew* there was magic and other beings like y'all existed, but I forgot I knew that. I guess I figured it was my imagination just trying to escape the bullshit that was part of my everyday life."

"Both you and Mel were like that, I bet," I said, trying to ignore the ache in my chest. Goddamn, I missed her like crazy.

"Yeah," Jeanie nodded, her eyes lighting up. "When everyone passed out, we used to play pretend all the time. Mel was always saving dragons and unicorns from evil. She talked to them like they were people."

I couldn't suppress the grin spreading across my mouth. *Just wait until you meet Razvan,* I thought.

"Dragons are totally real," Colt chimed in. "Your sister has one of those, too. Never seen a unicorn, but I wouldn't rule it out."

"Raz might be the last one," I added. "Unless others with the dormant shift pop up. His family thought they were humans for centuries."

"Jesus, *dragons?*" Jeanie slapped a palm to her forehead.

"Do you want to lie down?" Miriam offered. "It's been a long trek and I know this is information overload."

"Yeah, that might be a good idea, but," she hesitated. "Who's gonna watch the kids?"

"We will. Don't worry about it." Miriam stood, hovering over Jeanie like a mother hen as she prepared to lead her to a bedroom.

"I'm not tired. Can I play tag?" Bella asked, sliding off of her own seat.

"It's really okay," I said in response to Jeanie's worried look. "All the open space around the house is ours. We'll keep an eye on them, promise."

Jeanie finally resigned with a nod, her eyelids drooping like she hadn't slept in days, and got up to follow Miriam. Once the two of them ascended the stairs, Rinna grabbed Bella's hands and squealed excitedly.

"You guys know the rules." Colt leaned down to playfully tap Rinna's nose. "Human form only and don't go past the treeline. We'll be watching. I'll drag you back by your scruff if I have to."

"Humans don't have scruffs, Uncle Colt," Rinna giggled.

"You will after I'm done with you," he teased, tickling her sides and blowing raspberries on her cheeks until she ran away laughing. With the kids outside and the ladies gone, it was just me and Hunter's dark-haired brother left in the room.

"Coming around to humans, are ya, Colt?" The question was casual enough, but I wanted him to know I hadn't stopped keeping an eye on him and Gabe. This was still *my* house, and Jeanie was *my* mate's sister. I let the brothers know when they first showed up they had only one chance to disrespect us and they'd be gone, regardless of how they felt about humans.

"I've never been against humans as a whole, Connor," he answered. "Do I have some resentment? Some grudges toward certain individuals? Yes, of course. But I'm not a puritan. I've never been against human and shifter pairings, or even interspecies-shifter pairing. That puritanical way of thinking is dying out. At least, the few remaining wolf packs need to see that if they want to survive."

"What about Gabe?" I asked. "Haven't even seen his face since we got back."

"Gabe is... conflicted," he sighed. "Typical youngster, always having an identity crisis. He's completely in love with Miriam, but hates himself for it. He's afraid of wanting to be okay with how the world is changing, so he's spent the last couple days in wolf form trying to ignore that it's happening."

"How is the world changing?"

He lifted an eyebrow. "Don't you know?"

"I want to hear it from your perspective." I leaned back in my wheelchair, wishing I could prop my legs up, but settled for lacing my hands behind my head. "Humor me."

Colt rubbed his chin, thinking for a moment before speaking. "If shifters could be summed up in a single word, it would be pride. We're proud of being part of the animal kingdom in ways that normal humans have broken away from. But that pride has also been our downfall. It might be what wipes us out."

"Why do you say that?"

"Because we're too proud to ask for help," he said with a small smile. "To reach out to others outside of our species and especially to humans. Our ancestors said we didn't need shamans anymore, so they stopped passing on their gifts. As the number of shaman dwindled, shifters became even more closed off to humans and isolated themselves in their own communities. Without shaman, the general human population became less educated about shifters. Which is why we're hunted down to the extent that we are today."

He punctuated his monologue with a shrug. "At least that's my theory, anyway."

"So Mel is leading a new movement, in a sense." I rubbed my jaw. "She's saving shifters and also taking them as mates. That would probably blow the socks off the general human population if they knew."

"Shifters *and* normal humans as mates." Colt motioned toward me. "But yes, she's already normalizing shifter-kind. We're animals, but we're also people. Ultimately, we're not that different."

"Be honest now," I told him. "How would you feel if Miriam started seeing another human?"

He made a displeased face that made me laugh out loud. "No offense, Connor. But most humans aren't like you. All I can think of is some fuckin' redneck hillbilly sweating and moaning on top of her."

"What about another shaman?"

He shrugged, his face resuming a look of neutrality. "It's not very likely. Shaman are so few and far between now. Plus, most of them are female." He grinned. "That might be fun, but I don't think she'd like us taking attention away from her. It would depend on the situation, of course."

"Definitely. Hey," I directed my wheelchair to the fridge and opened, pleased to see that no one had touched my six-pack. I grabbed one beer and tossed it to Colt. "We have some kids to watch, don't we?"

"We do," he chuckled, leading the way out to the back porch and holding the door open for me. "Listen, Connor," he began, pausing to open his can and sip the foam that bubbled over the top.

"Yeah?" I watched him curiously.

He took a seat on the lawn chair next to me, resting the beer on his knee as he watched the kids run across the lawn. Even the littlest one, Riley, shrieked with laughter as she chased a grinning Roo. He kept his pace slow and let her tag him. He then gave her plenty of distance as she tore off on her chubby, wobbly legs before giving chase.

For the hundredth time that day, I wished Mel was here. She would have died from happiness seeing this.

"I respect the hell out of you," Colt said finally. "And Mel. It doesn't matter to me one bit that y'all are human. I'm glad it was you two that saved Hunter. So thank you for that."

"Sure thing, Colt." I held out my fist for him to bump. "I respect you too. Gabe, though? I dunno about that guy."

"He'll come around," Colt laughed, flicking his long, dark hair back with one hand. "Once he extracts his head from his ass."

"Let's hope that happens before I knock his damn head from his shoulders."

"I don't blame you one bit," he chuckled.

We sipped and made commentary on the kids' tag game like a couple of sports announcers until the sun dipped low behind the trees. Cicadas sang their mating call and mosquitos came out in full force, but we couldn't bring ourselves to call the children inside yet.

Exhausted from their game, they sprawled out on the grass and watched the stars come out. Roo and Rinna pointed out constellations and star names they knew to Mel's siblings, telling the myths and stories behind the characters in the sky. Colt and I were also content to sit and listen.

"Damn, they're smart," I muttered, draining the last of my beer.

"They are," Colt agreed proudly. "I didn't even know Hunter taught them all this stuff. He always did love night runs and stargazing though."

I tried not to feel uncomfortable that he had used the past tense, and crushed my beer can in my hand as I turned to go inside.

"Lord almighty, I hope they're all okay down there," I muttered.

17

MELODY

Lhozen wasn't in his office when my guards dragged me back to that fancy, wood-paneled room. Instead, I found a note on the couch where I first woke up that said,

Melody,

I understand seeing your mates in that state was disturbing for you. Feel free to draw yourself a bath to relax. Then my guards will escort you to dinner, where we will talk more. -Lhozen

What the Jesus jumping fuck?

I tore my eyes away from the note, then noticed on the end table next to the couch was a folded bathrobe and a varied selection of bath bombs. Against my better judgement, I reached out to touch the dense and insanely soft terry-cloth robe. Yup, definitely never worn before and most likely expensive.

What the hell is his end game here? He can't seriously be trying to bribe me?

I must have stood there for a handful of minutes trying to figure this all out, re-reading the note and looking at the bath stuff like I would find a clue. Nothing came to me, though.

What if I just refuse?

The guards escorting me to dinner sounded like his posh, British way of telling me I had no choice in the matter. Even so, what the hell was up with the bath stuff?

Like they were covered in some infectious disease, I lifted the robe and bath bombs off the table. No matter how badly I wanted to burn this place to the ground, it would be easier for me and everyone else involved if I played along. At least for now.

I tried a few different doors in the office. Most of them didn't budge, but the bathroom opened easily. It was just as luxurious as the office—an open floor plan with a clawfoot tub, spotless white tiles and plush bath mats under foot.

I scanned the room for anything that might resemble a camera lens. Lhozen didn't seem like *that* kind of pervert, but I wouldn't rule it out.

When nothing stood out to me, I turned the handles on the tub and removed my clothes. Deciding not to use the bath bombs in case they were laced with a poison or some type of drug, I set them aside and turned to hang the bathrobe on the door. To my surprise, the door already had an outfit hanging on the hook, and the sight of it made me stop in my tracks.

It was a red dress. Not just any dress, but an evening gown. It was strapless, the bodice form-fitting like a corset with a skirt that flares out at the hips. My heart sank. I had no doubt Lhozen wanted me to wear it to dinner. The strappy black heels on the floor confirmed it like the final nail in my coffin.

I sank into the scalding water of the tub when it filled, keeping my back turned to the door so I wouldn't have to look at that dress. I scrubbed at my skin, trying to erase the disgusting feeling that came over me. It felt just like when I performed with Syko for the first time. Like I served no purpose but to be arm candy. I had been nothing but a dolled-up prop for the most vile human being on earth.

I stayed in the tub until the water got cold. If I was late or early, I had no idea. Lhozen's note never specified a time, and I wondered if he'd want to punish me for making him wait.

Better me than my guys, I thought as I slowly toweled off. As if he didn't have the ability to hurt all of us at the same time. The despair began as a tiny doubt that snowballed, growing more and more as I took the dress off the hanger and stepped into it. I couldn't bring myself to look in the mirror, not even when I brushed my hair or applied lotion from an unopened bottle on the vanity. Lhozen's fancy bathroom didn't seem to supply makeup, so I didn't bother with any.

The dress and shoes fit perfectly, which only made me feel shittier. How could he have known my size? Maybe he was a god, and we were all just fooling ourselves.

Despite the perfect fit, I couldn't twist my arms enough to finish zipping up the damn thing. Sighing heavily, I opened the bathroom door only halfway zipped. When I returned to the office, my guards were waiting.

"Can you zip me?" I asked, turning around and lifting my hair off my neck.

Nothing happened for a long moment. I almost thought they would keep standing there like a statue, but soon felt leather-gloved fingertips skim the small of my back in search of the zipper. They snapped it up so hard I thought the zipper might break. And then thankfully the feeling of leather was gone.

"Thanks," I muttered, turning around.

The guard gave a curt nod and, for the first time, I looked at his face. Like, really looked at him as a person. He wasn't ugly. Probably in his early forties, clean-shaven, with hard, stern eyes. His cheeks were tinged with pink, probably at having to touch me.

The thought of trying to seduce him crossed my mind and made me recoil instantly. Even if it was a successful means to an end, I couldn't look my men in the face after betraying them like that. My mom and older sister used sex to get what they wanted. I would never be that person.

"Are we done here?" snapped the other guard by the door.

"Yeah," I drawled in the same indignant tone. "We're done."

The guard who zipped me took hold of my arm. My fresh bruises stood out in reddish purple welts on my pale skin, and I noticed he avoided closing his hand over them. He also didn't squeeze as hard as the other guy, who made me hiss in pain from his yanking my arm. Yup, that was the shoulder that had almost been dislocated. Left Guard was a grade-A asshole.

As they led me out of the office and into the now-familiar hallway, my eyes flickered to Zipper Guard on my right. Seducing him was out of the question, but maybe befriending him wouldn't be a bad idea. Surely not everyone here agreed with whatever Lhozen's sadistic plan was, right?

"What's your name?" I tried.

"Don't get chatty, bitch," barked Asshole Guard. "You stay quiet unless you're spoken to, understand?"

"I wasn't talking to you," I retorted cattily.

He replied with a yank on my arm that had me yelping and fresh tears springing to my eyes. He pulled so hard, my other arm came out of Zipper Guard's grip, and Asshole shook me like a rag doll.

"Bitch, say one more goddamn word and I swear to God, I'll—"

"Renson, stop." Zipper braced his arm between us. "If she talks, just ignore her. We need to take her to him in one piece."

Asshole released me with a growl, grinding his teeth with a wild look in his beady eyes. Something was wrong with that guy. He wanted to hurt something just for the sake of hurting it; he obviously liked inflicting pain.

"He's right," Zipper muttered once we resumed our walk. "You're better off not asking any questions."

THE WALK ENDED through one of the many unmarked doors in the hallway. I had no idea how any of Lhozen's minions kept from getting lost in this maze, but what laid out on the other side was unlike anything I'd ever seen.

It reminded me of the dining room from Beauty and the Beast. A long dinner table with elegant chairs and a chandelier overhead.

Lhozen was already seated, while wait staff whisked in and out of the room.

"Your chair, miss?" A man in a tuxedo swept his hand toward a chair directly next to Lhozen and looked at me expectantly. I returned his look with one of, *what the fuck is going on?*

This place almost felt like a twilight zone with rooms like this, and his office hiding behind metal doors. Was any of this actually here, or were these things more of Lhozen's illusions? Was this whole compound based on something that wasn't real? My head pounded with trying to make sense of what was real or fake.

My guys. Their lives and their safety. They're real and that's what matters.

"Melody, please sit," Lhozen motioned toward me. It sounded like an invitation, but I heard the undertone of a command. "You must be starving."

I had no appetite, actually. I was pretty certain my stomach was empty, and I still wanted to vomit all over this dress that probably cost an arm and a leg.

Nonetheless, I marched over and took a seat while the man in a tuxedo politely pushed my chair in. Immediately, a stemmed glass was placed in front of me and wine began pouring into it.

"I don't drink," I said, holding my hand out. "I'm too young, anyway."

"Ah. A pity." Lhozen signaled to the waiter, and the glass was whisked away. "But you are just in time for the main course."

A steaming plate was placed in front of me and despite my lack of appetite, my mouth watered. My plate held the juiciest steak I'd ever seen, cooked to a perfect medium, flanked by buttered potatoes and roasted vegetables. It looked too good to eat.

That's because it's not real, I reminded myself. It can't be real. Nothing he offers you is real.

I could feel Lhozen's eyes on me as I stared at my plate. The whole situation felt very Hannibal Lecter to me. What was *really* on my plate? Just to be safe, I picked up a fork and poked at the vegetables.

"You're suspicious," Lhozen observed. "Very cautious. That's one of the reasons why I chose you to receive the gift of the shaman. The best casters of Semblance also know how to look for illusions."

I brought a carrot to my mouth and chewed slowly. Holy shit, it was really good. Coated in some kind of glaze and cooked to perfection as it melted in my mouth. Maybe it *was* real?

"But you're still young and your power is unrestrained," he went on. "You need more training and I need my work to continue while I am not long for this world."

That took me by surprise. I swallowed the carrot and tried to regard him calmly, as difficult as it was. My other hand clenched in my lap, because it was all I could do not to reach across the table and choke him.

"What do you mean by that?" I asked.

"It means I don't have long to live, dear." He gave me a sad smile. "Although I've lived many lives, as you know. I'm quite certain I've seen the world through the eyes of every creature imaginable. From a praying mantis to a blue whale. It's simply marvelous this magic we have." He paused and gave me a strange look. "But I've seen nothing more lovely than looking through the eyes of a certain wolf, tiger, and dragon."

My hand froze in shock as I was moving a piece of potato to my mouth. Only through sheer force of will did I continue its trajectory past my lips. I chewed as slowly as I could with my pulse hammering in my veins.

So he *was* that kind of pervert. Only instead of looking through hidden cameras, he looked through the eyes of shifters. And not just any shifters. Mine. Private moments with my men and he was there like a sick little peeping tom. I don't know how I didn't throw up right then.

This information was important. My brain buzzed for a moment, trying to make a connection, then it hit me.

Arjun knew.

Of course, that brilliant, beautiful tiger fucking knew.

He couldn't tell me directly, not with the risk of Lhozen seeing through him and hearing his words. That was why he wouldn't do anything beyond kissing me. He didn't want to give this pervert the sick satisfaction of seeing us together. It had to be why he said that ringmistress stuff. I still didn't know what that meant, but I finally knew something I didn't before. Lhozen's ego was just too big to keep it to himself.

I forced a smile at him, hoping he didn't see the epiphany that just went off in my head.

"You saw through my men, intentionally?" I asked, forcing my voice not to shake.

"I did. And what a sight it was."

"How?" I propped my elbow on the table and rested my chin in my hand, hoping I made a convincing show of looking interested. "I've never been able to control the shifters I see through. Sometimes I'm watching a hunt. Other times I'm witnessing a private moment between two lovers that should only be between them."

I probably shouldn't have been snarky, but I couldn't help it.

"Under my training, you'll learn all that and more," he promised, ignoring my snark. "What do you say, Melody?"

"You ask that like I have a choice in the matter," I remarked.

"Because I'm a gentleman," he said with a smile. "But truthfully, no. You don't."

18

MELODY

"So what is the alternative?"

Lhozen gave me an eerily calm, patronizing smile. "My dear, if you truly had any idea, you would not dare to ask that question."

I set my fork down and brought my hands to my lap, trying to look as docile and cooperative as possible.

"Can I just ask... that you please not hurt them?" My lip wobbled. "Don't drug them. Don't force them to shift. If you could even consider letting them go—"

"Now why would I do that?" he mused arrogantly. "When they've so eagerly returned to me?"

The silence stretched between us. His glassy blue eyes never left mine, daring me to challenge him. With every interaction we had, I was beginning to see there was no reasoning with him.

"Don't hurt them then," I relented in a small voice. "Please."

"Since you asked so nicely, I'll consider it." He rose from the table, his dismissive tone made it perfectly clear he would do no such thing. "Now, come with me to the parlor, dear."

He held his arm out to me, bent at a ninety-degree angle. I swallowed my discomfort as I pushed my chair back and stood, my food mostly untouched while his plate was empty. The wait staff immediately swarmed in like an ant colony to clear the table. After placing my hand on his awaiting arm, Lhozen wasted no time in leading me away through another door.

This one led to another room of old-world elegance, just like the dining room. A classical quartet played soft background music in the corner. An elaborate bar made of glossy dark wood stood against one wall, surrounded by glittering crystal bottles of every size and shape imaginable. This room was, for the most part, empty and open. There were a few plush couches and armchairs scattered around, but the massive size of the room made it feel sparsely decorated.

"Dance with me." Lhozen turned me around and placed a hand on my waist. He made it clear that it wasn't a request.

I followed his lead to the middle of the room, then again as he took my hand and began moving to the classical music.

His eyes were half-closed, top lids lightly fluttering as we moved around the room. I could only guess he was focusing hard on some illusion, but what? And for what purpose?

My eyes slid around the room as we twirled. Aside from us, the band, and my guards, no one else was in the room. No one was watching. Why cast such elaborate illusions if there was no one to impress?

"You're a natural dancer," he murmured, extending his arm out to twirl me away. I played along, even flashing him a smile as I twirled back into his arms. I always was good at fake smiles when I was uncomfortable.

The music picked up speed and Lhozen went right along with it. I did my best to keep up, my mind still reeling as I tried to make sense of this whole act. He at first maintained a polite distance between us. Still, the longer we danced, I realized he drew me in closer and closer.

My belly brushed against his, and that hand on my waist pressed into me like a wall. I started to panic, my eyes darting about the room, hoping to catch the eyes of the others here. *Zipper Guard, my friend! Help me!*

Our gazes did meet as Lhozen continued twirling me around the room, but there was something weird about both of my guards.

Their eyes followed me watchfully, but instead of expressing anything, they stared with empty, hypnotic gazes.

I looked back at Lhozen, his face inches from mine now. His eyes were opened wider than before, but held the same blank stare as my guards. He wore a relaxed half-smile, as if sitting back on a sunny day and watching clouds go by.

Now thoroughly freaked out, it took me a full minute of twirling for it all to fall into place in my brain.

I was a ringmistress.

And this was just another performance.

My mind flew back to my burlesque dance when Raz and I rescued Arjun. Everyone watching me perform had been caught in a trance. They had been oblivious to anything else until Arjun jumped off the stage and mauled half the people watching.

Now the exact same thing was happening. I took my hand off Lhozen's shoulder and snapped my fingers in front of his face.

Nothing. His body kept moving us through the dance, but his eyes saw nothing but me.

Arjun, I will do so much more than kiss you when we get out of here.

Lhozen released me to do another twirl and this time I put extra flair in it, kicking one leg up to show off my calf under the puffy red skirt. At the same time, I looked around the room for a more thorough inspection.

Only the band in the corner didn't seem affected by my dance. Their eyes remained focused on their instruments as they played tirelessly. They had to be an illusion. There was no other explanation, even if they seemed so lifelike. Even if I was wrong, I had to risk it at this point.

Spinning around, the room with Lhozen, my eyes settled on the tranquilizer guns in my guards' holsters. That was it. My only shot.

I didn't dare interrupt the flow of the dance for fear of taking them out of their stupor, so I waited. We did three more rotations around the room before circling back to where we were closest to the guarded doors. My heart nearly vibrated from pounding so fast and my feet were starting to protest. I wondered if I let this go on, if Lhozen would keep dancing until he dropped dead.

But I couldn't wait that long, nor risk dropping dead myself. So when he extended his arm to let me twirl away once again, I took my chance.

I pulled my fingers out of his grip and continued twirling on my own, flashing him a flirtatious smile as I spun closer and closer to Asshole Guard. Looking back over my shoulder, he watched me with a dazed smile, and my heart leaped with victory. The trance was holding.

My spinning stopped directly in front of my guard and I extended my palm to him with a smile, as if asking him for the next dance. He returned the smile, removing his hand from his belt to accept the invitation. And then I shattered the illusion like a rock through a window.

My hand dove for his holster, wrapping my hand around the grip of the gun, and pulled. It came out easily, thank Jesus, but felt as heavy as a brick in my small, shaking hands.

Asshole Guard only had a moment to blink dumbly at me before I pointed at his chest and squeezed the trigger. A dart shot out, hitting him right in the pectoral muscle with nothing more than the sound of a small puff of air.

I didn't wait for his reaction, but stepped out of his reach and spun around to point the gun at Lhozen. My second shot hit him in the stomach, which he looked at in confusion. A thump behind me confirmed that the guard went down, and I glanced over my shoulder at Zipper Guard.

He still seemed dazed, blinking rapidly as his hands hovered over his own gun as if to pull it out.

"Sorry," I muttered, before aiming and pulling my trigger for a third time. The dart hit him in the shoulder.

"Shit," he groaned before slumping against the wall, fighting to keep his legs under him, but the tranquilizer was already circulating through his system.

When I turned back to Lhozen, he was on his knees and struggling to stay conscious. I didn't know how many darts were left in the gun, but would they kill him if I emptied the rest into him? Tempting as it was, I still had to free my guys. Plus, he was Arjun's to deal with.

"You...won't..." he slurred, fighting the sedative to lift his head up and shoot me a look of pure rage.

He finally collapsed, and the whole room shifted, like looking at a holographic image from another angle. The quartet band had disappeared, replaced by a vintage record player. A slow spinning vinyl album that played the same classical music as the illusioned band had been.

The bar, furniture, and all the elegant touches of the room disappeared, exposing the cold, empty room underneath. It looked like some kind of hospital storage room, stark white and sterile, with a few stainless steel cabinets, but not much else.

Unfortunately, my ridiculous dress and shoes were very real.

After spending precious seconds just staring at my new surroundings, I grabbed Zipper Guard's gun from his holster. In a moment of quick thinking, I grabbed his access badge too and shoved it down the front of my dress.

Now unguarded with two heavy-as-fuck tranq guns and standing out like a sore thumb in my puffy red dress, I pushed the door ajar with my shoulder. Poking my head out to look both ways down the hallway, I walked out when the coast was clear.

My heels clicked softly, echoing off the metal doors and walls as I headed back to the caged area. I held both guns at my sides, index fingers on each trigger and ready to pull.

Don't worry, guys, I thought. Your shaman's coming.

✣ 19 ✣

MELODY

I walked the hall alone in silence until I reached the long window that looked down over the warehouse full of cages below. Pressing myself to the wall, I had to bunch up my skirt so none of the humans would see it as I peeked through.

Only four humans in lab coats were down there, sitting around the metal table in the center. Two were typing on laptops, one flipped through charts, the other just leaned against the table, chatting. He was the least distracted and, therefore, the biggest threat.

I spotted Raz and Hunter in their cage, pushed back into a dark corner. Raz, still covered in black scales, was barely visible in the shadows. Hunter's form stood out as stark white, with a dark, shadowy form wrapped around him.

Raz, Hunter, I thought. *Don't react, but I escaped. I have two tranq guns and an access card. I can see you guys through the top window.*

My eyes fluttered halfway closed as I sent my presence to them. My dragon and my wolf received my presence in their heads with a flood of relief and warm, loving emotions.

Steluţa, I've never been so happy to hear you and feel you, Raz returned.

Are you guys okay? How's Hunter?

We're both okay. They haven't given us anything since the forced-shifting

827

drugs when you were last here. We still can't shift either way, though. This shit lasts around twenty-four hours.

Are those four humans the only ones here? What's the best way for me to get you guys out?

Yes, but you need to get them away from the desk. There's an alarm button underneath. If they push that, everyone in this compound will come running. I saw them test it last time I was here.

Okay. Can you guys distract them? Maybe get at least one of them to approach your cage?

I'll do what I can, but they might stick us with more drugs.

I have an idea. Just get one of them to approach you.

Okay, my love.

I pulled away from the window, flattening myself against the wall to take deep breaths. As I heard the loud clang of bars down below, I closed my eyes and focused on the illusion.

My red dress became dark green fatigues from head to toe, the strappy black heels shifting into combat boots. And on my belt, an empty holster where I could pretend to fit one of my guns. I pulled the brim of the matching green hat low over my eyes and walked confidently in front of the window.

All four humans now had their attention focused on Raz, banging on his bars and snarling. His jaws gnashed, showing off his pointed dragon teeth as he let out incomprehensible grunts and growls. Knowing him, he was throwing out curses and insults, but because of his partial shift, they couldn't understand him.

"Jesus, will you make it shut the fuck up?" one of the humans said as I reached the top of the stairs and began my descent.

"Happily," another one muttered, reaching for the tranq gun at her hip as she approached the cage. "How many should I empty into him?"

"Give him at least four," laughed another, the one who had been standing and talking.

"No way, he's a dragon. If he dies, our asses are on the line."

They bickered and bantered as I descended the staircase with the softest steps I could manage, desperate to not make my heels click and ruin the illusion. None of them paid any mind as I approached the table, running my fingers just underneath the lip until I found the button. The fucking chatty guy was standing right next to it.

"What's up?" he said, turning to me with a curious look. "Aren't you supposed to be guarding the chick?"

I lifted my gaze to his, ensuring that he saw my face under the brim of the hat, but didn't wait to see his expression transform. I pressed the barrel of the gun against his chest and squeezed the trigger. The moment the dart released, I shoved him backward and took his place to stand right in front of the alarm button.

"Guysssss...," was all he could get out before going down.

The remaining three turned back to me. One guy took off running, and I shot at him twice, the darts going wild. Shooting again, the third one sank into his back.

"Aaaahh, no! Let us go!"

The other two, both women, had gotten close enough to Raz's cage for him to grab them through the bars. They struggled and fought, but my dragon held an arm around one's waist and the other's neck. I lifted my gun and aimed, but the trigger clicked uselessly when I pulled.

"Fuck." I dropped it on the table and raised the other one, catching each of them in the chest with a clean, single shot.

You're good with that thing, steluța, Raz praised.

"Thanks, dragon." I shoved the slumped bodies of the humans out of my way as I unlocked his cage with my stolen access badge.

We barely had time to open the barrier between us and fall into each other's arms when my head was assaulted with voices and visions.

IS THAT THE SHAMAN? IS SHE GOING TO SAVE US?

SHAMAN! LET US OUT!

SHAMAN, MY CHILDREN! PLEASE SAVE MY BABIES!

"Agh, God!" I collapsed into a crumpled heap, my guard illusion now gone as I clutched my head. Every voice was like a hammer cracking through my skull.

Steluța!

"No, don't!" I cried, shaking my head. "Don't talk to me in my head! Fuck, it hurts so fucking bad..."

I wanted to throw up. To bang my head against the bars. To shoot myself with the tranq gun just to make it all stop. Every time this had happened before was nothing compared to this. Every single cry and plea, every desperate voice felt like a sledgehammer was splitting my brain apart.

Somehow, I saw through the unfathomable pain to put the key card into Raz's scaled, clawed hand.

"Get Arjun," I whimpered. "Get him out."

Then I pressed the tranq gun to my chest and fired.

ARJUN

When the flames on the floor of my cell disappeared, I didn't stop holding my breath. Lhozen liked to play games. He liked to *test my strength,* as he called it.

Even after Mel proved to me the flames were an illusion, I couldn't make myself face them. My closet-sized prison cell was four blank walls and those flames. There was nothing else to focus on but them and my fear.

I tried to remember jumping through Raz's fire onstage with him—real flames. Granted, he cooled their temperature and taught me to jump safely, but every practice run with him was a leap of faith. A headfirst jump directly into my fear.

The difference was, I trusted Raz. I could face my fear, because I knew my friend would be on the other side.

I used to trust Lhozen too, but not anymore.

He used these flames as a weapon against me, a tool to break me, to make me an obedient little cat. I wanted to laugh. To tell him to his face that he'd never break me down again, because I found someone to lift me up.

A girl born in a trailer park in Alabama, who had a stick up her arse at my sense of humor and made tea in the fucking microwave.

She wasn't the mate I had expected, but the gorgeous shaman from the shittiest upbringing was more than I could have ever dreamed of. I loved Melody and would never get the chance to show her.

Because as the hours rolled on and those imaginary flames rose higher, my stepfather succeeded in breaking me down.

I curled into a pathetic little ball in the corner of my cell as they stretched across the floor. The heat licking at my skin was too much. I had already screamed my throat raw and couldn't wrap my arms any tighter around myself. My sanity was unraveling.

When the flames disappeared, I knew it was only a matter of time before they'd return. Lhozen would wait until I was lulled into a false sense of security before bringing them back—probably directly on my skin next time.

The minutes ticked by and my paranoia grew. I could hear what sounded like yelling on the other side of my metal door, but chalked them up to hallucinations. Frightened out of my mind of what might come next, it made sense for my brain to create distractions.

When I heard the telltale beep of an access card and my door began sliding open, I knew I was losing it.

"Arrrj." The black, demon-like hallucination growled as he approached.

"Well done, Lhozen." I brought my hands together in a half-hearted clap. "You've won. If Hell exists, I hope demons just like this one fuck you in the arse for all eternity."

"Arrrj!" The creature roared more insistently as he stopped right in front of my face. Damn, he certainly looked real. His clawed, scaly, black hands grabbed my shoulders and gave them a solid shake. Then he slapped me.

It wasn't hard, but was familiar enough to make me look up at his face. He had done it almost in an affectionate way, like a friend would.

Those eyes. Why did this reptilian creature look so familiar?

"Arrrj!" He shook me again. "Sss-raz. Merrrl-dee heerrr."

"Raz?" I blinked. "Raz, that's you?"

He slapped me again and roared victoriously as he pulled me to my feet.

"Wait." I braced against his arms, holding myself up. "Why aren't you using Mel's Speak?"

He stretched his jaws, flashing teeth that rivaled the ferocity and deadliness of my tiger.

"Seee hurrrr." He formed one hand into a gun and pointed it directly at his own chest.

"She's hurt?"

He nodded emphatically. "Shuffft-terz." He clapped his clawed hands to the sides of his head and made a display of being in great pain.

"Of course, the shifters," I breathed, following him dumbfounded out of the cell. "She would feel them right here stronger than at any point before."

He led me to where she laid motionless and propped up in the furry white arms of Hunter, who rocked her gently.

My heart stopped as I ran over to them. "Gods, no! Is she...?"

"Sllleerp." Hunter pointed to the tranquilizer gun, and I sagged with relief.

"Fucking hell. This place is hard enough to escape without her knocked out and you two sounding like cave trolls."

"Narrllawffuh, Arrrj."

"I know it's not your fault, mate," I answered Raz as I inspected the rest of the humans lying on the ground. All out cold. "Would just be a lot easier if I didn't have to infer what the bloody hell you're saying."

I checked over a guy who looked about my height and proceeded to strip his pants off his legs. *Sorry mate, I need these more than you.* "How the hell did you knock all of them out?"

"Merrll drr," Raz inclined his horned head toward Mel. I only then noticed she was in a bright red ballgown. The puffy skirt spread about her and Hunter like a cloud.

"Right." I shook my head, still in disbelief that I hadn't been burned alive. "They must have adrenaline here to counteract the sedatives. No idea if they have anything for you blokes, sorry."

"Serrkuh."

He was either saying *it's okay* or *suck my dick*, neither of which warranted a response as I scanned the shelves lined with small glass bottles. Most of their labels had long pharmaceutical names, and I didn't have a clue how they worked.

All the while, I felt the intensity of hundreds of eyes staring at me. I couldn't hear them, but I knew the shifters in this room were mentally screaming at Mel, pleading for their lives. The moment I saw the adrenaline, I grabbed the whole case of bottles. They would fit into the same cartridge as the tranquilizers for the guns.

"Listen up," I said, turning to address the audience of caged shifters in the room. "There's no time for pleasantries. The lot of you need to shut the fuck up."

I got some head tilts and pawing at their bars, but whatever response they had, I couldn't hear.

"The girl is a shaman and we will all help you escape," I went on. "But you can't bombard her head with pleas and cries and begging. You must trust us. You must allow her to focus on her abilities. But I promise you, we will leave no one behind."

With that, I popped the adrenaline cartridge into the empty gun on the table and returned to where Mel was slumped against Hunter in the cage.

I pressed the gun to her chest and hesitated. "I'm sorry if this hurts, dove." And squeezed the trigger.

Her eyes shot open after a few seconds and her hands immediately went up to the sides of her head. "No, no, I can't be awake."

"Easy, dove." I dropped the gun and pulled her forward, immediately shifting to allow my purr to calm and soothe her. "You're alright. I told them to shut the fuck up. If they're still bothering you, Raz and Hunter will give them something to be scared of."

"Arjun?" she looked up at me, blinking as if unbelieving I was there.

"Yes, it's me, my love."

"You're free!" Her arms wrapped around my neck and her lips found mine.

Kissing her erased the last of my fear that still lingered from my metal box. I crushed her to my chest, feeling her heart against my own, and just relished in the joy of tasting her. My mate. My love.

But I couldn't let go and enjoy her as fully as I would have liked, knowing he could be seeing through me, Hunter, Raz, or any shifter in this place.

"Mel," I rasped, pulling away with regret. "Where's Lhozen, dove? What happened?"

"I knocked him out," she told me, a slight pant in her voice. "He's in a room upstairs, unconscious. I shot him and my guards with tranqs."

"Good girl," I praised, smoothing her hair away from her face. Unable to help myself, I kissed her again before resting my forehead on hers. "I knew you could. As cynical a bastard as I am, I knew you'd find a way."

"Arjun." Her expression turned grave as she licked her lips. "Something's... wrong with him. I don't know what, but he's completely delusional. He dressed me up like this, made a show of a fancy dinner and dancing for no reason. It's almost like he lives entirely in illusions and has forgotten about reality."

"I see." I measured her words carefully. "But you left him alive for me?"

"I did." A wicked grin came across her beautiful face. "He's all yours."

"Good. Up you go. Our work isn't done here."

Mel, Hunter, and I exited the cage to find Raz loading more tranquilizers into guns and setting them on the table.

Found their stash, he chuckled amusedly, then gave me a pointed look. *Can you hear me now?*

"I can, Raz." I answered, squeezing Mel's nape. "I had a hell of a time trying to communicate with these wankers while you were out, dove."

"Sorry I missed that," she muttered, dark eyes flashing as she watched me load another adrenaline cartridge into the gun I had just used on her. "You going to wake him up?"

"Yeah." I double checked the weapon before observing all the guns and cartridges laid out on the table. "Think you three can hold the fort here while I'm dealing with him?"

We have enough tranquilizers to bring down a herd of buffalo, so I think we can manage any more humans wandering in here, Raz observed.

"So we'll start unlocking cages and giving First Aid to those who need it," Mel said before glancing back at me. "And finding a way for everyone to get out of here, while you're busy."

"It's a plan." I slid a hand across her lower back and pulled her in for another kiss, sending my tongue past her lips this time, now that I knew Lhozen was unconscious and couldn't see.

"Be careful," she told me solemnly, giving me a hard look. "And don't hesitate to call me if you need backup." She tapped her temple, and I kissed her there, too.

"I will," I promised her. "But I'll tell you right now, I'll be taking my time with him. There are things he needs to answer for."

She nodded in understanding and let me go to start removing access badges from the unconscious humans.

Shove a sword down his throat for me, Raz called after me as I jogged up the stairs.

"Oh, I'll make him wish for that," I promised.

❧ 21 ❧

ARJUN

I pulled open five of those bloody metal doors before I found him. He and the two guards were lying where Mel left them, sprawled out on the floor. Standing over his body, I took a moment to look at my stepfather before shooting him full of adrenaline.

He definitely looked older than when I last saw him. I remembered my first few months in captivity, yearning for the days he'd sit with me and Mum over tea. He told stories of the shaman from years before and their shifter companions. One thing I always remembered vividly was how strongly he felt about humans and shifters coexisting peacefully.

He adored and loved Mum so much. My own father left our family to pursue another tigress who he felt was his true mate. Lhozen never treated me like a member of a different species. He affectionately called me son and filled every role that a father should.

At least he did until Mum died.

I yanked the empty tranquilizer cartridge out of his belly and pressed the gun against the same spot. The trigger pull made his whole body jerk from the impact. Then I sat back on my heels and waited.

His eyes shot open, blinking rapidly before he rubbed them with a heavy groan.

"Hello, Lhozen," I greeted.

"Arjun," he said with what almost sounded like pleasant surprise as he pushed himself up.

With a quick shove to his shoulder, I laid him flat on his back again with a grunt.

"I like you better like this, I think." My teeth ground together as I spoke and my index finger danced along the trigger of the gun. How tempting it was just to make his heart explode with adrenaline and end this bullshit now.

"This isn't exactly proper, is it?" he complained, but didn't try to sit up again. "Why don't we chat over tea like adults?"

"Why don't you stay exactly where you are?" I suggested, waving the gun in front of his face. "And explain to me what's proper about rounding up shifters, keeping them in cages, and pumping them full of drugs?"

"Really now, Arjun?" he sighed as if incredulous.

"Yes, really," I demanded, willing my voice not to crack. "How could you love Mum and treat others like this? How could you call me a son and do this to *me?*"

"Because you're being short-sighted and not seeing the whole picture!" he spat. "You don't see the vision that I do, the world in which your kind become the saviors of humanity."

Mel was right. He really was delusional. "What the bloody hell are you talking about?"

"Come on, Arjun. You're not daft. Look at the numbers, the data. The number one killer of humans is heart disease. Then diabetes, then cancer. How many shifters have died from those diseases?"

"Probably none because humans kill us first."

"Exactly, none! When was the last time you had a cold? The whole time you were in captivity, did you ever fall ill?"

My stomach seemed to turn in on itself, bile building up in my throat. "That's why you did it? As an experiment?"

"The human race is killing itself, Arjun. Shifters are thriving and hiding in plain sight. We can coexist, but us humans must save ourselves first."

"By enslaving us?!" I demanded. "What about Razvan the dragon, remember him? Hunter the Wolf Man? What's the greater good for exhibiting them like freaks?"

"Not all experiments are successful. The... uncooperative ones cannot be returned home, for risk of retribution against me from their communities."

I shook my head, unable to believe this was a real conversation happening between us. "You've truly lost your mind. Mum would be horrified at what you've done. I can't make heads or tails of whatever you're trying to do."

"Your mum," he whispered, his eyes becoming watery. "She would be proud of me."

"No, she fucking wouldn't."

"I miss her so much," he went on as if he didn't hear me. "When I gather enough data on shifter genetics, I may be able to bring her back."

My eyes nearly fell out of my head. "You what?"

"I still have a lock of her hair," his hand clamored up to the breast pocket of his jacket. "Cloning is more difficult with a mixture of animal and human DNA. I've already tried a few times. But when she returns to us, Arjun," he swept a hand, and the room transformed into an elegant parlor, the mirror image of the one we used to have back at home, "everything needs to be as it was before she was taken from us."

I could only gawk at my stepfather in disbelief. The only explanation I could fathom was that he snapped after she died. Like Mel said, his whole life became one big illusion. Coupled with his drinking, it must have driven him to avoid his grief, his new reality without her.

And hundreds, if not thousands, of shifters had suffered for it.

"You cannot get in my way, Arjun," he said, pushing himself up to sitting once again. "I've always loved you like my own son, but you and that girl cannot stop what must be done."

Something bright flickered at the corner of my eye and I yelped, dropping the gun and jumping away as my whole left arm became engulfed in flames.

I slapped my arm against the floor and rolled around desperately in my panic. *No, no, no! Put it out, I'm going to die!*

Even in my crazy desperation, my mind registered seeing Lhozen climbing to his feet, and it jogged a recent memory. Large dark eyes, raven black hair, and gentle hands on my skin. A voice telling me it wasn't real.

Only my fear made it real.

I forced myself to be still, holding my arm out in front of me. The flames danced and flickered, casting light and heat, but my arm was not burning.

Mel, you amazing, beautiful woman, you've saved me. You've saved us all.

My other hand unsnapped my pants, and I stepped out of them. I didn't even have to think about shifting. My tiger rose to the surface as easily as breathing. His was the blood we needed to spill since the beginning. Vengeance for our kind and our family.

"Lhozen," I growled, striding toward him while I could still walk upright. My teeth already pointed past my lips and stripes erupted on my skin.

He turned, nearly falling on his ass again when he saw that preying on my fear didn't work. My arm, now fire-free, lifted and pointed a long, curled claw at him.

"We arrrre stopping you," I said around my long teeth and tongue. "This ends with *yourrrr* blood."

I completed my shift and pounced.

My paws on his back sent him crashing down with a pitiful scream. I extended my claws and raked downward, enjoying the stretch while I turned his skin to bloody red ribbons.

He screamed so fucking loud, wailing like a banshee, but I didn't want to bite his throat yet. I wanted to make him feel just an ounce of the suffering he imparted on me for four long years. For everything he had done to Raz. And to Hunter. To Roo and Rinna. And every shifter that hadn't survived his cruelty.

I grabbed his ankle between my jaws and thrashed my head back and forth. Something snapped and his screams took on a new, higher pitch while his leg flopped around uselessly.

Shaking him until I was bored, I licked my lips and purred contentedly as I walked a slow, lazy circle around him. *What shall I break next?*

"Your soul will never be saved for doing this," he whimpered.

"You'll be reborn as a parasite. You'll never undo the harm you've done!"

It's already too late for me, I thought. *But it fills me with joy to know you'll never be saved, either.*

I meant that in the spiritual and physical sense. His screams could be heard across the compound, yet no one had come running to his rescue. Granted, any remaining humans were probably lying unconscious in the cage room.

The thought made me pause before taking another bite out of Lhozen's other leg.

I shouldn't be enjoying this alone, I realized. *The others deserve to take their own vengeance, too.*

With that, I grabbed his trouser leg between my teeth, careful not to pierce his flesh, and began dragging him toward the door.

"No, no! Where are you taking me?" he cried pitifully.

I ignored him, leaving a trail of blood as I pulled him along the floor to the hallway. He was not a small man and dragging him was somewhat cumbersome, but I reached the top of the stairs within a few minutes.

Down below, the scene was chaos.

Birds screeched and flew in circles around the room. A bear stood on her hind legs and roared, her cubs greedily nursing from her. Lynxes and foxes yowled as they ran around the room. Mel sat at the center table, tending to some minor wounds on a coyote; Julian, I presumed.

Lhozen let out a cry of pain and the room went silent, all eyes turning to me. Mel smiled, but her eyes held questions.

I placed a paw on Lhozen's shoulder and let out a victorious roar.

I had my words with him, I told Mel. *And spilled the blood I needed to spill. I thought it only fair to share with everyone else.*

None of the shifters responded, so I had no idea if they heard me or not. But Mel turned to address the room and repeat my words.

"Arjun's done with Lhozen," she declared. "He's free for all of you to take a swing, bite or scratch."

"NO! NO! PLEASE!"

His cries were drowned out by the cacophony of the jungle. Even Hunter howled and Raz managed to breathe small puffs of fire. I roared once more. Had I been in human form, I might have beaten my chest. *We won.* I could hardly believe it.

With one shove of my paw, Lhozen went swiftly down the stairs and the mob descended on him. To my surprise, everyone took a turn delivering a non-fatal blow. The larger animals waited patiently for their turn while the smaller ones gnawed, scratched, and swiped at him.

Blood dripped down the stairs, and Lhozen's cries soon turned to meaningless gurgles. I wasn't sure, but I thought one of the birds removed his tongue.

Finally, the she-bear hovered over him after her cubs were done gnawing at his fingers and toes. She stared at him for a long moment, then looked at me and shifted to a blonde woman with a strong, muscular build.

"You deserve the killing blow," she said. "I don't want to take that honor away from you."

I've already taken what I needed. Please, go ahead. Remembering she couldn't hear me, I lowered my head and inclined it to her, prompting her to go ahead with it.

"No, tiger brother." She smiled. "I heard the shaman say he raised you as a father. For you, this won't end here. You may carry his betrayal as a scar on your heart for the rest of your life. Begin your healing now, by taking away his power."

She stepped away, gathering her cubs to her, and I lowered my head even further in respect. Then I slowly padded down the steps.

Lhozen's face was unrecognizable. His breathing came out soft, wheezing and weak. Whether I finished him or not, he would die soon.

I lifted my gaze to Mel, and she gave me a small, encouraging nod. With a pleased, rumbling purr in my chest, I opened my jaws wide and closed them over his windpipe.

MELODY

The compound turned out to be a maze of hallways and tunnels, but with the help of the shifters, we were soon able to locate a discreet exit.

It had been set up to look like a sewage drain that emptied not far from the beach. That only showed how far Lhozen's delusions went. He constructed this whole elaborate place to secretly move shifters in and out, even without using Semblance.

Most of the shifters left immediately, eager to get back to their families, loved ones, and simply enjoy their freedom. A few lingered behind, like Julian and Anya, the she-bear with her cubs.

"Thank you," Julian said shyly for perhaps the hundredth time. "And sorry again, for uh, freaking out while you were talking to me with your mind."

He was utterly adorable. Tall and thin, with a mop of dark hair falling into his eyes. I wanted to adopt him as an older brother.

"Of course. Don't mention it." I said, hugging him around his waist. "If you ever come to Georgia, look me up. We have a big house and will be happy to host you. You too, Anya."

"I'm heading to Canada," she replied with a hint of apology. "Perfect weather up there, plenty of food. Wide open wilderness with fewer humans. No offense."

"None taken," I told her. "Have a safe journey."

"You as well, Melody. Thank you for being one of the good ones. I'll tell my grandchildren about you."

Raz and Hunter were still stuck between their shifts, so I used the last remaining mental focus I had to make them invisible on our walk back to the hotel. Arjun kept mostly silent after killing Lhozen. I wondered if it was bothering him more than he wanted to admit.

My wolf and my dragon collapsed together on the couch the moment we reached the room. With Raz's black scales and Hunter's white fur, they looked like polar opposites, but so perfectly together intertwined. Seeing them together made my heart want to burst. I got so close to losing them, but now they were safe. We were all safe.

I could have watched them happily or jumped into the middle of their cuddle pile if I wanted to. But right then, I wanted to check on a certain tiger.

Arjun remained silent and detached. He stood in the middle of the living room like he no longer knew what to do. He still wore the pants he had stolen from a human and Lhozen's dried blood on his neck and chest.

"Hey," I said, running my hand along his arm as I approached him carefully. "You okay?"

His arm wrapped around my shoulders, pulling me into his side as that ocean-colored gaze lowered to mine.

"I was just wondering what airline we should fly home on. It's been so long since I flew first class, I forgot which one has the best tea."

"What?" I blinked.

He chuckled, kissing my hairline. "I'm ready to get the fuck out of dodge, dove. As soon as those two can shift, I want to go home and I want to be bloody comfortable on the way there."

"Me too," I admitted. "I wonder if everything went okay with Connor. God, I'm dying to see my siblings again. But," I chewed my lip, blushing. "I've never been on a plane before."

"Ah, yes. I should've known." He squeezed my shoulder affectionately. "First class is going to ruin you, then. You'll never go back to economy seating."

"What's that?" I purposely widened my eyes as big as they could go. "Has Hell frozen over? I just told you something I've never done, and you didn't give me shit for it."

"Because I'm not that thick to take the piss out of a girl when I'm trying to figure out how to get in bed with her."

Now my eyes were wide out of genuine surprise. "You... what?"

"I'm rubbish at this whole seduction thing," he muttered, looking away from me. "I've never really done it before. I'm not brash and outspoken like Connor, silver-tongued like Raz, or cool and aloof like Hunter."

"No, you're not any of them." I brought a hand up to his cheek to make him look at me again. "You're Arjun. You faced your worst fear and taught me everything I knew to bring down evil today. We never, in a million years, could have pulled this off without you." My heart slammed into my throat, but I wouldn't let the rest of my words go unspoken.

"And I love you."

He sucked in a sharp breath as he turned to me, holding my shoulders with both hands.

"Mel—" I raised a hand to cut him off.

"I know you're not into the whole sharing thing and I get that. I don't want to make anything weird for you so I—"

He cut me off with a kiss, hard and possessive, that made me weak in the knees. His tongue forced its way past my lips in a way that felt just as intimate as sex. He didn't kiss or love freely, so my head was completely spinning as I came up for air.

"I told you, you are my mate," he said gruffly. "So what if you're the others' mate, too? You're still mine." His hand released its firm grip on my shoulder and moved up to caress my neck. "And I'm yours, dove. All of me is yours."

"You mean that?" I asked. "But you were so against it before—"

"Because I'm a fool," he muttered, running a thumb across my cheek. "The human side of me is, anyway. My tiger knew all along. Since I first heard your voice in my head. You saved me, my love. Not just from captivity, not just from my fear, but from dying a lonely old man because I was too stubborn to see what was right in front of me."

"Arjun..." I breathed his name as I curled my fingers into his skin. His muscles flexed beneath my hands, matching the needy pulse in my core. I wanted him. I wanted to feel alive with him and never take life or freedom for granted again.

Bits of dried blood flaked under my fingers and I couldn't help laughing as I rubbed it off his chest.

"Rule number one of seduction," I teased, "you should be showered and clean before trying to get a girl in bed with you."

"Right," he chuckled, inspecting himself. "You'd think that'd be common sense, yeah?" he said, wiping at the remaining blood on his chest.

"Rule number two," I said, stepping away as I slid my hand into his. "Showers are much more fun with a partner."

A beautiful grin spread across his face as his eyes lit up. "I like where this is going."

He followed me to his room, bypassing Raz and Hunter, who had fallen asleep in each other's arms. My poor boys had to be exhausted. I was too and a hot, relaxing shower sounded amazing, even when I had taken a bath just a few hours ago. Being with Arjun was just a bonus.

It wasn't until I turned on the hot water and we stood in front of each other that I realized I was still wearing the ridiculous red dress.

"Unzip me?" I turned my back to him and lifted my hair. My skin was practically vibrating with anticipating another touch from him. He finally touched me after what felt like thirty seconds, but nowhere near the zipper.

"It looks beautiful on you," he observed, his palm against the nape of my neck. The other hand came around the front to hold my jaw as he rasped into my ear, "but it would look better on the floor."

"Where'd you hear that one?" I laughed at the cheesiness of the line, but my breath quickly turned to gasps and soft moans as he covered my neck and shoulders with kisses. When he finally unzipped the dress and pulled it down, the kisses continued in a slow, sensual trail down my spine.

A question came to me as I turned around, pulling him toward me with the waistband of his pants. "Have you done this before?"

"Have sex?" He looked surprised, then embarrassed. "Yes. Why?"

"You just seem to know what you're doing." I flicked open the button, then unzipped him slowly. "For someone who was raised to take this stuff so seriously."

He chewed his lip, looking away and letting out a breath as if ashamed. "I had a... friend with benefits, you could say. We were both set up in arranged marriages and kind of commiserated over it. We got along and had physical chemistry, but were never in love. We kept it a secret, because of the shame it would bring to our families."

"Arjun." I said his name as I reached into his pants and filled my palm with him, enjoying the change in expression on his face. "You don't have to be ashamed of having a past. I have one too. Even before I met the other guys."

"I know, it's just," he sighed, rolling his eyes upward. "Mum never knew. She would have been so disappointed. I know it's dumb and doesn't really matter, but I still feel guilty that I wasn't the son she could be proud of." He drummed his fingers against the glass wall of the shower, now filling up with steam. "And especially now that I've killed her husband."

I opened the shower door and stepped inside, pulling him after me. His hands slid around my waist as we stood under the stream of water together.

"If she is watching, I'm sure she's proud of you," I said, watching the rivulets wind down the hard contours of his body. "You saved so many lives today. You overcame your fear. Hell, even if she's not, *I'm* proud of you, Arjun."

"Thank you, dove," he murmured, his pupils large as he looked at me. "She would've liked you, I think," he added with a small smile. "If you were Indian and living in England, she might even approve of me marrying you."

"Hah," I scoffed. "Well, I'm not, and I never was." My hands tangled in his hair, enjoying how the thick, dark tresses moved across my palms from the force of the water. "But I'm here. Right now."

"Yes," he agreed. "You are. And you're *mine*."

His next kiss pushed my back against the marble-tiled wall. I swore I heard a feline growl as his mouth devoured mine. Both of us slippery and wet, he kept me pressed to the wall as he slid down my body.

Kneeling in front of me, he kissed my vulva with just as much passion and hunger as my mouth. A moan escaped me as his tongue parted my folds, one hand reaching up to tease my nipple between his fingers.

I had to take a moment and silently thank his old friend with benefits. He *really* knew what he was doing.

Jolts fired through my limbs as his skilled tongue lashed at my clit. With one large hand, he pressed my hip back, preventing me from bucking against his face as much as I would've liked. So I settled for running my fingers through his hair while he ate me like a fine meal.

And as cats tend to do with their meals, he played with me. Tortured me. He took me to the edge of release, panting and trembling, before moving away to kiss my thighs or the crease in my hips.

"You're the worst," I moaned when he denied me once again, his teeth tracing the edge of my hipbone.

"Oh? Do the others give you what you want so easily?" he smirked, thoroughly enjoying my torment.

"Not always," I admitted reluctantly. "I should've known you'd be such a tease."

"Remember this, dove." His fingertips traced across my inner thighs, swirling and moving over the sensitive skin for the sole purpose of making me quiver. "I didn't fall under your spell like the others. You don't have the same power over me as you do them."

He brought his mouth and fingers right up against my pussy. My tender flesh ached for contact, pressure, sensation, anything.

"What do you mean by that?" I asked, fighting to make words through my brain being a jumbled mess.

"It means you can't tame a tiger."

With that, he sealed his mouth over my clit and pressed two fingers inside me at the same time. I gasped at the sudden fullness, the pressure I'd been craving building up faster than I could handle.

My release came explosively. I shook so hard, he had to press me against the wall to stay upright. Even after coming down from the high, my legs wobbled to the point of sinking to sit on the shower floor.

With a chuckle, Arjun shut off the water and wrapped me in a fluffy, luxurious towel. He carried me to the bed and laid me down gently. When he moved to get up, I grabbed his arm and pulled him back, wrapping my legs around his waist to prevent him from leaving.

"What makes you think you can tame *me*, tiger?"

23

MELODY

Arjun's grin was somewhere between shy and wily. The water droplets clinging to his skin defined his already breathtaking physique even more, and I didn't want to waste one second of not seeing him.

"I'm still wet," he said.

"So am I."

I wrapped a hand around his neck to pull him down to me, not caring that he dripped more water onto my bare skin. The towel underneath me would suffice.

His mouth captured mine as he hovered over me, and I caught the light, musky scent of my sex on his face. I let out a little growl of my own and kissed him harder. Despite not being a shifter, something about my own scent on my man felt animalistic and primal. I had marked him. He was mine.

"Maybe you do have a little tiger in you," he murmured, nipping at the column of my throat as he settled between my legs. His muscular thighs pushed mine apart, and his hands ran down the sides of my body like he was just in awe of me.

I explored him the same way, closing my eyes to relish in the feeling of what his mouth was doing to me. My fingers traced the ridges of his chest and abs like my eyes had done so many times before. I felt where his skin texture changed from the burn scars and had the overwhelming urge to kiss them.

"Roll over," I told him, tapping his arm.

"Why?" His voice was muffled in the crook of my neck as he planted lazy kisses there.

"Because I want to be on top."

"Mm. I'm quite comfortable here, though."

"Really, Arjun?" I sighed, raking my nails up his back. "Is this how it's gonna be every time?"

"Hmm, scratch me again like that and I might reconsider."

Digging in harder this time, I ran my hands slower up that wide, broad landscape of muscle and skin. His response was absolutely erotic, arching under my touch and releasing the hottest sounds, something between a growl and a moan. Jesus, I couldn't get enough of this man. Even if he was infuriating sometimes.

"Fuck me," he groaned, shuddering deliciously. "I should call you kitten instead of dove."

I forgot all about fighting him to get on top, because he started rolling forward, pressing his solid cock against my flesh that was still so sensitive from his teasing earlier. He slid against me a few times without penetration. Again with the torture.

His shaft rested, hot and heavy, on my clit, slowly moving back and forth. He watched me silently, hovering above me as he worked my body into a frenzy with just the slightest movement.

"Enjoying yourself?" I huffed, frustrated and vulnerable under the intensity of his gaze. My thighs squeezed around his hips. My hands grabbed the sheets, his forearms, anything they could. My pussy closed around nothing. And yet, he watched me unravel while practically being as still as a statue.

"Yes," he answered softly. "I could watch the woman I love writhe in pleasure for days. I've never seen anything so beautiful."

Those words made me pause and stare up at him. He returned my stare with a kiss that pressed me down into the pillows, then he pressed forward into me.

The sudden fullness of him forced me to break the kiss with a gasp.

That upward curve I saw in the cell was now stroking my inner walls in ways I didn't know could feel so good. My moan echoed around the room as I clung to him, digging my nails into his back again.

His growls were soft, but intense, right next to my ear as his thrusts steadily deepened. To hear his desire without words, that primal expression of pleasure rumbling deep in his chest, was hotter than any dirty talk. It made my legs quiver again, my toes curling into his calf muscles as he filled me to the brim.

"Jesus, Mel," he rasped, pausing while fully seated inside me. Again, he watched in fascination as I shook and convulsed around him. This time I saw his jaw clench against losing his precious control. His dick felt like a hot iron inside me, flexing with the effort to hold back his own release. It made that delicious curve press against me harder and extend my pleasure.

"God, stop that," I laughed. "I can't catch a breath."

"Neither can I," he mused, skimming a palm up the side of my ribcage. He cupped my breast briefly before moving on, caressing my neck and looking at me like I was some kind of wonder of the world. "You're absolutely breathtaking."

Heat rushed through me from head to toe, and it had nothing to with sex. "Aww, I like you when you're sweet." Damn, why were compliments hard for me? Especially from him. Ever since I met him, I wished he would stop fucking around and just say what he meant. Now, after falling for him, hearing words like that were almost overwhelming.

"And you love me every other time?" he teased, nipping my earlobe. "Especially when I'm an arse?"

"Oh, especially then," I groaned.

He slid his arms between my back and the bed, bringing my chest to his with a warm, passionate kiss. In the next moment, we went rolling across the mattress until I was straddling him.

"You wanted to be on top?" he grinned, smugly placing his hands behind his head.

"That doesn't mean I do all the work, tiger," I retorted.

He was still seated inside me and I began a gentle rolling of my hips, enjoying the view from where I sat. His eyes were half-closed and his teeth dug into his bottom lip as I rode him. His biceps bulged from the placement of his arms behind his head and I skimmed my hands down those hard surfaces. Exploring him like he had done me, I smoothed my palms over his chest, pressing into them as I raised and lowered myself on his thick shaft.

When I found that scar tissue along his ribs, I lowered my mouth to kiss him there. Grazing my lips and tongue across the ridges of his abdomen, I kissed the one on his opposite side.

"Why are you doing that?" His tone was curious, not accusatory.

I braced my forearms on his chest, still riding him at a slow, leisurely pace. "Because I like your body and I want to kiss it?"

"But why my scars?" He brought his arms down to push hair back from my face and caress my neck and back. His blue-green eyes were dark, dilated with lust.

"I don't know," I admitted. "They'll always be a part of you, a reminder of what you went through. It's a painful memory for you but maybe if I kiss them, the memories will hurt a little less."

A breath hitched in his chest as he cupped my face. "Gods, I love you, Mel. What did I ever do to deserve you in my life?"

Our mouths came together in a crash of passion and need. His hands went to my hips, supporting me as he thrust upward. My whole body surged with the pleasure of each impact of him into me. I couldn't control myself and neither could he.

I could only feel, take, and give. I felt him in my fingertips and toes with each hard inch he gave me. When I heard his growls, felt his fingers digging into my flesh, tasted the sweat on his skin, I wanted to give him more. More pleasure, more of me. My brave, beautiful tiger deserved nothing less.

At some point we rolled over again, and he held nothing back, pounding into me and filling me with a delicious ache that I couldn't get enough of. We didn't speak aside from groaning, kisses, and gasps. This was raw and primal, but still so human.

This wasn't a meaningless fuck to further our species, we were lovers. We faced death today. We faced losing each other before we had a chance to begin.

I couldn't speak for Arjun, but I would look back on this every time we came together as one again. I'd kiss him with everything in me and sink into bliss every time he sank into me. I'd kiss his scars and remember how close I came to losing him. And no matter how much he pissed me off, I'd never take my tiger for granted.

His thumb pressed to my clit the moment I started quivering again, and his mouth swallowed my moan. My release came like a tidal wave crashing and he followed, filling me with warmth as he roared into the pillow next to my head.

His heart hammered against mine, his chest a heavy weight on top of me, but I loved the safety and solidness of him. My hands remained wrapped around his back, my thighs attached to his hips.

We stayed like that, kissing and intertwined long after we came down from our highs, as if to make up for all the times we wanted to before, but didn't.

24

CONNOR

"I need to go back."

Miriam, Colt, and Gabe all stared at me, dumbfounded across the table.

"You can't," Miriam said, her voice wavering with concern. "It's too dangerous, Connor. I've seen—"

"Exactly *why* I need to go back," I interrupted her. "I can't just sit around with my thumb up my ass while Mel and the guys are risking their lives. It's been three days. I'm going fuckin' nuts."

"Connor, you're not a shaman or a shifter," she protested, her voice pleading. "You'll be walking into that situation completely unprepared. Do you even know how to get into the compound?"

"I'll figure it out," I said, rising from the table. "I'll go to the hotel first, see who's there and get updates."

"And if no one's there?" The inquiry came from Gabe. "What'll you do then?"

"Why, you volunteering to come with me, Wolf Boy? You gonna help me out by following their scent trail? No? Then don't fuckin' worry about it. Keep staying all tucked in and cozy in *my* house while I'm out checking on *your* brother."

"It's a valid question, Connor," Colt said, watching me cautiously.

"It's not wise to go back there alone with no plan. You have no idea what you're up against."

I kind of do, actually—Arjun's stepfather. The whole thing threw me for such a loop, I couldn't bring myself to tell Miriam, Lhozen's former apprentice. If he was as bad as Arjun said, who knew how far his illusions extended? I couldn't get her involved while the others were dealing with him.

"And what about the four other kids you brought home?" Gabe wouldn't let up. "You're just gonna up and leave them in our care?"

"Jeanie's not a kid. She's been taking care of them since she was, though," I shot back, fighting the urge to punch him in his face. "She's got it handled. They don't need a babysitter."

Finished with the conversation, I hurried out to start the RV. Damn, in times like these, I really needed a smaller vehicle. Now that we had money coming, I could actually think about that stuff. Not that I planned to drive across state lines to rescue my woman with any regularity.

Once the engine roared to life, I propped my prosthetic feet on the dashboard and double checked to make sure everything was secure. I went back to Dr. Selow yesterday, and he made a few minor adjustments. Now the prototypes felt perfect. For a moment at the breakfast table, I had completely forgotten that I didn't have my own legs anymore.

With Mel's gorgeous face in my mind, I tapped my shirt pocket to ensure the document I got from the doctor was still there. I couldn't wait to see her face when I showed it to her.

Because I *would* see her again. Despite the heart-crushing, shitty feeling that something had gone terribly wrong, I knew my girl wouldn't go down without a fight. And she had a lot of fight in her.

After letting the engine run for a few minutes, I brought my feet down, checked my mirrors, and started driving onto the gravel path.

I had just reached the edge of the property line, where the gravel road became paved again as it wound around the pristine FDR building when I saw them.

Four figures walked alongside each other through the FDR Center grounds. Two tall men, one starkly pale and the other with medium brown skin. Between them, a man with short, dark hair had a tattooed arm over the shoulders of a woman.

My woman.

I'd recognize that raven black hair, doe eyes, and creamy skin from a mile away. My mouth dropped open and I don't know how I didn't have a heart attack right then. They were home, and they were okay.

Thankfully, my brain worked enough to hit the brakes and put the RV in park before stumbling out the door like a drunken sailor.

"Mel?" I hollered as my legs carried me to them, blinking rapidly and rubbing my eyes to make sure it wasn't an illusion. "Babe? Guys, is that you?"

"Going on a camping trip, Con?" Raz joked. He released his arm around Mel's shoulders as she leaped forward, clasping her hands tightly around my neck and her legs around my waist.

"Thank God. Thank fucking God," was all I could utter at feeling her warmth and love wrapped around me.

"Jeanie?" she asked me, eyes wide. "The kids? Are they...?"

"They're all here, babe. Safe and sound," I assured her, taking in her smile, her eyes, and her heart beating against mine. It felt like she'd been away for months instead of mere days. "Fuck, I missed you so much."

"I missed you, too." Her lips found mine and nothing in my life ever tasted sweeter. I wanted to drink her in until my last breath.

Her legs eventually slid down to the ground and our lips parted, though her head stayed firmly attached to my chest. I had no intention of untangling our physical contact today. Maybe not even tomorrow.

"Fellas," I said, holding my arms out to the guys. "It's good to see y'all too. I take it you have a hell of a story for me."

"Like you wouldn't believe, mate," Arjun muttered, clapping his arm around me in a bro hug. I noticed how he touched Mel's waist too and looked at her adoringly. A world of difference from the sneaky looks and pretending to ignore her from before.

Ah, so that finally happened. I lifted an eyebrow at her and she confirmed it with a small nod, a grin threatening to spread across her face.

"Did the pups behave?" Hunter asked when he came in for his hug.

"No," I laughed. "But it's okay. They shifted right in front of Mel's siblings before we had a chance to explain anything. We had an interesting discussion but everything worked out."

"Really?" Mel's brow knitted worriedly. "Jeanie is so protective of the kids. I figured it would be weeks before she warmed up to the idea."

"That might have been ideal, but not practical, with two rambunctious pups running around," I winked at Hunter, who rolled his eyes.

"I'm gonna kill them," he groaned.

"No need. Jeanie had her reservations, but after that talk, she's really warmed up to the shifters. And the kids? They were running around and playing with the pups immediately. It was like they didn't even care. They were so excited just to have new friends to play with."

"Aww, good! They've really needed that." Mel pressed her face into my chest and squeezed around my waist. "They need friends and a real family. A normal life."

"Same with the pups," Hunter agreed, kissing the top of her head. "Having friends, especially."

"Ain't nothing normal about this family," I chuckled, turning around to head back to the RV. "But that's what so great about it."

"Have fun turning that bitch around," Raz laughed. Fucking dragon. I missed him, too.

"Kiss my ass, man. I'll have you know I do beautiful thirteen-point turns in this thing. Babe?" I squeezed Mel into my side. "Ride with me?"

"Sure," she laughed. "All the way back to the house—ahhh!"

I picked her up and threw her over my shoulder caveman style as her screaming-laugh rang out across the landscape. The RV door slammed behind us and I didn't waste any time. I threw her down on that tiny mattress where we made so many memories, and kissed my woman with everything in me.

"God, I missed you so much," I murmured against her skin, kissing every square inch I came across. "I was heading back to Florida because I couldn't stand not knowing if you were okay."

"We had good timing then," she breathed, sliding her legs up around my waist.

I lowered my forehead to hers, watching her face carefully try to hide her expressions. "How crazy was it?"

"Just as Arjun said," she sighed. "Like you wouldn't believe. I don't even know where to start."

"So you and him." I kissed her neck, breathing her in. "How long did it take for that to happen?"

"Well," she laughed lightly. "We got captured, and it technically didn't happen until after we got out."

"Captured? You?"

"All of us." She smoothed her hands up my chest and pushed gently. "We'll tell you everything, but let me up. I want to see my sister."

"Fine," I groaned, pressing her down into the mattress with another hard kiss before releasing her. She joined me in the passenger seat a second later, face flushed and lips swollen. Just how I liked her.

The RV barely got rolling on the gravel path when two blurs raced past us like a pair of bullets toward the house.

"The fuck—"

"It's Arjun and Hunter," Mel laughed. "They shifted and looks like they're racing. Shifters, always competing against each other."

"Fair enough, but where's Raz?"

Tap-tap-tap.

A black claw surrounded by obsidian scales clicked against my driver's side window. Grey eyes and a toothy grin greeted me in my peripheral vision.

"Looks like he gave the others a head start," Mel observed. She leaned over and blew a kiss at the dragon flying alongside us. He responded by licking my window.

"I swear to God, Raz," I yelled, rolling down the window just a crack. "If you make me run over one of these potholes, you're buying me a new car."

He let out a series of grunts that sounded like cackling laughter before flying away, easily beating the running shifters on the ground.

"Oh my God." Mel covered her mouth, blinking away tears as we pulled up to the house. Jeanie stood on the porch with Riley on her hip, the two of them looking skyward and pointing at the dragon flying overhead.

"It's okay, babe." I reached over and squeezed her knee. "She knows about Raz, too. Seriously, she's taken to everything really well. So have the little ones."

"I know, it's just…" she paused to wipe her eyes, then jumped out of her seat, and went running up to the porch the moment the RV stopped. "Jeaniiiiieee!"

Not wanting to intrude on them, I watched through the windshield as the girls hugged each other, both of them crying. Bella and Joey, who'd been playing with the pups, screamed Mel's name as they ran to the porch.

Even I had to wipe a tear as I saw them all together. The relief and joy was clear in their tear-streaked faces, how tightly they held each other, and how they laughed uncontrollably with joy.

This was all that Mel had wanted from the beginning. A safe, loving home for her family. She just happened to take a few detours and met four handsome knuckleheads along the way.

But I had a few more surprises for her and waited until she and her siblings were done hugging.

"Short trip, huh?" Gabe cracked at me as I exited the RV.

"Uh, yeah." I couldn't bring myself to still be pissed at him. Not after witnessing a moment like that.

"Look, sorry about before," he muttered. "I'm glad she's back, and that everyone's okay."

I lifted my chin in surprise. Maybe there was more to the young wolf than being an immature dick. "Thanks, man. I appreciate it."

"Miriam and Colt and I'll be heading home soon," he added, shoving his hands in his pockets. "We'll let y'all have some family time."

"Thanks," I said again. "See you around, Gabe."

"See ya, Connor."

Mel, Jeanie, and the younger ones were making a racket in the kitchen by the time I headed inside.

"We wanna make a cake!" Joey declared.

"Oh, but we need cake-making stuff," Mel answered, lifting her gaze to me and playfully mouthing, *help me.*

I curled my finger at her to beckon her closer, drawing her into the empty theater room.

"Told you they were well-adjusted."

"I'm so relieved," she sighed. "I was worried about how they'd react to... everything."

"Shifters, four boyfriends." I lifted my hands as if weighing both options. "There's probably weirder shit out there."

"Connor." Her smile fell. "How long will we be able to stay here? I know Dr. Selow said as long as you're using their services but with four more people now—"

"I'm so glad you asked, babe." I grinned, fishing the document out of my shirt pocket and waving the papers in front of her face.

"What's that?"

"The deed to the house," I told her. "Dr. Selow gifted it to us. It's ours outright."

"He...what?!" She snatched the papers from me and scanned over them. "How?"

"I'm afraid I'll have to retire from carnival work, babe," I said apologetically. "It won't be feasible with my new job."

Her eyes lifted from the papers slowly, so big and wide I could see myself in them. "What new job?"

"I'm going to be a mentor for the FDR Center," I told her. "They need people to help vets transition to civilian life while taking their disabilities into account. I figure I managed mine pretty well with your help, so..."

"Connor." Mel clasped her hands around my neck. "That's amazing! I'm so proud of you."

"I couldn't have done it without you, babe." I pulled her tight against my chest, loving how perfectly she fit against me. "Fuck, I wouldn't even be standing here if it wasn't for you."

"Neither would I," she whispered. "If it wasn't for you."

I lifted her up as we kissed, spinning her in a circle until she threatened to puke on me.

"Fine. Now get back in the kitchen and make that cake," I said with a slap to her ass when I set her down.

"Jesus, Connor," she groaned, but couldn't fully hide her smile as she rejoined her siblings.

"Oh, what are we making now?" Arjun asked, striding into the house and sliding a hand around her waist. She leaned into him and it filled my heart with joy. About damn time they set aside their differences and realize how good they were for each other.

"A cake!" Riley exclaimed, holding up a wooden spoon.

"Hey, do you turn into a wolf too?" Bella asked him.

"No, young lady. Even better." He stretched a hand out toward her. "I'm a tiger."

His arm grew stripes, fur, and claws right before everyone's eyes.

"Holy shit!" Jeanie cried.

But all the kids just said, "Whoooah!" and reached out to touch him with curious, gentle fingers. Mel beamed brighter than the sun as she watched them.

I couldn't wait to see her like that every day. Not worried or concerned constantly. Of course, she'd still have those days, and I'd be there for her in any way that she needed. But I knew from that point on, as long as her family was safe and she had us to love her, she'd find it so much easier to smile.

EPILOGUE

MELODY

I woke up needing to piss like a racehorse.

I was alone in bed and sunlight filled the bedroom, meaning I had slept in. And goddamn, did it feel good to sleep in my own bed again.

My feet hit the floor, and I almost made it to the bathroom before doubling back to grab the pregnancy test on the nightstand. Connor did not forget after we came home, and apparently did a bunch of research while we were in Florida. He insisted I take the test first thing in the morning because of the higher concentration of pregnancy hormones or whatever.

I just knew he'd be crabby if I forgot, because then he'd have to wait another whole day to find out.

After doing my business in the bathroom, I busied myself with picking up clothes from the bedroom floor and other random little tidying things while I waited for the results to show on the stick. My stomach did flips as I watched the clock on the nightstand once all the clothes were picked up. Three minutes might as well had been three hours.

Finally, I returned to the bathroom and picked up the stick from where I left it on the counter. I looked at the results, then at myself in the mirror.

I could barely breathe. *I need to tell Connor. No, everyone!*

"Babe?" I called down the stairs, but no answer. Only my voice echoed off the ceiling and walls. Not even the kids were making a racket downstairs, which was especially weird.

"Connor?" I made my way down the stairs, clutching the test tightly in my hand.

An empty house greeted me. Not a soul was in sight.

"Jeanie?" I called. "Where the hell is everybody?"

A flash of movement in the backyard caught my eye. I saw my four guys standing together in a row, the pups and the kids fidgeting and squirming off to the side while Jeanie talked to them.

Confused, I opened the sliding glass door and stepped out onto the patio.

"What are you guys doing?"

"*Steluța*, come here," Raz smirked mischievously. "We want to ask you something."

I shoved the pregnancy test in my pocket as I walked out onto the lawn, narrow-eyed and suspicious. "What are you guys up to?"

My heart stopped when they all dropped to one knee.

"Melody," Connor began. "You saved me from poverty, a life of pain, and from myself. You pushed me to be the man you knew I could be, and I will never stop loving you for that."

"It goes without saying that you saved my life," Hunter said. "And for as long as we've known each other, you've been the most patient and kind person I've ever met, human or shifter. You showed me family isn't dictated by blood or species and I will always love you for that."

"You trusted me," Raz said next. "When I know it wasn't easy for you to do so. When my life felt meaningless and dark, you, my *steluța*, showed me the light of your love. I want to spend the rest of my life proving that I'm worthy of your trust because I love you." He turned to Hunter, pressing a kiss to his cheek. "And you."

If my heart wasn't already overflowing, seeing that display of affection between them would have done it for me. I had to admit it softened the anticipation of turning to the beautiful tiger shifter with the ocean-colored eyes and waited for him to speak.

Like when we made love, he did nothing, but look at me for a long moment, saying nothing.

"There are no words," he said with a small shake of his head, never removing his gaze from me. "I could be cheeky or romantic, but none of it would do justice to how I feel about you. Yes, you saved my life. Yes, you helped me face my worst fear. Yes, you gave me the courage to confront the hidden evil I grew up with, but," he paused, "it's not enough just to tell you. I want to spend every minute of every day showing you how much I love you." He broke eye contact with me for the first time, looking at the three men kneeling next to him. "So on that note, we wanted to ask you..."

"Will you marry us?" the four of them said in unison.

"Yes!" I cried. "Of course, I will. Jesus Christ, I wanted to say that a whole five minutes ago!"

"That's what you get when you love four men, *steluţa,*" Raz laughed, rising to his feet. "We all wanted to say our piece."

They all stood and gathered around me for hugs and kisses, but I couldn't wait to tell them my news any longer.

"I'm pregnant!" I yelled, raising the pregnancy test aloft like a wand.

"What?!" Jeanie shrieked, who had been filming the whole proposal on Connor's phone. "You're having a baby?!"

"Don't worry, Jean," I laughed joyously as my men smothered me in kisses. Someone snatched the test from my hand and they all clamored at each other to see it. "All four of these baby daddies ain't going nowhere."

"Why would we?" Connor voiced huskily, tears glittered in his eyes. "You're our bride. The love of all our lives. So perfect for us in different ways." His hand smoothed over my belly. I laced my fingers with his, soaking up his strength, his protection, his love.

My Marine, my first love, and the father of my child, pressed his lips to my forehead, murmuring gently over my skin, "And this baby will show humans how to love shifters as you have."

THE END...ish

BACKSTAGE AT THE FREAK SHOW
EXTENDED EPILOGUE

I

SIGHT OF THE SHAMAN

I

MIRIAM

Snow fell all around me as tiny, glittering specks across the dark gray landscape. My paws, despite being the size of motorcycle tires, barely made a sound as I lumbered on toward my destination.

It was bitterly cold. Far too cold for humans, but my thick fur kept me at a comfortable temperature. Excitement brimmed within me and I picked up my pace, my breath creating soft puffs of vapor in front of my snout.

A wedding! Perhaps the first wedding between a shaman and her *ila* in a generation. There was hope on the horizon yet for our kind.

I let out a brief howl as I ran. Crossing thousands of treacherous miles in a single night was no hardship for me. Soon the temperature would rise and the snow would melt. Sun and heat were not part of my typical environment, but I could adapt.

A new scent on the breeze made me growl. Gunpowder, quickly followed by the stench of human fear.

What are you doing out here, little human? Surely you know better than to hunt alone at night?

A shot rang out, going wild and harmless over my head, and I came to an abrupt halt. Lifting my nose in the air and swiveling my ears, I pinpointed the foolish human's location within seconds.

Perfect. I needed a snack for the long journey.

He made a hell of a racket, scrambling out of the bushes he was hiding in.

"Holy shit!" he cried out, stumbling backward in the snow like a newborn deer. "It's real! Oh my God, it's real!"

I roared in his fear-stricken face until the smell of piss reached my nose. He held his gun but seemed to completely forget how to use it while he cried and pleaded. Hungry and bored with his whimpering, I swiped a paw and knocked him into a nearby tree.

Finally silent, he laid in a crumpled heap at the base. My stomach growling, I ambled over and tore off his clothing with my teeth and claws for easier access to his flesh.

I always hated getting fabric stuck in my teeth.

"GUH!"

Cold sweat bathed my body as I jolted awake, sitting straight up in bed as my heart raced like I just ran a mile. My stomach sloshed dangerously, already queasy from the never-ending flow of champagne from last night's bachelorette party. Now I had the taste of human flesh in my mouth to go along with it.

"Mir?"

Colt stirred next to me, barely awake, but still wrapped an arm around my waist protectively. "Another vision?" he asked, gently pulling me back down onto the mattress until I laid next to him.

"Someone's coming to the wedding." My whisper came out hurriedly as I struggled to catch my breath. I never saw through the eyes of a shifter like that before and struggled to make sense of what I just experienced.

"Lots of people are," he chuckled, pressing a kiss to my temple. "I hope Mel's ready. It's going to be quite the affair."

I turned on my side to face him and nuzzled my head under his chin. My handsome wolf shifter enveloped me in a cocoon of warmth and strength. He was just what I needed to chase away the intense sensations of cold and bloodlust from what I just saw.

"This one is different," I muttered against his throat. "He's dangerous. He's on his way to the wedding right now and attacked a human so... casually."

Colt's arms tightened around me. "Do you think Mel's in danger? Or you?"

"I don't know," I admitted. "He seemed... excited about the wedding. I don't think he has anything against shaman. But he killed and started eating a human like it was nothing. Ugh, I can still taste it..."

"There's going to be lots of guests with open disdain for humans," he reminded me. "Many who have no problems doing unsavory things to them. In their eyes, it's justice. But this wedding is going to be symbolically about bridging the divide between us. I think lots of guests are looking forward to seeing that progress."

"God, I hope so," I sighed, leaning my cheek against his heart. "I am a little worried, though. I mean, most of the wedding guests are strangers. We don't know what they're capable of."

"It's a risk," he agreed, smoothing his hands down my back. "But Mel and the guys insisted on doing it this way. It's their wedding and we have to trust their judgement."

"You're right," I sighed, trailing my fingers along his biceps."

"We'll let the security team know," he kissed the crown of my head. "What kind of shifter was he?"

I thought for a moment, recalling all the sensations I felt while in this shifter's consciousness. "I don't know."

Colt pulled back, his golden eyes quizzical as he stared at me.

"He wasn't like any animal I've ever heard of before," I said. "In some ways, he felt like a wolf. Dense fur, ran on four legs, an excellent sense of smell. But he was gigantic. I mean, the adult human he killed was child-sized from his perspective."

Colt's brow furrowed. "A dire wolf, maybe? Those supposedly went extinct, but I mean, we are seeing a dragon shifter get married today."

"He was alone," I said. "That's what makes me think he's not a wolf.

I didn't get any sort of pack mentality from him. He's definitely a solitary hunter and prefers it that way."

"Huh," Colt laid back in his mess of pillows, staring at the exposed wooden beams in the ceiling as he thought. "I have no idea, Mir. We can ask Arjun, maybe? Although he's busy as fuck today."

"Arjun doesn't know anything that I don't know," I smacked Colt playfully, but my heart gave an uncomfortable twinge in my chest.

The English tiger shifter and I had an icy relationship, which was thawing, but not particularly quickly. His stepfather Lhozen taught me everything I knew about becoming a shaman, a human with special abilities to communicate with and see through the eyes of shifters. In a world where humans profited off of exploiting and experimenting on shifters, we shaman were essential in protecting and guiding them in a world that treated them as sub-human.

Unfortunately, Lhozen also turned out to be a leader in a shifter-trafficking ring. All three of Mel's shifter fiances had been captured by Lhozen's operative at some point. Including his own stepson, Arjun, and Colt's brother, Hunter.

Because my shaman training began shortly after Arjun's mother died, he believed Lhozen took me in not only as an apprentice, but as a mistress. Which couldn't be further from the truth, but there was no reasoning with a young man filled with grief.

Now, Arjun would become my brother-in-law, of sorts.

"Where's Gabe?" I asked, lifting my head off of Colt's chest to see that his youngest brother, and my other lover, was not in bed with us.

"Off brooding somewhere, like usual," Colt scoffed. "Probably trying to convince himself not to attend this wedding out of principal or whatever."

I sighed in response, dropping my ear back to the watery thud of Colt's heartbeat. People thought dating two men was complicated. Just being with Gabe on his own was like dating ten guys. I never knew who I was going to see. And one of them was always pissed off at me.

"Don't go looking for him," Colt protested as I started to get up. He pulled me back down to his chest and wrapped me in a bear hug. "Let him hear what he's missing out on."

The sultry whisper in my ear was accompanied by his cock

twitching against my thigh. Heat flooded my body as I involuntarily arched against him, his eyes dark with lust as he held me flush against his firm body.

"Colt, I need to get ready," I halfheartedly protested. "Makeup is in a couple of hours."

"Won't take that long," he murmured, lips trailing down my jaw. "It's going to be a long day. I just want a taste of my woman before she's whisked off for bridesmaid duty."

His mouth was hot and decadent on my skin. Accented with the sharpness of his teeth, he made me shiver despite being wrapped up in warmth.

"Colt," I sighed with a big breath of air, my resolve waning.

"Miriam," he answered, gently sucking on my collarbone as he rolled us over lazily. His mouth claimed mine as he pressed me into the mattress, lowering his long, lean body to drape over mine. Supposedly, these wolves didn't have magic, but they seemed to have me under a spell all the same.

I pushed back his hair, a rich dark brown that was almost as long as mine, and arguably prettier, as I responded to his kiss. Biting his lip playfully, I elicited a soft laugh from him as he pulled away, looking down at me adoringly.

"I thought I might have breakfast in bed," he whispered naughtily, lips now ghosting a trail over the swells of my breasts.

"Mm, how nice for you," I sassed back, my breath hitching as his tongue circled around one of my nipples.

"Have I ever left you unsatisfied?" His mouth lifted away from my skin as he reached up to lift my chin. "Answer me."

My teeth dug into my bottom lip. My body loved his dominant streak. It was like a language he spoke that only my heat and desire could understand. But every time he did something like this, I wanted to push his buttons. To see how far he would go if I didn't obey.

"Miriam." The way he spoke my name carried a dark hint of warning. A flush of heat ravaged me without a single touch.

"No, of course not," I told him, my voice meek and submissive. "You've never left me unsatisfied."

A half-smirk quirked on his lips. "So you know my breakfast will be just as good for you as it is for me."

His hand trailed back down my body, never stopping, but he flattened his palm and touched me with slow sensuality and intention. He gazed at my breasts, hypnotized as he kneaded the sensitive flesh before moving on. He traveled across my belly, following the curve of my waist and filling his hand with the roundness of my hips before venturing between my legs.

"Fuck, you're so perfect," he whispered in a soft growl as he caressed my folds, his fingers already slick as he teased me. "I can't believe you're ours."

"I can't believe you're mine," I mewled, my back arching off the bed as I raked my fingers through his hair.

His teeth teased my nipples into aching peaks before soothing them with his tongue. As his kisses moved lower, my hips raised off the bed, chasing the delicious pressure of his hand and sweet release. The moment his mouth reached the crease between my pelvis and thigh, he removed his hand from my pussy and wrapped his arms around the outsides of my thighs.

"That's a greedy little clit," he looked up at me wickedly, hot breath fanning over me as he placed the softest of kisses on my hood. "But I'm going to take my time enjoying breakfast."

"You're evil," I moaned, curling my fingers into fists around the bedsheets at my sides as I thrashed.

"Pout all you want, Mir," his lips grazed my inner thighs, sending my whole body into trembles of anticipation.

"Colt," I groaned, my voice dark and needy.

He alternated kisses and nibbles on my thighs, moving lower until I could no longer reach his hair. It was the most blissful torture I ever experienced. He took his sweet time alright, kissing his way all the way down to the sides of my knees before starting his journey back up.

My breaths became shallower and more ragged, my pulse accelerating as his hot, wicked mouth made its way closer to my center again.

"Mm, that's how I like my girl," he said, less than an inch away from my quivering flesh. "Teetering on the edge for me so beautifully."

Finally, his mouth pressed flush against me, tongue lashing up and down to taste me fully.

A scream escaped my mouth at the sudden intensity shooting from my limbs, radiating from my core. I started bucking against Colt's mouth, but he held my hips down, looking up with a gleam in his eye as he devoured me.

His eyes closed in the next moment, moaning as his lips and tongue drank me in, like I was the most succulent meal he ever had in his life. The vibration of his voice over my clit sent the pressure building like a volcano within me.

He released my lips after a long, sensual suck and took away one of his hands that held me down. In the next moment, I felt something long and rigid press into me. At the same time, his mouth pressed a hot kiss to my clit before his tongue began lashing at the hard nub.

"Fuck!" I groaned like an animal, my head tossing from side to side wantonly as his fingers massaged the inside of me, while his mouth worked tirelessly at my clit.

After such a long, drawn-out beginning, the buildup of my release came almost too fast for me to handle. My thighs clasped around Colt's head like a vice, but he never stopped, not even when my release came explosively.

I must have screamed, but barely heard myself over the jolts of pleasure shooting through me. Colt drew it out even longer, continuing to massage my channel and circle my clit with gentler pressure so it didn't become painful. It was still intense, but pure bliss, even through the aftershocks of the main release rocking my body.

He only stopped, withdrawing his fingers from me, and kissing my thighs again, when my breathing and heartbeat finally began to slow down.

"Mm," he sighed contently, looking up at me. "Most important meal of the day."

2

MIRIAM

After showering, I found Gabe in the kitchen, looking at his phone with a cup of coffee in front of him. He was shirtless, only wearing lounge pants with his feet up on the kitchen table. Colt hated when he did that, which was the main reason why he kept doing it.

In our modest two-bedroom cabin in the Georgia wilderness, there was no way Gabe didn't hear what Colt, and I were just up to.

"Hey," I greeted him, making my way to the counter where the full French press called to me like a caffeine beacon. "Ready for today?"

"You mean ready for a bunch of strange shifters to overrun the place like a convention of weirdos?" he scoffed, not looking up from his phone screen. "Sure. Guess I'm as ready as I'll ever be."

I went to pour coffee for myself before noticing my favorite mug was missing from the cabinet.

"Have you seen my—"

"Right there." He glanced up for half a second to nod at my mug, a handmade ceramic piece covered in a bright purple glaze, sitting at the far end of the counter.

It had already been filled with coffee, and was accompanied by a plate of grapes, scrambled eggs, and slices of breakfast sausage.

Looking back at him, Gabe's attention returned to the phone as if I wasn't in the room.

"Thanks." I carried the mug and plate to the seat next to him at the table.

"Mm," was his reply.

After a moment of thought, I leaned over and kissed his cheek. His expression didn't change, but I saw the flush creep up his neck.

Once I started eating, he put his phone down and stretched his muscular arms over his head. "Just didn't want you to end up hangry," he groaned through his stretch.

Gabe and Colt couldn't be more opposites, both in looks and demeanor. While Colt was tall and lean with a dancer or swimmer's build, Gabe was broad and a few inches shorter, like a wrestler. Both had hair down to their collarbone and otherworldly, modelesque facial features. Colt's hair was darker and Gabe's was a reddish auburn.

Colt was also the open book while Gabe was a locked down fortress. Falling for Colt had been easy, with his charming wit and smile, and being so openly affectionate toward me. While he did mourn the loss of his pack, he looked toward a new future of shaman and shifter working together, with open arms.

Gabe, on the other hand, resisted every increment of change in his new life. Humans hunted down his pack to the point where they had to separate. Colt and Gabe stayed together, but their third brother, Hunter, was captured along with his two pups.

My two wolves had never heard of shaman, but I knew exactly what they were the moment they started sniffing around my old butcher shop for scraps. Sensing nearby shifters was the first training point for a shaman, but I had to earn the wolves' trust before revealing that I knew their secret.

Every day with Gabe was a hot and cold game. He kept his feelings guarded behind that painfully handsome face, showing the briefest moments of warmth in gestures like this morning's breakfast, or the way his body curled around mine at night.

I couldn't entirely blame him. Wolves were raised in very rigid, old-school traditions. They were protective of their pack families for good reason. It was all that Gabe knew, and what he prided himself on. He was raised not to trust humans and in an instant, his pack was gone and he'd resorted to scavenging for food.

Even for a wolf shifter, Gabe was proud. He seemed allergic to smiling or admitting being wrong about something. He seemed content to sleep with me, even sharing me with his brother, but the moment any deeper feelings were breached, he pulled back like a hand on a hot stove.

And yet, I stayed hopeful that he would open up to me one day. Maybe I did so foolishly. But every time I got frustrated to the point of wanting to give up on Gabe, he showed me there was more to him.

When I first met him, there was no way he would have approved of his brother of marrying a shaman. In his eyes, wolves only needed each other. Not humans. But after spending more time with me, and seeing how happy Hunter was with Mel, he seemed to slowly be coming around.

Slowly being the key word.

"When are you guys heading out?" I asked before a hearty gulp of coffee.

"Whenever Colt's thoroughly washed and done in the shower," he smirked. "I'm gonna go nuts if I have to smell you on him all day."

"Nothing stopped you from joining," I pointed out. Truthfully, I was a little hurt that Gabe hadn't joined us in bed. He seemed to be avoiding group dynamics for a few days.

He shrugged in reply. "I don't feel much like sharing lately."

My stomach dropped. It wasn't like he sought me out on his own, either. What was he really trying to say?

"Any particular reason why?" I dropped my eyes to my eggs, circling them around my plate with my fork.

Another shrug. "Just a lot on my mind."

That you won't ever tell me.

I didn't even bother asking. I knew it would be a fruitless attempt and just continued eating my food. With him and Colt being groomsmen and me a bridesmaid, it was going to be a long day for all of us.

"THERE SHE IS!" Mel, in a beautiful lavender silk robe with *Bride* embroidered in golden letters, wrapped me in a hug. "You're just in time, Mir. The makeup artist just got here. Miriam, Lara. Lara, Miriam."

"Hello!" A woman with frizzy red hair, black-rimmed glasses, and wearing an apron stuffed with makeup brushes waved at me. "Nice to meet you."

"Likewise," I smiled at her. In my mind's eye, I saw large, brown eyes, a plush, furry body, and delicate, leathery wings. It seemed Lara was a bat shifter, a flying fox of some kind.

"Miriam, keep that door cracked, would ya?" I turned to see Connor, Mel's only non-shifter husband to be, peeking around the corner with a grin on his face.

"Excuse you!" Mel laughed, pulling me into her master bedroom. "No peeking before the ceremony!" She slammed the door closed to Connor's protests and locked it for good measure. "Jesus, he's the worst of them today. How are your two behaving today, Mir?"

"Nothing out of the ordinary." I plopped down on a corner of the bed. "Colt is lovely. Gabe is a stone wall. You know, the usual."

"So dump his ass and just go steady with Colt," Mel's sister and maid of honor, Jeanie May, suggested, putting their youngest sister Riley on the floor so she could crawl around. "You know, like normal people," she teased.

"It's not that simple," I sighed. "I've fallen for Gabe too, and I just *know* he has feelings for me. He does little sweet thoughtful things for me, but getting him to express anything is like pulling teeth. I think it's just hard with how he was raised."

"Hunter and Colt were raised in the same way too, you know." Mel took a seat in the makeup chair while Lara set up her kit. "At some point, you've got to put your foot down, Mir. He's allowed to feel conflicted, but that doesn't give him a pass to make you feel like shit."

"I know," I sighed, running my hands through my long, dark hair. "Did you get the same kind of shit from Hunter?"

"No, it was actually Arjun who gave me the most shit," Mel smirked, closing her eyes as Lara began her work on her face. "They've all been pains in my ass for various reasons, but I've learned to deal with them all. Sometimes it took patience and compassion, other times I had to stand up and tell them when shit wasn't acceptable. Such is life when you're marrying four men," she sighed.

"I don't know how you do it," Jeanie chuckled.

"It's work, but it has its perks." Mel's grin grew broader. "Loving so many different personalities and feeling how much they love you back all in their own unique ways. There's nothing else better in the world."

"Where do I find men who would be willing to share?" Lara joked.

"I don't recommend traveling and performing in carnivals run by shady humans," Mel laughed. "Even if you find good men, you're bound to find lots of trouble along the way."

"Don't feed hungry wolves meat scraps either," I added. "Then you'll be in my situation."

"This wedding seems like a good place to start," Jeanie scrolled through her phone while keeping an eye on Riley. "The guest list came out to fifty people. Nearly all of them shifters."

"Any shaman RSVP?" I asked.

"Doesn't look like it, though not everyone specified."

I hesitated before asking my next question. "Any unusual or mythical shifters?"

"You mean like dragons?"

"Yeah, just curious."

Mel's eyes slid over to me, but I kept my gaze trained on Jeanie as she scrolled through the list.

"I don't think so. A lot of these look pretty standard. Lion, wolf, bear, an arctic fox, a few elk, eagles. Oh, an elephant! And uh," Jeanie frowned. "What's a cassowary?"

"A flightless bird from Australia," Lara said. "Mean motherfuckers. Hopefully, they behave."

"Oh, we're pretty well prepared for scuffles," Mel laughed. "The security team's been hand-picked by Connor and you know how he gets. Short of a bunch of dragons torching the place, I think we'll all make it out alive."

"Interesting choice of words on your wedding day," Jeanie snorted.

Mel shrugged. "Making shifters feel like they're included and belong somewhere is important to me. I'm not naïve enough to think that everyone will get along swimmingly, but I want them to see this wedding as bridging the gap between humans and shifters. If they go home after enjoying a party with humans in the mix, I've done what I wanted."

We small-talked and speculated more about the guest list as we each took turns getting our makeup done. As I sat in the chair, I was dying to tell Mel about what I saw. She had the same Sight ability, and would know where I was coming from. Our abilities weren't a secret to her sister or most shifters, but I itched for a private conversation with my fellow shaman all the same.

But this was her wedding. She would be surrounded by loved ones constantly, as she should be. All I could do was hope the gigantic, mysterious shifter on his way here wouldn't pose a threat. And if he did, that the security team would be ready for him.

A headache flashed across my forehead as I zoned out in the makeup chair. *Shit, right now?* I thought, trying not to move my head.

Here was where my Sight ability was different. These headaches marked when I would see events that had not yet come to pass.

In my head, I saw Mel smiling in her wedding dress, tears glittering in her eyes as her four men looked at her like she was the only woman in existence. Looking past them and at the rows of wedding guests sitting in attendance, one man stood out.

Even while sitting, he was shoulders taller than most people. Standing, he had to be at least 6-foot-seven. A broad, muscular body strained under his suit. He gazed straight at me with one brown eye and one pale gray eye. Black eyebrows quirked as if amused. His clean-shaven face carried a bemused smirk on full lips, a straight nose and strong jaws. Black hair pulled back into a tight topknot completed his look.

The flash of his face was gone in an instant but still left me breathless, as all my future visions did. My heart drummed like I just sprinted up a flight of stairs as the echo of the headache slowly faded away.

"Mir, you okay?" Mel's large brown eyes focused on me, wide and concerned.

"Yeah," I flashed her a strained smile. "Just shaman things, you know."

She frowned, glancing up at Lana and Jeanie. "Hey girls, can I get five minutes with Miriam?"

"Mel, you don't have to—"

"Yes, I do or I'm going to worry about you all day." She ushered Lara and her sister out of the room before spinning the makeup chair to make me face her. "What did you see?"

I blew out a long breath, knowing she wouldn't let up until she knew. "I saw through a shifter early this morning, nothing like I'd ever seen before. That was why I asked about the guest list."

"And just now?"

"I saw, I think it was him. A few hours from now at the ceremony. Just sitting there and smirking at me." I wrung my hands in my lap. "He seemed excited about the wedding but I watched through him while he killed a human on his way here."

Her eyebrows lifted. "For what?"

"Nothing. Just for being in his way. But," I grabbed her arms, "I told Colt, and he's telling the security team."

She nodded, her expression thoughtful. "Now that you've seen him in human form, maybe tell security what he looks like. We don't have many humans involved with the wedding, but can't be too careful."

"Connor," I breathed. Mel hired almost all shifters in the wedding, from the catering to the photographer. Her fiance, Connor, was the only human present who wasn't also a shaman.

Mel threw her head back and laughed at that. "I'm not worried about Connor. He'll have this guy dancing like a drunk fool before the end of the night."

3

GABE

"Ow! Geez, pierce my damn nipple, why don't you," Hunter growled, flinching as Razvan pinned the boutonniere to his suit jacket.

"I could if you'd like," the dragon shifter grinned, securing the purple lily with his tattooed hands before straightening my brother's lapels. "I did a brief piercing apprenticeship back in Romania. Did one of the studs through my cock myself."

"Every time I see you, Raz," Colt laughed from his spot on the couch, "I learn something new about you."

"I've led an interesting life, what can I say." The small tattoo near the dragon shifter's eye compressed as his gray eyes roamed over Hunter. "And now I'm marrying the two loves of my life."

"You guys nervous?" Colt looked over all four of the grooms—Raz, Conner, Arjun, and our middle brother, Hunter.

"Not about getting married, no," Connor, the only non-shifter, fiddled with his cufflinks. "About some of the guest list? Absolutely." He gave a hard look to Colt and I. Colt told him about Miriam's vision the minute we arrived at their house.

"Whose bright idea was it to invite a bunch of strangers to our wedding again?" Arjun clipped in his posh English accent. The tiger shifter was of Indian descent and was the only one to wear a non-traditional tuxedo, although his colors of purple and pale gray matched the other grooms. Rather than a jacket and tie, he wore a slim-fitting *Jodhpuri* suit with ornate buttons and a relaxed collar that made me envious. Mine felt like a fucking dog collar in this heat.

"Your future wife's," Raz jabbed at him. "A little late to worry about it now."

"Mel insisted on it and we all understood her reasons, despite the risks. She always thinks of others first. It's how she is," Hunter added warmly.

"You're quiet today, Gabe," Connor observed, fixating his dark green gaze on me. "Aren't you thrilled? A celebration with 99% shifters and one human. Seems like your kind of party."

My wolf wanted to snarl, but I forced him back down. It was true that I didn't care for most humans, he and a select few others being the exceptions. I personally wasn't a fan of a bunch of strange shifters congregating in one area either, but this wasn't my wedding.

I was admittedly rude to Mel when I first met her, and Connor never seemed to let it go. We weren't buddies by any means, but over time developed a cordial, mutual respect for each other. Still, he never failed to bring up my feelings toward humans as a dig at me. And still he wondered why I continued to not be a fan of them.

"Strangers of any kind are a risk," I responded coolly back to him, keeping my face blank.

"I'm glad we agree on something," he replied.

"Hey, so what's up with you two and Miriam?" Hunter changed the subject. "Is she going to be front and center for the bouquet toss?"

"We're not anywhere near ready for that," I scoffed before Colt could jump in and say anything.

"Maybe you're not," my oldest brother bristled. "But honestly, I've given the whole marriage thing some thought."

"Yeah well, it's not all about you, bro," I pulled at the collar of my shirt, already getting hot under it. "The three of us are a package deal. That's what we decided."

"You've got a funny way of acting like it," Colt's tone turned accusing. "Where the hell were you this morning? Then you blow her off and tell her you're not in a sharing mood? What gives?"

"Can we not do this now?" I growled through my teeth. "We're celebrating Hunter and the guys today, not bickering about our own shit."

"You're the only one making this difficult, Gabe." Colt would just not let up. "I love her. She loves both of us and you're just being a dick for no reason."

"Guys, come on." Hunter stood between us. "Gabe's right. Not here and not now."

"Hey." Raz went to the liquor cabinet and pulled out a bottle of something before setting up six shot glasses. "It's a new day, gentlemen. For us four, it's the start of our new lives. Let's wash yesterday away with a toast, ah?"

"Is that some kind of Romanian proverb?" Arjun cheeked, his blue-green eyes flashing as he picked up a shot glass filled with amber liquid.

"Fuck nah, I just made it up," the dragon laughed.

Standing reluctantly, Colt and I were the last to grab our shot glasses. His tight frown told me he wasn't done interrogating me with this stuff today. Hopefully, we made it past the ceremony, at least. The six of us held our shot glasses as Connor cleared his throat.

"To love, patience, and kindness toward all creatures," he began.

"Boooo," Raz teased under his breath. "You suck."

"Sorry, man. That was just a practice run." Connor side-eyed him and began again. "To the best damn party on this side of the Mississippi with hopefully no assholes to ruin it, and to the amazing woman who brought us together and puts up with us for God knows why."

"That's more like it," Hunter grinned.

All six of us clinked glasses and threw back our shots. The whiskey burned a delightful trail of fire from my throat to my belly and seemed to have a similar effect on the other guys. Raz even blew out a small flame as he exhaled.

"Not bad, Arj," he mused, looking down at today's date on the engraved glass. "You hooked us up with good stuff."

"Only the finest for us, lads." The tiger shifter grinned down at his glass as well.

I ran my finger over the engraving on mine, already knowing what it said. Melody, Connor, Hunter, Razvan and Arjun. Shifted into marital bliss July 25th, 2019.

"Looks like some of the first guests are here," Colt mused, looking out the window as sharply-dressed people strolled onto the lawn.

A few couples, groups of friends, and some single people milled about. There was nothing unusual about them to any human observer, but with one sharp inhale, I picked up multiple animal species. A few wolves and felines, some avian, and another I couldn't quite place.

"Where's a damn shaman when you need one?" Arjun chuckled. "I want to know all about these people."

"Ours is probably getting into her dress now," Connor glanced at his watch. "God, I can't wait to see her."

"The next time you do, she'll be your wife." Hunter slapped his back excitedly.

"And yours," Connor grinned back.

Just then the grooms got called away for pictures, leaving Colt and I alone again.

"Shall we walk around and mingle for a moment?" Colt pulled on the sleeves of his suit jacket. "We're not needed with the grooms until a bit later."

"Sure," I grumbled, twisting open the bottle of whiskey to pour myself a second shot. "Why not?"

Colt waited for me at the door, a scowl on his face. "Can you at least pretend to be happy today? Or a few notches above moody asshole, at least?"

"What are you talking about? I'm thrilled. Our brother is getting married to a human and a few dozen strangers now know where he lives."

"You're fucking unbelievable, you know that?" he hissed through gritted teeth before smiling tightly at a pair of guests walking by. "Sometimes I wonder why you stick around with Miriam if you think so lowly of humans."

I stayed tight-lipped but silently wondered the same thing, but for different reasons. It wasn't that I thought poorly of Miriam or Mel. They were brave, strong women who loved fiercely. Miriam and I hadn't exchanged any words of love yet, but I could feel it in the way she touched me, kissed me, and spoke to me. How deeply and genuinely she cared was just one of the many reasons why I held her at arm's length.

If I allowed myself, I could love her back. I craved the easy connection she had with Colt, the sweetness and flirtation between Hunter and Mel. Miriam deserved to be surrounded by men who adored her, but was I meant to be one of them?

To give myself to her, to claim the beautiful shaman with long dark hair and make her my mate, would mean admitting I'd never be part of a wolf pack again. I'd never hunt an elk or run through the woods under the moonlight with my mate. And I'd never raise pups of my own.

Hunter got lucky. He had a mate and two pups before meeting Mel. His first mate died from gunshot wounds, then he and the pups were captured a few years later. Now he was in love with both a female human and a male dragon shifter. None of us would have seen that coming. Hunter said he loved both Mel and Raz more than his former mate, but at least he had a true pack life first. At least he had his pups.

I loved my niece and nephew dearly, but it wasn't the same as having my own. Miriam was an amazing woman, and her abilities were awe-inspiring. But a human and a shifter could never produce a child.

The old school wolf pack mentality we grew up with also frowned upon species intermixing. Sure, we were all human in one way, but a wolf and a platypus usually didn't have much in common. Hunter felt this way at one point, but I guess being captured and put on display as a carnival freak changed his perspective.

Colt never cared. He never intended on settling down and always seemed happy with a bachelor lifestyle. As the wild one of the three of us, he dated anyone from normal humans to bird and horse shifters, much to our alpha's chagrin. It honestly surprised me how smitten and dedicated he became to Miriam. To hear that he'd been thinking about marriage was a shock.

Me, I couldn't decide how I felt about this whole wedding business. Mel, Hunter, and the rest of the guys seemed happy, but I wasn't sure if it was right for Miriam, Colt, and I. Just sharing a woman with my brother was enough to wrap my head around, but being legally and spiritually bound to both of them? It ran a little too close to comfort for me.

I people-watched with Colt idly, already bored with everyone who arrived. Thankfully, they all looked well-behaved and eager to witness the nuptials. Around me I could feel the other guys' relief, like a weight off their shoulders. All the guests seemed normal so far.

The four grooms and Colt stepped out to greet people, shake hands, and small talk while I hung back. I wasn't the most social person and preferred to observe instead. Once I got a few drinks in me at the reception, maybe I'd strike up a conversation with someone.

A peculiar smell in the air had my neck snapping to one side. I never picked up a shifter scent like this before. It was like a wolf's, but different. My nose picked up salt, blood, and something else I couldn't identify. This scent also felt cold, although I had no way of describing how I knew that.

The strange scent had my hairs standing on end and my wolf snarling. This had to be the shifter, Miriam saw. Nothing else stood out like this bastard, whoever he or she was.

"Colt," I barked under my breath.

"Yeah, I know," he answered gruffly. "It's great to meet you, thanks for coming!" He finished chatting with one couple before turning to me. "Keep your eyes sharp," he muttered under his breath.

"No need," I breathed as the hulking figure, tall and dark like a shadow, came into view. "Found him."

4

COLT

He came alone, standing head and shoulders taller than any normal man in attendance. Hunter and I were among the tallest guys here and this one seemed to tower over us, the topknot at the crown of his head making him seem even taller.

I almost missed his odd-colored eyes, one gray and one brown, if he didn't give a polite nod at us as he walked by on legs that looked like tree trunks. His gray suit fit him well, if a bit snugly. This guy was well over six and a half feet tall of pure muscle.

"What the fuck is he?" Gabe growled under his breath.

I couldn't help but glance sideways at my brother. He acted like he didn't give a fuck, but when it came to Miriam's safety, he turned into a ruthless guard dog.

"Only one way to find out," I muttered, following the guy's movement with my eyes.

Everyone openly stared at the large man, but he breezed through the yard without a care in the world and took an empty seat near the back row of chairs. The ceremony wouldn't begin for another half-hour, but he seemed content to sit and wait.

He stared straight forward, hands folded calmly in his lap. Up ahead, at the decorated arch, the bridesmaids and flower girls posed for the photographer. Miriam looked gorgeous in her purple, strapless bridesmaid dress as she held the hand of Bella, one of Mel's younger sisters. My cock and heart pulsed at the same beat as I watched her smile and laugh.

I couldn't wait to take that dress off her, and from the way Gabe looked at her, he felt the same way. We momentarily forgot about the large man in the audience until Miriam looked out across the lawn. Her smile faded and her hazel eyes went wide. He was hard to miss and from the look of stunned recognition, he was exactly the person we thought he was.

"Go tell John." I nudged Gabe with my elbow. "Tell him we have our guy."

"What? You tell him!" my brother hissed. "I'm not taking my eyes off that giant."

"Just go," I shoved him more forcefully toward the head of security. "I'll handle it. You're not exactly Mr. Charisma."

He walked off grumbling, watching the back of the big dude's head until he no longer could. I straightened my tie and wished I helped myself to a second shot of whiskey as well, before ambling over to the mysterious stranger.

"Hi! How are you?" I plastered a smile on my face and sat in the chair next to him, holding my hand out. "I'm Colt, one of the grooms-men. Thanks for coming."

He leveled his odd-eyed gaze at me, keeping his face neutral as he slowly extended a massive hand to accept mine.

"Taqqiq," he replied in a deep tone that was warmer than I expected. "Most call me Tak."

I nodded, turning over the unusual name in my mind. "Where you from, Tak?"

"Alaska," he replied with a hint of a smirk. "The great frozen north."

"Yeah? The South is pretty different from where you're from, huh?" I tugged at my collar. "I've lived here my whole life and still can't get used to this heat. At least it's not the middle of summer anymore."

"I'm used to a wide range of temperatures." Tak chuckled politely.

Confusion swirled inside me. I didn't get a dangerous vibe from this guy at all. The girls moved to a different place for more photos, with Miriam still sending us nervous glances between her poses and smiles. But Tak's eyes didn't linger on her, nor on anyone. He was acting like any wedding guest who came alone.

"Are there many shaman in Alaska?" I asked. "Or shifters?" I silently wondered if he would reveal his shift without me asking directly.

"Shaman? There used to be, generations ago." His voice carried a hint of sadness and longing. "My people had one of the highest populations of shaman before settlers moved in and annexed Alaska to the United States, second only to the native tribes in the lower forty-eight. They slowly stopped passing on their gifts so as to not be persecuted." Tak tilted his head toward me. "I'm sure you know the general history."

"I do a little," I said. "From what my ah, girlfriend told me."

"You're a lucky man, Colt." Tak smiled as he looked over the outdoor ceremony area, eyes pausing on Miriam for a moment before moving on. More people began taking their seats as the time drew near. "As are the four men marrying their shaman today. It's a blessed day."

"You do know one of the grooms is a human?" I asked, closely gauging his reaction.

"I could smell him, yes," Tak remarked casually before turning to look at me with those odd eyes. "We call humans like him an *arviq* in my language."

"What does that mean?"

He stroked his jaw as he thought. "Loosely, it means fortunate one. He is extremely fortunate to have been chosen as a shaman's consort, but it's not all about that. It can also mean blessed in a way. He was born differently than other humans, to live so seamlessly among shifters without prejudice. A higher power gave him this ability, so he is also blessed." Tak gave me an odd look. "Do you not support a shaman choosing a fellow human to marry as well as shifters?"

"No!" I barked out a laugh. "Not at all. I love Connor. He's like a brother to me. I like him more than my own brother sometimes, honestly."

"Ah," Tak nodded at the archway, where the grooms began gathering. "The pale wolf is your brother, correct?"

"One of them, yes." We watched as Raz stepped up close behind Hunter, resting his head on my brother's shoulder as the photographer snapped photos. Hunter looked back at the dragon shifter and murmured something before giving Raz a quick kiss as the camera clicked away.

"That is also rare to find," Tak chuckled good-naturedly. "Grooms finding love between each other. I've never seen a harem work so well together."

"Colt!" Hunter yelled at me while waving his arm for me to come over. I almost forgot I had to be in pictures, too. Gabe was already there, scowling away.

"It was nice talking to you," I clapped Tak on the shoulder as I rose from my chair. "We'll see you at the reception?"

"You will," the large man nodded. "I look forward to it."

I walked up the aisle to the five, no, six, men in matching tuxes waiting for me. Mel's little brother, Joey, clung shyly to Connor's leg.

"Well?" Gabe wasted no time in whispering harshly under his breath. "What did you find out?"

"Not much," I muttered before smiling at my reflection in the camera lens. "He seems like a nice guy, actually."

"A *nice* guy?! Fucking shit, Colt..."

"He has no problem with Connor, or any human that gets along with shifters, it seems."

"That's comforting," Connor muttered.

The photographer motioned for me, Hunter, and Gabe to pose for a photo, so we moved to the side and stood as instructed.

"What's his shift?" Gabe grumbled.

"Smile for me, honey!" the photographer cajoled. "Thank you!"

"No idea." I flashed a smile when instructed, throwing my arms over both of my brothers' shoulders.

"You're fucking useless," Gabe whined.

"Whatever. I guarantee it wouldn't have gone any better if you talked to him. We'd have to kick your ass out for brawling."

"Hey," Hunter thumped my chest. "Seats are filling up. We're getting started. Don't kill each other before you walk down."

"Not me you have to worry about," I muttered, following Gabe inside the house to line up. He'd be walking out first with Mel's sister, Jeanie. I was to follow him with Miriam.

"Holy shit," I breathed, stunned for a moment when I saw Mel at the far end of the room.

Her ivory gown had purple accents and pooled around the floor in silky waves like a magic potion. Even her veil was a gradient of white, slowly transitioning to a deep purple hue for a dark, almost gothic vibe.

She was far from a traditional bride, four grooms notwithstanding, but still added her dark touches to the classical bridal look.

"Mel, you look stunning," I told her. "They're going to be fighting over you before you finish walking down the aisle."

"Thanks, Colt," she smiled shyly under her veil. "I hope they like it."

I spotted Miriam near the front door and took my place at her side.

"Doesn't Mel look amazing?" she asked, wrapping her slender hand around my bicep.

"She's not the only one," I growled under my breath, not-so-subtly letting my eyes roam over her bridesmaid's dress.

The strapless style accentuated the feminine curves of her neck and shoulders, the fabric clinging to the rest of her body like a glove.

"You're shameless," she teased, quirking a smile up at me as the music started. Gabe and Jeanie walked arm in arm as the grooms and guests looked on.

"And you love it," I told her as we stepped up to our spot. "By the way, I talked to the big guy. He seems harmless. Even nice, I'd say. Of course, that was just my first impression, but who really knows."

"Thanks." she squeezed a little tighter around my arm. "Something feels off to me, though, and it has to do with him. I just can't put my finger on it."

Gabe and Jeanie reached the archway where the grooms stood, and it was our turn to walk out.

"We're staying vigilant, Mir," I whispered as we stepped out. "Both of us," I added.

She nodded curtly before flashing a bright smile for the photographer and wedding guests. Even if he was an ass sometimes, I felt it was important for her to know Gabe was watching out for her, too. He'd protect her with his life if it came down to that.

Connor and Hunter stood to one side of the archway, the officiant in the middle, and Raz and Arjun on the other side.

I kissed Miriam's cheek before reluctantly removing her hand from my arm and went to stand with Gabe while she went with Jeanie. Everyone immediately stood as *Here Comes the Bride* kicked on, and let out a soft collective gasp as Mel began her walk.

She held the arm of her little brother Joey, who barely came up to her shoulder, but he stood tall and proud as he prepared to give his sister away to the new men joining their family.

They turned to each other and hugged tightly upon reaching the end of the aisle. Wedding guests were already dabbing their eyes as Mel handed her bouquet of white and purple lilies to Miriam.

She reached out with both hands to take those of her four grooms, who were stunned into breathless silence at their bride.

"My fellow shifters and friends from all walks of life," the officiant began. "Today is one of many new beginnings. For these five people, today marks the beginning of a lifelong commitment to not only care for and comfort their one partner, but each other. Today, these people acknowledge that together they are greater than the sum of their individual parts. As a single unit, they have the strength to overcome all obstacles, both internal and external."

"Today also marks a new beginning for all shifters," he continued. "As the first wedding between shaman and shifters in generations, this holy union represents a new age of love and tolerance. May this proclamation and commitment of love between human and shifter inspire all of you here today, so that we may look toward a brighter future."

Mel pulled her hands away from her guys to start clapping, and the grooms quickly followed. In moments, everyone stood up and joined in thunderous applause for the officiant.

He smiled humbly, lowering his head, but he was right. *That* was why Mel and her guys invited shifters from all over to attend. To be here was to witness history.

"And now," the officiant said after everyone quieted and sat down. "I'll hand it over to one of the men of the hour," a soft chuckle arose from the guests as that, "to say the vows they have prepared."

A microphone was passed to Connor, who pulled a velvety ring box from his pocket with his other hand. The mic picked up the tail end of his long breath before he began speaking.

"I'm not a shifter. There's nothing special about me—"

"Shut up," Mel interrupted, earning a laugh from everyone in attendance.

A massive grin of joy erupted onto Connor's face. "Clearly, I'm wrong about a lot of things, but you're the one thing I got right. I'll always cherish you, babe, through the highs and the lows. I'll be the shield that protects our family, whether shifter or human, for the rest of my days."

Blinking tears away, he passed the mic and ring to Hunter, who took a long moment to gaze at his bride before speaking.

"Some wolves believe in fate," my brother began. "I never did until I met you. My children are yours. My heart and soul are yours." He paused to glance at Razvan, the tattooed dragon shifter returning his gaze with wide, dilated eyes. "I'm blessed with two incredible mates I'd do anything for. This is the pack I was meant to have. I'll always put our children and you two first."

Mel sniffed, blinking rapidly as Raz took the mic and ring next.

"What can I say, *steluta*, that I haven't already promised you before?" His Romanian lilt was low and thick with emotion. "You have my loyalty, my love, and my trust for the rest of my days." Looking at Hunter, he continued, "And you're just as much my mate as Melody is. I'll light up any motherfucker stupid enough to come near either of you."

A few laughs, gasps, and wide-eyed looks from children came over the crowd as he passed the ring and mic to Arjun. But it just wouldn't be a Razvan wedding without some expletives and threatening to set something on fire.

"I'm going to be a massive pain in your arse," the tiger shifter smirked. "I'll take the piss out of you every day because that's how I show I love you. But I'll also make you a proper cup of tea and purr you to sleep every night. I'll love you to the end of my days, dove, and I promise you'll never have a dull moment with me."

The vows of each man seemed to soak into everyone attending as the mic was handed to Melody. She drew a shaky, emotional breath before her voice rang musically from the speakers.

"I would make vows to you all individually, but our guests need to eat and drink before the day is over," she joked. "So my promise to you, the four loves of my life, is that my heart will always have room for each of you. I'll never pick favorites or pit you against each other. I'll always make time. I'll always listen and give you someone to lean on the way all of you have done for me. I have a unique story with each one of you, but the greater story of *us* is just beginning."

Barely any eyes were dry by the time Mel finished speaking. Even Gabe sniffed in front of me and wiped his eye as if the wind blew something into it.

"You may now exchange rings," the officiant said when the mic returned to him.

Arjun, the last to hold the ring box, slid a white gold band onto Mel's left ring finger. Miriam and Jeanie then stepped forward, holding two rings each on velvet pillows. One by one, Mel took a band and slid it onto the ring finger of each of her grooms. When she finished, Arjun and Raz clasped her left hand while Connor and Hunter held her right. "I now pronounce you husbands," the officiant smirked at the pluralized word, "and wife. Y'all may kiss your bride."

There was a moment of pause, followed by a giggle from Mel. In the next instant, her four husbands surrounded her, playfully shoving and fighting each other to land a kiss first as the crowd stood and gave a roaring applause.

❧ *5* ❧

MIRIAM

After another hour of pictures, hugs, and happy tears, we were finally able to sit down.

Colt and Gabe wolfed down their food and guzzled drinks until they were talking excitedly with the other guests at our table. Seeing Gabe laugh and smile was a rare treat.

I ate slowly, sipping my champagne while keeping my eyes sweeping across the entire reception hall. We moved from the ceremony in Mel's backyard to a banquet room in the neighboring campus of the FDR Center for Disabled Veterans.

After retiring from carnival work, Connor worked for the Center as a counselor. He moved so flawlessly on the dance floor with his bride, some of the wedding guests would never know he had two prosthetic legs.

The banquet hall had open, slanted ceilings with exposed beams, floor-to-ceiling windows, and was nestled into the surrounding woods. It gave the reception an outdoor private party feel, which seemed to put many of the shifters at ease.

The bride and grooms couldn't stop smiling at each other and kissing. Guests got a kick of tapping their silverware to their glasses for more kisses, while poor Mel tried her best to be fair and kiss each man an equal amount.

The pure love and happiness was palpable in the air, especially when my two wolves finished their conversations and sandwiched me between their firm bodies. Still, no matter how much they made my pulse speed up, or how infectious Mel's smile and happiness was, I couldn't shake the feeling of something being off.

And it had something to do with *him*, the powerfully built man with odd-colored eyes chatting at a neighboring table.

"You're quiet lately," Gabe murmured in my ear, his fingers skimming along my waist while Colt kissed the shell of my opposite ear.

"I could've said the same to you this morning," I replied icily.

Colt stifled a chuckle while his younger brother pulled away from me in surprise.

"Are you upset about something?"

"Are you, Gabe?" I retorted. I must have drank more champagne than I thought, because I wasn't normally so quick to pick a fight. "I never know if you're going to be sweet to me like this or a stone wall like this morning. I'm kind of sick of it, frankly."

He pulled even further back, brow furrowed in disbelief. "You really want to get into this now?"

"Yeah, why not?" I pulled my napkin off my lap and whipped it onto the table. "It's a beautiful night. Love is in the air. But I already know. For how much you're going to be all over me tonight, you're going to ignore twice as much tomorrow. I feel like a guilty pleasure to you, Gabe. A dirty little secret that everyone already knows about."

"That's not true," he choked out.

"It's what you act like." I shoved my chair back abruptly and rose to my feet. "I'm going to the ladies' room."

"Mir--"

I ignored him while fighting to keep my cool. Thankfully, most guests were fixated on watching the dance floor to notice me. Hunter and Raz slow-danced together while Connor and Arjun swayed with Mel sandwiched between them. Peals of laughter made me look before entering the restroom. The guys had switched places and now Arjun danced with Raz, holding the dragon shifter an arm's length away.

I spent a few minutes in front of the mirror, just taking calming breaths. The last thing I wanted to do was make a scene at Mel's wedding. Gabe was right about one thing. Now was not a good time to talk about us. I should've waited until I was more sober and there were fewer people around.

But deep down, I was glad that I told him. Those feelings had been bubbling since we met, and now they were out there. He knew without a doubt how I felt about him. If he wanted to keep me, he needed to realize his actions had consequences.

I touched up my makeup and straightened my spine before returning to the reception. Mel wouldn't accept this from any of her men, so why the hell would I?

"Excuse me," said the deepest, most masculine voice I ever heard in my life.

I turned to see a large, looming figure leaning casually against the wall right outside the restrooms. His jacket was gone and his tie loosened, but there was no mistaking him. He towered over me, gazing at me curiously with two different colored eyes.

"Yes?" my voice unintentionally came out a breathy whisper as my heart lodged in my throat. There was a cruel, masculine beauty to him. I didn't know whether to be afraid or intrigued.

"I was wondering if you'd like to dance." He straightened, moving away from the wall and closer to me.

My gaze slid to the dance floor, now filling up with tipsy guests as upbeat pop music filled the room.

"Yes, I would."

I didn't know what made me say it. Maybe because I knew it would get under Gabe's skin. I also needed to know *why* I saw flashes of this man in my mind. And anyway, why the hell not? He was hot, and it was a party.

"Your men won't mind?" he asked with a cocky smirk, eyes flashing with victory.

"It's not their decision, is it?"

He chuckled amusedly as he led me to the dance floor. "I'm glad I asked the right person."

"What's your name?" I twirled around to face him. He was too tall for me to reach his neck, so I placed my hands on his forearms. His hands almost enveloped my entire waist.

"Taqqiq. Call me Tak, it's easier."

"I'm Miriam."

"Miriam," he repeated, as if tasting what my name sounded like.

"Your name's unique," I observed as we moved together across the floor. "What does it mean?"

He pulled me just an inch closer in a way that was intimate, but not invasive. I realized my sense of unease was gone, like being so close to him made me feel safer than I had been all night.

"It means moon," he said in a low voice near my ear. "In the Inuit languages."

"You're from the far north, then?" I asked, remembering how softly the snow fell around him in my vision.

"The land of ice and snow," he chuckled before pulling back to look at me, creating some distance between us. "You ask a lot of questions. Are you this curious about everyone you meet?"

I hesitated before answering. "No." With a newfound boldness, I stepped in closer and slid my hands up to his biceps. "I'm very curious about you, though."

He looked surprised, but a pleased smile lit up his hard, rugged face. "That's a refreshing change. A lot of people are afraid of me."

"Why?"

"Because of what I am," he answered softly. "And what my species is purported to have done in the legends of the Inuit humans."

My curiosity overwhelmed me, threatening to spill over. I was brimming with excitement that this man was a creature out of a legend, probably one rarely heard of this far south.

But he was also a person, and I had to check myself. Shifters hated being treated like zoo animals on display, especially if they were a rarer species. Right now, Tak was a man dancing with a woman at a wedding and nothing else. He was essentially a guest in my home, and I wasn't about to be rude by asking invasive questions.

"I'm not afraid of you," I told him. "I'm happy you came all this way to celebrate my friends' love."

His gaze heated as he tentatively pulled me even closer, his forearm wrapped entirely around my waist now and my hands nearly braced against his chest.

"You're an interesting shaman, Miriam," he breathed. "And if you don't mind me saying so, absolutely lovely. Your men are lucky."

"You're sweet, Tak," I smiled. My cheeks heated as I watched his lips move. "Do you have someone back home?"

"No, I don't." He said it lightheartedly, but I didn't miss the longing in his voice.

"Well, maybe you'll meet someone special here."

He said nothing for a moment, his eyes flickering to mine before glancing away. "Maybe I already have," he murmured so low I nearly missed it.

I'd been so mesmerized by the movement of his lips, I didn't notice when the music stopped. My peripheral vision told me we were standing at the edge of the dance floor, but I barely paid attention to my surroundings. My focus was all on him.

His two different colored eyes were fascinating to look at and I couldn't tear my gaze away. He radiated strength and power, still holding my waist in a firm, but not restrictive, grip. I didn't even know what this man shifted to, but just the human side of him drew me in like a moth to a flame.

"Miriam," he voiced in a low growl after what had to be several minutes of just holding and staring at each other, "can I—"

"Please, Tak." I breathed eagerly, standing on tiptoes as I fully braced my forearms on his chest now. For some reason, this man was a mystery I was dying to uncover. I barely scratched the surface and needed to explore him deeper.

His hand on my waist slid up my back to palm the nape of my neck. I leaned into the rough, callused skin of his thumb, tracing light circles at the base of my skull.

I lifted my face to his and watched his lips lower to mine through heavy eyelids. In that tense, brief moment before our mouths would meet, a hard banging sound made me shriek and jump against him.

Both arms closed around me like a shield as the exit door down the hallway burst open from the outside. A human, rage etched onto his face to match the guns, knives, and various homemade weapons strapped to his body, came toward us.

"I'm going to kill all you dirty animal fuckers and send you straight to Hell!" he screamed.

❧ 6 ❧

MIRIAM

Tak shoved me behind him, completely blocking my view of the human with his body. "Tak, no!" My voice rose to a panic. The human had enough weapons on him to arm at least ten more people.

"Miriam!"

I heard my name from behind me, then someone jerked me into their chest. The familiar smell told me it was Gabe, though it barely registered in my mind.

Where the hell was security? Tak getting killed to protect me was all I could think about.

"Tak!" I screamed again, fighting to reach him, but strong arms held me back.

The large man's shift was immediate. His suit fell apart in ribbons as he stretched to the height of the ceiling. Black claws extended from his hands as gray, black, and brown fur covered his body.

"Holy..." Gabe whispered, unable to finish the thought as we just stared at him.

Tak looked exactly like a wolf, but was the size of an elephant. He fell to all fours, arms and legs the length of my body, and roared in the terrified human's face.

With one massive paw the size of my torso, Tak pinned him against the wall. Jaws gaping wide with rows of dagger-like teeth on display, the gigantic wolf almost seemed to be smiling.

Don't you know you shouldn't go hunting at night, little human.

Tak's voice rang with a calm, almost soothing quality in my head. Gabe and I stared at each other, our looks confirming that we both heard it. I never heard anyone but Mel communicate like that.

The stench of piss filled the air and Tak seemed he had enough. Bringing his paw to the human's face, he gripped his whole head, claws curling around like that of a human hand.

With one quick snap, the human's head jerked to the side like a Ken doll, then he slumped to the floor as Tak released him.

Colt and the security team came running just as the large man began shifting back to human.

"Nice of y'all to show up," Gabe spat.

"What the hell happened?" Colt pulled me to him, squeezing me tightly as his fingers closed possessively in my hair. "I heard you scream, Mir. Fuck—"

"Tak saved us." My own voice sounded far away as I turned to look at the large, now naked man. "He probably saved everyone here. That guy was armed like a terrorist and said he was going to kill everyone."

"We'll take care of this," John, the head of security, tapped Colt on the shoulder as he and his guys went to remove the body.

"Normally, I spill more blood, but," Tak looked at the human's body, then us sheepishly, "I didn't want to create a mess to clean up."

"What the hell are you?" Gabe demanded. Normally, I would have chastised him for being rude, but the shock left me stunned.

"I'm an Amarok," Tak replied calmly. "My species used to roam the most frozen parts of the northern hemisphere. Now we're monsters in Inuit legends."

"Cool. Next question," Gabe said dryly. "What the hell were you doing with Miriam?"

"Hey," I spun to face him. "I'm right fucking here, you know."

"Alright, fine." He crossed his arms, turning his gaze on me. "What the hell were *you* doing with *him*?"

"Dancing," I fired back. "And talking. You know, stuff people do at weddings. Not that it matters to you, anyway."

"Of course it matters to me," he huffed, eyes narrowing. "You're with *us*. And it looked like you were about to kiss him."

"So?" I challenged. "At least he wanted to kiss me."

Gabe's expression sent a crack shattering through my heart. After all this time, I finally saw what he kept hidden so far beneath the surface.

"I do want to kiss you," he breathed in a pained voice. "Constantly. It's all I think about, Mir. I just—" he raked a hand through his auburn hair. "I just don't want to lose you like I lost my pack."

A pin could drop in that hallway, and it would be deafening. Colt stared at him with a dumbfounded expression, and I knew those were the most honest words Gabe had spoken in a long time. To me, maybe ever.

"Then why are you so hot and cold with me?" I asked, holding onto this raw, honest moment like it might be the only time I see it. "Why do you act like I don't matter to you, but do sweet little things that no one else would think of?"

"I can't lose you if I tell myself you're not mine," he muttered, eyes flickering down in shame. "But no matter what, I love seeing you light up. I live for the smile on your face when you're happy, then die a little at the thought of someone like that," he nodded at the human now being zipped into a body bag, "taking you away from me."

"Gabe," I voiced more breathily than I intended. "Then what's with the interrogation about Tak?"

"I don't know, I—" he sucked in a deep breath. "I fucked up, Miriam. I'm sorry. I've been such a dick, and I thought you wanted to replace me with him." He looked at Tak. "Sorry, dude. You did a good thing here. We all owe you our thanks."

"I'm just glad the two shaman are safe," Tak looked at me before raising his eyes to the main room where Mel's men fawned over her, blissfully unaware of the fact that someone just burst in to kill them.

All the better. No one needed that stress on their wedding day.

"I'm not replacing you, Gabe," I said, returning my attention to the wounded wolf. "But I was fully intending on kissing Tak, and that's something I should've brought up with you two first." I looked up at Colt, still wrapped around me protectively. "I was acting out of frustration and I'm sorry for that. It's not fair to any of you." I lifted my eyes to Tak, indicating I was referring to him as well.

He was still completely nude and not in the least bit shy. Leaning one large shoulder against the wall, he watched our conversation passively with broad arms crossed in front of an even broader chest. Black line tattoos arranged in intricate geometric patterns decorated the thick, corded muscles of his forearms. Keeping my eyes on his face and not anywhere lower was the biggest challenge of the night.

Colt pulled my attention away from the muscle-bound Amarok, lifting my chin up to make me stare into his gorgeous, golden eyes.

"Do you still want to kiss him, Mir?"

My whole body lit up like a match. I knew exactly what he was asking between those words and wanted to kiss him just for asking. Colt just understood me. There was no game with him, which was what I loved about him.

I nodded yes at his question, my throat too thick with desire to speak.

A naughty smirk pulled at my handsome wolf's lips. "Go get him, then."

I turned to face Tak, whose grin now echoed Colt's. With his clothes gone and the adrenaline still pumping through me at what just happened, I approached him until his arms dropped to his sides. His odd-colored eyes captured me, and his clean, masculine scent was intoxicating.

"Did you want to finish what we started?" My voice was low and husky. I'd never done anything like this before and probably never would have without Gabe's honesty and Colt's encouragement.

Tak's answer was a sexy, animalistic groan as his arm shot out to wrap around me. In the next moment, I was crushed to a hard chest and the mouth I'd been aching to taste came crashing down to mine.

❈   7   ❈

TAQQIQ

Miriam tasted just as sweet as she looked. Her lips parted for me like the petals of a flower. She melted against me, releasing soft moans and sighs as our tongues became acquainted in an erotic dance.

My hair came loose from my topknot after shifting back, and her soft hands threaded through my locks to scratch over my scalp.

I moaned at the delicious tingling sensations and deepened the kiss as I pulled her tighter. She tasted like spring after a long, cold winter. I'd never been with a shaman before and my cock sprung to life like I was a teenage virgin again.

Oh shit!

Breathless, I jerked away, momentarily forgetting that I wasn't wearing anything.

"I'm sorry," I panted, covering my cock and balls with my hand. The damn thing all but stabbed her in the thigh.

"Don't be," she said with a foxy smile. "I'm flattered to have gotten such a reaction."

Her tall wolf, Colt, cleared his throat as he turned to look back at the reception hall.

"The party's winding down. We'll be seeing the bride and grooms tomorrow for brunch, so I'm sure they won't mind if we skip out early."

"What are you suggesting?" the shorter, muscular one, Gabe asked.

"I'm suggesting we take this party back to our place." Colt grinned wolfishly at Miriam. "Unless you'd prefer some alone time with Tak."

Miriam turned back to me, closing the distance once again. She skimmed a hand across my chest, fingertips resting over my heart that threatened to break out of my ribcage.

"Tak, I'd love to continue this," she whispered huskily. "Would you be alright with my men joining us?"

"Of course," I growled eagerly. "Whatever brings you pleasure."

Colt and Gabe wasted no time in loosening their ties and untucking their shirts, their wolf features already taking over.

"Follow ursss," Colt instructed as his jaws elongated into a slender muzzle, lips pulling back into a toothy smile.

Miriam rode on my back as I followed her wolves through the forest. In my Amarok fur, we had a silent conversation, completely with our thoughts.

Do you often take a third lover to join you with your men? I asked.

No, she admitted. *You're the first, actually.*

I'm honored, I told her. It was the truth. Shaman were sacred to my species. They were the only kind of human who could understand and communicate with us. To be invited to one's home, much less to their bed, was considered a great privilege.

I'm sorry for airing out our relationship struggles in front of you like that, she said after a moment of companionable silence. *I don't usually do that, but I guess everyone was feeling intensely emotional today.*

You don't need to apologize, I said. *I was happy to witness a turning point for your Gabe. I hope he appreciates you more.*

Her fingers clutched tighter around my fur and my heart skipped a beat.

Can all Amarok talk like this? she asked. *Mel, my shaman friend who got married today, is the only one I've heard speak with her thoughts to other shifters.*

Yes, we speak to each other and humans this way when we can't use our mouths, I explained. *I didn't know other shifters couldn't.*

You're fascinating. Miriam's mental voice brimmed with awe. It would have made me blush if I were human. *How much longer are you staying?*

I don't know, I answered honestly. My original plan was to head home immediately after the reception, but the pretty little shaman on my back threw quite a wrench into those plans.

Well, you won't leave too soon, I hope, she said. *I'd love to learn more about you, Tak.*

A growl of desire rumbled deep in my chest. *I feel the same way, Miriam.*

Her wolves led us to a modest, but comfortable cabin deep in the woods. The air was cooler and wilder out here, which made it feel more like home.

Miriam slid off my back after I trotted up to the front door. Her men had already gone inside and a warm, yellow light filled the windows.

With a smile, Miriam took my hand and pushed the door open to bring me into her home.

"Miriam," I hesitated at the door while she shot me a quizzical look.

"We Amarok look like wolves, but we don't hunt in packs," I told her. "We're solitary animals, for the most part. I've never been part of a shaman's... harem." I swallowed. "If something is off-limits, or I act out of line in any way, please tell me. I'm truly honored to be invited into your home, and I only want to make you feel safe and plea—"

She cut me off with a kiss, taking a small jump to reach my lips, which forced me to catch her. I held her flush against my body once again, forgetting all my reasons for hesitating the moment I tasted her on my tongue.

When we finally parted for a breath and she led me inside, I followed without question. Colt and Gabe waited for us in the bedroom, naked as the day they were born. Colt sat in an armchair by the window. Gabe laid back on the bed, leaning against the headboard. They stroked themselves idly, eyes focused on Miriam.

"You take the lead, Mir," Colt said, his voice already tight with desire. "You and Tak get to know each other. Bring Gabe and me in whenever you're ready."

"You guys are the best," she cooed before turning back to me with a smile. "Does that sound good to you?"

I lifted her off the ground in reply, securing her against me with my hands cupped around her ass. Her thighs squeezed around my waist, forcing the hem of her bridesmaid dress up higher. I took in her classical beauty—long dark hair, caramel skin, hazel eyes filled with lust, and the sexiest smile—before kissing her again like I needed her mouth to breathe.

I lowered us to the bed slowly until her back arched up from the mattress. Nudging her dress higher up her thighs, I kissed my way down the side of her graceful neck. The sweet sharpness of her nails dug into my back, accentuating her little gasps and moans every time I sucked her tender skin.

Somehow, I found the zipper on her back and yanked the flimsy thing down. All patience and coolness left me as I pawed at the bodice, eager to free her breasts and taste more of her delectable body.

"Gabe," I heard Miriam purr as my lips trailed down her chest. "How you doing, baby?"

"I'm so fucking hard watching you," was his throaty reply. "Does he make you feel good?"

"Mmm!" she moaned, sucking in a small gasp as I grazed over her pert nipple with my teeth. I, too, was hard as a rock and let her know it by letting my erection drag against her inner thighs.

"Colt?" she threw her head back as she reached an arm over to stroke Gabe next to us.

"You sound so fucking hot," her tall wolf growled from across the room. "Keep going, gorgeous. I'm here when you need me."

After peeling the dress all the way off her curvy hips and down her long, shapely legs, I dragged my fingertips slowly back up. Starting at her ankle, I watched her shiver as I traced over her calf muscle, then the inside of her thigh before I caressed her swollen, soaked folds.

"Mm!" Her mouth now filled with Gabe's cock, her hips lifted off the bed at my touch, pink lips glistening with arousal.

My mouth watering at her gorgeous pussy, I simply couldn't stop myself from taking a taste. I leaned down, lapping up her sweet juices as her muffled moans grew louder. Gabe kneaded one of her breasts while I cupped the other, rolling her nipple under my thumb until the stiff peak stood at attention.

As she greedily slurped on his cock, my hand explored her luscious curves on its way down her body to meet my mouth. I released her lips and moved my focus up to her clit, lashing my tongue on her swollen little bud as I pressed a finger inside her.

Her hips wanted to buck against my face, but I held her down, adding a second finger to stroke her channel. Her moans grew desperate, frantic and frenzied as her orgasm built. I sealed my lips around her clit and sucked her little hot button while my fingers tapped on it from the inside.

She came explosively, her pussy closing like a vice around my fingers as her thighs trembled so beautifully. By all the gods in the sky, there was nothing more beautiful than watching a woman come undone with pleasure.

From the sounds of Gabe's moans, he came as well. His chest rose and fell with exertion as Miriam licked and swallowed him.

I drew out her orgasm as long as I could, dragging my tongue all over and around her pussy until she twitched with sensitivity and the aftershocks. Sitting back on my heels, I took a moment to just look at this woman, flushed and sated.

"You're so sexy, Tak," she panted, her eyes drinking in my scars of battles past, my tattoos, until her gaze settled on my cock, engorged, stiff, and ready.

"Miriam," I rasped, tracing the curves of her waist to her hips in wonder. "You are the very definition of sexy."

"Tak," her arms reached for me, "God, I fucking want you."

With a groan, I lowered myself back down to her, claiming her mouth in a kiss as my cock nudged itself between her slick thighs.

"Colt?" she called for her tall wolf again as I tasted her sweet neck.

"I'm here, love," he said gruffly, somewhere closer than before.

Miriam's head tilted up, and he kissed her waiting mouth. Sitting up near the headboard, he directed her hand to his shaft as he swallowed her sweet moans.

I pressed up to my hands, fisting my cock and stroking the head between her folds as Gabe came to her other side. He kissed her neck and caressed her pillowy, gorgeous tits as I slowly pressed inside her.

Her pussy hugged so tightly around my head, I stopped moving. She pulled away from kissing Colt to stare up at me.

"Fuck, you're big," she breathed.

"I'll go as slow as you need," I assured her, although my jaw was tight. She was so hot and felt so good wrapped around the most sensitive part of me, I'd pop off too early if I wasn't careful.

I circled my thumb over her clit, watching as she turned to kiss Gabe, her hand stroking Colt in a steady rhythm.

After a few moments, her walls relaxed enough to let me further inside. Every inch felt better than the last. Pure pleasure radiated from the tip of my cock all the way to my toes. She felt so incredible and looked so fucking hot between her two men. I already knew I wouldn't be going back to Alaska tomorrow. Maybe not even next week.

The wolves teased, touched, and kissed her upper half until I was fully sheathed inside her. A deep growl escaped me as I began my thrusts, watching her for any signs of pain or discomfort.

"Do you like Tak's cock, baby?" Colt asked as her moans matched the impact of my thrusts. "You like how he fills your pussy up?"

"Yesss," she hissed, her eyes meeting mine through her thick eyelashes.

That only spurred me on to thrust harder, crashing my hips to hers while our gazes remained locked. My eyes, being two different colors, often made people uncomfortable, but ever since we first spoke today, she maintained eye contact with me. It was a small thing, but it made me feel like she accepted me. Now, in her bed, with her two mates, the least I could do was please her into another dimension.

I brought my hand to where our bodies connected, strumming her clit to coax another orgasm out of her.

"Tak," she gasped, gripping my forearms as her pleasure heightened, her pussy closing in around me on all sides.

For a moment, it was just us. There could have been a hundred naked men standing around, and it wouldn't have broken through the intimacy, the intense chemistry locking our eyes and our bodies together.

My mouth fell to hers. Claiming her, tasting her, needing her. My fingers threaded through her hair until my palms cradled the back of her head. Her hands slid from my arms to my back, pulling me to her until skin kissed skin.

My thrusts became wild and uncontrolled, but she took it all and begged me for more. Just on the edge of my release, her orgasm shattered around me. Milking my cock with fierce convulsions, she drew my come almost violently from my balls. Spilling inside her, both exhausted and exhilarated me.

But apparently, she wasn't done yet.

Rolling up, she pushed me back to kneeling, then got on all fours in front of me. I groaned and shivered as her soft tongue gently licked me, cleaning me off while the intensity of my orgasm subsided.

Colt kneeled behind her as she did so, making her cry out as he slid into her in one powerful thrust. The tall wolf liked to dominate, I noticed. He fucked her hard, pulling her hips back as he crashed forward against her. Gabe remained off to the side, caressing and kissing her back. I reached under and played with her breasts when she finished licking me. Colt's punishing thrusts rocked her beautiful tits right into my awaiting palms.

I watched her face as he made her come a third time, stroking her cheek and neck as I thought how much I'd like to watch face contort like that in morning light.

Following Colt's release, we all collapsed in a sated pile. To my surprise, Miriam placed her head on my chest and snuggled into my side. Gabe curled up behind her and Colt scooted further down to rest his head on her thighs.

"So, think you might stay a little longer?" Miriam murmured sleepily right above my heart.

I caressed up her arm that draped across my body, stopping at her shoulder to rub small circles there.

"I think you've convinced me," I chuckled with a kiss to her forehead.

❧ II ❧
A HAREM OF FREAKS
HONEYMOON

❧ 8 ☙

MELODY

"Romania better be as amazing as you are." I caressed the back of Raz's neck, digging my nails lightly into the dark, buzzed hair on his scalp. "It's gonna take a lot to make me want to get off this plane."

"I knew flying first class would ruin you," Arjun teased, looking up from his magazine across the aisle from me. "You're such a princess now."

"A *pregnant* princess," I corrected him, sticking out my tongue. "And now that you've said your wedding vows and I'm growing your baby, you have no choice but to obey my every whim."

"Grand," my tiger shifter huffed, returning his attention to his magazine, but I didn't miss the smirk playing on his lips.

Next to me, Raz chuckled as he leaned into my head scratches, draping an inked hand over my thigh. Seeing the fresh tattoo of my name around his left ring finger made my heart skip a beat. He preferred to wear the ring I gave him at the ceremony on a chain around his neck. I'd never tire of seeing the symbols of my men's love and devotion to me.

"You'll never want to leave Romania once you see it, *steluta*," he assured me. "My home country has a dark, ancient beauty to it.

Despite everything that's happened in my past, I've honestly missed it."

"I'm surprised you wanted to come here for a honeymoon." I curled my feet underneath me on the spacious plane seat, careful not to kick Connor, who was sound asleep on the other side of me.

"I wanted you to see where I came from," he squeezed my knee affectionately. "As a way of getting to know me better, I guess."

"Aww, you're sweet, Raz," I leaned over the armrest to kiss him, savoring the intoxicating smoky scent of my dragon shifter.

"I have my moments," he grinned back, pushing up the armrest to secure his arm around me and pull me closer.

"I can't wait to see your homeland," I told him, snuggling into his side. "I'm sure I'll love it almost as much as I love you."

"You'll definitely love it more than England," Arjun piped up. "My country hasn't got much going for it aside from our tea and fish and chips."

"What are you talking about?" I demanded. "There's got to be lots of great stuff about England!"

"I'm a tiger shifter, dove, in case you forgot," he answered with snark. "I'd take a spooky dark forest over a ride in a London cab any day of the week."

"Fine." I rolled my eyes at him. "I would like to see your home too one day, though."

He looked thoughtful for a moment. "I'd rather take you to India, I think. For some reason, I've always felt a closer connection to my mum's homeland than my own."

"We'll plan on it, then." Partially because I wanted to but also just to annoy him, I stood from my seat, removing myself from Raz's embrace to cross the aisle into my tiger's lap.

"Hello," Arjun breathed softly, his ocean-colored eyes bright with pleasant surprise.

"I'm sorry, am I disturbing you?" His magazine fell forgotten into the empty seat next to him as I straddled his thighs, purposely situating my chest at eye level with him.

"Yes, always," he sighed, fingertips skimming along my hips to my waist. "My gorgeous, cheeky wife is such a bother."

"What are wives good for?" My lips hovered just above his as my hips began a slow roll, grinding into his lap.

My tiger let out a frustrated growl as I pulled away when he lifted his mouth to kiss me. "You want to play that game, dove?" His powerful arm wrapped around me, holding my lower body down in his lap with no room to escape. "You really want to play cat and mouse with a *tiger*?"

Behind me, I heard a dry chuckle and the unclicking of a seat belt, followed by booted footsteps walking away. I figured Raz was getting up to look for some action with Hunter. Good thing we had this first class suite to ourselves.

"What if the flight attendants come through here?" I leaned my head back, giving Arjun access to the full column of my throat.

"Let them." He placed hot, lingering kisses under the length of my jaw. "I'm sure it won't be the first time they walk in on honeymooners who couldn't wait to land."

With a bold yank, he shoved my bra and blouse up high on my chest, letting my tits spill out. I was still in the first trimester of my pregnancy, but the damn things already went up a cup size. Of course, none of the guys complained.

Arjun's eyes remained glued to mine, daring me to stop him as his hands smoothed up my thighs next, hiking my skirt up. I sucked my bottom lip between my teeth, urging him on. To be honest, messing around up here, with the danger of being caught, thrilled me.

Still, a rustling sound behind me made me freeze, much to Arjun's amusement.

"Why does all the fun stuff happen while I'm asleep?"

I looked back across the aisle to see Connor sitting up and rubbing his eyes.

"You're not missing anything, grumpy," I giggled. "Get over here."

He stepped across to our row of seats in one long stride, a wicked gleam in his forest green eyes as he took the seat next to us.

I leaned over to kiss him, Arjun taking one of my nipples in his teeth as I did so.

"Mm!" The light sting made me jump, almost losing my balance if my men weren't so quick to hold me up.

Connor held my nape and my upper back as his tongue dove into my mouth. I wrapped my arms around his neck to avoid tumbling into his lap.

Arjun seemed to enjoy my leaning over sideways position. His large hands skimmed over my ribs and waist, followed by his teeth grazing over my skin and making me shiver.

Shifting my weight, my hands dropped to Connor's lap to stay balanced. He was already tenting his jeans, a sight that thrilled me even more now that we were on a plane.

"Need that taken care of?" I asked in a breathy whisper, dragging my fingertips over his zipper.

"Babe, you can put googly eyes and craft paper outfits on my dick if you want to. As long as you're touching me, the answer is always yes."

"For fuck's sake, Connor," Arjun groaned. "The last thing I want to think of is your cock in a fucking tiny bowler hat and waistcoat."

"I bet I know what you do wanna see, RJ."

"Hmm?" My tiger long gave up on telling Connor not to call him that nickname. He was too busy kissing the side of my breast right then, anyway.

"Our wife's lips wrapped around it." Connor's gaze heated. "I bet you want to make her moan as loud as she can with her pretty mouth stuffed full."

"You're not too far off," Arjun purred, grinding his own erection into my core. "But I want to leave some fun for when we arrive at our destination."

"Take it as far as y'all want." Connor licked his lips. "But I've always wanted to get sucked off over a mile high."

"Is that so?" I eased his zipper down and undid the top button with two fingers. "How come I never knew that?"

"Because it's a minor fantasy compared to the one thing I really wanted." He cupped my face and pressed a tender kiss to my lips. "Finding the woman of my dreams and raising a family with her." His hand fell to my lower belly.

"Well, I'm here to make all of your fantasies come true." I nipped his earlobe and began a slow trail of kisses down his neck. "Until death do us part."

"Fuck, babe," he groaned as my hands slipped inside his boxer briefs, stroking his already thick, hot length.

Arjun's hands kneaded my ass and inner thighs, getting me thoroughly worked up until I was practically dripping in his palm when he pressed it against my core.

"Fuck," he growled, echoing Connor. "You really love being shared, don't you, dove?"

"Mmm." I had kissed my way down Connor's chest and abs and just took the crown of his dick into my mouth. To further illustrate my point, I rolled my hips against Arjun's hand.

"Goddamn." Connor pushed my hair out of my face as my tongue swirled around him. "Look how bad she wants it, RJ. She's dying for your cock."

"And she'll get it," my tiger quipped as he moved my panties aside. "Later."

He pressed one finger into me and then another, stroking my channel in such a way that almost felt like his thick cock was inside me. I rode his hand as I sucked Connor sloppily, high on this lust for two of my husbands. I didn't care if anyone came in and saw. We were newlyweds and couldn't stop ourselves. And there just happened to be five of us.

"You're so fucking sexy," Arjun rasped, grinding the heel of his palm against my clit as I brought Connor to the back of my throat again and again. "Such an incredible fucking woman. I want you to come for me."

"Mmm..." I was already so close. My thighs quivered every time his hand fucked me. Connor rolled my nipples between his fingers, piling on more intensity to my building orgasm as he began thrusting into my mouth.

"Oh God, babe. Yes, take my cock," he hissed. "Take it all while your tiger makes you come."

Arjun's fingers thrust into me one, two, three more times before my pussy convulsed around them. My release sent me squirming across both of their laps. Connor let out a string of unintelligible curses as his cock stood erect like a steel beam and sprayed the back of my throat.

I swallowed every last drop of my Marine husband and lapped at him for more.

"Holy fuck," he panted, glancing over at Arjun. "We are some lucky sons of bitches."

"That we are," my tiger agreed, withdrawing his hand from me. I could feel that he was still as hard as a rock.

"Aren't you frustrated, tiger?" I rolled my hips against him again, enjoying the conflict in his blue-green eyes.

"Oh, painfully so, dove," he grinned at me. "But I'm fond of a little delayed gratification."

❊ *9* ❊

RAZVAN

With my *steluta* busy playing with Arjun, I went to find a plaything of my own.

I found Hunter alone in the next row of seats in our private first-class section. As usual, he was video chatting with the pups.

"Are you doing everything Uncle Colt and Gabe are telling you to?" he asked sternly.

"Yes, Dad," they said in unison. "Hey Daddy Raz!" Rinna squealed when she saw me lean into the frame.

"Hi, love," I smiled at her. The pups had taken extremely well to Mel as a stepmother and her three other mates as father figures. Adopting them was all but official. We were just waiting for the paperwork to be processed, but I already thought of those pups as my own kids. I loved their father and their new mother in the deepest parts of my black, fire breathing soul.

"Dad, we wanna play tag with Bella and Joey," Roo pouted. "Can we talk to you tomorrow?"

"Fine," Hunter sighed. "But be good. When Auntie Jeanie says go inside, you do as she says. You hear me?"

"Yes, *Daaaad*."

925

"Okay. I love you guys."

"Love you too. And you too, Daddy Raz!"

"Have fun, guys. Love you."

Hunter ended the call and leaned his head back with a sigh.

"You worry too much about them." I leaned in to kiss his pale, unblemished neck. The bites I left on our wedding night had already healed.

"I've never been this far away from them," he said. "Or away for this long."

"They're in excellent hands," I assured him, caressing his chest. "And two weeks will fly by before you know it."

"You're right," he admitted with an affectionate squeeze of my knee. "As usual."

"I have my moments," I grinned, kissing his neck with more force.

"What's gotten into you?" his breath hitched as my teeth dragged along his throat.

"*Steluta's* messing with Arjun." I cocked my head, listening to the muffled sounds of moans in the next aisle up. "And Connor too, sounds like."

"Sheesh," Hunter chuckled. "We haven't even landed in Romania."

"You know we have a saying in my country." I turned his mouth to mine. "It roughly translates to, 'we can die at any moment, so make love as often as you can'."

Hunter narrowed his golden eyes suspiciously. "Is that true?"

"Nah, I just made it up."

With that, I grabbed the back of his neck and pulled him in for a rough kiss. His teeth came down on my lip, making me moan and my cock jolt to attention. My split tongue caressed the inside of the pale wolf's mouth as he shoved me down on the seat.

I wrapped my legs around his waist and pulled his hips to mine just as he pinned my arms down. His cock felt just as hard as mine through our jeans, heavy, thick, and so fucking good as we rubbed against each other.

He bit my neck with a growl and my dragon roared back, fighting to dominate this wolf as wisps of smoke escaped my mouth.

This was what I loved about being with a man. We could release aggression in a healthy way and play rougher than we usually could with women. I loved Mel and would've been happy enough just to be with her. But she encouraged Hunter and I to explore our attraction to each other. Before I knew it, I found myself in love with two people. She fell in love with four. Now, I couldn't imagine my life any other way.

"You drive me fucking crazy, you know that," Hunter rasped against my throat. "Almost as crazy as her."

"You're a bigger cock tease than her," I ribbed him back, loving the heat and weight of his hard body on top of me. So different from the softness of a woman, but still enough to make my dragon claw at the surface. I claimed both of my mates, but yearned to do it again and again. I wanted to leave no doubt in Hunter's brain that he was mine.

"Because I *have* a cock," he grinned slyly. "I know a thing or two about teasing them."

I wrestled my arms free from his hold and bucked my hips to send him tumbling to the floor. I was on top of him in a flash, pinning him flat. Already, our chests heaved with ragged pants, our hearts pounding in tandem as they pressed against each other. If someone from the cockpit heard our tumble, they smartly didn't come out to investigate.

"What are you two doing?"

We looked up to see Mel standing on her long, shapely legs, hands on her hips. Her cheeks were flushed and clothes rumpled, eyes dilated with lust. I could smell her arousal like the sweetest nectar.

"Waiting for you, *steluta*," I grinned at her. "Seems you still want to play."

"With you guys?" she smiled back. "Always."

She took a seat, looking at us on the ground like a queen ruling over her subjects. I released Hunter to lean over in front of her and give her a long, languid kiss. Her moans from my split tongue caressing hers drove me wild. When she reached for the bulge in my jeans, her soft touch couldn't come soon enough.

Hunter moved to the seat next to her, kissing her neck and spreading open her beautiful legs. I went to sit on her other side, my pants already down to my knees with my pierced head poking out of the top of my boxer briefs.

She took the moment to turn and kiss Hunter, melting under his touches as I lazily stroked my cock over my underwear. When his hand slid up her thigh to tease her clit, she practically hit the ceiling as she jolted in response.

"Someone's jumpy," he teased, kissing the tip of her nose.

"I'm really sensitive." She was already panting. "Arjun…gave me one that was intense."

"Damn pussycat," I yelled loud enough for him to hear in the next aisle. He didn't respond, but I could just picture him rolling his eyes and sipping his tea with a smug grin.

"So we get to just tease you, rile you up?" Hunter's eyes flashed excitedly, his hand moving under her blouse. "Until you're ready for some intensity again?"

"I was thinking," she said coyly, fingers trailing down his arm, "I could let you guys sit back and relax. Get in the right mood for your honeymoon."

She slid off the seat, kneeling in front of him as she pulled apart his belt. My cock twitched, and I pulled my hand away from it, or else I'd be too close to the point of no return already.

"Come here, Raz," Mel patted the seat next to Hunter, then slid his pants down to his knees.

"Ah, remember when we first did this, wolf?" I smirked at him as I scooted over, my tattooed thigh pressing against his pale one. "Feels like it just happened."

Hunter chuckled, which turned into a moan as Mel dragged her soft tongue down the length of his shaft. "I was terrified of touching you back then," he murmured to me. "I knew once I did, there would be no going back."

"And look at us now." I cupped the back of his neck and pressed my forehead to his. "Fucking marital bliss."

He smiled before our mouths crashed together. I closed my eyes as I tasted him, soon feeling Mel's soft hand wrap around my thick base. The only sounds I heard were Hunter's moans and our wife's wet mouth sucking him greedily.

"Oh, God." Hunter's mouth broke away from mine to watch her bob up and down on him. "You're so good at that, beautiful."

I bit his shoulder, thoroughly enjoying his face, and the hitched breaths he took. Mel's hand gently stroked me from root to tip, and I wrapped my hand around hers to make her squeeze harder.

She released Hunter's dick with a wet pop of her lips and smiled up at me as she moved over to my cock.

"Is my dragon asking for more attention?" Her tongue circled my head, flicking at the three piercings on the flared edge.

"Always," I stroked her cheek. "I can never get enough of you."

My wife swallowed me into her mouth, and my head slammed back against the headrest at the sensation. Her lips and tongue were fucking heaven. How could such soft body parts get me as hard as a steel rod?

Hunter grabbed my face for another rough kiss, Mel's hand working his long, gorgeous cock in my peripheral vision. She went back and forth between us for ages, sometimes taking a break to stroke both of us while we kissed each other and her.

"I love you," I murmured to her, leaning over to cradle her face as I kissed her. *"Te iubesc, steluta,"* I repeated in my mother tongue.

She was the first person I fell in love with, and Hunter, the second. I'd known casual sex and debauchery with both genders all my life. Everyone wanted to hook up with the tattooed bad boy with the split tongue, but no one ever cared about me like these two did. And once I found them, I swore I'd never let them go.

"I love you, my dragon," she smiled against my lips.

"Hey." Hunter leaned over and placed an uncharacteristically soft kiss on my cheek. "You're my mate and I love you too."

I grinned like a six-year-old on his birthday. No shifter ever claimed me as a mate before and I loved that Hunter reminded me I was his. I went through being drugged, beaten, caged, forced to swallow swords and every form of torture imaginable. I thought I'd die forgotten and discarded in a seedy roadside carnival, not live happily ever after with two amazing mates.

"I love—ughhh."

Mel swallowed me again, and when my cock hit the back of her throat, I forgot how to form words.

"You want my come, *steluta?*" I asked her, thrusting into her sweet mouth. "'Cause that's what you're gonna get if you keep deep throating me like that."

"Mmm!" she replied enthusiastically, taking me deeper. Her hand slicked faster up and down Hunter's shaft.

"Fuck." Hunter squirmed next to me, his cock turning red as he neared the edge. "How close are you?"

"Not much longer," I panted.

"What if we both go at the same time?"

"Then you'll have a mess to clean up," I smirked at him.

"Dick." He punched me in the arm, so I grabbed a fistful of his long, platinum hair and pulled.

When our mouths crashed together again, he bit my lip so hard, I tasted blood.

That little bit of pain and male aggression was all I needed. My orgasm ripped through me, shooting out the tip of my cock to paint Mel's tongue.

"Holy... fuck!"

Her hand stroked me, milking my rigid cock like her pussy would to drain my balls and take everything I had.

She licked her lips and smiled as she released me, spent and conquered. As she moved to Hunter to finish him, she kept one hand on my thigh and I locked my fingers with hers.

Hunter released a deep sigh as her mouth covered him, taking him down her throat with no sign of fatigue, her hand massaging his balls to tease him even more.

"How did I get so lucky?" our wolf mused dreamily as he watched her please him.

"I think everyone here has wondered that at one point or another." I brought Mel's hand to my lips and kissed the back of her palm, my pulse still racing.

"*I'm* the lucky one," she declared, winking at me before descending on Hunter's cock again.

"That's what you think, beautiful." Hunter stroked her face. "But you have no idea."

"We have our whole lives to prove it to her, though," I leaned my head on his shoulder, watching her with him.

"Fuck," he hissed, grabbing a fistful of Mel's raven black hair, thrusting deep into her mouth. "I'm so close. Right there. Oh, God..."

Curious if it would have the same effect on him, I turned his head to face me and gave him a hard, biting kiss. The way he spasmed, stiffened, and moaned told me all I needed to know. I skimmed a hand over his chest to feel his heart beating wildly like a drum.

Just as Mel finished swallowing his load and licked him clean, we heard the speakers crackle over our heads with an announcement.

"Ladies and gentlemen, please take your seats and fasten your seatbelts as we make our descent into Bucharest, Romania."

MELODY

"Wait, why aren't we staying in Dracula's castle?" Connor demanded as we piled into the Mercedes SUV.

"Because it's a fucking tourist trap," Raz huffed from the front seat before speaking in a rapid string of Romanian to our driver.

I clamped my thighs together and tightened my grip on my purse strap. It was unbelievably hot listening to him speak his native language. Even when I just had his cock down my throat, I couldn't get enough of my dragon shifter.

"So? It's *Dracula's* fucking castle!"

"You do realize it wasn't *really* his castle?" Arjun said. "It just inspired the story, and even that is debated. Bram Stoker supposedly never visited Romania."

"What?!" Connor rocked dramatically in his seat. "I've been lied to my whole life!"

"No, you've just been thick as a brick the whole time."

"I mean, sure I have, but not in the way *you're* thinking, RJ."

"For fuck's sake," Arjun groaned, throwing a heavy arm over my shoulders. "Save me from his antics, dove."

"Too late." I kissed his cheek. "You're stuck with him for life."

"Damn." A lazy smile spread across my tiger shifter's face. "I suppose some sacrifices are necessary in the name of love."

His tongue swiped across mine in a slow, sensual kiss. I shivered with anticipation, knowing how much passion and intensity he was capable of. My tiger was holding back, waiting for the opportune moment to sink his teeth and claws into me.

As we drove through quaint villages and picturesque forests, Connor continued being a loudmouthed tourist in the row behind us. Next to him, Hunter was his usual quiet self, while occasionally laughing at something Connor said. Raz barely spoke a word of English as he conversed with the driver up front. I bet he was happy to speak his mother tongue again, as he rarely got the opportunity back home.

And in the middle row, Arjun continued to tease me with hot, slow kisses on my lips, face, and occasionally, my neck. I tried to distract myself with the beautiful scenery, but my tiger knew exactly how to pull just enough of my attention back to him.

After a few hours of driving, the villages grew few and far between, and the forest became denser and wilder. We pulled up to a gray-bricked home sprawling out through the trees and with one tower reaching at least four stories high.

"Aww, it's a mini castle!" I beamed at it out the window.

"Sort of," Raz grinned back at me from his seat. "This was a royal steward's summer home in the Middle Ages. He was a favorite of the *voivode* of Transylvania at the time."

"Dracula?" Connor asked excitedly.

"No," Raz barked back. "Vlad Dracul didn't have any favorites. He impaled people for fun."

The guys and our driver helped carry our luggage into the foyer. The ceilings were high and slanted with thick wooden beams. Intricate rugs covered the rustic hardwood floors, and a fire roared in the massive stone fireplace.

Further back through a wide doorway, another smaller fire crackled in an open brick oven. Cooks chatted in Romanian as dishes and cutlery clinked together. The smell of hearty meat and exotic spices made my mouth water.

"Buna ziua!"

I turned to find a young man, maybe sixteen years old, with dark hair and a shy smile approaching me.

"May I take your bags to your room?" he asked with a strong accent.

I quickly wracked my brain for the few Romanian words I knew. *"Da, multumesc!"*

He bit back a laugh and I wondered how badly I screwed up that pronunciation.

As he whisked my bags away, I felt a squeeze around my waist and a hot mouth against my ear.

"It's so hot to hear you speak my language," Raz purred.

"I was just thinking the same thing about you." I turned to plant a quick kiss on him. "It's a beautiful language. I just wish I could say some of the words better."

"Ah, I'll have you fluent by the time we leave." He nuzzled me and kissed my temple. "The kitchen staff are preparing dinner for later. Hunter and I are thinking of shifting and exploring the forest a bit to stretch our legs. Will you be alright?"

"With Arjun and Connor?" I rolled my eyes. "How will I ever survive?"

"You have to survive," my dragon chuckled, wrapping his tattooed arms around me. "You're carrying our baby."

He pressed a deep kiss to my mouth, forcing my lips open. That split tongue against mine made my knees weak to the point of nearly collapsing against him.

The thought occurred to me that I might *not* survive all the sex and attention from my four husbands on our honeymoon. If I had to go home in a sexed-out coma, I was okay with that. As long as I woke up in time to meet our baby.

"Let's check out the room," Raz grinned slyly as he pulled away. "I think you'll be pleased."

There were elevators going up to the tower, but we opted for the narrow, winding staircase. Raz and I paused at every window on the way up, taking in the breathtaking view of the Romanian countryside. I swore this place was magical. It felt like I was in a fairytale.

The others were waiting for us in the honeymoon suite when we arrived. Connor had taken off his prosthetic legs and sprawled out on the massive four-post canopy bed that looked like it could fit all of us. A large bay window looked out over the wild forest. This room had its own massive fireplace, already lit and bringing warmth and coziness to the ancient stone walls.

It was the epitome of medieval romance. In one word, perfect.

"Look, babe." Connor scooted to the foot of the bed, where a bottle of champagne sat in a metal bucket of ice. "They got non-alcoholic champagne for you."

"Read the label, *steluta*," Raz urged me gently.

I picked up the bottle and read aloud, "Congratulations, Melody, Connor, Hunter, Razvan, and Arjun. Enjoy your honeymoon and may it be the start of a wonderful life together. Oh, my..." I quickly wiped away a tear, emotions flooding me. "How did they know?"

"I arranged it." Raz hugged me from behind, kissing the back of my head. "Let's make a toast."

Hunter retrieved chilled glasses from a mini fridge that had more champagne and wine inside, while Arjun opened the bottle and poured. Once we all had glasses, Connor cleared his throat and raised his.

"To the incredible love of this woman who brought us together, who picks no favorites except me."

"Bollocks." Arjun jabbed him hard in the ribs, much to the amusement of everyone.

"To many years of love, laughter, and kinky sex ahead."

I snorted. Connor winked at me before continuing.

"On a serious note, I never thought I'd find myself in a group marriage," my Marine paused, his voice tightening with emotion. "But I'm so happy it's with you, babe, and that you have three other good men to protect, love, and cherish you. God knows you deserve every bit of it."

"Hear, hear." Hunter raised his glass and grinned.

"To our honeymoon," Arjun agreed. "And to Raz, especially for arranging the trip of a lifetime for us. Well done, mate. This is simply the dog's bollocks."

"*Noroc*, eh, cheers," Raz smiled. "Happy to do it for you, *steluta*, and even you three dicks. I love you all."

We drained our glasses, and I found myself kissing three different mouths in rapid succession. First Raz, then Connor, then Arjun. This time, all the soft teasing from the car was gone.

My tiger held me flush to his hard body, his kisses deep and hungry. I heard Hunter and Raz murmuring softly to each other as they kissed, so the person lifting my shirt and kissing my back could only be Connor.

"I need you," Arjun whispered harshly against my lips, his cock stiff and erect between us. "Christ almighty, how I fucking *need* you, woman."

"You're not the only one," Connor murmured behind me, lips ghosting a trail across my skin.

"You've already had her," Arjun said with a possessive growl, pinning my hips to his.

"I had her mouth," Connor argued, his hand traveling over my ass to cup between my legs. "But not here."

"You all enjoy yourselves," Raz chuckled. "We'll be back."

I looked up just in time to see him open the bay window and step one booted foot on the ledge. Even though I knew his abilities well and had seen him shift dozens of times, I still gasped when he stepped out into nothing and dropped out of view.

Not two seconds later, a dragon with shiny, obsidian scales and a wingspan nearly as wide as the room, hovered in front of the window with a powerful beat of his wings.

"Be back in time for dinner," I told him.

Raz's lips pulled back in a toothy grin and he beat his wings again, this time taking off toward the forest.

A tongue licked my hand, and I looked down to see a gorgeous white-furred, golden-eyed wolf staring back at me.

"You too, Hunter." I scratched his neck and planted a kiss on his head. "I love you."

He licked my face before turning to run down the spiral staircase, claws clicking on the stone.

"That'll make the staff scratch their heads," Connor laughed.

"Like the dragon flying overhead won't?" Arjun quipped.

"News of shifters and shaman have been spreading ever since our wedding," I reminded them. "It's about time people started seeing them out in the wild."

"Yes, but what I haven't figured out," Arjun placed my hand over his thick shaft, "is what position I'll take my wife in first."

"Smart man, getting back to what's important." Connor unzipped my skirt and let the fabric pool around my feet. "Jesus, babe, you're still soaked."

"Not my fault—"

Arjun cut me off with another hard kiss, palming each of my breasts in his large hands as I did away with his pants and underwear. My tiger purred delightedly as my fingers wrapped around velvety skin, stroking upward on his rigid shaft.

Connor pressed down on my back, asking me wordlessly to bend over while he peeled my panties down my legs. Arjun removed my top and his own as I did so, meeting his cock at my eye level.

Just as I slid my lips over his head, Connor's tongue dragged along my slit, helping himself to a full, luscious taste of me.

"Mmm," his voice vibrated along my most sensitive parts, sending tendrils of pleasure throughout my whole body.

I stole a glance up at Arjun as I continued stroking him, giving him small licks and sucks. His caramel skin looked delicious, and I wanted to lick every last inch of him. His abs flexed with each heavy breath as he watched me please him.

"Turn around, dove," he commanded with a growl.

"I'm not done back here, buddy," Connor protested.

"You'll get yours. I told you I need her." Arjun reached out and spun me around with one strong hand on my waist.

Now on my hands and knees in our luxurious bed, facing Connor, my cry echoed off the stone walls as Arjun entered me from behind.

"Fuck me," he hissed, pressing all the way in to sheath himself inside me.

After all the messing around on the plane, *this* was what my pussy was begging for. To be filled and fucked by one of my animalistic men.

My walls hugged around Arjun as he slid in and out, his grip like a vice around my waist. His hipbones bounced off my ass and his balls hit my clit with each deep thrust. All too soon, he pulled out of me completely.

"I need to pace myself." He gave me a sheepish grin when I looked over my shoulder, his muscular chest rising with every labored breath.

"Well, shit. Scoot over, RJ."

A new rush of heat filled my core as Arjun stood up, stiff cock jutting straight ahead, and Connor took his place.

Something about two, or multiple, men fucking me turned me on like nothing else. My back arched like a bow as Connor slid into me, my head thrown back far enough for him to kiss me.

"God, you're the sexiest woman alive," he groaned, slapping my ass with hard cracks until I whimpered from the delicious sting.

"Look at me, dove."

I gazed in front of me to a gloriously naked and hard Arjun. His cock glistened with my wetness.

"Clean me off with that pretty little tongue," he rasped.

I licked my own juices off of his shaft, getting every last drop as Connor pounded into me. It felt absolutely filthy, and I loved every bit of it.

With each hard thrust, my sexy Marine marched me closer and closer to an explosive orgasm. But then, he too, pulled out completely.

"Guys, I'm so close," I whined, my thighs quivering as I struggled to stay up on all fours.

"Mm, poor little dove," Arjun cooed. "Coming on the plane wasn't enough for you?"

I shook my head, my bottom lip stuck out and pouting.

"She's been pleasing her men so selflessly, like a good girl." Connor stroked my back, planting kisses all the way up my spine to my neck. I felt like I would explode any second.

"Lie back, love," Arjun kissed my lips, his eyes hooded. "Let us take care of you."

I flopped over onto my back, spreading out like Connor had earlier. Staring up at the rich, red canopy, I wondered how I became a princess in a castle with not one, but four princes.

Arjun hooked my legs over his thighs as he lined up to enter me.

His eyes locked onto mine as he pressed forward slowly, keeping his body upright.

Connor laid on his side next to me, his hands skimming over my body as Arjun built up a steady rhythm with his thrusts. My Marine caressed my waist, pinched my nipples, and kissed my belly. He did everything but touch my clit.

"Babe," I moaned, rolling my head around. All the sensations buzzing through my body had me just shy of the peak. "I can't stand it. I need..."

"What, this?" he pressed two fingertips to that tiny nub and circled.

"Oh, God, she just got so tight," Arjun groaned. He grabbed my hips and fucked me harder, pounding me with all his strength.

Connor kept the pressure steady on my clit, and I nearly jolted off the bed when my release came crashing down on me.

"Fuck," Arjun choked out as his release spilled inside me. I swore feeling his pleasure made me come again, drawing his cock deeper into me until he looked like he might collapse.

When he did, falling next to me on the bed, Connor swiftly took his place at my entrance.

"Can you handle a little more, babe?" he grinned down at me, stroking my thighs as his cock flexed against my tender flesh.

"Fuck me," I demanded through my panting. "Now."

"Yes, ma'am."

He filled me up smoothly, my pussy still eager and waiting for him. My Marine thrusted slower than Arjun, but rolled his hips to ensure I felt every inch of him deep inside.

"You feel incredible," he groaned, leaning down to kiss me.

"Mm, I love how you feel." I lifted my hips to meet his, thrust for thrust. "And you, my tiger." I turned my head to kiss the beautiful man lying next to me. Arjun's contented purr rumbled from deep in his chest and vibrated against my lips.

"You're so beautiful," he whispered, sliding his arm under my head. "I can't believe you're mine."

"I love you, Arjun." I kissed him again, melting like putty as his hands roamed my body. I only broke away to gasp as his fingers went to my clit, and my eyes snapped open to see his smug cat grin.

"You wouldn't mind another orgasm, would you, babe?" Connor picked up the speed of his thrusts, filling me in a way that felt so different from Arjun, yet just as delicious.

"Oh, God, you guys..."

Words escaped me as my eyes rolled back, losing myself to the hands, mouth, and cock all with the same goal in mind—to pleasure my body.

"Fuck, I'm almost there."

Connor sounded so far away through the blood pounding in my ears. The first jolt of release struck me like lightning, and then I felt him spill inside me. Each convulsion after that felt like another orgasm, again and again.

The next thing I knew, I woke up burning hot and sweating.

"Welcome back to the world of the living." Arjun unstuck himself from my left side, his ocean-colored eyes shining like two gemstones.

"How long have I been out?" I rolled to unstick myself from Connor, who laid sleeping on my other side.

"About a half hour. Raz and Hunter just got back. They didn't want to disturb you, so they're having pre-dinner cocktails downstairs."

"I suppose we should join them." I stretched and yawned.

"I'll get the shower started." Arjun dropped a kiss to my shoulder before climbing out of bed and heading toward the ensuite bathroom.

I watched his gloriously tight ass walk away before rolling back to Connor.

"Hey babe," I whispered, planting kisses on his face and neck. "Want to head down for dinner soon?"

"Mm," he threw an arm over me and pulled me close. "I love you so fucking much, baby."

I knew he was sleeptalking. As a heavy sleeper, he said hilarious nonsensical things sometimes, but right then, I could only smile.

"I love *you* so fucking much," I whispered back. "More than I can ever express."

"You're the woman of my dreams and the best wife a man could ask for. And you're going to be an amazing mother to our son."

Son?

I lifted an eyebrow. "How are you so sure it's a boy?"

Connor jerked and snorted, his eyes fluttering open.

"Hey babe," he yawned. "Is it dinnertime yet? I'm starving."

"Almost." I barely held back my laughter. "Raz and Hunter are downstairs. Arjun just turned on the shower."

"Perfect." He slapped my ass and rolled out of bed, walking on his hands toward the bathroom. "I can't wait for some shish kebabs or whatever the hell Romanians eat."

I just laughed as I followed him, ready to spend the next two weeks basking in the love and adventures of my honeymoon.

II

MELODY

"Where's Raz this morning?" Hunter looked at each of us at the breakfast table, the tattooed dragon shifter's place noticeably absent.

"He took off early for Bucharest." Arjun stirred a sugar cube into his tea.

The pale wolf frowned. "Why? He didn't say anything to me."

"He went to see his friend, remember?" I grabbed Hunter's hand and pulled him down next to me at the table. "The one who split his tongue and gave him all the tattoos? They haven't seen each other since before Raz got captured and shipped to the States. So they're off catching up."

Hunter nodded and didn't say anymore, but the wrinkle in his brow didn't go away as he buttered a slice of bread. Connor slid him a cup of coffee and patted his shoulder. I kissed his opposite shoulder before digging into my own breakfast.

After eating, Connor and Arjun decided to take off for some castle tours and Hunter mumbled something about running through the woods. His mood didn't seem to improve, so I cornered him outside before he could shift and take off.

"What's really bothering you?" I slid both arms around his slim waist, propping my chin on his chest to look up at him.

He sighed and tried to force a smile. "It's nothing, beautiful. Just my own stuff."

"Tell me," I urged, squeezing around him tighter.

It seemed like my shaman senses began picking up on subtler emotional shifts between my shifter men ever since we got married. I wasn't sure if it was the ceremony that seemed to strengthen my abilities—a lot of my own magic was still mysterious to me. But there was a definite shift between the time before, and after we declared ourselves husbands and wife. And right then I picked up a sense of woundedness from my gorgeous wolf shifter.

"It's just…" he sighed deeply, wrapping his long arms around my shoulders. "This is *our* honeymoon, and it feels like he's ditched us."

"Oh, love." I nuzzled my face into his chest. "He hasn't. This is just his first chance to see his old friend in years. Bucharest is at least two hours away by train, so he had to leave early to spend the day and make the most of it."

"But he couldn't take any of us?" Hunter frowned. "What if you or I wanted to check out the city?"

"We can, but then he'd be interpreting for us and doing all the touristy stuff without getting time with his friend." I played with the strands of long, platinum hair falling down his back. "This is his country, Hunter. His home."

"His home is with us."

"It is now, but he was taken from here forcibly. He didn't leave by choice and never thought he'd get a chance to come back. Now he has. So give him a day, love, just to speak his language, see a friend from his past, and just be a regular, Romanian dude."

Hunter snorted, but a wry smile pulled at his lips. "He's way too hot to be a regular anything."

"You got that right," I giggled, bringing my arms up to loop around his neck. "Anything else bothering you?"

"It was mostly that, feeling like we're all here to celebrate being together and he just took off on us." His hands dug into my shoulders, massaging gently. "What you say makes a lot of sense, though. I'm still kind of bummed and I miss him. But I understand better."

"He'll be back." I pressed a soft peck to Hunter's lips. "Do you want alone time with him when he's back?"

"No." His smile grew, golden eyes lighting up wolfishly. "But alone time with you and him, yes."

"Done." Our smiles touched, and then our lips opened up for a deeper kiss.

Our chests pressed together, hearts beating as one while our tongues mated and bodies heated. I had half a mind to get a quickie started right here, just a little warm-up for when our dragon returned, when a door slammed open and I jumped nearly a mile in the air.

"It's just the kitchen staff," Hunter laughed, pressing a kiss to my forehead.

Sure enough, our hosts came out of the side door speaking in rapid Romanian as they tossed kitchen scraps to the chickens behind our villa. We waved and smiled, saying good morning in our clumsy Romanian before Hunter tugged my hand toward the woods behind the property.

"Oh no," I said in mock despair. "A big bad wolf leading me to his lair in the deep dark forest."

"All the better to ravage you, my dear." He grinned and kissed my hand. "Raz and I found this spot the other day. It's not far, but there's a little clearing that's beautiful." He leaned close to my ear. "And private," he added in a husky whisper.

"Oh, lead the way, handsome wolf," I smirked back.

He kissed me once more before shifting. I ran my hand along the white fur on my husband's back while he trotted at my side. When I scratched his head, he looked up with the same golden eyes full of love and adoration.

The Romanian wilderness was magical. It felt ancient and untouched as Hunter and I walked through, the air tingling with life and mystery. Not that I didn't love being surrounded by my four husbands, but it was nice being alone with him. Just us and the sounds of the forest.

Goosebumps rose on my skin as the trees grew denser, blocking out the sun as the air grew cooler and damp.

Hunter nudged his nose against my elbow as I rubbed my arms. *Cold?* he asked with a soft lick and a whine.

"I'm okay." I carefully stepped over a decomposing log, wishing for a moment that I wore pants instead of a dress.

My white wolf rubbed against me like a cat, offering warmth in his dense fur. *Not much farther now,* he promised. *The sun will be out again in the clearing.*

"How is it you already know me so well?" I joked, scratching over his head.

You're my wife. He pressed his head into my side, tongue lolling out with a smile. *My mate.*

I paused in my walk to place a kiss on his snout. "I'll never get tired of hearing you say that. Any of you."

He licked my face before I could pull away. *And we'll never get tired of saying it.*

I ROUSED from my nap in the middle of the clearing to the beat of leathery wings.

"Raz's back," Hunter murmured sleepily. He'd shifted back at some point during our nap, and now my head rested on his human chest instead of his furry side.

The span of Raz's dragon wings blocked out the sun as he made a slow, careful descent. I felt the heat emanating from him like he was a miniature sun himself. Steely gray eyes watched us stretch and come up to sitting. Raz shifted in midair, dropping lightly on his feet with a devilish smile.

"Little risky to fly out here, don't you think?" I said with a frown.

"I was well into the forest before shifting," he assured me, planting a fast kiss on me before moving to sit beside Hunter. "No one saw, *steluta*. Promise."

"How was the city?" Our wolf curled into Raz, nuzzling and kissing the dragon shifter with all the affection and love of a puppy.

"Good," Raz leaned into him, soaking up the affection. "It was good to catch up with Luca. I missed my loves, though." He grabbed Hunter's hair in his fist, hard enough to make the wolf whimper slightly, before kissing him hard and aggressively. "Sorry to take off like that. I just had a very narrow window of when I could see him."

"It's okay." Hunter was panting slightly from the kiss, golden eyes sliding over toward me. "Mel made me understand."

I grinned at them together, my chest buzzing with love at their connection. Perhaps it was a shifter or scent thing, but they seemed so in tune with each other's smallest shifts in emotions.

The sly grin returned to Raz's face as he lifted the hem of his shirt. "Look what I got done."

He pulled the shirt all the way off, tattooed flesh already golden with a light tan. My eyes traveled over the designs, hunting for a new addition to the art on his body. It took a good several seconds before I spotted it.

"You pierced your nipples!" I said, already salivating at the new metal bars on his chest.

"They look good, don't they?" He looked down, turning from side to side like a woman checking out her cleavage.

"You always look good," Hunter growled softly, leaning in to kiss him again.

"What, *steluta,* you don't want to be in the middle of this?" Raz grinned lazily, spreading his hand behind him on the ground as Hunter peppered kisses on him.

"It's not that I don't want to." I stretched out on my side, propping my head on my elbow. "I just love watching you two."

My dragon let out a pleased hum at that, catching Hunter's jaw in his hand to kiss our wolf again. I clamped my thighs together in a futile attempt to stave off the friction that my body craved. But it was no use, watching my two shifter lovers kiss and touch with abandon. It was only us out here, no one to judge based on sexuality or shifter species.

Hunter resumed the path he started kissing down Raz's neck. The dragon shifter caressed his face, pushing his pale hair back as the kisses moved down his chest. He let out a groan as Hunter's mouth covered one of his freshly-pierced nipples.

"Does that hurt?" Hunter glanced up at him.

"No," Raz grunted. "Feels fucking good. Should've pricked those ages ago. Don't stop."

With a grin, Hunter's tongue flicked out to move the metal bar through the sensitive bud. He looked over at me with those golden eyes, and I had to check myself for visible drool.

"You should play with the other one, beautiful. It's fun."

Raz sucked his lip between his teeth as a grin threatened to split my face. "Don't mind if I do."

I scooted over to sit next to Raz, first losing myself in his gray, lust-filled eyes. "Hi, my handsome dragon."

"Fucking kiss me, my sexy wife," he moaned with a lopsided grin.

Our lips crashed together, the heat of fire within him filling my mouth and drenching my core. His split tongue fluttered around mine, always such an odd but addicting sensation. By the time my kisses fell to his neck and started down his chest, Hunter was already at his navel.

"God." Raz's head rolled back on his neck. "You two, just...fuck."

"Mm-hm," I agreed with a light tug of his nipple bar between my teeth.

His tattooed hand ran along my side, then underneath to grope my breasts. "Would you get some piercings here for me to play with?"

"Nope." I looked up at him with my cheek on his abs. "Not in a million years. Pain is your thing, fire boy."

"Fine," he chuckled. "Your nipples are perfect as they are, anyway."

I kept my kisses at his chest and neck level, giving into hungry clasps of his mouth on mine when he begged for it. That split tongue would undo me if I let it, a seductive serpent flicking out for a taste. If I didn't keep my head on straight, I'd stand up and let that flexible muscle work my clit into a greedy frenzy of orgasms. But it wasn't all about me. Right now, I wanted to assist two of my men in enjoying each other.

Raz let out a heavy groan the moment Hunter freed his cock, heat lighting up in my dragon's throat with his desire. Soft wisps of smoke escaped his lips and nostrils as our wolf lover wrapped his mouth around him, tongue flicking over the metal balls piercing the flared edge of Raz's crown. I caressed down his stomach, resting my head on Raz's shoulder as we watched Hunter suck him, his palm sliding up and down the rigid length.

"Mm." Hunter released our dragon's dick with a pop of his mouth, resting his head on Raz's thigh with a dreamy smile. "Share his cock with me, beautiful."

"You don't have to ask me twice." I slid down with a grin, keeping my eyes locked on Raz's until the last possible moment when I lowered my mouth over him.

"Fuck...me."

"We'll get there," Hunter chuckled, dragging his mouth over the V-line in Raz's hips as I devoured him.

Our dragon cursed and groaned and writhed beneath as we passed his dick back and forth like an ice cream cone. When one sucked him down, the other massaged his balls, our favorite way to make him squirm.

"I'm not kidding. I need to fuck one of you," the dragon shifter rasped. "Decide in five seconds or I'll pick someone at random."

"Greedy dragon," I teased, lifting back up to kiss him.

"I'm not known for being patient," he growled against my lips. A rough smack on my ass made me gasp. "Hop on, *steluta*."

I threw a leg over to straddle him, tattooed hands immediately pulling the top of my dress down to my waist before surrounding my breasts. Hunter was kind enough to bunch up my skirt and pull my underwear to the side.

Sharp wolf kisses blazed a trail from my shoulder up my neck. A soft tongue, split down the middle, caressed my nipples before licking a path to my throat. I leaned forward to suck on Raz's neck, scooting forward to glide my sex along his length, still wet with a mixture of my and Hunter's saliva.

His moan cut off thanks to a kiss from Hunter. I giggled into Raz's neck and sucked on his earlobe, making his hips buck underneath me. I absolutely loved it when they kissed each other with me in the middle. Their attraction and love for each other was one of my favorite parts of our relationship.

I slid up Raz's length until his tip met my entrance. He let out a tortured sound as I rubbed over his head, teasing him. He thrust up to enter me and I moved away. The dragon shifter was usually the top in his and Hunter's relationship, so I liked to take his control sometimes—make things a little more balanced.

"*Steluta*," he growled. "You're not being very nice."

"Dragon," I mock-growled back. "You did leave us for the entire morning."

"Is that what this is about?" he whined.

Hunter chuckled and pulled away, his kisses returning to my back. "I felt a little jilted earlier but Mel talked sense into me. I guess this is how she expresses missing you though."

"I won't go again," Raz groaned. "I'll never leave your sight. Tie me to the bed if you want," he smirked. "Just sink that sweet pussy onto me, please."

"How about this?" I licked his ear, eliciting a shiver. "Take us next time."

"Take you?"

"Yes. I'd love to see Bucharest, and to meet your friend."

"Me too." Hunter leaned over my shoulder to plant another kiss on him. "We're married now, sharing all of our lives. I'd love to see the people and places of your childhood that made you happy."

"You would?"

I answered by sinking down onto his stiff length, taking all of him within, as I was more than ready.

"We love all of you," I breathed into his ear as I seated myself. "We accept and love every piece of your past, present, and future. You're ours."

Raz cupped my face, kissing me deeply as he reclined slowly onto his back. He propped himself on one elbow while I braced my hands on his chest.

"My beautiful wife." His gaze was hooded, voice low with the embers always burning somewhere in his body. "*Te iubesc*."

"I love you."

His piercings rubbed my front wall with each delicious slide in and out. Behind me, Hunter's fingers trailed down my spine and paused at my ass.

"Yes," I told him before he could ask the question. "I want you too, Hunter."

"Just fingers, or...?"

"No, you."

The wolf shifter nipped my shoulder with a delighted growl, then I heard him dig through my purse for our travel-sized bottle of lube. With four husbands who loved spontaneous sex, such a thing became necessary to keep on hand. And for the past few weeks, we'd been easing into anal with toys and fingers. It was a regular thing between Raz and Hunter and they were especially careful with me, if even too much.

Raz cupped a hand around my neck, pulling me down for another kiss. "Now this is a fucking honeymoon."

I continued to ride him slowly while Hunter gently stretched and prepped me. The wolf shifter unzipped, and his cock dropped on my ass with a soft slap. He began lubing himself up, the head of his cock resting on me as he stroked himself with sexy breaths.

"I want you both so bad," I whined, pressing down harder on Raz with each downstroke of my hips.

"You need to come first." Hunter's hand slid around to my front, reaching down to strum my clit where Raz and I conjoined. "Need to get nice and relaxed."

"I am relaxed!"

The guys laughed together, Hunter's teeth teasing the shell of my ear, while Raz's tongue moved to the nipple he neglected earlier.

"The more relaxed, the better." Hunter's breath teased my neck as he expertly strummed my clit, his hand moving with the rise and falls of my body.

"The better what?" I looked over my shoulder, daring him, my sweet and polite wolf, to say it.

"The better it is to take a cock in your sweet little ass and pussy at the same time." He didn't hesitate, and an extra strong jolt shot through my clit. It was so hot when he was unexpectedly dirty.

"Oh, she's close." Raz's lips trailed up the column of my throat, my breasts filling his hands. "Yes, squeeze my dick, my perfect little wife."

I crashed down on him once, twice, three times before my orgasm rocked through me like lightning. Raz lifted me off him but replaced his cock with his fingers so my convulsions wouldn't close around nothing.

"Give me her." Hunter's grip went to my waist and pulled me back onto his cock.

Iron-solid and slick with lube, he slid into me easily. I whimpered as he fucked me through the aftershocks, setting off a series of mini-orgasms.

"God, I love watching you two fuck." Raz reclined all the way back, his own cock slick and pulsing on his lower stomach while he took a breather.

He teased my nipples as they rocked back and forth from Hunter's thrusts, before running his touch down my body to my clit.

"Again?" I gasped, heat and sensitivity already spreading from my core.

"We do want you very relaxed," my dragon shifter reiterated.

He stroked another orgasm out of me within seconds, my walls fluttering around Hunter's length before he reluctantly pulled out.

"I promise I'm relaxed enough," I panted.

"I guess we believe you, beautiful," Hunter chuckled, sliding his cock down the cleft of my ass until his head met my opening.

He pressed against the tight ring of muscles, adding more lube to where we connected and pushed forward another inch.

"Doing okay, beautiful?"

"Yes, yes..." The stretching was different from in my pussy, but I still wanted it. And I wanted my sweet wolf more than anyone in a taboo, forbidden part of my body.

My fingers curled into Raz's chest as Hunter inched his way in, adding more lube the whole time. Raz reached his hand between my legs, steely eyes watching as our lover eased himself into my ass.

"Mm, fuck," Hunter cursed behind me, and I realized Raz was massaging his balls from between my legs.

"Just walking you back from the edge, wolf," the tattooed man grinned, sliding his hand back to stroke my folds and my wetness. "How's it feel back there?"

"You asking me or him?"

"You." Metallic gray eyes bore into mine. "I know he's in absolute heaven, but what matters most is our wife is happy."

"I love it when you say that word," I cooed dreamily at him. "And I'm good. It's...intense, but it doesn't hurt."

"Good." He leaned up and kissed me, split tongue caressing inside my mouth. "Are you ready for me?"

"Always."

Hunter paused in his slow thrusts to let Raz enter me from below. When his pierced head pressed through my entrance, I almost thought he wouldn't fit. I was so completely full of Hunter already, but Raz watched my reactions as he eased himself in slowly.

"Oh...God...fuck..."

"You okay?" Raz nipped kisses at my lips. "You need us to back off?"

"No, just slow at first."

They alternated thrusts, making small movements in and out of me. I leaned forward until Raz cradled me on his chest, his smoky scent warm and soothing like a campfire. It was surreal, having both of them in my body.

"Fuck, wolf, I can feel you through her," he growled beneath me.

"Same here." Hunter's voice was tight, his breaths ragged. "You're making her ass feel even tighter and it's too fucking good."

"More," I whimpered, unable to move without losing one of them. "I need more of you both."

They picked up speed together, stuffing me full, my senses overwhelmed. Pressing in together was almost too much, but when one pulled back, I needed more. It was such deliciousness in excess.

"Hunter, come here," Raz groaned with a rare use of our wolf's real name.

I rested my cheek on Raz's chest so Hunter could lean over my shoulder. They kissed in a hard clash of lips and teeth, their animal sides growling with need as they shared my body.

"Don't exclude yourself, beautiful." I lifted my head, allowing Hunter to kiss one corner of my mouth as Raz kissed the other.

Our three-way kiss was sloppy, uncoordinated, and so perfect and passionate. All discomfort was gone, and I eagerly whimpered for more from them. Hunter crashed his hips against my ass, fucking me there with full force now, while Raz slammed into me from below. We shared kisses, licks, bites, and moans as an explosive orgasm started building in me.

I thought there was no way my pussy could close tighter around Raz's cock than it already was, but the shock waves rippling through me proved me wrong. Waves of pleasure hit me so hard, it almost felt like drowning. I forgot which ways were up, down, or how to breathe. All I knew was my nerves were alight with mind-tingling pleasure, shooting the sensation to every cell in my body.

When my men spilled their releases into me, it set me off again. This time it was their pleasure getting me high like a drug. I collapsed on top of Raz and Hunter rested his chest on my back. Feeling three rapid, sated heartbeats as one was such a beautiful thing.

III

FUCKING HORMONES

12

CONNOR

I looked up from my news article, immediately alert at the sound of the tiny sob that Mel tried to smother. "Babe, what's wrong?"

"Nothing. It's nothing." She wiped at her eyes, but the tears and sniffles just kept coming.

I scooted closer in the wide bed, my hand instinctively reaching for her belly. I was no shifter, but the urge to protect my wife and unborn son was primal, animalistic. I'd give a slow, painful death to anyone that made her cry, destroy anything that put even the slightest amount of stress on her body that currently housed a tiny person.

"It's obviously not nothing. What—"

Looking down at the tablet resting on her belly, I saw a video playing of a puppy.

"His back legs are paralyzed, so they gave him a wheelchair!" Mel was full-on sobbing now. "That's *sooo* sweet."

I looked at her. "This is why you're crying?"

"It's just so cute...I can't..." she drew in a deep breath, wiping her eyes. "Sorry, you know my hormones are all out of whack."

"Don't be sorry," I chuckled, dropping a kiss to her shoulder. "I just want to protect you whenever you're upset." My hand slid across her belly, feeling for any kicks from our boy. "Both of you."

Her lips turned to me, finding my mouth. "I love you, Con."

I closed my eyes, savoring her kiss like it was our first one. "Love you, babe."

"Hey!"

A loud thumping up the stairs startled her, switching on my protective instincts again. Wrapping an arm around her entire belly, I looked at the door to see all three shifters—Arjun, Hunter, and Raz, shoving their way into the bedroom.

"What is it?" Raz was already puffed up, his dragon lungs ready to breathe fire at any threat. "We thought we heard crying."

"She's watching cute animal videos again," I explained.

"Sorry guys!" Mel was laughing now, her face flushed with embarrassment. "You know I get weepy when I watch that stuff."

"Don't be sorry." Hunter slid into bed on the other side of her. "It's really sweet that you get moved by that stuff."

The other two gathered around near her legs, Arjun immediately starting up a purr as he nuzzled the outside of her thigh. Raz caught her ankle and kissed her other leg, making her giggle and squirm as his split tongue danced over her skin.

"How's the pup?" Hunter caressed her belly just over my arm, leaning down to place a kiss on her gorgeous bump.

"Cub," Arjun corrected jokingly, and leaned up to kiss the underside of her stomach.

"He's calm so far today." Mel stroked her fingers through Hunter's platinum hair, while scratching the new scruff growing on my jaw with the other hand.

"Can I try something, love?" Arjun peered up at her, his smile cunning.

"What?"

He pressed the side of his face to her belly and amped up his purr. The vibration carried throughout her whole body in a steady, crackling rhythm. Within a few minutes, I felt small kicks fluttering against my palm.

"I saw that!" Raz cried out, crawling up to get closer. "Keep doing it."

Arjun kept his purr going while the rest of us gathered eagerly around Mel's belly.

"You think he likes it?" I wondered, watching the flurry of movement with awe. "Or is he kicking and punching like, 'cut that shit out!'?"

"Of course he likes it," Arjun grumbled. "Everyone likes purring."

"Sweet boy," Raz said, his voice thick with emotion as he nuzzled Mel's belly. "*Te iubesc, fiul meu.*"

After telling our son he loved him, he continued whispering in Romanian. I couldn't understand all of it, but I got the sense that it was full of promise and praise.

Hunter lifted his head, looking toward the open bedroom door. "You guys can come in here."

Roo's head poked through first, then Rinna's. "We can? I thought the bedroom was for adults only."

"Just this one time you can," the white wolf grinned at his pups. "Your little brother is moving around in Mel's belly. Come see him!"

They didn't need a further invitation than that. The kids sprinted toward the bed and tumbled onto the mattress.

"Easy," I warned them, still protective of Mel's condition.

"Gentle, guys," Hunter added. "Give me your hands."

Together, his pups stuck their palms out. Mel grabbed Rinna's and Hunter took Roo's.

"You can feel him," Mel smoothed our stepdaughter's hand over her belly. "Right about here."

"Ah! Is that his foot?" Rinna squealed excitedly.

"I think so," Mel smiled. "Your turn, Roo."

Hunter's son opted to press his ear to Mel's belly, acting dramatically like he was getting kicked in the face. Eventually, the kicks calmed down and Mel was no longer teary-eyed. The pups remained snuggled up to Mel's belly, gently nuzzling against her and talking softly to their new sibling. No one seemed eager to leave her side, so it was a good thing our bed was big enough to fit everyone.

"Need anything, babe?" I slid an arm around Mel's shoulders, rubbing out the tension in her neck as she began sinking into the pillows.

She turned her face toward me with a sleepy smile. "I have *every-thing* I need."

"Look at you," Arjun breathed softly as he lifted up to his knees, staring at her and all of us surrounding her. "I wish you could see your-self like this. You're a fucking goddess."

"Oh stop," Mel laughed.

"It's true," Raz chimed in, stroking an affectionate hand down her leg. "You're so beautiful. So perfect for us, it's unreal."

"That's what I've been trying to tell you for nearly a year." I dropped a kiss on her cheek.

"I still can't believe this is real, sometimes." Hunter clasped his fingers between hers, their rings making a soft, metallic clink. "Some days I still expect to wake up in a cage, stuck between shifts."

"But Mellie and Connor saved us!" Roo declared, crawling over to his dad.

"And us." Raz nudged Arjun.

"Ditto here," I sighed, resting my head on Mel's shoulder. "From myself, my demons, everything imaginable."

"You guys, seriously!" Mel fanned her face, tears welling up in her eyes again. "Stop, my fucking hormones—"

"Mellie said fucking!" Rinna cackled, falling over.

"Shit." Mel bit her lip, catching herself again, which got Roo started on the laughing.

Raz tickled the bottom of Rinna's foot while Arjun pretended to bite Roo's arm, amplifying their giggles, which spread laughter across the whole bed like wildfire.

"Hey!" I clapped my hands once loudly. "I have something to say."

Everyone quieted, confusion on some faces at the sudden serious-ness in my tone. I waited a few tense moments before speaking.

"I love this fucking family. That's all."

The kids collapsed into giggle fits again while the adults tried to keep their disapproving faces on, but it didn't last. Through the smiles and the way everyone piled around together, I knew we all felt the same.

IV
THE CIRCUS OF PARENTHOOD

❧ *13* ❧

ARJUN

The thought of home tugged at my once closed-off heart. Years ago, I never thought I'd make it to this age. Every now and again I had to sit back and just absorb that, not only was I alive, I had a *good* life.

I had a wife who I missed terribly while away. I had a son, my little tiger cub in every way but blood, which didn't matter to me in the slightest. He was every bit mine just as the humans who created him, even the animal instincts deep within me recognized that. I'd tear out hearts and entrails without a second thought to protect him and his mother, my mate.

Eagerness drove me to press down on the gas pedal, to drum my fingertips on the steering wheel as I wound through the twists and turns heading back to our house. I waved at the landscaper, knowing he'd be stern with me if I drove too fast past the veterans' center where Connor worked. I already made that mistake once.

Once our charming home came into view, I felt a pull like Mel herself had her little fists clutched at my shirt as she yanked me down for a kiss. I'd been away at a Shifter-Shaman conference for a whole weekend, and while the time spent was good and productive, it would have been better with Mel with me.

963

Everyone knew who she was. Stories spread like wildfire of the young shaman woman who rescued her own shifter harem and busted an entire underground trafficking ring of shifters who'd been sold and experimented on. Her presence at the first organized convention of people like us, now that we were slowly emerging out of secrecy, was sorely missed.

But there would be others in the future. Mason was just too young to travel, and Mel wasn't yet ready to leave him.

I parked the car and hurried into the house, not bothering to grab my luggage from the trunk. It could wait until after I saw my mate and son.

The front door was locked, a bit unusual for a house with so many adults and children coming and going constantly. I fished for my keys and eagerly unlocked it, stepping into the foyer. Immediately, I heard Mason's cries, but didn't see anyone.

"Mel?" I shrugged off my coat and hung it on my hook. "I'm home, love."

Mason's cries intensified at the sound of my voice, and the first spark of worry hit me. Our home was usually as busy as a beehive, but it seemed empty today, with the exception of his cries.

"Melody!" My tiger's instinct rose to the surface as I walked deeper into the house. Not full-on predator mode, but caution and spatial awareness were at their heights.

I followed the sounds of my son into the theater room, which we had half converted into a playroom for him. Relief flooded through me when I saw both of them.

Mel stared out at one of the windowed doors leading out to the woods behind our home, holding and bouncing a red-faced, wailing Mason.

"Love, are you okay?" I came up behind her and put my hands on her shoulders.

She turned around slowly. "Oh, you're home."

"Yes, you didn't hear me come in?"

"Not over him."

As she sniffed and seated Mason higher on her hip, I got my first look at my wife in just over three days. Her nose and eyes were red, with dark circles to match. Her normally glossy, black hair was unbrushed with several knots, probably where our boy got his sticky fists in it. The shirt she had on was the same one she wore when I left, only now it was covered in an array of food stains.

"Mel!" I pressed the back of my fingers to her cheeks and forehead, projecting my voice over Mason's wailing. "What's wrong? You look exhausted."

"I *am!*" A cry escaped her now, one of frustration and utter weariness. "And I don't know. He just won't stop crying."

"Is he changed? Fed?" I ran a hand over my son's bottom to check his diaper.

"Yes! Also bathed, also played out. He won't take a nap, I just don't know."

"Where is everyone?" A growl rose in my voice. "Why isn't anybody here to help you?"

"Connor's at work. Hunter and Raz went off to the woods to shift and hunt with Hunter's brothers."

"And your sister?"

"She's on a field trip with the kids." Mel's face crumpled and my heart nearly broke. "I told the guys to go shift, they hadn't in over a week. And I didn't want to bother Miriam. I—I thought I could handle it..." She trailed off into quiet sobs, still bouncing Mason on autopilot.

"Here, love. Give him to me." I took my screaming, red-faced son from her and nestled him against my side. "Now, young man," I murmured against his dark, feathery soft hair, "what's got you all tossed about, hmm? Your poor mum needs a nap, you know."

I started pacing back and forth, holding his squirmy body against my chest. I patted his back a few times, but no burps came up.

"Maybe we should take him to the doctor?" Mel watched us with her nervous, tired expression, wringing her hands in front of her.

"He doesn't seem sick." I kissed the side of my son's head. "Just very upset about something."

"I've done *everything.*" Mel flopped down into an armchair, sinking deep into the cushions. "I just don't know what he needs and I feel terrible."

"What he needs is to stop being a brat," I chuckled, nuzzling into him. "If he were an actual tiger cub, I'd swat his little arse with my paw."

"That's not funny, Arjun."

"Yes it is, love. You're just exhausted." I turned to look at her. "When did you last sleep? Or shower?"

Mel sighed, bringing a hand to her forehead. "I don't even remember. I napped a little here and there? Everything's just kind of run together since you left."

"You still have a whole bloody household to help you while I'm gone! What happened to them?" I demanded irritably. "This is exactly why you have four husbands, love. So we can *all* make this easier for you."

"Don't be mad at them," she sighed. "I told them I wanted to give them a break. He's *one* kid! I thought I could handle it." Her lip wobbled. "I'm just a bad mother."

"Melody, no." If I wasn't holding Mason, I would have yanked her into my chest with a growl, but settled for stroking the back of her neck. "You know that's not true."

"Then why can't I calm him down?"

"Babies are hard in the best of times, love. And you're exhausted, just take a breath."

She turned into me, slumping against my shoulder while Mason continued to cry and fuss in my other arm. I hated that both of them were upset. The others would be sure to get an earful from me when they got back. They should have known better than to leave her completely alone.

My purr started low, barely noticeable as I stroked Mel's hair, kissing her forehead while just trying to keep my boy from tumbling arse over kettle out of my grip. Mel sighed and nuzzled into me, the vibrating in my throat growing louder. I knew it comforted her, and at the moment, it seemed like nothing else would help. After a few moments, the weight in my opposite arm began to still.

"Look at that," she whispered, reaching out for Mason's chubby foot.

He was calmer, now snuggled up to my shoulder like she was. His fist was in his mouth, drool puddling on my shirt as his eyelids started drooping.

"Keep purring," Mel whispered. "He's gonna knock right out."

I turned it up to a loud rattle, enveloping my son in the rhythmic vibrations that seemed to calm him just as much as his mum. Even after his eyes closed and his fist slid limply out of his mouth, I purred while carrying him all the way to his bassinet across the room.

"Sleep deeply, little cub," I whispered over my purr as I slowly lowered him down.

"If I had known that was all it took," Mel grinned at me, "I'd have recordings of it since he was born."

"We can record the next one," I told her, pulling my shirt out of my slacks. "Now," I leaned down over the armchair, hovering my mouth above hers, "I'm drawing a bath and putting you in it."

"Mm, tell me more," she smiled.

"It's going to be hot and bubbly, with one of those wretched bath fizzer things."

"Bombs," she said. "They're called bath bombs."

"Of course, love. Then while you're in there," I skimmed my fingertips over her jaw, tracing down her neck. "I'm going to make dinner. How does a tikka masala sound?"

"Ugh, amazing," she moaned, leaning into my hand. "I've been living on whatever chips I can get out of the cabinets."

"Oh no, crisps won't do. My wife needs a full meal." I pulled her from the chair, scooping her up into my arms to carry her to the bath upstairs. "And then," I brushed my lips across her forehead, my purr returning, "I'm going to make a meal out of her."

An hour later, Mel was clean, relaxed, and refreshed. She happily sat at the table while I doled out dinner for us.

"They're out really late," I remarked, eying the setting sun. "I really can't believe they'd leave you alone for this long."

"It was my fault," she sighed, fiddling with the baby monitor. "I insisted they go. Hunter almost didn't, but Raz was itching to get into his dragon form. I just," she took in a shaky breath, "got overwhelmed so quickly and felt like a failure."

"You're not." I dragged her chair close to me with a growl, bringing a nip down on her shoulder. "The first few months—the first year, really—is the hardest. Even if I didn't come home when I did, he would have exhausted himself and fallen asleep eventually. There's no way you could have known, love."

Her eyes were still downcast, fork picking through her food absently as I massaged my fingers into her nape. "Is there anything else bothering you?"

"I don't want to be like *my* mom," she admitted in a tiny voice. "I guess I...wanted to prove to myself that I could be better, but—"

"Hey." I lifted her chin to make her face me. "That woman who spat you and your siblings out is no mother. She used you. She is nothing. You?" I pressed a kiss on her mouth, my tiger already roaring to protect his mate from her own insecurities. Thankfully, Mel's incubator was already serving time for drug trafficking and child endangerment, but I hated that the woman still affected my wife's sense of self-worth.

"You are the most powerful shaman seen in generations," I whispered against her lips. "You have driven peace between shifters and humans. You saved my life. You gave me my son. You have a man, a wolf, a tiger, and a *dragon* who worship the ground you walk on. My love," I sipped another kiss from her, all but pulling her into my lap, "you are nothing short of extraordinary."

Her dark eyes blinked away tears, lips pulling into a grateful smile as she held my face in her palms. "I love you so much," she sighed. "Sometimes it still doesn't feel real, that I have all of you. So many people search for one soul mate to complete them, and I have four."

"You deserve a hundred soul mates if that would make you happy."

"No way!" she laughed. "Now *that* would be a full house."

"It would mean you're never alone with the baby." I pressed a kiss to her palm.

"Are you suggesting I add to my harem?" she teased. "Maybe a lion, or someone from Tak's tribe—"

My tiger bubbled to the surface, releasing a possessive growl to her laughter.

"You don't seem hungry, so maybe I'll just convince you that we're enough." I turned her chair to me, grabbed the waistband of her leggings, and proceeded to yank them down her hips.

"I don't need more convincing after that lovely bath and dinner," she giggled, squirming in my grip but not putting up much of a fight.

"Well, I'm starving for you." I kissed the exposed flesh on her hip, working the stretchy fabric down lower. "I haven't touched or tasted my wife in too fucking long."

Mel's hand covered mine, stopping me. "What if Mase wakes up?"

"That's what the baby monitor is for." I looked up at her quizzically. "Love, do you not want me to?"

"It's just..." she sighed with a small shake of her head. "It's stupid."

"Surely it's not, whatever it is."

"I'm still, you know." She gestured with her hands, but not in any way that I could interpret.

"I'm afraid I don't, love. That time of the month?"

"No, I'm still just..." she blew out a breath. "I'm all, you know, stretched-marked down there."

A laugh burst out of me, and I dropped a kiss to her belly. "Oh, you gorgeous woman. You had me worried."

"It just...doesn't look very nice. We can turn the lights out—"

"Melody." I captured her lips with mine, positioning my body between her legs. "I'm a man and an animal. I love you, and lust for only you. I'm well aware that having a baby changes some things—"

"It's just not like before." She chewed her lip nervously. "I'm only nineteen now, but my body doesn't look like it..."

"You know what you look like?" I yanked her leggings forcefully down her thighs, exposing the parts of her she wanted to hide under the kitchen lights. "You look like my mate. A tigress with stripes to match mine." I leaned down, covering her pussy with my mouth before she could argue, groaning with need as I savored her sensitive flesh.

"Arjun!" she gasped, but the hand in my hair held me in place rather than shoved me away.

Her knees found their place on my shoulders as I devoured her, sucking her lips into my mouth and taking long, decadent licks of her sweetness. My hands roamed her body, making sure to touch those places she was insecure about.

Maybe it wouldn't all go away tonight, but I was determined to do everything in my power to make my wife feel sexy and desired again. Another note for the guys—we needed to stop fucking her in the darkness of the bedroom. It would be difficult with so many kids in the house these days, but for Mel, we'd make it work.

I paused for a breath, bringing a hand down to stroke in and out of her pussy while I spent more time telling her what I really thought of her body.

"I thought you were beautiful before having Mason." I kissed her navel. "But I swear to all the gods you're even more beautiful now."

"Wha, what?" she panted, gorgeous breasts heaving. I leaned up to caress one while I fingered her, making sure to be gentle amid all the breastfeeding.

"You carried my son in here and that's a beautiful thing." I kissed her belly again. "But the main reason it is that I know you better now. I'm more in love with you every day. And the more I fall in love with you, the sexier you become."

"Arjun..."

"Yes, say my name, dearest wife," I commanded, dragging my fingers along her sensitive walls. I never minded sharing her, not one bit, but I enjoyed the selfish satisfaction of my name on her lips as she bucked and squirmed under my touch.

My mouth ghosted a trail down toward her center, trailing over every perfect piece of her until I found her clit. Just a few light sucks and rumbles of my purr had her spasming, climbing fast toward a peak until she crested it so beautifully.

Her fingers yanked on my hair as she came, seizing up with stiffness before relaxing into utter bliss. I wanted to hear her scream but she bit it back, only a strangled whimper leaving her mouth. We wanted the baby to stay asleep, so I didn't mind.

I stroked and licked her until she couldn't stand it anymore and shoved me away, with aftershocks running through her body.

"When the guys get home," I said with a kiss on her thigh. "I'm going to make them eat you out, one by one, as an apology for leaving you alone."

"Arjun..." she protested weakly, eyes hooded with sated pleasure.

"No sucking cock and no touching unless it's to please you." I rose up from between her legs, wearing her scent and wetness on my face proudly. "They need to be reminded of how to appreciate you."

Mel rocked forward, reaching for the back of my neck with a lazy grin. "But kissing is okay?"

"Yes." I rested my forehead on hers. "Kissing will be permitted."

She sighed dreamily, lips hovering over mine. "Thank you, my tiger."

I hugged her close, pulling her sweet body against me. "Thank you, my beautiful wife."

🦋 14 🦋

MELODY

I headed for the side exit the moment the stage went dark.

"*Steluta?*" Raz called after me, his breath coming in soft pants from the exertion of the performance.

The audience was going nuts and didn't hear his pet name for me, but he was close enough that I heard him just before going down the narrow stairs. He'd figure out where I was going, eventually.

My legs hit a solid wall of fur after only a few feet. Arjun's massive feline head pressed against my hip, rubbing affectionately with that deep, rumbling purr.

What's wrong, love? His mental voice was full of concern.

"Nothing." My own lungs labored for breath, pulse still beating wildly.

Raz and I finished off the show with a sexy dance number, complete with his fire and knife tricks, of course. We rehearsed it for months under a world-class choreographer. This was supposed to be our big comeback after taking time off from my pregnancy. But all I could think about while on stage was my son and two other mates back home.

It's obviously not nothing, so try again. Arjun nipped my hand playfully. Anyone else would have been terrified to have their hand anywhere near a Bengal tiger's mouth, but I trusted my mates implicitly. Which meant I had to come clean about this too.

"Mel?" Raz's footsteps echoed softly down the side stairs behind me. The use of my real name and not my nickname showed he was also worried about me. "They're expecting an encore. Are you okay?"

"Yes." My dragon slid an arm around my waist, dark tattoos blending with the fleur-de-lis pattern on my corset. "I just need to talk to them real quick." My fingers closed around Raz's, my other hand stroking down the side of Arjun's neck. "I miss them. I haven't been able to stop thinking about them all night."

"I miss them too. But if we call now, will you want to go back out there when we hang up?"

I turned around to face Raz, finding the warmth in his metallic gray eyes. "How do you think we did out there?"

"Honestly?"

I nodded, working the nervous swallow down my throat.

"*Steluta*." Raz gripped my shoulders, squeezing gently. "We were incredible. It was like we never left."

"Really?" I squeaked out. That was not what I expected to hear.

Listen to them, love. Arjun head-butted my lower back. *Feel them.*

I did. I heard the collective shouts of, *"Encore! Encore!"* as one voice. I felt the stomping of feet traveling up my legs through the floor. The claps of hands made the air vibrate like it fizzled with magic.

"But I didn't feel it like before," I confessed to my mates. "I felt distracted and just went through the motions. I felt like I was faking it."

"You're a different person now." Raz lowered his forehead to mine. "Your priorities have changed. The stage isn't an escape for you anymore, because there's nothing to escape from. It's a means to an end. A way to support your family, and there's nothing wrong with that." His hands slid down my arms to clasp loosely around my fingers. "Let's finish off strong, ringmistress. Then let's call home so we're not rushed."

I pulled in a long breath. He was right about all of it. The audience couldn't see it, but everything was different. Ever since having Mason, my abilities seemed more honed and sensitive. I could smell as well as

Hunter now, was in control of my reflexes, like Arjun. When I was pissed or frustrated, I swear I felt fire building in my chest like Razvan. And when I was away from Connor, Mason, or any of my loves, my heart felt stretched too tightly, like they were holding it from a distance and waiting for me to come back.

But was that shaman or mom instincts? I should probably make more mom friends either way. This was my first time being away for work since early in my pregnancy, so my hormones and maternal urges were probably just going nuts. But Raz had a good point. If I called Connor now, I'd want to curl up with the phone in the hotel room and never go back onstage.

One more show for tonight. Just one.

Arjun's presence behind me morphed, stretching taller as he shifted to human. Standing buck naked without a care in the world for whatever the stage assistants saw, he pressed his broad chest against my back as large hands came around my waist.

"It's your decision, love." His ocean-colored eyes were devilish. "I certainly wouldn't mind cutting this evening short."

I looked up at him, my head barely hitting the top of his chest, even with heels on. "One more?"

My tiger grinned and dropped a fast kiss to my mouth. "One more. You want me out there?"

"Yeah," I grinned back. "Let's do shifter magic."

He chuckled against my lips, then patted my butt as he stepped away. "We really are ending this with a bang now, aren't we?"

"No better way to do it." Raz was already twirling his knives.

I quickly checked my makeup, my clothes, then nodded to the stage managers that we were going back out. The crowd went from stomping and chanting to loud cheers and whistles as the dark stage once was bathed in bright lights.

Alone, and with my wide ringmistress smile, I walked out in front of the curtain to address the smiling, cheering faces.

"What's that, you say?" I bowed forward with my hand cupping my ear. "You want more?"

The screams and energy lifted several notches. The air crackled with so much sound and magic, it could have been solid enough to walk on. I was never fully convinced that non-shaman humans didn't have magic on some level. Connor didn't have my abilities, yet he was so in tune with me and my shifter mates. I always knew there was something extraordinary about him, even if his magic didn't present itself like mine.

Most humans would run and scream in terror at the sight of a shifter. That, or try to capture and exploit them like my mates had been. But if Connor could be the exception to the rule, surely others could, too.

I straightened up, velvet-gloved hands on the hips of my corset and my grin turning satisfied.

"Oh, I missed you too, my friends," I said to the audience, channeling the longing for my son into my words. "And if more is what you want, that is exactly what...you'll...get!"

On my final word, flames shot up next to me on the stage, making the front row pull away from the heat before they went absolutely nuts. The fire was fake, of course, an illusion thrown by my abilities. But it looked and felt real, and that it came from absolutely nowhere.

Raz jumped down from the stage supports right on cue, two swords in his hands. Together, we spun and twirled in another dance that looked both seductive and dangerous to the audience. We moved together, our bodies in perfect tandem, as he threw swords in the air and caught them behind his back. His arms came around me, blades pressed to my throat or against my back. My leg wrapped around his hip as he teased the blade against the hosiery on my thigh for everyone to see.

Of course, I was completely safe with him, and this illusion of danger was just as much foreplay for us as it was for the audience.

We separated, making our way to the opposite ends of the stage. He pulled in a big, exaggerated breath and blew out a massive ball of fire, earning more gasps of awe from the crowd.

Normally his fire was real, but for this bit, it was an illusion, too.

I stretched my arms out like I was going to catch this fireball, but instead, morphed the illusion into a ring shape at the center of the stage. Raz began a lazy, easy sword juggling routine, a practiced bored expression on his face as he walked in and out of the fire ring hovering just above the stage floor.

As I lifted my arms, the ring gradually rose up with my movement. Raz had to do bigger, more elaborate jumps back and forth. Eventually, he graduated to flips and somersaults—all while still juggling his swords. The crowd went nuts as he topped himself again and again, jumping higher than any mere human could.

What they didn't see was him getting a bit of lift from his dragon wings, which I made invisible with my powers.

On his final jump through, he caught his swords and took a deep bow, but the applause was short-lived. Screams and shrieks rang out as Arjun stepped out, the massive Bengal tiger stalking just behind the ring. Raz feigned ignorance, waving and blowing kisses as Arjun stalked closer.

I made a big show of trying to wrestle with the fire ring, contorting my hands as if trying to manipulate my power, then put on a shocked face as a dozen more fire rings popped up on stage. All smaller, and they all started moving.

Raz turned to me with a puzzled expression. And that was when he saw Arjun.

The tiger pounced through the first fire ring, the biggest one, and the chase began. Raz dodged, jumped and dived through the fire rings floating and dancing on stage, the tiger right on his heels.

When I heard Raz's feet running over the wooden stage floor, I realized it was because the audience went silent. As one entity, they held their collective breath as man, tiger, and fire moved across the stage. The silent, deadly animal grew closer with every precise leap through the fire rings, the stakes growing higher.

At precisely the right time, I clapped my hands together, bringing all the fiery rings to converge into a single giant ball again in the center of the stage. With Arjun and Raz right in the middle of it.

Then the stage went dark, the audience too stunned to even breathe.

When the warm glow of the overhead lights returned, the three of us stood side-by-side. Raz and I each placed a hand on Arjun's back and bowed low from the waist, arms sweeping out to the sides.

A thunderous noise swept over the auditorium as thousands of people jumped to their feet, and then their deafening applause followed. Arjun roared and bowed his head low, earning even more enthusiastic applause from our audience.

We stayed up there for what had to be several minutes, but they would just not stop shouting and clapping!

Finally, I broke away, heading toward the side exit with a final wave, already feeling like I'd been away from the rest of my family for too long.

The moment Arjun shifted back to human form and pulled clothes on, I went up to him.

"How was that?" I asked, searching his blue-green eyes. "Were you okay?"

I wasn't asking about our performance this time, but *him*. My gorgeous tiger shifter had been forced to perform with real fire when I found him. The burn scars on his ribs weren't the only damage done to him in that time. This comeback tour was originally going to be just me and Raz, possibly Hunter, but Arjun stepped up saying he wanted to be part of it.

It made sense. He and Raz had performed in sideshows together many times. As two prized, rare shifters, they bonded over necessity, survival. While Raz learned to accept and eventually embraced a life of theatrics as long as it was on his terms, turning tricks on stage only seemed painful for Arjun.

"I'm your husband that's gotten the least time with you," he'd told me back then. "Let me stick to you like a barnacle on your arse for a bit longer. I'll even be happy to go onstage and earn my keep."

As long as I used my shaman ability to mimic fire, and not the actual substance that would burn him, he seemed fine. But now I really wanted to know. Even for fake fire, it was real enough for the audience and there was a lot of it.

"My love." Arjun cupped a large hand around the back of my neck and lowered a hot kiss to my mouth. "In your hands, I'm more than okay. Always." He grinned at me, still feline and mischievous with human teeth. "You did amazing, Mel. I'm so proud of you."

"I think we set some panties on fire tonight," Raz agreed, kissing the back of my head. "The venue owner is probably clutching his insurance papers now, but I bet we'll get a bonus."

"Honestly," I kicked my heels off, opting to walk barefoot to our backstage dressing room, "none of it matters. I'm just glad it's over with." Grabbing both of their hands, I made for the door with my name taped on it. "Let's call home."

15

MELODY

All the pressure and stress of the evening melted away the moment Connor's face popped up on my phone screen.

"Hey, babe." He spoke softly, his grin tugging at my heart from thousands of miles away. "It was getting late. I wasn't sure if you'd call."

"They demanded an encore." Raz rested his chin on my shoulder. "Hey, Con."

"Pfft, of course they did," Connor replied. "It's been almost two years since y'all have put on a show."

"We'll get you a video." Arjun squeezed my opposite shoulder. "Our girl was incredible."

"Knew she would be." Connor's pride beamed through the small screen and the ache to curl up on my Marine's chest was fierce. "How do you feel, Mel? Victorious?"

"I was just dying to get it over with and talk to you," I confessed. "I miss you."

"We miss you more, babe." Connor blew a kiss at the screen.

"Where's Mason?"

"Right here." Connor tilted the phone down to point at our sleeping sixteen-month-old, dead to the world on his chest.

"Fuck," Arjun sighed. "Miss my little cub."

"How's he doing? Has he been fussing at all? Eating okay?"

"Babe," Connor laughed lightly at me. "He's fine. The first day you were gone he was a little fussy, but Hunter and I are loving on him a ton. Wolf man's been able to bond with him more and I think he's relieved about that."

"Roo and Rinna aren't upset about him being with the baby?"

"Nah, they're independent and don't want to spend all their time with Dad, anyway. They've been spending time with Miriam and her guys."

"And Jeanie?" I just could not stop asking about everyone in our busy household. "How are she and the littles?"

"Fine." I could tell Connor wanted to tease me, but he reeled it in and answered me with patience. "We're helping her out, too. And she's watching Mason when we need a break. Seriously, babe. All is well and everyone is stepping up when others need a hand."

I breathed a sigh of relief, and Raz pressed a reassuring kiss to my neck. Old habits died hard. Being far away from my family, when they didn't need rescuing, wasn't a feeling I was used to.

"Okay. I'll let you go so he doesn't wake up."

"Can't wait to see your beautiful face in person." Connor stared at me dreamily. "I got dibs on you first when you're back."

"Have fun fighting a wolf for that," Raz cackled.

"I will," Connor joked back. "He's no alpha, I can top him."

"Hey," Raz leaned over my shoulder to get closer to the camera. "We share her, but the wolf is mine."

"Calm your scaly ass down, you know I'm joking."

"This has been lovely to catch up," Arjun now leaned in, "but we're coming home bright and early tomorrow, and I'd like to make the most of our time with our wife before you hide her away to yourself."

"Aw, way to rub it in, RJ," Connor snorted. "I get it, though. Y'all have fun."

"I love you." I made a kissing face at the screen, prompting a heart-melting smile from Connor. "See you soon."

"I'm counting down the minutes. Love you to pieces, babe. Guys?"

"Hm?" Raz was already flicking the sides of his split tongue against my earlobe.

"Don't wear her out too much."

"Just for that, we'll send her to you in a misshapen puddle," Arjun grinned. "Goodnight."

"Nigh—"

My tiger pressed the end call button on the screen before Connor finished talking and laughed at my ensuing glare.

"Oh dear, have I made you cross?" He spun my chair to face him. "That won't do at all."

"Arjun..." I couldn't even finish the thought as he kneeled on the floor, separating my knees so he could wedge his way between them.

"What do you think, Raz?" My tiger's large hands skimmed up my thighs, pausing just under my skirt where my stockings clipped to my garters. "Should we keep the outfit on or off?"

"Definitely on." Fingers toyed with the corset strings running down my back. "I've been thinking of bending her over in this outfit all night."

"At least loosen the strings back there so I can breathe." It was already hard enough to take a deep breath just from two of my hot shifters closing in on me.

"That I can do, *steluta.*"

Raz's serpent-like tongue flicked its way from my ear down the back of my neck as his fingers deftly untied the ribbon at the base of my spine. He left the most sensuous, wet kisses along my shoulders and upper back, my ribs finally free to expand. In front of me, Arjun's hands continued slow, hypnotic movements across my thighs. His fingers teased my bare skin just over the top of my stockings, but not going any higher.

I scooted toward Arjun with impatience, leaning my head back on Raz's chest, which was now bare. He cupped a hand under my jaw to make me look upward, then kissed me with all the heat and ferocity that only a dragon shifter could. His tongue caressed the inside of my mouth while Arjun's hands pulled my legs even further apart.

Then he started vibrating.

"Oh, God." I thrashed in my seat, to no avail. The tiger's heavy palms locked my lower body down. "That's so not fair."

"Oh, making complaints, are we?" Arjun's purr abruptly stopped, looking up with his predatory grin between my thighs. "I thought women enjoyed those little vibrating contraptions?"

"Yeah, I just mean…" Between Raz's tongue and now Arjun, using his purr as a sex toy, I found it hard to breathe again. "It's not fair you're going to make me come so fast."

The deep, vibrating rumble started up again, loud and powerful as a motor in a car. "Well, I did promise to send you back to Connor thoroughly worn out."

His purr was so loud it even drowned out his voice. He dipped his head between my legs again, the vibration setting off the nerve endings in my inner thighs.

"Ohh—mm!"

Arjun pressed a kiss against my panties, and his face might as well had been a Hitachi wand. My hips jerked against his mouth, already eager for more of that delicious sensation. He clamped down on my thighs to hold me still, a low chuckle changing up the rhythm of his purr.

Raz's mouth found mine just as Arjun hooked my knees over his shoulders. The moment Arjun moved my panties aside, and I felt both of their tongues on me, I nearly came right then and there.

"I almost regret wanting to leave this on," Raz rasped, tugging a few more strings loose on my corset. "I love your skin on mine too much."

The corset was loose enough then that he could reach inside, his tan skin and dark tattoos sliding over my shoulder and chest to grab my breasts. His fingers rolling my nipples weren't the same as his tongue, but Arjun's purr traveling over my skin reached up to there, and then some. I felt the vibration in my toes and my lips. I swore I felt it through the finger he pressed into me as his tongue teased and danced around my clit.

"Please, Arjun," I panted, sending one hand down to tangle in his silky black hair, while the other wrapped around Raz's neck behind me.

"Please what, love?" He pulled away, placing an infuriatingly chaste kiss on my inner thigh.

"Please let me come!" The bastard knew exactly what he was doing.

"At first you said it was unfair that you'd come so quickly with my purr, now you're begging for it." He grinned up at me. "Funny how that works, eh?"

I let out a frustrated noise, my whole body teetering on the edge, which Raz promptly silenced with another hard kiss.

"I think she needs something else in her mouth, mate."

"I think you're right."

Raz stood and moved to my side. He didn't have to do a thing but stand there, because I attacked his belt buckle and zipper like they were my sworn enemies. He was already thick and scorching hot, the piercings sliding past my teeth as I took him in my mouth.

"Oh, fucking..."

He let out a hot string of Romanian profanities, which just encouraged me more. I dragged my lips up and down his shaft, his hand reaching into my corset to play with my nipples again. And finally, Arjun returned to focusing on my clit.

My tiger stopped messing around and curled his fingers inside me as he sucked soft kisses at my clit. His tongue swiped at that sensitive bundle of nerves, hitting it again and again as I moaned around Raz's shaft until I shattered.

"Oh yes, yes," my dragon breathed as I shuddered and convulsed with release. "Fuck, that's beautiful."

I barely came down from the aftershocks rolling through me when Arjun lifted up from my pussy. He pulled me forward with one swift movement and impaled me on his cock. I cried out at the impact with my fist still wrapped around Raz.

"Someone's gonna think we're murdering you," Raz chuckled, moving closer so I could still reach him with my mouth.

"Or giving her the fucking of her life," Arjun pressed all the way in, then withdrew to leave me painfully empty. "In which case, they'd be wise to not barge in."

His grin was cocky, watching my face as he sped up and slowed down his thrusts, always teasing me. He loved my whimpers as he pulled out and savored every inch of me sheathing him as he returned home.

"Would you like to come again, my darling wife?" His hand reached between us, thumb circling lazily around my clit in time with his thrusts.

I released Raz's cock with a sucking pop of my lips. "Yes," I panted.

Arjun lifted an eyebrow, apparently unsatisfied. "Yes, what?"

"Yes, please."

"Fuck me," the tiger growled, picking up his pace and keeping his hand between us as he leaned down to kiss me. "Your voice...your body...your eyes when you look at me." His forehead leaned on mine. "You fucking undo me."

He slammed into me more forcefully now, thumb pressing down on my clit until another orgasm sent waves of toe-curling bliss over every inch of me. My pulse pounded so hard in my ears, I barely heard Raz's question with his mouth right against it.

"Can I have your ass, steluta?"

"Yes," I moaned deliriously. "Yes, please."

I hadn't had two of my men at the same time since our honeymoon with him and Hunter. Once I got later in my pregnancy, the logistics of it became too cumbersome. Then afterward, with kids at home at any given time, it became more difficult to have group fun in general. We stole moments when we could, but never found the right opportunity to double up.

Arjun pulled out of me and grabbed my hands. "Stand for a bit, love."

I rose on wobbly legs while Raz grabbed lube from his duffel bag, then returned to sit in the chair I was just in.

"Have a seat, *luv*," he mimicked Arjun's accent with a playful swat to my ass.

I lowered onto his lap, leaning forward to kiss Arjun while he got me ready. The cool, slippery liquid slid down the cleft of my ass, meeting Raz's fingers resting on the tight ring of muscles.

He kissed my back, reaching around me to caress my breasts as he gently began working his fingers in and out of me.

"You good, *sotie*?"

He used the Romanian word for wife and it made me utterly melt. I was beyond good. I had four of the best, sexiest, most loving men in the world to call my husbands.

"More than good."

I blinked away tears, suddenly moved beyond words at the love and tenderness they showed me.

Arjun cupped my chin, his brow furrowed at seeing my eyes welling up. "What is it?"

"It's you." I kissed his palm. "It's Raz. Hunter. Conner. You all take such good care of me and I love you so much."

"Oh, my love." Arjun cupped my cheeks with both hands and kissed me sweetly. "It would be shameful for us to love you any less."

Grabbing hold of his wrists, I captured his lip with my teeth. My tiger's smile pressed to mine before our tongues swept across each other. He slid into me again, still holding my face and kissing me. Raz lifted me in his lap, Arjun pausing his movement as the dragon shifter nestled his slick cock against my ass.

"Put your feet on the floor and press back on me." Raz's lips moved against my back as he gently pulled my hand behind me to press on his torso. "Then lower yourself on me as you're ready."

Arjun held me steady, hands on my waist and thick cock inside me. With my tiptoes on the floor, I slowly lowered my heels and, thus, my ass onto Raz's cock. His head slipped in and I stopped, hissing at the hard pressure of his piercings on my tight entrance.

"Relax." He kissed and massaged my back. "I'm adding more lube. Then when I push in a little more, you won't feel them as much."

Arjun pulled my attention away from the discomfort with a kiss, his hand sweeping over my clit as he flexed his hips forward. He wasn't really thrusting, just moving enough to make me focus on the pleasure.

When Raz pulled me down another inch, I broke the kiss to roll my head back with a moan. I forgot how full I'd feel with two thick cocks inside me.

"Better?" My dragon kissed my shoulder blade with a raspy chuckle.

"Much," I panted, my heels dropping to the floor as I lowered myself all the way onto him.

"Ohh fuck me, you're tight." Raz's forehead pressed to my back as his hands swept forward, finding my breasts.

He let me control the movement at first, letting me bounce on my toes to ride him until my legs gave out. Then he slid us forward until he was halfway out of the chair and nearly reclined on his back.

"Tell me if it's too much." I felt another kiss on my back as he locked a hard grip on either side of my waist. When he thrust into my ass, it felt like all the air pushed out of my lungs.

"*Steluta?*" He paused, seated all the way inside me, Arjun still resting inside my pussy.

"Don't stop," I begged. "Both of you, fuck me, please."

Hot, masculine moans filled my ears as my lovers moved, filling and stretching me to the max. Arjun planted his hands on either side of the chair, on his knees between Raz's and my legs as he drove into me. The pressure of Raz in my ass made my pussy hug around Arjun tighter, his thickness dragging against my walls in the most achingly delicious way.

"Beautiful," my tiger purred, leaning in to hover his full lips over mine. "Now if only you had something for your mouth, eh?"

I grabbed his jaw, feeling so full and drunk on their bodies and sensations I could hardly speak, and pulled him in for another biting kiss. He growled against my tongue and thrust into me harder, his behavior shifting from loving to rough. My tiger—all of my men really —were so careful not to hurt me, but I loved seeing their animalistic sides come out during sex.

I knew Arjun's tiger was roaring with need just below the surface. I could feel the animal's power, the desire to mount and dominate his mate. The beautiful man's intense rutting, his harsh breaths and growls were the only parts he dared let creep to the surface, and I loved seeing that grip of control slacken.

The heat of Raz underneath me and the scent of smoke in the air told me he wrestled with his dragon in the same way. Still, he never broke his rhythm, gliding in and out of my ass as he dragged his mouth along my back. His teeth and split tongue moved across my skin, feverishly whispering curses in both Romanian and English.

Every sense was amplified as my two lovers fucked me, my skin a true living, breathing organ that was hungry for them. My clit tingled with every slam of Arjun's body into me. They let out a mutual moan together as I tightened around them, my body climbing high to chase release.

"Fuck, that's so good…" Arjun's whole body seemed to vibrate now, his purr and growl blending into a sexy crackling sound just under his voice.

"She's so close," Raz groaned, his mouth like liquid fire on the nape of my neck. "And I am too. Fuck, my dick can't handle it."

"Right there with you, mate."

Arjun's hand returned to my clit, and I knew I was done for. Those last few swipes were the cherries on top of the layers of touch, heat, their sounds, and their hard cocks penetrating me. I exploded into a shaking, shivering mess, my throat going raw from screaming the release of pleasure. And just as the wave crashed, it rose again as my men emptied themselves into me, their muscles stiffening and hard grips making my skin red.

Raz released me, his breaths deep and greedy for air as he realized his fingers left marks curled into the flesh of my waist. "Sorry, *steluta*."

"Don't be." I turned, bringing one arm to wrap around his neck as I kissed him deeply. My other hand reached forward for Arjun, who caught my fingers and placed a breathless kiss on my palm before placing my hand over his stampeding heart.

When Raz and I separated, I breathed out a small plume of my dragon's smoke. We wore matching grins as our foreheads rested on each other, my fingers caressing over his scalp.

"Don't ever be sorry for loving me the way you do," I whispered.

V
GIRLS' NIGHT

16

MELODY

"Stop checking your phone, girl." Jeanie May playfully slapped her hand down on the screen I was staring at. "You too," my sister jokingly chastised Miriam, who had snuck a peak on her own device. "Forget your men for once. It's a girls' night out!"

"It's not the guys I'm worried about," I told her. "But the baby."

This wouldn't even be my longest time away from Mason—Raz, Arjun, and I did four more Vegas shows in the past six months. But even still, that was work. This, going out for happy hour with my sister and friend, was supposed to be...fun?

"Who is under the watchful eye of four fathers who will tear a man limb-from-limb, then light his corpse on fire, if he so much as smells suspicious. Relax, Mel."

"Don't tell me you don't get nervous about being away from the littles," I shot back at her, sliding into a barstool at a pub table. We were still underage, me at twenty and her almost nineteen. But neither of us would drink booze and this divey place wouldn't care about checking our IDs.

"Melody, how do you think I fed them? Kept a roof over our heads?" A waiter dropped a basket of chips and salsa on our table, and

Jeanie crunched loudly on a chip. "I left them alone all the time. They knew how to fend for themselves."

I nodded knowingly. Jeanie and I learned how to fend for ourselves too when we were Bella and Joey's ages. We got creative with our hiding places, with barricading the flimsy plywood doors so our mother's boyfriends wouldn't stumble drunk and high into our rooms. We took that knowledge and passed it down to our siblings for their own survival. They never got a chance to be kids. It was slow-going, but now I was hopeful they had a chance to relearn childhood in our home, with my guys as examples of good role models, of a healthy family.

Miriam came back from the bar, precariously holding three drinks in her hands. A virgin daiquiri for me, an Italian soda for Jeanie, and the only drinker out of all of us, a mojito for herself.

"How are things going with the wolves, Mir?" my sister asked the other shaman, our neighbor, in a relationship with Hunter's two brothers, and some kind of situationship with a curious shifter she met at our wedding.

"Fine." Miriam sucked loudly at her straw, obviously not fine. She drained half of the mojito in a single gulp.

"Tak still hasn't gotten back to you?" I asked as gently as I could.

She shook her head, long dark waves shimmering over her shoulders. "Today marks a week. He's never gone so long without contact before."

"No wonder you wanted to go out and drink." Jeanie rubbed her back sympathetically. "What do Colt and Gabe think?"

Miriam blew out a long breath. "Gabe wants me to write him off. He's cutthroat like that. Colt says don't lose hope, that he loves me and wants to be with us. He just needs time to get his shit settled back in Alaska first. Sell his house and stuff." She propped her elbows on the table and dragged her fingers through her hair with a groan. "I swear those two are like my heart and mind arguing with each other."

"Hey, no matter what," I placed my hand on her arm, "at least you still have them. They'll support you through this, whether Tak comes back or not."

"I know you're right," Miriam sighed, poking at the ice in her drink with a straw. "It just sucks so bad. Tak and I just had this instant chemistry from the beginning."

"He scared the shit out of everyone at the wedding," Jeanie chuckled. "Looking back, though, it was crazy hot. Watching you two dance and everything, whoo!" My sister fanned herself dramatically.

Miriam smiled at the memory. "That was an amazing night. For multiple reasons."

"Sure was." I gazed down at my wedding band, resisting the urge to check my phone again should Jeanie take it upon herself to steal it.

"He told me he was serious about us," Miriam pouted over her drink. "That his home was with me. Everything he's ever told me is just running through my head and I'm wondering if it was all true."

"You'll find out," I told her. "Whether or not he comes back, you will get your answer."

"I guess you're right," she sighed.

"Quit moping, Mir," Jeanie said in her tough-love but still upbeat tone. "You're gorgeous, you're powerful. You have two sexy wolves who worship the ground you walk on. You've got everything going for you and if Tak can't see what a prize you are, it's his loss."

"Ditto," I said, giving her a quick hug around the shoulders. "Forget about him. Just for tonight at least."

"You guys are right. I will." Miriam perked up slightly, angling her eyes at me with a smirk. "Want to play spot the shifter?"

"Ohh, yes, I love this game!" Jeanie clasped her hands together excitedly, her eyes darting between me and the other shaman.

"Sure," I grinned, choosing not to let on that I'd already sensed all the shifters in the bar when we walked in.

"I'm picking up three. How about you?" Miriam waited smugly as she sucked at her drink straw.

"Five."

"Really?" Miriam coughed in surprise. "Who?"

"Two felines at the bar," I muttered, subtly angling my head to the two black men sitting with their backs to us. My senses gave me flashes of a strong family unit with strong ancestral pride, wise golden eyes, and rippling, predatory power. "Lions, most likely. The big one is the leader."

"Yeah, I got them," Miriam answered. "The big guy who's supposed to be checking IDs at the door, but flirting with the hostess is a moose. Who else?"

"There's two more who really don't want to be detected." I bit my straw playfully, grinning at her. "You can sense them, though. I know you can."

Miriam narrowed her eyes in concentration. "Hmm, you're right. I feel something else there, but..." Her eyes snapped open. "The two girls!"

"Yup."

"Aww." Miriam clenched her hands, resisting the urge to turn around and look at the women curled up together in a corner booth. "They're so cute."

"And unfortunately a double-target, especially down here," I said. "I can totally understand their caution."

"What animals are they?" Jeanie asked. "Can you tell?"

"Birds," Miriam and I answered in unison. "I'm getting..." Her brow pinched in concentration. "Really bright, beautiful feathers, but I don't know exactly."

"Yeah, flying over a tropical rainforest," I added. "The Amazon, probably. It's breathtaking. They've been in the highest treetops, hanging out with monkeys, other gorgeous birds." I shrugged. "Who knows, exactly? They're trying to stay hidden, so I don't want to dig too deep."

"They're just lovebirds," my sister smiled. "That's so sweet."

"Five is a lot for shifters to be in one place," Miriam mused.

"It's working," I sighed happily. "Slowly but surely. They're finding their place among the general population."

"So what's a girl like me gotta do to nail a man with an animal half?" Jeanie waggled her eyebrows suggestively. "Are they different in bed from regular human guys?"

"Jeanie!" My laugh turned into a cough, frozen strawberry slush going down the wrong pipe.

"What? I've always wanted to know!"

"I don't really have an answer."

"What do you mean? You have Connor to compare!"

"That's not a fair comparison," I laughed.

"Why, 'cause he's your baby daddy?"

"Connor is an exceptional human." Warmth spread through my chest at the thought of my Marine husband. "Not just in bed, but who he is."

"You're no help." Jeanie dismissed me and turned to Miriam. "What do you say?"

"Sex with shifters is one-thousand percent better," she grinned. "But all the humans I've fucked have been mediocre. I've never had anyone exceptional to even the odds." She squeezed my knee teasingly.

"Talk louder, why don't you? So the guys at the bar can hear us," I giggled, watching one of them straighten up and casually look over his shoulder.

"Does the animal play any part in it?" Jeanie asked. "Like, do predators like it really rough? Mel, does Raz shoot fire out of his—"

"Jeanie May!" I gasped.

"It's just a question!"

"N-no, he doesn't," I stammered, equally out of laughter and embarrassment.

"Here's what I want to know." Miriam bit the corner of her smile. "Does he have tattoos down there too?"

"Um, yeah." My face grew uncomfortably hot. "And piercings."

"I knew it!" She pounded a fist victoriously on the table.

My sister's eyes widened. "How does *that* feel?"

Part of me wanted to sink into the floor. The other part couldn't resist the smugness spreading across my face.

"Intense, but really, really good," I said. "When the angle is just right, the uh, friction is just explosive."

"I need to have Colt get one of those," Miriam sighed dreamily. "Gabe would never, but I bet Colt would be down."

"Okay, now it's easy for us to jump on Mel since she has such variety." Jeanie leaned across the table. "But Miriam, tell us all about what it's like to fuck a couple of wolf brothers. In excruciating detail, please."

Miriam chuckled, the perfect image of coolness and confidence as she swallowed her drink. "It is so. Fucking. Good."

"Details, woman! I said details!"

"Colt is the suave one." Miriam leaned back in her seat. "He's charming and flirty. So damn passionate. He doesn't hold anything back. Gabe?" She paused to suck her lip between her teeth, pondering on Hunter's youngest brother. "He can still be kind of closed off just day-to-day. You know, moody and kind of sullen."

"Because he doesn't like humans?"

"He didn't use to," Miriam corrected. "He's come around a lot, especially since the wedding. But in bed, he's..." she smiled, her mind off somewhere else. "He's such a teddy bear. He's cuddly and sweet and affectionate. Outside the bedroom, he can be so guarded but when we're intimate, it's like he can let all of that go and just *be* with me."

Jeanie and I let out an "Aww," together. I thought of my own gorgeous, sweet-natured wolf. Hunter had his own struggles with not only humans, but his dual nature of being attracted to men and women. It was so beautiful to see his and Raz's relationship bloom alongside our own.

"What's something shifter men bring to the bedroom that human men don't?" Jeanie was like a gossip column reporter. I half-expected to see her taking notes at any second.

"They're definitely not as selfish, for one thing," Miriam scoffed.

"They're very..." I searched for a word. "Instinctive? Like they're so in tune with everything—sounds, smells, body temperature and breaths. All those little subtle changes when you feel yourself getting close to orgasm? They know it right as it's happening."

"Totally agree," Miriam nodded. "Even before the sex actually happens, they know. I can just walk outside, see Gabe cleaning up after a hunt and think, damn that's hot. Next thing I know, Colt is grinding on my ass and whispering he can smell how aroused I am."

"Fuck. Me." Jeanie fanned herself.

"That's Arjun with me," I laughed. "He loves to mess with me when I'm caught up watching Hunter and Raz make out. He can usually get Conner roped in too."

"You lucky bitches." Jeanie shook her head. "I'd love something like that, but you know." Her eyes slid over to me. "Before Connor whisked us away, I thought good men didn't exist. I'm still not sure if they do, since y'all have snatched up six of them."

"There's someone out there for you, sis." I clasped her hand. "Maybe even multiple someones. But you are so young—"

"Yeah, I still got my whole life ahead of me. I get it." She waved a hand in my face. "It's a good thing though, because now I know what healthy relationships look like."

"Exactly!" I beamed at her. "And we won't let you settle for less than you deserve. We have an army of claws and teeth at our disposal."

"Plus your grumpy Marine." Jeanie rolled her eyes. "I'm never finding a man. You're all gonna scare them away!"

"You don't want someone who won't fit in with our crazy family anyway," Miriam laughed.

"Cheers to that!" I agreed.

The three of us threw back our drinks, and Miriam slid out of her stool. "Another round, ladies?"

"Hell yes!" we shouted.

"Oh, and Jeanie." Miriam leaned over to whisper as she gathered our glasses. "The lion shifter that keeps looking over here is hot and young. Like twenty-five at the oldest. Want me to wingwoman?"

"No!" Jeanie looked horrified, clasping at the woman's arm. "Don't you dare say anything. You know I can't control what comes out of my mouth!"

Miriam just pulled away, grinning deviously as she headed to the bar.

17

HUNTER

"**W**hat do you think, Mason?" I turned to my youngest son in his high chair. "Do you think this is enough butter for popcorn?"

He smiled and cooed, arms and legs flailing animatedly as he banged his plastic spoon on the tray in front of him.

"You're right, it definitely needs more." I drizzled another helping onto the fresh popcorn, sealed the container and shook it to distribute evenly, which Mason seemed to love watching. "Check for me, little guy. Did I get it over every piece?"

"What's the holdup in there?" Raz called from the theater room.

"Mason's inspecting the popcorn!"

"Well, let me inspect it with my mouth!"

I peeked over from the kitchen, the sight before me sending the best kind of ache through my chest.

Raz was stretched out on the longest part of our sectional sofa, shirtless and barefoot, with only black sweatpants on. His feet were crossed at the ankles as he flipped through movies for us to watch while Mel was out with the girls. But the best part? He was cuddled up to my children as if they were his own.

Roo nestled into Raz's side, talking softly as Raz's remote arm settled around my son protectively. My oldest pup was getting too old for cuddling with Dad, but gravitated toward my dragon mate like he was a second father. Which was exactly what I'd hoped would happen.

Wolves needed packs and large family units. It was in our DNA. And our blended pack, with a variety of shifter species and the most amazing human woman at the center of it all, could not be more perfect.

Rinna curled up to Raz's other side, her fingers curiously tracing the tattoos on his ribs while he and Roo talked over the movie selection.

"Ahhh." Raz squirmed with a grin and plopped a kiss on Rinna's head. "That tickles, wolfling."

I turned back into the kitchen with a huge goofy grin on my face, just as Connor came down the stairs.

"Heard from Mel yet?" He breezed through the kitchen, heading straight for the fridge for a beer.

"No. She just left an hour ago." I gave the popcorn one more good toss.

"Maybe I should text her." He opened a bottle, then left it on the counter as he went to Mason's high chair. "What do you think, boy? Hm?" He leaned in, kissing Mason's cheeks. "Should we send Mommy a picture of you?"

"Leave her alone." My voice carried a slight growl. "She deserves time away from all of us."

"I know, but look how cute this guy is! Huh!" Connor groaned as he lifted a squirming, giggling Mason out of his high chair, smacking kisses and blowing raspberries on the toddler's face as he nestled him to his side. "Spittin' image of me, don'tcha think?"

"I dunno." I leaned against the counter, looking at the two of them together. "He has your eyes but I think he looks more like Mel."

"He's got her hair, for sure." Connor ruffled the downy, dark strands with a big palm. "And those damn eyelashes, Jesus!"

"Hey, where's the popcorn?" Raz bellowed from the other room. "We're waiting on you guys!"

"Worthless husband." I rolled my eyes as I headed in with the bowl of buttery perfection. "Where's Arjun and the littles?"

"Right here."

The big tiger shifter strolled in from the adjoining den, which he had turned into a workout room. Well, as well as one could stroll in with a child clinging to his back and two more around his legs.

"How's weightlifting been?" Connor snickered, preparing Mason a bowl of baby food while I settled with Raz, my pups, and our popcorn.

"Excellent," Arjun huffed, wiping sweat from his brow. "Why, it feels like I'm still lifting weights." He placed his hands on his hips, paying no mind to Mel's youngest siblings trying their best to hold in their giggles as they dangled off of him.

"Hm, wonder why that would be." I mused, stealing popcorn kernels from my daughter, who growled at me.

"I haven't the faintest idea," Arjun sighed. "Well, I'm off to shower—"

"We're right here!" Bella cackled, unable to contain it anymore.

"What?!" Arjun feigned shock as he made a big show of looking down at her, then at Riley clinging to his other leg. "Are *you* the reason why my legs are so heavy?"

"And Joey's on your back," Bella informed him.

Arjun whipped around, making Joey laugh and scream like he was on the rollercoaster of his life, until Arjun slowly slid him down.

"Can we ride on Arjun too?" Rinna started climbing over the back of the couch.

"Not tonight, honey." I pulled her back down. "Let's watch the movie."

"Tomorrow, my little wolfling." Arjun bent over the back of the couch and kissed her forehead. "I'll need your help with my deadlifts."

"Okay!" She plopped back down happily, narrowly missing the bowl of popcorn.

"Can we be wolflings too?" I heard Joey ask behind us.

"You're my tiger cubs!" Arjun answered without missing a beat. "You're big and fierce like tigers, grrr!"

He chased them around the room, encouraging them to growl and snarl like him until they collapsed on the far end of the couch.

"You guys want popcorn?" I passed the bowl down to them.

"They're exhausted," Raz chuckled. "Probably need something to drink. Arj knows how to tire them out."

"Already got it." Connor walked in, somehow carrying Mason, Mason's food, a beer, and three child-sized plastic cups, which he set on the coffee table in front of the TV. "Have some juice, kiddos. And help yourselves to popcorn."

Bella, the bravest of them, slid off the couch first and grabbed a cup to drink from, followed by Joey, who helped Riley, the youngest. Arjun took off to shower, so we three guys all exchanged a satisfied look. We knew Mel's youngest siblings wouldn't be affected by their old home life as much as Mel and Jeanie. There may even come a time where they barely remembered it. But it still felt incredible to see them coming out of their shell, hanging out with us and trusting us a little more, bit by bit.

They trusted Connor the most, since he was the one who took them away from the shelter, once Jeanie escaped with them from the trailer park. After Connor, they gravitated most toward Arjun, and seemed most wary of me and Raz.

"Thank you for sharing your popcorn," Bella mumbled shyly.

"You're welcome," I beamed. "I'll make another bowl if you want."

Roo leaned across Raz's far side. "Do you want to watch a movie with us?"

"Yeah!" Riley was already crawling across my and Raz's laps to sit next to him.

I swelled with pride and Raz acknowledged he felt it too, with a light brush of his hand on my leg. My pups never had any other kids to play with until the littles came to live with us. I was so proud my kids were doing their best to include them in our family. Our pack.

The kids finally settled on Zootopia while I got up to make a second batch of popcorn. Just as the movie was winding down and most of them were nodding off, four cell phones went off at the same time.

"That's probably Mel," I whispered, not wanting to wake Bella asleep on my right side, nor Joey on my left.

"Mm-hm," Conner confirmed, his face lit up with his screen while he cradled Mason on his shoulder. "Look at our girl."

He turned his phone to show Raz and I. Mel had sent a selfie of her, Jeanie, and Miriam—all beaming beautiful smiles and their heads tilted toward each other.

"Did she say anything?" Raz asked. The two of us were pinned beneath sleeping children and couldn't reach our phones.

"She's on her way home." Connor's thumb swept over the screen as he wrote out a reply to her. "Say cheese, guys."

He angled his phone up high to take a picture of us. It was easy for me to smile. I knew Raz wore a similar one as he propped his chin on my shoulder. Connor snapped it and sent it to her, then all of our phones dinged with an immediate reply.

"She says, 'oh-em-gee, my babies are the cutest. See you soon, heart-eyes-emoji'."

"You're such a fuckin' dad," Raz snorted.

I couldn't bring myself to scold him for swearing in front of the kids. It had been a simple, easy day, but these were my favorite. Just a day and a movie with my family.

"I love you," I whispered, giving Raz an abrupt kiss.

His surprise turned into pure elation. "I love you, Hunter." He grabbed my chin and pulled me into another kiss. "I love our kids and our family."

"Where's my kiss?" Connor grumbled jokingly from his end of the couch.

"Walking through the door in a half-hour," Raz laughed, nuzzling my cheek. "You can't handle a dragon, Con."

"You're probably right," Connor laughed in response.

With that, we started rousing the kids for bed in anticipation of our wife coming home.

18

MIRIAM

"Night, girls!" I waved to Jeanie and Mel in the car.

"You gonna be alright, Mir?" Jeanie frowned out the passenger window.

"Fine," I assured her. I was a little tipsy, but I really was fine.

I actually enjoyed walking through the woods myself. The trees, the ground, and all the hidden critters seemed to tickle my shaman abilities. It wasn't silence but like a wordless conversation with nature that gave me peace. The cottage I shared with Colt and Gabe was under a quarter mile away, anyway.

"I can walk with you," Mel offered.

"And walk back by yourself?" I shook my head. "Trust me, girl. I'm good."

The other shaman didn't look convinced. "Well, text me as soon as you're home."

"Aye-aye." I did a clumsy salute that morphed into a wave as I headed into the wilderness.

The sounds of night insects, owls, and my own shoes crunching over the ground were comforting. These late night walks through the woods used to calm me. But tonight, now that girl time was over, nothing could calm my racing thoughts about Tak.

I looked again at my phone with no calls or messages, the questions running through my head. Did he change his mind about wanting to be with me? And if so, why wouldn't he tell me? He promised to always be honest.

"You're my heart, Miriam," he told me with that sexy growl and possessive kiss right before he left. I could still feel his teeth on my skin, how passionately he fucked me on our last night together.

Tak was an Amarok shifter, an enormous wolf-like creature from Inuit legend. Unlike normal wolves, they were solitary animals. He'd never had a pack, or any kind of community. I always wondered when he left if he preferred it that way. If sharing me, if having a steady partner, was just not in the nature of someone who spent so much time alone.

"Maybe, but why would he lie?" I asked the dark forest. "Why would he make promises only to break them?"

I didn't.

Startled, I whipped around, despite the voice coming from inside my head. Gray and black fur looked silver in the moonlight, covering a wolf the size of an elephant stalking toward me.

"Tak?" I gasped, briefly wondering if it was my drinking that caused my eyes to play tricks on me. But mojitos didn't make me hallucinate voices in my head.

His shoulders pushed trees aside as he came closer, his massive body blocking out the moonlight. A black nose the size of my face dipped low, his pale blue eye and dark eye both full of sorrow in his wolf face.

I'm sorry I let you down, Miriam. The massive wolf lowered to his belly, head resting on paws the size of car tires. *Will you let me explain?*

Seeing him in his animal form was always incredible. He looked like a creature from a fairy tale. But I knew animal forms were also a type of shield for shifters. It created a barrier, keeping them from dealing with more human issues.

"Shift to human, please," I said, trying to keep my voice firm. I would hear him out, but his disappearance had hurt me. "And talk to me, man to woman, please."

He hesitated only a moment before his form shrank down, fur

disappearing into human skin, snout and paws becoming a human jaw and hands.

I clenched my fists at my sides, fighting the urge to run to him and bury my face in that broad chest. Tak's silky black hair was loose, falling over his shoulders instead of his usual topknot. His almond-shaped eyes were crinkled, strong brow furrowed in concern.

"You wanted to explain." I crossed my arms. "So explain."

"I was captured," he said softly. "By humans."

The shock was clear on my face. "*You?* How?"

Amarok were skilled hunters, known in Inuit legends to have humans as their preferred prey. I knew Tak had eaten his fair share of them.

"They had a shaman with them," he frowned. "He used his magic to lure me into a trap. They took all of my belongings, so I couldn't call you. I'm so sorry, my heart."

"Tak." All restraint gone, I ran to him, my hands flying to his face. "Did they hurt you?"

"Not badly."

Up close, I could better see the pain etched in his face, the fatigue from running all the way from Alaska to Georgia.

"Where?" I demanded.

"It really isn't bad, just—"

"Fucking tell me where!"

He sighed, a ghost of a smile on his lips as he lifted his shirt. Bruises and burns marked him from the abdomen up to his chest.

"It was mostly injections," he said, wincing slightly when I touched him. "Experimental drugs. I'm sore, but I'll be fine."

"We have to tell Mel." I stood on tiptoes, reaching to wrap my arms around his neck as I buried my face in his shoulder. "She and her guys escaped from people like this. They—"

"They're gone, my heart," Tak said sadly. "I had barely escaped when they set their own lab on fire. They destroyed the evidence and will lay low until they can resurface." He slid both large arms around my back. "It's the nature of being out as a shifter. They'll keep coming after people like me. Like Colt, Gabe, and Mel's guys."

"Then you need to stay with me." I brought my hands to his face and pressed our foreheads together. "No more trips back to Alaska." I felt like a wilted flower at his silence in response. "Unless you don't want to be here?"

"My heart," Tak growled, caressing up my spine. "With you is the only place I want to be." His fingers wound through my hair. "This was my last trip back. I didn't get everything settled that I wanted to, but," he shrugged. "None of it matters, anyway. What matters is this."

His lips slid over mine with gentle pressure, far gentler than what I wanted. "Taqqiq," I whispered his full name against his lips. "If you don't kiss me like you mean it, your furry ass is welcome to return to the frozen north."

He laughed, deep and rumbling through his chest, then crashed his lips to mine, tongue invading my mouth and stealing my air.

We started lowering to the forest floor, our kisses hard and desperate and starving.

"Do you want to, uh, fuck yes," Tak groaned as I attacked his neck, biting and sucking hard in the rough way he liked. "Want to go home first?"

"No," I murmured against his hot skin, tugging hard at his clothes. "I need you. Right fucking now."

He didn't need any more prompting after that. Large hands slid under my dress, caressing sensitive flesh that had been aching for him for days. The friction against the ground already had my straps coming off my shoulders, and he sucked a hot trail down my chest.

"I want to go slow with you." His mouth nudged against the swells of my breasts. "To savor you after being without you for so long but—"

"Don't," I begged, nipples and core, hell everything, aching for him. "I need you, Tak. We can make love later. Just fuck me, please."

His growl was animalistic and so fucking hot. I heard the odd crunching and snapping sound of shifting, and then sharp claws against my thighs under my dress.

"Don't be scared," he urged when I froze, then smiled gleefully as his claws tore through my panties.

I couldn't even bring myself to be mad at him, instead reaching and fumbling desperately at his zipper as my skirt hiked to my waist. His cock, long and thick, tumbled out. Just feeling him in my palm, hardening by the second, was such a relief. I still needed more, but stroking him there, listening to his groans and breaths, made it all sink in. My gentle—sometimes rough—giant wolf was home. And this time, he wasn't leaving.

"Miriam," Tak shuddered my name out as my palm slid up and down his stiff length. He yanked the top of my dress down, sucking a nipple into his mouth and grazing the stiff peak with his teeth as he teased the other one with his fingers.

I made him stop for a moment just to get him out of his shirt. I loved fucking him outside and seeing the moonlight on his naked skin. Hell, I loved having all my men out in the woods. They seemed to get more pleasure out of it and were wilder, uninhibited. Maybe something to do with nature tapping into their animal sides, but whatever it was made the sex extra fucking hot.

My dress now bunched up material around my waist, Tak closed my legs and placed them against his shoulder. I braced myself for the impact of his cock, but he pulled the fabric over my hips and up and over my legs first. Then he slammed into me.

"Oh, fuck!" My scream echoed off the trees at the sudden intrusion. He felt bigger, thicker than I remembered.

"Miriam." Tak moaned my name again, drinking me in as he hugged my legs to his chest. His hips rolled, dragging his cock out of me before pressing in again.

"Tak," I groaned back, my hands scrambling for purchase on the ground, on his thick thighs. "More, baby. I need to feel you."

He separated my legs, moving them to his sides so I could wrap around him, then he leaned over me, pressing his palms into the ground as his gaze locked on mine.

"This is what kept me going, you know. When I was captured." His flesh slapped mine with every thrust. My hands flew to his arms, flexed and strong. I could only marvel at his powerful body moving through me.

"Fucking me?" I asked with a breathless laugh.

"Fucking you, smelling you, touching you." He lowered further over me, catching my mouth in a rough, possessive kiss. "Hearing your laugh and your sexy moans." His lips ghosted a trail down over my chest, thrusts slowing down to long, deep strokes in and out of my pussy. "Feeling your heartbeat." He pressed a kiss on my left breast. "Because my heart doesn't beat without yours."

"Tak," I gasped, bringing his face back up to mine.

I kissed my big, beautiful lone wolf with everything in me, locking my ankles behind his back to pull him in deeper, to feel every inch of him. Mindful of his injuries, I ran my fingers over every part of him that I could reach, memorizing him with my touch. He lowered his body over me, bare skin rolling and kissing as his thrusts deepened, stretching and filling me to the brim.

"I love you, Tak," I whimpered, nails clawing across his wide back, the pleasure coiling in my clit from the friction of his heavy body on top of me.

"I love you," he rasped against my throat. "My heart, there's no me without you."

"Never leave me again." My plea was breathless against his ear.

"Never," he promised with a groan, his thrusts picking up speed as he sensed my pleasure.

"Tak..." My fingers and toes curled into his flesh, the tension winding up in me like a compressed spring.

"Yes, my heart," he purred, anchoring my hip down with a large hand as he crashed into me, hitting my clit in the way that was just fucking right. "Come on my cock."

I was wound up so tight I couldn't breathe through his next few thrusts that sent me hurtling over the edge. Only when my release shot throughout my whole body did my breaths come in ragged, desperate gasps.

"Oh, Miriam," Tak groaned as he pulsed and swelled inside me, heightening the sweet aftershocks rippling through me.

"Yes, come for me," I whimpered. "I want to feel you."

But he held back, pausing while seated deep inside me to kiss me with a week's worth of longing, love, and passion. Only after we came up for air did he start moving again, with his thumb against my clit, to coax another orgasm out of me.

My next release spurred his, arms and torso stiffening as he came, the muscles sexy and sculpted in the moonlight.

Tak rolled off of me, then promptly pulled me on top of him, hands caressing naked skin as our heartbeats stamped against each other.

"Your back is covered in dirt," he chuckled, wiping clods and blades of grass off of me.

"You're the one who took off my dress," I retorted, tracing lines down his skin as I nestled into his shoulder. "Could've just left it on."

"Never," he scoffed, fingers grazing the side of my breast as he caressed me. "Sex should always be completely naked. That's my only rule."

"Mm-hmm." I hummed happily, gazing up at the stars glittering above us when a question struck me. "How did you escape?"

Tak's arms tightened around me, his lips brushing my forehead as the silence stretched on between us.

"There are some bad humans that are no longer alive," he said finally. "I know I can't hunt them like I used to, but—"

"Tak, it's okay." I kissed his neck. "You were defending yourself. You had to get out."

He cupped my face, eyes finding mine in the dark. "I know, but I also know the effort you're all trying to make in working with humans. I had to leave the bodies and run. It won't look good—"

"I don't care." I silenced him with a kiss. "They'll spin it and try to demonize you in any way possible, but I don't care. You have teeth and claws for a reason. I'm glad you used them."

He sighed and let the back of his head hit the ground. "I was so worried you'd turn me away."

"I got worried when I didn't hear from you. And then confused," I admitted. "I should have asked Mel or Arjun's contacts to check on you. I should have known—"

"Don't blame yourself, my heart." He stroked my cheek. "I was too careless. But it's over now. I wasn't sure if you'd take me back, but I'd find my way here even if all my paws were amputated just on the chance that you would."

"No more talk of that," I said with a soft thump to his chest. "Let's go home and surprise the guys."

He grinned, bright and toothy as he rolled us up to sitting. "Forget the clothes, let's go back naked."

"And they'll just want to fuck again," I laughed.

"That's the idea." Tak nuzzled me. "Maybe in the stream where we can wash this dirt off." His mouth traveled down my chest. "Where the cold water will make your nipples all tight and sensitive while your men keep you warm."

"Hm, you make a tempting offer," I grinned, sliding off his lap. "And I sure would kill to see their reaction."

"Let's do it." He jumped to his feet, powerful legs pushing up to his imposing height as he took my hand. "Again and again, until you can't stand us anymore."

I grinned back, skipping on bare feet and buck naked under the moonlight as we headed toward the cottage. "It'll be a long time before that happens."

THE END

ALSO BY CRYSTAL ASH

Say Your Prayers

<u>Shifted Mates Trilogy</u>

<u>Unholy Trinity: The Complete Series</u>

<u>Harem of Freaks series</u>

Steel Demons MC

Lawless

Powerless

Fearless

Painless

Helpless

Heartless

Senseless

Ruthless

Merciless

For a complete list of books by Crystal Ash, visit her Amazon page.

ABOUT THE AUTHOR

Crystal Ash is a USA Today Bestselling Author from California. She loves writing steamy, heart-wrenching romance with tortured heroes, especially if they're in a reverse harem. Crystal's other loves include animals, mythology, and well-crafted alcohol, most of which can also be found in her stories.

When she's not writing, she's probably drinking craft beer with her husband or trying to coax her feral cat into accepting affection.

crystalashbooks.com

facebook.com/Crystal.Ash.Romance
instagram.com/crystalashbooks
amazon.com/author/crystalash
bookbub.com/profile/crystal-ash

www.ingramcontent.com/pod-product-compliance
Lightning Source LLC
Chambersburg PA
CBHW020335010826
48970CB00012B/766